THE SCARLET RUSE
and
Two Other Great Mysteries

JOHN D. MACDONALD

THE SCARLET RUSE
and
Two Other Great Mysteries

LIPPINCOTT & CROWELL, PUBLISHERS
New York

contents

The Scarlet Ruse

To all McGee's lost ladies,
and the few he has yet to find.

I have learned that the countless paths one traverses
in one's life are all equal. Oppressors and oppressed
meet at the end, and the only thing that
prevails is that life was altogether too short for both.
—Don Juan as quoted by Castaneda

Oh, goddammit, we forgot the silent prayer!
—Dwight D. Eisenhower
(at a Cabinet meeting)

1

After seven years of bickering and fussing, the Fort Lauderdamndale city fathers, on a hot Tuesday in September, killed off a life-style and turned me into a vagrant.

"Permanent habitation aboard all watercraft within the city limits is prohibited."

And that ordinance included everything and everybody, from the Alabama Tiger aboard his plush *'Bama Gal,* running the world's longest floating house party, all the way down to the shackiest little old pontoon cottage snugged into the backwater mangroves.

It included Meyer, the hairy economist, living comfortably aboard his dumpy little cruiser, *The John Maynard Keynes,* low in the water with the weight of financial tomes and journals in five languages and chess texts and problems in seven.

It included me and my stately and substantial old barge-type houseboat, *The Busted Flush.* The edict caught me off balance. I had not thought I was so thoroughly embedded in any particular environment that being detached would be traumatic. Travis McGee is not hooked by things or by places, I told myself.

But, by God, there had been a lot of golden days, a lot of laughter and happy girls. Moonrise and hard rains. Swift fish and wide beaches. Some gentle tears and some damned good luck.

Maybe that is what made the gut hollow, an old superstition about luck. Long long long ago I stepped on a round stone in darkness and fell heavily at the instant that automatic weapons fire yellow-stitched the night where I had been standing six feet four inches tall and frangible. I had two souvenirs from that fall—an elbow abrasion and the round stone. I still had the half-pound stone after the elbow healed. I kept it in the side pocket of the twill pants. Then they leapfrogged two battalions of us forward by night to take pressure off some of our people who'd dug in on the wrong hill.

Our airplane driver didn't care for the attention he was getting and kept his air speed on the high side as he dumped our group. I came to the end of the static line with one hell of a snap, and there was such a sharp pain in my ankle I thought I'd earned another Heart. I pulled the shrouds around, landed on shale, favoring the right leg, rolled and unbuckled, unslung the piece, and listened to night silence before I felt my ankle. No ripped leather or wetness. Pain lessening. Then I missed the round rock. When the chute popped, the rock had popped the pocket stitches, and it had gone down the pant leg, rapping the anklebone on the way out, hurting right through the oiled leather of the jump boots. And I felt at that moment a terrible anxiety. "My rock is lost. My luck is lost. Some bastard is sighting in on me right now."

Later I realized that I had made some bad moves during those next five days before they pulled us all back.

This was the same feeling. I'd clambered up onto the sun deck of the *Flush* so many mornings at first light and had looked out at my world from the vantage point of Slip F-18 and known who I was. True, the great panorama of the sky had been dwindled over the years by the highrise invasions. But it was my place. I'd taken the *Flush* out a hundred times and brought her back and tucked her, creaking and sighing, against the piers, home safe. Safe among her people and mine.

I guess there weren't enough of us, all told. The city commissioners authorized a survey and found out there were sixteen hundred people living on boats within the city limits. That isn't much of a voting block in a place the size of Lauderdale. And boat people are not likely to act in unison anyway.

We'd all been pretending it would be voted down, but they made it unanimous.

So all day Wednesday, little groups formed, reformed, moved around, broke up, joined up again, aboard the watercraft at Bahia Mar.

Meyer lectured an embittered audience aboard the *'Bama Gal,* standing on the cockpit deck amid a decorative litter of young ladies, quaffing Dos Equis, spilling a dapple of suds onto his black chest pelt.

"They say we have added to the population density. Let us examine that charge. Ten years ago perhaps a thousand of us lived aboard cruisers and houseboats. Now there are six hundred additional. During those ten years, ladies and gentlemen, how many so-called living units have appeared in this area? Highrise, town houses, tract houses, mobile homes? They were constructed and trucked in and slapped together and inhabited without thought or heed to the necessary water supply, sewage disposal, schools, roads, police and fire protection. All services are now marginal."

"Fiffy thousand more shore people, maybe, huh?" said Geraldine, mistress of the old *Broomstick*.

"They say we have created sewage disposal problems," Meyer intoned. "Doubtless a few of the live-aboard people are dumb and dirty, emptying slop buckets into the tide. But for the majority of us, we have holding tanks, we use shoreside facilities, we want clean water because we live on the water. Thousands upon thousands of transient cruisers and yachts and houseboats stop at the area marinas every year. Hundreds of millions of dollars' worth of marine hardware, paying a high ticket for docking privileges and bringing ashore a lot of out-of-town spending money. And we all know, we have all seen, that it is the transient watercraft which cause a sewage disposal problem. They do not live here. They take the easiest way out. They do not give a damn. But will the city commissioners pass a law saying transients cannot stay aboard transient boats? Never! Those transients are keeping this corner of Florida green, my friends."

He was applauded. Yay! We would march on City Hall. They would see the error of their ways.

But Johnny Dow put the whole thing in perspective. He cleared his throat and spat downwind, turned away from the rail, and said, *"Ad valorem,* goddammit!"

"Speak American," said one of the Tiger's playgirls.

"They hate us. Them politicals. You know what they make their money on. They come from the law and real estate and selling lots and houses. *Ad valorem.* We not putting dime one in their pockets. They drivin' past seeing folks live pretty free, not needing them one damn bit, and they get scalded. We're supposed to have property lines and bushes and chinch bugs and home improvement loans. Jealous. They all nailed down with a lot of crap they don't like and can't get loose of. So here we are. Easy target. Chouse us the hell out of town forever and they don't have to see us or think about us. Figure us for some kind of parasite. Scroom, ever' damn ass-tight one of them. Can't win this one, Meyer. We're too dense, and we make sewage. Easy target. Neaten up the city. Sweep out the trash. *Ad valorem.*" He spat again, with good elevation and good distance, and stumped across the deck and down the little gangway and off into the blinding brightness of noontime.

Meyer nodded approvingly. "Scroom," he murmured. The end of an era.

We walked together back to the *Flush* and went aboard. We sat in the lounge, frowning and sighing.

Meyer said, "I saw Irv. He said something can be worked out."

"Something can always be worked out. Sure. If a man wants to live aboard a boat, something can be worked out. If he can pay the ticket. A man could buy a condominium apartment right over there in that big hunk of ugly and make it his legal and mailing address and stay there one night a month and aboard all the other nights. Can something be worked out for all the people who get hit by the new law?"

"Hardly."

"Then it isn't going to be the same, old friend. And do we want any part of it, even if I could afford the ticket?"

"You short again?"

"Don't look at me like that."

"You in the confetti business? You make little green paper airplanes?"

"I have had six months of my retirement in this installment, fella."

He beamed. "You know, you look rested. Good shape too. Better and better shape this last month, right?"

"Getting ready to go to work, which I seem to remember telling you."

"You *did. You did!* I remember. That was when I asked you if you would help an old and dear friend and you said no thanks."

"Meyer, dammit, I—"

"I respect your decision. I don't know what will happen to Fedderman. It's just too bad."

I stared at him with fond exasperation. A week ago he had tried to explain Hirsh Fedderman's unusual problem to me, and I had told him that it was an area I knew absolutely nothing about.

Meyer said, "We have thirty days of grace before we have to move away, boat and baggage. I just thought it would be a good thing to occupy your mind. And I told Hirsh I knew somebody who maybe could help out."

"You got a little ahead of yourself, didn't you?"

He sighed. "So I have to make amends. I'll see what I can do by myself."

"Stop trying to manipulate me."

"What are you talking about?"

"Take a deep breath and say it. If it's what you want, take a deep breath and say it."

"What should I say?"

"Take a wild guess."

"Well . . . Travis, would you please come with me to Miami and listen to my old friend Hirsh Fedderman and decide if you want to take on a salvage job?"

"Because you ask me so nicely, yes."

"But then why was it no before?"

"Because I had something else shaping up."

"And it fell through?"

"Yesterday. So today I need Fedderman, maybe."

"He is a nervous ruin. He's waiting for the roof to fall in on him. If it would be okay, how about this afternoon? I can phone him?"

2

Fedderman asked us not to arrive until quarter after five, when both the female clerks in his tiny shop would be gone for the day. I put Miss Agnes, my Rolls-Royce pickup, in a parking lot two blocks from his store. He was in mainland Miami, a dozen blocks from Biscayne and about three doors from the corner of Southwest Eleventh Street.

There was a dusty display window, with a steel grill padlocked across it. Gold leaf, peeling, on plate glass, said ornately, FEDDERMAN STAMP AND COIN COMPANY. Below that was printed RARITIES.

Meyer tried the door, and it was locked. He knocked and peered into the shadowy interior and said, "He's coming."

I heard the sound of a bolt and a chain, and then a bell dingled when he opened the door and smiled out and up at us. He was a crickety little man, quick of movement, quick to smile, bald rimmed with white, a tan, seamed face, crisp white shirt, salmon-pink slacks.

Meyer introduced us. Fedderman smiled and bobbed and shook hands with both hands. He locked the door and led us back past dim display cases to the small office in the rear. There was bright fluorescence in the office and in the narrow stockroom beyond the office. Fedderman sat behind his desk. He smiled and sighed. "Why should I feel better?" he asked. "I don't know if anybody can do anything. The whole thing is impossible, believe me. It couldn't happen. It happened. I can't eat. I can't sleep. I can't sit still or stand still since I found out. Mr. McGee, whatever happens, I am glad Meyer brought you to hear this crazy story. Here is—"

I interrupted him. "Mr. Fedderman, I try to recover items of value which have been lost and which cannot be recovered by any other means. If I decide to help you, I will risk my time and expenses. If I make a recovery of all or part of what you have lost, we take my expenses off the top and split the remainder down the middle."

He nodded, looking thoughtful. "Maybe it wouldn't fit perfect, because what is lost isn't mine. I understand. Let me tell you."

"Go slow because I don't know a thing about stamps and coins."

He smiled. "So I'll give you a shock treatment." He took a desk-top projector with built-in viewing screen from a shelf and put it on his desk and plugged it in. He opened a desk drawer and took out a metal box of transparencies and fitted it into the projector. He turned off the light and projected the first slide onto the twelve-by-fifteen-inch ground-glass viewing area.

A block of four stamps filled the screen. They were deep blue. They showed an old-timey portrait of George Washington. The denomination was ninety cents.

"This was printed in 1875," Fedderman said. "It is perhaps the finest block of four known, and one of the very few blocks known. Superb condition, crisp deep color, full original gum. It catalogs at over twelve thousand dollars, but it will bring thousands more at auction."

Click. The next was a pair of stamps, one above the other. Four-cent stamps. Blue. They pictured three old ships under sail, over the legend "Fleet of Columbus."

"The *only* known vertical pair of the famous error of blue. Only one sheet was printed in blue instead of ultramarine. In ultramarine this pair would be worth . . . twenty-five dollars. This pair catalogs at nine thousand three hundred and will bring fifteen at auction. The top stamp has one pulled perf and a slight gum disturbance. The bottom stamp has never been hinged, and it is superb. Quite flawless."

Click. Click. Click. A couple of crude bears holding up an emblem, with "Saint Louis" printed across the top of the stamps and "Post Office" printed across the bottom. A block of six brownish, crude-looking five-cent stamps showing Ben Franklin. There were no rows of little holes for tearing them apart. A twenty-four-cent stamp printed in red and blue, showing an old airplane, a biplane, flying upside down. And about a dozen others, while Fedderman talked very large numbers.

He finished the slide show and turned the bright overhead lights back on. He creaked back in his swivel chair.

"Crash course, Mr. McGee. I've showed you nineteen items. I've bought them for a client over the past fifteen years. Right now there is another twenty thousand to spend. I am looking for the right piece. Another classic. Another famous piece."

"Why does he want them?" I asked.

Fedderman's smile was small and sad. "What has he put into these pieces over fifteen years? A hundred and eighty-five thousand. Plus my fee. What do I charge for my time, my advice, all my knowledge and experience and contacts? Ten percent. So let's say he has two hundred and three thousand, five hundred dollars in these funny little pieces of paper. I could make two phone calls, maybe only one, and get him three hundred and fifty thousand. Or if I spent a year liquidating, feeding them into the right auctions, negotiating the auction house percentage, he could come out with half a million."

Meyer said, "As the purchasing power of currencies of the world erodes, Travis, all the unique and the limited-quantity items in the world go up. Waterfront land. Rare books and paintings. Heirloom silver. Rare postage stamps."

"Classic postage stamps," Fedderman said, "have certain advantages over that other stuff. Portability. One small envelope with a stiffener to prevent bending, with glassine interleafs for the mint copies, you can walk around with a half million dollars. These classics, you can sell them in the capital cities of the world, cash money, no questions. Well, some questions for these items because all the old-timers like me, we know the history, which collections they've been in over the years—Hines, West, Brookman, Weil. We know when they changed hands and for how much. For each item here there is a certificate from the Philatelic Foundation saying it is genuine. The disadvantage is they are fragile. They've got to be perfect. A little crease, a little wrinkle, it would break your heart how much comes off the price. These, they never get touched with a naked finger. Stamp tongs if they ever have to be touched. They are in a safety deposit box."

Meyer encouraged Hirsh to tell me how he operated. It was intriguing and simple. He and any new client would take out a lockbox set up to require both signatures and the presence of both parties before it could be opened. He used the First Atlantic Bank and Trust Company, four blocks from his store. When he made an acquisition, he and the client would go to the bank and put it in the box. The reason was obvious—as soon as Fedderman explained it to me. He made a formal legal agreement with each client. If at any time the client wanted to get out from under, Hirsh Fedderman would pay him a sum equal to the total investment plus five percent per year on the principal amount invested. Or, if the client desired, he could take over the investment collection himself, at which point the agreement became void.

"It's just to make them feel safe, is all," Fedderman said. "They don't know me. They don't know if the stamps are real or forgeries. I started it this way a long time ago. I've never closed one out the way it says there in the agreement. But some have been closed out, sure. There was one closed out six years ago. About fifty thousand he had in it. I got together with the executor, and we auctioned the whole thing through Robert Siegel Auction Galleries, and a very happy widow got a hundred and forty thousand."

"They can get big money that easily?" I asked.

Fedderman looked at me with kindly contempt. "Mr. McGee, any year maybe twenty-five millions, maybe fifty millions go through the auction houses all over the world. Maybe more. Who knows? Compared to the stock exchanges, very small potatoes. But if the merchandise was available, the stamp auctions would be twice as big. Three times. That is because shrewd men know what has happened to classic merchandise during forty years of inflation. They'll buy all they can find. You put money in a Swiss bank, next year it's worth five percent less. The same money in a rarity, it *has* to be five percent more because the money is worth less, and the demand adds more percent. So in true rarities these days, the increment, it's fifteen to twenty percent per year."

"How many clients do you have right now?"

"Only six. This one and five more. Average. Sometimes ten, sometimes three."

"How much do you invest in a given year?"

He shrugged. "Last year, over five hundred thousand."

"Where do you find the rare stamps to invest in?"

"All over the country there are dealers who know I'm in the market for the very best in U.S., British, and British Colonials. Those are what I know best. Say a dealer gets a chance to bid on an estate. It's got some classics which make it too rich for him. He phones me and he says, 'Hirsh, I've got here in a collection all the 1869 pictorials in singles used and unused, with and without grills, with double grills, triple grills. I've got special cancellations on singles and pairs, and I've got some blocks of four. Some are fine, some superb, average very fine.' So maybe it's Comeskey in Utica, New York, maybe Tippet over in Sarasota, I fly there and figure what I can use and maybe I add enough to the pot so he can bid in the whole collection, and I take the '69s and he takes the rest. Or I get tipped about things coming up at auction and move in and make a buy before they print up the catalog. Or there is a collector tired of some good part of his collection, and he knows me. Or a dealer needs some ready cash on stuff he's had tucked away for years, watching the price go up. I deal fair. I never take advantage. Three years ago a collector wanted to sell me his early Bermuda. He had some fakes of the early Postmasters' Stamps from Hamilton and St. George. At eighteen and twenty thousand each and looking like some dumb kid printed them in a cellar, no wonder there's fakes—lots of them—around. He threw in fifteen or so fakes he'd picked up over the years. I sat right here and went over them. One bothered me. It was Stanley Gibbons catalog number 03, center-dated 1850. The W. B. Perot signature was way off. Too far away from the original. Know what I mean? The rest of it was so damned perfect. Would a counterfeiter be so stupid? Not with several thousand dollars at stake. Okay, so maybe Perot was sick or out of town or had a busted hand that day. It took six months, but I got an authentication out of the Royal Philatelic Society, and I sent the collector my check for nine thousand, which was the best offer I could get for the stamp at that time. I put the stamp in a client investment account. You wouldn't believe the kind of word-of-mouth advertising I got out of that."

The whole thing seemed unreal to me. He claimed to have made fifty thousand last year as a buying agent for the investment accounts. But here he was in a narrow little sidestreet store.

"Your problem, Mr. McGee, I can see it on your face. You think all this stamp stuff is like bubble-gum wrappers, like maybe baseball cards, trade three of your players for one of mine. It doesn't seem like grown-ups, right? Let me show you how grown-up it can get, okay?"

He opened an old cast-iron safe, took out a little file drawer, took out some glassine envelopes. With small, flat-bladed tongs he took out two stamps and put them in front of me.

"Here, look at these two through this magnifying glass. These are both the five-dollar Columbian Exposition of 1893, unused. Printed in black. Profile of Columbus. Catalog seven hundred. For stamps like these, the retail should be a thousand each. Quality. Perfect centering. No tears or folds or bends. No short perforations. No perforations missing. Nice clean imprint, sharp and bright, no fading. A fresh, crisp look. Right? Now I turn them over. Keep looking. See? Full original gum on each. Nobody ever stuck a hinge on either one and stuck it in an album. Perfect? You are looking at two thousand dollars retail? Wrong! This one is a thousand dollars. This other one is schlock. I'll show you."

He got out a pistol-grip light on a cord, turned it on, and turned off the overheads. We were in almost complete darkness. "Black light," he said. "Look at the stamp there." Two irregular oval areas glowed. One was the size of a lima bean, the other the size of a grain of rice.

Fedderman turned the lights on again. "Let me tell you what is maybe the history of this piece of junk here. Back in 1893 maybe some uncle goes to the Exposition and he brings back a fine gift, all the stamps, and maybe a souvenir album. So a kid licks this one like putting it on an envelope and sticks it in the album, along with the others. This one maybe had one straight edge, where it was at the edge of the sheet when it was printed. Okay, maybe it spends thirty, forty years in that album. Finally somebody tries to soak it off. Hard to do after the glue has set. They don't get it all off. Some of the stamp comes off on the album paper. That leaves a place called a thin. A nice centered stamp like this with no gum and two thins and a straight edge, nothing else wrong, it goes for maybe a hundred and fifty, hundred and a quarter retail, perhaps ninety bucks wholesale. Okay, last year or the year before, somebody buys this dog along with some others of the same kind of high-value dogs. They take them to Germany. Right now, working somewhere in West Germany, there is a pure genius. He makes up some kind of stuff to fill the thins. He gets the gum from low-denomination Columbians. He puts it on perfect, no slop-over between the perfs. And he reperfs the straight edge perfect as an angel. I'm telling you, back around World War One, Sam Singer was the stamp doctor in this country. Then there was a fellow in Paris named Zareski who was pretty good, especially faking cancellations. But this German is the best yet. Very dangerous. And I'm showing you why I'm worth the ten percent I get for doing the investing."

Suddenly he slumped, sighed. "Sure. Hirsh Fedderman is so damned smart. When you think nobody can take you, somebody takes you."

"Tell Travis what happened," Meyer said.

It took Fedderman a few moments to pull himself together. "Eighteen months ago, a little longer ago, I guess, this man phones up, his name is Frank Sprenger, he wants to have a talk with me about investing in stamps. He says he heard about me from so and so. I knew the name. Excuse me, I don't like to give out names. It's a confidential relationship. So I drove over to the Beach, and he's got a condominium apartment, like a penthouse, in the Seascape. It's in the afternoon. There is a party going on, girls and laughing and loud music and so forth. Sprenger comes and takes me into a bedroom down a hall and shuts the door. He is big and broad, and he has a great tan. He has a great haircut. He smells like pine trees. He is not going to tell me what he does for a living. It is entertainment, maybe. Like with girls or horses or importing grass. Why should I care who I deal with? The protections are there. I do a clean business and pay my taxes. I give my sales talk. He listens good. He asks the right questions. I show him a sample of the agreement and a sample receipt like I sign to show the total investment and a sample inventory list like he can have if he wants. He says he will let me know. He finally lets me know it is yes. We meet at the bank and set up the box, and I sign the agreement, and we get it notarized. He says he can't say how much or how often, but it will usually be cash and is that okay? I tell him okay. He gives me forty thousand in cash in a big brown manila envelope right there, and I put it in my business account. Who wants to walk these streets with money like that? He had the two fellows who came with him waiting in the car. I'm alone. The items I showed you, that's not Sprenger's account. Sprenger said he didn't want anything well known, any special item that dealers would know on sight. I said it would make a little more volume. He said okay, but keep the volume down."

"Did his request mean anything to you?" I asked Fedderman.

"What do you mean?"

"He planned to turn over cash in unpredictable amounts for merchandise which couldn't be traced. Did you make any guesses about him from that?"

"Guesses? A man can do a lot of guessing. Why should I care? I can prove the money turned over to me from my copy of the receipt and from my deposit record. I can show where it went, show my percentage for my own taxes. Suppose it isn't his money. Suppose he's getting ready to run. Any time he wants, he can meet me at the bank, give me back my signed agreement, take the merchandise home."

"What did you invest in?"

"Superb unused blocks of four without plate numbers. High values. Columbians, Trans-Mississippi, Zeppelins. Some larger multiples, like a beautiful block of nine of the two-dollar Trans-Miss, mint, sixty-five hundred it cost me. Same kind of purchases of Canadian Jubilee in the high-dollar values. Also some older stuff when they were perfect singles, used or unused, like a nice mint copy each of Canada numbers one, two, five, seven, nine, and thirteen. Twelve thousand, five hundred right there. Value." He leaned toward me. "It is the most valuable stuff, Mr. McGee, on a size and weight basis, the world has ever known. Some years ago Ray Weil and his brother, Roger, bought a Hawaiian stamp at auction for forty thousand. Very thin paper. Some newspaper guy in New Orleans, I think it was, figured out that it came to one and a half billion dollars a pound."

"I'm impressed."

"It doesn't come with bubble gum."

"I said I'm impressed, Mr. Fedderman."

"Call me Hirsh, please."

"Hirsh, I want to know what happened. How did you get taken? Or did you get taken?"

"You know those early Canadas? The way I came onto them, there was this old guy up in Jacksonville, he—"

"Hirsh!"

"Okay, I'm sorry. They were switched."

"What do you mean?"

"I mean what I said! Sprenger did a lot of business with me. A *lot!* I had to really hustle to find the right stuff. I know the figure by heart. Call it nineteen months. Three hundred and ninety-five thousand. My ten percent on top of that. Four hundred and thirty-four thousand five hundred, that's what he has in it. Cash every six to eight weeks. Right now I've got about nineteen hundred and fifty dollars of his money to spend. It can't come out perfectly even, right?"

"It was switched, you say?"

"Let me show you something," he said. He got up and trotted out of the office into the store and came back in a few minutes and closed the door again. He put a slim, handsome album in front of me. It was in a black-fiber dust case. The album was of padded blue imitation leather. The pages had transparent slots for stamps and Mylar interleafing.

"This is a brand made abroad. Lighthouse. Same color and size as Sprenger's. I provide it, after making the first investment. Right here on the front bottom corner, in gold, his book says Frank A. Sprenger. I get it done at the luggage place in the next block. This size fits nice in a middle-size safety deposit box. Here is the procedure. I buy something for Sprenger's account. Mary Alice keeps the records on the investment accounts. Mary Alice McDermit. Missus, but separated. She's been with me almost five years. Very sharp girl. Okay, I turn the item over to her, and she fixes up a Hawid or a Showguard mount or mounts and posts the price from the invoice in the ledger, on the page for Sprenger's account. She puts the item in the safe, and then when Sprenger can meet me at the bank, Mary Alice comes along too, and we take the box into one of the bigger rooms where there is room for three to sit down at a table. I show Sprenger what I bought for him and answer questions if he has any, and Mary Alice puts the item or items in the album just like this one as we sit there. Then it goes back in the box, and we get an attendant, and it gets locked into the hole in the wall and we leave."

"He comes alone?"

"He comes alone into the bank. Yes. There is usually somebody else in his car."

"The stamps were switched?"

"Listen. Almost two weeks ago, the seventh. Thursday. He was able to make it at eleven in the morning. I walked over with Mary Alice. I had some Zepps and some early colonials. Barbados and Bermuda. Solid investment stuff. Thirty-three thousand worth. Too much to keep here. Okay, it was like always. We went in. I showed him what I had. No questions. Mary Alice put them in the stock book. She wondered if she should put the Barbados on an earlier page with other Barbados. She looked back at that page. She had to turn some pages to find what she wanted. I got a look at the pages. Meyer, like I told you, I thought my heart was going to stop. I've got eyes like an eagle. Fifty years I've been looking at stamps. Across a room a diamond dealer can tell a good stone. Right? I'd bought prime merchandise for Sprenger. And I am looking at junk. It is not so obvious Mary Alice could tell. Sprenger couldn't tell in a year. What am I looking at? Bad centering. Some toning and staining. Some pulled perfs. Instead of very fine to superb, I am looking at good space fillers, if that. I felt for a minute like the room was spinning. What saved me, I didn't have any breath to say anything. Then my mind is racing, and I get hold of myself. When Mary Alice has put the new buys in, I take the stock book and leaf through it, saying something about Sprenger will never be sorry he made the investment.

It is worse than I thought. Blocks reassembled from singles. **Repairs.**
Scratches. Little stains. Not counting what Mary Alice had just put in, I
had bought three hundred and sixty-two thousand dollars' worth of
standard classics. Mostly superb condition. Total catalog would run
maybe three hundred and twenty-five. I was looking at stuff that was
one fifth and one sixth and one tenth catalog anywhere. Sixty-five thousand at the best. Somehow I got the strength to walk out of there on my
own legs. You think I've had a night's sleep since then?"

Meyer said, "Hirsh got in touch with me."

"It had been too long since I saw you last," Fedderman said. "What
is the matter with the world? Old friends don't see each other. What I
wanted, Meyer, was to borrow your mind. Such a logical mind! I get excited, and I can't think two and two."

"I listened to the story," Meyer said, "and it made me wonder if
Frank Sprenger might be the kind of barracuda who'd steal his own
property and make Hirsh pay him for the loss. The deposit box is in a
busy bank. Hirsh here is not an unusual type. His signature isn't complex or ornate. Sprenger would know the way Hirsh usually greeted the
different vault attendants. Sprenger had an inventory list of everything
in the investment collection. I asked Hirsh if defective duplicates would
be hard to find. He said some of them would take a while, mostly no.
So it began to seem plausible that Sprenger had somebody accumulate
the same items, and then they went to the bank together and switched,
took the good ones out of the stock book, and put the defective ones in.
Somebody successfully passed as Hirsh Fedderman."

"You like that assumption?" I asked Meyer.

"I don't like it any better than you do. It is a very touchy thing.
Hirsh goes there often. Somebody gets uneasy and steps on the silent
alarm, and Frank Sprenger is in a special kind of trouble. Anyway, it
didn't happen."

"Vault records?" I asked.

Fedderman beamed at me approvingly. "I keep a careful record of
every time I go to the vault. I made a list. I went to see my friend Mr.
Dobson and gave him the list and asked him to find out if I'd been there
more times than on the list, because maybe I had forgotten to write
down a visit, and that's why my inventory was sort of messed up. There
was no extra visit at all."

"And your next guess?" I asked Meyer.

"Hirsh's practice is to turn the items over to Mary Alice McDermit. She keeps the records, puts the items in mounts. I suggested the switch took place in this shop, item by item, before they even got to the bank. Hirsh went up in blue smoke."

"Not her. Believe me! Anyway, I always personally showed the new items to Sprenger. I couldn't help seeing if they had turned to some kind of junk. Could she make the switch right there in front of both of us? No! A stock book like this one has double-sided pages. It holds a lot. Here is the inventory list. To add up to that much without buying well-known pieces, there are almost seven hundred items. No. That's ridiculous. Even if she wanted to do it, there's no way."

"Next guess?" I asked Meyer.

"The next thing was try to talk you into taking a look. You said no. Today you said yes."

I frowned at Fedderman. "What happens if Sprenger decides to ask you for cash money, according to your agreement?"

"Don't even say it out loud! I have to find four hundred and fifty thousand. Where? I can sell out my investments. I can empty the bank account. I can borrow. I can liquidate inventory. Maybe I can make it. Then I can get some salvage from that junk, pay back the loan. Maybe I end up naked like the day I was born."

"What if he wanted to cancel and the stamps hadn't been switched?"

"No problem. You have no idea how hungry the auction houses are for prime merchandise. I could borrow, interest free, seventy-five percent of anticipated auction prices. That would be close to four hundred. I would come out ahead on the whole deal. The older an investment account is, the better off I am if the client wants out. If a client wanted out, I would have to advise him he'd be better off selling the items on the open market. I'd handle that for him without commission. It's part of the agreement. I'd get him the best price around."

"When did you look through that stock book previously, Hirsh? Can you pinpoint a date when everything was in order?"

"I tried. Four times this year I met Sprenger there. February, May, July, September. It was in February, or it was November last year, I looked through the book. Everything looked good. I think it was February, but I can't be sure."

"So . . . it couldn't happen, but it did."

"I . . . I just don't know what I . . ." His voice got shaky. His face started to break up, and he brought it under control, but for a moment I could see just how he had looked when he had been a boy.

"I'll think about it and let you know," I told him. It wasn't what I had opened my mouth to say. Meyer knew that. Meyer looked startled and pleased.

3

Meyer and I strolled through the golden sunshine of evening, and through the residual stink of the rush-hour traffic, now considerably thinned out. We walked a half-dozen blocks to a small, dark bar in an old hotel. Elderly local businessmen drank solemnly, standing along the bar, playing poker dice for the drinks. At first glance they looked like an important group, like the power structure. But as eyes adjusted to the dimness after the hot brightness outside, the ruddiness became broken veins, collars were frayed and dingy, suits cut in outmoded style, the cigar smoke cheap, the drinks especially priced for the cocktail hour.

They talked about the market and the elections. Maybe once upon a time it had been meaningful. They had probably met here when they had worked in the area, when the area had been important, when the hotel had been shining new. So now they came in from their retirement at this time of day, dressing for the part, to nurse a couple of eighty-five-cent drinks and find out who had died and who was dying.

We carried our drinks over to a table under a tile mural of an improbable orange tree.

"So Fedderman got in a bind, a bad one, and he took Sprenger's money and bought junk and pocketed the difference," I said. "All along he knows there is going to be a day of reckoning, and because Frank Sprenger sounds hard case, it could be a very dirty day. If, by getting help, he can give himself the look of being a victim, he could save his skin."

Meyer smiled. "I went down that road. It doesn't go anywhere. Not because he is an honest man, which I think he is, but because he is a bright man. He buys for old customers, not under any special agreement. They take his word on authenticity. He could slip junk into those collections, and there would be no recourse against him. He is bright enough to know that you don't fool around with the Frank Sprengers of this world. Maybe you shouldn't deal with them at all. He rationalizes by saying that what he does is honest. He likes action. Sprenger is a lot of action. Fedderman likes having big pieces of money to invest. He likes phoning London and talking to his friends at Stanley Gibbons."

"How do you know him?"

"Ten years ago I invented an economic indicator I called the Hedge Index. Activity in works of art, antiques, gold, silver, coins, rare stamps. I felt it could be done on a sampling basis. Fedderman was one of the people who agreed to help. He was absolutely candid. No tricks, no lies, no exaggerations. When I had the bugs ironed out, I ran the index for two years and then published a partial report. There was a direct correlation between rate of inflation and hedge activity, with the hedge activity being a lead indicator of major rises in the announced cost of living by about ninety days. It's been picked up by the big boys and refined. I wanted the kind of built-in warning they used to have in France. When the peasants started buying gold and hiding it, you knew the storms were coming."

"Are they coming, O Great Seer?"

"What do you think we are standing out in the middle of with neither spoon nor paddle? Anyway, I've dropped in on Hirsh when I've been in the neighborhood ever since I gave up running the index. I said something to him once about having a friend in the salvage business. It was in connection with a customer whose valuable collection had been stolen. That's why he phoned me when this came up."

"If he's such a specialist and so bright, why isn't he rich?"

"He's seventy-two years old. His wife died of cancer twenty years ago. He gives a lot of money for cancer research. Both his sons emigrated to Israel and married there. He has seven, I think, grandchildren. He visits once a year. He gives to Jewish Relief, Bonds for Israel. He's set up an educational insurance policy for each grandchild. He's big in the temple. Special work and special gifts. He runs the store because he likes it. He's used to it. His work is his hobby. He's very proud of his reputation for fair dealing. He's proud of having so many good friends scattered around the country. He overpays his help. He lives in an apartment hotel, so called. He knows everybody within four blocks of his store in any direction. Why isn't he rich? I think maybe he's as rich as he wants to be."

"Maybe he ought to sell the business and retire and leave for Israel next week."

"That's the last thing Hirsh would ever do."

"If he could do it, he would have already done it."

"Right."

A huge old man came lumbering over to our table. "Don't tell me," he said. He bent over and peered into my face. "Don't tell me. You were six years wi' the Steelers. Then you got traded to the Eagles. This your second year wi' the Dolphins, right? Like fourteen years in pro ball. You lost the speed, and you're not as big as the ones coming up, but you got the cutes, boy. You got the smarts. You got those great patterns and those great fakes. In a minute I'll come up with your name. You'll see. Who's this with you?"

"One of the trainers."

"Trainer, eh? Good! Wors' thing you can do is consort with a known gambler, right? They'll throw your ass out of the league."

When he reached for a nearby chair, I stood up quickly and said, "Nice to meet a knowledgeable fan, sir. See you around."

"Any minute now I'll remember your name, fella."

"Want some help?"

"No. I don't need any help. I know you good."

The sun was gone when we went out into the muggy evening. Meyer sighed as we started toward the parking place and said, "You look like a hero, and I look like a known gambler."

"Nature plays fair. You're the one with the good head."

"The good head says you are going to try to get a line on Sprenger first."

In September the Amalgamated Lepers of Eurasia could negotiate special convention rates at any one of fifteen brassy hostelries along Collins Avenue. Bellhops even smile when tipped.

I found a handy spot for old Miss Agnes and told Meyer to be patient. I could work it better alone, and it might mean several hotel lounges before I could put anything together. I tried the Fontainebleau first, that epic piece of decor a *Saturday Evening Post* journalist once described as looking like "an enormous dental plate."

When my eyes were used to the gloom, I spotted a bar waitress who used to be at the Eden Roc. Kay. Nice eyes, big smile, fat legs.

"Hey, where you been hiding, McGee?"

"What are you doing working here?"

"Oh, I run into kind of a personal problem the other place. It was better I should try somewhere else. It's okay here."

"How are the twins?"

"In the second grade! Would you believe?"

"I bet they're beautiful."

"They are, if I say so myself, but they're hellers. Look, I got to take care of my station."

"Come back when you get a chance. I want to ask you something."

"Sure."

When she came back to the bar and touched me on the shoulder, I turned on the stool and said, "I was trying to get a reading on somebody. I was looking for somebody like Brownie."

She leaned warmth against the side of my thigh and said, "I know. But they say he's dead."

"How long?"

"A year, maybe. He just stopped showing, and when somebody checked his place, there was nothing there. So nobody got a postcard even, and they say he was dropped in the ocean, and somebody cleaned his place out so it would look like he left. Maybe he had too many readings on people. You know."

"Is Willy still over at the Contessa?"

"Sure. He knows all, that guy. But he won't say."

"Maybe he owes me one."

"If he does, he won't remember. You know how he is."

"I'll give it a try."

"You come back, hear? I'm off at nine tonight."

"Wish I could, Kay. I really do. But this one is priority."

The desk tried to brush me off. I told the cold-eyed old man to check with Mr. Nucci before he made it final. He went over and murmured into the phone, studying me as he talked. He hung up and came over and told me that if I would go to the Winner's Circle Bar, Mr. Nucci would join me there in a few minutes.

It was more like twenty minutes before he slipped onto the stool beside mine. He wore a brown denim suit with lots of pockets and ropes and zippers, and a yellow velvet shirt, open to the umbilicus. His face was bland-brown, hairless as his brown smooth chest. Sleepy eyes, languid manner, a thin little mouth, like a newborn shark.

Willy Nucci started as a busboy and now owns more points in the Contessa than anyone else. This is an unlikely Horatio Alger story along the oceanfront. He managed it by making various pressure groups believe he was fronting for other, just as deadly, pressure groups. He did it by expert intelligence work, brass, guile, persistence, and hard work. Nearly everyone thinks he is a front for New Jersey money, money that comes down to be dry-cleaned and flown back or flown abroad. I am one of the very few people who know Willy is clean and that he owns the biggest piece of the hotel. Maybe the IRS knows.

The motif of the bar is horse. Everything except saddle horns on the bar stools. In season it is a good place for the winners to spend and the losers to cry.

"I kept you waiting," Willy said in a flat voice. Statement of fact. I nodded. Silence is the best gambit with Willy Nucci, because it is one of his useful weapons. He makes people edgy by saying nothing. It's always handy to use the other man's tricks, because he never knows if he is being mocked.

I outwaited him, and finally he said, "It's your dime, McGee."

"Look at the edge of my glass."

He leaned toward it, tilting his head, and saw the little pale pink smear of stale lipstick. He called the barman over and chewed him in a small terrible voice. The man swayed and looked sweaty. He brought me a new drink, delivering it with a flourish and a look of splendid hatred.

"What else is bothering you?" Willy asked.

"I have a name, an address, a description, and I want a fill-in."

"I don't know many people anymore. The Beach keeps changing."

"You *have* to know, Willy."

"All I *have* to do is run this place and turn a dime on it for the owners."

"Willy?"

He gave me a quick, sidelong glance. Silence. A barely audible sigh.

"Willy, there is a young lady with a lot of energy on the paper in Lauderdale, and she keeps after me, saying she wants human interest stories about playtown, USA. She digs pretty good. She knows how to use courthouse records."

He got up slowly, looking tired. "Come on, damn you."

We went out past the guard and the empty pool and up the stairs to the roof of the cabana row of the Contessa Hotel. These are the days of exotic bugs, induction mikes, shotgun mikes. People like Willy Nucci talk in the open, at night, near surf roar or traffic roar. Or they rent cars and turn the radio volume high and drive around and talk. They never say anything useful over the phone, and they put in writing the bare minimum information required by the various laws and regulatory agencies.

We crossed the recreation roof to the ocean side and stood side by side, leaning on the railing. Freighters were working south, inside the Stream. The sleepy ocean whacked listlessly at the little bit of remaining beach, with a small green-white glow of phosphorescence where it tumbled.

In my newscaster voice instead of my Travis McGee voice, I said, "When Willy Nucci quietly acquired his first small percentage of the Contessa Hotel, it was laboring under the crushing burden of a sixth and a seventh mortgage. Today, hiding behind a bewildering maze of legal stratagems, Mr. Nucci is not only the principal owner, but he has managed to pay off most of the indebtedness—"

He responded, his voice rising with exasperation. "Look. Okay. I wanted to tell *somebody*. I wanted to brag. We had a lot of time and nothing to do, and neither one of us figured we had a chance of getting out of there once it was daylight and they could use those goddamn rifles."

"Wouldn't you like other people to know?"

He calmed down. "Sure I would. But it would cost me. I get nibbled pretty good. The unions, the assessments, the graft, the public servants on the take, the gifts you make like insurance premiums. But there's restraint. They have the idea that if the bite gets too big, some very important muscle is going to come down here and straighten some people out. If they knew it was just Willy Nucci, owner and operator, there would be a big grin, and they'd smack their lips and move in very tight and close. I don't have much margin to play with. I've got sixteen years invested. The books look good right now. Last season was good, and this one will be better. You might as well know this too. I'm going to try to move it this season. I can come out well. And cut out of here. How come I always run off at the mouth to you, McGee?"

"I win friends and influence people."

He frowned at his private piece of ocean. "You could have used what you know, but you haven't. Except you use it to leverage me."

"Not often."

"I make this the third time. In three years. Maybe this time I can't help you."

"The man is big and broad and suntanned. Officially or unofficially, he's in a penthouse at the Seascape. He moves around with some fetch-and-carry people. Frank Sprenger."

Silence. He pinched the bridge of his nose. He looked up at murky stars.

"Willy?"

"I don't know how much you know about the way things are. For all I know you think that soft, romantic crock of shit, *The Godfather,* was for real."

"I thought it was real, like a John Wayne western."

"There's hope for you. All the action is divided up. There are independents, and when they get big enough, they are absorbed or smashed. There are three neutral areas. Places where anybody can go who is part of the national action and not get pressured. Sanctuaries. Miami, Vegas, and Honolulu. There are hits sometimes, but outsiders, amateurs. Discipline situations. 'Do not crap in your own nest' is the motto. There's enough for everybody in the sanctuaries. That's how come you have maybe nine different groups from elsewhere, owning lots of pieces of property and pieces of action along the Beach here. Like there are twelve groups operating side by side in Vegas. Other areas are strictly territorial. That's how come all the trouble in New York lately. Now suppose every one of the nine organizations operating here sent down their own bagmen and bankers and enforcers? It would get too hairy. People would start pushing. People would push back. It would stop being a safe place for the topside people to come and relax, and it would hurt trade. So there's been a working arrangement for maybe thirty years. The local group has their own operations, like a franchise area, but you can see how it wouldn't be fair to cut the out-of-town groups out of the picture entirely because a certain substantial piece of business comes through their owning certain situations here."

"Example?"

"Okay, say that Minneapolis has substantial points in a couple of hotels and owns a steak house franchise and a taxi company. The local group will be scoring from every part of the operations. Hookers and games and drugs at the hotels on top of linen service, union dues, kickbacks, dozens of angles. And they will work the steak houses and the taxi company pretty good too. So it works almost like a money-room skim. The extra costs of doing business get built into the books as legitimate expenses, and then out of the unrecorded cash flow, an equal amount gets bundled up and couriered to Minneapolis. The profit is minimized, which cuts taxes, and the rebate is under the table, ready for more investment."

"And somebody has to be the bookkeeper and enforcer, somebody everybody agrees on, to see that the skim is honest?"

"For the last six years, Frank Sprenger. Phoenix. Before that it was Bunny Golder, for years and years. He died of a stroke. I heard that some kinky girl friend got him smashed and then ran a sharpened piano wire into his brain through the corner of his eye, but nobody ran an autopsy to check it out."

"What is Sprenger like?"

"I'll tell you what he's like. He's like exactly the right man for the job. He doesn't use anything, not even booze or tobacco or coffee. He's a body freak. Not muscle building. Conditioning. He lives like a good heavyweight six weeks away from a title shot. Except for women. He takes care of more than his share. He spends a lot of time cross-checking the action. He's found some people clipping off a little as the money went by them, and they are not seen around anymore. I hear the local group has stopped trying to con him, because it isn't safe or healthy."

"What's his cover?"

"Investment consultant. He has a second-floor office on Lincoln Road. He's in the yellow pages. He pays his taxes. I think maybe he has some legitimate clients. He's a careful man."

I waited until I thought of the right kind of hypothetical question. "Willy, I want you to listen to some stuff I am going to make up and tell me if it could happen. Let's say that in the past year and a half Frank Sprenger has been buying important paintings. He has been using an expert and paying a fee for his judgment. Four hundred thousand worth of art. It's been going into a storage warehouse. Possible?"

"Sure," Willy said. "Especially if it's on a cash basis."

"Say it is."

"Money makes more problems every day. You hear how they want banks to report everything over five thousand? Now they are beginning to crack the Swiss and get the numbers. The islands used to be good, but what's going to happen to the Bahamas, the Caymans, Jamaica, the next couple of years? It's very hard to set up a corporation and feed cash into it in such a way you can get past an audit. You put cash in a jar in your backyard, it isn't working for you. It's shrinking all the time it's buried. Dry-cleaning money gets more expensive all the time. One way they are using lately is you buy yourself a broker, one who'll fake back records for the sake of the commission and a little present. Then you set up a buy five years ago for something that has gone up like eight hundred percent. Then you have the sale records faked too and pay capital gains, and what you have left is legitimate and you can invest it legitimate. You have to be your own fence, for God's sake. So why not paintings? I like it. He would be handling it for one of the out-of-town groups or individuals. He handles investment money right here. The local group has legal talent he can use. Raw land has been good. Pieces of home-building outfits have been good. In-and-out marinas have been good."

"How much would he be supervising in a year? I mean, how much would the total skim be, the amount he'd be watching?"

"McGee, this has to be absolutely horseback. I could be off, way way off."

"Take a guess."

"Well . . . working it backward and saying that the total take for the Florida group in this area is seventy-five million with fifteen million expenses, and maybe twenty-five percent of the net is reimbursed on account of special ownership . . . Sprenger keeps an eye on maybe fifteen million."

"And *invests* that much?"

"Oh, hell no! The groups mostly have their own way of handling a cash rebate. It goes back by messenger. Frank might have to find a home down here for one mil, or one and a half, or even two."

"Okay. Now here is the final suppose. Suppose that right now all those paintings in that bonded warehouse are fake."

He snapped his head around, eyes wide open for the first time that evening. "You have some weird sense of fun there, McGee."

"Think out loud."

"Well . . . Sprenger wouldn't know it. He wouldn't get into that kind of a con. Unless, of course, he had orders to spoil somebody's day. But I don't think they'd use him for that. He's too good doing what he does. Okay. Sprenger doesn't know. Then he's dead."

"Literally?"

"Literally. Because there are only two choices when the news gets out. Sprenger is either getting cute or getting stupid. And they can't take a chance either way. The only reverse leverage he has is what he knows. So he has to be taken dead before he can get a chance to use it. It's a standard risk. A man like Sprenger makes as much money as the president of Eastman Kodak. He accepts the occupational risk. If he goofs, he gets more than fired. And if he goofs and has any small chance of covering himself before the news gets out, he would gut his brother, peddle his sister, and feed his father and his godfather to alligators, a hunk at a time, to earn that small chance."

"Why are you so sure Sprenger will do what he's told to do?"

"Where have you been? They never let anybody close to the money unless they've got a good lock on him. Sprenger will always be some kind of errand boy. Somewhere there is something in writing or on tape or on film that some prosecutor can't ignore. Like with the talent they own. Nobody goes looking for a new manager if the one you already have owns your ass."

In silence he looked down at the eroded beach. He said dolefully, "They want to pump umpty-seven billion yards of sand in front of all the hotels, a big beach like in 1919 they had. Bond issues, big assessments, more taxes, just so all the clowns can go parading by on public beach land for maybe two years before a hurricane takes it all back out to sea. And after next season this old crock hotel will need a quarter mil of maintenance and redecorating. With luck I'm out by April."

"Willy?"

"Uh?"

"You've got me wondering. You have to get a rebate from Sprenger."

"I should sidestep it and give up the edge?"

"But how?"

"Maybe there is a little spin-off group of investors in St. Louis, and maybe they have sixteen points. So a hundred percent of the skim goes there, and they take twenty-two percent instead of sixteen, in return for running it in and out of some accounts before it ends up in something which could be called maybe Acme Management Associates or Scranton Development Corporation."

"Which could be you?"

"Not entirely, but mostly. There's no other way I can go and still make out. You can't fight the establishment."

"Funny thing to call it."

"Why? It's the way things are. They put a night bell captain on. I don't have to pay him a dime. What's your pleasure? Hash-candy from Calcutta? A Greek virgin? Table-stakes poker? Cuban cigars? A quick abortion? Mexican gold? An albino dwarf? If you can afford the ticket, you've got it. I can't get rid of him. The cops probably know he's dealing. But if they charge him, if the case is airtight, it still goes all the way to jury, and after the jury is picked, it takes two phone calls. Or three. Cash money if you vote to acquit, Pancho. And if Alfred gets convicted, you'll come home from work some day and find something that'll give you a weak stomach the rest of your life. Who stands up to that? Nobody. The klutz with no connections cops a plea, and they process him into the slammer. Alfred, my special employee, will never do a day of time unless he gets smart-ass and they want to settle him down. Nobody really gives a goddamn anymore, McGee. Everybody wants to keep his own ass safe from harm." He paused and made a sound which was like a suppressed gag. Maybe it was laughter. I'd never heard Willy Nucci laugh before, so I couldn't tell. "Even me," he said. "Especially me."

4

I felt guilty about leaving Meyer alone for so long. I had no way of knowing Willy was going to make Zsa Zsa sound like a mute. I always feel guilty when I keep Meyer waiting. And there is never any need for it. He never paces up and down, checking the time. He has those places to go, inside his head. He looks as if he were sitting and dozing, fingers laced across his middle. Actually he has walked back into his head, where there are libraries, concert halls, workrooms, experimental laboratories, game rooms. He can listen to a fine string quartet, solve chess problems, write an essay on Chilean inflation under Allende, or compose haiku. He has a fine time back in there. If you could put his head in a jar of nutrient and keep him alive forever, he would wear forever that gentle, contented little smile.

He came reluctantly back to the lesser reality of here and now and, as I drove north up A-1-A, he told me he had had a confrontation with urchins. They had a needle-sharp icepick and thought a protection price of five dollars per tire was a good place to start the bargaining.

"We had a nice conversation," Meyer said.

"You had a nice conversation."

"I told them that theirs was a profession mentioned in the first writings of mankind over thirty centuries ago. Roving bands of barbarians would demand that a village pay tribute, or they would sack it."

"They listened to the lecture?"

"A discussion, not a lecture. Questions and answers. There is a parallel, of course, in Vietnam, where the Viet Cong would spare villages in return for food, shelter, and information. And I told them about the Barbary pirates extracting tribute from our merchant vessels. Then they went away finally. After they were gone, I remembered we hadn't decided on any dollar figure. I guess they forgot."

"Three of them."

"Age twelve, thirteen, and fourteen."

"Meyer, did it ever occur to you that one of those half-size hoodlums could have shoved an icepick into you?"

I could sense he was genuinely startled and upset. "Into me? But why?"

Why indeed? Conversely, why not? I don't know exactly what it is about Meyer. Sometimes, for fun, when we have been at someone's home, I have seen him do his St. Francis bit, when there has been a bird feeder visible from a window. Meyer goes and stands a few feet from the feeder. The birds come back. They look him over. They talk about him. And in a few minutes they start landing on him. Once when we took a runover dog to a veterinarian, the man told Meyer he had good hands. Meyer could hold the dog still. It snapped at the doctor. I have been on the beach with Meyer and five hundred other people and had a frantic girl run directly to Meyer to tell him she was hallucinating and please help me, please. It is a rare attribute, but not all that rare. Lots of people have it in varying degrees. Maybe it is an echo of the remote past when we all lived in the peaceable kingdom. We should find out what it is, how to increase the aptitude, how to teach it to others. It is symptomatic of our times that no one is studying this wild card, nobody thinks it important. In an icepick world, any kind of immunity is crucially important. Any avenue of loving-kindness needs some directional signs.

I went up A-1-A looking for a place I had not been to in a long time. Meyer had never been there. It was near Hallandale. I know I made the right turn. I cruised a few blocks. Everything looked strange. I put my old electric-blue pickup truck next to a gas island where electronic pumps squatted like skeptical Martians. After extravagant admiration, and several questions about Miss Agnes, the attendant let me ask my question.

"Huh? Oh sure. Hell, it's been maybe two years. That old house was right down there where that big red and white chicken is flapping its wings. Chicky-Land. Let me see. It was Rosa and . . . and . . ."

"Vito."

"Right! I took the old lady there plenty of times on special occasions. They could handle maybe twenty-four people, tops. Reservations only. You never knew what you'd get for dinner, but by God it was always delicious and always more than you could eat. They treated you like guests in their home."

"What happened?"

He frowned as he cleaned the high windshield. "Something about the zoning and all. They started giving them fits. Rewire the place, then redo the plumbing, then put in some kind of sprinkler system. Then change the kitchen over somehow. They say somebody wanted that land. Every time something had to be done, they'd have to close until it was all okay and approved. Then Rosa had some kind of breakdown, and Vito went down to a meeting and broke the nose on one of the commissioners. They jailed him, but some of his old customers with clout got him out and got it all quieted down. They went away someplace. I heard one of the commissioners was in the group that bought up that whole two blocks for the shopping plaza and Chicky-Land."

"If you wanted to find a meal that good right now, where would you go?" I asked him.

He took my money and made change as he thought it over. Finally he said, "Damn if we just don't eat that good anymore anywhere. Funny, sort of. Big, rich country like this. Everything starting to taste like stale sawdust. Maybe it's just me."

"We are all living in chicky land," I told him.

Back in the car, heading home, I told Meyer about the little sculpture garden Vito and Rosa Grimaldi had fixed up. White cement statues of swooning maidens and oddly proportioned animals. With a dozen complicated floodlights, which all kept changing color, focused on the statuary and the three small fountains and the plantings. "So incredibly vulgar, it was somehow very touching."

"As vulgar as that big red and white electric chicken?"

Meyer is often unanswerable, an annoying habit.

We ate in one of the less offensive steak houses, at a table made from an imitation wooden hatch cover. They are sawing down forests, strapping thick green planks together with rusty iron, beating hell out of them with chains and crowbars, dipping them in a dark muddy stain, then covering the whole thing with indestructible transparent polymer about a quarter inch thick. Instant artifact.

We talked our way up, over, across, and around the Sprenger situation, after I had given him the Willy Nucci perspective.

It was agreed that Sprenger had the contacts to get an accurate reading on Hirsh Fedderman before opening negotiations. So it was possible that he could have set Hirsh up, that by devising a way of switching the rarities, he had invented a way of doubling his money. The stuff had a ready market. And Hirsh would pay instead of run. But it did not seem to be Sprenger's style, even without knowing the man. If he wanted to play tricks and games, wouldn't he rather play them in his own jungle?

We decided that if we could figure out how the switch had been made —and that might involve walking Hirsh and Miss Mary Alice through a typical bank visit complete with philatelic props—it might be possible to work backward from the method to the conniver.

Which would mean letting Mary Alice McDermit know for the first time that important stuff was missing.

"I'd say she's about twenty-seven," Meyer told me. "One of those big, slow, sweet, gentle girls. You know the type? Dark hair, fair skin, blue eyes, expression always on the edge of a smile. A beautiful disposition. Five years with Hirsh. I think I heard him say the other woman had been there fifteen years. She would be close to forty. Jane Lawson. A service widow. Teenage kids, I think. Small woman, quick and cranky and very smart. I don't think Mary Alice has any children. I'm sure of it. She is separated from her husband. This is the way I read that store and the relationship. They are dependent on Hirsh and on the job. He pays them more than they could get elsewhere. So between them they make it up to him by making that little store pay off. It's kind of a family, the three of them. They take care of each other."

We both agreed that any frontal approach to Frank Sprenger had an unhealthy flavor. Nucci had marked him high for hard, high for smart. He was in a slot where he had to be suspicious of any approach from any direction.

Meyer came up with one faintly promising thought.

"Even though those aren't famous rarities he bought for Sprenger, not things any dealer would recognize on sight, maybe there is some kind of way of identifying them. I don't know enough about it. But did you notice that Philatelic Foundation certificate he showed us? There was a photograph glued to it, and an embossing seal used. If just one of those things can be traced . . ."

"There were numbers in the margin of those blocks of four and six he showed us."

"We need to know more about it, Travis."

"Do we?"

He leaned forward and peered at me very intently. "Hmmm. A kind of disapproval? That's what's bothered me most. Why should Travis McGee give a faint damn what happens to an elderly party who isn't too careful whom he deals with and inevitably gets stung? The desirable quality of shining innocence isn't there this time. And is it a total disaster? He has a place to go, people to look after him. You could get involved, but it would be going through motions."

"Sometimes it isn't any more than that."

"Are you saying no?"

"Not quite yet."

"But you might?"

"It is a distinct possibility."

He looked tired. He sighed. He pushed a piece of gristle around his plate and finally hid it under his potato skin. I caught the eye of the redcoat who had served us. He had saved up all his cordiality for the critical moment of check and tip. The service had been indifferent, the orders not quite correct. What do you do? If you are cross, tired, and immature, you take it out on the waiter. The world is not enhanced to any measurable degree by one, or by one million, confrontations with venal, lazy waiters. And it impedes the processes of digestion. So you compute the tip and leave in good order and try to remember never to return.

But it had been one more smear on an already dingy day. All day I had been trying not to think of the eviction notice. But it was in the back of my mind. Willy Nucci had depressed me more than I had been willing to admit. He wanted to get out, and he was not at all sure he could. So, out of accumulations of anxiety, he had talked and talked and talked. The old men in the old bar had depressed me. And children with icepicks are not amusing. And I wished I'd gone to eat at Grimaldis' when Vito and Rosa were in trouble. I might have been able to help. It was easy to see that I had a new remorse. It was one of the night thoughts of the future. If I had only . . . I have a long list of those.

After Meyer had gone to his home afloat, I made myself a hefty nightcap and turned the lights off and went up to the sun deck in a ratty old blue robe and sat at the topside controls, bare feet braced on the dew-damp mahogany. It was a soft night. Car lights, boat lights, dock lights, starlight. Sound of traffic and sound of the sea. Smell of salt and smell of hydrocarbons. The *Flush* wind-swayed under me and nudged against a fender.

"Hey, McGee? McGee?" she called from the dock.

I got up and went aft and looked down at Jenny Thurston under the dock lights, in basque shirt, baggy shorts, baseball cap, and ragged boat shoes.

"Hey, is it really true?" she asked.

"Come on aboard. Want a drink?"

"I got most of this here can of beer, thanks."

She came up topside and took the other pilot chair, beside me, and swiveled it around to face me in the night. "I got back around five, and they showed me in the paper, and all of them were bitching about it. I looked for you to check it out."

"It's true enough, Jen."

"Well, goddamn them! Nobody is going to move me ashore, McGee. I was born on a boat. We'll have to find a place where they're not trying to iron everybody out flat. Maybe down in the Keys?"

"Maybe."

"But it won't be the same as here. Never."

Jenny lives aboard a roomy old Chris and paints aboard her. Jenny paints three paintings. One is of a beach with a long cresting wave, sandpipers, and overhanging palms. One is of gulls in the wind, teetering over the abandoned, stove-in hulk of an old dory on a rocky beach. The last is of six old pilings at low tide, with weed and barnacles on the exposed part, with four brown pelicans perched on individual pilings, and two more sailing in to land on the empty ones. She paints them in varying sizes and frames them in different styles, in order to have a useful range of prices. They all sell. They hang in untold hundreds of northern living rooms, all signed in the bottom right corner: Jennifer Thurston.

She is chunky, forthright, salty, and loyal to her friends. She paints as many paintings as she needs, in order to get along. She has pretty eyes and good legs. From time to time, sturdy young men move in with her, aboard the *West Bank*. The average tour of duty has been about three months. The old-timers have learned to estimate the probable date of departure very accurately. They detect in the young man a certain list-lessness, a sallowness, a general air of stupor.

So we sat in the night and talked about old times and people long gone. Sam Taggert. Nora Gardino. A girl named Skeeter. Puss Killian. Remember when . . . ? Hey, what about the time . . . ? Were you around when . . . ?

It was all nostalgia, sweet and sad, and it was good therapy. Some-times you need that special kind of laughter.

I went down the ladderway with her and walked aft to the gangplank. I bent and kissed her and felt her mouth sweeten and flower under the pressure when she grabbed hold to make it last longer. She sighed as I straightened, and she said, "Sometimes I wish I didn't have my rule about sleeping with my friends."

"A lot of the trouble in my life has come from not following your rule, Jen."

"It's always better when you don't have to give a damn."

"Take care of yourself."

"Let's try to see if we can find a place most of the old hands can tie up permanent. You know. Enough room and everything."

I watched her walk away. She slapped her old boat shoes down with stumpy authority. Her hair had smelled fresh and sweet. I needed a lady to be happy with. Not that lady, though. It had been a long time be-tween amiable ladies. Chauvinist pig yearning for new play toy, new love object? Not so as you would hardly know it. Reverse of Jenny's dictim: It's always better when you give a damn. But how do you tell a genuine damn from one you muster up to justify tupping the wench? Well, you can tell. That's all. You can. And so can she. Unless, of course, she is just a female chauvinist pig yearning after you as a play toy, a sex object, and drumming up *her* little rationalizations.

I dreamed about a lady I saw on one of those stamps. Antigua. 1863. Lady in profile in rosy mauve, with an elegant neck, a discreet crown on her pretty head. She turned with a half smile, looking out of the stamp at me, then shook her head, frowned, and said, "Oh, golly. *You* again, huh?"

5

The First Atlantic Bank and Trust Company occupied the first two floors of its own office building on a noisy corner. The four of us walked from Fedderman's shop to the bank. Meyer walked ahead with Hirsh. I followed with Mary Alice McDermit. Anyone would probably mention that she was tall enough for me. In hardly any heels at all, she came close to six feet. It was a stifling Thursday morning. September can be a seething bitch in Miami. She wore some kind of sunback dress. Her glossy black hair bounced to her free stride. Her fair skin had taken a tan the color of weak butterscotch. Her face had good bones, but it was slightly plump, and something about her expression and the way she dressed made me think of a very large twelve-year-old girl.

"I can't believe it," she kept saying. "I just can't *believe* it."

"Hirsh believes it. He got a good look two weeks ago today. The good stuff is gone, except what you put in that day."

"We knew something was awfully wrong. The way he's been acting. Jane and I talked about it. We tried to find out from him. I just can't believe it."

It felt good to walk with a girl who matched my stride, nice brown knees alternating. Any kind of a close look and that twelve-year-old impression was gone all of a sudden.

She said, "It wasn't any of your really great stuff. You know. Like one-of-a-kind or tied to historical covers or anything. But it was all really first-class, high-catalog material, the kind you can depend on to hold value."

"You like futzing around with postage stamps?"

She gave me a blank, frowning look. "What do you futz around with, huh? Hitting an innocent little white ball with a long stick? Soldering wires together and playing four-track stereo? Slamming some dumb little car around corners, upshifting and downshifting? Are you a gun futz or a muscle futz?"

"I think I know where you're going with that."

"Where I'm going is that there's no list to tell you where you rate on some kind of scale of permanent values and find out how unimportant you are. But I can tell you what nobody ought to be doing."

"What's that?"

"Nobody ought to be sneering at anybody else's way of life."

"Mrs. McDermit?"

"Mmm?"

"Could we set our personal clock back and start over again?"

Her smile was bright, vivid, personal, merry. "Why, you dummy? We're getting along pretty remarkable."

"We are? Good."

"I like people. I really do. Here's the bank."

The safety deposit vault was in the back left corner. There were three people on duty there. Hirsh Fedderman signed the slip and put down the number of his own personal box. They let us all in, and had the three of us wait in the corridor off to the side which led to the private booths and little rooms. Hirsh joined us, with his box under his arm. The attendant led us back to one of the little rooms. There was a table, three chairs. The attendant said he would bring another chair. I told him thanks, not to bother.

The table was butted against the wall. It was narrower than a card table and about half again as long. They moved the chairs to where they had been in an identical little room on September seventh. As I stood with my back against the closed door, Hirsh and Mary Alice sat at the right, Mary Alice nearest me, facing Meyer across the table—Meyer, of course, representing Sprenger.

I said, "Try to make as exact a reconstruction as you can. I'll stop you if I have any questions."

Hirsh said, "I put the box right here, against the wall, nearest me, and I opened it like this and took the stock book out. Okay. Here is the stock book I brought, so . . ."

"Put it in the box and close the box and then take it out as you did before and do with it exactly what you did the other time."

Hirsh took it out and put it in front of Mary Alice and said, "Other clients, I hand them the book. They want to take a look at their money. Not Sprenger. I tried at first. He wouldn't take it. He'd just shrug."

Mary Alice said, "That was when I was taking the new purchases out of my purse, like this. And the inventory sheet. I gave the inventory sheet to Mr. Sprenger, and I put the new stamps, in their mounts, right here, where they would be handy for Mr. Fedderman."

"I took a copy of the list out of my pocket," Hirsh said. "I put it here in front of me, like this. Then I read off the items and found each one and showed it to Sprenger and then pushed it toward Mary Alice."

"By then," she said, "I'd taken the book out of the slip case and opened it up, and as Hirsh pushed them toward me, I would pick them up and slip them into the book like this, into these transparent strips. I used these tongs because you have to have something to lift the edge of the strip. The stamps were in mounts like this, so it was just because it's easier for me, not to protect the stamps, I used stamp tongs."

"Is that the same inventory list?" I asked.

"Exactly," she said. "And I fixed up the right number of mounts and the right size. But these stamps I just put in are junk from the new issue service."

"Go ahead just the way you did with him," I said.

Hirsh tried to smile. "I try to give a little spiel. Clients like it. I couldn't tell if Sprenger did or not. We never got loosened up with each other. He'd grunt. He always seemed bored, like I was taking too long. Okay. I'll say the sort of thing I said to Sprenger. It won't be exact, but it will be close."

I watched intently. I had them do a repeat of Mary Alice looking back through the book to see if there was room on a prior page to put the new Barbados stamps with the previous Barbados stamps. I had Hirsh take the book and leaf through it and give it back to Mary Alice. She put it in the fiber dust case and handed it to Hirsh. He opened the box and put the stock book in and closed the lid.

"Then I picked up the box and started to stand up, but he said he had some money. I thought he had it with him so I sat down, but he said he would be in touch and get it to me soon. I haven't seen it yet. We left the room. When I came out of the vault, he was gone. Mary Alice was waiting for me. We walked back to the store. Like always, I would have been kind of depressed. He never said, 'Very nice. Very pretty.' Nothing. You like people to take an interest. But I was too scared to be depressed. I was terrified. My head was spinning. I almost told this girl."

"You should have told me, Hirsh. Really."

"I should worry your pretty head with total disaster?"

She looked at me. "Did you see anything?"

"Nothing at all. Did you always do it that way?"

"Always," she said. "With him and the other clients too. Just like that. Except it's more fun with the others."

Meyer said, "Do either of you remember a distraction? Did anybody yell fire, drop anything, fall off a chair?"

They remembered nothing like that. They had been buoyed by a fragile hope. It seeped away. Hirsh went from looking sixty-two to looking ninety-two. Meyer was somber. The girl bit her thumb knuckle and blinked rapidly.

So we all got out of there. We went back to the shop. Jane Lawson looked at us with anxious query when we all walked in. Hirsh and Mary Alice shook their heads no. Jane looked bitterly depressed. An old man with hair like Brillo sat erect on a stool, using gold tongs with great deftness as, one by one, he examined stamps and replaced them in the stock book in front of him.

"Fedderman," he said, "everything here is perfectly ordinary, quite tiresome, exceedingly unremarkable."

"Colonel, if I had looked through them, I would have known that, right?"

"Yes, but—"

"And then if I told you I had not looked through them, I would be lying. Right? Believe me, that book is exactly the way I found it, in one of the cartons. If it's tiresome, I'm sorry."

"Huh!" said the colonel.

"What?" asked Fedderman.

"Nothing. Nothing at all."

"Wait. You put this one back crooked. Let me help you. What do you know? Look, Mary Alice. A nice double surcharge on Canada C3. Doesn't that go pretty good?"

"Like about seventy dollars in Scott, Mr. Fedderman."

"See, colonel? In the middle of all this junk, a nice little error. Let me see. Original gum. Never hinged. Nice centering. To you, colonel, only forty dollars."

"Forty!"

"I know," said Mary Alice. "That surprises me too, sir. It ought to be fifty-five at least."

"Well . . . put it aside, dear girl," said the colonel.

They meshed smoothly and well, did Fedderman and Mary Alice. She went behind the counter. Meyer and I went back to Fedderman's office with him and closed the door.

"Now what?" Fedderman asked out of the depths of his despair.

"One thing I know," Meyer said. "The impossible doesn't ever happen. Only possible things happen."

"To me the impossible happens," said Fedderman.

"If it isn't you and it isn't Sprenger," Meyer said, "then it has to be Mary Alice."

"Impossible!"

"So we are comparing two impossible things, and it being Mary Alice is not quite as impossible as what happened."

"Maybe I follow you," Hirsh said. "My head hurts. I hurt all over. I'm coming down. I should be in bed with a pill."

"Did she bring that same purse?" I asked Fedderman.

"Purse?"

"The one she had today is like a picnic basket made of straw painted white. Did she have the same purse the last time?"

"Yes. No. How should I know? There are five clients. What difference does it make?"

"I wish I knew *if* it made any difference. That junk you saw in the Sprenger collection. Could it have come out of your stock here in the store?"

"What I saw? Some of it, maybe. Very little. I didn't have long enough to study it, you understand. A dealer has a good memory for defective pieces. No, I'd say probably none of it from my stock, or I would have recognized one piece anyway. Besides, it was higher catalog value than what I stock here."

I remembered Meyer's interesting thought. "Hirsh," I asked, "suppose whoever switched the goods has sold the Sprenger items to the trade. Could you identify them?"

He thought, nodded, and gave me a show-and-tell answer. Once again the projection viewer came out. He put a slide box in place and in the darkened office clicked through a half-dozen slides and stopped at a block of four blue stamps imprinted "Graf Zeppelin" across the top. They were a two-dollar-and-sixty-cent denomination.

"This is one I picked up for Sprenger. It was in a Mozian auction catalog last year. It is absolutely superb, and I had to go to fourteen hundred for it. I take an Ektachrome-X transparency of everything I put in an investment account. I use a medical Nikon, and I keep it right here on this mount. Built-in flash. Now you see where the perforations cross in the middle of the block, those little holes? They make a certain pattern. Distinctive. Maybe unique? Not quite. Now look out at the corners. See this top left corner? That paper between the perforations, right on the corner, is so long, it looks as if maybe there was a pulled perforation on the stamp that was up here, in the original sheet. Okay, add that corner to the pattern in the middle, and it *is* unique. Any dealer could look at this slide, go through a couple dozen blocks and pick this one out with no trouble. Individual stamps would be a lot harder, especially perforated. Imperforate, usually they are cut so the margins are something you can recognize. Of course, postally used stuff, old stuff, the cancellation is unique."

As he put his toys away, I said, "Could you get prints made from the slides of the most valuable items and circulate them to your friends in the trade?"

"A waste of time and money. These days, believe me, there are more stamp collections being ripped off than ever in history. Information comes in all the time. Watch for this, watch for that. Hoodlums come in here to the store, and they tell me their uncle left them some stamps in an album, do I want to take a look, maybe buy them? I say I've got all the stock I want. They'll find people who'll buy. But not me. I don't need the grief. After fifty years in the business, I should be a fence? Am I going to look at the stamps the hoodlum brings in and call a cop? Who needs a gasoline bomb through the front door?"

"Then there's no way?" Meyer asked.

Fedderman sighed. "If all that stuff goes back into circulation, a lot of those pieces *have* to find their way into the auction houses. Every catalog, there are pictures of the best pieces. Like if there are two thousand lots listed in the catalog, there could be a hundred photographs of the best items. One day last week I sat in here, I went through a couple dozen catalogs to try to spot any item from the Sprenger account. H. R.

Harmer, Harmer, Rooke and Company, Schiff, Herst, Mozian, Siegel, Apfelbaum. Nothing."

"Oh," said Meyer, his disappointment obvious.

"I think I am going home to bed, the way I feel," Fedderman said. "What are you fellows going to do now?"

I said, "I am going to get Mary Alice to help me."

"How do you mean?" Hirsh asked.

"If she knows more than she's told us, the only thing she can do is play along with me."

"But that kind of person," Hirsh said, "she would help if you ask. It wouldn't prove anything."

"Suppose I get to the point where I ask something or do something which would make her back away fast if she was innocent, and she doesn't back away?"

He stared at me, uneasy and upset. "She is a good person. She isn't used to anything rough."

"Rough?" I asked him.

"No offense," he said.

Meyer said, "You look terrible, Hirsh. Travis will drive you home."

"It's not even as far as the bank, but the other way. So I can't walk it?"

"I'll walk with you," Meyer said.

"Why should you bother?"

"Why shouldn't I?"

On the way out through the store, by prearrangement, Hirsh told his two ladies that Mr. Travis McGee was going to do what he could to help out in this terrible situation, and he would appreciate it if they would answer questions and show him things and so on. Meyer told me he would go his own way, do a little research maybe, take a bus probably, and see me at Bahia Mar.

6

Jane Lawson went off on her lunch break about fifteen minutes after Meyer and Hirsh left. A man came in to buy a beginner's stamp-collecting outfit for his son's birthday. I imitated a browser, leafing through big glassine pages on a countertop easel, looking at incredibly florid stamps from improbable countries, like Ajman, Zambia, and Bangladesh.

I liked the way Mary Alice handled the customer. She was plugging an outfit which, with stamps, album, manual, hinges, and so on, came to $24.95. The man finally said he couldn't go over fifteen dollars. She told him there was a $14.95 kit, but she could assemble something better for him. She took items from stock, added them up, and told him it came to $14.50. Then she threw in another packet of stamps as a birthday present from Mr. Fedderman. She did not patronize the man. She made it seem like a better deal than the more expensive spread.

The narrow store seemed jammed full of merchandise in a bewildering confusion. But as I got used to it, I could see there was a logical order to the storage and display, and see that everything was bright and clean.

After the man left, she moved over to where I stood at the counter and said, "It's sort of a policy in the trade, you know, to encourage kids to collect. But look at what some of these countries are doing. This stuff is just a bunch of . . . gummed labels. And they grind it out in such millions, they'll never be worth more than what they're worth this minute. I've told Hirsh I wish they'd all get together and boycott the countries that take advantage." She turned a page. "Look here. This is a new issue for Grenada; it's an island near Trinidad that used to be part of the British Empire. They've got a contract with some company that grinds out stamps and sends a few of them to Grenada for postal use and sends the rest directly to dealers like us and splits the profit with the government in Grenada. It's just a racket. Gee, I guess we're no better. Our government encourages collectors. Every stamp that isn't used means no postal service is required, so it's practically all profit. People buy all the commemoratives as they come out, in whole sheets, and tuck them away like an investment. Some investment! You go to sell them, somebody will take them off your hands like for seven percent discount off face value. That's because they print hundreds of millions of every one." She hesitated. "I guess you don't want to know about stuff like that."

"Why not? If I was looking into a theft of paintings, I'd want to know something about art."

"What are you? Some kind of investigator? I know you are Meyer's friend. He's such a dear, sweet man. We all love him."

Before I could answer, a man came in and was greeted by name. She went back to the safe and brought out five little brown envelopes. The man sat on a stool, took out his own magnifying glass, and, one by one, inspected the gold coins. Big coins. Mary Alice waited patiently. Finally he said, "Okay, dear. These three. Tell Hirsh this one is a slider, and I don't like the strike on this one. That makes six hundred and twenty, doesn't it?"

She used scratch paper and said, "Six forty-four eighty with tax, Mr. Sulzer."

He produced six hundreds and one fifty. She made out a receipt and gave him his change. He said, "When are you going to change your mind about some nice Sunday?"

"If I do, I'll let you know, okay?"

"How is he doing locating a 1930?"

"Gee, I don't know. He was complaining about finding one that wasn't the quality you want. I really don't know much about coins, like I keep telling you. If he finds one, I'm sure he'll phone."

Sulzer left. She made a face at me. "He collects double eagles. St. Gaudens, not the Liberty Heads."

"What's a slider?"

"He won't buy anything except B.U. or better. That means Brilliant Uncirculated. The only things better are choice, gem, and proof. This one here, he thinks it could just as well have been called A.U., or Almost Uncirculated. So if a coin is sort of in the middle, where you could maybe honestly call it one or the other, it's what a dealer calls a slider. I don't feel a thing for coins. I mean they're valuable, and they keep going up and all, but I don't want to own them. Let me get these back in the safe with the money."

When she came back I said, "What about some nice Sunday?"

"Oh, he's got a sailboat. And a lot of ideas."

"And you've already got somebody you'd rather go sailing with?"

"Yes, but not the way you mean that. You didn't tell me what kind of investigator you are, Mr. McGee."

"Travis or Trav, Mary Alice. I'm not any kind. I just try to find things people lose. On a percentage basis. Salvage consultant."

"I hope you find the stamps."

"You'll probably be able to tell me where they are."

She bit her lip and tilted her head. "Now that's kind of a rotten thing to say."

"How so?"

"I wouldn't do anything like that!"

"Like what?"

"Steal anything."

"You, dear? I mean you are a bright woman, and you probably saw something or heard something or know something which doesn't seem important at all, but is really very important. When you and I find out what it is you know, then it will tell us where the stamps are."

She frowned at me. "I don't like cute."

"What?"

"You said that the way you said it so I would take it wrong. You wanted me to. You wanted to see me react. Okay, I'm reacting. I don't like that kind of cute. Don't play little games with me. If I'm waiting for you to play games all the time, I won't be thinking of how to help, will I?"

"Good point."

"You did it on purpose?"

"Certainly. Can I take you to lunch?"

"She'll be back in ten minutes. Sure."

"Seems quiet around here. Don't you get bored?"

"Bored! I'm about ten thousand jobs behind right now. I've got a whole mess of new issues to mount. Our mailing is going to be late this month. It goes to six hundred people. I've got three appraisals I'm working on, for estates. I took two of them home to my place, because they aren't all that important moneywise. But the other is back in the safe, and it's pretty nice. It's nicer than Hirsh said it was going to be."

"And if you wanted to, you could pull a nice item out of it and replace it with something cheaper, and nobody would know?"

She turned away from me and began straightening albums on one of the shelves behind her.

"What's the matter?" I asked.

"I'm waiting until I can say something."

I waited. She turned back. "Here is the only way I can say it. Excuse my French, I don't give a goddamn what you would do or wouldn't do. Or what anybody else in the world does or doesn't do. If I steal, somebody knows. Me! That's why I can't, won't, or don't. And I am going to have lunch alone, thanks."

"I guess you should. I guess nobody is really worthy of breaking bread with you, dear. We ordinary mortals are unable to tell at first sight just how totally honest and decent and virtuous you really are. At first glance, you look like a sizable and pretty lady, and I have the vague feeling that many pretty ladies have done unpretty things over the last few thousand years. By all means, lunch alone and think clean and honest thoughts, dear."

She went white and then red with anger. She slapped her palm on the plate glass counter top. "But I am getting so goddamn tired of you accusing me of things!"

I yelled too but just a little louder. "So move the scenario elsewhere, you silly bitch! Move it to Chicago. Mr. X, the expert, buys for Mr. Y, the investor. Miss Z keeps the records and handles the merchandise. X, Y, and Z go to the bank a dozen times. The merchandise is stolen and replaced by cheap goods. Who do we blame, dear, X, Y, or Z? You were there! Who? Who? Who?"

She blinked and blinked, and the tears welled and spilled and trickled. She made an aimless gesture, and I took her hands and held them. She looked down and said, "I guess I just . . . I don't . . ."

The door opened, and the pressure on the mat bonged the overhead bell. Jane Lawson peered at us.

"What's going on? Are you crying, Mary Alice?"

"We were just going to lunch," I told Jane.

"Let go and I'll get my purse," Mary Alice said.

***

After we'd ordered a drink, Mary Alice went to the women's room to repair the tear damage. She came back smiling and sat and sipped and said, "You're kind of wearing, you know? Or maybe it's the whole rotten day. I feel ragged around all my edges."

"It doesn't show."

"On me it never does. I could be dying, and people would tell me how great I look. I always wanted to be one of those mysterious little girls with the hollow cheeks and the sad eyes. I wanted to have a kind of accent. You know. Like Hungarian."

"And all the sad-eyed little Hungarian girls want—"

"I know, I know. You've got a funny look on your face, Trav."

"I just found out I don't have to wonder about one thing that didn't fit too well. I don't have to accuse you again."

"Thanks for practically nothing."

I reached across and touched the bridge of her nose and pulled my hand back. "The answer is right there."

She looked puzzled, took out a mirror, and turned her head toward the light. "Oh. The little groove place, huh? From the glasses. But why would . . . oh, I think I see. If I inventoried all those things and cut the mounts to size and put them in the book, wouldn't I see they weren't the same when I looked back through the book that day? The answer is, I don't wear my glasses in the bank. The close work is all done. The answer is vanity. Okay. No matter what kind of frames I get, I look like a big goggly owl."

"How about contacts?"

"I can't adjust to the hard ones. You can't get bifocals in soft lenses. I wear them to see close, and then I'd have to take them off to see across the room or drive my car or cross the street. Or wear glasses for distance when I was wearing them."

"Oh."

"Jane says the only thing faster than light is me whipping my glasses off when a customer comes in. I know it's silly. I think my husband made me sort of supersensitive about them."

"How?"

"I shouldn't mention him because I don't like answering questions about him, and so I hardly ever do."

"No questions."

"Thanks. We better order, maybe?"

We ordered. After the food came, I said, "I know you didn't find out until this morning, but you must have *some* idea of how it was done."

"I can't believe it really happened. I keep thinking Hirsh has to be wrong. He's really old. Don't old people get weird ideas sometimes?"

"That would be a pretty complicated fantasy."

"But for me it's easier to believe."

"Why do you say that?"

"Look, it's the detail, the volume. If I had no interruptions and everything right there, it would take a *long* time to take the good items out and put the bad items in. There are thirty-six double-sided pages in that stock book. Seventy-two pages and about ten to go. Okay, that means about ten items per page. I'm pretty quick with my hands. They're kind of big but quick. So I have to take an item out of the horizontal strip and put it aside and then select the item that goes there and put it where it should be. Ten seconds to switch one? Fair guess? So six hundred single stamps, pairs, blocks, and plate blocks all in mounts would take six thousand seconds, or one hundred minutes, or an hour and forty minutes. And if I could get very whippy and do it in five seconds, it would still take ten minutes less than an hour. Just exactly how am I going to do that sitting practically touching two men at a little table under a bright light? The goodies *have* to be right there in that book! Or the bank is crooked. Take your choice."

"Would you be able to remember the arrangement, the way you put the items in the book?"

"Sure."

"And you could see well enough to—"

"I'm not *that* blind. I found the Barbados page, and it was too full to take the ones we'd brought that day, even if I'd moved the items closer together. And I like to arrange the stamps on the pages. You know. Spaced to look nice. It doesn't matter to Sprenger. He wouldn't care if we put them in a cigar box, I guess. But they are nice, and they represent a lot of money, and it is sort of . . . a response to the quality and the money to arrange them nicely."

"Do you think if you had your glasses on that day in the bank, you would have seen something was wrong?"

"From what Hirsh said this morning I should hope so! Bad centering. Stains and toning and fading. But not in every case."

"Why not?"

"Well . . . take Barbados, for example. Scott 53, the four-penny rose, is worth about fifty dollars unused, for a real good one. But Scott 53b in the same condition is worth fifteen hundred dollars anyway. Know what the silly difference is? Well, 53 is perf fourteen on all sides, and 53b is perf twelve and a half on the sides."

"What do those numbers mean?"

"Like fourteen. Those little holes so you can tear the stamps apart, it means there are fourteen holes in a space two centimeters long. You use a gauge to measure, something with the different gauges all printed on it. So you couldn't look in the stock book and tell with the naked eye if you had the ordinary 1875 four-penny rose or the special one. The special one is worth so much more because there were so few of them printed."

"And you certainly have one fantastic memory, Mary Alice."

She laughed. "I'm showing off. My memory isn't so great. I remember that one because I found one. Hirsh bought a collection of Colonials. It was so neat and orderly and well-labeled and mounted that we sort of took for granted the collector had really studied them. Well, it was just sort of luck. I took an ordinary one we had in stock and put it beside the one in the collection because I wanted to see which one was really best, for a customer. And the perforations didn't look right. I used the one stamp to measure the other. After the customer left, I used a gauge. Then, on my own, I sent it off to the Philatelic Foundation in New York, with a fee in advance, and in six weeks it came back with the certification it was 53b. So I put it on Hirsh's desk as a surprise. He put it in Sprenger's investment collection, and he gave me a hundred-dollar bonus. It's really *fun* to find something like that, you know? Like mining for gold, I guess."

Though I had no empathy for her excitement, I liked the expression on her face, the look of enthusiasm. To each his own. I wondered why some man hadn't made a lot of extra effort to keep hold of this girl. The special, bonus size. A lifelong supply of goodies. But she had warned me nicely about asking questions.

I decided abruptly that I was going to take the lady at her own valuation. It is a process of logic, I guess. If she had the art, the style, the exquisite ability to project a total plausibility regardless of what stress I'd put on her, then she would not have spent five years in a funny little stamp store in Miami. Pretense requires vast expenditures of energy. That much guile would have sought better stalking places.

Besides, I liked the neat little creases at the corners of her mouth. I liked that tricky blue shade of her iris. I liked the genuine big-girl hunger with which she stashed away the medium-adequate meal. I liked the way the black hair had a coarse, healthy gloss and the way she tossed and swung it back out of her way.

"Okay," I said, "you are no longer on the suspect list."

"Are you sure you want to do me such a big favor?"

"I know how impressed you must be."

"Are you suspicious of practically everybody?"

"Practically."

"That must be a hell of a way to go through life, fellow."

"It's only when I'm working. The rest of the time I'm an amiable, trusting, innocent slob."

"Isn't it steady work?"

"It could be, but I don't let it. When I get a few bucks ahead, I retire. Retirement is more fun at my age than it would be later."

"You've got a point. Also, you don't look married. Which makes it easier, huh?"

"Just one thing about you raises a question."

"Such as?"

"You have a sedentary job, Mary Alice, and from what you said, I guess you work at home too. But I know good conditioning when I see it. You walk around on springs."

She grinned, clenched her fist, and made a muscle. At her invitation I reached over and prodded it with a thumb.

"Very substantial," I said.

"I have to live with it, Trav, or give up. I'm big, and I've got good coordination. I ran with a pack of boys from the time I could run. I played all their games and all the girl-games too. I can win canes and boxes of taffy at those weight-guessing places. What would you guess me at? Don't try to flatter me."

"Hmmm. Between a hundred and thirty-five and a hundred and forty?"

"One fifty-six this morning, stripped, on my very good scales. I've got big heavy bones, and I grew a lot of muscle tissue at all the games. So I'm in training always, because if I let things go, they really go. The muscles turn to lard, and everything starts to sag and wobble around, very nasty. I do the Canadian thing. And I make all my points—men's points, by the way—every week of my life. I've done it so long, I *love* it."

"I dog it. I get soft enough so that it bothers me, and then I have to go to work on it."

"You look in real good shape, you know?"

"I've been working on it."

We looked at each other. The blue eyes seemed to get bigger, just big enough to let me in. I had the feeling I was reaching down into that blueness, to where something had gone *click,* startling both of us. I heard her breath catch, and then she took a deep deep breath, looking away as she did so, breaking the unexpected contact. I signaled the waiter, making a writing motion in the palm of my hand. He nodded and came toward the table, sorting through his checks.

We walked back side by side and about twenty inches apart.

"Thank you for a very nice lunch, Travis."

"You are most welcome, Mary Alice."

"Like Hirsh said, I want to help you any way I can."

"You've been a lot of help."

"Have I?"

"That estimate of the time it would take to change the items in the stock book was useful. It helps me see the whole picture."

"I'm glad."

"Perhaps when we get back to the store, you can let me inspect one of those books."

"Of course."

"My car is over there in that lot. Would you like to look at it?"

She stopped and frowned at me. "Why should I want to look at your car?"

"Maybe because it is older than you are."

"It is?"

"It's a pickup truck."

"Really?"

"Do you want to look at it?"

"Why not?"

As we neared it, I pointed it out. "Yech," she said, "what a frightful shade of blue." And then she said, "But it's a homemade pickup truck!" And then she said, "My God, it's a Rolls-Royce." Then she braced herself against it and laughed. No silvery little tinkly giggle. "Haw ho haw hah haw. Oh, God. Oh, ho haw!" A bray. A contralto bugling.

"If you think Miss Agnes is funny, you should see my houseboat, where I live."

"Whu-whu-whu-what's funny about *that?*"

"I can't explain it. I have to show you."

"Yuh-yuh-you *do* that. Oh, dear." She found her Kleenex and wiped her eyes and blew her nose. We headed for the office.

"Is it really *that* funny?"

"No. I hurt your feelings or something?"

"No."

"It . . . it was relief, kind of. When you said look at your car I thought, Oh, God, another of *those*. You know. You'd have some kind of nasty little thing about two feet high and ten feet wide and twenty feet long, with fifty dials and a speedometer that goes up to two hundred. And I'd have to admire the ugly damn childish thing or even ride in it if you insisted. Then you'd show me your key that fits every Playboy Club in America and overseas, and then you'd try to do the old magic trick."

"What old magic trick?"

"You know. All of a sudden you turn into a motel."

"And you laughed because none of that is going to happen?"

"And because that Miss Agnes is a very *dear* automobile," she said, pushing open the door to the shop.

7

On Friday morning I cleaned up after my breakfast, took a couple of overdue loads to the Laundromat, and sat and peaceably watched some women get their loads whiter than mine. I was not torn with jealousy. I wished them well. On the way back a fat man on a rackety little trail bike nearly ran me down, then yelled out his estimate of my ancestry and lineage. I smiled and nodded and wished him well. I remembered vaguely that the city fathers had put the roust on me. Move off your boat or leave town. I wished them well too. Nourish yourself well at that public trough, boys. Gobble any goodies which happen to float by.

Meyer was sitting on the dock, legs swinging, waiting for me. He came aboard. He stood behind me as I stowed the laundry.

"How did you make out?" he asked.

"Beautiful."

"What?"

"This is the best time of year. Right?"

"I stayed and talked to Hirsh for a while. By the time I got around to calling the shop, you were gone."

"We left early. Mary Alice and me."

"Turn around, Travis."

"What?"

"Turn around a minute and look at me."

"Sure."

He stared and nodded. "I see."

"What do you see?"

"That you're going to try to help Hirsh Fedderman."

"What? Oh, sure. That's right. As right as—"

"Rain?"

"Whatever you say, old buddy."

When my chores were done, we had a talk. I pulled my wandering attention in from somewhere out beyond left field and tried to settle down to the task at hand. I remembered what Mary Alice had said about how long the switch would take and how incredible it seemed to her, how she wondered if any switch had really taken place at all. I tried her approach on Meyer.

"I have to believe Hirsh," Meyer said. "If he saw it, he saw it. His mind is very quick and keen."

"She really knows all that stuff."

"What?"

"All that stamp stuff."

"I would think it would be more remarkable if, after five years, she didn't know all about it."

"What?"

"Never mind. Good God!"

"I wanted to give her a ride in Miss Agnes. It was a slow afternoon. Jane told us to take off. I followed Mary Alice to her place, in her old yellow Toyota. We had a drink in Homestead and dinner in Naples."

"Naples?!"

"I know. We were just drifting along, talking about this and that, and Naples seemed like the closest place. So we came back across Alligator Alley and came here, and I showed her the *Flush*. It knocked her out, like Agnes did. I like the way she laughs."

"You like the way she laughs."

"That's what I said. So then I drove her home and by then it was too late to even stop in for a nightcap."

"How late is too late?"

"Quarter past five."

"No wonder your face looks blurred."

"Meyer, the whole twelve hours seemed like twenty or thirty minutes. We just hit the edges of all the things there are to talk about."

"Are you going to be able to think about Hirsh Fedderman's problem?"

"Whose what?"

He went away, shaking his head, making big arm gestures at the empty space ahead of him. If he had come back, I would have told him that I had almost decided that there was no problem at all, that Fedderman had been mistaken. If there is no way at all for something to have happened, the best initial assumption is that it didn't happen.

On that Friday I arrived at the store at closing time and drove Jane Lawson back to her place, a so-called garden apartment in a huge development of yesteryear, about a half-hour bus ride from Fedderman's store.

She sat erect on the edge of the seat and said, "Our gal was pretty punchy all day, Trav."

"I haven't been exactly alert."

"Now turn left again and here we are. I hate that miserable bus, but it would be a worse bus ride for Linda, so she takes the car." She had already told me that Linda was the elder of her two, a scholarship freshman at the University of Miami in Coral Gables. Judy was a junior in high school. Sixteen and eighteen. I had noticed she talked about Linda quite a lot and had very little to say about Judy.

She tried the door and then got out her keys and said, "Excuse the way the place will probably look. Working mother and two teen gals. I've tried. But they have a tendency to hang their clothes up in midair."

The living room was small and oven-hot. She hurried over to a great big window unit and turned it on high cool, and then raised her voice to carry over the thunder of compressor and fan. "The house rule is the last one out turns the beast off. It eats electricity. But it will chill this place fast, and then I can turn it down to where we can hear ourselves think. Isn't it terrible? Fix you a drink?"

"If there's a beer?"

"There could be. Let me look."

She came smiling back with a cold bottle of beer and a tall glass and excused herself to change out of her working clothes. There was too much furniture in the room. The fireplace was fake. There was a double frame on the mantel, and in one side of it was an incongruously young man with a nice grin, Air Force uniform, lieutenant bars, pilot wings. In the other half was a picture of the same lieutenant in civilian clothes, sports jacket, and slacks. He was holding a baby and looking down into its invisible face while a Jane Lawson, eighteen years younger, stood by him, no higher than his shoulder, smiling up at him.

There was an alcove off the living room with some high-fidelity equipment, with racks of tapes in bright dog-eared boxes, with tilted stacks of records. The room was getting cool very quickly. I went over and checked the controls on the beast and cut it from high cool to cool, from max fan to medium. It shuddered and smoothed to about the sound of a good chain saw on idle. I was back looking at the pictures when she came out in an overblouse and faded blue shorts and sandals. She was a slight and pretty woman, with the residual marks of old tensions in her face, with a firmness to her mouth and corners of her jaw.

"That's Jerry," she said. "It's seems incredible. He was stopped right there in time, just thirteen months after this picture. In another year Linda will be as old as I was when I met Jerry."

"Combat?"

"No. He was trade school. He wore the ring. They used to have more flameouts in fighter jets back then. He was on a night exercise, just two of them. That particular model, the way it worked, there was an interlock so that if you didn't jettison the canopy first, you couldn't eject, you couldn't make the charge go off to blow the seat out. It was supposed to be a safety thing, so a green pilot couldn't get nervous and blow himself through the canopy. But his canopy release jammed and all the way down he told his wingman exactly what he was doing to try to free it. No messages for anybody. Just technical information. A real pro."

"They must have to take a special course in cool."

"If I sound bitter, it's because they were already turning out a better canopy release thing and making the change in the field as the kits came in."

So I told her about the radio tape years ago, made in Lauderdale and broadcast only once before NASA came galloping in, all sweaty, and confiscated it. The interviewer had asked one of those good and tough-minded and freethinking men of the early days of space orbiting how he felt as the rocket was taking off. Maybe it was because he had heard that question too many times. He answered it with a question. 'How would *you* feel, taking off, sitting up there on top of fifty thousand parts, knowing that every one had been let to the lowest bidder?' "

"Grissom?" she asked. I nodded. "I thought so. It sounds like Gus. I knew those guys. I came close to marrying one. The girls were little. They liked him. I was half in love and telling myself the girls needed a father. So maybe the new father was going to end up frozen hard as marble, circling us all forever, haunting us all forever. I dillydallied and

I dithered and shillyshallied and all those words. And the train left the station before I could make up my mind whether to buy a ticket. Maybe it's best. Who knows? Well, my troubles aren't what you came to talk about."

"This problem could give you trouble you don't need. If the investment items are gone, Hirsh is going to have to make it good with Sprenger. With a man like Sprenger, I don't think there'd be a choice, even if Hirsh did want to look for an out. It might clean him out. It might take the store and the stock to do it."

She was sitting in the corner of the couch. She pulled her legs up under her and made a face. "That would really be rotten. For him, I mean. He's been so good to me. I can't believe I've been there fifteen years. I answered a blind ad, and when I found out what it was, I didn't want it at all. He liked my letter. He begged me to try it. He offered me too much money. I couldn't even type. I thought somebody was going to take advantage of this crazy little man, so it might as well be me. I didn't find out until later he'd interviewed at least thirty-five girls before me without finding anybody he wanted. He was looking for a nut who'd go to a business school nights and learn to type just because it would make things easier for him. Trav, don't talk about the troubles I could have. I'll manage. With the pay and the pension and being able to use the PX at Homestead, I've stuck rainy-day money away. Jerry's folks have helped some, and they'd help more if I had to let them. The thing is to help Hirsh so he doesn't have to sell everything."

"That's what Mary Alice says too, but she can't really believe the good stuff isn't still in that book in the safety deposit box."

"Hirsh doesn't imagine things like that. Know what I keep thinking?"

"What?"

"Don't tell Hirsh. If one investment account could be cleaned out like that, so could the others, couldn't they? He hasn't had a chance to look at any one of the other five during the past two weeks."

"You certainly know how to relax a person, Jane."

"You thought of that already, huh?"

"They're all handled alike, pretty much, aren't they?"

"Yes and no. The oldest account is Mr. Riker Benedict, and that was started about the same time I came to work. In fact, it was the first account Hirsh set up that way, mostly because Mr. Benedict couldn't really believe that the things Hirsh wanted to buy for him would keep going up in value year after year. He's bought nineteen classic pieces in fifteen years, famous items. And he's looking for another one now. The collection is worth so much more than Mr. Benedict put into it, there's really no point in keeping on with it in the same way. But it's a ceremony, adding a new piece. The two of them will spend half a morning in the bank going over the great rarities, one by one, whether they are adding a new one or not. With the other accounts I would say that sometimes they go over the things previously purchased and sometimes they don't. The Sprenger account is the one where he never looks at the old purchases or the new ones either. He just sits there like so much dead meat. He nods, shrugs, grunts, and that's that."

"What would happen to those accounts if anything happened to Mr. Fedderman?"

"That's all worked out in the agreement. It's clear that he has no ownership interest in anything in the investment accounts, and his lawyer has a power of attorney in the event of Mr. Fedderman's death, and I think it's on file at the bank with a signature card. In the agreement the lawyer and the investor meet at the bank along with an appraiser certified by the APS, and the investment account is appraised, and if the current estimated resale value is higher than the breaking point in the agreement, the account is then accepted by the investor, and the agreement is surrendered. If the resale is less, the difference between it and the guaranteed price becomes a claim against the estate. But there would be no question of a claim of any kind on five of them. And on the stuff Hirsh has bought for Sprenger, I think Hirsh would come out a little bit ahead, actually, the way the market is going. You see, he hasn't really been taking any risk at all. This was just an easy way of easing the fears of people with risk capital. Sort of satisfaction-or-your-money-cheerfully-refunded. You can do that when the product is really tops."

"Unless the product mysteriously disappears."

"It's made him sick. It really has. Physically sick."

"I keep wondering how come Mary Alice keeps all the records and does all the work on the investment accounts."

"Because I've been there longer? I used to do it, and then when Moosejaw retired and Mary Alice came on, I taught her the routines."

"Moosejaw?"

"Excuse me. Miss Moojah, a maiden lady with a very strong personality. A creature of legend. She didn't believe in the alarm system. There are eight buttons in handy, inconspicuous places. She kept a toy baseball bat under the cash register. Twice when she was alone, a would-be robber aimed a gun at her. Twice she picked up her bat and let him have it. One needed two lumps before he went down, and one collapsed on the first one. Then she'd push the button. It made Hirsh so mad he couldn't speak. He just made gobbling sounds. He was so afraid the next one would kill her. Anyway, I'm glad to have Mary Alice do the scut work. I'm sort of more into decision-making."

"Such as?"

"Well, the routine things, of course, that Hirsh hasn't time or patience for. When to reorder and how much. Albums and packets and mounts and so on. But the part I like best is watching the market and studying it and advising Hirsh. It's a lot of work, but he says I have a real talent for it. I study the changes in the catalog prices as they come out: Scott, Minkus, Stanley Gibbons, Sanabria. Also, I get the list of prices realized from all the leading auction houses and find out what the lots are bringing in New York and on the West Coast and in London. It isn't all up, you know. I saw some little early warnings three years ago on Italian issues. They'd moved up or been pushed up too fast. So we had some pretty good things in counter stock, and some real good things in the investment accounts, and Hirsh moved everything out quickly. He lets me run a little risk account, like speculation in inventory. I saw that early Canada was looking active, so I put the money in those issues, and they've really moved. They were always good, but sort of stodgy. Now they're glamour. I think that—Do you *really* care about all this?"

"Would Mary Alice rather be making decisions?"

She pursed her lips. "No, I don't really think so. I'm more the cerebral type, and she's the manual type. That's oversimplifying. She loves to cut mounts and fix up pages. She loves to appraise estate stuff, item by item, and bring out the watermarks and count the perforations and check the color charts. She'd rather not have me handling any of the really good things. She got *furious* at me last year. When there is envelope paper stuck to the back of a stamp, you put it in a little wet box called a Stamp Lift, and after a while you can peel that paper right off the stamp. The old gum softens in the dampness. It was a pretty good Columbian, a four-dollar denomination with a light cancel. I took it out too soon, and I peeled part of the stamp right off. That's like making confetti out of a couple of hundred-dollar bills. She got so mad she wouldn't talk to me for hours."

"But usually she's easy to get along with?"

"A personal or official question, sir?"

I wondered if my ears looked as red as they felt. "It has to be personal, doesn't it?"

"Who should blame you? That is a pretty vivid hunk of lady. And you seem to have that old familiar look."

"Fox in the henhouse?"

She laughed. "More like a pro linebacker trying to line up on the wrong side. But on the personal side, I can't tell you much. She's fun to work with. The three of us make a good little team. I don't see her after work. Maybe there have been a lot of men trying to get close to that. If it works out the way it works out with the customers and the guys who work near the store, then they don't get anywhere either."

"How am I doing?"

"Who knows? It's early. I shouldn't give advice. I would go very very slow."

"What's her trouble?"

"I don't really know. I don't know a thing about her marriage. She won't talk about it at all. And as far as I can tell, she has absolutely no sex life at all, and that is a lot of big healthy girl with a lot of little motors running. From a couple of casual remarks I'd say that she certainly was turned on to it at one time. The only thing I can think of is that it was such a rotten, hideous marriage that it somehow turned her all the way off. And she keeps herself quieted down with all that exercise. The impression I get, the minute the man makes the first grab, she's off and running, and he never gets another chance. You spent a lot of hours with her. What did you really find out about her?"

I went back over it in my mind. "Not a hell of a lot. No family, apparently. And she lived in Philadelphia when she was a kid."

"And also in Scranton. I've asked her direct questions. She says, 'Jane, someday when we have a lot of time, I'm going to tell you all about it.' But we haven't had enough time yet."

The door opened onto the shallow hallway, and a young girl came in. She was slender, taller than her mother, with brown hair darker than Jane's dark blond. Her hair was long and lifeless, half hiding a sallow and strangely expressionless little face. She wore missionary-barrel work pants, too heavy for September in Florida, a soiled body shirt. Her feet were bare. Her hands were as grimy as her feet. She carried a notebook and two schoolbooks in the crook of her arm.

She gave us one swift, opaque glance and headed past us toward the rear of the apartment.

"Judy!" her mother said. She stopped and turned slowly.

"You want something?"

"This is Mr. McGee. My daughter, Judy."

"Hello, Judy."

She gave me a briefer taste of that original look. She swept it across me. I was absolutely without meaning to her. She was something in a forest, aware only of other creatures like herself. I was a tree, and she did not give a damn what brand of tree. She half nodded and made a small sound and turned back on her way. I sat down again.

"Judy?" her mother said.

She stopped in the doorway. "Now what?"

"I want to talk to you."

"So talk."

"Not this minute. I'm talking to Mr. McGee. I just don't want to come looking for you and find you've gone out again."

"They're waiting on me."

"Go tell them to be patient then."

"Screw that. I don't want you hassling me. I told you that already."

"Go to your room and wait right there!"

"Is that an order?"

"What does it sound like?"

"Shove it, you silly old bitch. Phone the probation officer and tell him I've gone out. Okay?"

Jane Lawson started up when the girl left and then sat back down again. She put her fists on her bare knees and bent forward at the waist and rested her cheeks on her fists. In a little while she straightened, blinking, and gave me a frail smile. "Sorry."

"There's a lot of it going around."

"Judy . . . is at a difficult age. It's very difficult for young people these days."

"Don't you want to go talk to her?"

She gave me a grateful and appreciative look. "I'll just be a minute."

Very difficult for young people these days. Or any days. In what golden epoch was being a teenager a constant joy? There has always been a generation gap. It is called twenty years. Too much talk about unresponsive government, napalm, irrelevant education. Maybe the real point is that young lives have no accepted focal point. The tribe gives them no responsibilities, no earned privileges, no ceremonial place. In the family unit they do not fit into a gap between generations, because the generations are diffused. Maybe that is why they are scurrying pell-mell back to improvised tribal conditions, to communes. The schools have tried, *in loco parentis,* to fill a vacuum, condition the young on a fun-reward system. It has been a rotten try. The same vacuum spawns the rigid social order of the Jesus freaks, another try at structure and meaning. The communes themselves are devices of the privileged, because if everybody went into communes, the communes would become impossible.

So the kids float. They ram around, amble around, talk and dream, and rediscover all the more simplistic philosophical paradoxes. And the ones in the majority who make it (as apparently Miss Linda Lawson was making it) find some bottom within themselves. A place to stand. A meaning derived from fractionated nonsense. They are not a brighter generation than ever before. They have been exposed to more input, so much they have been unable to appraise and assimilate it but are able to turn it into immediate output, impressively glib and commercially sincere.

And the few that can't make it, like the younger daughter, exude the ripe odor of the unwashed as opposed to the animal tang of healthy sweat. Their tangled and musty locks make the shining tresses of the others repugnant to all those Neanderthal spooks who would hate and resent youngness no matter how it might be packaged. The lost ones, like Judy, get so far into the uppers and the downers and the mind benders—hardly ever knowing what they are taking, seeking only something in the blood that will bring the big rush, and warp the world—that if told it would make a nice high, they would stuff a dead toad into their ear. The lost ones trade the clap germs back and forth until they cultivate strains as resistant to penicillin as were the Oriental brands of yore.

It is relaxing to climb down off the egomanic pedestal of guilt and blame and shame and responsibility and say, "Who told me I have to understand the causes?" There are bad kids. There are bad trees in an orchard, bad apples on any tree, sick worms in any decaying apple. A world of perfection would be absurd. Even Doris Day couldn't sustain that kind of concept. Who needs it? We need the flawed ones, the lost ones, as a form of emotional and social triangulation, to tell us if we've gained an inch since Hammurabi. Rough rough rough on the people who love them, but by some useful design in the human fabric, the rejects manage to kill most of that love by the time they are grown. Think of it, dear Jane Lawson, as a trick of nature whereby some great smirking cowbird came long ago and laid its egg in your nest.

She came back in and said, "Thanks anyway."

"Something wrong?"

"She'd gone out the back way. I . . . had to check up on one of my sneaky spy tricks. That green rubber band around her books. I put a hair from my head under it the day before yesterday. It's still there. If she's not going to school, they're going to pick her up. They'll put her in a state school for girls."

"Probation for what?"

"I'd rather not say. She's in my custody, but I can't control her." The tears threatened to come again. "My lawyer said if we could find a place that would take her, we could jump the gun and go to the judge and get a transfer of custody. A private place. But either they won't take her or the cost is so fantastic. . . . He's still looking." She hit her knee with her fist. "What am I supposed to do? Chain her to the wall in her room? Beat her senseless?"

What do you say? My best guess would do Jane Lawson no good whatsoever. My best guess was that the girl was on the edge of leaving for good. And in some city as yet unknown, she would be studied with great care by experts. And if they were to decide it was merchandise worth salvage, she might indeed be beaten into total submission, cleaned up, dressed up, trained, and marketed for a few years. The merchandising experts cruise the bus terminals, and they watch the downtown streets for young girls carrying suitcases or packs. Impersonal appraisal. No uggos, no fatties, no gimps, no rich kids, nothing too too young.

"You didn't come here to get involved in a family problem," she said. She sighed. "Maybe in time she'll straighten out."

"Sure," I said. We smiled at each other. It was that special social smile people use when they don't believe anything they are saying.

8

When I phoned Mary Alice early on Saturday morning, she said that I'd caught her just before she went out the door. She said she was going to stop and see how Hirsh was and then do some shopping, and then she was going to her health club and work out, like she did every Saturday. What did I have in mind? Nothing special and nothing in particular. I had noticed the ocean was flat calm, and the weather people said the wind out of the west would hold all day, and I'd had a runabout tuned, and it was running well. So, running down outside, I could make it in very good time, and I knew a place that put up a good lunch, and I thought maybe we could run down the bay to a place I knew where we could have our own private patch of Atlantic beach for a swim and picnic. What she could do would be set the time when I could pick her up, say at the Royal Biscayne Yacht Club. She could leave her car there. I could drop her off there from the *Muñequita* later, or if she wanted, she could come back up to Lauderdale with me, and I'd get her back to Miami somehow.

She thought about it and decided that maybe the health club could be canceled out with no problems. That left the necessary shopping and seeing Hirsh and how about noon at that yacht club, okay? I told her twelve thirty would be better for me, and she said fine.

I phoned the lunch order and told them when I would pick it up. I was unsnapping the big tarp cover off the *Muñequita* when somebody called my name. Two men stood on the dock, silhouetted against the glare of blue sky, looking down at me. I said I was indeed he. I freed the rest of the snaps, folded and stowed the tarp, climbed up onto the side deck of the *Flush,* and went aft, wanting a better look at them before deciding whether or not to ask them aboard.

"Permission to come aboard?" one of them said.

"Please do." They came onto the shallow aft deck. Solid handshakes. One was Davis and one was Harris. No first names volunteered. I have spent a lot of years making quick guesses, and at times my health has depended on accuracy as well as speed.

Both in their thirties, both of a size, six feet or a hair under, both somewhere shy of two hundred pounds, both softening in the middle and around the jaws, but not too much. The dark one had a Joe Namath hairdo and a villain's mustache. The other was red-brown and crinkly, with a swoop of sideburns.

The first impression was that they were used to working together. Men who do not know each other well express an awareness of each other in body movements and expressions. Familiar partners act more as if each were alone.

I couldn't put any geography together. The voices were Everywhere voices, like the men who do local news on television. Mustache was tanned, and Sideburns was permanently burned several shades of red, several degrees of peeling. Big hands. Old nicks on the knuckles. A very intent expression in the eyes, at odds with casual stance. I could read it very close to cop, but a few things canceled that out. The teeth were the persuasive, gleaming white you get from expensive show-biz caps. Twenty-dollar haircuts. A drift of male cologne, leather and pine and fresh paper money. Summer-weight knits, both slacks and shirts, and shoes so funny-looking they had to be very in. Mustache had a fat gold seal ring on his pinky with a green stone in it.

In the back of my head all the troops hopped up out of the sack, grabbed weapons, and piled into the vehicles. They raced out to the edge of camp and set up a perimeter defense and then lay and waited, weapons off safety, loaded clips in place, grenades handy.

"Can we talk, Mr. McGee?"

"No reason why not," I said. I sat on the rail, one leg swinging free, the other foot braced, the knee locked.

Mustache was Davis. Memory trigger: Jeff Davis, dark hair, mustache. Harris: Harris tweed, tweedledee and dum. I didn't believe either name. I made no suggestions about where to sit. There was no awkward social hesitation. Davis folded himself into the deck chair, and Harris sat on the curve of railing six feet from me.

"We're representing somebody," Harris said. "He doesn't want his name brought into the deal yet."

"What deal?"

"There's a situation he wants you to look into," Davis said. "He thinks he's been had. He thinks he got tricked into the short end of a deal."

"You're confusing me, gentlemen."

"What's to confuse?" Harris asked, faking bewilderment. "He may want you to take a shot at salvaging the deal for him, getting back what he got conned out of. Isn't that what you do?"

"Do what?"

"*Salvage* work!"

"I don't do anything. I'm retired. Oh, sometimes I do a favor for a friend. I think the man you represent needs a licensed investigator."

"No, Mr. McGee," said Harris. "He needs you. He was very firm on that particular point. The way this thing is shaping up, he maybe might need you at a moment's notice. So he would be very grateful to you if you would just sit tight and wait to hear." He reached into his pants and took some bills folded once out of his side pocket. He pulled the bills out of a gold clip which said "After Tax" in block letters. He crackled and snapped five one hundreds, one five hundred free of the pack, reclipped the rest and put it away, folded the bills and took a long reach and shoved them into my shirt pocket. "Just to show he isn't kidding around."

"I couldn't help anybody I don't know."

"If he needs your help, you'll *get* to know him."

I pulled the money out and held it toward Harris. He pulled back. I tossed them into Davis's lap and said, "Sorry."

"You busy or something?" Harris asked with just a shade too much casual innocence.

"I'm doing a favor for a friend of a friend. Trying to, at least."

"What I think you should do is drop that one," Davis said.

"Should I?"

"The man we're talking about," he continued, "he heard about you someplace or other, and he got a good impression. He's not used to asking people for help, and they say they're busy or some damn thing."

"We all have these little disappointments in life."

"Is that smart-ass?" Harris asked.

"I didn't mean it that way. Think of it this way, gentlemen. If we all got exactly what we wanted all the time, wouldn't life get very dull?"

"This man gets what he wants," Davis said.

"Not this time."

"Suppose he wants to give you a choice, McGee," Harris said. "Suppose he keeps the deal open, and when you get out of the hospital and you can move around again pretty good, he sends somebody to ask you again."

I stared at him and then at his partner. "Now come *on!* What's your script anyway? Kick my spine loose and drive away in your 1928 La-Salle? You two looked and acted and talked like you know the names and numbers of all the players. All of a sudden, Harris, you open up with this hospital shit, and you sound like somebody got you from Central Casting."

Davis in the deck chair gave me the smile of a lazy hyena. "Every once in a while he does that," he said. "Remember that old movie *The French Connection?* Want to know how many times this crazy turd went to see it?"

"Oh, come on, Dave," Harris said petulantly.

"The thing is," Davis said, "he gets hung up on some kind of image thing, and he likes to use it when he talks to civilians, because if they've been to all the same movies, they almost wet their pants when Harry comes on hard."

"You should learn to read people," I told Harry Harris.

Harry shrugged. "So it worked. That was one of the questions, right? To find out if McGee was—"

Davis cut him off. He evened the edges of the six pieces of money as he spoke and folded them once lengthwise. "Suppose you happened to be nibbling around the edge of something where this man we're talking about has an interest, and so he gets a reading on you, and he gets some kind of idea of what you do. So let's imagine that having you in the picture makes him back up and take another look at that particular deal. So not knowing how you fit, he thinks the easy way is to give you a retainer so you would come in on his side of it if things are getting fancy, if somebody has been stupid enough to play games with him, even though that somebody came highly recommended."

"How would this man think I'd fit?"

"What he said was you might even be trying to work out a way to give him the short end of that deal."

"I'm only interested in getting back something someone has lost. When there's no other way to get it back."

"The man could have thought you were trying some kind of Robin Hood bit. Or he might think you could be conned."

"Can we start using his name?" I asked.

"It's better we don't," Harris said. "Dave and me, we might not even know his name. Lots of things go through channels."

Davis said, "I can tell you one thing. The man would feel better about this trip we took if you would take this round one." He held the money out. "Kind of like a sign you're not trying to slip it to him. You don't have to back off from anything you have going on. It would make him keep on wondering about you if you don't take it."

I took a step and took the bills and put a haunch back onto the railing. They both looked relieved. The jargon changes constantly due to the telephone taps. Ten bills made a round one. Five round ones to a victor. When we first heard that, Meyer deduced that it came from V for Victor, V being the Roman five. Two victors make a spot. X marks the spot, maybe? Ten spots make a big round one. Ten big round ones make a mil, and thus we are back into English.

I was not certain about my own judgment in taking it. It set up a dependency relationship. If you take the money of a man like Sprenger and then work against him, they can find you behind a shed in Tampa in the trunk of a stolen car, shot-gunned and six days dead in the bake-oven heat, a silver coin in the rotting mouth.

We shook hands again. Away they went. Dave Davis. Harry Harris. I saw them stop and admire a big new Rybovitch fishing machine, looking like a pair of mod Indiana businessmen hunting for a charter. Dave Davis and Harry Harris?

I went below, up to the bow and down through the service hatch into the bow bilge. I opened the false hull and stepped back from the slosh of seawater that spilled down and started the automatic bilge pump. I reached in and got my waterproof box, opened it, and put nine bills in with the dwindling reserve fund. It fattened it a little, but not enough.

I was beginning to run late. On the way over to pick up the picnic lunch, I wondered just what micro-percentage of the thousand dollars I had taken came from the pocket money and lunch money of Judy Lawson's high school class. I wondered what kind of little death they were peddling in the girls' rooms this week.

I buttoned up the *Flush,* tight and secure. I wanted to talk over the visit with Meyer and get his opinion, but there just wasn't time. All the required gear was in the *Muñequita.* She burbled her way past the moored fortune in transient and local cruisers and motor sailers and elegant houseboats. A few friends hallooed. Teak baked in the sun, and brightwork shimmered, and toilet paper danced in my wake in the bourbon-colored water of the boat basin. I went down past the gas docks and under the bridge, nudging the throttles up as I went through a little tide chop in the pass. I turned her south short of the sea buoy and angled out. The port engine coughed out at three thousand rpm, kept dropping below two thousand, building up to three, and coughing out again. I called Davey some unhappy names. He swore he had them both running perfectly. I pulled them both down to idle, waited a few minutes, and then popped them up to full throttle. Little doll came surging up onto her plane and scooted, with rpm moving up into the red.

I backed them off to thirty-eight hundred rpm, listened, made my apologies to Davey Hoople, master marine mechanic, age nineteen. A half-millimeter nudge on the starboard throttle put them into final perfect sync. I was out far enough to make my straight shot to the Miami ship channel, so I held it on the heading and threw it into automatic pilot. I watched the needle as it searched. I had it about a degree too much west, so I took it out and tried again and hit it perfectly. I took a brew out of the cooler and stood on the pilot seat and sat on the backrest part, sea wind in my face, the horizon misty-pale and glassy, the *Muñequita* doing her thirty-eight knots without effort, the wake straight as a line on a chart.

I kept trying to sort out my guesses as to how and why Sprenger had sent a couple of members of the first team, but some bottomless blue eyes kept getting in the way. Fine day, fine boat, fine beer, and it had been a long long time since blue eyes. So I wrapped up the whole problem and shoved it into a cubicle over in a side corner of my mind and slapped the little door shut. A man should have his weekends, no matter what he does.

I tried to spot a yellow Toyota in the parking area as I came easing down the line of private markers into the protected basin of the Royal Biscayne Yacht Club. The smallboat area was off to the left beyond the rows of yachts and was built of those floating slabs of aluminum and flotation material which moved up and down with the tide, simplifying access and mooring. A young Cuban, uniformed in the club colors, came running out, waving me off. "No, no, no!" he yelled. "Ess private! Ess cloob."

"*Soy socio, hombre.*"

He looked startled and uncertain. He looked back over his shoulder for help. "*¿Eh? ¿Nuevo possible, señor?*"

"*No. De muchos años.*"

"*Pero—*"

"*Momentito. Ayúdame, por favor. Tengo mi tarjeta de socio.*"

He hesitated, then took the bow line and made it fast. I swung in and cut the engines and jumped out with the stern line. After I made it fast I went back aboard and opened the shallow drawer under the chart bin and found my card. I handed it to him.

He frowned and then smiled. "*Ah. Especial. Bienvenido,* Meester McGee."

I read his name on the pocket. "Thank you, Julio." I dropped the card back in the drawer. I told him I was looking for a tall, dark-haired lady who was to meet me at twelve thirty. It was now twelve forty-five. No, he had not seen such. Would I please come to the small house of the dockmaster and sign the boat register? It would be my pleasure. He hoped he had not offended me. I said that it pleased me to see such care and diligence.

A few years back the cloob had a very ugly problem, and a member had asked me to help them deal with it. I posed as a guest and, with a little good management and a lot of good luck, solved it without confrontations or publicity. The Board of Governors wanted to give me some special token of appreciation. They knew I had as much chance of slipping through their membership committee as a hog of entering heaven. So at the next meeting they amended the bylaws to permit one special membership, without initiation fees or dues, to be awarded by the board. I was nominated, seconded, and voted in, and then they voted to rescind the amendment to the bylaws. I seldom use it and knew it was childish to use that way of impressing, or trying to impress, Mary Alice McDermit.

I walked up the steps from the dock area to the edge of the lawns that slant down toward the water and the seawalls. A walkway and avenue of coconut palms led up to the main buildings of the club. The old

Moorish portion has two new wings attached, wings as stark and modern as anything by I. M. Pei. So all of it together looks like a wedding cake for the Arabian bride of a suitor from Stonehenge. I could walk up there to the lofty paneled coolth of the men's bar and order one of the finest planter's punches known to man and sign for it. The bill would come in due course, on thirty-pound parchment with an engraved logo. I could stand and drink my drink, looking out through high windows at a dancing pool full of wives and children and daughters and grandchildren.

At least half the tennis courts were being used by hot-weather maniacs, out there going *pung . . . ponk . . . pung . . . ponk,* yelling insincerities at each other and screaming of love.

The yellow Toyota came past floral plantings and parked in landscaped palm shade. Julio appeared beside me and said, "Ess your she?" When she got out and stood erect, dwindling her auto with a lot of female stature, I said, "Yes. Ess." And Julio went bounding toward the parking area to help with her gear. A very obliging young man. Very earnest. Very dedicated and doubtless very ambitious. He was bounding proof of the fact that the Cuban colony in Miami has the most upwardly mobile young people and the lowest crime rate of any ethnic colony in the U.S. east of San Francisco's Chinatown.

My she wore a big floppy fabric hat in a big white and yellow check. She wore a yellow top and a short white skirt so slit that her stride revealed the matching yellow shorts. She wore huge glasses with lavender lenses. She had a big yellow Ratsey bag and a big white shoulder bag. Julio took the beach bag from her and went on a dead run to stow it aboard the *Muñequita.*

"I'm so sorry I'm late, Trav. Traffic and bad planning. But, my God, this is some place to wait, if you have to wait. Wow! I got stopped at the gates, and I had to sign a guest thing and write in the name of the member I was meeting. I was positive you'd just picked this as a handy place. But he looked on a list. You *are* a member, huh? This is really some kind of incredible. There must be an army of guys just to keep the flowers looking so great."

Maybe it was better than a pretense of total cool, all this happy, awed enthusiasm. But I found myself wishing her approval wasn't quite as total and quite as genuine.

My twenty-two-foot runabout gave her some more pleasant astonishment. "I thought you had some kind of outboard thing. Hey, this is more like they race to the Bahamas."

"Same hull design they used a few years ago, but they had a lot more muscle than the pair of one-twenty-fives this one is wearing."

She hopped aboard, very lithe and springy for the size of her. She stooped and looked forward, under the bow deck. "Say, you've got mattress things and a toilet! It's all so neat!"

Julio nearly fell in while freeing my lines, because he couldn't take his eyes off Mary Alice. He radiated a worshipful approval. She had about seven inches and thirty-five pounds on him, and he was doubtless imagining walking her through his neighborhood on Sunday morning, dressed in her best, as if Snow White had finally made up her mind and decided on one of the dwarfs.

As I chugged, dead slow, past yachts looking like ponderous caparisoned elephants in gleaming outdoor stalls, Mary Alice moved close to me and hooked her left hand over my near shoulder and made a laughing sound of delight. Her hip bumped me. I had the feeling that exact place where she put her hand would turn into a raised, radiant welt showing the precise shape of fingers and palm.

"You know what?" she said.

"What?"

"I shouldn't even tell you. I figured that this time of year, what happened was the owner hired you to stay aboard *The Busted Flush*. I mean, a lot of guys want a woman to believe things. You never really said it was yours. I mean, from the dock it looks kind of lumpy and funny. But that great kitchen and that huge living room and that tub and the shower big enough for four people, practically, and that crazy bed in the main bedroom, like one I saw in a magazine, you know, why should I believe it, Trav?"

"But now you do."

"You just don't look as if you belong to great clubs and own great boats is all. Or act like you do."

"What do I act like, Mary Alice?"

"I don't know. After I moved into the place I'm in now, a guy came around to hook up my phone. He got a thing about me, and when he has service calls in the neighborhood and he sees my car, he stops to find out if my phone is working. As if I wouldn't report it if it wasn't. He's almost as big as you are. A little younger. I mean, if he tried to make me think he owned *The Busted Flush* . . ."

"I won her in a poker game."

She hit me in the ribs with her elbow. "Oh, sure. I *bet* you did. You're funny, you know. I can't tell what's a joke and what isn't. We can go fast now? How fast will this go anyway?"

"It's tuned right now, and the bottom is clean, and I put a new pair of wheels on her, so she should do very close to fifty, but I don't like to hold her there more than a few minutes because I don't like to buy new engines every year. Wait until we get past Dinner Key and I'll show you."

When I got past an area of prams and sailfish and little cats, I pushed it to full, with both mills yelling in full-throated unison. She stood tall above the top of the windshield, the wind snapping her black hair. She was laughing, but I couldn't hear her, and she had me just above the elbow in an impressive grasp. The reading was a full forty-four knots, which is a respectable fifty and a bit. I pulled it back down to cruising speed.

She roamed the walk-around and found the slalom ski stowed up under the gunwale overhang, zipcorded to bronze eyebolts. She wanted to know if we had far enough to go so she could ski. I said yes, if she didn't keep falling off, and she said she was the kind of freak who does all the physical things well after a few tries, and she'd had more than a few tries at the skiing. She went under the foredeck and pulled the privacy curtain, taking her beach bag with her, and in a little while she came out in a plain, businesslike, off-white tank suit, her hair pulled tightly back and fixed there with a silver clamp. I had gotten the tow line out and clipped it to the ring bolt in the transom and held it clear of the slowly turning wheels.

She grinned, threw the ski over the side, and dived after it. When she had the ski and had worked her feet into the slots, I pulled the bar past her at dead slow, and she grabbed it and turned to the right angle and nodded. I pushed both throttles, and she popped up out of the water and the *Muñequita* jumped up onto the step in perfect unison. After she made a few swings, I knew she was not going to have any trouble. She gave me the pumping sign for more speed and then the circle of thumb and finger when it was where she wanted it. It translated to thirty-two miles an hour.

She was not tricky. There were no embellishments. All she did was get into the swooping rhythm of cutting back and forth across the almost-flat wake, far out there in the expanse of Biscayne Bay, far from land, far from any other water craft. She edged the slalom ski as deeply as the men do, laying herself back at a steep angle, almost flat against the water, throwing a broad, thin, curved curtain of water at least ten feet into the air at the maximum point of strain. At that point before she came around and then came hurtling back across, ski flat, to go out onto the other wing, the strain would sag her mouth, wipe her face clean of expression, and pull all the musculature and tendons and tissues of her body so taut she looked like a blackboard drawing in medical school.

She took it each time to the edge of what she could endure. It was hypnotic and so determined that it had a slightly unpleasant undertaste, like watching a circus girl high under the canvas, going over and over and over, dislocating her shoulders with each spin, while the drums roll and the people count.

I put it into autopilot so I could watch her. From time to time I glanced forward to make certain no other boat was angling toward us. I knew she would have to tire soon. I tried to calculate her speed. She was going perhaps twenty-five feet outside the wake on one side and then the other. Call it fifty feet. I timed her from her portside turn back to her portside turn. Ten seconds. For a hundred feet. Miles per hour equals roughly two thirds of the feet per second. Ten feet per second. Add seven miles an hour then to the boat speed. Very close to forty miles an hour. At that speed, if she fell, the first bounce would feel like hitting concrete. Water is not compressible.

I heard a thick, flapping sound over the boat noise and looked up and saw a Coast Guard chopper angling across at about a thousand feet.

I saw us for a moment the way the fellow up there saw us. Gleaming boat. Deeply browned fellow in blue swim trunks running it at speed, watching the graceful girl swinging back and forth, girl in a white suit, with a light, very golden tan.

For all he could tell, the girl was eighteen, and the man was twenty, and somebody's father had bought the boat.

Suddenly I felt bleak, oddly depressed. It took a moment for me to realize that one of Meyer's recent lectures on international standards of living was all too well remembered.

". . . so divide everything into two hundred million equal parts. Everything in this country that is fabricated. Steel mills, speedboats, cross-country power lines, scalpels, watch bands, fish rods, ski poles, plywood, storage batteries, everything. Break it down into basic raw materials and then compute the power requirements and the fossil fuels needed to make everybody's share in this country. Know what happens if you apply that formula to all the peoples of all the other nations of the world?

"You come up against a bleak fact, Travis. There is not enough material on and in the planet to ever give them what we're used to. The emerging nations are not going to emerge—not into our pattern, at least. Not ever. We've hogged it all. Technology won't come up with a way to crowd the Yangtze River with *Muñequitas*.

"It was okay, Travis, when the world couldn't see us consuming and consuming. Or hear us. Or taste some of our wares. But communication by cinema, satellite, radio, television tape, these have been like a light coming on slowly, being turned up like on a rheostat control in a dark cellar where all of mankind used to live. Now it is blinding bright, cruelly bright. And they can all look over into our corner and see us gorging ourselves and playing with our bright pretty toys. And so they want theirs now. Just like ours, God help them. And what is the only thing we can say? 'Sorry. You're a little too late. We used it all up, all except what we need to keep our toys in repair and running and to replace them when they wear out. Sorry, but that's the way it is.' What comes after that? Barbarism, an interregnum, a new Dark Ages, and another start a thousand years from now with a few million people on the planet? Our myth has been that our standard of living would become available to all peoples. Myths wear thin. We have a visceral appreciation of the truth. That truth, which we don't dare announce to the world, is what gives us the guilt and the shame and the despair. Nobody in the world will ever live as well, materially, as we once did. And now, as our materialism begins to sicken us, it is precisely what the emerging nations want for themselves. And can never have. Brazil *might* manage it. But no one else."

Good old Meyer. He can put a fly into any kind of ointment, a mouse in every birthday cake, a cloud over every picnic. Not out of spite. Not out of contrition or messianic zeal. But out of a happy, single-minded pursuit of truth. He is not to blame that the truth seems to have the smell of decay and an acrid taste these days. He points out that forty thousand particles per cubic centimeter of air over Miami is now called a clear day. He is not complaining about particulate matter. He is merely bemused by the change in standards.

Now, as I watched the tireless lady zoom back and forth, he had made me feel like one of those regal jokers of olden times who could order up enough humming bird tongues for a banquet. What's your message, Meyer? Enjoy?

She slid back to a straight track behind the stern. She smiled and rolled her shoulders. She cocked her head and then tried some signals on me. First she held her left hand up, finger and thumb an inch apart. Then she pulled her hand across her throat, in the cut-power signal. Then as I started to turn toward the controls, she shook her head violently and held her hand out, palm toward me. I waited, puzzled, and she pointed toward the water off to the port side of the boat, and then she bent her knees and swung her fanny out to the right. So I had the message. I decided I'd better leave it on pilot but be close enough to take it out in a hurry.

She moved out to the side and gave me her signal and swung wider for speed. I pulled the throttles halfway back, and she tossed the line clear, into the wake, and came angling in too fast toward the port side, amidships. I moved quickly to grab her, but she yelled me off, turned parallel to the direction of the boat, slowing, and just as the speeds were identical, she gave a little twisting hop which hoisted her rear onto the flat gunwale and would have been perfect except she was overbalanced. The slalom ski went up, and she fell over backward into the cockpit. I wasn't close enough to break her fall, and I heard the thump her head made against the deck and felt it through the soles of my bare feet. She scrambled up and went to the stern and brought the tow line in, and then I cut the power all the way back. In the semi-silence I said, "You are totally mad. Miss the edge and you'd get swept right into the port wheel."

"That's how come I jumped too far."

"Did you ever try that before?"

"Onto docks. It's trickier because you have to get it just right, ending up at the dock just when you stop and start to sink. So this is easier. You can kind of adjust because it's like the dock is moving too."

"And that makes it easier?"

"You're cross because it scared you, Trav. Well, I'm a little scared too. I always get scared *after* I try things."

"You thumped your head pretty good."

"All this hair worked like a cushion. It's my elbow that hurts."

She showed me. She had knocked a flap of skin loose. I got out the kit and disinfected it and put a Band-Aid patch on it. She stretched and then squatted on her heels and bounced a few times and came up slowly. "You know, that's *really* a workout," she said. "I wish I could do that every day. I'd get hard as rocks. It would really firm me up."

"I didn't notice anything very loose."

"Then you weren't looking."

"I'm pretty sure I was looking."

She gave me a quick sidelong glance, not at all flirtatious. It backed me off from whatever was about to come into my mind. She said, "Pretty soon I am going to start eating those life jackets."

I looked ahead and picked out the familiar island shapes. I established my location and knew the water I could trust. I said, "You'll be eating in fifteen minutes, and you can start drinking right now, if you're up to it. Look in the ice chest over there. I laid aboard some of those cocktails in cans. Take your pick. Give me a vodka martini, please."

She picked a marguerita, pulled the tabs off the cans, and handed me mine, then clinked cans. I was glad to note I did not have to tell her why we don't throw the shiny tabs overboard.

"I feel great," she said over the engine noise. "Everything is pulled loose, sort of. All stretched. I want to have two drinks, eat myself blind, go to sleep in the sun, and then have a swim, and then ski all the way home."

"So be it," I said. "Won't you burn?"

She poked at her thigh. "My skin is thick and tough, like some kind of plastic. I don't burn at all. After I get pink about nine thousand times, then I gradually turn the color I am now, and then nothing else happens, no matter what."

I read the shallows ahead and slowed down and eased up to them and then along the edge until I found a notch deep enough to get me close to shore. I cut everything and put a couple of hooks over and slung the boarding ladder.

Then we off-loaded everything and, in two trips, carried it up over the dune and down to the little cove on the Atlantic side, dispossessing a pale and malevolent crab when we spread the two giant beach towels in the semi-shade of a pair of wind-torn old casuarinas. We had more of the extravagantly convenient drinks-in-a-can. (Were the emerging nations targeting on this delight in their misty futures?)

I went back and checked the hooks, reset one and trod it into better bottom, and brought back the battered and eroded old battery radio. It brought in the most useful Cuban station, playing, on this Saturday afternoon, a concert of symphonic pieces for Spanish guitar. With very few commercials.

We had a short swim before lunch. The drinks were making the bright day faintly, tantalizingly unreal. I caught her looking stealthily at my ugliest and most impressive souvenir of old trauma, the long deep one down the top of the thigh. I told her it was surgical. A wound had become infected, and they had chopped around in there three times, planning to take the leg off if they had to schedule the fourth. She asked if it was something that happened in some war, and I said no, it had been a civilian difference of opinion. There were some less impressive marks from one of those wars, and the rest of them were either bad luck or good luck or bad judgment. She swallowed and said she couldn't stand the thought of being hurt. She simply couldn't stand it. Oh, not the little bangs and bumps and sprains you get from athletics, or even a couple of busted ribs and a broken collarbone, which she got when she fell from the rings in a gym one time. She meant really really hurt, with stitches and drains and operations and needles and all that. She swallowed again. She said she had never even been really sick, not ever.

Having seen her eat and knowing that outdoors improves appetites, I had ordered enough for four. Hunks of sharp cheddar, cucumber salad, giant roast-beef sandwiches on dark bread, corned-beef sandwiches, big crisp kosher dills, a big thermos of iced coffee, two big pieces of tart deep-dish apple pie. It was successful. She kept making little humming sounds and small chuckling sounds. Through the dark curtain of hair I saw the solid jaw muscles bulging and sliding under that golden hide as she chomped away. I warned her about the horseradish but she slathered it on the roast beef anyway, yelped when she got into it, and then finished the sandwich, eyes tearing, snuffling as though with a head cold.

She yawned and lay back on the big towel I had provided her. She put a forearm across her eyes. In the middle of a sentence her voice dwindled and blurred and stopped. I saw the deep, slow, diaphragmatic breathing of heavy sleep, lips apart, edge of white teeth showing. Her upflung arms revealed the faint, sooty shadow of the shaven stubble. Her palm was turned to the sun, fingers curled. Her other hand, almost a fist, rested against the flattened, muscular belly. Tiny round beads of perspiration, the size of the heads of the pins they put in expensive shirts, clung to the pale fuzz of her upper lip.

I looked at the angle of the sun and got my watch out of the side pocket of the canvas bag I had brought from the boat. A straight shot to the Royal Biscayne would take forty minutes. And I wanted to be coming into Lauderdale past the sea buoy no later than eight fifteen. So, to have some of the day left for more swimming, more skiing, I wouldn't want to sleep more than about a half hour. I set the alarm. Meyer had given the watch to me because it amused him. It does not make a sound. At the specified time, a semisharp little metal nub starts popping out of a little hole in the underside of it, stabbing you in the wrist.

9

On Sunday morning after ten o'clock I got around to hosing down the *Muñequita* with fresh water from the dockside connection at Slip F-18. After I wiped the water spots off the brightwork, I checked the batteries and the oil level in the engines, used a dip stick to check the level in the two tanks against the fuel gauges, greased the linkage in the power lift, and carried the picnic items aboard *The Busted Flush*. By then the cockpit deck had dried, so I did a better job of making her white rubber fenders fast in the right places before I snapped the big custom cover in place all the way around. As I clambered up onto the *Flush*, I heard Meyer calling my name. He was coming along the dock at an unaccustomed briskness, and I went ashore and met him with a suggestion he buy me some coffee aboard his boat, mine having run out.

"And what was the big hurry?" I asked him.

As we strolled back toward his dumpy cruiser, he said, "There's something I never thought of before. When you want to deliver surprising news, your first impulse is to do it in a hurry. If it's good news, the second decision is to slow down, take your time, savor the pleasure of delivering it. But with bad news, you keep hurrying. You want to get it off your hands. Share it."

"Which means yours is bad?"

"Bad. Sad. It's nothing I want to hang onto for the pure relish of it. Jane Lawson was killed yesterday."

I stopped.

He kept going for three strides and turned and looked at me and said, "I know. She was more alive than most."

"Vehicle?"

"No. From what I understand from Hirsh, somebody trashed her house. The police think it was high school kids. The younger daughter runs with a batch of kids who have been feuding with other gangs of girls. They think it was revenge of some kind. The girl's possessions were pretty much destroyed, and it looks as if perhaps Jane came back while the damage was happening. She would have run into her place and tried to stop them, of course."

"If it was a gang of girls, yes. I'd buy that."

"It doesn't look intentional. It looks as if she could have been grappling with someone, trying to restrain them, and someone else grabbed her from behind by the hair to pull her away and broke her neck."

"Jesus God!"

"When she went down, they got out of there in a hurry. The other daughter came home and found her late yesterday afternoon. Hirsh woke me up at eleven thirty last night, phoning me to tell me about it. For a while I could hardly understand him."

"Do they have a time of death?"

"They say between one thirty and three, preliminary. The electric clock in the younger daughter's room stopped at two fifteen when somebody threw it against the wall."

"Do they have the younger daughter, Judy, in custody?"

"Maybe. Hirsh said they were still looking for her at ten last night. Apparently neighbors are no help in that place. It's designed for a kind of privacy, so it is difficult to see people come and go. There are no community areas or activities. People are moving in and moving out frequently. With all the window air conditioners on and the televisions and radios and all the children in that development, nobody hears anything. And if there was some suspicion of something unpleasant going on, the neighborhood reaction would be to turn up the volume on the set and not check the time. Otherwise one might become involved. If you get involved, you can spend untold hours sitting around, waiting to be called into court."

"Meyer?" I said.

He gave a little start. "Sorry. I got sidetracked. Come along. I do have coffee made. I'll have to suggest a study of why people become involved and why they don't."

"Like the forward pass."

"You lost me, Travis."

"When you pass the ball, six possible things can happen, and five of them are bad."

He was silent until he handed me the mug of black coffee, reaching out over the stern quarter to hand it to me where I sat on the dock. "Five things can go wrong?" he asked.

"One, incomplete. Two, intercepted. Three, caught and fumbled. Four, penalized for offensive pass interference. Five, caught for no gain or for a loss."

"I forgot about the penalty."

"Also, they can smear your quarterback just as he unloads and put him out for the rest of the season. That makes six bad things out of seven chances. Why are we doing this, Meyer?"

"So as not to discuss Jane Lawson."

"Let's let her wait in the wings while I tell you about Dave Davis and Harry Harris."

He listened and had no comment until I requested one. And his comment was a pass. He said it needed thought. The alternate assumptions put it into the province of symbolic logic.

I said, "Jack does the family marketing whenever it rains in the afternoon, if it is not one of Jill's bridge days, provided it is not one of the Tuesdays or Fridays when Jack rides to work with Ben."

"Scoff, if it amuses you."

I gave him back his empty mug and stood up. "I have the feeling that nothing is going to be able to give me much amusement for quite a while."

When I was two steps away, he said, "You had your phone turned off last night?"

"I do believe I did."

I went back home and sat in the lounge and thought about Jane Lawson for a little while and looked at my watch. Twenty-five minutes before noon. I went to the master stateroom and opened the door. Mary Alice had shifted position since I had crept out. There was a faint breath of coolness in the air conditioning—she did not like it turned high —and she lay face down, diagonally asprawl across the big bed, sheet down to her bare waist, one hand under her cheek, the other fist clenched close under her chin. One tangle of black hair was sheafed across her sleeping eyes, and shining strands hung down over the side of the bed.

I eased myself stealthily onto the bed to sit and look down at her. There was her own mix of scents in the cabin air, a smell of sleep and girl and Mary Alice, a sort of smoky smell, pungently sweet, with an undertaste of tart, like a wine just turning.

I had not believed she would be in my bed. Not after I had defied Jane's warning about her. When the watch had stabbed me awake on the beach, I had leaned and propped my arms on either side of her and bent to her lips and kissed her awake. Her lips rolled softly open, and then she pushed me away and stared at me, pulled me back down very strongly for about a low four count, then shoved violently and rolled away, rolled up onto knuckles and haunches and stared at me through dark hair. I reached out and caught her arm and said, "What is it with you?"

She tossed her hair back, yanked her arm free. "I don't want to get into that anymore. I really don't."

"Never?"

"Never," she said and stood up.

I got up too and said, "It's . . . an unusual decision."

"Now you can tell me it's ruining my health. Anybody can look at me and see I'm a wreck."

"Mary Alice, it's your body and your decision to make. I'm not going to argue and pressure you. I didn't mean to upset you. I'm sorry."

"Why should you be sorry?" she said. "I'm . . . going for a walk, okay?"

She went down the little stretch of beach. She went as far as she could go without swimming, which was about a hundred feet. She picked up a handful of small shells from the tide line and stood plunking them out into the sea. I found a piece of driftwood, a flat board off somebody's dock or beach steps, and used it as a shovel and dug a hole deep enough to bury our debris above the tide line, with about eighteen inches of sand stomped down on top of it. When I looked at her again, she was sitting on the little slope of beach, arms around her legs, chin on a knee, staring toward Africa. I could tell that it was a time of thought for her, a time of decision. When at last she came back, she was determinedly merry and carefree. I could not read her at all.

There was time for another swim. We swam around to the bay side, and I got two sets of masks, snorkels, and swim fins out of the locker.

We swam to a place where boats had anchored, and we found rare and unusual treasure on the bottom. Genesee and Blatz and Pauli Girl. Coors and Utica Club and Hockstein brewed in Rollie, Alabama. Vintage aluminum. Rare brands brought from afar.

Her forced jolliness seemed to become genuine later on. We frolicked and raced and startled some small fish. Then it was time to pack up and run for it, with no time for skiing on the way back to the Royal Biscayne.

Then she stopped me as I was slowing to make the turn between the club channel markers. She wanted me to wait a minute, right there. So I got myself opposite the tide and held it in place with just the port engine turning softly in gear. She stood in balance, her back to me, and then turned and came over and stood close in quarter profile.

"Would they mind my leaving my car there?" I had to lean close and make her repeat it.

"No. They wouldn't mind. Is it what you want?"

She turned her face farther away. "I don't know what I want. I'm stuck. Right in the middle. Dammit, when I *want* somebody to hustle me . . ."

I pulled her chin around and uptilted it, but she would not look at me. Her glance slid down and away, off to the side. I put the starboard engine in gear. I turned the boat until she was headed northeast, toward the channel. I took Mary Alice's hand and put it on the starboard throttle. I took hold of the port. I put the loop of line over the spoke to lock the wheel.

I said, "Okay. As I push this throttle, the port engine is going to pick up speed, heading for the channel, heading for home. Let's say that is my intention. But the wheel is locked, so if the starboard throttle stays right where it is, all I am going to do is make one hell of a big circle and end up aiming back into the yacht club."

She didn't say anything. Her hand was slack on the throttle. I slowly pushed mine up. We went almost straight and then began to turn more and more easterly. I could see I was going to have some problems with water traffic if I waited too long for her. She took her hand off, and as I was about to accept that as her decision, she hit the throttle with the heel of her hand, banging it all the way forward. She sat in the copilot's chair. The maneuver gave me a couple of very busy seconds flipping the loop off, yanking the throttle back, turning the wheel.

I said, "When you make up your mind, honey, you—"

"Shut up and drive," she said.

I went outside, got on my heading, and put it on pilot. She did not want a beer. She did not want a drink. She did not want any conversation, thanks. So I took a beer back and sat on the engine hatch as we roared through the calm sea, tipping and lifting a little in the swell that was just beginning to build. She stood up and leaned her folded arms on the top of the windshield, staring ahead for a long time, standing hipshot with ankles crossed. The light of the dying day was gold and orange. The shore was turning blue-gray, the sea to indigo.

I guessed that in another five minutes I would take it out of pilot and turn toward the sea buoy and the early lights of Lauderdale. She came striding back, losing her balance and catching it, looking angry, and said, "Can you turn everything off and sort of just float out here? Please?"

Done. A sudden silence until ears can find the smaller sounds. Dip and pitch and roll, water slapping the hull, something rolling and thumping in a gear locker, water sloshing the cooler.

She went back and sat on the broad transom which was also the engine hatch, swiveled to hang her legs over the stern. I sat beside her, facing inboard.

"I don't talk about my husband," she said.

"People have noticed."

So she talked about him. She hopped back and forth in time and space, with silences between. I didn't come in with questions. She had to set her own tempo of revelation. She had gone steady with a boy for several years. She'd caught the eye of an older man, one of the McDermit brothers who had a lot of food-service companies in Pennsylvania and New Jersey, catering airlines, operating coffee-break concessions and cafeterias in factories and offices, owning vending machines and warehousing facilities. He had big cars, phones in his cars, a duplex apartment with a staff, an executive jet.

She had played one against the other, in a girlish mischief. Then abruptly Tom, the boyfriend, had died in a one-car accident, lost control at high speed on the interstate. McDermit had been gentle, understanding, comforting. She had married him.

"Then it all turned so rotten," she said. "They owned race horses, those brothers. I was another thing, like a horse that costs so much to keep, you can do any damn thing you want with it. He liked to hit. He liked to hurt. He couldn't really make it any other way. He was trying to break me. We had a big fight, and I told him Tom had been a man, and he wasn't a man. He said he had a specialist put a gadget inside the wheel cap on Tom's right front wheel, set so that at seventy it would push a weight against a spring thing and blow the lugs off. He said Tom was dead meat. I said he was never going to touch me again, and I was getting a divorce. He said nobody was ever going to touch me again, so I didn't need a divorce. He said to get out if I wanted to, but if I let anybody have me, he'd have both of us killed."

She hadn't really believed him. She'd gone to a lawyer who accepted the divorce action eagerly, then suddenly cooled off. When she insisted on knowing why, he took her into a little conference room and closed the door. He was sweaty. He told her she should go back to her husband. He said the brothers were always involved in legal actions, and sometimes they were indicted, but nothing had ever gone any further than that. He told her he didn't want her business, she didn't owe him a dime, please leave.

She tried another town and another name, and McDermit had phoned her at work to say hello. He found her more quickly the second time. So she had come to Miami and gone back to her own name. "His people check on me. Somebody comes around every couple of months. You get used to it. Five years, practically. It isn't all that rough, getting along without. It isn't that big a part of life."

"Why now and why me, Mary Alice?"

She sighed. "I hope you can find your way in off this ocean in the dark."

"No problem."

"Look at all the stars! You can see them better out here."

"Evading the question?"

"No man in his right mind is going to take a chance on getting killed, just to get one specific piece of ass out of all the ass there is floating around. And besides, I'm not all that great in bed. I'm a big healthy girl, but I'm just sort of average sexy, like you'd find anywhere."

"Question still pending, lady."

"I'm saying it *isn't* now and it *isn't* you, because it could have been if I decided, but instead I've told you why it shouldn't happen. It would be stupid of you. And it would be stupid of me to let myself get into it. I've had it all pushed down out of sight, and I'm okay. I get along fine."

"Then let me ask it a different way. Why did you *almost* decide on now and on me?"

"Not because you are so absolutely irresistible, believe me. If I was inventing a guy to . . . break my fast with, he would sort of be like Michael Landon, only a foot taller."

"Like who?"

"If you don't know, never mind. I think that the way it started, I had the idea that if I ever got the nerve to take the risk, it should be with somebody who'd be awfully damned hard to kill, and then maybe he could keep me alive too. It was just . . . what is the word when you think of things you aren't going to do?"

"Conjecture?"

"Right! I conjectured about us. Then I woke up on the beach, and you were asleep, and I looked at you and kind of wanted you. Still conjecture. Then you kissed me, and I was having a dream it fitted into. Then I went down the beach and thought about it, and then I began playing some kind of fool game about it, but you have to come to the end of games, right? Something to get killed over? Who needs it? Come on, dear. You better start aiming me toward home. I'm sorry. I really am."

"And you don't play quickie games, do you?"

She snapped her head around. "You better not be asking me to."

"I'm not."

"If I wanted to sneak it, I could have had all a girl could need."

"I know."

"It would have to be something that starts and keeps going until somebody finally says whoa. Out in the open. People would know just by seeing me look at the guy."

And now, in the shadows of the curtained master stateroom, I wanted to see that look. I slowly ran the ball of my thumb down the crease of her back, from shoulder blades to the little knobs in the small of her back. She sighed and moved slowly and made a small murmur of complaint. Then suddenly she stiffened, sprang up and back and away from me, eyes wide and blank in terror, as she grasped the sheet and pulled it up across her breasts.

She expelled the frightened in-suck of breath in a long grateful sigh, hooked her hair back out of the way with curled fingers, gave me a small and uncertain smile, and said, "Talk about having a heart attack, darling."

"Bad dreams?"

"Mmmm. Hold me, huh?"

I stretched out beside her, atop the sheet, and put my arms around her. She put her face in my throat. She chuckled.

"What's funny?"

"A dirty joke a girl told me where I have lunch. It sort of fits. You know. I'll mess it up if I try to tell it."

"Try."

It was the one about the doctor with the gorgeous girl patient who comes in with a hangnail and has to strip for the complete physical, and it ends with the tag line, "Don't be silly, Miss Jones. I shouldn't even be doing *this!*"

And she didn't tell it very well.

"Darling?" she said.

"Wha'?"

"Tell me exactly what you promised and exactly what you are going to do."

"Hmm. Let's see. I am going to put extra drums of fuel aboard this here vessel. I am going to equip her and provision her for a voyage of uncertain duration. And at the first hint that your freak husband is after us, whenever you say go, we go, taking the *Muñequita* in tow. If the weather is good enough, we see if we have enough good luck and good management to get over to the islands. If not, we lie at anchor somewhere down Biscayne Bay or in Florida Bay until we get the right weather."

"When I say we're leaving, what do you do?"

"I do not argue. I do not discuss. I do not negotiate. I hang up the phone, start the engines, and wait for you."

She gave me a very strong hug. "That's our deal."

"That's our deal, M.A."

"Time is it?"

"Moving up onto noon."

"What! Good Lord!"

"Something must have relaxed you, honey."

"Sure didn't look like anything was going to at first. I was absolutely hopeless. I was just too tense and nervous and scared to be worth a damn. You are a very patient guy."

"In a self-serving kind of way."

There was a long silence and small motions finally, body language involved in question and answer, query and response, trick or treat. And off in the side of my mind was a fleeting recap of Meyer's insight, that we all tend to save good news as long as we can. But sometimes, with a little tickle of guilt, we find a compelling reason to save the bad for a little while too.

She was still taking her long sloshing steaming soapy noisy shower when I took her Bloody Mary into the head and yelled to her that she would find it on the counter beside the sink. She yelled her thanks.

Aboard the *Flush,* under a bunk, there is a big storage drawer full of lady items which have been left behind or bought for emergencies or donated to the cause. No point in even looking, because had there been a previous lady of these dimensions, I would remember. But her yellow top and shorts were still fresh enough.

The very best eggs and country ham and toasted English muffins with strawberry jam. We sat in the booth next to the stainless steel galley, and she was right about that blue-eyed look of hers. She looked at me often, during and between the forks of egg, the bites of muffin. Anybody intercepting that look would have wondered if it was melting the fillings in my teeth. Bloodhounds look at the moon that way, and kids look into candy stores that way, and barracuda look at baitfish that way.

We shared the cleaning up and took final cups of coffee into the lounge. So I took a deep breath and looked over her shoulder, out the port, at the sunny gleam of the row of boats, and told her about Jane Lawson. Glassy shock. Exclamations of disbelief. Yawls and yawps of grief, pain, and anger. Reddened, streaming eyes, considerable nose-blowing, and then she wanted to be held, patted, comforted as the residual snuffles and snorts became less frequent.

She went and fixed her face and came back and phoned Hirsh Fedderman. He had to tell her all he knew about it. She made wordless sounds of shock and sympathy. The tears began running again, and she made frantic motions at me. I put the box of tissue within reach. She asked questions in a torn and tearful voice and honked into the wads of Kleenex. After that was over, she had to have another session of holding, patting, comforting and then go fix her face again.

She came back and plumped herself down. "I'm exhausted," she said. "I felt so marvelous, and now I'm pooped. It makes my problems seem like nothing at all. Hirsh is really down. The poor old guy. The last straw, sort of. I don't know what he's going to do now. I know what I better do. I better go and be with him. He hasn't really got anybody else. Not nearby."

She got her things. At the doorway from the lounge onto the aft deck, we kissed. For a casual kiss, she felt big and hearty, solid and tall, practically eye to eye with me on her tiptoes. For what she considered any important kissing, she had a strange knack of dwindling herself. She curved her shoulders forward, let herself cling, but without much tangible weight, delicately in fact.

She looked up at me. "We're some kind of special."

"That's what people keep saying about us, all over town."

"Can I be kind of a coward?"

"How?"

"Don't come to my place. That's asking for trouble. Don't phone me, there or at the store. Just to play safe. Okay?"

"Don't call us, we'll call you?"

"Constantly. You won't believe how often. I'm going to walk all tilted over from the weight of the dimes."

So I locked my floating house and went on ahead. I went and got Miss Agnes and came back around and picked up Mary Alice. She nipped in and slunched down, saying, "All of a sudden this is a pretty conspicuous car."

"And no matter what you ride in, you are a conspicuous lady."

"Isn't *that* the damned truth."

"Would you feel better if I wore a dress and a blond wig?"

She turned and stared at me. "You would make the most incredibly ugly woman in all Florida."

"Just stop being so edgy."

"I'll try. But he's a sick, murderous, tricky bastard."

10

I drove her to the club. The man at the gate remembered Miss Agnes far better than he remembered me. And as before, he looked as if it took a great effort of will for him to keep from asking to please never bring such an ugly old handmade pickup into paradise.

There was a slot where I could park near her Toyota. She got in her car, and I put her beach bag in. She gave me a shy, nervous, quick little smile and said she'd phone or maybe just drive up there, if that would be all right. I told her anything would be fine. She hit her brakes a foot shy of a lot of sedate gray Continental as she backed out and then thumped over some curbing as she made her turn. Good-bye, dear girl. And take care of yourself. And Hirsh.

I retraced the route I had used when driving Jane Lawson home. We had been talking. I had followed her instructions without paying too much attention to the turns. So I got partially lost at about the halfway point and nearly lost when I was almost there. When I came upon it, there were two cars in the drive with that vaguely official look. There was a rental Oldsmobile at the curb, and a burly brown man with a shaved head was leaning against the front fender with his arms folded, managing to look patient and impatient at the same time. He wore a white short-sleeved shirt and blue sailcloth Bermudas. His calves and forearms were thick, sinewy, and very hairy.

I parked twenty feet in front of the green Olds and came walking back. He said, "There is absolutely nothing to see here. Get back into that . . . vehicle and drag ass."

I took the final six slow strides that put me in front of him. He was fifty at a distance and early sixties close up. But he was fit. Very fit. He even seemed to have muscles on his forehead. I couldn't fit him into any part of the picture until I noticed the ring on his finger.

"Are you Jane's father-in-law, sir?"

"I'm General Lawson. Why? Who are you? If you are another goddamn newspaper—"

"My name is McGee. Travis McGee. I'm a salvage consultant. I drove Jane home Friday after work. She asked me in. While we were talking, Judy came in and left with some friends. I found out about this terrible thing this morning. I live in Fort Lauderdale. It is reasonable to assume that in the course of questioning Mr. Fedderman, her employer, and Mrs. McDermit, her co-worker, they would ask them when was the last time they saw Mrs. Lawson, and they would say when she left with me. So, in a spirit of cooperation, I thought it would be well to report to whoever is investigating the case. General, I am very sorry about this. I also wish to point out that all of this is none of your goddamn business, and I am humoring you because I hear the habit of command is hard to shake."

He unfolded his arms, and his chin moved six inches toward me. "What's that? What did you say?"

"I said I gave you more answer than I had to."

"What were you to Jane?"

"I'll even answer that, sir. An acquaintance."

He closed his eyes for a moment. "They've been coming by. Creeps. Sickies." He tilted his head, frowning, staring at me. "They go by nine times at three miles an hour, or they stop and get out and stand and gawp at the door with no more expression on their face than a ball of suet. Families with little children, standing and staring, with God only knows what kind of dim thoughts moving around in their empty skulls. I've sent a lot of them on their way. The sun is hot, and I've got a cheap lunch sitting like a stone in my stomach, and the law is hunting down my granddaughter. In other words, I apologize."

He put his hand out. I took it without hesitation.

He opened the car door and sat sideways on the seat and looked up at me. "Pride is so goddamned wickedly expensive. I have been waiting here, thinking about pride."

"Sir?"

"Three sons. Jerry was the only one who went into the service and the only one who died. The other two are doing fine. I retired early. Heart murmur. The second star was a going-away present. Bought a little grove in California. Take care of the trees. Gardening. Golf. Bridge. Am I boring you?"

"No, sir."

"I'm boring myself. Somebody has to get stuck with listening. They paved a road near my place. I went and watched them every day. Isn't that fascinating? Old fart watching the big yellow machines. Made myself agreeable. Asked questions. Never saw such a crowd of fuckups, pouring money down the sewer. Found a couple of my retired NCOs and officers, as bored as I was. All put some money in the pot. Rented equipment after we bid low on a culvert. Made out. Plowed it back in. Every one of those other six old farts have taken at least two million out of it. And I kept fifty percent of everything. Seven corporations. Factory structures in Taiwan. Flood control in Brazil. Bridges in Tanzania. Pipelines in Lousiana. Shrewd old bastard, right? Wrong. Just bored doing nothing. Horse sense and energy and being fair. Nothing more. There's a Christ-awful shortage of horse sense in the world. Always has been. Ask me where the pride comes in. Go ahead. Ask me."

"Where does the pride come in, General?"

"Me beginning to make money hand over fist, and Jerry's widow with two little girls. I had to travel a lot, leaving Bess alone. Lots of room in that house, and if there wasn't, I could build more onto it. No, she was too proud. She wanted to make her own way. Raise Jerry's kids without help from anybody. Bess wanted to come down here and visit her and talk her into it and bring her back. She was sure she could. So my pride got in the way. If the damned girl wants to act like that, let her. Jane's pride and my pride. Send too big a check along with the Christmas stuff, and she'd send it right back. Oh, shit, isn't pride wonderful? She stayed right here in this half-ass place leading a half-ass life, when if she'd wanted to spend a thousand dollars a day of my money, it would have tickled but not pinched. So she's gone down the drain after a lot of scruffy little years, and the younger girl has gone sour. For what? There's no meaning to it at all. None." He put his elbows on his knees, his face in his hands.

I gave him ten seconds and then said, "Are you waiting for them in there?"

He looked at me as if he had forgotten who I was. "Oh, they're supposed to be finishing up. I can go in when they're through, they told me." He patted his shirt pocket. "Linda is over at the hotel with Bess. I've got a list of things. I don't want that little girl to have to come back here even one more time. She had one look. This was her home. She shouldn't remember it like the way it is now."

I excused myself and went up the steps and pushed the buzzer. I told my story to a fat young man with a guardsman mustache. He took me back through litter and ruin to a bedroom where two technicians were working in a perfume stink, patiently dusting the large fragments of glass. A large man sat on the bed, murmuring into the bedside extension. He had a big head and golden locks and a great big face and jaw, with fleshy, regular features. He hung up and stared at me with a look of total, vapid stupidity. It did not change as I went through my little account for the third time.

He said, "My name is Goodbread, and so far I'm making the file on this one. What I hope, McGee, is that you are one of the kinks we get now and then, they kill somebody and come back and say they just happened to know that somebody and how are you boys making out catching the killer, heh?"

"Sorry I can't help you that way."

He favored me with a long, stupid stare. "I might anyway have Arn run you down and check you through everybody's computer file."

"There's somebody you could ask."

"The mayor?"

"Captain Matty Lamarr."

"Your first name again? Travis? Stand easy." He phoned again. He had a very soft telephone voice. He held the phone in such a way that half his big hand formed a cup around the mouthpiece. I guess he was getting the home number. The captain was a few years past pulling Sunday duty. He held the bar down, then dialed again. Big swift nimble fingers. He spoke, waited a time, then spoke again. Listened a long time. And another question. More listening. Expression of gratitude. Hung up.

"The captain didn't say you are his favorite people."

"He's not one of mine, but we got along all right one time."

"He says there's no use asking you what kind of an angle you are working."

"If any."

"He says he thinks you stay inside the law, just inside, most of the time."

"I try, lieutenant."

"Sergeant. And he said you answer questions right, or you clam up, and you can be a help if you want to be."

"I liked the woman. I didn't know her well, but I liked her."

"The captain says that the only handle he could find to use on you was that you don't want your name in the paper."

"There's a point where that handle breaks right off, sergeant."

His long stare was lethargic, his eyes sleepy. "So let me know if you feel anything starting to give, McGee."

"Can I suggest something to you?"

"You go ahead, and then I'll tell you if you should have."

"The woman's father-in-law is waiting out at the curb in a rented car. He wants to pick up some things for the older daughter."

"And?"

"If you know who you are keeping waiting, okay. But I read an article about him in a magazine a couple of months ago. That is Major General Samuel Horace Lawson, and Lawson International is listed on the big board, and in his line of work I would guess that he gives a bundle to both political parties, and if he gets annoyed enough, he is going to—"

"Arn!" Sergeant Goodbread roared. The fat young one with the guardsman mustache came in almost at a run, his eyes round.

"Arn, fill me in on that guy you talked to out front."

"Uh . . . he's related. Lawson. Old folks. He just wants to get some stuff out of here when we're through. For the daughter. Why? He'll keep."

"Did he call himself General Lawson?"

"Sure. But you know how many old generals we've got around this state—"

Sergeant Goodbread went out and brought the general into the house, apologizing for the delay. He helped Lawson with the list of items and had Arn carry them out to the Olds. Goodbread talked for about ten minutes to Lawson in the living room. I could hear the voices but not the words. The air conditioner was too loud. I sat on the bed. The technicians kept going listlessly through the broken glass looking for clean fresh prints. Or even fresh smudges. Many many police officers have worked in criminal investigation until retirement without ever working on a case where a fingerprint made one damned bit of difference one way or the other. A skilled man knows a fresh print or smudge the instant he brings it out by the way the natural oil from the skin responds.

Lawson left. Goodbread came to the doorway and beckoned me into the living room. A chair and the end of the couch had been cleared off. A plastic tape box crunched under his heel and some brown stereo tape caught around his ankle. He motioned me toward the couch, and he bent and plucked the tape off his ankle before he sat in the chair. He took a stenopad out and opened it and put it on his heavy thigh and said, "Description of Judith Lawson, please."

I shut my eyes for a moment and rebuilt her, head to toe. I started to give it to him slowly, but I saw he was using some form of speedwriting or shorthand, so I delivered it more quickly. I gave him the conversation as I remembered it, not word for word but reasonably close.

He closed the pad and said, "Thanks for your cooperation."

"Can I ask some questions?"

"What for?"

"I want to waste your time with my idle curiosity, Sergeant. Like I wasted your time telling you about General Lawson."

"He mentioned . . . Captain Lamarr mentioned you get kind of smart-ass."

"Is the reconstruction that she came home and found persons unknown busting up this place?"

"No way to check it, but she was wearing street clothes, and her purse was found beside the body. Without a dime in it."

"And where was the body?"

He hesitated. "In that doorway there to that hall, legs in this room, head in the hall."

"Was the air conditioner on when the body was found?"

He looked at the ceiling, and for a moment that massive face firmed up, losing the practiced and deceptive look of the dullard. "On when I got here. Which seems several days ago and was yesterday. Linda Lawson said the only things she touched were the front door, which wasn't locked, and her mother and that telephone. Why?"

"When we got here Friday, the heat would knock you down. She apologized. The house rule was last one out turns it off, first one in turns it on. It made a hell of a noise on high, but cooled off the place fast."

He went over to the door and walked back into the room. He came back and sat down. "So the kids were busting up the back of the place when she came in, and this room was okay, and so she went over. . . ."

He paused. I said, "If you hear a noise, you don't turn on something that makes it harder to hear."

He nodded. "And if you are going to sneak in and bust a place up, you don't turn on a lot of noise that would keep you from hearing if anybody is coming. And the daughter would have had to walk farther to turn it on than to get to her mother."

We sat in silent contemplation. He tapped the stenopad and said, "Unless this little chickie was part of the group."

"For what reason?"

"Do they need reasons?"

"How did they get in?"

"Awning window in Judy's room was open wide, screen pushed into the room. A small person could wiggle through and go open the back door or the front."

I looked at the floor, at thin shards of picture glass and at a triangular piece of the face of the long-dead Jerry Lawson, a piece containing one eye looking up at me. Next to it was a tape cartridge, multi-track, plastic cracked, tape dangling from it. The color picture on the plastic housing was of a young girl, smiling mouth agape, eyes half-closed in song. The press-apply label on the tape box read $7.79. The broken box and label looked fresh and neat.

I picked it up. I handed it to Goodbread. He threw it on the floor and said, "I know, I know. Dammit. What kids wouldn't rip off new tapes? Take the money in the purse. Leave perfume. Smash everything in the kitchen, including bourbon, one bottle, seal intact. What kind of kids, everybody puts on gloves in the summertime before they touch anything? Something else too."

He got up and went into the next room and came back with a nine-by-twelve manila envelope. He undid the clasp and looked through glossies and selected one and handed it to me, saying, "You never saw this."

I studied it. At first it made no sense, and then I saw what he meant. It was a picture taken with a wide lens and flash, looking down at the doorway where the body had been. There was a ghost outline of a woman lying on her side, head tilted back.

He bent over me, pointed with a thick finger. "Along here some kind of bag or box of some kind of cake mix or cookie mix hit the wall and exploded and came sifting through the air. Then along here, where the side of this leg was, are pieces of a blue and white vase, very small pieces. When the examiner started to roll her over, I saw the clean floor underneath her, so I had them lift her off it very careful."

I looked up at him. "So what kind of glove-wearing kids, who wouldn't rip off tapes, perfume, or booze, broke her neck and went right on trashing the house?"

He sat down. "If you take total freaks, if they did not give one damn about anything, where do the gloves fit the pattern?"

"Where are the dirty words?"

"The what?"

"With paint, catsup, lipstick, anything. On the walls. Where's the big pie? Don't they always think of putting all the clothes in the middle of the kitchen floor or in the bathtub and pouring everything liquid on top of the mess?"

"I never thought of that," he said. "It's kind of orderly. Wrong word, I guess. Break everything breakable. Tip all the furniture over. Dump all the drawers. Slash the clothes and bedding." He tapped his notebook again. "Mama came home and had another fight with this kid. It got physical, and mama got killed. So the kid trashed the house to make it look as if she didn't do it. She trashed her own stuff."

"Or someone was in here looking for something to steal when she came home, sergeant. Lost his nerve. Tried to grab her when she ran. Broke her neck. Then tried to make it look like kids."

"Except where is the girl? Why doesn't she show?"

"But if it was *your* way, she would have to show up to make it work, wouldn't she? Running would spoil her idea."

He wiped the lower half of his face with a big slow hand. He looked tired. "I've got more to think about than I need. I want to decide whether or not I want to stay on this. I can get off in thirty seconds, risking nothing."

"I don't understand."

"The general doesn't want publicity. The press hasn't made him yet. I told him I want to keep it that way as long as I can because, without him, this one is low priority. Three column inches on page thirty-one. An indoor mugging of a middle-aged widow. If whoever killed her keeps on thinking it's handled on a routine basis—which means only so many man hours, lab hours, legwork, and then into the open file— maybe that person won't do such a good job of covering as they would if they knew all the pressure there is behind it. I can get departmental priority, quietly, on the basis of who he is, and it improves my chances of a wrapup on it. But if I tip the press, if I made a private call, say, to Gene Miller on the *Herald,* then it moves from page thirty-one to maybe a big story on the first page of the second section. It hits a lot of sensitive areas. It gets political. The person or persons we're looking for are alerted, and so they go back and put a lot more braces and rivets on the alibi. And as I told the general, they will cover Judy Lawson's trouble with the law, because when something gets big, on the days when there's nothing new, they go back and dig up the old and print it, because if it isn't known, it's new. And official sources get into the act."

"What do you mean?"

"Official sources revealed today that the persons who murdered Jane Lawson may have in fact been looking for her younger daughter Judy, arrested seven months ago by vice-squad undercover agents—"

"Vice squad!"

"She was fifteen then, working with two older boys. There was a rash of it at the time, kids working the parks and working over the tourists. The girl smiles and wags her little behind and tells the mark she'll give a ten-dollar treat over in the bushes or over in that camper or van. He goes for it, and the boys jump him and pick him clean. Maybe one mark in ten files a complaint. A lot of them are users. Maybe the others are behind in their car payments. They ran Judy through medical, and she wasn't using, and she wasn't dosed, and it was first time, so she got two years in the custody of her mother. The boys were already in the files and legally adults, so they didn't make out that well. Anyway, if it should break, they would take me off and give it to somebody with a lot more rank. The general has given me a deadline to come up with something promising, and if I don't, he's going to break it himself by coming up with such a reward for information it will clog the switchboards for a week."

"How much time?"

"Not enough."

"Where is he staying?"

"In a hotel."

"Thanks. Thanks very much."

"I've stopped being an information service. Where can I find you if I want you?" I told him, and he wrote it down. "And if you think of anything McGee, get in touch right away. Don't try to decide what is and what isn't worth telling me. Get in touch."

He stood up. I was dismissed. When I looked back, before closing the door, he was staring into space, big face slack, mouth sagging open, eyes sleepy and lifeless. It was a *shtick* I'd never seen before: Here is a cop so stupid you don't have to keep your guard quite so high. Here is a cop who needs help finding his way out of a phone booth. Somebody's dumb brother-in-law. Sure. I could see how that style would fit a lengthy interrogation. Long pauses. Simple questions. A lack of comprehension requiring endless repetition. "And what was it you said you did after that?" Then the eventual, inevitable, fatal contradiction, because the one thing successful lying requires is total recall of all the details of the structure of lies, and that is rare anywhere, even among men who face prison if they fumble just one critical question.

11

I drove over to the beach and put old Ag into a private fenced lot which bragged of its security measures. On the way I had stopped at a mainland shopping center and was now the owner of a red and white flight bag containing shorts, socks, shirt, and precuffed slacks which were going to be too short. I carried the cheap sport coat over my arm. The rest of the overnight essentials were in the new flight bag. Thai International.

The same cold-eyed man was on the desk. I told him to tell Mr. Nucci that Mr. McGee wanted to check in. He once again muttered on the phone, hung up, spun the visitab index, turned, and picked a key out of the mail rack.

He put a card in front of me and said, "Please."

I hesitated and could think of no reason why I shouldn't be exactly who I was and so signed in. A bellhop took me on a long easterly walk to far elevators. We rode up to eighteen and walked farther east, to the end of the corridor. He turned on all the lights. It took some time. He had to work his way around a big room. He finally left, with tip, and I was alone with my big bed on a circular platform, with my electric drapes, my stack of six big bath towels, my balcony overlooking the sea, my icemaker, my sunken tub, my coral carpeting six inches deep.

I phoned Meyer aboard the *Keynes*. I told him that I was in 1802 at the Contessa, and it seemed a convenient temporary refuge. I asked him what he did when he knew he had heard something that meant something, and he should be able to remember what it was, and he couldn't.

He said he usually walked back and forth and then went to sleep. I asked him if that did any good, and he said practically never.

I tried Mary Alice and hung up after the tenth unanswered ring. There was a tapping at my door. A waiter brought in a tray with a sealed bottle of Plymouth gin, a double old-fashioned glass, a large golden lemon, and a tricky knife with which to cut slices of rind. Willy Nucci followed the waiter in and waved him back out and closed the door.

Willy came over and shook my hand. He smiled at me. "How do you like this room? All right?"

"Willy!"

"Want me to fix you one of your crazy gin on the rocks, or do you want to do it?"

"Willy!"

"What I can do, pal, I can send up this Barbara I've got doing some PR for the place, living here in the house, little bit of a thing, she learned massage in Tokyo, and it's the damnedest thing, she uses her feet. She walks on your back. You wouldn't believe. Let me send her up, you'll never regret it. Pretty little thing."

"Sit the hell down!" I roared.

He backed up and sat down and wiped his mouth. "I was only—"

"Willy, the room, the bottle, a girl walking on me . . . What in God's name has gotten into you?"

"Anything you want in this hotel is yours. It is only to ask. Okay?"

"What makes me so important all of a sudden?"

"You've always been important to me, McGee."

Then light dawned. I stared at him. I laughed. He didn't. I said, "Willy, your grapevine works too fast."

"I hear what I have to know."

"Like I'm working for Frank Sprenger?"

"Remember one thing. This is the first time his name has ever been mentioned between us."

"Why should you and I have ever talked about Sprenger?"

Some of the tension went out of him, and his shoulders came down about an inch. "I'm not asking you what you're doing for him, am I?"

"I'm not doing anything for him, Willy."

The shoulders went up again. "You took his money. That I know."

"I took his money."

"Some of the things you've done haven't been all the way bright,

McGee, but if you are saying what you seem to be saying, then you are being a hundred and ten percent stupid. If you take Sprenger's money, you do something he wants done. If you don't do it, you don't get to give the money back. You don't jerk around with any Frank Sprenger."

"We're involved here in semantics, Willy."

"You said you're not doing anything for him."

"I'm not doing anything against him."

Shoulders went all the way back to normal. "Oh! Then that's what you're doing for him. Not doing anything to screw him up. Which means he thinks you can or will be able to."

"One small item and not much money."

He nodded. "Like that thing we—" He stopped himself. "Like if he was involved in some kind of investment and didn't get what he thought he was buying, and somebody wanted you to help with the real stuff."

"Are these rooms bugged without you knowing for sure?" I asked him.

"People are in and out all day. I do the best I can for the owners. And the owners would want me to tell you this, Travis. And you tell Frank Sprenger for me. Any friend of his, any time, the best we got is what he gets. I personally guarantee it."

"I'll tell him what a damned good job Willy Nucci does for the owners. But I'd wager he knows that already."

"I try my best. What do you want? Just ask."

"I might want something later. Maybe later we could take a little walk together by the ocean and talk."

"I'll tell the switchboard, when you phone me it goes through right away."

"Thanks, Willy."

At the door he paused and turned. "Even if the only part you want is the massage, I'd recommend her. You'll sleep like a baby." I declined. He shrugged and left.

I tried Mary Alice for ten more rings. I tried Hirsh Fedderman. The woman said, "This here is Mrs. Franck speaking, a neighbor, I am sitting with Mr. Fedderman who is now sleeping at last, thank God."

"Was Mary Alice McDermit there? Or is she still there?"

"Here there is only me, Mrs. Franck, and there is Mr. Fedderman, like I said already, sound asleep. Who did you ask?"

"Mrs. McDermit. She was there today. When did she leave?"

"How should I know if I don't know her? I didn't meet everybody that comes here. This dear old man, he is blessed with friends. All day long too many people coming to see him, tiring him out, bringing enough food we could feed Cuba maybe."

"Mary Alice works for him. She's a young woman with long black hair, six feet tall."

"Ah! Oh! You should say so. That one. Yes. Such a size person they are growing these days. It is something in the food. What time is it now? Nearly nine? So she left at four o'clock, five hours ago. You missed her by a little. If she ever comes back, who shall I say is calling?"

"Thank you, never mind. How is Hirsh?"

"How do you think he is? That nice woman being killed in her own home by wicked children, fifteen years she worked for him, a faithful loyal person. His heart is broken in two. That's all that is wrong."

"I know it would be wrong to wake him up, and you wouldn't even if I asked you. So would you happen to know if a woman who used to work for him is still alive? I think her name is Moojah."

"Of course Miss Moojah is alive! Wasn't she here today, bringing a hot casserole? She's in the book. Why don't you look? How many Moojahs are there going to be? She lives in Harmony Towers, that has a three-year waiting list for senior singles. Miss Moojah will be alive when all of us have passed away, believe it."

After I hung up, I checked the directory. Yes indeed. A. A. Moojah. I wrote the number on the phone-side scratch pad, just as the phone rang.

"Hello?"

"Oh, great! Just dandy!"

"I called you twice. No answer. How did you find me?"

"Meyer told me."

"Meyer phoned you?'

"I didn't say that, sweetie. Meyer is sitting smiling at me like some kind of an owl."

"An owl. You mean he's here in . . . oh."

"Yes indeed. Here I am in all my pretties, making my poor dear little yellow car go seventy-five on the turnpike."

"It always seems to me like downhill from there to Miami."

"If and when I feel like, I'll check that out."

"When do you expect to feel like it? I have some things I want to talk to you about."

"Meyer is a wonderful conversationalist. I'm going to have another delicious drink, and then we're going to go eat somewhere nice. So don't wait up for me."

I started to explain that so many things were happening, it was too inefficient to try to commute, but I realized I was talking to an empty line.

I broke the seal on the bottle and was pleased to find that my personal icemaker made those nice little cubes the size of professional dice. After one sip I got out the card which one of my two visitors had given me—either Harry Harris or Dave Davis. The unlisted phone number was written on the back in red ballpoint.

When the phone was answered, I could hear music and laughter in the background. The girl said, "Whatever you were looking for, we got it."

"What I am looking for is Frank."

"We got . . . oops. Wrong way to go. Whom is speaking?"

"McGee. T. McGee."

"Just stand there," she said. She did not cover the mouthpiece perfectly, and I heard her bawling over the background noise. "Frank, somebody name McGee. You wannit?"

She came back on and said, "He'll come onto an extension in just a sec."

"Hello?" he said. "Let me hear you hang up, Sissie."

She let us both hear it, like a good rap on the ear with a tack hammer. "Sorry about that," he said. It was a deep, easy voice. "And sorry I couldn't come to see you the other day. I got tied up. I told them not to give out a name. Just the number where you could get in touch with either of them."

"They didn't give out any name, Mr. Sprenger. If it was in connection with something I was involved in, concerning a Mr. Fedderman, then I could add two and two, but I wasn't sure, of course. Then something made me sure."

"Such as?"

"I was over on the Beach, and I stopped at the Americana for a drink, and somebody I know came over and said she understood I'm working for you now."

Five seconds of silence. "I find that *very* interesting. You wouldn't want to give me the name?"

"No, I wouldn't. But she doesn't work for you, as far as I know. I didn't appreciate it."

"How am I supposed to take that?"

"I don't know how you want to take it, Mr. Sprenger. I just don't want any confusion in anybody's mind about whose problems I'm supposed to be taking care of."

"Why don't you come to my office tomorrow, say about ten o'clock, and we can discuss your investment problems?"

"I found your Lincoln Road address in the book. About eleven would be better, I think."

"I'll see you whenever you arrive. Right now you and I are even with the board. I consider it full value received. Okay?"

I said everything was just fine. I hung up, smiling. It was worth a thousand dollars to him either way. If I was trying to con him into thinking there was a leak in his administrative apparatus, it was worth it to know I was dull enough to try to con him. On the other hand, if there was a leak, he was tough and smart enough to find it. I knew there was a leak. And I knew that if it was a plant, my friend Willy Nucci was too shrewd to set himself up by letting the plant know where the information was going. One thing seemed reasonably certain. Frank Sprenger would have it sorted out by the time I met with him on Monday. And be duly grateful. I could guess how his mind would work. Absolute loyalty, absolute silence, these are required, are so critical they are seldom even mentioned. Any violation of this credo is a form of voluntary suicide. The reason is that if the unreliable one talks to someone who intends no harm, and if someone who *does* mean harm can learn of the defection, then the threat of exposure is deadly enough to extract the same information for other uses. There are two reasons why they use the same sort of cell structure as do intelligence apparatuses. It limits the availability and dissemination of potentially damaging information. And it makes it a lot easier to track down any leak.

I stretched out on a chaise, drink at hand, scratch pad at hand, and began working my way through a tangle of phone lines toward Sergeant Goodbread. I finally persuaded a communications person to patch me through to Goodbread's vehicle.

"McGee, I can't make any kind of statement. You know that."

"This is sort of personal. When you can get to a phone, call me. The sooner the better."

It took him six minutes to get to a phone. "It better be good," he said. "I still haven't been home yet. I'm dead on my feet."

"I want to give you some information, but I don't want to give you all of it."

"Have you lost your mind?"

"What I want to do is get you all the way off that idea of the daughter being involved or kids being involved."

"We've got Judy. She came home this morning and saw a police car and thought her old lady had turned her in, so she and her friends drove right on by. Friday night she and her friends drove up to Orlando to go to Disney World. They looked so scruffy they couldn't get in. So they drove over to Rocket Beach and spent the day, six of them, in an old VW camper and tried to stay overnight, but the law took them in to see if they were on any wanted lists, then rousted them south out of the county. It looks as if it will check out all the way, if we have to. After they drove by the house, they went to a friend's place, whose parents are off at some kind of convention. Anyway, at about six this evening, some other friend called up that house to ask the girl if she'd heard about Mrs. Lawson getting killed and the cops looking for Judy. So the kid got smart and phoned in, and I had her brought in. It really shook her up. It's violation of probation, and nobody in custody of her. What would happen, she would go to the state school."

"If it weren't for the general?"

"He and his wife and the sister came in and talked to the girl. He wanted to bust her right out, right now, but the only way he could do it, it would turn into news. I want it to stay quiet. If the man who did it suddenly hears there is going to be every kind of heat and pressure he ever heard of, he could be long gone."

"The man?"

"She came home with him yesterday, say. She brought him to her place. They hassled. She started to try to run. He grabbed her by the hair to yank her back, not meaning to kill her, but he was too rough. Broke vertebrae. The spinal cord was pinched and lacerated. The time of death they say was maybe about two thirty, but the injury could have happened then or earlier. There would be a lot of paralysis, but the heart and the breathing could have kept going an hour after the neck was snapped, maybe longer. She went down, and he probably started to get out of there, then decided to confuse everybody. I had a hell of a job convincing that old man to lay back. Judy's release can be arranged quietly tomorrow."

"Where are they staying?"

"Now it's your turn, McGee."

"I'm not pleading or begging. I'm just telling you that it would be a very nice gesture on your part, sergeant, if you would accept what I want to tell you without going after what I really have to hold back."

"I'll decide after I hear the first part."

"There is a good chance that some person or persons unknown believed that Jane Lawson might have something very valuable hidden in her apartment."

"How valuable?"

"Four hundred thousand, maybe."

"Is there a chance they got it?"

"If there is a chance it was there, there is a chance they got it."

"Is it bigger than a breadbox?"

"That's as far as I want to go right now."

"The *hell* with that, McGee. Come in or get brought in. What are you trying to do to me, giving me such crap?"

"You are a good officer, I think. And if I get clumsy and walk in front of a city bus, I want you to have some kind of a starting place."

"Then *give* me one! The general is at the Doral."

"I did."

"Is it gold coins, McGee? Is it? Hey! McGee! Is it?"

Slowly, gently, I replaced the phone on the cradle, and its little night glow went on glowing.

I checked the time and wondered about the Doral. If one wanted to get anywhere at all with the general, it wouldn't be over the phone. Probably not in person either.

I wondered about breadboxes and gold. What were they getting for it lately? More every day. Too much an ounce. I scribbled an estimate. A hundred and twenty pounds of gold should be worth about four hundred thousand. Considerably smaller than your standard, everyday breadbox. But one hell of a lot more comprehensible than Fedderman's little squares and oblongs of antique paper.

He had showed me one in a catalog. British Guiana. Scott catalog number 13. One-cent magenta. Valued at $325,000. Unique, meaning there is only one in the world. Also, 1856. It is Stanley Gibbons catalog number 23 valued at £ 120,000. Crude printing in black on reddish purple paper and initialed in ink by a postmaster long dead.

So, to paraphrase Mary Alice, just what preoccupation of man *is* worth futzing with? Anything which relates to survival is acceptable on the basis that survival is both possible and laudable. Survival of self and species and environment.

Everything else then becomes a taste. Taste of the humming-bird tongues, taste of gold in the vault, taste of Barbara Barefoot, taste of uniqueness of oneself, because if there is only one British Guiana 13 in the world and you own it, you walk about with the knowledge of being the only man who owns it. You are unique. If you have the biggest pile of throwing stones in the tribe . . . whoa, that goes back to survival.

So what packrat preoccupation did I have? What special artifacts does McGee fondle?

As I was about to pronounce myself immune, I suddenly realized I am the worst possible kind. I collect moments of total subjective pleasure, box them up, and put them in a shed in the back of my head, never having to open them up again but knowing they are there.

So what would be a gem in the collection?

A time when I am totally fit and I have just come wading through one of the fringes of hell, have been stressed right to my breaking point, have expected to be whisked out of life, but was not. I am out of it, and if there is any pain, it is too dwindled to notice. I am in some warm place where the air and sea are bright. There are chores to do when I feel like it, but nothing urgent. I am in some remote place where no one can find me and bother me. There is good music when and if I want it. There is a drink I have not yet tasted. There is a scent of some good thing, a-cooking slowly. There is a lovely laughing lady, close enough to touch, and there are no tensions between us except the ones which come from need. There is no need to know the day, the month, or the year. We will stay until it is time to go, and we will not know when that time will come until we wake up one day and it is upon us.

And that is a McGee catalog 13, unique, shameful, and totally hedonistic. Misfit. An ant with a grasshopper syndrome. Rationale: One turn around the track.

I decided I had better take the whole thing and drop it in front of Meyer, like a crock of snakes, and let him do the sorting and prodding. Meaning, he says, is what somebody finds meaningful.

The phone rang, and she said, "Just to be sure you're alone in your broom closet, luv."

"What else? You're downstairs? Go back through to the second batch of elevators."

"Just as soon as you take care of this man's problems."

"Bell captain here, sir."

"Mmm. Alfred?"

"Why, yes sir!"

"Any dear friend of mine is, by definition, a dear friend of Mr. Nucci's. Send Mrs. McDermit up, please. Cordially."

"Sir, I was only—"

"You were only trying to put a body block on any freelance hooker trying to work your house, Alfred. And no one can tell by looking at them anymore, can they?"

"Sir, I—"

"Find out what she would like to drink and have it sent up, please. And have the waiter bring a dinner menu, please."

"Right away, sir!"

Her little glass jug of margueritas, sitting embedded in a bowl of shaved ice, reached 1802 about fifty seconds after she did, and just as I was explaining to her that any pretty lady coming alone into a Collins Avenue hotel after dark, carrying a purse as big as a bird cage, would be under suspicion of entrepreneurism.

We tried to be jolly and gay, but it kept fading off into a minor key and into silence. The conductor raps the stick on the podium and starts the music again.

Even the absolutely superb steaks did not get us back into our own places. An ugly death had bent our realities, and we were each on our separate journey to Ixtlan because it meant different things to each of us. We ate by the light of candles in hurricane globes, guttering and flickering in front of the open balcony doors, in the moist warm wind that came off the sea. I wheeled the dinner equipment out into the hall and chained the door before we moved the candles to bedside, and even the strokes and promises, the rituals and releases of love did not pierce that curious, deadening barrier between us. We did what seemed expected and what seemed the momentary imperative, each living inside the ivory round of skull, looking out of it with night eyes at the shifts and shadows of conjoining.

12

I awoke, and the candles had burned out. I could hear the sea and, approaching across the sea, a hard night rain, a bumble and thud of thunder. As I sat up, a vivid green-white flash filled the room, leaving me with the afterimage of her pillowed head beside me, eyes awake and looking toward the dark ceiling.

I got out on my side and went around the bed to the big doors. The first driving rain came just as I was closing the second one, spattering and bouncing as high as my belly. The doors closed out the rush of wind, the storm sounds, and muted the thunder. I found the pulls and slid both sets of draperies across the doors. The storm was no longer something alive. It was on tape on a television set next door.

I put a breath of air conditioning back on to keep the air in the room from turning stale, and when she called me, I went to her side of the bed. She found my hand and tugged at me. When I bent to her, she pushed and said, "We didn't talk."

She hitched over, and I sat on the bed, against a solid warmth of hip under percale. She said, "Over the phone you said you wanted to talk. We didn't talk that kind of talk, did we?"

"No. We talked bad lines from old movies, I think."

She was in a total blackness. When I closed my eyes, nothing changed. She said, "It's funny. You know? They've all said so many things so many ways, there's nothing left for people to really say to each other. I mean I can say things, but behind it I can hear Cher saying it to Sonny." She changed to a thin, squeaky little voice. "I am Gabby Gabriele, your very own talking doll. Pull my string and I'll say anything you want."

I said, "Sometimes Jack Lemmon is speaking, sometimes Jack Lord, sometimes George Peppard, sometimes Archie Bunker."

I heard and felt the depth of her sigh. "That's it," she said. "Nothing is really real, and then Jane Lawson is dead, and that is very very real. She'd talk about her kids and the house, and she'd sound like Erma Bombeck, and that wasn't real. You wanted to talk about Jane, and then you didn't, and I didn't ask you."

"Sooner or later, Mary Alice, we have to talk about her, so I guess now is okay. I've got some facts. You have to help me put them together."

"Me help?"

"The damage to the house was done *after* somebody cracked her neck."

"After! But how—"

"Let me cover the ground first. It wasn't kids, because too many of the things kids take were still there. The trashing didn't have the usual pattern. It was imitation trashing, a diversion. The person involved wore gloves. There wasn't even a fresh oil smudge on all the glass and pottery things that were broken. The trashing could have been a diversion for another reason too, to cover up evidence of careful search. Whoever did it came through the front door, I think, with Jane. Then later they blew more smoke by making it look as if some small person had wiggled through an awning window in the bedroom. Judy is in custody. She was a couple of hundred miles away."

She squeezed my hand in the darkness. "How could you get to *know* all these things, darling?"

"I took a deep breath and walked right into the middle of it, using the excuse I took her home Friday. If I'd found somebody too rigid and dumb running the show, I would have left it at that. There are only two kinds of people you can con. Greedy people and bright people. The greedy ones want to use you, and the bright ones want to see how far you'll take it."

"But what does it all *mean?*"

"Lots of guesses. Maybe it's as simple as it looks. Somebody came to the door. Pushed his way in. Killed her and took what she had in her purse and looked for more. Then take it through all the shades and gradations right up to the way out, where she was the one who somehow got her hands on the rarities Hirsh bought for the Sprenger account, and maybe somebody in Sprenger's organization knew about it and went after her."

"But Mr. Sprenger doesn't even *know* anything is missing!"

I thought that over and decided not to go into it with her. Give Sprenger credit for a good intelligence system. When you put a lot of eggs into a lot of different baskets, you watch all the baskets. McGee starts hanging around Fedderman's shop. Let us say I do not look as if I collect stamps or coins. I am conspicuous. It is a handicap, professionally. So he gets a line on me through the plate on Miss Agnes. Or, an ugly concept to swallow, Jane Lawson tells him I am interested, having previously told him his expensive rarities have turned into junk. Or there is some kind of conspiracy involving Fedderman and Sprenger which I have not yet been able to figure out. I can start with the only point I am sure of—that Davis and Harris approached me with the idea that the man they represented had a hunch he had been taken but was not really sure.

Too many ifs and whereases to inflict upon the lady who lay close at hand, warm and invisible in the smaller hours of Monday, on one of the twenty-fifths of the many Septembers of my life. Should a man reach eighty, he has only had eighty Septembers. It does not seem like many, said that way. It seems as if there are so few each one should have been better used.

Meyer made one of his surveys of the elderly couples in the Fort Lauderdale area, the ones being squeezed between the cost of living and their Social Security. They were very bitter about it. They were very accusatory about it. Amurrica should give them the financial dignity they had earned. Meyer's survey was in depth, relating income over the working years to the pattern of spending. Meyer radiates compassion. He is easy to talk to. He ended his survey after forty couples chosen at random, because by then the pattern was all too clear.

He said, "I'll put it all into appropriate and acceptable jargon later, Travis, but the essence of it is that all too many of them were screwed by consumer advertising. Spend, spend, spend. Live for today. So they lived out their lives up to their glottises in time payments. They blew it all on boats and trailers and outboard motors, binoculars, and hunting rifles and department-store high fashion. They lived life to the hilt, like the ads suggest. Not to the hilt of pleasure, but to the hilt of spending. They had bureau drawers full of movie cameras, closets full of record players and slide projectors. Buy the wall-to-wall carpeting. Buy the great big screen. Visit all the national parks in America. Funny thing. They had all *started* to lay away some dollars for old-age income, but when the Social Security payments got bigger and the dollar started shrinking, they said the hell with it. Blow it all. Now their anger is directed outward, at society, because they don't dare look back and think of how pathetically vulnerable they were, how many thousands they blew on toys that broke before they were paid for, and how many thousands on the interest charges to buy those toys. They don't know who screwed them. They did what everybody else was doing. Look at the tabulation on my last question. 'If you had to do it over again, how much would you put aside each month, expressed as a percentage of income, and what would you give up?' Read the things they'd give up, my friend. It would break your heart."

I am no living endorsement for prudence and thrift. My grasshopper excesses are worse than theirs. Yet mine are deliberate. I do not expect to have the chance to become very old. And though my chance is perhaps less than theirs, to think that way is romanticism, like that of the seventeen-year-old who vows no wish to live past thirty. I hobble down the raw streets of some unimaginable future, cackling, soiling my garments, trying to stop the busy people striding by so I can show them the dead bird I am wearing around my withered old neck. Not an awesome and magnificent albatross. A simple chicken.

"Where did you go, darling?" she asked.

I came back to the reality of my hand taken to her unseen lips, each knuckle slowly kissed. A coolness moved across my naked back, coming in silence from the unseen vent on high, drying the last of the sleep sweat.

"I went roaming in my head. It isn't very orderly in there. A lot of brush and jungle trails and no signposts. So I get lost in there sometimes."

"I came after you, huh?"

"Thanks."

"That makes me feel spooky, thinking of the insides of heads like that. I don't go back into mine. It's full of dull junk. Old cardboard boxes from supermarkets, packed with old clothes and schoolbooks. It's full of things that are all over."

"Are you tidy? Is everything labeled?"

"No. Why should it be? I'm never going to go poking around in there. It's all throwaway. I ought to have a truck come and get it. I don't think back. Neither should you, dear. And there isn't any point in thinking ahead, because nothing ever comes out the way you expect it will. So what I do is think of right now, and I do what I want to with it."

"I'm thinking of right now."

"Good. We weren't real good before, were we? Like yesterday, all except the first time yesterday. Jane dying made things strange. For us."

"She has to be involved with Hirsh's problem somehow, but certainly not out of any need for the money."

"Why do you say that? Why not any need for the money?"

"If she really had to have the money, if she was desperate enough to try to steal from Hirsh, long before she got to that point, she would have asked her father-in-law for it."

"What if she needed a lot?"

"How much is a lot, Mary Alice? I would imagine he could have moved a million dollars into her name in that First Atlantic Bank and Trust within an hour of her phoning him."

Her breath whistled. The bed shifted, and the hip warmth pressure went away. Her grasp tightened on my hand, and I sensed, without seeing her, that she had hitched herself up to face me. I felt against my throat and chest a subtle radiation of the heat of her body, and the humid scents of her came clearer to my nostrils. Her voice spoke from blackness at my throat level and not far away. "Are you sure? She never said *anything* like that!"

"I'm very sure. I met the man. I've read about him. He's very impressive."

"But I don't understand."

"Why she didn't tell you about it?"

"Not so much that. Why she lived so small and so shabby. Once Linda started going to college, Jane took that rotten bus every school day. I can't remember her going to a hairdresser. She was always letting her skirts out or taking them in. What kind of a weird kick was she on anyway?"

"Living her own life, maybe."

"If you want to call it living. I never knew she was such a freak."

"Apparently you and she didn't exchange life stories. You didn't tell her things either."

"That's sort of different. I could have gone back to McDermit, maybe. I don't know. I never asked. If I did, I'd have lived rich. If I could have stood it, I'd have stayed. But what kind of grief would she have had to take? Nothing at all. Just a nice life."

"Maybe she thought this was a better way to raise her kids."

"Do you mean that? Judy sings in the choir, maybe? And gathers wildflowers for mama dear?"

"She did all right with Linda."

"And she thought a five hundred average was okay? It seems to me that . . ."

After a long silence I said, "Seems what to you?"

"Forget it, huh?"

"Sure."

"Oh, God, Trav, I don't want to talk about Jane or think about her or Hirsh or Frank or anybody. I just want to make love. Okay?"

"I can't think of any good reason why not, girl."

"You seem to be thinking clearly, dear."

It was better between us. The curious feeling of apartness was gone. She was not a strenuous partner. We slowly and gently and with mutual consideration sorted ourselves out so that there was no strain of support or numbing weight for either of us. In that perfect ease, that sleepy, lasting luxury, I drifted in and out of those fantasies which are neighbors of sleep. In one of the fantasies I was holding a gigantic and disembodied heart, holding it in that precise posture, moving against it in that precise rhythm which was the only way in the world it could be made to keep on beating with that small, deep, and solid rhythm, and could be kept alive.

13

She was all combed and showered and lipsticked and dressed when she woke me up and said that she was leaving to go back to her place and change and then go to the store.

My mind felt like glue, and I wondered if I was duplicating Sergeant Goodbread's habitual expression. "But Hirsh wouldn't want business as usual, would he?"

"Of *course* he wouldn't, silly man! But there's always the mail, and the things I haven't finished, and I want to see what Jane was doing that somebody else will have to finish. I won't open the place up. I'll print a sign and put it on the door. If there's anything Hirsh has to decide, I'll take it to his place and ask him. I hope there is. It will be the best thing in the world for him to start making decisions."

"Say hello to him for me."

"Get some more sleep, darling. I'd give odds you're going to need it."

She gave me a pat and went off to the door, springing along on those Olympic legs. She undid the chain and left, the latch clacking shut. I remembered how (only the day before yesterday) the webbed, interwoven muscles of her thighs had bulged when the full strain of the slalom cutback clenched her whole body. Visible at such times but never discernible to any loving touch, not on the shoulders or back, the arms, or legs. Firm, yes. But so sweetly sheathed by the resilient softness of the woman-padding of the little layer of subcutaneous fat. Grasp her more strongly, and the firm underlayer of muscle was then tangible, sliding and clenching and relaxing. And the tone and control of the athlete muscles was apparent whenever she moved, whenever she bent, flexed, twisted, or lifted, and apparent in the tirelessness of her repetition of any stressing motion.

I bobbed across the surface of sleep, sinking and pulling myself away from it, and at last stood up and creaked a hundred muscles in gargantuan stretching, padded in and adjusted the four shower nozzles to soft thick spray for all the soaping and rinsing, and then to hard fine stinging spray for the cold that finally woke me up all the way. I brushed with the new brush, shaved with the new tools, put on my supermarket socks and shorts and slacks and shirt, my shoes from a previous life where I had lived aboard a houseboat somewhere, and went down to find a place in the hotel to have breakfast. The basement coffee shop had the windowless fluorescence of a bus station at midnight, so I went back up and was led across fifty feet of carpeting to a window table and handed a menu as big as a windshield—twice as big when opened. Three copywriters had swooned while trying to describe the taste of eggs scrambled with roe.

When I lowered the menu, Willy Nucci was sitting across from me. It gave me a start, so visible he said, "I could wear a bell, like a leper."

"I should have been able to hear your shirt."

"This was a gift, handwoven in Guatemala."

"By parrots?"

"You are very funny today. You are killing me."

The man came up and bowed and took my order. A large fresh orange juice. Blueberry waffle. Double on the Canadian bacon. Maybe some cinnamon toast. Pot of coffee. Willy ordered coffee. After the captain left, Willy said, "From what Alfred said, I guess you got to regain your strength."

"I thought he was wished on you. I didn't know he reported to you."

He glanced around nervously. "Why should I ever say he was wished on me? He's a good night man. When he isn't sure, he checks with me. I was making a joke."

"You were? Ho, ho, ho. What did he check with you?"

"If you were throwing my name around or you were okay and he should drop it right there. Drop it there, I told him."

"What if I was just using your name in vain?"

"He wouldn't have broke up any romancing, just had some hackie tail her to wherever when she came out, then depending if it was town or beach, a couple of friendlies would have picked her up for soliciting, and then it would have been put to her as either a hundred bucks and ninety days as a free-lance, or case dismissed if she wanted to join up and pay her dues and learn the rules."

"How about a perfectly legitimate girl friend?"

Willy almost smiled. "Unless a girl has very heavy connections, what difference does it make, after all? And if she's got the connections, she'll start naming them the minute she's picked up, and then it's a judgment call on the part of the friendlies."

"So he described her to you?"

"Long black hair, blue eyes, and tits that came up to his ears. She got a little pissed off at how he acted and wouldn't give him a name, so he tried the description on me because he said he thought he'd seen her someplace."

"Where?"

"He couldn't put his mind to it. I told him to forget it, all and any part of it. He said she was built for heavy duty, for a man and a half. But a little too old to be a bonus item for anybody who turns her over to the union."

My juice came. I tasted it. I pushed it over to Willy, to taste. He made a face and said, "Yech. Know what does that?"

"What does that, Willy?"

"The oil in orange rind is practically the same molecular structure as castor oil. So whatever clown ground this fresh, ground right past the juice and pith into the rind. Be right back."

And that is why it is a good hotel. Willy knows everything. He checks every incoming purchase. He reaches up and runs his fingers along ledges. Fifty times a year he picks a room at random and sleeps in it and makes sure that every little thing he finds wrong is fixed.

He came back with fresh juice in a taller glass. He watched me taste it, relaxed when I pronounced it delicious. He said, "Who can knock the woman who did it wrong? A little round Cuban woman, she does the work of three people out there. God grant I shouldn't lose her and the union shouldn't slow her down."

"Before you sell the place."

"Sell! Sell what I don't own? Are you dealing off a short deck?"

"Sorry, Mr. Nucci."

"Here's your breakfast, McGee. Enjoy."

***

Sprenger Investment Associates was five blocks west of Collins on Lincoln Road, on the second floor in the middle of the block on the wide pedestrian mall. The big glass door hissed when I pushed it open. It was a combination reception room and bullpen, with a deep blue rug and gauze green draperies, big Formica desks in kindergarten colors. A broad tape machine in a decorator housing was against the wall at the left, demonstrating its inhuman typing skill. A table contained stacks of literature about municipal bonds. One floor man was on the phone, another talking to an elderly couple, a third reading *The Wall Street Journal*. They were young men, expensively dressed and coiffed. Over on the right a computer printout station was making a subdued roar as the interleaf printout sheets came folding down into the bin. A girl who seemed to be fifty percent thighs stood at a waist-high counter deftly separating and binding a previous printout. Another girl was having a doughnut and coffee. The third girl stared at me from the reception desk, making her decision not to get up and come around the desk with welcome smile after she had given me a quick inventory, from shoes to sun-parched hair.

"May I help you?" she said, in a voice which indicated she thought it was most unlikely that she could. It was cold in the room. She was pretty. There were goose pimples on her upper arms.

"Mr. Sprenger said he would see me whenever I got here."

"Are you sure he said that?"

"Why don't we try him on it, little chum?"

"I couldn't interrupt him, really."

"The name is McGee."

I saw at once that she had been instructed. But she had not been prepared for somebody who looked as if he had come to fix the wiring. Her eyes went round. "Oh, of course! I remember now. Mr. McGee." Her smile became very wide. Unreal, but wide.

"That's a dead tooth," I said. "Just beyond the canine on the upper left. A pretty girl should get that fixed."

Her smile shrunk enough to hide the gray tooth. She wanted to be offended but couldn't risk it. "I keep trying to get an appointment." She trotted back and through a door made of blond wood, her hair and her little rump bouncing.

She came out, and very close behind her there was a tall frail old man, erect and handsomely dressed. Frank Sprenger, looking just as I expected him to look, had a big brown hand on the old man's arm just above the elbow. He took him over to one of the young men and got him seated and told the young man to brief Mr. Sumner on the new issues on the recommended list, nothing less than Standard and Poor double A. He came back and nodded to me and stood aside and let me go first. He was big and he was broad and he was brown. He had black, straight, coarse hair that looked as lifeless as hair on a museum Indian. His face was a chunk of bone with the skin taut over it. He had simian brows under an inch and a half of forehead. The skin folds around his eyes had a reverse slant from that of the Japanese, and embedded in there were little bright intense blueberry eyes. He was dressed in a way that made him conspicuous in Miami in September—beautifully tailored banker's gray in summerweight weave, a white shirt custom-made for what looked to me like a twenty-two neck and forty-inch sleeves, a blue silk tie, a gold stickpin, gold cuff links.

His office was just as anachronistic. It was like a small library-study in an English manor house, and it looked out upon what seemed to be a ground-floor garden, surrounded by a stone wall. But as I sat in the leather chair he offered me, I saw that though the plantings were real, the turf was Astro, and the stone facing on the wall was by Armstrong.

His voice was a bit high for the size of him, and he projected it with very little lip movement and no animation on his face at all. It is characteristic of people who have either been in prison or who live in such a manner that their total environment becomes a prison of sorts, a place where communication can be a deadly risk.

"Thanks for seeing me," I said.

"Think nothing of it. You found a problem I didn't know I had. I appreciate it."

My chair was carefully placed. Before him on the desk was one of those brass and mahogany gadgets which are supposed to tell you the time, temperature, humidity, and state of the world, as well as play music for you, FM, AM, or taped. I could not see the dials. His glance kept straying to it, and I realized I was probably being scanned. The world of electronic bugging has gotten so esoteric that the best defense is a receiver of great precision and limited range which constantly scans all frequencies on which a concealed mike could be broadcasting, and translates anything it picks up into a visual signal.

A quick run up and down the scale would not be enough, because the casual visitor might be set up to activate his sending equipment once things got interesting. Also there are some bugs, slightly more bulky, which can be activated and deactivated by an outside incoming signal. The best defense, of course, is to never say anything of use to anybody. The second best defense is the offensive technique of transmitting an overwhelming blast of white noise, a smothering hiss, on all frequencies, whenever you say anything you'd rather not hear played back some day.

I said, "A friend told me about a brand new development, a new way to bug a room, Sprenger."

He showed no surprise, only a mild interest. "Yes?"

"Everything is a sounding board. Every word we are saying moves the glass in that big window there. There is a transparent substance somebody can put on the outside of that glass that will reflect a certain kind of laser beam. The beam transmitter has to be in a very solid mount. It reflects back to a receptor, very sensitive, which translates the minute differences in the angle of the beam into fluctuating electrical impulses which can be translated into sound. They can do it from half a mile away, and there isn't any device you can use which will detect it."

"Pick up the voices, the words?"

"A speaker is a diaphragm that moves back and forth like the head of a drum and changes electrical impulses into sound."

He got up and went over to his window, tested the yield in the center of it with big spatulate fingers.

"Could be," he said. "But nobody can see into this window from anywhere because of the wall. So they couldn't hit the window with one of those." He came back and sat at his desk.

"You live in this room? Or don't the other rooms you live in have windows?"

He rubbed his bumpy nose, closed his blueberry eyes for a few seconds, then said, "I'll check it out. You are doing me some good, maybe. You checked me out?"

"Enough for my purposes. I didn't know about this operation."

"It isn't a cover. It's a legitimate outlet for municipal bonds. Home base is in Memphis. We do three hundred million a year in face value right out of this office. We service the municipal bond portfolios of over forty smaller banks."

"But you're not regulated like regular brokers."

His deep tan turned to red tan, and his voice got louder, and he used more lip movement. "We have an association of municipal bond dealers pledged to clean our own house and eliminate the bad practices of the past and drive the shysters out of—What the hell are you laughing at?"

"I couldn't help it."

"What's so funny?"

"You're wired into every kind of hustling there is. Protection, franchises, smuggling, drugs, gambling, broads, unions, extortion, and you get all huffy about your clean bond business."

He thought about it. He tried a small smile which lasted almost a microsecond. "Maybe it's funny. It started as a cover. We bought somebody out. I got interested and built it up. Some of the skim goes away and comes right back into good bonds. I ask them, if the money comes back clean and it is supposed to go into legitimate investment, which would you rather have—a shopping center giving you a taxable ten percent return or bonds giving you five and a half tax free that you don't have to wake up in the night and wonder about?"

"You have a point."

"What bothers me about you, McGee, I can't read you getting into this strictly as a favor to Fedderman. Where's the connection?"

"I owed one to a friend, and he called me on it and said help Fedderman." I knew he would accept that kind of reasoning and thought I saw acceptance in those small eyes. "How did you make me?" I asked.

"In nineteen months I put a good piece of money into that little old man's action. He checked out as an okay old man. He's good for his guarantee. But I wouldn't want to find out some day—he's gone, and there's a jewelry store. Also there is another thing, I wouldn't want that little old man to have a big mouth and say Frank Sprenger is giving him bundles of cash, and having all of a sudden some kind of audit that spreads from his book to mine. I could give all the answers, but it still wouldn't look good. I'm supposed to keep my head down at all times. So I arranged to have people keep an eye on the little old man. Any change in his pattern. I heard over two weeks ago he was getting to work earlier, staying longer. Maybe he's packing? He starts to get appraisals on a lot he owns, on some securities, on the retail business. So when you came onto the scene, we were already at battle stations, so I got a fast reading on you, and it shaped up this way in my mind. The little old man is very nervous lately. You try to get things back when people lose them and the law can't help them. I'm not his only account, but maybe the stuff he bought for me is missing? If so, I am the injured party. Fedderman will have to make it good, if that's so, but I would rather have the items he bought."

"Why?"

"If I wanted money, I already had money. I wanted the stamps."

"That's what I mean. Why did you want the stamps?"

"Personally? I didn't and I don't. A certain associate is under very close surveillance. He made a mistake and didn't cover it well, and he thinks they are maybe building a very tight case against him. He's old and he's tired and he won't last long locked up. Anything he tries to cash in, they'll know it. He has some action going down here, and so he asked me to put his end into something small you can carry in a pocket, as good as money. It used to be stones. They're too big a markup even wholesale and too big a discount elsewhere. I heard of Fedderman, so we had a nice talk, and I tried to see if it would work."

"Tried it?"

"He sold me four stamps from Grenada. From the island. Two pairs they were. One-penny green. Fifteen hundred bucks. I had a courier going to West Berlin, so I told her to sell them there for whatever she could get, and she got forty-eight hundred West German marks, no questions asked, and about a five-minute wait for the money. It worked like he said it would, so I went his route. When that certain associate wants to make his move, he can slip away and get down here. I give him the merchandise and get him onto a freighter with new papers, and he can live nice in a warm climate until he is dead. As a matter of fact, it's too bad the stamp thing isn't a market that will absorb money faster and easier."

"What am I supposed to be doing for you?"

"Is my merchandise missing?"

"Out of a lockbox in a bank?"

"I don't see how it could be. Maybe it didn't get into the box."

"I don't know for certain if it's missing. Fedderman thinks something is wrong. But he's old. He could be wrong."

"He'll have to make it good. That's the agreement."

"He intends to live up to it."

"So if the merchandise is missing, you're trying to find it for Fedderman? You can be trying to find it for me too."

"It would be the same thing. He'd turn it over to you. If it's missing."

"I don't know what he's been putting in the book. I get these lists. They don't mean a hell of a lot to anybody except somebody in the same line of work as Fedderman. If anything has happened, it's more inconvenience to me than anything else. You let me know how you're getting along."

He counted out some money and leaned and put it on the corner of the desk near me. I said, "I don't want to be on the payroll, Mr. Sprenger."

"I wouldn't put you on. That's expenses, nothing else. Expense money saves a man time and trouble and makes him more efficient. That's a policy of mine."

"Well . . . just for expenses then."

"You have anything, you use the number Dave gave you. There's always somebody at the place."

"I think Harry Harris gave me the number."

"Harry who?"

"Harris. Reddish-brown kinky hair, sunburn, sideburns."

"I don't have anybody like that working for me."

"Oh."

"Nobody who does work for me would ever remember anybody who looks like that."

"Now that you mention it, Dave was alone when he came to see me."

"What if I got in touch with you about some other kind of a problem sometime?"

"I seldom take on any work."

"It wouldn't be often. You could be on a retainer."

"I travel a lot. I might not be where you could get in touch."

"For your information, maybe seventy-five percent of what I do is all legitimate business affairs and management problems."

"I didn't mean I was making moral judgments."

"Then what?"

"I'm no damned good at taking orders. You get that way, working for yourself long enough."

I saw his interest fade. "Suit yourself then. Thanks for stopping in."

I didn't stand up on cue. "Too bad about that other clerk in Fedderman's shop."

"I would have missed that entirely if the name Fedderman didn't catch my eye. It jumped out of the print at me. Lawlor? Lawrence?"

"Mrs. Lawson. Jane Lawson."

I was trying to watch him closely without being too obvious about it. He seemed awfully plausible. I picked the words with greatest care. "Frank, you bother me."

The blueberries turned to pebbles. "I *bother* you?"

"One little old man and two women in that shop. So they are involved, the women are, in all his accounts in some manner. So in effect they are handling four hundred thousand of money entrusted to you. You think there has been some hanky-panky. The senior of the two clerks gets killed. Somebody got too rough. You read it, but you never stop to wonder if there is any connection at all. Is that logical? What's my other guess, Frank? What comes next?"

He frowned at me. "Now, come *on! I* sent somebody to shake the merchandise out of her if she had it? Why take a risk like that?"

"It turned into a risk when somebody got too rough."

He shook his head. "No, McGee. No, no, no. Your head is full of smoke. That was a nice little woman. You can smell the ones who will and the ones who won't."

"But you never went to the store?"

"She came to the bank once with Fedderman."

Suddenly that little itch in the back of my mind stopped itching, and I stopped finding some way to scratch it. I heard Jane Lawson's voice. *The Sprenger account is the one where he never looks at the old purchases or the new ones either. He just sits there like so much dead meat. He nods, shrugs, grunts, and that's that.*

"When did she come to the bank?"

He took an appointment book out of the middle drawer and leafed back through it. "May twenty-second. After lunch. The big girl came back from lunch and started throwing up. It was too late for Fedderman to reach me, so Mrs. Lawson came with him. I don't know why he apologized. What difference is it to me which woman puts the stamps in the book? Fedderman wants to make a big thing out of everything. Maybe you've got the same problem. Some freak got into the house and broke that little woman's neck."

I left with money in my pocket and vague unrest in the back of my mind. The pretty little receptionist was prodding at her dead tooth. She snatched her hand away and gave me more smile on one side than on the other. I stopped and looked at the broad tape. Brownsville, Texas, was coming out with a twenty-million-dollar general obligation issue at five and a half percent to expand their sewage disposal system. Sharon, Pennsylvania, was assuming seven million dollars more of public debt for roads, bridges, and flood control. That was nice. I wondered how many Sprengers and friends of Sprengers had their hands cupped under the faucets, waiting for the honey.

I walked a block and took a beach cab over to the mainland. On the island of Miami Beach, all you can legally get is a beach cab. If he takes you to the mainland, he is supposed to come back empty. The mainland cabs taking fares from the airport to the hotels along Collins have some of the doormen well enough greased so they can beat the system. Sometimes I wondered how much Sprenger and his pals had to do with the weird cab system that was suddenly costing me about seven dollars. But Sprenger had covered expenses.

It was almost noon. I peered into the shop and saw Mary Alice and rapped on the glass. She stared toward the door and then smiled and came quickly and let me in, locked the door, gave me the close and hearty stance, the hearty jolly kiss.

"Did you sleep all this time?"

"Me? Heavens! I was up practically before you got the door shut."

"That isn't going to do either of us any good, buddy."

"I came to see about taking you to lunch and—"

"I'm *so* glad you came here, Trav, really. There's something that really bothers me. I just don't know what to think. It seems to . . . I don't want to say anything until you see it."

It was back in Hirsh's office, on his desk. I sat in his chair and examined it carefully. She stood beside me with her hand on my shoulder. It was a white cardboard box, about twelve inches long, eight inches wide, an inch and a half deep. There was wide brown mailing tape affixed to it, running around it the long way and then around the middle, overlapping. Where the tape crossed, there was a mailing label: Mrs. Jerome Lawson. Correct address. It was stamped in big red rubberstamp letters, BOOK RATE. The return address was Helen's Book Nooke.

"The bookstore is two blocks from here," Mary Alice said.

There were three eight-cent stamps on the package, not canceled. There was heft to the package, as if it contained a book. When I shook it, the book slid back and forth. The box was a little too long for it.

I examined the ends with care. The tape seemed to be slit very inconspicuously at one end. I fiddled with it until I found that the end could be pushed inward. It folded down reluctantly against the resistance of some kind of very strong spring. Once it was folded down and the box tilted until the contents were beyond the edge of the folded-down part, the contents could be pulled out of the box.

The contents was an album or stock book just like the one I had been shown previously as being identical to Sprenger's. But this one was green. Mary Alice pulled it out of its fiber slip case and showed it to me. There was a name in gold on the bottom right corner: J. David Balch.

"Who is J. David?" I asked.

"One of the investment accounts. See. There's nothing in here. This is a new stock book. I found this by accident. It's so weird. We each have a little space for personal stuff under the counter near the back. Like cupboards with doors. This was in a brown paper bag, and it was wrapped in a sweater of hers. But it was too heavy for just a sweater. So I started monkeying around with it, wondering if I could open it or maybe pry it open a little way to look in. Know what I thought? That maybe she hid it because it was a very dirty book. That Helen sells things that you wouldn't believe, if she knows you."

I looked at the box again. There seemed to be some reinforcing glued to the back of the flap and to the bottom of the box so that the springs would not push through the cardboard.

She said, "I feel like such a great big dummy. I just never thought of changing the whole damned book."

"You are not alone, M.A. This thing is a shoplifter's gaff. They usually make them in handier sizes, without such a strong spring. And usually they are tied with string. If you glue the string to the paper, you get a very convincing look. The professional shoplifter buys an item from a good store. She takes it home and doctors the box and then takes it to other stores. Put it down on a counter and you can shove things through the end flap very inconspicuously. They have purses that are gaffed. They can put them down on the counter on top of merchandise and reach down into the purse and pull stuff up into the purse from underneath, through the bottom. I guess this had strong springs because it had to go through the mail. We didn't think of changing the whole book because they are personalized and arranged in a certain order."

"I can figure that out too, Trav."

She went and got a three-ring notebook and opened it up at the index tab which bore the initials F.A.S. "These are the inventory sheets for Mr. Sprenger's account. I haven't kept this in the safe or anything. Why should I? Now look at these little figures I wrote in. There are thirty-six double-sided pages, and seven transparent pockets across each page. I number the pages in ink up in the top corners. Okay. Take this stamp here." I read: US # 122a* 90c car. & blk, w/o grill, VF $1500 ($1375) 28–6–4. The last three figures were written in.

I looked up over my shoulder at her. "Twenty-eighth page, sixth row down, fourth stamp over?"

"I don't want to seem like I'm accusing Jane."

"Build the case and I'll try to tear it down."

"Okay. When she was alone here, she could bring these pages back to this little duplicating thing and run off copies. They give her exactly what had been bought for the Sprenger account and the exact order in the book."

"And then she—"

"Let me do it. If I'm going to. Hirsh let her run that little speculative account, bid things in at the auctions, buy things from other dealers. It was like some kind of a joke between them. So she could have bought junk and put it into a duplicate stock book in the same order. And she always got the names put on the books."

"At a luggage store?"

"Luggage and leather goods. Cerrito's. We walked past it going to the bank."

"So she could get a second stock book labeled Frank A. Sprenger without you or Hirsh knowing?" She nodded. I said, "I wonder if they keep any record."

"Could you go find out? Please? Now? I have to be sure. I just can't stand . . . thinking about it and not knowing."

14

When I got back, I noticed her eyes were red. She snuffled and smiled and said, "I'm okay now. What did they say?"

I told her that they liked Jane Lawson at Cerrito's. Quite a few years ago, knowing that they were giving Hirsh a very special price on imprinting, she had asked if she could do it. The press was in the back room. She had become adept at locking the pieces of type into the press, aligning the album properly, and pulling the handle to give it the right pressure to impress the gold leaf letters into the leather. They were happy to have her do it. They enjoyed having her come in. They were shocked at her death and at the suddenness and the ugliness of it.

At M.A.'s suggestion, I took her into Hirsh's office and held her in my arms.

"Now I know the ugliest thing of all," she said. "The last and ugliest thing about it. She had to poison me."

"What!"

She pushed me away and stared at me. "You better believe it. We went to lunch together that day. That was because I was going to eat earlier so I could go to the bank at quarter to one. You know, I'd forgotten about it until today? That was back in May. I don't know the date. I could look it up. We had exactly the same thing. Exactly. That's what was so strange about it. I'm never sick. But coming back I told her I was feeling very very peculiar. By the time I got here, I was *really* sick. At the restaurant I went to the girls' room after our lunch came. That's when she must have put something in my coffee to make me toss up everything. You see, Trav, that's when she must have had the book full of junk all ready, in this box or one just like it, and she knew that Hirsh wouldn't go to the bank alone because he likes to make a little ceremony out of it. She had to know he'd take her. I didn't remember that one time because there are a lot of other times I went on the other accounts. And she went sometimes when I couldn't for one reason or another. You know what? I bet Mr. Sprenger would remember because that would have been the only time he saw her."

"But wasn't there another time you went to the bank to put things in Sprenger's book? July?"

"Right. But there was no reason to look at the old pages, like with the other investors. So nobody noticed. Trav, while you were gone, I've beat my brains out trying to remember if she had a box like this that day I was sick. I don't want to be unfair. I don't want to imagine anything that didn't really happen. But I keep thinking she had something she said she was going to mail. A package of some kind."

"How could she work the switch?"

"I'd guess maybe she'd go in there with the box empty and the duplicate stock book in her purse. She'd have a chance to slip the stock book full of junk from her purse to her lap, under the table. At the moment Hirsh would be showing Mr. Sprenger the first item, they would both be looking at it, and she could take the book out of her lap and open it on top of the good book and edge the book off into her lap. Probably with one hand she could shove it into the box, past the spring. I mean in *that* way, there would always be the book on top of the table. The table wouldn't ever be empty. Hirsh might remember if she mailed anything."

She sat on Hirsh's desk, and I stood frowning in front of her. "And I'm supposed to shoot it down?"

"I hope you can. I really hope you can. She . . . just wasn't that kind of a person."

"In May she scores. Big. In September she's still here?"

"I know. Mr. Balch's account must be worth at least two hundred thousand market value."

"Hirsh leafed through the book, and he guessed that the stuff that was substituted was worth about sixty-five thousand."

"What? Oh, no. You must have misunderstood. I think he included the good stuff we just added that day." She turned and indicated her notebook. "Jane was here a lot longer than me, but I bet I could take Sprenger's list and go up to New York with fifteen thousand dollars, and I could buy stuff that would look okay maybe to Mr. Sprenger or to you but not to a dealer. And . . . Hirsh sent Jane to New York in April to bid on some things when he couldn't make it."

"So where would she get fifteen thousand?"

"I don't *know*. I just don't *know*."

"Why do you say it that way?"

"Well . . . because we both do appraisals. You get so you know what to look for. It wouldn't be any big deal to see something really good and slip it out of the collection and put in something cheap that looks like it. They are estate things usually. The collector is dead. So it just looks like he made a mistake in identification. And it would be a hundred dollars here, fifty dollars there, two hundred in the next place."

"She'd have no trouble selling them?"

"Why should she? It's like they say, I guess. People start taking a little bit and then more and then a lot. Like a disease. If it was like that with her, Trav, then it wouldn't make any difference about her in-laws having money, would it?"

"Every big city has rich shoplifters. Kleptos. But the shrinks say they do it to get caught and punished."

"Don't you see? If something hadn't happened to her, she *would* have been caught. You would have found out."

"I would?"

"Hirsh said Meyer told him that you have a kind of weird instinct for these things, that you have your own way of finding out who took what. I guess he's right. Look what's happened."

"Part of it has happened. Where did the Sprenger collection go? Who has it? Did somebody take it from her house or take the money she got for it? And are the other investment accounts okay?"

She stared and swallowed and put her hand to her throat. "Oh, God, I hope so. I hope Mr. Benedict's collection is okay. If anything ever happened to those, it would kill both those old guys, I think." She hesitated, tilted her head, "No, maybe Jane was pretty shifty, but she wasn't stupid. You just couldn't sell those nineteen things anywhere. They're all famous. They've all been written up."

"If somebody wanted to get caught, though?"

"Maybe it wasn't like that with her."

"What do you mean?"

She got up from the edge of the desk and hung her arms around my neck. "I'm getting so I'm imagining things, maybe. I guess it could have been a year ago. Jane got real strange. Jumpy and nervous. She told me confidentially not to tell Hirsh, but she might quit and move away. She got some phone calls here she didn't want to talk about. They left her real quiet and shaky. And then after a couple of weeks she was herself again. But not really like before. She seemed . . . resigned and bitter. I was wondering . . ."

"Wondering what?"

"There are an awful lot of ways somebody could threaten a couple of young girls. She was always terribly concerned about them. If somebody wanted her to steal from the shop . . . I guess it's a dumb idea."

"We need all the ideas we can—"

Her fingers dug into my wrists. Her face changed. "Shh! Listen!" she whispered.

She tiptoed to the doorway to Hirsh's cubicle office and looked stealthily around the doorframe toward the front door.

"I thought I heard somebody," she said in a normal tone.

"Speak of being jumpy."

"Don't make fun, huh? I have this sixth sense pretty well developed after five years. I've had the idea the last few days that McDermit is having somebody make the usual check on me. It's about that time. Are you getting that boat ready like you promised?"

"Progress is being made."

"Like what?" she demanded, cool-eyed and skeptical.

"There are blocks that bolt to the deck just forward of the side deck, close to the pilothouse. There are ring bolts outside, bolted through the pilothouse bulkhead. Two fifty-five-gallon—"

"I just wanted to make sure—"

"Two fifty-five-gallon drums fit behind those blocks on the port and two on the starboard. A friend named Johnny Dow is bolting the blocks down where they belong. He'll put four clean empty drums in place—"

"Darling, please!"

"—clean empty drums in place and use braided steel cable with turnbuckles to make them secure, using the eye bolts. Meyer, who has the keys and knows the security systems aboard, will open up the *Flush* this afternoon, and Johnny will move it to the gas dock and get the drums filled with diesel fuel and get my tanks topped off and bring it back to the slip. Meyer has the list of provisions and maintenance supplies and will see that they are brought aboard and stowed today. I have a hand pump that starts a siphon action to transfer the fuel from the drums to the regular tanks."

"Please, dear."

"At the most economical speed, the additional two hundred and twenty gallons builds the maximum range, without safety factor, up to eleven hundred miles. I have not told Meyer why I wanted him to do me these favors, and I imagine he thinks it is busywork I have invented to keep him out of Miami."

"I'm sorry."

"I was damned reluctant to make that promise to you, M.A. But you wanted it made, and I have made it. Having made it, I would not dog it."

"If I ever say 'Like what?' to you again, the way I said it that time, wash out my big mouth with yellow soap."

"I promise you that too."

"Brutal male chauvinist pig?"

"Well, if you put up a fight, I'm not sure I can manage the soap part."

She grinned, assumed the stance, jabbed with a long left, and then hooked off the jab, a respectable whistler missing by a calculated inch.

"My very best punch," she said.

"You keep impressing me in new ways, Mary Alice."

"Darling, what are you going to do? Stay in the same place again tonight?"

"Join me?"

"Too many eyes are watching me. At least, I have the feeling they are. I think somebody saw me get home this morning. I tried to be sly, but it turned out stupid. I left my car home and took a cab. And so, of course, arriving home at eight something in a cab looks worse than if I'd had my car. No, honey, much as I need you, I'd be too jumpy. Where are you going to be the rest of today?"

"Here and there."

"But what is there you can possibly do?"

"Once in Vegas I saw an old lady in the Golden Nugget, absolutely totally broke. The slots had cleaned her. So she was sidling around pulling at the handles on the off chance some idiot left a coin in one of them. I saw her find a handle that she could pull, and she hit three somethings and got about twelve dimes down the chute. She got a half hour out of those dimes before she was broke again and started to pull at the handles on the idle machines. That's my mysterious system, M.A. I go around pulling handles in case some idiot forgot he left a dime in the machinery."

"What if I have to get word to you?"

"Leave a message at the Contessa for room 1802. This shop is letter A. Your place is B. If you are coming to the Contessa, it is C. If you are going to Lauderdale to wait for me, it's D. Use a last name that fits. Miss Adams, Miss Brown, Miss Carter, Miss Dean. So I'll check in for messages now and then. 'Miss Carter called and will call again' means I'll head for the hotel and see you there. Clear?"

"Sure. You do that pretty damned fast, you know. You must have had a hell of a lot of messages from girls in your day."

"In my day? Thanks. I had the feeling these were my days, somehow."

"If I let you live through them, maybe. I've got more work to do here. What'll I do with this funny box?"

"Put it in the safe for now."

"Should I tell Hirsh? I don't want to."

"Save it for now."

"Okay, dear. Please take care of yourself."

"I came here to take you to lunch."

"I don't want to be seen with you. And I'm not hungry. And you don't know how unusual that is. I'm always hungry."

Harmony Towers had all the exterior charm of a women's prison. But inside the colors were bright and cheerful, and the people at the main desk were helpful. Miss Moojah was expecting me, and I could find her in Community Room 7, down that corridor to the end, through the fire door, and up the stairs one flight, and I couldn't miss it.

Fifteen old people were sitting in a circle in Community Room 7, and a swarthy young lady was saying, "Weeth the irregular verps, Mr. Lewis, you muss memorize, eh? *Traer*. To breeng. Breeng me a drink. Imperative. *Traigame una copita*. Eh?"

They all stared at me, and a woman hopped up, excused herself, and walked briskly to the doorway, motioning me back out into the hall. She was medium tall, erect, stick-thin, with penciled brows and hair dyed mahogany pink. She had a massive, jutting, macrocephalic jaw. Out in the hall she looked me over with great care and then said in a deep, metallic contralto, "Around here one gets so accustomed to seeing withered little crickety old men or fat wheezing sloppy old men, one tends to forget how they must have once appeared, Mr. McGee."

"I could have come later, after your class."

"I would rather you took me away from it. It is a matter of duty and conscience to attend. There are seven dolts holding the rest of us back. I have petitioned to have the class split in twain. I am so far ahead of the lesson schedule right now, it is pitiful. Come along. We can talk in here. A waiting room. There are dozens in the building. Waiting for what? An absolute waste. Please sit down. Hirsh told me you are a friend of Meyer, and you are trying to help him. He was reluctant to tell me why he needs help. But with a bit of urging he gave me the whole story."

"Did you really bash two holdup people with a toy baseball bat?"

She looked astonished. "What's that got to do with anything? There were three. I didn't have to hit the third one. I told him that I would, and he believed me and left. Why do you ask?"

"I was curious. It seems to be just about the most stupid kind of behavior possible."

"You certainly say what you think."

"I'm trying to figure out how much weight I should give to anything you tell me."

"It was stupid behavior. The bat was a gift for my grand-nephew. Still wrapped. I snatched it up out of terror, certain the man was going to kill me. I hit him, and he fell down, and I became notorious. I was interviewed. My picture was in the paper. So I bought another bat for the little boy. When the second holdup attempt occurred, I felt I was in a dream. I had to retain my reputation as a character. I hit him in slow motion. His eyes rolled up out of sight, and he still stood there until I hit him again. More publicity. On the third attempt I told him I would hit him. He left. After he left, I looked for the bat. It was gone. Hirsh had disposed of it. I fainted dead away. Stupid, Mr. McGee? No. Not stupid. Silly. Very very silly."

"I had to know. Sorry."

"I understand. My mind is quite clear."

"Do you think Hirsh is right? Is the Sprenger stuff gone?"

"Yes."

"Have you wondered about how it could have been done?"

"Young man, we are all fascinated by larceny. Fortunately for civilization, most of us merely think about it. Obviously the entire album was taken and another substituted. It is equally obvious that Mr. Sprenger managed it by devising some diversion, some alternate focus of attention. Had I still been employed by Mr. Fedderman, he would never have taken on the Sprenger account."

"You made the decisions?"

"Of course not! I would have let Hirsh know I did not approve. Then he would know that if he went ahead with it, I would make his life totally miserable, and he would have decided it wasn't worth it. A man like Sprenger would find it amusing to steal his own property and then make Mr. Fedderman reimburse him for his investment."

"I see. Then there is no connection, you feel, between the theft and the death of Jane Lawson?"

"Did I say that? Did I even imply it? Then how do you infer I would believe that? Last Thursday morning those two young women learned what had happened. Jane Lawson had a lot of time to try to work out the puzzle. You were all trying, were you not? I imagine she devised a theory of how it was done and felt compelled to test it before reporting it. She had a very good mind, you know. Quite logical."

"Could she have been involved, on her own or as an accomplice?"

"Jane Lawson? The question is grotesque. It is . . . fifteen years ago he employed her. She seemed very pleasant and plausible. We had to teach her everything about the business. She learned quickly. A good memory. I am a very skeptical old woman. I set some traps which looked like the most innocent of accidents, where she could profit without any possibility of detection. She did not hesitate a moment. She is the sort of person who, if she were using a pay phone and found a quarter in the coin drop, would feel very uncomfortable about keeping it. With some people, with too many people, conscience is the still small voice that says maybe someone is looking."

"What if somebody put heavy pressure on her, like threatening her kids?"

"I think she'd pack them up and go to her in-laws and ask for help. And get it."

"She told you about the general?"

"Privately, in confidence. We worked together there for ten years, remember. I tend to pry a bit. Of course, I'm going to go back now and fill in until he can find someone. I let her know I did not think her decision was entirely rational, but I respected her for it. She should have married again, of course."

"Did you help train Mary Alice too?"

"Are you asking about her in the same way? Maybe not exactly in the same way? A personal relationship exists? I stayed on for two weeks after he hired her. She was, and is, a very troubled person, I think. She was quite depressed when she first came to work. She never discusses her background. I had thought her a fugitive in the legal sense. Now I think she is a fugitive from emotion. She has visited me here many many times. She brings little problems to me. Problems of identification. She hated to ask Jane or Mr. Fedderman to help her. She is not really highly intelligent. She has a high order of native animal shrewdness, perhaps. In time she became fascinated by the high-value rarities. There is something touching and childish about her enthusiasms. I do not believe—in fact, I am quite positive—Mary Alice could not plan anything very complicated and carry it out."

I thanked her for her time. I said I would probably see her in the store. She said Hirsh was going to open up again on Wednesday, the day after tomorrow. She went back to her class, and I phoned the hotel from the downstairs lobby. I had checked at two thirty. Now it was quarter to four.

A Miss Dunn had phoned at five after three and left word she would phone again. She did not leave a number.

I phoned Meyer, caught him aboard his boat. It was too soon for Mary Alice to arrive. I told Meyer she was on the way, ETA unknown. Keep an eye out for her. Put her aboard the *Flush*. Lock her in. Then wait for me aboard his boat. I taxied back to the hotel, packed in fifteen seconds, and tried to pay my bill. But it was courtesy of Mr. Nucci, who wasn't in the house at the moment.

I walked to the lot, repurchased my old pickup, and took the fastest route through a light rain toward the Sunshine Turnpike, swallowing the little bits of acid that kept collecting in the back of my throat.

15

I jumped down onto the cockpit deck of the *Keynes* and went below into the very cramped quarters where Meyer lived like a bear in a cave. A very clean bear in a very littered cave.

"She's aboard," he said. "With three suitcases, a hatbox, and a train case. Your enchanted barge is all fueled, furbished, and provisioned, sir. May I offer my best wishes for a happy voya—"

"Knock it off!"

I do not talk to Meyer like that. It shocked and annoyed him. Then he got a closer look at my expression.

"She gave me the keys to her car," he said. "When she parked, she backed it in to hide the plate. She asked me to drive it away from here and leave it in an airport lot. Miami, if I want to be very obliging."

"Leave it right where it is for now."

"Okay."

"I want to ask you to do something without giving you any of the reasons or background. But there's a risk."

"A big risk?"

"I don't know how big. Maybe there's none at all. Tomorrow morning I want you to go to this address and see Frank Sprenger. Use my name to get to see him. Play it this way. You are very angry at me. I let you believe we were going to make a very nice score out of Fedderman's problems, share and share alike. In fact, I told you that we'd stay healthier if we got out of Sprenger's area until things quiet down, and at McGee's request you got *The Busted Flush* all ready for a long cruise, maybe over to the Islands, so bring your passport. So tonight McGee smuggled a woman aboard the *Flush*. You didn't see her. You don't know who she is. But from something I said while drunk, you think she came to the Contessa late last night and stayed with me in my room overnight. Tonight I told you your trip was off. I got ugly about it. I said I had better company. I said Frank Sprenger was almost as dumb as Hirsh Fedderman."

"Sprenger . . . and *Mary Alice!*"

"I don't know what he'll do. Maybe there'll be no reaction at all. Right now I'm . . . trying to work out a jigsaw puzzle where every piece is square, and when I get them in the right places, they make an abstract painting. But they also make an abstract painting any way I fit them together."

"If he's interested?"

"Remember No Name Island?"

"Of course."

"Find it by yourself?"

"No problem."

"You are going to tell him that my plan, when the two of us were going, was to take the *Flush* down into Florida Bay and lie behind No Name and wait for a good five-day forecast before running across to Nassau. You can take him to the place. For a fee. Just him. The two of you can drive down to the Keys and rent a skiff and go on out to No Name. Are you sure you can find it?"

"My God, Travis. It's—"

"All right. You can find it. It isn't on any chart, so he can't find it alone. Of all the ways I can read this puzzle, if I'm right at all, he'll be willing to come alone. If it's a mob scene, forget it. Be sure you aren't tailed by his people or anybody."

"How do I let you know if—"

"I'll listen to Miami Marine tomorrow afternoon from three fifteen to three thirty, four fifteen to four thirty, five fifteen to five thirty. If you don't come through with a call, I'll come in and come after you."

"But won't she be able to—"

"Once we're well out of here, I'll tell her I asked you to keep tabs on anybody who might come looking for me. If he doesn't bite, just tell me everything is quiet. If he reacts but the time isn't set yet, tell me you heard somebody was looking for me but you didn't get a chance to see them or talk to them. If you are set up with him and know about when he might come visiting, say a man with a beard came by and wouldn't give his name, but he's going to come by again at such and such a time."

"And come back at you the next day when it's definite?"

"I'll monitor at the same times. This is a big tricky bastard, Meyer. Don't listen to any lullaby from him. I think he might make you sit while he goes and gets a description from the night man at the Contessa, the night bell captain."

"Isn't that a little too tricky, the part about the hotel?"

"Suggestion?"

"I didn't see her, but I saw her car and went and wrote down the plate number, and I know where it's parked."

I thought it over. "I like it better. What I don't like is the way I keep thinking of reasons why, if I'm right, Sprenger would like to leave all three of us in deep blue water."

"If it works out and we drive down there, the two of us, and get the skiff from . . . what's that place by the drawbridge?"

"Regal Marine."

"On the way out I can mention I gave somebody a letter to mail for me if I don't reclaim it by such and such a day. Who would I be writing to, Travis?"

"Two letters. Our friend Captain Matty Lamarr, who has never been bought or scared, and to General Samuel Horace Lawson at the Doral." I thought about my luck. Our imminent eviction from what I had begun to feel was safe sanctuary had torn a hole in the bottom of the luck feeling. I sensed emptiness and a cool feeling at the nape of the neck. "Have you got paper and envelopes?"

"When this noble vessel, *The John Maynard Keynes,* sinks, it will be because of an overburden of paper bound and unbound. Here you are. May I read over your shoulder?"

"Meyer, will you accept the premise that the less you know, the more plausible Sprenger will find you?"

"A subjective judgment. But okay. Who will I leave these with?"

"Jenny Thurston. Allow room for delays."

Two short letters. All I had to give was my guess as to who and why. The combination of Matty's professionalism and the general's massive leverage would open up all the rest of it. I put them in the envelopes and handed them, unsealed, to Meyer. "You were reluctant," I said. "Chance to overrule."

He sighed and licked the flaps and sealed them tightly. He said, "Interesting analogy, about the jigsaw with square pieces and nonobjective art. So you put them together in a way, I suppose, that pleases you, and so you call it the only logical arrangement."

"That's what I seem to be doing."

"It is also an analogy for a madman's view of reality. No rules restrict his assemblage, because they're all square pieces. So he makes a pattern that pleases him, and then he tries to impose it on the world, and they lock him up."

"Thanks, Meyer."

He put his hand lightly on my arm, his wise eyes very sober and quiet. "Quixote, my friend. It has been too long for you, too long since there was a woman who moved you, who made magic. It started to be very good, and some automatic relays in that skeptical skull broke the connection. A sense of what-might-have-been can make a man very vulnerable. Suspicion can become one hell of a big windmill. And some kinds of windmills can break your ass."

"Contents noted," I said.

There was a pale pink scrap of day left when I unlocked the *Flush*, noting with approval that Meyer had unhooked the shoreside umbilical cords for phone, water, and electric and had taken off the spring lines and the heavy weather fenders. I didn't want to use any interior lights unless I was on engines or on the alternate one hundred and ten system off my generator.

In the gloom Mary Alice rose up from behind the far end of the big yellow couch and said, "Where the *hell* have you been?"

"Taking care of this and that."

"Don't you know you've got to get me *out* of here."

I moved closer to her and checked on the validity of her anxiety by saying, "Settle down, honey. We'll be on our way in the morning."

Her voice got very thin. "In the *morning!* I can be *dead* by morning! Now. Please. Can't we just go a little way? Please."

I saw the dark shape in her right fist, pointed down at the deck. I took her arm and pulled it out of her hand. She resisted and then let go of it. I took it over to the light of a port. A little Colt .25 automatic, about as small as you can get and stay reasonably lethal.

"Where'd you get this?"

"Can we talk about where I got things when we're *moving?!*"

I handed it back to her. Maybe it would make her feel a little bit better. Her anxiety was genuine, or she was a great loss to the theater.

I went to the topside controls and cranked her up. When she settled down from the indigestion and flatulence that afflict her whenever I rouse her from indolence, I went down and cast off the lines, moved her ahead a bit, and left her teetering against a piling. I brought the *Muñequita* close with a boathook, jumped onto her bow, took her lines off the dock, and scrabbled back aboard with her bow line, snubbed her close, and bent the line around a stern cleat. I cut the timing very close. By the time I got back to the controls the bow was swinging very very near the bow of an old and very well maintained Consolidated in the nextdoor slip. The unfriendly old man who owned her stood by his railing with a big fender, ready to lower it to where I might crunch into him.

"Watch it!" he bawled, just as I gave it hard right rudder and gave my port diesel a hard quick jolt of reverse. It held me against the piling and stopped the swing of the bow and started it moving out.

"Sorry," I called to him as I eased out of the slip. No point in trying to reply in kind. He had enough trouble in the form of a wide wife with a voice like a bearing about to go. He worked on the boat all week long with her telling him how to do what he was already doing. On Sundays they took a picnic cruise of three hours, and you could hear that voice of hers all the way out to the channel, telling him to watch out for the things he was already watching out for.

After I was under the bridge and past Port Everglades, heading south inside, in the Waterway channel with the running lights on, a healthy arm snaked around my waist, and the big lady pulled us close together and said, "Wow."

"I'll put it in the log. One heartfelt wow."

"You better believe it."

I showed her a distant marker to aim at and gave her the wheel and went aft and gave the *Muñequita* a little more line until she towed steadily without wallowing. Mary Alice was very anxious to give the wheel back to me.

"Makes me too nervous," she said. "Where are we going?"

"I know a good place about an hour and a half down the line. We can anchor out. It's good water and out of the traffic."

"You tell me how I can help, huh?"

"You might be able to find your way below and come back with a pair of drinks."

It took a while. She had to hunt for things. She apologized. It was full dark. I was using the head spot to pick up the reflectors on the unlighted markers. I was aware of her near me in darkness, sitting in the starboard chair, aware of how quiet she was.

"And about the automatic?" I said.

"Oh, a friend gave it to me. He was worried about me. He thought it would be a good thing for me to have."

"Ever fire it?"

"I drove way out into the country one time, to sort of ranchland. I found a beer can in the ditch and put it on a rock. I had a box of fifty shells. It didn't make as much noise as I thought it would, but I kept flinching. I had a newspaper in the car, and I stuck it onto a stub sticking out of a big pine tree. Then I could see where the bullets were going, and I figured out how to work it. If I didn't know when it was going to go bang, I flinched after it happened. Then they went where I was aiming. Then I could hit the can pretty good. Every other time at about twenty feet."

"That's pretty good."

"If I had to shoot somebody, I'd imagine his head is a big beer can."

"The torso is a bigger target."

She was quiet for about thirty seconds and finally said, "I'd shoot somebody who wanted to hurt me, right? So I think it would be better to shoot him in the part that does the thinking."

"I can't fault you for logic."

"What?"

"Do you think Jane Lawson switched the stamps in any of the other investment accounts?"

"Darling, can I make a new rule for us?"

"Such as?"

"You come to a point when . . . you want one life to end and another life to begin. I don't want to talk about any of that. It's all over now. I'm somebody else. So are you. We're both new people."

"What are these new people going to live on, M.A.?"

"I haven't seen you hurting for money. Not the way you live. You certainly had the sense to bring along a bundle, didn't you?"

"Even what they call a goodly sum runs out."

"In cash?"

"How else? And safely aboard."

"And we can get to the islands, can't we?"

"Slowly, in the very best weather. Sure."

"We can make the money last a long long time in the islands, living on this boat, can't we?"

"What islands did you have in mind?"

"You practically *have* to go to the Bahamas first, don't you?"

"Correct."

"Well then?"

"Well what?"

"We can just sort of poke along down the islands to the end of them and then wait for good weather, like you say we need, and go across to the next batch. If we kept doing that, where would we end up some day?"

"Trinidad. Venezuela."

"Is there anything wrong with that?"

"These two new people are going to have a long and intimate relationship."

"From the samples, you haven't anything against that, have you? As any fool can plainly see, *I* like the idea. A crazy man has run my life for the past five years, and now he'll never find me again. He'll never have a chance to kill us, will he?"

"When we run out of funds, we'll seek honest work?"

"You're getting stuffy, you know that? What you should do now is just live. Right? It's a big adventure, and we're together, lover. We'll be in love and have fun and swim and eat and laugh and all that. You're the captain. You can marry us. Let's think up a new last name for the happy couple."

"McWorry?"

"Mister, I am *really* going to cure you of that."

I found my little parking lot, circled on three sides with mangrove. I checked the time and the tide chart and laid her just where I wanted her, cross-hooked so she would swing properly on the tide change. I pulled the *Muñequita* up onto the starboard quarter and made her fast there against fenders so she would not nudge us all night. I started the generator and checked the bilges and put Mary Alice in charge of the galley. I sat in the lounge with my drink, moving those square pieces around atop the game table in my mind, finding damned little to please me.

16

We got an early start in mist that soon cleared, and by eleven in the morning we were well down the length of Biscayne Bay in the most oppressive heat I could remember. We were making a stately six knots, but there was a steady six-knot breeze from behind us, so we moved in a pocket of airlessness, in a reflected dazzle that stabbed up into the shade of the tarp I had rigged over the topside controls.

I kept it on automatic pilot most of the time, taking it out now and again to make a correction for tide drift. She sat in the white copilot seat in a salmon-colored bikini, slumped, with her heels propped atop the instrument panel, her legs apart, her fanny on the edge of the seat, the nape of her neck against the top of the back. She had piled her black hair into a half-knotted wad on the top of her head. Sweat trickled down between her breasts, down her belly, and into the top edge of the bikini bottom, darkening the fabric. She had exposed almost every optional inch of skin area to the breeze that never happened.

The heat made her cross. "Jesus, McGee, is it *always* like this?"

"This is very unusual weather we're having."

"Ha, ha, ha. Can we stop and swim or something?"

"Not through here. Have another cold beer."

"I don't want another cold beer. Heat makes me feel sick."

"When we change direction, we'll get some breeze."

"Like how soon?"

"Hour. Hour and a half."

"Dear Jesus. I just can't take much of this."

"Complain, complain, complain."

She snapped her head around and stared at me, her eyes narrow and furious. "Do you want me to make a list of *everything* I want to complain about?"

"If it would make you feel better, go ahead."

"Maybe my nerves are on edge for a lot of reasons."

"Could be," I said. No argument. I let the discussion die. It wasn't going to do either of us any good to talk about it.

Last night she had decided we would have a very busy bed, and she began to do a lot of flapping and roaming and rambling, changing from here to there, and changing back, apparently trying to express a special gratitude with a lot of extra-strenuous work. I stayed with her for a time, and suddenly it was all rubbery fakery, smack and slap, grunt and huff, like a pair of third-rate wrestlers in some lunch-bucket town practicing for the evening's performance for the nitwits who think it quite real.

As soon as I got that image of it, both the spirit and the flesh became weak. She settled down, still breathing hard.

"Did I do something wrong, darling?" she asked. "Did I move wrong and hurt you or anything?"

"No. No, it wasn't that."

"What then?"

"I don't know. It just happened."

"Does it happen often like this with you?"

"I wouldn't say so."

"You want I should help you? Here, let me help you."

"No, honey. Let's just wait."

"Wait for what? Violins?"

"Let's just take it easy. That's all."

"That's easy for you to say. What about me? You don't give a damn how I feel, do you?"

"Sorry about all this."

"It was going to be really great."

"Next time."

She made a sound of exasperation and moved away from all contact with me. From time to time she sighed. Then she got up and went across to the smaller stateroom and slammed the door, leaving behind a faint effluvium of perfume, exertion, and secretions, leaving behind some bedding for me to untangle, leaving behind that strange male guilt and shame impotence creates. The female and the male are both victims of the male sexual mythology. If I do not achieve, or if I prematurely lose that engorgement which creates the stiffness required for penetration, then my manhood is suspect. My virility is a fiction. I have been unable to give or receive satisfaction. The act has not been carried to its compulsory conclusion. Once any element of doubt enters the equation, then the male erection, that font of aggression and mastery, becomes as vulnerable, as delicate, as easily lost as a snowflake over a campfire.

She left me there alone, full of self-pity and yet with a sense of relief. There was just too damned bouncing rubbery much of her, and nothing anywhere that one mere hand could cup. I had all the self-derision of the suddenly gelded stud. I would auction off the *Flush* to some Burt Reynolds type and pursue the quiet life. Some gardening. Gourmet cooking. And a little philately. Or some numismatics, for a change of pace.

I thought of paying a call upon her, but instead I went to sleep. I was more apprehensive than curious.

Now, forced to recall how miserably I had disappointed the lady, I wondered if I might find a clue to a repetition of failure if I were to look upon her and try to summon erotic dreams of glory and see if I could detect the promise of some small physiological response.

Now, in the blazing shimmer and the white needles that came sparking up off every ripple I looked sidelong and quickly at her sitting there and felt awe and a little stirring of alarm. There was so bloody much of her, all so firm and fit. A yard and a half of great legs, boobs like two halves of a prize honeydew, a mouth from here over to there, hands and feet almost as big as mine, a powerful-looking neck full of strings and cables and muscles which moved into a different and visible pattern each time she changed the position of her head. I was aware of all her hidden engines, all working away, from the slow hard *kuhdup* of her heart to all the other hidden things, absorbing, nourishing, fractionating, eliminating.

"If you don't mind too much," she said. She made a nimble reaching flexing motion and dropped a damp wad of salmon-colored fabric onto the deck. "This is a monokini," she said. She stood up, eeled the rest of it down her hips and down her legs and stepped out of it. "And this is a nokini at all. And automatic pilot or no automatic pilot, this is not invitational. It's to keep from dying."

I pointed to the thunderhead building in the southeast, lifting into the sky. "With any luck," I said.

"Can you drive over that way and get under it?"

"If you look over in that direction, like two hundred yards, you will see some birds walking. Never drive the boat toward where the birds are walking. First rule of navigation."

"Oh, great!"

"Whether we get it or not, it'll change the wind."

"How soon?"

"Maybe an hour."

"Why do I bother to ask anything at all? *Why* can't you use the air conditioning while you're running?"

"It has to run off the generator. There's something wrong with the wiring. There's some kind of crossfeed somewhere. If I start the generator, everything will be fine until I cut in the air conditioning. Then it blows about seven fuses, and we're dead in the water until I replace them. On every boat everywhere, dear, something is always wrong with the wiring."

"Why does it have to be the air conditioning?"

"Because God hates us both."

"Don't say that!"

"Offends you?"

"Just don't say it. Okay? It isn't something to be funny about. That's all. It doesn't offend me. It just makes me feel strange. Crawly."

The *Flush* waddled along, the long V of her wash fading into the hot ripply dance of the big bay. The lady stood up between the pilot seats, brace-legged, letting her black hair down and rewinding it to bind up the strands which had escaped. Sweat made oiled highlights on the long curves of her body.

My concealed amusement at myself had a very acid flavor. Here was the libertine's dream of glory, the realization of all the night thoughts of adolescence: a handsome, lithe, healthy superabundance of naked lady in her prime, alone with our hero aboard his crafty craft, stocked for weeks of cruising about, a lady as infinitely available as the very next breath or the very next cold beer or hot coffee, and our hero was wishing she had stood on the other side of her chair because he found her overheated towering closeness oppressive, yea, even approaching the vulgar. It made me remember the time I went to the performance of a Spanish dance troupe, hoping there was a ticket left at the box office.

There was, way way down front. It was so close I could smell the dust they banged up out of the stage. I could see soiled places on the costumes. I could smell the fresh sweat of effort mingled with the stale sweat of prior engagements, trapped in gaudy fabric, released by heat. I could hear the dancing girls grunt and pant. I could see dirty knuckles, grubby ankles, and soiled throats. They were very very good. Ten rows back the illusion must have been perfect. But I was too damned close to the machinery, and it killed the magic.

Okay, hero. You are a sentimentalist, a romanticist. A throwback. You want all those tricks of a bygone culture—the shy and flirtatious female, the obligation for pursuit, retreat, the ultimate capture. Pretty chauvinistic, buddy. This is the new casual world of equality. You are both made of the same order of meat. Should she have a yen for a beer, she can go get it and open it. Should she have a yen for an interlude of frictive pleasure, she can turn and swing astride you as you sit, and you can keep an eye on the channel ahead over her shoulder. Contact and excitation create a natural physical release. It is no big wondrous emotional complicated thing. The new message is that sexual mystery causes terrible hang-ups which create neuroses which destroy lives.

It all made me want to move to a small town in Indiana and start a little factory where I could make buggy whips, stereopticons, and hoop skirts, and sit in the glider on the porch on the summer evenings and hear the children at play and finally go inside and, by gaslight, read that Admiral Dewey had been placed in command of the fleet.

A world I never knew. Maybe the worlds you never knew are always better than the ones you do.

She sat again and swung her feet up. "Won't this thing go any faster than this?"

"Not enough to matter. It's a displacement hull. It has to push the water out of the way. I could get three more knots out of her and use twice the fuel I'm using now."

"It's a real crock."

"But it's my real crock."

She shrugged and was silent. I tried to put my finger on what it was about her that was battling me and irritating me. It seemed excessively childish for her to complain so constantly about being mildly uncomfortable aboard a houseboat taking her away from something that really terrified her.

Children lack empathy about how the adults around them feel. Children have a tendency toward self-involvement which makes them give too much weight to trivia, too little weight to significant things. If the house burns down, the charred sister and the charred kitten are equally mourned.

I had believed her empathetic, sensitive, responsive. I had enjoyed being with her. This female person did not seem at all responsive in the same way. I went back over the relationship. A cartoon light bulb went on in the air over my head. At all prior times, up to last night and now, my involvement had been in exactly the same track as her self-involvement. So of course she had been responsive, in the way a mirror is responsive.

If you go to a play which is concerned with a dramatic relationship you have experienced, you are deeply moved. The actress will speak the lines in a way best designed to move you. But take the lovely, talented thing to dinner, and she will bury you in the debris of her tepid little mind, rotten reviews in London, the inferior dressing room on the Coast, the pansy hairdresser's revenge, her manager's idiot wife, the trouble with talk shows, and who has stopped, or started, sleeping with whom or with what.

I had listened to drama and believed it. And now I could not believe that this was the actress.

I saw the squall riffle approaching way off the port bow, making a busier calligraphy on the water. It covered so large an area it could not miss us. I told her to prepare for sudden comfort. While she was looking at me with blank incomprehension, the rain breeze swept us, a coolness with a smell of rain and ozone. She made a glad cry and stood to face it, arms out in pleasurable crucifixion. It died away, and she said "Nooooooo" in a long descending mournful minor.

"More on the way and rain behind it."

It was more than I expected. The strong gusts threatened to whip the tarp away, and I took it down, folding it with difficulty, stowing it under the instrument panel. Electricity winked and bammed around us as the rain came in silvery, wind-whipped sheets, heeling us to starboard, obscuring the far markers. The rain was unseasonably cold, and abruptly it turned to hail, the size of puffed rice, whipping and stinging us, so that she yelped with pain and surprise and ducked down below the rail on the port side, behind me, for shelter. Then more rain came, heavier but with less wind. I had backed the *Flush* off to almost dead slow, so that if we wandered from the channel we would nudge the shallows instead of sticking fast. Mary Alice gloried in the rain, upturning her face to it, laughing at the pleasure of it streaming down her body. Her hair was soaked and flattened. The deck ran with water. She picked up her bikini parts, wrung them momentarily dry and put them back on. But we had both started to shiver. I was going to switch to the pilothouse controls when suddenly the rain ceased, and I could hear it steaming on across the bay toward the mainland. The depth finder was reading eleven feet, and I had to move easterly about fifty feet to get the distant markers lined up.

Cloud cover moved west, and soon we were in hot sunlight that made the deck steam as it dried.

She toweled her hair half dry, flung it back, and said, "I'm *starving*, darling. I really am. After I eat, I'm going to chop my hair short."

"What?"

"It's too much of a damned nuisance on a boat ride. You could probably cut it better, huh? How about when we get to the place you said? Will you?"

"Reluctantly."

"Why reluctantly? Oh, could it help you turn on, if it's long?"

"I think long hair is becoming to the shape of your face."

She frowned. "I mean chop it off to only about here, not like when it was all shaved—"

"All shaved off? Why?"

"It was sort of like an initiation."

"Sounds like a very unusual club."

"I'll tell you all about it sometime, honey."

"We've got nothing else to do right now. Why not tell me?"

"Right now I've got to fix something to eat. You want to eat now too. Samwiches?"

After we ate, I said, "Okay. The story of the shaved head."

"I don't feel like telling it now."

"But I feel like listening to it now."

She stared at me. "Are you going to be like that? I don't *like* to be pushed around, Travis. I've had enough of it all my life. If you muscle me, I can't feel loving toward you. You understand what I'm saying?"

"I don't think I could ever adjust to a reward-and-punishment system of lovemaking."

"I have news for you. You're going to have to."

"Really?"

"When I'm happy, I'm the best thing that ever happened to you, and when you make me unhappy, I'm just no good at all. Sorry, but that's the way I am."

"I wasn't trying to muscle you."

"I accept your apology."

"I just wanted to know if you were in a home or a prison when they shaved your head."

"Oh, you are such a smart bastard! You just cut off the supply, friend."

"Prison then?"

"No, goddamn you to hell! It was a school for girls."

That was the forlorn tipoff. The ones which are attended voluntarily are called girls' schools. I asked no questions. I could feel the radiations of her anger. At last she sighed. "They caught me and a boyfriend with the whole trunk of the car full of radios he'd taken out of parked cars. We'd both been in trouble before. I was fourteen, and he was twenty. I was in a foster home, and those people didn't give a shit about anything except the sixty-two fifty a month they got for letting me sleep there. At the school we were in cottages. Twenty girls in a cottage. A matron was supposed to run the cottage, but ours was a wino, so two butch girls ran it. I wouldn't let them into my bed at night, so one of them stole a gold locket from one of the black girls and hid it on the underside of my bed with tape. They found it in a shakedown looking for some missing table forks, and so then they all jumped me and shaved my head. It took a lot of doing. I tore them up pretty good. Afterwards I used to jump the ones who did it, one at a time. They locked me up alone a few times, but I kept going until I got every last one. I guess I'll keep my hair long the way it is. It isn't all that much trouble."

"When did you get out?"

"This isn't the confession hour. Some day I'll tell you all that stuff. When I feel like it. Right now I'm going downstairs. You just drive the boat, huh?"

Her voice was weary rather than angry. It seemed quite pleasant being alone. I put the sun tarp back up. I took a beer out of the cooler. A ray leapt high and came down, slapping his wings hard against the water to stun enough minnows for an afternoon snack. Over to my right, in the shallows near a mangrove island, a mullet made three leaps. Mullet come out gracefully enough, then land flat out, on belly or side. They are vegetarians. They graze the undersea meadows where parasites fasten to their skins, and so the mullet leap and knock them loose and go back to grazing. Flying fish leap to glide away from the teeth of the predator fish. Dolphins leap for the pleasure of it. Sailfish leap to shake free of the steel hook.

So why, after the five quiet years in the depths, did my bikinied creature leap free? To knock away the parasites, to stun something she wanted to feed on? To escape the predator or the hook? Or for the pleasure of it?

I shuffled all the square pieces and put the puzzle together again. The trouble with square pieces is that there is no way to know if any are missing or how many are missing. Or many pieces do not belong in the puzzle at all.

I checked the next marker number against my Waterway chart and found we were making better time than I had estimated. We would be there in time for me to monitor the Miami Marine Operator frequency for Meyer's call.

17

There are long expanses of tidewater flats north of the main channel through the eastern part of Florida Bay. Once long ago, when it had been imperative to find a safe place to stash *The Busted Flush,* a friend, now dead, had gone ahead in the dinghy, using a boathook to take the soundings, while I followed at dead slow, taking bearings on other islands, marking down the coordinates. There were several false turns, but at last he found a way around an island about a hundred feet long, forty feet wide, shaped like a lima bean, where by great fortune there was good water close in to the muddy shore. Then he and Meyer and I worked like madmen, hacking mangrove branches and wateroak branches, trying to cover the bulk of the *Flush.* We were not more than half done when we heard the little red airplane coming and had to dive for cover. They should have seen it from the air, but they missed it.

I got out the chart to refresh my memory of the old channel. I had inked it in. It looked like a lumpy run-over snake. I had enough tide to make it, and the slant of the sunlight helped me read the water ahead. Even so I nudged the mud several times where the turns were sharp, where I had to back and fill, like a tractor trailer truck threading a Mexican alley.

I laid the *Flush* close in, close enough to spit into the mangroves, killed the engines, and threw over a bow hook and a stern hook, planning to go over the side and walk them into better position and make them firm, but something changed my mind quickly. Three somethings. A sky-darkening cloud of ravenous mosquitoes, sand flies, and stinging gnats. As I bounded down the ladderway, Mary Alice came out onto the stern deck, knuckling a sleepy eye. Then suddenly she began dancing, hollering, flailing her arms, and slapping herself heartily. We both tried to get through the doorway at once. We got in, and I slammed it and went looking for any open, unscreened port. They were coming into the galley. I slid that screening across and got out the bug spray and gave them a taste of civilization.

"*This* is your goddamn paradise?" Mary Alice yawped. "*This* is where we are supposed to wait for good weather?" She looked down and whacked herself on the thigh. "You are some kind of dummy, you know that?"

There were little ones coming through the screening. I told her to shut up and close all the ports while I started the air conditioning. Soon, after we had killed off the last of the invaders and the moving air began to feel cool, it began to seem better to her. I told her we were lucky there were no dive bombers, a kind of fly half as big as a mouse that folds its wings on high and comes arrowing down to take an actual piece of flesh out of your body, leaving a hole and a trickle of blood. He takes it away with him and sits in a tree and eats it like an apple. She wanted to believe I was kidding. I was, but only by about ten percent.

I explained to her that the wind had died, and when it came up again, it would be out of the north, and we could go out on deck without being dragged away and eaten. But for now I was going to assume the anchors did not need moving and the *Muñequita* did not need attention. I was not going out there. No.

Her disposition began to show considerable improvement, and suddenly it was time to gear up and listen for Meyer. She followed me into the pilothouse, asking too many questions.

"Okay," she said, "so what good does it do if you know that somebody has come around looking for you?"

"Or you. Wouldn't you want to know who?"

"Knowing why is all I need to know. Anyway, what makes you think you can trust that hairy son of a bitch?"

"I don't think about it. I just trust him."

"If you've got somebody under the hammer, you can trust him. Otherwise, forget it."

"Another of Mary Alice McDermit's delicate aphorisms."

"Afor what?"

"Hush."

I tuned the channel another hair and got rid of some of the blur. We listened for the full fifteen minutes. There were calls for other boats and calls from other boats, but no traffic for us. She'd had a nap. She was getting hungry again. She was bored. She wanted a drink but didn't know what. There was a whiny sub-tone in her voice. I let her play with the radio, and she found some country music and turned it too high. It wasn't worth trying to get her to turn it down. She sat cross-legged on the floor, swaying back and forth, singing the lyrics she knew, scratching her bites.

He didn't phone on the second segment either. She was tired of the radio. She went in and changed her clothes and came back in a yellow terry thing like a body stocking that she said was too tight in the crotch. She kept tugging at it. It made her cross. She rummaged through the cabinet over the wall desk and found some cards. The only game we both knew was gin. She didn't give a damn what I might be holding and paid no attention to what I picked, so she constantly discarded right into my hand, and she constantly lost. She turned the radio on again and played solitaire on the floor in front of it. I don't know what her rules were, but she went out every time.

On the third and final fifteen minutes of monitoring, the marine operator came up with a call for "the motor yacht *Busty Flush*." She had a short list, and I came in and identified and took the call. Meyer sounded as if he were calling from the bottom of a big laundry bag. As soon as he'd start to come in clear, they'd dump in more laundry. But I managed to extract from the blur that there had been a fellow looking for me. I felt my pulse give a hefty bump. I waited for the next part of our little code. Mary Alice stood at my elbow, listening to the insectile low fidelity of my tin speaker and, with her thumb, trying to relieve the undue stricture of the nether end of her yellow garment.

It was sick excitement to know that I had placed a bet on a three-legged horse and every other horse had fallen down on the clubhouse turn and my choice was lumping home at historic odds.

Yes, the fellow had a beard. "His name is George Sharsh. He said you know him. Do you know him?"

"George who?" This was beyond the limit of our code, and I was puzzled.

"Sharsh. S as in sniper. T as in telescope. A as in arson. R as in rage. C as in careful. H as in hide. Sharsh."

"Starch?"

"Right!"

"Sure, I know him."

"He said he'd be back tomorrow in the late afternoon or early evening."

"Tomorrow? Thursday?"

"Right. What will I tell him?"

"Stall him." I hesitated. That was wrong. Meyer might think I wanted him to try to delay Sprenger. "No. Just find out what he wants and see if you can take care of it."

Out of the depths of the laundry he said good-bye. I hung the Bakelite mike back on the hook and flipped the set off.

"Who is this George Starch guy?" Mary Alice asked.

"Oh, he comes around with a problem now and then."

"Like what?"

"Well . . . like a disposal problem."

"I don't get it."

She followed me back to the lounge. I had an urge to experiment. "George is sort of an agent. Somebody might be holding stock certificates that don't belong to them. George finds a way to unload them."

"He comes to you with stuff like that?"

"Once in a while."

I stretched out on the yellow couch. She leaned on the back of it, standing behind it, looking down at me. "I got this idea you were straight, sort of. What do you do, work both ends?"

"I do favors for friends."

"But Meyer wouldn't get involved in anything like that."

"Like what?"

"Fencing anything."

"Last night before I came aboard, I saw Meyer. He had a suggestion about your car. By now some friends of ours are baking a different color onto it, and they'll put Alabama tags on it and sell it right in Miami. Alabama tags make it easy. There's no title certificate. Meyer will probably clear three hundred."

"*He* suggested it? I'll be damned! Gee, you never know, do you? Whyn't this George Starch move things through . . . you know, regular channels?"

"That's like selling to a supermarket, M.A. They're so big they beat the price way down. I'm a corner grocery store, and I can make better deals."

"Unless they find out you're making better deals."

"I'm not a total damn fool, honey. If some hungry clown contacted me with a problem about a couple of barracks bags full of grass from Jamaica or Barbados, fresh off somebody's Piper Apache, I would route him to Frank."

She swallowed and licked her mouth and started to speak and had to speak again, the first attempt was so ragged.

"Frank? Frank who?"

"Frank Sprenger. What Frank do you think?"

"How would I know what Frank? How would I know?"

I reached up and patted her hand. It felt damp and cold. "Sorry. That's right. How would you know? He isn't in operations. He's just a guy who's acceptable to all parties at interest, and he works as a sort of traffic manager and resident auditor. I guess because you saw him all those times at the bank, I had the idea you would know what he did."

"Investments," she said in a small voice.

"All kinds, dear. All kinds. I never got to ask you this question. It's been in my mind. Frank is very very heavy with the ladies. You are far from being dog meat. I imagine he made his move. What happened?"

"He . . . isn't the sort of person who appeals to me."

I laughed. She asked me what was so humorous. I said it was like a deer in deer season refusing to be shot by a hunter in the wrong shade of red hat.

"Okay, so maybe he doesn't like girls as big as me. Some men are really turned off by tall girls."

"If everything else is in the right place, I think Frank might start to get turned off if a girl was fifteen feet tall and weighed four hundred lovely pounds."

"Well . . . he never tried anything. I had *no* idea you knew him at all. You never *said* anything about knowing him."

I stretched and yawned. "It was sort of a confidential relationship. He gave me a little fee to sort of represent him in the Fedderman problem. I wouldn't have fooled with it otherwise."

She gasped and stood erect. She ran around the end of the couch and came thumping down onto her knees on the floor beside me, sat back on her heels, and stared at me. "He *paid* you!"

"A token. Two round ones for expenses. What's the matter with you anyway?"

She thumbed her hair back. "Exactly what did he tell you to do?"

"Why are you getting so churned up?"

"This could be very important. Please."

"He told me he heard that Meyer wanted me to help Fedderman, who thought that the properties in Sprenger's investment account had been switched. He said he heard that it didn't appeal to me. I told him that it didn't appeal because I thought he could handle his own problems better than I could. He asked me, as a favor to him, to check it out. To keep my eyes open and his name out of it, insofar as our private agreement was concerned. I'd say he took care of it himself without my help. You and I know who made the switch."

I waited for a reply, but I had lost her. She was still there, but her eyes were focused on something farther than the horizon. She was chewing her underlip. Her eyebrows went up over the bridge of her nose, separated by two new deep wrinkles.

I wondered if I was wearing an identical pair of wrinkles. Good ol' Meyer had found a Meyer-like way of imparting ugly information. Frank Sprenger was enraged. And I had better be very careful and do an efficient job of hiding, because Sprenger was planning to take care of things with a rifle with telescopic sights and then burn my house to the ground. I could not imagine Sprenger, no matter how enraged he might be, confiding his battle plans to Meyer, no matter how much Meyer encourages confidences.

But I could imagine Sprenger asking specifics of the location of the *Flush,* the terrain, the cover, and asking details of her construction and fuel, enough to enable Meyer to make one of his intuitive yet logical series of guesses.

"So he knows you then," she asked. "He knows where you live and how you live?"

"Certainly. Dave Davis and Harry Harris have been aboard this houseboat. You wouldn't know them, I guess. They work for Frank."

"If he came looking for you or sent somebody, would they ask Meyer where you are and if anybody is with you?"

"I would imagine so. But Meyer would say he doesn't know."

"Would Frank know Meyer would probably know?"

"I guess so."

"Oh, dear Jesus God."

"You better tell me your problem, girl."

"He can make Meyer tell him."

"If Meyer sees that Frank is serious about it, he'll tell him. He'll tell him the *Flush* is set for long cruising and you're aboard with me."

Her face crumpled. She toppled onto her side and wound her arms around her head. She began to sob.

I sat up and reached down and patted her. "Hey! Hey, what's wrong?"

She sat up snuffling, eyes streaming. "Wrong! I'm dead, that's what's wrong. You killed me, you dumb son of a bitch!"

She scrambled up, stumbled and nearly fell, and ran back to the stateroom and slammed the door behind her.

I leaned back and closed my eyes. Now I could sit at the game table and take some of the square pieces and turn them the way they belonged and glue them to the table. Too few to be able, from them, to discern all of the pattern.

The brain is a random computer. Fragments of experience, sensation, distorted input, flicker across multiple screens.

. . . The last time I felt I had lost my luck, I made some bad moves which should have cost me more dearly than they did.

. . . None of Fedderman's older investment accounts would have been likely to know Sprenger or to put him in touch with Fedderman. Sprenger could have used a name given to him by someone else.

. . . Meyer's first instinct was that Frank Sprenger had been setting Fedderman up, using the inventory lists Fedderman gave him as a basis for buying substitute junk, using a double for Fedderman to make the switch easily.

. . . Willy Nucci had been very emphatic about how eager Sprenger would be to cover up any personal goof before it became public knowledge.

. . . When Meyer and I had talked about Sprenger at the steak house that night after I saw Willy, we had agreed that, on second thought, it did not seem to be Sprenger's style to try to go for a double by cheating Fedderman, when it would be easier to play the tricks and games he was used to. Easier and safer.

. . . "I like people. I really do." Mary Alice had said that as we walked to the bank. The people who really like people are so genuine about it they are unable to imagine how it would be *not* to like people. And so they don't go about proclaiming.

. . . Mary Alice had leafed back through the book, looking for the page which had Barbados stamps to see if there would be room for more from the same island on that page. She did not have her glasses. Hirsh often bragged about his vision. She knew he could see the pages. Hirsh was volatile. Was he expected to react, to reveal the discrepancy then and there, so that Sprenger could demand that Hirsh live up to his guarantee?

. . . In the store last Thursday, I had believed her declaration of honesty. But she had wept more readily than I would have guessed. Meyer had called her amiable and gentle. She had become just what I wanted her to be. For just long enough.

. . . Had her explanation at lunch that day, of how long it would take to switch the stamps from book to book, been designed to induce me to have the brilliant thought that maybe the whole book had been switched? If so, I struck out.

. . . My decision at lunch that day, to trust her and believe her, had been based upon my assumption that if she had the art, the guile, and the energy to project a false image so skillfully, she would not have spent five years in that little store.

. . . Had she sensed when I was vulnerable enough so that she could play that old game across the table, the blue eyes which become trapped in the silence of the stare of realization, widening in a kind of alarm, then, with obvious effort, breaking contact?

. . . Why would Jane Lawson wait fourteen years before stealing anything? Why would she wonder about the authenticity of the items in the other investment accounts when Mary Alice didn't, not until much later? Jane Lawson was a very bright woman. If she had planned the action and made the switch the one and only time she filled in for Mary Alice, she would know that eventually I would find out about it. I would ask the right question of Hirsh or Mary Alice, and they would remember. So wouldn't she look a lot better if she casually volunteered the information? If she had done nothing wrong, she might not think of bringing it up.

. . . After five years of working with Mary Alice, it was Jane Lawson's diagnosis that Mary Alice would rather work with her hands than make decisions. They were close during working hours, but after working hours Jane never saw her. In the politest way possible, Jane had said she thought Mary Alice to be a little bit on the dumb side. Today I could agree. But not until today.

. . . Jane had called the device of putting a hair from her head under the rubber band around Judy's books one of her "sneaky spy tricks." It showed a certain talent for subterfuge. Would she mention the rubber band trick if she had used that same talent more profitably?

. . . Harris and Davis got to me much too fast, much too soon after I became involved. And their first objective was to sideline me, to pay me to back away from Fedderman's problems and wait for word from my anonymous employer.

. . . I remembered Harris being silenced by Davis. Harris had said, "That was one of the questions. To find out if McGee was—" Was what? Susceptible of being scared off? Too committed to the Fedderman problem already? Apparently if I couldn't be bought off or scared off, the third step was to clue me in by saying their boss was interested in the Fedderman situation—which was the same as naming him—and wanted to be certain I was not going to help somebody pull something dumb and fancy which would leave Sprenger on the short end. I could not have let them go back and report that I knew how to keep a good scorecard and I'd refused the money. To Sprenger that would have been tantamount to saying I was out to try to clip him.

. . . Mary Alice had reacted all too greedily to the ripe and pungent smell of money within the restricted tailored gardens of the Key Biscayne Yacht Club. She had almost visibly salivated. And when she got over believing I was probably the caretaker on the *Flush,* the touching began. Hand on my shoulder, hip bumping into me. People establish private space around them and do not move into yours or let you into theirs unless you establish intimacy or the promise of it. She had abruptly diminished the spaces we both maintained, moving into mine, letting me into hers. There must be a mutual willingness to reduce the space, or one person becomes uneasy and uncomfortable. Meyer uses that phenomenon to rid himself of the very infrequent person who bores him. He moves inside their space rather than trying to back away. When he stands with his nose five inches from theirs, they begin to falter and move back. Meyer keeps moving in, smiling. They see somebody across the room they want to talk to and excuse themselves. Or remember a phone call they have to make. With Meyer it is a deliberate kindness to do it that way.

. . . Out there afloat in the night off Lauderdale, she had told me that if she ever did want to take the risk, it would be with somebody so hard to kill that maybe he could keep her alive too. And after soliciting me, she tried to turn me off again, with both of us knowing it was too late at that particular time and place for any stopping.

. . . She had wept very quickly and abundantly when I had told her about Jane Lawson last Sunday. As she had wept easily in the store. As she had wept not long ago, right here, when she had toppled over. In the kind of early life she had, of foster homes and the school for girls, could the luxury of genuine tears be sustained, or would tears be one of the weapons of survival?

. . . "Don't come to my place. That's asking for trouble." I'd never been inside it. When I'd first seen it, she had answered my unspoken question, saying that there was a lot of difference in size and in rent between the big apartments on the top floors in front, and the little studio apartments on the lower floors in the rear. "Don't phone me there."

. . . Willy Nucci heard of my new relationship with Sprenger very quickly. But not too quickly for Willy. His network is all over the beach. Switchboards, housekeepers, doormen, car rental girls, apartment managers, bartenders. I'm only guessing. There is probably an unlisted number to call, an anonymous voice, and cash money in a plain envelope, enough to keep the flow coming in, as much cash as the information is worth. Willy wouldn't be so stupid as to be known as the destination of the flow. Then sharpsters would start feeding bad information, to con something out of Willy. Probably somebody close to Harry Harris told her hairdresser about the fabulous old houseboat some fellow in Lauderdale named McGee owns. Harry saw him on business. Which, to Willy, who might have heard it within twenty minutes, meant I was on Sprenger's team.

. . . In the thunderous night, in the darkness, she had lain naked under percale, squeezing my hand and saying oooh and ahh at my modest account of my deductive brilliance. She said she didn't want to go rummaging around inside her head. She said it was all junk, all throwaway. The news of Jane's in-law wealth had galvanized her, lifted her up out of the bed. In alarm? And she could not comprehend why Jane had never gone after that money. She thought it freak behavior. I thought it odd. But I could understand. The next morning she was up unexpectedly early and diligent and brisk.

. . . Alfred, the night bell captain, thought he had seen Mary Alice somewhere before. And she would not give him her name.

. . . When I had asked Sprenger, in his office, how he had gotten onto me so quickly, his explanation was detailed, garrulous, and unconvincing. So was his explanation about the source of the investment money. I think that what made both stories unconvincing was the ease with which he could have sidestepped my questions. How did you get onto me? I keep good track of things. Where did the money come from? An investor. Sprenger had not gotten where he was by saying one word more than required in any situation. And the explanation about the test with the courier in West Germany seemed more as if he was trying to sell me on how good an idea it was.

. . . I'd believed Sprenger when he said he had not gotten agitated when he learned Jane Lawson was dead. Yet he should have been. If he believed his investment account was intact, he might not have reacted at all. Yet he *knew* something was wrong. The only answer was that he knew Jane Lawson was not involved. That meant he had to know who was.

. . . I went from Sprenger's office to the shop, where she had been working diligently all morning. And suddenly there were a lot of things pointing right at Jane Lawson. But when was the label on the gaffed box typed? And when and why were new albums imprinted in gold for Frank A. Sprenger and J. David Balch? Sprenger's, at least, had only a few pages left empty. "Jane, honey, while you're over there, whyn't you take these two and make me up the blue one for Sprenger and the green one for Balch, okay?" Had the figures written on the inventory sheets been for simplicity in finding a specific stamp or to make it easier to make up a whole duplicate book?

. . . Hirsh might remember if Jane Lawson had taken a package along that day and mailed it. She could have been given the package by a girl too sick to go to the bank that day. "Please mail it for me, Jane honey."

. . . The poisoning episode was increasingly hard to buy. She had to claim it happened, because that meant Jane Lawson had arranged it when she was ready to make the switch. How do you measure exactly how much emetic to give a big healthy girl, an amount that will render her too ill to go to the bank but not so ill as to have to be taken home? Banks have phones. Fedderman would have left a message for Sprenger. Sickness is easy to fake. A hunk of soap slides down easily. Send Jane off to the bank this time, and make the switch in July, at the next visit. Sprenger would probably call the signals. Easy for him to lean across the table and point down to one of the new purchases and ask Fedderman a question about it. Plenty of time for her to switch the books.

. . . Miss Moosejaw had said Jane Lawson would have added up how it was probably accomplished and tried to test her theory. By asking a question? And the old lady had not thought Mary Alice morally incapable of robbery that devious, just mentally unable to plan and carry out something so complex. But with Sprenger to plan it, could she carry it out?

. . . If Sprenger was worried about somebody trying to get cute, was it hard to figure out who he had in mind?

I stood up. I wished I could somehow stand up and leave myself still stretched out on the couch. I wanted to shed myself, start brand new, do better.

Had I been spending the last many years selling real estate or building motels, I could not be expected to recognize that special kind of kink exemplified by our Mary Alice McDermit. There are a lot of them, and they come in all sizes, sexes, and ages. They are consistently attractive because they are role players. Whatever you want, they've got in stock. They are sly-smart and sly-stupid. They would much rather tell an interesting lie than tell the truth. Never having experienced a genuine human emotion, they truly believe that everybody else in the world fakes the emotions too, and that is all there is.

I once knew an otherwise sane man who became hopelessly infatuated with the peppy, zippy little lady with the bangs who used to do the Polaroid commercials on television. He bought every kind of camera they make. He took pictures of her picture on the tube. He cut her picture out of magazines. He wrote and wrote and wrote, trying to get a name and address. He went to New York and made an ass of himself visiting advertising agencies and model agencies. It took a long time to wear off. It was totally irrational.

I had seen somebody I had invented, not Mary Alice. I explained away her inconsistencies, overlooked her vulgarities, and believed her dramatics. And so it goes. It is humiliating, when you should know better, to become victim of the timeless story of the little brown dog running across the freight yard, crossing all the railroad tracks until a switch engine nipped off the end of his tail between wheel and rail. The little dog yelped, and he spun so quickly to check himself out that the next wheel chopped through his little brown neck. The moral is, of course, never lose your head over a piece of tail.

Goodbread merely pretended a vast stupidity. Mine, nourished by the blue eyes and the great body, had been genuine. But last night some strange kind of survival instinct had taken over. The body seems to have its own awareness of the realities. In the churny night, the tangly bed, abaft that resilient everlasting smorgasbord, body knowledge said "Whoa!" And whoa it was, abruptly. One just doesn't do this sort of thing with monsters. Not with a big plastic monster which would kill you on any whim if it was certain it would never be caught, and if it anticipated being amused by the experience. Body knowledge said she'd killed Jane Lawson. Not at the moment of Whoa. Afterward, in a growing visceral realization.

She had mousetrapped Sprenger somehow, and it was probably within her power to make him look like such a fool, the people he served would feel a lot better if he was on the bottom of the Miami River. Willy Nucci had explained the occupational hazards to me and to what lengths Sprenger would go to cover up any indiscretion, any violation of the code. The parties at interest had brought in the hard man from Phoenix to police one of their neutral areas, and after six years of service, he had gone sour. Over a woman. And that was his vulnerable area, right? Right.

I had set it in motion, knowing that if Sprenger ignored Meyer's information, all my guesses were wrong. So I could wait for him or run. I could bring Mary Alice into it all the way or use her as bait. I could try to negotiate with him or hit first.

I tried to guess what I would do if I were Frank Sprenger, but I found I did not know enough about the situation, the relationships. Mary Alice could tell me, but I did not like to think of the ways I might have to use to make sure she was telling me all of it. There was no way to appeal to her, except through her own self-interest. She was afraid of being hurt. She had said so after I had mended the flap of elbow skin. Not the casual bumps and bruises and abrasions. But really hurt, with infections and drains and IVs. And that I could not do.

18

I found her snapping the catches on her train case. She had changed to pale pink jeans and a light blue work shirt with long sleeves. She had tied her head up in a blue and white kerchief. She wore new white sneakers.

She straightened and looked at me almost expressionlessly. There was a little contempt there. Not much else.

"I'm splitting," she said.

"You've thought it all over, eh?"

"You blew it, baby. You really blew it. It could have been okay for us. Frank will have guys watching every place for five hundred miles where you could dock this boat. I don't give a damn *what* you do."

"Where are you going?"

"You know something? That's dumb. That's really dumb. All you are going to know is that you put me ashore back by that bridge where the cars were. When Frank wraps wire around your dingus and plugs it in and starts pushing the button, you're going to wish to God you had something you could tell him about where I went."

"Why should he care where you go?"

"Oh, boy. He can talk his way out of how I could run when he wasn't looking and how he'll find me and so forth. But he can't risk what I'll say to the McDermits about him. How long before it gets dark here?"

I looked at my watch. "Little over an hour."

"How long would it take the little boat to get back to that place where the bridge is?"

"Fifteen minutes."

"I'm taking the train case and this suitcase and leaving this other junk. I want it to be a little after dark when you let me off. You better put on better clothes for the bugs out there. You got some kind of repellent to put on?"

"What's he got to do with the McDermits?"

"Huh? Oh, I'm married to Ray. He's the middle brother. They got him on tax fraud and conspiracy and a couple of other things over five years ago, and he's in Lewisburg. He's doing easy time. Except he can't do any balling in there, and he's as spaced out on it as old Frank is. Ray was going to get out last year on parole. But the silly jackass got into some kind of mess, and it will be at least another year. Maybe two. Are you going to change?"

"This is probably as true as the last version you told me."

"So forget the rest of it. All right?"

"And forget the boat ride, M.A."

She had the little automatic tucked into the waist band of her jeans on the left. It was not an especially deft draw, that cross-draw recommended to FBI agents, but it was fast enough for somebody six feet away too stupid to anticipate it.

"We will definitely not forget the boat ride, friend," she said. She backed away, aiming more carefully. "I can't run the damned thing, and I am definitely not going to ruin you so bad you can't run it. Unless you get cute and I make a mistake, and then I'll try to run it. It can't be a lot different than a car. I'd rather you run it. What's the best place? Right up there over your collarbone, maybe. Through that big muscle that comes down from the side of your neck? You want to hurt while you run the boat, or do you want to be okay and feel good and say good-bye nicely?"

"You read me wrong," I said. "I said forget the boat ride, because according to the tide tables, there shouldn't be anything out there now except mud flats and sand flats and a trickle of water here and there. Can't you feel how solid the deck feels under your feet? And the little list? We're aground, and so is the *Muñequita*."

I watched her expression and her eyes. She glanced toward the port. She couldn't see from that angle. She sidled to her left, and the instant her eyes swiveled away from me, I took the long step, the long reach, caught her by the wrist and by the elbow and gave the funny bone a powerful tweak. She yelped as her hand went dead and the gun fell. I yanked my eyes and face back just in time, and her hooking slash with her left hand left four bleeding lines high on my chest and packed her fingernails with tissue. I shoved her onto the bed so hard her legs rolled high and she almost went over the other side. I picked up her automatic and swiveled the little safety up into the notch on the slide and put it into my pocket.

She sat on the side of the bed, and the tears rolled as she looked dolefully at me. "I'm sorry. I'm so s-scared, honest, I don't know what I'm doing. I'm sorry, darling."

"That doesn't work either."

"What?"

"Sprenger wants you. So if I want to maintain good relations with him, the easiest thing to do is wrap you up and hand you to him. I'll say, 'Frank, old buddy, she conned both of us, but here she is.'"

The tears had dried and stopped in moments. She sat scowling in thought, nibbling her thumb knuckle. "No. I'm trying to give it to you absolutely straight. It would finish the both of us, not just me, because he couldn't be sure of how much I told you. He can't afford any part of it getting out."

"So the more you tell me, M.A., the more dangerous I am to Frank, and the more chance I might want to play it your way."

She studied me and then gave a little nod as something seemed to go click way back in those blue eyes.

After Ray was sentenced, she said, it became obvious that there were some people in Philadelphia who believed he had done some talking to make his sentence lighter, and they were willing to get back at Ray McDermit through his young wife. Ray didn't want her visiting him. He said it drove him up the walls. Sprenger kept an eye on the McDermit interests in the Miami area. He was new then, about a year in the area. He flew up and brought Mary Alice back down. She was to find a job where she would stay out of trouble. The McDermits provided rent on a handsome apartment and the utilities, a car, but no cash in hand. Ray had said it was his wish that if he wasn't getting any, he wanted to be certain Mary Alice wasn't giving it to anybody else. She said he was called "the crazy brother." He wasn't crazy, but it was hard to guess what he would do. From inside prison he exercised a lot of power with the threat of revealing the damaging information he had in his head.

"I thought I could cut it," she said. "Besides, Sprenger wasn't about to get careless about keeping an eye on me. And if I goofed, I had no idea what Crazy Ray would want done to me. But I knew it would get reported back and whatever he wanted done would get done. I got to like the store and the stamps and all, sort of. And I practically killed myself at the Health Club, but I got awful restless. I really did."

She had figured out, finally, that Sprenger was the key to her personal freedom. She worked on him for a long time. He was very cool and cautious. Finally desire was stronger than circumspection.

"Those cats that have the choice of a couple hundred girls, the one they want the worse is the one they shouldn't have," she said. "I knew the leverage it gave me once we started, and so did he. What I was afraid of, he'd have me killed and have it look as if I just packed and left. He couldn't be expected to be able to keep me from splitting. He set up our dates, you'd think it was a CIA operation. If it ever got back to the McDermit brothers, you can imagine. A man who'll rip off your wife when he's supposed to be keeping her on ice will cut a piece of your money too. I was afraid once he had all he wanted, I was going into a canal, car, clothes, and everything. So I told him I had confided in a certain person, who would never never tell, unless, of course, I disappeared or something. And then I had him between a rock and a hard place. If he hurt me to make me tell who, I'd make a phone call to Philadelphia, and he was dead. He was right on the hook, and he knew it, and he had no way of stopping anything I wanted to do. And what I wanted was money of my own, and I told him if he'd become a client of Fedderman, between us we could take him for what he was worth, which I figured at four hundred thousand, from things he had said. He explained to me he was supposed to have good judgment, and I wanted him to make a stupid, dangerous, amateur investment in postage stamps, for God's sake. He said Fedderman would go to the law if he got swindled, and the name of Frank Sprenger would come into it, and some people would come and take him swimming. I made him talk to Fedderman. I made him check it out that there's a steady market for rarities. He found out there's no duty hardly anywhere in the world on importing or exporting rare stamps. I had the leverage, and I kept at him. He had to use his own money. He went over just how I wanted to do it, and he figured out better ways. After we started, I found out Ray wasn't getting out and might even have to go the whole ten years. Which would make me an old bag, thirty-three damn years old, and the hell with *that* noise. So it made it more important for me to take Fedderman."

I could see how neatly she had trapped Sprenger. But I wondered that he had not arranged a fatal accident or a fatal illness so plausible the confidant would have felt no need to make a report.

I could guess at his dismay in investing a fortune in little colored bits of paper.

She got up and went and looked out the port. "There's enough water out there to run the little boat, right?"

"Right."

"You're pretty tricky."

"Keep talking."

She sat on the bed again, choosing her words carefully, explaining to me that it was her guess that by now Frank Sprenger had reported her missing, and with whom and how, to the McDermits. He would have to do that to take the edge of plausibility off any report the confidant might make. There wasn't one, but he had no way of knowing. Or maybe now there was one. Me. The only way Sprenger could feel completely safe would be to arrange the private, efficient, anonymous deaths of Mary Alice McDermit and Travis McGee and recover the fortune in rarities with which Mrs. McDermit had fled.

"They're aboard?" She nodded. "Show me."

She snapped the train case open. I went over and stood over her, tensed for any unpleasant surprise she might bring out of the dark blue case. She took out the top tray, and under it were three six-by-nine manila clasp envelopes, with cardboard stiffening, each filled to about a half-inch thickness. She opened one and eased some pliofilm envelopes out and spread them on the bed. I saw blocks of four and six stamps, still in Hawid and Showgard mounts, showing old dirigibles, old airplanes, black cattle in a snowstorm, portraits of Chris Columbus, with and without Isabella.

"All here," she said. "Years and years of the good life. It will last forever in the right places. I cleaned some goodies out of the safe too, stuff he has for stock."

"Where'd you get the junk you substituted?"

"Indirectly, by Frank, through an independent agent in New York. I made new inventory lists without any description of quality. He bought junk. Stained, torn, thinned, repaired, regummed, faded, rejoined, even forgeries. They cost a little over twelve thousand, I think. I took them to my apartment and mounted them and put them into the duplicate book. Then when we were close enough to all the traffic could stand, Frank distracted Hirsh, and I switched books and shoved the good one into that box Frank got me that I showed you. We went out together, and I mailed it. Frank thought it was coming to him, but I'd changed the label. God, was he ever irritated! But what could he do?"

"What could he do?" I wanted to go further with it, but sensed that this was not the time to push. I picked one of the transparent envelopes up and looked at a block of six showing a mob scene around Columbus in chains.

"Careful!" she said. "That's thirty-five hundred at least."

"Anywhere?"

"Practically." She gathered the stuff up and put it back into the envelope. She closed it, hesitated, put the other two back into the train case, and handed me the one she had just closed.

"What's this?"

"It's worth about forty percent of the whole thing, that envelope. I think we should be entirely honest with each other. You've got to forgive me for trying to do a stupid thing. I need your help. Do you have a passport?"

"Yes. Aboard."

"And some money?"

"Yes."

"I can really be a very loving person, dear. That's at least a hundred and sixty thousand dollars in that envelope in your hand."

"You mean, leave us flee together, Mrs. McDermit?"

She looked annoyed. "Well, why the hell not? What else have you got working for you? It's what we were going to do anyway."

"Only at some port of call with an airstrip, I was suddenly going to find you missing."

"I thought of it. I thought I might, after a long long time alone with you."

"With me, the great lover?"

"That would probably never never happen again, and if it does, you shouldn't be so silly about letting a person help."

"But now we start going by air right away?"

"What's the best way to do it?"

"Oh, probably take the *Muñequita* right across the stream to Bimini. It might jar your teeth and kidneys loose. Top off the tanks and run to

Nassau. Tie up at Yacht Haven and take a cab into town and get a visa for London or Rome or Madrid and go out to the airport and wait for something going our way."

"That easy?"

"The first part of anything is usually easy."

"I always wanted to see the islands. I really did. I just hate missing the islands. Maybe we can come back some day."

Yes indeed. I would have truly enjoyed showing her the islands. How the big aluminum plant and the oil refinery of Amerada Hess blacken the stinking skies over St. Croix. Maybe she'd like the San Juan Guayama and Ybucoa areas of Puerto Rico where Commonwealth Oil, Union Carbide, Phillips Petroleum, and Sun Oil have created another new industrial wasteland where the toxic wastes have killed the vegetation, where hot oil effluents are discharged into the sea and flow westward along the shoreline in a black roiling stench, killing all sea life.

She might be impressed were I to cruise into Tallabea Bay and describe to her the one and a half billion tons of untreated wastes from Commonwealth–Union Carbide which put a two-foot coat on the bottom of the bay. Or we could take a tour up into the mountains to watch how the trade winds carry the bourbon-colored stink of petrochemical stacks through the passes all the way to Mayaguez, ninety miles from the refineries. While in the hills, we could check and see if Kennecott Copper and American Metal Climax have started to strip-mine the seven square green tropic miles of high land which they covet.

It might have made quite an impression.

"Can we start now? Can we?"

"It's full dark on an outgoing tide. The morning is good enough. In the morning I can take the *Flush* back out the way we came and leave her in storage at Regal Marine. Abandon her and it attracts too much attention. The Coast Guard would get in the act and Civil Air Patrol and guide boats and so on. Then we can go on from there."

"Okay. I feel so much better. I'm so glad we had this frank talk, darling."

"I guess we accomplished a lot."

"Oh, we did!" She lifted the train case back out of the way and hitched over to me and put a shy kiss near my mouth. I held her and looked past her hair at the manila envelope I still held in my right hand.

Pore helpless little critter. Sharing her wealth, but only on a temporary basis. Only until she could find the right time and place to slip an icepick into my brain through whatever orifice seemed handiest.

"Shouldn't we have a drink to celebrate?" she asked.

Of course, of course. She trotted to the galley to make the drinks. I changed into khakis and a white T-shirt and went to the lounge. As she came smiling in with the drinks, I said, "If Frank were to come here tonight . . ."

She jerked and lost some of my drink on the back of her hand and on the carpeting as she was handing it to me. "Jesus! Don't come on like that, will you?"

"Hypothetical question. Would he come alone?"

She sat opposite me and pondered it. "I don't know. It depends. He's the kind of guy who likes all the odds his way. I'd say this. If he didn't come here alone, he'd leave alone. There isn't any such thing as trusting people, not when it's worth money to them to put a knife in your back. What he'd probably do, he'd fake one of his slobs into thinking it was some other kind of deal, and when it was done, he'd drop the slob right beside us."

"Is he really as rough as you seem to think?"

"You've got me nervous. Is it okay to pull those curtains across? I don't like all that black looking in at us."

"Go ahead."

She pulled all the heavy curtaining and turned off two of the four lights. She sat beside me and said, "That's a lot better." She touched my glass with hers. "Happy days," she said.

"Happy days, Mrs. McDermit."

"Is it like a joke, the way you keep calling me that?"

"I guess it's like a joke."

"The best thing would be if Frank *did* come here and we were ready and waiting and we took him."

"Would he be hard to take?"

"You better believe it. He's a freak. He knows it all—judo, knives, guns, everything. Like a hobby. And he is fabulously strong. Not just ordinary strong, but special, the way some people are. He can hold his hand out like this, all his fingers spread, and put four bottle caps between his knuckles, here, here, and here, and the last one between his thumb and the side of this finger. Then he can slowly make a fist and bend every cap double. Don't look at me like that. It isn't a trick. He has to be careful to place them right, or they can cut into his flesh. There's another thing he does. You know the kid game, you put both hands out palm up and the other person puts their hand palm down on top of yours and tries to yank them out of the way before you can turn your hands over and slap the backs of their hands? I've never seen anybody fast enough to slap him or fast enough to get out of his way. And, wow, does he ever slap! He told me once that when he was fifteen years old, he was a bouncer. He never had to hit anybody, he said. He just took hold of them above the elbow and walked them out, and they always went. They couldn't use that arm for a few days either."

"Good with guns?"

"Not fast-draw stuff. Not like that. He has these custom guns, like he had one in the car he showed me once, like a rifle, with a place for his hand to fit perfectly, carved out to fit his hand. And a telescope fastened to it, with a lot of straps and gadgets. He said he makes his own loads. He belongs to clubs where they shoot at targets, and he wins cups and medals. Do you know what he told me? He said he could put a ten-penny nail into a tree, hammer it in and leave a half-inch sticking out, and he could stretch out on the ground a hundred yards away and drive it in with his first shot every time. I said I didn't believe it. He said he'd show me, but he never did."

"He may yet."

"Will you please *stop* that! It makes my skin crawl. And it's getting too cold in here. Can you do something about it before my teeth start chattering?"

I went over and turned the thermostat down. The deeper voice of the compressor stopped. The generator chugged on. I heard a wind sound and a faint shift of the bulk of the *Flush*. I took Mary Alice out onto the deck to prove to her the bugs had been blown away. We went up onto the sun deck. There were ragged clouds obscuring and revealing a third of a moon. I could see a considerable distance by moonlight. The flats stretched out in every direction, mud flats, sand flats, grass flats, dotted with the mystery shapes of mangrove islands, from handkerchief size on up to fifty acres.

It was not a reassuring vista. It was not terrain I could protect easily. The obvious way to get at me would be to keep in direct line with the nearer islands, pick a close one, come up behind it, wade out the flats to the edge of the mangrove, and then settle down and wait, with a clear field of fire through the shiny green leaves and the gnarled branches and roots.

I would be able to tell better by daylight, but the nearest one big enough to use as a screen for a long approach seemed to be at just about nail-driving distance.

"I don't like places like this," said the lady.

"You won't be here long."

"Hurray."

I went back down the ladderway and out to the aft deck. I stripped down to my boat shoes and went over on the shallow side and walked the bow anchor and stern anchor out to a better angle. I climbed aboard the *Muñequita* and unsnapped part of her cover, enough to get a small hook out and make it fast to a stern cleat before I walked it back to where she would ride quickly.

I got back aboard the *Flush* by getting up onto the diving shelf permanently affixed to the transom just above water level, then climbing up the two folding metal steps and swinging over the rail. She watched me dry myself on my T-shirt and said, "How can you stand to go down into all that black guck? There could be stuff down in there that bites."

I pulled the T-shirt back on and picked up the pants. They had lost some weight. I spun her and got her throat into the crook of my arm and felt around until I came upon the outline of the little automatic, pouched down into her groin. She stabbed back at my eyes, and I tightened up on her breathing until she was pulling at my arm with both hands. I slid my free hand down inside the jeans and found the gun and pulled it out. I spun her back away from me. She thumped into the bulkhead, coughed until she gagged, and said, "I'll feel better if I've got it. Please?"

"Sorry."

"You creaked my neck. You know that?"

"Sorry."

"I wouldn't shoot you with it. You know better than that."

I went in. She followed me, complaining. Now her throat felt sore. I didn't have to be so rough. Some kind of bug had bitten her on the forehead out there. See the lump it made? Why are you carrying your pants? Put them on. You look ridiculous. I went to the head to get away from her, picking up my manila envelope en route. It was the same heft, but I looked inside, just in case. All apparently in order. All yours, Hirsh, *Deo volente*.

Ever since one Boo Waswell nearly brought me and friends to an un-
timely end aboard this same *Flush,* Meyer and I have improved many
an idle hour trying to add surprises to the furnishings. They have to be
unexpected and not complicated. Meyer is very good at it. I opened one
of his. It is quick and easy. You open the medicine cabinet. It is set
into a double bulkhead. The bottom shelf seems to be a part of the
outer frame of the cabinet itself. But if you take the stuff off it and push
it up against the pull of a friction catch, it opens like the lid of a box. I
reached down in there and took out the oily Colt Diamondback,
checked the load, put it back, and put its far smaller and weaker cousin
beside it. The recess was deep enough to stand the envelope on end
where it would not touch the weapons. I slapped the lid down, put toilet
articles back on it, and shut the cabinet. Invisible hinges, a very sturdy
catch, a nice deep dry hole. One of the better efforts.

I had to do some thinking before I got back out in range of Mary
Alice's noisy petulance.

I knew she had no idea of where we had come from, what our direction had been coming in. So if I headed in the wrong direction, she
would not object. I wanted more open space than I had. If I could go
gently aground, or appear to be aground, with a half mile of open flats
on every side, I might lure the marksman close enough to equalize our
skills. Like within ten feet? Topside, in the bin, on its brackets, was the
old Springfield shark rifle with the four-power scope, but the barrel was
slightly keyholed and the slugs had a tendency to tumble.

She made him sound like he kept popping out of a phone booth in a
funny cape and zooming into the sky. I had seen him. All right, so he
looked very impressive. Our very short acquaintanceship had been interesting so far. Especially the way I had kept taking his money. And
his girl.

He could use an island for a screen, and he could use Meyer, just to
see if he could verify Meyer's ill will toward me. He might bring Davis
along, the one with the dark mustache. Expendable? Who knows?
Murder and arson. Boats burn hot. Four can fry as cheaply as three.
One good thrust with a gun butt or a solid smash with a piece of pipe
and you can forget about using the family dentist to identify his work.

No, stasis was not my style. The more I thought of ways and means,
the less I liked it. Running is no good either, unless it is the kind of running where you circle back and come out on the trail right behind the
hunter. So tomorrow I take the *Muñequita,* and I wait just as close to

Regal Marine as I can get. Hello there, Frank. Looking for anybody in particular?

She rattled the latch on the door to the head. "What are you doing in there anyway?"

"Thinking."

I heard her mumble as she walked away. I came out and made another drink and fixed us something to eat. She had stopped complaining. She looked thoughtful. No thanks, she did not want to play any music. No, no gin rummy, thanks.

"Trav?"

"Yes, honey."

"You don't want to ask me anything else about anything?"

"I don't think so."

"It's all cleared up in your mind?"

"I think so."

"Well . . . okay."

She began yawning. She came over and wanted to be taken off to bed. I told her to take herself off. She went pouting away to her own bed. I stayed up a little while trying to tell myself that everything was going to work out just right, like everything always had, almost.

But I could not get into it. I am apart. Always I have seen around me all the games and parades of life and have always envied the players and the marchers. I watch the cards they play and feel in my belly the hollowness as the big drums go by, and I smile and shrug and say, Who needs games? Who wants parades? The world seems to be masses of smiling people who hug each other and sway back and forth in front of a fire and sing old songs and laugh into each other's faces, all truth and trust. And I kneel at the edge of the woods, too far off to feel the heat of the fire. Everything seems to come to me in some kind of secondhand way which I cannot describe. Am I not meat and tears, bone and fears, just as they? Yet when most deeply touched, I seem, too often, to respond with smirk or sneer, another page in my immense catalog of remorses. I seem forever on the edge of expressing the inexpressible, touching what has never been touched, but I cannot reach through the veil of apartness. I am living without being truly alive. I can love without loving. When I am in the midst of friends, when there is laughter, closeness, empathy, warmth, sometimes I can look at myself from a little way off and think that they do not really know who is with them there, what strangeness is there beside them, trying to be something else.

Once, just deep enough into the cup to be articulate about subjective things, I tried to tell Meyer all this. I shall never forget the strange expression on his face. "But we are *all* like that!" he said. "That's the way it *is*. For everyone in the world. Didn't you know?"

I tried to believe him. But belief is a very difficult feat when you crouch out here in the night, too far from the fire to feel its heat, too far from the people to hear the words of their songs.

19

Something woke me, and I rolled out of the bed and stood half crouched in darkness, head cocked, listening. There was a whisper and slap of very small waves against the hull, and a softer and equally regular sound of the waves slipping up into the mangrove roots and sliding back. Nothing else. I had turned the generator off before midnight.

I have learned to trust my undefined anxieties. They are sentinels standing guard. I must find out if they are being alerted by shadows or by reality. If they cry wolf nineteen times and on the twentieth time it is a real wolf, it is better to check every time than roll over and go back to sleep and lose your throat.

I moved naked through the familiar degrees of darkness of the known spaces of my home place. The door to the other stateroom stood open. I moved two steps into the room and listened and heard a small snorting sound at the end of each inhalation and a long flaccid rattle of the soft palate during exhalation. She was in sleep. A man will sometimes imitate snoring to feign sleep, a woman never. My eyes were used to the darkness by then, and in the faint starlight of the port I could make out the dark blur of her hair on the pillow, then a suggestion of profile. She was sleeping on her back.

Before going to bed, I had checked all the locks, all the security devices. There was no way to deactivate them without starting up a klaxon that would whoop the birds awake three islands away. I wondered if someone had come aboard over a side rail and the shift of weight had turned on my silent, subjective alarm system.

In retrospect, Frank Sprenger seemed strangely more impressive. The blueberry eyes stared out from the sun-browned folds of skin. His neck seemed broader than his skull. I went back to my stateroom and pulled a pair of shorts on. It is strange how a man, totally naked, feels a little more vulnerable. It seems to be a distraction, an extra area to guard. Cloth is not armor, yet that symbolic protection makes one feel at once a little more logical and competent. Doubtless the hermit crab is filled with strange anxieties during those few moments when, having outgrown one borrowed shell, he locates another and, having sized it carefully with his claws, extracts himself from the old home and inserts himself into the new. The very first evidence of clothing in prehistory is the breechclout for the male.

When I had rolled from the bed, I had plucked the Airweight from its handy bedside holster without conscious thought. I put it back where it belonged and got the M35 Browning out of the locker. It is a 9mm automatic pistol with a staggered box magazine, so that it has a fourteen-round capacity. It fits my hand, and I like it. It goes where I point. The way to get that instinctive relationship with a handgun is to tape a pencil flashlight with a very narrow beam to the barrel, exactly in line with it, and rig it so that you can comfortably turn the beam on for an instant with thumb or finger. Then stand in a room in the dusk, turn and fire, spin and fire, fall and fire, at the lamp, the corner of the picture, the book on the table, a magazine on the floor. Point naturally as if pointing the forefinger, arm in a comfortable position, never bringing it up to the eye to aim. An hour of practice can develop an astonishing accuracy. After that you practice in a secluded place with live rounds.

I am being turned off handguns. Meyer did it. He made three casual statements, apropos of gun legislation. He said, "The only two things you can kill with a handgun are tin cans and people." And he said, "Way over half the murders committed in this country are by close friends or relatives of the deceased. A gun makes a loud and satisfying noise in a moment of passion and requires no agility and very little strength. How many murders wouldn't happen, if they all had to use hammers or knives?" And he said, "Studies have shown that if a person is not a psychopath, not a soldier, not a cop, there is only a one in ten chance they can bring themselves to fire a gun directly at a robber."

So there has been a diminishing pleasure in the look and the feel of handguns and in the ability to use them. I am even beginning to dislike the shape and feel and smell of them. But as long as I pursue a career in my version of the salvage business, I am going to affront people who yearn to read my obituary. So the weapons are tools of a precarious trade. Just as, I suppose, a carnival fire-swallower might find it useful to keep some fire extinguishers handy. He might even hate fire extinguishers because they are reminders that something might go wrong, but unless he is an idiot, he will keep them within reach, fully charged, and know how to use each one.

Out on the deck I was in a brighter world. I kept to the heavier patches of shadow. I made two circuits, stopping, listening, waiting. The damp wind was out of the north, warm and steady. A nightbird went by, shouting of doom in a hoarse, hopeless voice, even laughing about it.

I eased back into the lounge and reset the master switch and listened again. It was almost four in the morning. I tucked the pistol into the belly band of the shorts, the metal slightly cooler than the night air. I knew I had taken on a load of adrenaline that would take an hour to be so totally absorbed I could sleep. As I neared my bed, I heard her speak in her sleep. "Marf? Shugunnawg. Whassawhummer?"

I went in. She whined, rolled her head back and forth, whined again, and turned onto her side. So one of those words had probably alerted the sentinels and turned on the alarms. She was down inside her head, asking questions.

I sat on the bed, put my hand on her shoulder, and shook her. She came fumbling up the dark ladder. "Whashawanname, Frank? Crissake. Oh. Whassamarra?"

"You were having a nightmare."

"Come *on*, McGee. I never even dream."

"Everybody dreams, M.A. Some people remember more than others. You were talking. You woke me up."

"Talking? The *hell* you say. What about?"

"Asking questions. But not in any language the world has ever known."

"How do you know they were questions?"

"Rising inflection. Marf? Whassawhummer?"

"Oh, boy. Marf. Where are you? Oh. Well, anyway, I asked questions. You certainly didn't ask many."

"What do you mean?"

"You're looking down at me from somewhere, and I can't see you.

Come down here some." She pulled at me. I stretched out and put my feet up. She put her head on my shoulder and rested a fist on my chest. "You know what I mean about questions," she said.

"Do I?"

"You're so tricky. You know? You left me waiting for the other shoe to drop. Like anybody would think you would ask about how come Jane got the other stock book printed with Frank's name."

"I assumed you asked her, saying you'd run out soon."

"Sort of like that. I asked for spares for all the investment accounts, because Lighthouse stopped making that kind, and if they had names on, we wouldn't make a mistake and sell them out of stock. Well . . . what about me telling you she poisoned me?"

"Window dressing. You were sick one day. And remembered it later, when you needed more window dressing. And those numbers on the sheets to indicate arrangement were for your own benefit in making up the junk book. And you invented that bit about how upset she was long ago and about her talking about going away. You can't check anything out with a dead lady. She can't verify conversations. And people *have* smashed up a house to conceal a search."

"Okay. You're so smart about everything, aren't you? You didn't even have to ask me about how much more I knew about the whole thing, did you?"

I stopped breathing for about two seconds and hoped that it had not been noticed and interpreted. If I were to ever be certain, I had to make the whole thing seem casual, unremarkable. I had to make my indifference persuasive. So I yawned widely and noisily and turned toward her, stripping the coverlet down below her hips, the better to hold and stroke and caress her.

"Hey, no problems, huh?" she said.

I slipped the pistol under the pillow. I yawned again. "No more questions about old Jane, honey. I know you killed her."

She turned her mouth away from me, stiffened, caught my moving wrist, held me still. "You are so damned sure," she whispered.

"Forget it," I said. I worked on her, trying to bring her along, trying to soften her tensions.

She pulled back again. "Why are you so sure?"

"I told you all the reasons it wasn't kids."

"But if it was a person trying to make it look as if kids had done it, why me?"

"Does it matter one way or the other? Forget it, honey."

She tried to forget it. I could feel her trying to let go, trying to let her body take over. She pushed me away. "Wait a second. Please. Look. Is there any proof?"

"When Fedderman finds out the good stuff is missing out of stock and finds out you are gone without saying good-bye, what do you think it's going to look like?"

She tried to shake me in her exasperation. "But proof, damn you!"

"Relax. Nobody saw you coming or going. You didn't leave anything behind. They are even buying your version of when it happened."

"*My* version?"

"You set the electric clock in the bedroom ahead to two fifteen, then you yanked it out and heaved it at the wall." I wanted to hold my breath again. Instead, I gathered her close, kissed her throat. She sighed.

"The thing about it, darling," she said. "I *really* liked her. I really did." She sighed. Her breath had a trace of the staleness of sleep. "What do people expect a person to do when they don't leave you any kind of option at all? Know what she was going to do?"

"No. Who cares?"

"Stop a minute. Put yourself in my place. I didn't go to her house on my own. She asked me to come there. To talk. Or else. The way she sounded, I parked a ways off. She got hold of me at Hirsh's. Okay, so I cut that sort of short and went to her place. She was waiting for me, very cold and unfriendly, all dressed to go out. Know where she was going? To tell Hirsh and make him phone the police. Oh, she'd figured it all out that it had to be me. She knew how. Not exactly, but too close. Stop a minute. I made some offers. I begged her. I pleaded. I turned on enough tears for a fountain. And then she saw what was going to come next, so she ran, and I caught her and grabbed her, and we both fell down in the doorway. I was very mad at her. She was underneath, on her face, and I got up and pushed her back down and kneeled on her back and got hold of her hair and yanked up and back. It made kind of a crunchy little sound, and she went soft as butter. Yech. All loose, sort of. I thought she was dead then, but I guess she lived a while. I sat down and thought it all out, and then I found red rubber gloves under her sink. I took the money out of her purse and wrecked the whole house and left."

"How did you keep from getting all spattered with all the stuff you broke?"

"I didn't. What I did first was take everything off and put a shower cap on my hair. I just wore that and the gloves, and took them with me when I left. I got splattered. After I was through, I took a shower and got dressed. I tried not to look at her at all the times I went past her. I *really* was awfully fond of Jane. Do you forgive me?"

"Do I *forgive* you?"

"Oh, I knew you'd understand, my darling. You scared me, being so sure. I tried to think of everything, even that back window to make it look as if a small person had gotten in that way. There was so much to do and to think about, that's why I was late getting to your yacht club. I was late and very nervous and scared."

"Nobody would have known it."

"Remember when you kissed me for the first time and I went off down the little beach to think?"

"I remember."

"Right up until then I was going to keep on with Frank. Then I realized that I had really bitched him up, the way that trouble with Jane came out. What I should have done was tell Frank right away and let him handle her. Being so very cautious about things, the way Frank is, I knew just what he would do to keep from being linked up in any way with Jane's death. I knew the son of a bitch was going to try to make me switch back, put the good book back, and sneak the junk out of the bank. Then he would cancel the deal, take the good stuff and arrange to have it sold, and try to come out practically even. Where would that leave me? I decided it better be you from then on, not Frank. It was the only way I could keep the whole thing. Poor Frank. By now, from the way I ran, he's figured out that I killed Jane and I've got the goodies. He knows that Fedderman will probably yell swindle and report me missing. And there is no way in the world Frank can keep from being brought into it. Even if he keeps it quiet that he knew me outside the bank, he is going to have to explain where all that cash came from. I guess he can, but he's going to look like a very dumb person. I don't think Hirsh is going to have to pay him back. I don't think Frank will live that long. I guess I love you, McGee. Do you love Mary Alice?"

"Immeasurably."

"Well . . . now you can prove it. With—oh, goddammit, you're gone again. What the hell is the matter with you?"

"I think I know what woke me up."

"I can tell you something that didn't."

"You can't set a trap to catch a trap."

"What is that supposed to mean?"

"I can't very well surprise your chum by getting to him a lot earlier than scheduled, because that is exactly what he is doing. This is important to him. Why should he give a stranger a schedule and stay with it? Besides, if he is a marksman, why should he come in at dusk, with night coming on? Dawn is better. And not far away. Welcome, Frank boy." I was thinking aloud.

She was gone, abruptly. She knocked the shade off the fixed lamp, found the switch, ran around the foot of the bed to my side, made some small gobbling sounds, and ran back to her side.

"Frank?" she said. "Here? Soon?"

"Settle down. We'll play it as if he were going to show up about dawn. Today. Every day. You cooked him. You cooked him as many ways as there are."

"What have you got there?"

"What does it look like?"

"It's a gun, dammit. I meant, where did it come from?"

"Put some clothes on."

"What am I going to do in them? Are we leaving? Or what?"

"Put on the pants and the long-sleeved shirt again."

"If you think I'm going out into those bugs, you're—"

"Shut up, will you? Just get dressed and shut up."

"You can't tell me what to—"

"I can take you out onto the bow, with a deck chair, and tie your arms to the arms and your feet to the footrest, and your neck to the backrest and leave you there and see how good a shot he is."

"Now come *on!* I don't mind jokes, but when you—"

I stood up. "No joke. The more I think about it, the better I like it."

She let her mouth sag open as she looked at me. And then she swallowed without closing her lips, an effort that made her throat bulge and convinced me she was taking me seriously.

"You *mean* it!"

"Just shut up and get your clothes on."

She did. It did not take her long. She went into the head and came out with her hair brushed glossy and a new mouth in place.

"Can I ask you something, Trav?"

"Like?"

"What makes you think he's coming here?"

"It's too long a story."

"Okay."

I put on khakis, and a dark green knit shirt with short sleeves, and old deck shoes. She followed me up to the sun deck. I went forward and stepped up onto the rail and hooked an arm around a stanchion for balance. I looked south through the nine-power Japanese glasses. Though there was a line of gray in the east and the glasses had good light-gathering qualities, it was like looking into a smudge pot. I couldn't even find a horizon line.

I dropped back to the deck, looked around, trying to organize something. Running would indicate to him that I'd guessed right. He would have to assume Mary Alice had told me everything useful. *Not* running would indicate innocence or stupidity or some of both. It might be the best answer. I discovered that I was trying not to think of Meyer. If my guess about Sprenger's actual schedule was right, Meyer could have been subjected to some sudden and very ugly persuasion. Stubborn old bear. Weird old economist.

Think, dammit! Like the little signs IBM used to distribute before they suddenly realized that if it were ever obeyed, if men everywhere really began to Think, the first thing they would do would be to take a sledge and open up the computers. A few are doing it already, sly seers, operating in sly ways. They have to guard the computer rooms these days. A little alnico magnet, stuck in exactly the right place with a wad of chewing gum, can erase a hundred thousand units of information before they find it.

Think! But the *Flush* felt like a ponderous toy, something in a foolish game for over-aged children. Meyer and I had been using it as a treehouse, hiding the secret words, the pacts, the membership list, the slingshots, and the Daisy Air Rifle. Now a real live man was going to come across the flats and blow the treehouse out of the water. Maybe I could get out the old bubble pipe and waft some soap into his eyes.

Prediction. He would have to have Meyer with him, because though Meyer could find No Name from the remembered shape of it, he certainly could not describe to anyone else how to find it.

Prediction. He would have someone with him. He would not want to rent a skiff with an outboard himself or send Meyer to rent it. The safe play would be to send a third man, with instructions to come back in the skiff from Regal Marine and pick them up.

So then, three of them. If he brought Dave Davis, which seemed possible, it would make a goodly weight of meat in the rented boat. He would want a good boat, for capacity and for speed. Regal Marine certainly catered to some very early-bird fish freaks. Predawn rentals, so you can get out to the feeding grounds by dawn, aching to hook into the King of All of Them.

Once he had found us and identified us, Meyer's function would be ended. Once Sprenger had killed us and located the investment account items aboard the *Flush,* the third man's portion of the job would be finished. I did not care to use up any mental energy speculating about how he would handle everything from then on. I would not be able to care.

The band in the east widened until it began to shine gray upon the world. The islands began to show, in a thin milky mist. So this one, No Name, was too close to the *Flush,* and we stood too tall beside it, to make it good cover for a boat moving toward us. It would have to be the island in front of us, over a hundred yards away.

It was light enough, or would be by the time I got the hooks in and the *Flush* cranked up, to retrace the winding, unmarked channel back south to good water. Live to fight another day or run again. Or meet up with Sprenger and company under the worst possible conditions. If there is anything more vulnerable to sniper fire than a pleasure boat in shallow waters, I would like to hear about it. Maybe those Texas sportsmen who used to shoot the sandhill cranes from cover as the big ungainly birds came gliding in for a landing had found something easier to kill. Suppose I did manage to disappear? What would then happen to Meyer? He could wear a sickly smile and say, "Mr. Sprenger, they were *supposed* to be here!"

So whether he came at dawn or at dusk, the problem was the same. Instead of having all day to think about it, I had a fraction of an hour.

Go wait for him in the mangroves? Set the scene here so he would . . . A rusty gear in the back of my mind groaned and turned. The dry bearings squealed.

"What's with you?" she said.

"Always try on the Indian's moccasins," I said.

"What?"

"You'll see what I mean when I get through. If I have time to finish.

Here. Take these. Use this to focus. You keep sweeping that area over there. If you see any kind of a boat coming toward us or moving across that area, sing out."

"Where'll you be?"

"Busy."

20

It didn't take too long to prepare the major elements of the scene. I warned Mary Alice to hang on when I backed the *Flush* off and then rammed her up into the mangroves, with a great crunching, crackling, settling, listing. I took the *Muñequita* away from the island, over to water the right depth, and pulled her plug. She had enough flotation so she would stay up completely awash, but I didn't want her drifting, so I put her on the edge of a sandbar. She ended up with water almost covering the pilot seat, the other seat canted up and out of the water. I smashed her windshields with a wrench. I had taken the Winslow life raft out of the hatch. I fitted the paddle together, popped the yellow raft as fat as the air from the cartridge would inflate it. I had to be very careful walking on the bar. It was love time for the stingrays, and they were thick, almost buried in the sand and matching it in color. They averaged eighteen inches across. There is never a bit of trouble if you scuff your feet. They shake themselves out of the sand and go skimming off, underwater fliers with leathery wings.

Halfway back to the *Flush,* I stopped paddling and looked at the *Muñequita.* Her plight touched my heart. She was abandoned, a derelict. The sun had changed from deep red to orange to a blazing white just above the horizon, promising a blistering day.

When I climbed aboard, she looked down at me from the sun deck and said, "What the *hell* are you doing?"

"You're supposed to be watching."

"Okay, okay. I'm watching."

"Have you got with you any kind of hat that Frank Sprenger would know and remember?"

"He isn't much for noticing clothes. Unless he's bought them for you. I like big floppy cloth hats with big brims. I've got a red one that's *really* red, and he kidded me about it."

I swarmed up and took the glasses and got up on the rail and searched. I saw a dot moving across the glassy sea a long long way off. I hustled her below, and she got the hat out of one of the suitcases she had planned to leave behind. It was more than red. It was a vivid scarlet. I dug around in a forward gear locker and found the old fenders I should have thrown away, but was saving in case I had to use them in a lock somewhere, with the sides of the lock black with oil. They were of ancient gray canvas, stained and worn, and filled with matted kapok. They were cylindrical, about thirty inches long and as big around as her head.

I tried the hat on one and it fitted.

"You have fallen out of your tree," she proclaimed.

"You are going to be hiding, minus the long black hair, and this is going to be your body, floating in that two-man raft."

Once she got the idea, she helped. She did give a small cry of desolation when I gathered all that hair into my left fist and then gnawed through it with the kitchen shears between hand and skull. She fastened it into a long fall with rubber bands. I taped it to the fender. I wanted a lot of weight in the raft. I checked on the distant boat and found it closer each time. I used a spare anchor, wired to all the fenders, and a lot of canned goods to overload the rubber raft. I threw a blanket over all the junk, tucked it down, shifted the stuff around to look like a woman's shape under the blanket. The fender with hat and hair was at one corner of the raft, shining, black hair spilling out from under the scarlet brim to lie in sharp contrast against the yellow rubber.

I took it out quickly, wading, swimming, pushing it, and used a small mushroom anchor to hold it into a very gentle tide current so that the red hat end was toward the island I thought he would use as cover when approaching.

When I climbed up onto the *Flush,* she was standing there, looking quite changed with her hair gnawed off ragged and short. She was staring out at the raft and held her clasped hands close to her throat. When I turned and looked, I saw what caused the curious expression on her face. It was better than I hoped. It was spooking her. She floated out there, dead in a raft. I wondered if she had ever really been able to comprehend the fact of her own eventual and inevitable death. Today, my friends, we each have one day less, every one of us. And joy is the only thing that slows the clock.

When I got the glasses on the boat, they brought it so close I had the startled feeling they could see me as clearly as I could see them. Three of them, in a pale blue boat, proceeding very slowly, angling from my left to my right. From there I knew they could see the white of the superstructure of the *Flush* through the trees on No Name. I estimated they were a little bit less than one mile away, and they were moving very slowly because they were crossing the shallows. The direction indicated they were moving over to where they could turn toward No Name in the concealment of the island a little over a hundred yards west of me. Yet I could not be certain they were not merely early-morning fishermen.

I went below and got back in a hurry, carrying the spotting scope. I turned the eyepiece to the sixty-power click and used the angle between the rail and stanchion as a rest. Sixty power makes an object at six thousand feet look one hundred feet away. The narrow field made it very difficult to track a moving object. They were coming into deeper water and picking up speed. I caught them in quick and momentary glimpses. It was one of the countless imitations of the Boston Whaler, with the central console where the operator can stand and run the big outboard by the remote controls. I could not catch the man running it. He seemed big enough to be Davis. The time I got him in focus long enough, he was looking south. I saw a planter's hat with bright band tipped forward, jammed down on his head to keep the wind from whipping it off. Yellow shirt.

Meyer sat on the stowage box in front of the console, leaning back against it, arms folded. Or tied? Folded. He wore his old souvenir hat from Lion Country. The white hunter variety, with a plastic band stamped to imitate leopard. Frank Sprenger was in the bow, sitting on the casting platform. He wore a black T-shirt, white shorts, a bright orange baseball cap with a long bill, and big dark sunglasses. He held a fishrod in his hand, pointed straight up. He wore binoculars around his neck.

When I saw those, I backed down and away. She was waiting for me on the side deck, swallowing frequently.

"On their way," I said, answering the question before she could ask it.

"What do we—"

"Now listen. Carefully. We've got ten minutes, probably more, before Sprenger gets in position. He'll leave his friend in the boat, and he'll wade to that end of that island, where the sandbar is. The other end is in water too deep, and this end is closer to us. Okay now, what he would want to do would be get comfortable, get a nice clear field of fire through an opening in the mangroves where they begin to thin out, and then wait until we were both on deck and then drop me first and then you. I think he would want information to keep from wasting time in search, so he would drop me with a head shot or a heart shot and get you through the legs."

"It makes me sick even to listen to—"

"So he is going to look and find the kind of ruin he might have caused himself. Both boats disabled and your body in that raft. Somebody got here first. That thing about moccasins, I was trying to say that it is the kind of thing he would accept, would believe had happened. His little world is falling apart anyway, and so this is one more rotten disaster he hadn't counted on. But it isn't going to make him reckless and impatient. He's a careful man. He'll wait quite a while, I think. He'll watch for some movement by that dummy in the raft. Sooner or later he'll have to satisfy himself. I think what he'll do is sink the raft. Then wait a while longer and finally come aboard, maybe alone, more probably with friend."

"Where will we *be?*" she demanded, her voice stretched thin.

I took her below. It was beginning to heat up below and would get considerably worse. I warned her to expect it and endure it. Silently. She wanted her little weapon, so I traded it for the other two manila envelopes and put them in the same hiding place as the one she had given me. No point in having Sprenger find her two and decide that was the batch and leave.

I took her down into the forward bilge and through the crawlway and up into the rope locker. Even though she was a big big girl, there was room for her and a lot of anchor line, and there was ventilation of sorts. I told her she could sit with her feet dangling, but when she heard anybody, or *if* she heard anybody coming through the crawlway, to pull her legs up inside and pull the door shut and slide the little bolt over to lock it from the inside. I made it emphatic. "Stay right here no matter what you hear, what you imagine, what you think. Don't try to think. Just stay until I come after you. Get cute and we're both dead."

"Where will you be? What are you going to do?"

"Take care of you. Shut up and wait. Not a sound. I've got a good place. I'll get the jump."

I left her there and went and opened up my good place, stocked it with what I thought I'd need, left it open and ready. I went to the galley and knelt and looked cautiously out of the lower right corner of the fixed glass opening by the booth that adjoins the galley.

I had thought it would give me a view of everything. The angle was slightly wrong. I could see the yellow raft and the wreck of the *Muñequita* and most of the nearby island, but I couldn't see the sandbar end of it. I could see to within ten feet of where I guessed he would take up his position. Now be as patient as he.

I could not have told Mary Alice the truth about what I wanted to do. I wanted the ruse of the raft, the red hat, the silence, the disabled boats, to lure them aboard, Sprenger and friend. I had the idea they would save Meyer for some conversations once they saw my stage setting. Tie him to the mangroves while they came aboard the *Flush*. And then, when I had my opportunity, I would merely pop out of my secret place, sap the nearer one behind the ear with a delicate twist of the wrist, hold the other one under the gun, and yell boo. Turn him around and darken his world too, then truss them both with utmost care and diligence. Go get the lady with the unusual haircut and add her to the stack. Go get Meyer and the boat and bring the boat around. Use the big anchor and the power takeoff winch to pull the *Flush* out of the mangroves. Cork up the *Muñequita* and rig a pump and float her. Take both small boats in short row and retrace the winding channel back to the main channel, and put Meyer, with a cold brew in hand, at the wheel, while I make a call through the Miami Marine Operator to one Sergeant Goodbread. Sergeant? This is McGee, I've got something for you.

No problems. Virtue prevails. A brisk encounter, made successful by the element of surprise.

Every ten minutes I looked at my watch and found that one more minute had gone by. I could hear a distant hysterical laughter of terns scooping up baitfish. I heard a jet go over, very high. I heard a drop of my sweat splat onto the vinyl floor.

My pants were dry, salt crusty, and now beginning to darken with sweat around the waist. The boat shoes were still damp. The wind was slacking off. I could see the water turning glassier. The bugs would come up out of the mangrove and grass marsh and shorten Sprenger's iron patience.

He would not be emotional now. Now it was a chore. He had been brought in from Phoenix six years ago on more of a basis than his pretty face. If punishment for trying cute tricks is quick, merciless, and permanent, fewer attempts are made, and the whole interweave of cooperation and concession runs more smoothly. If unaffiliated strangers come to the city to undercut the going street prices, and they are found long dead in an elegant apartment beside their long-dead girls, fewer strangers come to town to go into business. If a man testifies before the grand jury and they find his head in a hatbox in a coin locker at the airport, all grand juries accomplish less.

I changed position. My legs were cramped. Come *on*, Frank! I happened to be looking at the raft when I saw the scarlet hat leap into the air all by itself, along with the flat echoless smack of high velocity across water. The hat jumped up about a foot, leaping toward the middle of the raft. The impact knocked the fender forward, so that it slipped down below the round yellow bulge of rubberized fabric. It pulled the hair with it, so that only a small fringe still hung over the round of the life raft, visible from the island. I could not have hoped for a more realistic effect. The raft began to sink at the foot end. There were three more shots, spaced one second apart. The raft settled more quickly and almost level. It disappeared. Air bubbles belched up. Then there was just the red hat, floating high on the water, but beginning slowly to settle as the salt water soaked into the fabric.

There was a silence of perhaps five minutes, and then the spaced shots began again. Six of them. I saw where they were going when the second one sent red dust into the air from the lens of the port bow running light of the *Muñequita*. He shot her lights off and the little chrome knob off the top of the ensign staff and the little elbow off the top of the windshield wiper.

He certainly wasn't using any target rifle, not at that rate of aimed fire. The sound had a vicious, stinging quality about it. Six shots gave me a vague clue. It was probably a bolt-action, small-caliber, high-velocity load job, like that .243 Winchester Special, which dropped about a half inch in the first hundred yards, firing a seventy- to eighty-grain slug at a muzzle velocity of around thirty-six hundred feet per second.

Boats have a personality, a presence, a responsiveness. Little Doll had done her damned well best at all times for me, and I had sunk her onto a sandbar so somebody could shoot her bangles off. It had to be confusing her.

There was a shorter wait, and this time the six shots came smacking at *The Busted Flush*. I heard the ship's bell ring and the dying scree of ricochet off brass. Crash and tinkle and zing. Thud and whine and whizz of splinters.

Just about enough time for a reload and it began again. One got into the galley and clanked around among the pots. Then a lengthening silence. My cue to disappear. Tall white rabbit hops back into top hat.

I had bet Meyer that I could go aboard the *Flush* and hide and he could not find me in a two-hour search. He knew the old houseboat well. We bet one hundred dollars, plus welching privileges, which means that if you lose, you can buy the winner a very good dinner and try to renegotiate your loss.

He did not know that while he was up in Montreal for a week, listening to people read papers on international currency and exchange, I had found an exiled master carpenter from Cuba. When you open the door to the head, you are in a short corridor with the master stateroom at your right, the guest stateroom at your left. Affixed to the bulkhead straight ahead is a full-length mirror, already installed when I had won the houseboat in a poker game. I had done some measuring. The little Cuban was amused. He said it was possible. He moved the interior bulkhead out a few inches. He went around into the galley and made a tall provision locker a few inches shallower. He removed the mirror, cut a hole just a hair smaller than the mirror, put a brass piano hinge down one side of the tall mirror and reinstalled it. I tried it for size in there. If a man does not have a swollen gut, even a large man takes up surprisingly little space if you measure him back to front. Less than twelve inches. But it was too dark in there. I located a good piece of two-way glass at an exorbitant price, and he installed it in the mirror frame. It was much better that way.

The Cuban removed every trace of his highly skilled labor. He devised a simple but solid catch which would hold the mirror-door closed and could be released by inserting a long wire brad into an almost invisible hole on the right side of the mirror, in the bulkhead next to the frame. For the occupant there was a simple turn block on the inside. He did a lot of winking, because he thought it was where I planned to tuck the errant lady when the husband came storming aboard. I did not advise him that I had never gone in for the middle-America hobby of scragging the random wife at any opportunity. But there had been a lot of times when people had come aboard looking for other people, when it had been unfortunate all the way around to have no good stowage area for people who would rather not be found. And as long as I had it, I thought I would make Meyer pay for it. He lost the bet. He marveled at the ingenuity, the craftsmanship. He bought me a legendary steak, a great wine, and wheedled me down to ten percent of the original bet.

They would come aboard. They would search the *Flush*. And sooner or later, they would both be in the short corridor between the staterooms at the same time. At which time I would pop out, the Browning automatic in my right hand, the woven leather sap in my left, all ready and eager to thump their skulls with ten ounces of padded lead at the end of a spring.

I moved toward the lounge, staying back out of sight, listening. I had the shirts memorized. White shirt on Meyer. In case of bad trouble, fire at yellow shirt or black shirt. Soon, a little sooner than I expected, I heard the unmistakable sound of more than one man walking through thigh-deep water. I couldn't tell if it was two or three, only that it was more than one.

So I nipped back to my safe and secret place. I'd left the mirror-door standing open. It was still open. The mirror lay on the corridor floor, and the biggest piece was smaller than a dinner plate. One of those twelve shots had come angling down the corridor or had spun off something or . . .

What now, big white rabbit?

Terror is absolutely nonproductive. It is not worth a thing. So if it is new to you, you don't know how to handle it, and it can freeze you. But if you have felt it before, many times in many places, you know that if you can start moving it will go away. You can't spend time thinking, or you will freeze up again. You have to move without thought. It can be like shifting into some rare and special gear, some kind of overdrive seldom needed and seldom available. I dipped down and picked the pistol and sap off the floor of the useless refuge. They were going to come into the lounge from the aft deck. It was the logical approach for them. And it was the only belowdecks space that was large enough to improve my chances. I got there as fast as I could and as silently as I could. There was only one place in the room where I could not be seen from the doorway or from the ports. I crawled to it, to the shelter of the long curved yellow couch, and flattened out. I could look under it and see the sill of the open door. I could hunch forward a foot and a half and be able to see the whole doorway.

All right now, McGee. Forget the childhood dreams of glory. Have no scruples about firing from ambush and firing to kill. No Queensbury rules, fellow.

I heard the diving platform creak. Water dripped. There was a grunt of effort, slap of wet palm against railing, thud of rubber soles on the decking. Then the sequence was repeated.

"Goddamn the bugs!"

"Shut up!"

"There's nobody on—"

"Shut up!"

There were ten seconds of silence. And suddenly something came bounding into the lounge. I had the impression of some animal, some vast, vital, rubbery strength that covered fifteen feet and landed lightly, poised, every sense alert. Next, a pair of big wet tennis shoes stopped by the sill, just inside the room.

The voice by the door said, "There's nobody on this—"

I was going to have to get rid of that voice by the door to give all my attention to the animal presence over beyond the couch. I wormed forward and saw all of him, Davis, soaked to the waist, revolver in the left hand, the hand nearest me, the hand now sagging down to his side. I told the gun to go where I pointed it, as it always had, forgetting the first one was double action, missing the hand, putting the second one into the hand. He screamed and pounced for the dropped weapon, trying to grab it up with the other hand, and I hit that hand, and he went diving, tumbling out the doorway onto the deck as I spun, hitched back, looked up, and waited for the round target of the head to appear over the back of the couch. The three shots had been very close together, a huge wham-bamming sound far different than the whippy lick of the rifle, and leaving a sharp stink of propellant in the hot air.

The rifle cracked like a huge whip and laid its lash across the edge of my thigh. I suddenly had the wit to flatten out again and look under the couch. He wore white boat shoes. I had to turn the automatic onto its side to aim. I couldn't point it naturally. I had to aim it. The shoes moved closer. I had to aim again. The side of the shoe burst into wet red, and he made not a sound. I took my chance on bounding up rather than trying for the other white shoe and bringing him down. But as I swung the pistol, he fired without aiming, a snap shot, doubtless hoping to hit me, but it worked like one of those impossible trick shots out of a bad Western. It slammed the gun out of my hand and spun it into the far corner, leaving my hand and arm numb to the elbow.

Sprenger worked the bolt quickly and aimed at the middle of my forehead and then slowly lowered it.

"You're a damned idiot, McGee. And a damned nuisance."

"You haven't got a lot of options."

He tested the foot, taking a short step on it. He did not wince, limp, change expression. But pain drained the blood out of his face and made his tan look saffron. He had shed his sunglasses.

"Meaning I need you?" He waved me back and took another step and propped a hip on the corner of the back of the couch.

"Is Meyer all right?"

It took several moments for the implications of my question to get through to him. "You are some kind of people, you two. He's a bright man. He knows a lot about the tax future of municipals. We had a nice talk. I'm losing my touch. I can't read people anymore. That damned McDermit woman is insane. Was insane. Once she got leverage, it was like all she wanted was to get us both killed. I read you wrong. I read Meyer wrong."

"Is he all right?"

"So far. He probably isn't comfortable, but he's all right. Thanks for letting me know he's trading material."

"If you could get back there to the boat."

He looked at his bleeding foot. "Blow it off at the knee and I could get back there." I believed him. He shook his big head. There was a glint of rue in the little blueberry eyes. "I had nearly five hundred round ones stashed, in case I ever had to run and had a chance to run. *Postage* stamps! Dear Jesus Lord!"

"A sterling investment, Mr. Fedderman says."

"What could I do? She would have screamed to the McDermit brothers I was laying her."

"There wasn't any dear friend primed to make a report."

He thought that over. "I couldn't take a chance. You can see that. That woman would *rather* lie than tell it straight." He leaned back and looked out the doorway. He lifted the rifle slightly and said, "Something you should know. At this range, any place I hit you—"

"I'm dead from hydrostatic shock. It hits fluid, transmits the shock wave up veins and arteries, and explodes the heart valves. You came close. You put a skin burn on my thigh."

"You know a lot of things. Walk way around me slowly and take a look at Davis, from the doorway."

I followed directions. Davis was out. He was on his face, legs spraddled, one smashed hand under his belly, the other over his head. I could see little arterial spurtings from the torn wrist, a small pulsing fountain that was as big around as a soda straw and jetted about three inches. Blood ran into the scuppers and drained into the sea. His head was turned so I could see his face. His closed lids looked blue. His mustache was glued to white papery flesh. He had dwindled inside his clothes, but his big straw planter hat was still firmly in place. The small jet dwindled quickly. Two inches, one inch, nothing.

I turned around slowly and took a slow step back into the lounge. "He just bled to death."

He looked puzzled. "I thought you hit him in the hand."

"Both hands. He couldn't stop the bleeding, using the one that wasn't so bad."

"You were trying to hit him in the hands?"

"Yes."

"You're good with that thing. But you are an idiot. If you're that good, you could have popped up and hit me in the head and then him."

"Call it a natural revulsion, Frank."

"You've got first aid stuff aboard?"

"Always."

"You're going to get it and fix this foot."

"We're supposed to be in negotiation, aren't we?"

He looked at me and through me, at the narrow vista of his possibilities, his meager chances. He said in a tired voice, "I built that municipal bond business from almost nothing. It was supposed to be a front. But I *like* it. I'm *good* at it. It's what I really want to *do.*"

"Frank?"

"I know. I know."

"So the pattern was kill me and the woman and Davis and Meyer, burn this boat with all four bodies aboard, after retrieving the rarities Mary Alice ran off with, and go back and run a very good bluff and hope for the best, hope they don't find out Mary Alice killed Jane Lawson, and then tie you to Mary Alice in the Fedderman swindle. If you can get the goodies back, your best move would be cancel out with Fedderman and retrieve that junk out of the box."

He frowned at me. "How would you know about burning? Just how in hell would you know that?"

"You must have asked Meyer some questions about this houseboat that gave him the idea you were trying to figure out if it would burn well and if it was in a place where there was no chance of anybody putting the fire out."

He thought, nodded, and said, "Then he radioed you."

"So you're still on course, aren't you? Two down and two to go. Get me to fix the foot. Get me to tell you where she hid the stuff. And you should probably have me retrieve that body out there so it won't be floating around with holes in it, making people ask questions. Then we go over and bring the rental around, and you add two more bodies to the pyre and get out of here."

"You're very helpful. Why are you so helpful?"

I had to make it very good. He had to believe me. I had to be casual, but not too casual, earnest but not too earnest. "Haven't you had the feeling, Frank, I've been a half-step ahead of you?"

"Maybe. Until right now."

"Once I heard from Meyer that I could count on you making a try, why would I just sit here and wait for it? Would I be such an idiot that I'd figure I would be able to take you with no fuss? I have respect for you, Frank. As a fellow professional. I did what you'd do in my shoes. I took out insurance. I talked to Meyer late yesterday afternoon. I wouldn't exactly say we're going to hear bugles and look up and see the U.S. Cavalry come riding across the water, firing their Sharps rifles. But I wouldn't say that anything you do is going to go unnoticed."

"Then I've got no chance at all. End of the line?"

"Insurance can always be canceled. Maybe I wouldn't make a claim."

He swung his leg out, looked at his shoe. "Stopped bleeding, at least. If it can be canceled, McGee, I can make you tell me how to go about canceling it. I found one man once I couldn't make talk. He had such a low threshold, he'd faint at the first touch. That's the only time I've ever missed. And I've had more than a hundred people find out they had more to say than they wanted to."

"I'm terrified. I'm not trying to be smart. I really am. You could make me tell you. I'm sure. But it would take as long as I could hold out, and I don't think you could do it without leaving a lot of visible damage, and when you got all done, Frank, you'd find out that the only way it can be canceled is by me, in person, not on the phone, not in writing. By a personal friendly visit to my insurance agent."

"And you want to use crap like that to make a deal?"

"Why not? Disprove it. I can get Fedderman to market the stuff. I want exactly half. I'm a practical man. I'll put myself in your pocket to save my skin and my partner's. I'll write you a confession of where, when, and how I killed Davis and how I killed Mrs. Ray McDermit. I know an island near here high enough so we can bury the bodies, and I'll put that in the confession along with the chart coordinates. Then you own me."

"But you'll keep the insurance in force? We'll own each other, you mean. Can we get this foot fixed?"

"Is the negotiation all settled?"

"Half? Hell, I guess so. Let me see those damned postage stamps."

"Later. Last night I ran over to the village in the runabout and mailed them to myself. Three envelopes."

"Why didn't you start with that?"

"You wouldn't have bought it. But now you do, because if it wasn't true, I *would* have started with it."

He almost smiled. "Half. Harry Harris said he heard that was the way you go. It's a big piece. That dumb jackass, know what he was doing? Going home at night and telling his woman all about what he did all day. Like he was a bill collector or something. If you hadn't tipped me about the leak, I wouldn't be buying you now. Now will you *please* do something about my foot?"

That word was the one which unlatched half the springs which were holding my stomach up against the base of my throat. Please. A beautifully predictive word. Stomach moved halfway back to normal position.

"There's a first aid locker back—"

And Mary Alice thumped the doorframe with her left hand as she staggered and caught her balance. She was running wet with sweat, head to toe, her face pallid, mouth open, eyes dazed with the near-fainting state the heat had brought on. She had her little automatic in her big right hand, but it was at her side, pointing at the floor.

Frank Sprenger swung the rifle toward her, and she tried to lift the little automatic to aim it at him. The rifle shot whacked, and her blue eyes bulged and broke, and she dropped straight down, very strangely, as if she were a bundle of clothing slipping off a hanger. But the little gun was coming my way, floating in the air with the momentum from swinging it up to fire it. But instead she had released it. It was moving so slowly in the air that I had time to change my instinctive reflex to pick it out of the air with my right hand and try instead with my left. My hand was still numb, and some feeling was coming back, with enough pain along with it to tell me it was broken in some way.

I could see it turning, floating, and as I reached and took it out of the air, taking it properly by the grip, beyond it I could see Frank Sprenger, out of focus, standing transfixed with the rifle still aimed down the companionway, at the empty air where her head had been.

I pointed at him and the little automatic snapped a little louder than a cap gun, and he spun and yanked the trigger of the rifle while some spectator in the back of my mind peered at him and told me that the fool had forgotten to work the bolt action. Keep firing, the spectator said. Hurry!

He came at me. Bounding. Stone-brown face under the orange cap. Huge brawny arms reaching for me. A caricature of a muscled chest, carved of hickory, molding the black T-shirt. Bowed legs, massively thewed, bounding under the white shorts, springing him toward me, while his little nightmare blueberry eyes looked remote, impersonal, totally assured. No favoring of the smashed foot. I backed away, pointing my stupid left hand at him, the little automatic saying its futile *bang, bang, bang,* making no impression on him at all. He smashed me like a truck, bounced me against the bulkhead and off it, to fall under him and see that sledge fist rise high and come smashing down toward me. I rolled my head to the right, rolled it into blinding brilliance, and over and over and off the edge of the world and down, the brilliance turning to a tiny white dot way above me and then winking out.

21

I was in a big old bed that sagged in the middle. It had a tall dark head-board. There was a window over to my right. Double hung, with an area of flawed glass in the bottom pane that warped the green calligraphy of the banyan that reached so close to the window it muted the light in the upstairs bedroom.

The bedroom door was opposite the foot of the old bed. It was always open. The closet was off to my left. There was a chest of drawers beside it. There was a huge conch shell on top of the chest of drawers. There was a framed lithograph of Venice on the wall over near the window. With a gondola in the foreground. The bathroom was out the door into the hall and to the left, just before the stairs going down.

I had been there a long time. I had heard heavy rain on the roof and roaring down through banyan leaves. At every dusk the tree screamed with its full passenger list of small birds. Sometimes I could hear surf, far away. I could hear traffic, closer than the surf, high-speed trucks droning by in the night. Something with a noisy old engine came in and out during the day, dying somewhere below my window. I could hear outboard motors sometimes, much closer than the surf. Once a great blue heron landed in the banyan, so close I could see his savage yellow eye.

I could hear young voices in the house, laughing. They played music, banged doors, roared away on motorcycles. I saw and heard these things and accepted them. They were there. I had no question.

I could not open my mouth. My tongue tip traced the bits of wire and the new hole where it felt as if two teeth were gone in the upper row on the right, near the front but not right in front. And one tooth below them. That was where the glass straw went. It had a bend in it, to make it easier to suck while lying down.

For a time, vaguely remembered, there had been a broad starched woman in white, who had strong and gentle hands and clicked her tongue a lot. Bedpans, back rubs, changing dressings. And before that a different place, corridors, stretcher, shots.

Now there was only the small woman with the ruff of blond hair turning gray. Gentle brown eyes. When the wheelchair was first gone, I was afraid to lean on her as hard as I had to, when we made the endless journey down the hall to the bathroom. But she was strong, much stronger than she looked. I remembered that I used to see her in the night, in the rocking chair over there, always awake when I woke up.

It was my face in the mirror, but not my face. When the leg began to hold better under me and when the dressing was gone from my face, I would lean on the sink and try to decide just what was wrong. There were two long, healed incisions, stitch dots still apparent, dark red against the yellow pallor of the lost tan. It was something else that was wrong, not the red wounds. Something subtly out of balance, the way the bedroom was not quite true, with no corner exactly ninety degrees and the doorframe and window frame not parallel to either ceiling or floor.

I accepted, but I began to superimpose a question atop the acceptance. I had another world somewhere else, but the shape of it was murky. I did not want to try to bring it into focus. But it seemed to be coming nearer of its own accord.

It was easier to stay in this world. I knew what the little wire cutters on the bed stand were for. I had asked the woman, and she had said that if I vomited, I could choke to death unless she was there to cut the wires that held my jaw together. It had been broken in three places. And the cheekbone had been crushed.

It was easier to stay in this world where I knew that in the middle of the morning and in the middle of the afternoon, I had to sit in the rocking chair and slowly lift and lower my right leg. From ten times at first, with no weights, to a hundred times with the gadget she had made, a sailcloth wrapping with strings to tie it on and with pouches for the lead fish weights. The leg grew stronger, but it did not feel right. It felt numbed and prickly, as a limb does when it has gone to sleep and has started to come awake. Sometimes there were needles of pain from my toes into my hip. Sometimes the area around the ankle and the top of the foot would feel very hot or very cold or even as if it had a soaking wet stocking on it when it was dry and bare.

The doctor came. He snipped the wire. He made me work my jaw while he watched. He told me the woman would get me gum to chew. It would condition the jaw muscles. He shone a bright little light into my eyes. He made me strip and walk away from him and toward him while he watched my right leg. He told me to put the pajamas and robe back on. He said the leg was doing fine. He asked me my name. I told him it was Travis. He asked if there was more, and I said I wasn't sure. I didn't know my address. He made me count backwards, add figures in my head, spell long words.

One day she came to my room a little before dusk, as the tree was beginning to fill with birds. I had been sitting in the rocking chair by the window, watching the birds come home, watching the sky change. She pulled a footstool close to the rocking chair and put a hand on my arm and looked up at me in a way that was half mischief and half sadness. "Who am I?" It was her familiar question, and I knew the familiar response.

"You are Cathy," I said.

In the last of daylight I took her hand and looked at it, at the weathered back of it, the little blue veins, the country knuckles. It seemed a very dear hand indeed. She knelt on the footstool and was closer and taller. I kissed her and felt the ridged area where the inside of my mouth had been stitched. Her brown eyes glinted in the last of the light. It was all strange and sweet and unemphatic, as though it were an inescapable extension of this unquestioned world, as natural and inevitable as all the rest of it.

I looked at her and said in a shaking voice, "You *are* Cathy! My God, I have been . . . what has . . . oh, Cathy! Cathy!"

The whole back of my mind had been nailed shut. There was a creaking, straining, and the barrier tumbled, and it all came spilling out. The watery weakness ran out of my eyes and down my face, and I couldn't make words. But she knew what had happened. She hugged me, laughing, crying, snuffling.

Candle Key. Cathy Kerr. That sagging, weathered old bay-front house of hard pine and black cypress.

She said, "Your houseboat, it's tied up to our old dock out there like before. And like before, there's handyman stuff that's piled up, when you're feeling up to it."

"We used to go out in your skiff and take Davie fishing."

"Remember that day he caught into that shark and got mad at you for cutting it loose? He wasn't even in school yet." She touched her hair. "Now he's near thirteen. I'm an old lady now, way over thirty, Trav."

"Where's your sister? Where's Christine?"

"Just down the road. She married that Max fellow, and she had four more, six in all. The kids are in and out of here all the time. I tried to keep them quiet, but you know how it is. Max got into the land business, and you wouldn't believe what he got us for the land that Daddy left us the other side of the main road."

"How many times are you going to have to put me back together?"

"This is only twice. And it was both of us needing it the first time. It could be forty times and never make up to you for what you did for me and what you lost of your own a-doing it. I've got to call Meyer right now! I shouldn't even have waited this long. He was closer to believing that fool doctor than he was me. I said it would be just a little time, and the doctor said maybe never."

She gave me a quick kiss as she stood up.

"Because you had a terrible terrible concussion and they thought there could have been some bleeding inside of your skull that cut off what you knew before somehow. Meyer being here three times and you not knowing him was terrible for him."

She went swiftly to the door, and I saw the well-remembered way she moved, that quick light way of the professional dancer, quick of foot on those lithe, sinewy, lovely legs.

"What's the date?"

"Hmm. The man on the television said this morning it was nine more shopping days till Christmas."

She was gone, leaving me to try to fit my mind around that huge hole in time. Sprenger had killed me on the twenty-seventh day of September. Over two and a half months ago.

When she came back upstairs, she said Meyer said he would leave in ten minutes to drive down. The day was gone. She turned the lights on. I felt emotionally exhausted. I got into bed, and she sat beside me on the bed and held my hand and told me how Meyer had arrived in a rental boat the afternoon of that day with me in the bottom of the boat, wrapped in blankets with the left side of my face so horribly bashed in that my eye seemed to be out of the socket. I seemed to be alive but barely. Not alive enough to go through the routine of phoning an ambulance. They put me in her old pickup, and she had driven like a madwoman while Meyer had stayed back in the truck bed with me to keep me from bouncing around too much. They took me to Dr. Ramirez. The one who looked like a Swede. I suddenly realized it had been Ramirez who had been coming to see me here in Cathy's house. He remembered me from before. Back when he and I started putting Lois Atkinson's head back on. He treated me for shock. The three of them watched over me that night. The next day I was moved by ambulance to the little hospital in Homestead, where there was a surgeon Ramirez believed in, who could rebuild the left side of my face. Cathy told me I was full of alloy pins and plates and special wire. When I was well enough to be moved, I was brought back to her house by ambulance. She had quit her job in the village to take care of me.

"What did Meyer tell you about what happened? What did he tell Ramirez?"

She licked her lips. She wore an odd expression. "What happened, you and Meyer had come down into Florida Bay to do some fishing. You went out from the *Flush* in your fast little boat, and you went up on the bow to make something fast and gave Meyer the wheel, and he was going between some little islands when the steering cable broke, and he veered right into the island, you got threw headlong into the mangroves."

"What's the matter with my leg?"

"Your back got wrenched up, and it tore a nerve some. The sisciatic? That's it. But it's coming along real good."

"So where did Meyer get the rental boat?"

She straightened. "Any questions like that, you better ask him. I just wouldn't know a thing."

She fed me well, and I slept and was awakened at ten thirty when she and Meyer came into the bedroom. He was beaming like a pumpkin with big candle. I didn't want him to notice the damned water running out of my eyes again. He didn't notice because he kept turning his back to blow his nose.

Cathy left us alone and closed the door. He said, "The absolutely worst part of it, believe me, is to have nobody to tell."

Nothing could have stopped him from telling me. Davis had come aboard the *Keynes* at one in the morning, roused Meyer, and driven him down to Miami, where they picked up Sprenger and drove on down to Regal Marine. Sprenger and Meyer had waited near the public boat ramp while Davis drove to Regal and eventually arrived with the rental boat. Sprenger carried an elegant leather case, the shape of a gigantic dispatch case. It was custom fitted for two rifles, two scopes, ammunition, slings, cleaning equipment. Meyer managed to delay their arrival to No Name by routing them across flats where they could not risk planing speed. Sprenger had left Davis with Meyer in the boat behind the nearby island. He waded to the south end of the island and waited there a long time. He had fired one shot and then, at varied intervals, three series of six shots each. He came back to the boat and had Davis tie Meyer's hands behind him, with one arm through the steering wheel. They left him alone.

"Distant firecrackers," Meyer said. "And then nothing. One hell of a lot of nothing. Except heat. And bugs. Finally I wormed around and stood up on the seat and got my fanny on the edge of the steering wheel. I bounced on it three times, and on the third time it broke off. I got out of the boat and found a mangrove stub covered with barnacles and backed into it and rubbed until I frayed the rope in two. And lost some skin. There was an old gaff in the boat. I took it along. Where do those bluebottle flies come from? How do they know? They were so thick on Davis's face, I couldn't tell who he was until I scared them off. And the lounge was full of them. I thought you were dead. Sprenger was lying across you. Then I wondered why you didn't have your share of flies. I put my ear next to your mouth and felt the exhalation. So I lifted him off you."

"Thanks."

"Don't mention it. I wasn't tracking well. I didn't know where to start. I should have got on the horn and called a Coast Guard chopper in. I never even thought of it. Everybody . . . everybody was so damned *dead!* You know? It makes it hard to think."

"What killed him?"

"Five little holes in his chest, right through his black shirt. Centered, but just a shade to the right, I think. You could have covered them all with a playing card. Fantastic."

"He shot her. Where did he hit her?"

"I don't know. There was a hole right at the base of her skull, big as half an English walnut."

That fitted the way she had gone down. Her mouth had been sagging open. So that was where the little slug had gone, into the back of her throat and on out.

"I got the boat and had a hell of a job getting the steering wheel back on. I never did. I had to push down on it to turn it. I got you into the boat. I couldn't go back to Regal Marine. I hadn't rented it. I'd taken time out to pull Davis inside and close everything I could and shove clothes into the broken ports and spray those damned hungry flies. I remembered Cathy and figured I could find this place from the Candle Key water tower. So I told her—"

"She picked it up from there. I know about Ramirez and Homestead. But what did you do then?"

"Okay, I had the feeling then that you were going to live. But I couldn't think of any good way to explain what had gone on. I didn't even *know* what had happened. So on the way back from Homestead, I stopped at Regal Marine. They weren't worried about their boat, not with Davis's car parked in their lot. I told them I was a friend of Davis's, and we'd decided to keep the boat longer. I gave them two hundred dollars and said he was having good luck farther down the Keys and sent me up to get his car. I showed them his car keys. I said it might be another few days. I went out and told Cathy not to wait. I drove Davis's car to Miami and left it in a shopping center lot with the windows down and the keys in it. I took a bus to Homestead to see how you were and took another bus down to Candle Key. It was too late to do anything. I slept in this room, and in the morning I took the rental boat back out there. I tied a towel around my face. I had a little bottle with gasoline in it. It paralyzes the sense of smell. Every time it started to get through to me, I'd put a little on the towel. Even so, I wasted a lot of time running for the rail."

"Jesus, Meyer!"

"By then it was self-preservation. Where would I fit if it all broke open? I'd fit in a cell somewhere. I kept thinking it was what you'd do. It was a McGee solution. But not my kind of thing. I wrapped them in that blue canvas you had, that roll of it. I sewed them in with that curved needle and that waxed twine. I wired that big rifle case of Sprenger's to his ankles. After he was in the rental boat. Bodies are heavy. I cried once, Sprenger was so heavy, and I thought I couldn't get him out of the lounge even. Not tears of sadness. Tears of rage. I kicked him. That's a bad reaction. Were you saving that thirty feet of chain for something special, with the big links, this big? I wrapped it around and around her waist and wired it. It won't come off."

His voice was too thin and fast and high, and his eyes were strange. "Meyer, Meyer."

"The thing I used for the third one, Davis—you'd described him, the mustache, Joe Namath haircut—I don't know what it was, down in the aft bilge, heavy, like the end of an iron cage. Then when they were in the boat, I covered them with that big net, that gill net. I put two rods in the rod holders."

"Take it easy."

"I drank some of your gin. Out of a cup. Warm. A whole cup. I gagged and gagged, but I kept it down. Then I went across and under a highway bridge, and I went outside. I don't even know what bridge. I wanted it to be calm out there, but it wasn't. Whitecaps. I had to throttle way down, and it took forever to get out to where the Keys were just a line on the horizon. What do you say when you dump over three people in blue bags? My head is full of things. I couldn't find anything I wanted inside my head. Then I remembered something. I looked it up later. From the Book of Mormon, the Book of Ether, chapter one.

"'And the Lord said, For, behold, ye shall be as a whale in the midst of the sea; for the mountain waves shall dash upon you. Nevertheless, I will bring you up again out of the depths of the sea; for the winds have gone forth out of my mouth, and also the rains and the floods have I sent forth. Behold, I prepare you against these things; for ye cannot cross this great deep, save I prepare you against the waves of the sea, and the winds which have gone forth, and the floods which shall come. Therefore what will ye that I should prepare for you, that ye may have light when ye are swallowed up in the depths of the sea?' Why did I remember that? I wish I knew.

"So I said amen and tipped them over the rail, and they went down. That cage thing caught in the net, and it took it along too. I had some headway, and the steering was stiff, so it held into the wind until the last and it started turning. When I got to the wheel, the wheel came off and before I could get it back, a wave came in and filled it half full. The engine started missing, and I turned it toward land and opened it up. It drained the water out. I bit my tongue. I lost my lucky hat."

"The Lion Country hat?"

He tried to laugh, but his face twisted and broke, and he put his head down into his hands and sobbed. It is the gentle people who get torn up. They can cope. They can keep handling the horrors long after the rest of us fade out. But it marks them more deeply, more lastingly. This was role reversal at its most bitter. I knew what he had to have, and I wondered for a moment at my own hesitation. Life seems to be a series of attempts to break out of old patterns. Sometimes you can. I reached and touched him on the shoulder.

"You did well," I said. "You really did a hell of a job. You did exactly what you had to do. It was the right choice."

So he straightened up, dabbed his eyes, blew his nose, smiled in a wan way. In a level, unemotional voice he told me the rest of it. There had been time to intercept the letters he'd left with Jenny Thurston, but he knew I hadn't signed them. So let them go. Let the people look for Sprenger and Mary Alice. Take the chance that there were only five people who knew Mary Alice had left via Lauderdale aboard the *Flush*, and three of them were dead.

He had returned the rental boat, paying for the broken wheel, and had used Cathy's old skiff to get out to No Name, day after day, cleaning up the evidence of violence, repairing the places where bullets had struck. He got the generator and the air conditioning operational. He threw out the perishables, which had spoiled in the heat. He did not get rid of Mary Alice's belongings until he had found the treasure in the hidey hole he himself had invented. He had floated the *Muñequita* the hard way, with a hand pump. He had taken the lights off her, the fittings that had been damaged by Sprenger's sniper fire, deep-sixed them, bought replacements, and, with Davie Kerr's help, rewired them. They towed the *Muñequita* to Candle Key, to a small marina with a good mechanic. The engines had been in the salt water too long. He had pulled them, rebuilt one, was nearly finished with the other. On an especially high tide they had left Christine, Cathy's sister, to watch me, and Cathy, Davie, and Meyer had gone out and brought the *Flush* back and tied it up at the dock near the old house. He and Davie and Cathy had done a lot of work on it.

I asked him about Hirsh and the murder investigation.

He shrugged. "The guilty flee when no man pursueth. The law leaned on my old friend, but he had nothing to say. Yes, he had an investment arrangement with a Mr. Sprenger, who was in the bond business. The amount invested was a matter between the two of them. If Mr. Sprenger was dissatisfied, the money would be returned. Hirsh had to go to the bank when the tax people opened the box and took what was in it. He had to sign a release saying the contents were Sprenger's. He gathered from the tax people that every single piece of paper relating to Sprenger's personal affairs had disappeared along with Sprenger. When I gave him those three brown envelopes and he opened them and saw what they were, he asked me three times how I came to have them. I told him if he asked me once more, our friendship was over. He asked me what he was to do with them. I said that because, according to his own explanation, they were not sufficiently unique to be traceable as individual items, they should go back into stock. He said they would go into his box at the bank, in case somebody should come to claim them. He was eighty years old when I got there. When I left, he was fifty, going on forty-nine. He and Miss Moojah are running it alone."

"Didn't Goodbread come looking for me?"

"Oh, yes. And Captain Lamarr. They came down here together, the two of them, after you were out of the hospital. They went to the hospital too. They were sorry you were so badly hurt. I think I had to tell them six times how you got hurt. When they talked to Ramirez, he remembered picking mangrove bark and splinters out of your face. It was a big help to have him remember that. There was a big fuss about the murder. General Lawson made a thirty-second television spot, offering a hundred thousand dollars for information leading to the whereabouts of Mrs. McDermit and/or Mr. Sprenger. It's quieted down. It was a long time ago. The universe continues to unfold."

It was after midnight. We were both exhausted. He stayed over, sleeping aboard the *Flush*. When I saw him at midmorning, he showed me what he had forgotten to show me the night before. He had a little folding viewer in his pocket, and he unfolded it and put a 35mm slide in it. I turned it toward the segment of sky in the top corner of my window. It was Hirsh's photographic handiwork. It was the same lady I had seen in another world. In that world she had been in profile. On these three stamps, a strip of them without the little holes to tear them apart, she was turned and looking out at me. What had she said before? "Oh, no, *not you* again!" She was in a different color this time, curiously close to the same color as that hat Mary Alice said Sprenger would recognize.

The lady in the stamp had a small, sulky, oddly erotic mouth and an expression of arrogant challenge.

"Who is she?" I asked.

"A gift from Hirsh to you. A personal, private gift."

"I mean, did the lady have a name?"

"Are you serious? Her name was Queen Victoria!"

"Pardon me to hell, Queen."

"Here is the certificate of authenticity from the Royal Society. It's an unlisted error, a double error, the wrong color and printed on both sides."

I looked at the certificate. New Zealand Number 1, a horizontal strip of three, printed in scarlet vermilion instead of dull carmine. Recess printed. Fainter impression in same color on reverse. Unlisted. Unique. Authentic.

"What's it worth?"

"Ten years ago an appraiser from Stanley Gibbons said forty thousand dollars. Hirsh says if you want currency, there is an auction coming up where it should be entered. I forget the details. For a while I thought you really needed the money."

"You think I don't? I'm going to—"

"I know, I know. I was going to buy you an apartment near Bahia Mar. A legal address. Near where your roots are. We've both been there too long to get rousted now by politicians."

"Something changed your mind? You want to move away?"

"No. We had it wrong. You know how rumors are around Bahia Mar. It affects the squatters, that new ordinance. But it doesn't affect commercial marinas. It doesn't affect us. There's been a celebration ever since Irv set us straight."

"The *Flush* is at a good anchorage right here, Meyer."

He looked very thoughtful. "I know. A man in your condition shouldn't make too many decisions, maybe. Should I put Hirsh's gift in the auction?"

"I . . . I think I'll hang onto it for a while."

"That means you'll have to find a salvage job pretty soon, doesn't it?"

I sensed the very first small tingle of anticipation, very faint, buried very deep. But authentic. "I just might," I said. "I just might."

There came a cold day in January, cold and fiercely bright, when I put on the sweater and wool pants she had brought me from a clothes locker aboard *The Busted Flush,* and I went downstairs with her and out through the wind. I was lighter than I had been since the operations long ago on my leg. I felt as if I were made of cornflakes, stale rubber bands, and old gnawed bones. I had come out of an endless old movie into arctic glare.

We went out to the *Flush*. She wanted to get me inside, out of the wind, but I wasn't ready for that. I climbed the steep ladderway to the sun deck with convalescent care, crossed to the starboard rail, and stood looking out across the steel-gray bay under the hard blue sky. The old houseboat did not welcome me. It was not my boat. It had a problem in its guts, blood and stillness and bluebottle flies.

Cathy sensed something wrong and put her hand over mine where I grasped the rail. Something in her touch told me to remember the sweetness. I turned and looked down into those brown eyes, into that strange mix of humility and knowingness and pride.

I had to bend nearer to hear her as the wind tore at her words. "Like before," she said. "Like it was if that's what you want, what you need, when you're ready. I could say it didn't matter to me, I'd be lying." She lifted her chin a little. "But either way, it wouldn't be no obligation to you, Travis."

"Cathy, I—"

"Don't say about it now. Wait until you're up to it."

She heard her own words and looked startled and then blushed a marvelous pink and hid her face against my sweatered shoulder. It took her a few seconds before she could join my laughter. And right then I felt the deck change under my feet. The *Flush* seemed to shrug off her grisly preoccupation and look around and recognize me. She made us welcome. She had been as far away as I had, perhaps.

Cathy and I went below and had mugs of hot tea with cinnamon, and then she walked me back to the old house. Over the sound of the afternoon game on her television set, I could hear her out in the kitchen, singing as she fixed dinner, as far off-key as she used to be, the last time I had lived here on Candle Key.

The Deep Blue Good-by

For Knox Burger,
McGee's first editor

1

It was to have been a quiet evening at home.

Home is the *Busted Flush,* 52-foot barge-type houseboat, Slip F-18, Bahia Mar, Lauderdale.

Home is where the privacy is. Draw all the opaque curtains, button the hatches, and with the whispering drone of the air conditioning masking all the sounds of the outside world, you are no longer cheek to jowl with the random activities aboard the neighbor craft. You could be in a rocket beyond Venus, or under the icecap.

Because it is a room aboard, I call it the lounge, and because that is one of the primary activities.

I was sprawled on a deep curve of the corner couch, studying charts of the keys, trying to work up enough enthusiasm and energy to plan moving the *Busted Flush* to a new mooring for a while. She has a pair of Hercules diesels, 58 HP each, that will chug her along at a stately six knots. I didn't want to move her. I like Lauderdale. But it had been so long I was wondering if I should.

Chookie McCall was choreographing some fool thing. She had come over because I had the privacy and enough room. She had shoved the furniture out of the way, set up a couple of mirrors from the master stateroom, and set up her rackety little metronome. She wore a faded old rust-red leotard, mended with black thread in a couple of places. She had her black hair tied into a scarf.

She was working hard. She would go over a sequence time and time again, changing it a little each time, and when she was satisfied, she would hurry over to the table and make the proper notations on her clipboard.

Dancers work as hard as coal miners used to work. She stomped and huffed and contorted her splendid and perfectly proportioned body. In spite of the air conditioning, she had filled the lounge with a faint sharp-sweet odor of large overheated girl. She was a pleasant distraction. In the lounge lights there was a highlight gleam of perspiration on the long round legs and arms.

"Damn!" she said, scowling at her notations.

"What's wrong?"

"Nothing I can't fix. I have to figure exactly where everybody is going to be, or I'll have them kicking each other in the face. I get mixed up sometimes."

She scratched out some notes. I went back to checking the low tide depths on the flats northeast of the Content Keys. She worked hard for another ten minutes, made her notes, then leaned against the edge of the table, breathing hard.

"Trav, honey?"

"Mmm?"

"Were you kidding me that time we talked about . . . about what you do for a living?"

"What did I say?"

"It sounded sort of strange, but I guess I believed you. You said if X has something valuable and Y comes along and takes it away from him, and there is absolutely no way in the world X can ever get it back, then you come along and make a deal with X to get it back, and keep half. Then you just . . . live on that until it starts to run out. Is that the way it is, really?"

"It's a simplification, Chook, but reasonably accurate."

"Don't you get into a lot of trouble?"

"Sometimes yes, sometimes no. Y is usually in no position to make much of a fuss. Because I am sort of a last resort, the fee is fifty percent. For X, half is a lot better than nothing at all."

"And you keep it all sort of quiet."

"Chook, I don't exactly have business cards printed. What would I say on them? Travis McGee, Retriever?"

"But for goodness' sake, Trav, how much work like that can you find laying around when you start to get so broke you need it?"

"So much that I can pick and choose. This is a complex culture, dear. The more intricate our society gets, the more semi-legal ways to steal. I get leads from old clients sometimes. And if you take a batch of newspapers and read with great care, and read between the lines, you can come up with a fat happy Y and a poor X wringing his hands. I like to work on pretty good-sized ones. Expenses are heavy. And then I can take another piece of my retirement. Instead of retiring at sixty, I'm taking it in chunks as I go along."

"What if something came along right now?"

"Let's change the subject, Miss McCall. Why don't you take some time off, and make Frank highly nervous, and we'll assemble a little group and cruise a little houseboat party on down to Marathon. Let's say, four gentlemen and six ladies. No drunks, no whiners, nobody paired off, no dubious gender, no camera addicts, nobody who sunburns, nobody who can't swim, nobody who . . ."

"Please, McGee. I'm really serious."

"So am I."

"There's a girl I want you to talk to. I hired her for the group a couple of months ago. She's a little older than the rest of us. She used to dance, and she's working back into it very nicely, really. But . . . I really think she needs help. And I don't think there's anyone else she can go to. Her name is Cathy Kerr."

"I'm sorry, Chook. I've got enough right now to last for months. I work best after I begin to get nervous."

"But she thinks there is really an awful lot involved."

I stared at her. "She thinks?"

"She never got to see it."

"I beg your pardon?"

"She got a little drunk the other night and very weepy, and I've been nice to her, so she blurted it all out to me. But she should tell you herself."

"How could she lose something she never saw?"

Chookie wore that little fisherman smile which means the hook has been set. "It's really too complicated for me to try to explain. I might mess it up. Would you just do this, Travis? Would you talk to her?"

I sighed. "Bring her around sometime."

She padded lithely over to me and took my wrist and looked at my watch. Her breathing had slowed. Her leotard was sweat-dark and fitted her almost as closely as her healthy hide. She beamed down at me. "I knew you'd be nice about it, Trav. She'll be here in twenty minutes."

I stared up at her. "You are a con artist, McCall."

She patted my head. "Cathy is really nice. You'll like her." She went back to the middle of the lounge and started her metronome again, studied her notations, and went back to work, leaping, thumping, making small grunts of effort. Never sit in the first row at the ballet.

I tried to get back to channel markers and tide levels, but all concentration was gone. I had to talk to the woman. But I was certainly not going to be shilled into some nonsense project. I had the next one all lined up, waiting until I was ready. I had enough diversions. I didn't need more. I was sourly amused that Chook had wondered where the projects came from. She was living proof they popped up all the time.

Promptly at nine there was a bing-bong sound from the bell I have wired to a push button on the pier piling. If anybody should ignore the bell, step over my chain and come down my gangplank, the instant they step on the big rope mat on the transom deck there is an ominous and significant bong which starts many abrupt protective measures. I have no stomach for surprises. I have endured too many of them. They upset me. The elimination of all removable risk is the most plausible way of staying alive.

I flicked on my rear deck lights and went out the aft doorway of the lounge, Chookie McCall gasping behind me.

I went up and unsnapped the chain for her. She was a sandy blonde with one of those English schoolboy haircuts, where the big eyes look out at you from under a ragged thatch of bangs. She had overdressed for the occasion, the basic black and the pearl clip and the sparkly little envelope purse.

In explosive gasps Chook introduced us and we went inside. I could see that she was elderly by Chook's standards. Perhaps twenty-six or -seven. A brown-eyed blonde, with the helpless mournful eyes of a basset hound. She was a little weathered around the eyes. In the lounge lights I saw that the basic black had given her a lot of good use. Her hands looked a little rough. Under the slightly bouffant skirt of the black dress were those unmistakable dancer's legs, curved and trim and sinewy.

Chookie said, "Cathy, you can go ahead and tell Travis McGee the whole bit, like you told me. I've finished up, so I'll leave you alone and go back and take that bath, if it's okay, Trav."

"Please do take a bath."

She gave me a pretty good rap behind the ear and went off and closed the master stateroom door behind her.

I could see that Catherine Kerr was very tense. I offered her a drink. She gratefully accepted bourbon on ice.

"I don't know what you can do," she said. "Maybe this is silly. I don't know what anybody can do."

"Maybe there isn't a thing anybody can do, Cathy. Let's just start by assuming it's hopeless and go on from there."

"I drank too much one night after the last show and told her and I guess I shouldn't have been telling anybody."

In her light, nasal voice I could detect some of that conch accent, that slightly sing-song way the key people talk.

"I'm married, sort of," she said defiantly. "He took off three years ago and I haven't heard a thing from him. I've got a boy age of five, and my sister keeps him, down at the home place on Candle Key. That's why it's stinking, not so much for me as the boy Davie. You want a lot for a kid. Maybe I dreamed too much. I don't know, rightly."

You have to let them get to it their own way.

She sipped her drink and sighed and shrugged. "The way it happened, I was nine years old. That was in nineteen forty-five. That was when my daddy came home from the war. Sergeant David Berry. That's my maiden name, Catherine Berry. I named my boy after him, even though my daddy had been in prison a long long time when the boy was born. What I think happened, my daddy got onto some way of making money when he was overseas in World War Two. A lot of money, I think. And he found some way of bringing it back. I don't know how. He was over there in India and Burma. He was gone over two years. He was a drinking man, Mr. McGee, and a strong man and he had a temper. He came back on a ship and got off it in San Francisco. They were going to send him to some place in Florida to get discharged, and he was coming home. But in San Francisco he got drunk and killed another army man, and because he thought they would keep him and he wouldn't see us at all, he cut and ran. And he got all the way home. Running like that didn't do him any good at the trial. It was a military trial, like they have. He came home in the middle of the night, and when we got up he was out there on the dock, just looking at the water. It was a foggy day. He told my mother what happened. He said they were going to come and get him. I have never seen a woman cry like that, before or since. They came and got him like he said, and they put him in prison for life in Leavenworth, Kansas. It was an officer he killed. My mother took a bus out there to see him that Christmas, and every Christmas from then on until he died two years ago. When there was enough money, she'd take along me or my sister. I got to go twice. My sister went out there three times."

She went off into dreaming and memories. In a little while she gave a start and looked at me and said, "I'm sorry. The way it was, he thought he would get out sooner or later. I guess they would have let him out, but there was always some kind of trouble coming up. He wasn't a man to settle down to prison like some can. He was a very proud man, Mr. McGee. But here is the thing I have to tell you. Before they came and got him. I was nine. My sister was seven. He sat on the porch with his arms around us, and he told us all the wonderful things that would happen when they turned him loose. We'd have our own boats and our own horses. We would travel all over the world. We would have pretty dresses for every day in the year. I always remembered that. When I was older, I remembered it to my mother. I thought she might make fun. But she was serious enough. She told me I was never never to talk about it to anybody. She said my father would work things out in his own way, and some day everything would be fine for all of us. But of course it never was. Last year a man came to us, name of Junior Allen. A smiling man. He said he had spent five long years in that place and knew my daddy well. And he knew things about us he could only know if my daddy told him. So we were glad to see him. He said he had no family of his own. A freckledy smiling man, quick to talk and good with his hands at fixing things. He came in with us, and he got work over at the Esso station, and the money helped. My mother was started sick then, but not so sick she couldn't care for the kids by day, when Christine—that's my sister—and I were working. Her two, and my boy Davie, three little kids. It would have neatened out better if Junior Allen had took up with Christine, her husband being killed by the hurricane of sixty-one, when the cinderblock wall of the Candle Key Suprex blew over onto him. Jaimie Hasson his name was. We've had all this bad luck with our men." She tried to smile.

"Sometimes it comes in bunches," I said.

"Lord knows we've had a bunch. It was me Junior Allen liked best. By the time we took up together, my mother was too sick to care too much. As she got sicker she seemed to turn inward like some people do, not noticing much. Christine knew what was going on between us, and she told me it was wrong. But Junior said the way Wally Kerr took off and left me, I was as good as divorced. He said I couldn't even ask for a divorce until seven years went by without hearing from Wally. I since found out he lied.

"I lived like man and wife with Junior Allen, Mr. McGee, and I loved that man. When Mother died, it was good to have him close. It was near Christmas. She was washing greens, and she just bent over the sink and made a little kitten sound and slid down dying and she was gone. Christine stopped her job because somebody had to be with the kids, but with me and Junior Allen working, there was just enough to get by. There was one thing strange in all that time he was with us. I thought it was because he had gotten so close to my daddy in prison. He liked to talk about Daddy. He never stopped asking questions about him—about what things he liked to do and what places he liked to go, almost as if he was trying to live the same life my daddy had lived 'way before the war, when I was as little as Davie is now. Now I remember other things that didn't seem as strange then as they do now. I remembered about the fish shack my daddy built on a little no-name island, and I told Junior Allen, and the next day he was off he was gone all day in the skiff, and he came back bone tired and grouchy. Little things like that. I know now that he was hunting, Mr. McGee. He was hunting whatever my daddy hid, whatever it was he brought back that was going to give us those dresses and horses and around the world. Using one excuse and another, he managed to dig up just about every part of the yard. One day we awoke and Junior Allen was gone. That was near the end of this last February, and both the markers by our old driveway were tumbled down. My daddy built them long ago of coquina rock, too big and grand for such a little driveway, but built rough. Junior Allen tumbled them down and away he went, and in the ruin of the one on the left was something I don't know what it was to start. Scabs of rust and some rotten cloth that was maybe once army color, and some wire like a big clip, and some rust still in the length of a little chain, and something that could have once been some kind of a top to something.

"He took along his personal things, so I knew it was just like Wally Kerr all over again. No good looking for him. But he showed up again three weeks later, on Candle Key. Not to see me. He came back to see Mrs. Atkinson. She's a beautiful woman. She has one of the big new houses there, and I guess he met her when he was working at the Esso

and putting gas in her Thunderbird car. People told me he was staying
in her house, that he'd come down in expensive clothes and a big boat
of his own and moved right in with her. They would tell me and then
look at me to see what I'd say or do. The fourth day he was there I
came upon him in the town. I tried to speak and he turned around and
hurried the other way, and I shamed myself, running after him. He got
into her car and she wasn't there and he was pawing his pockets and
cursing because he couldn't find the key, his face ugly. I was crying and
trying to ask him what he was doing to me. He called me a busted-down
little slut and told me to go back and hide in the swamp where I came
from, and he roared away. Enough people saw it and enough heard it,
so it gave them a lot to talk about. His boat was right there, a big
cruiser, registered to him and owned by him, right at Mrs. Atkinson's
dock, and she closed the house and they went off in it. Now I know she
lived careful, and couldn't buy him a boat like that. And I know that
living with us, Junior Allen didn't have one dollar extra. But he looked
and looked and looked and found something and went away and came
back with money. But I can't see there's a thing in the world anybody
can do about it. Chookie said tell you, so I've told you. I don't know
where he is now. I don't know if Mrs. Atkinson knows, if she isn't still
with him someplace. And if anybody could find him, what could they
do?"

"Was there a name and port of registry on the boat?"

"Called it the *Play Pen,* out of Miami. Not a new boat, but the name
new. He showed a couple of people the papers to prove it his. I'd say it
was a custom boat, maybe thirty-eight foot, white topsides, gray hull
and a blue stripe."

"Then you left Candle Key."

"Not long after. There just wasn't enough money with just one of us
working. When I was little a tourist lady saw me dancing alone and
gave me free dancing lessons every winter she came down. Before I was
married I danced two years for pay up in Miami. So I came back into it
and it's enough money so I can send Christine enough and she can get
along. I didn't want to be in Candle Key any more anyway."

She looked at me with soft apologetic brown eyes, all dressed in her
best to come talk to me. The world had done its best to subdue and
humble her, but the edge of her good tough spirit showed through. I
found I had taken an irrational dislike to Junior Allen, that smiling
man. And I do not function too well on emotional motivations. I am

wary of them. And I am wary of a lot of other things, such as plastic credit cards, payroll deductions, insurance programs, retirement benefits, savings accounts, Green Stamps, time clocks, newspapers, mortgages, sermons, miracle fabrics, deodorants, check lists, time payments, political parties, lending libraries, television, actresses, junior chambers of commerce, pageants, progress, and manifest destiny.

I am wary of the whole dreary deadening structured mess we have built into such a glittering top-heavy structure that there is nothing left to see but the glitter, and the brute routines of maintaining it.

Reality is in the enduring eyes, the unspoken dreadful accusation in the enduring eyes of a worn young woman who looks at you, and hopes for nothing.

But these things can never form lecture materials for blithe Travis McGee. I am also wary of all earnestness.

"Let me do some thinking about all this, Cathy."

"Sure," she said, and put her empty glass aside.

"Another drink?"

"I'll be getting along, thank you kindly."

"I can get in touch through Chook."

"Sure."

I let her out. I noticed a small and touching thing. Despite all wounds and dejections, her dancer's step was so firm and light and quick as to give a curious imitation of joy.

2

I wandered through the lounge and tapped at the door and went into the master stateroom. Chook's fresh clothing was laid out on my bed, and her sodden stomp-suit was in a heap on the floor. I heard her in the tub, wallowing and sloshing and humming.

"Yo," I said toward the half-open door.

"Come in, darling. I'm indecent."

The bathroom was humid with steam and soap. The elderly Palm Beach sybarite who had ordered the pleasure barge for his declining years had added many nice touches. One was the tub, a semi-sunken, pale blue creation a full seven feet long and four feet wide. Chook was stretched out full length in it, her black hair afloat, bobbing around in there, creamy with suds, utterly luxuriant. She beckoned me over and I sat on the wide rim near the foot of the tub.

I guess Chook is about twenty-three or -four. Her face is a little older than that. It has that stern look you see in old pictures of the plains Indians. At her best, it is a forceful and striking face, filled with strength and dignity. At worst it sometimes would seem to be the face of a Dartmouth boy dressed for the farcical chorus line. But that body, seen more intimately than ever before, was incomparably, mercilessly female, deep and glossy, rounded—under the tidy little fatty layer of girl pneumatics—with useful muscle.

This was a special challenge, and I didn't know the terms, knew only that most of the time they are terms one cannot ultimately afford, not with the ones who, like Chook, have their own special force and substance and requirements. She had created the challenge, and was less bold with it than she wanted me to believe.

"How about that Cathy?" she said, her voice elaborately casual.

"A little worn around the edges."

"How not? But how about helping her?"

"There's a lot to find out first. Maybe too much. Maybe it would be too long and too expensive finding out what I'd have to find out."

"But you couldn't tell about that until you looked into it."

"I could just make a guess."

"And not do anything."

"What's it to you, Chook?"

"I like her. And it's been rough."

"The wide world is full of likable people who get kicked in the stomach regularly. They're disaster-prone. Something goes wrong. The sky starts falling on their head. And you can't reverse the process."

She sloshed a little and scowled. My left hand was braced on the edge of the tub. Suddenly she lifted a long steaming gleaming leg and put the soaking sole of her bare foot firmly on the back of my hand. She curled her toes around the edge of my wrist in a strange little clasp and said, her voice husky and her eyes a little alarmed at her own daring, "The water's fine."

It was just a little too contrived. "Who are you trying to be?"

She was startled. "That's a funny thing to say."

"You are Chookie McCall, very resolute and ambitious and not exactly subject to fits of abandon. And we have been friends for a couple of months. I made my pass, 'way back when, and you straightened me out very pleasantly and firmly. So who are you trying to be? Fair question?"

She took her foot away. "Do you have to be such a bastard, Trav? Maybe I was having a fit of abandon. Why do you have to question things?"

"Because I know you, and maybe there are enough people getting hurt."

"What is that supposed to mean?"

"Chook, dear girl, you are just not trivial enough for purely recreational sex. You are more complex than that. So this very pleasant and unexpected invitation has to be part of some kind of a program or plan of action or design for the future."

Her eyes shifted just enough to let me know I had struck home. "Whatever it was, darling, you've bitched it good."

I smiled at her. "If it's pure recreation, dear, without claims or agreements or deathless vows, I'm at your service. I like you. I like you enough to keep from trying to fake you into anything, even though, at the moment, it's one hell of a temptation. But I think you would have to get too deeply involved in your own justifications because, as I said, you are a complex woman. And a strong woman. And I am no part of your future, not in any emotional way." I stood up and looked down at her. "Now you know the rules, it's still your decision. Just holler."

I went back to the lounge. I examined my sterling character and wondered if it would be functional and entertaining to thud my head against the wall. My fingernails made interesting little grooves in the palms of my hands. My ears grew, extending to tall hairy points, and as I did a little pacing, they kept turning in her direction, listening for a shy summons.

When at last she came out, she wore white slacks and a black blouse, with her dark damp hair bound in a red scarf. She carried her dancing gear in a little canvas case. She looked tired and shy and rueful, and came slowly to me, meeting my glance with a multitude of little quick glances of her own. Clothing leans her, disguising ripeness.

I cupped my hand on her chin and kissed a soft, warm and humble Indian mouth. "What was it all about?" I asked her.

"A fight with Frank. Kind of a nasty one. So I guess I was trying to prove something. Now I feel like a fool."

"Don't."

She sighed. "But I would have felt worse the other way. I guess. Eventually. So thanks for being smarter about me than I am."

"My friend, it wasn't easy."

She scowled at me. "What's the matter with me? Why can't I be in love with you instead of him? He's really a terrible man. He makes me feel degraded, Trav. But when he walks into the room, sometimes I feel as if I'll faint with love. I think that's why . . . I feel so sympathetic toward Cathy. Frank is my Junior Allen. Please help her."

I told her I would think about it. I walked her to her little car, out in the sweet hot night, and watched her go sputtering off, carrying the ripeness, unimpaired, back to surly Frank. I listened for the roar of applause, fanfare of trumpets, for the speech and the medal. I heard the lisping flap of water against the hull, the soft mutter of the traffic on the smooth asphalt that divides the big marina from the public beach, bits of music blending into nonsense, boat laughter, the slurred harmony of alcohol, and a mosquito song vectoring in on my neck.

I kicked a concrete pier and hurt my toes. These are the playmate years, and they are demonstrably fraudulent. The scene is reputed to be acrawl with adorably amoral bunnies to whom sex is a pleasant social favor. The new culture. And they are indeed present and available, in exhausting quantity, but there is a curious tastelessness about them. A woman who does not guard and treasure herself cannot be of very much value to anyone else. They become a pretty little convenience, like a guest towel. And the cute little things they say, and their dainty little squeals of pleasure and release are as contrived as the embroidered initials on the guest towels. Only a woman of pride, complexity and emotional tension is genuinely worth the act of love, and there are only two ways to get yourself one of them. Either you lie, and stain the relationship with your own sense of guile, or you accept the involvement, the emotional responsibility, the permanence she must by nature crave. I love you can be said only two ways.

But tension is also a fact of life, and I found myself strolling toward the big rich Wheeler where the Alabama Tiger maintains his permanent floating house party. I was welcomed with vague cheers. I nursed a drink, made myself excruciatingly amiable, suitably mysterious and witty in the proper key, and carefully observed the group relationships until I was able to identify two possibles. I settled for a blooming redhead from Waco, Takes-us, name of Molly Bea Archer, carefully cut her out of the pack and trundled her, tipsy and willing, back to the *Busted Flush*. She thought it an adorable little old boat, and scampered about, ooing and cooing at the fixtures and appointments, kittenish as all get out until faced with the implacable reality of bedtime, then settled into her little social chore with acquired skill and natural diligence. We rested and exchanged the necessary compliments, and she told me of her terrible problem—whether to go back to Baylor for her senior year, or marry some adorable little old boy who was terribly in love with her, or take a wonderful job in Houston working for some adorable little old insurance company. She sighed and gave me a sisterly little kiss and a friendly little pat, and got up and went and fixed her face and crammed herself back into her shorts and halter, and after I had built two fresh drinks into the glasses we had brought from the other craft, I walked her back to the Tiger's party and stayed fifteen more minutes as a small courtesy.

When I was alone in darkness in my bed, I felt sad, ancient, listless and cheated. Molly Bea had been as personally involved as one of those rubber dollies sailors buy in Japanese ports.

And in the darkness I began to remember the brown and humbled eyes of Cathy Kerr, under that guileless sandy thatch of hair. Molly Bea, she of the hard white breasts lightly dusted with golden freckles, would never be so humiliated by life because she could never become as deeply involved in the meaty toughness of life. She would never be victimized of her own illusions because they were not essential to her. She could always find new ones when the old ones wore out. But Cathy was stuck with hers. The illusion of love, magically changed to a memory of shame.

Maybe I was despising that part of myself that was labeled Junior Allen. What an astonishment these night thoughts would induce in the carefree companions of blithe Travis McGee, that big brown loose-jointed boat bum, that pale-eyed, wire-haired girl-seeker, that slayer of small savage fish, that beach-walker, gin-drinker, quip-maker, peace-seeker, iconoclast, disbeliever, argufier, that knuckly, scar-tissued reject from a structured society.

But pity, indignation and guilt are the things best left hidden from all the gay companions.

Take them out at night.

McGee, you really know how to live, old buddy.

Adorable little old buddy.

It was to have been a quiet evening at home. Until Cathy Kerr came into it, bringing unrest. At last I could admit to myself that the rubbery little adventure with the Takes-us redhead was not because I had denied myself a sudsy romp with Chook, but because I was trying to ignore the challenge Cathy had dropped in my lap. I could afford to drift along for many months. But now Cathy had created the restlessness, the indignation, the beginnings of that shameful need to clamber aboard my spavined white steed, knock the rust off the armor, tilt the crooked old lance and shout huzzah.

Sleep immediately followed decision.

3

The next morning, after making laundry arrangements, I untethered my bike and pedaled to the garage where I keep Miss Agnes sheltered from brine and sun. She needs tender loving care in her declining years. I believe she is the only Rolls Royce in America which has been converted into a pickup truck. She is vintage 1936, and apparently some previous owner had some unlikely disaster happen to the upper half of her rear end and solved the problem in an implausible way. She is one of the big ones, and in spite of her brutal surgery retains the family knack of going eighty miles an hour all day long in a kind of ghastly silence. Some other idiot had her repainted a horrid electric blue. When I found her squatting, shame-faced, in the back row of a gigantic car lot, I bought her at once and named her after a teacher I had in the fourth grade whose hair was that same shade of blue.

Miss Agnes took me down the pike to Miami, and I began making the rounds of the yacht brokers, asking my devious questions.

After a sandwich lunch, I finally found the outfit that had sold it. Kimby-Meyer. An Ambrose A. Allen, according to their record sheet, had bought a forty-foot Stadel custom back in March. They had his address as the Bayway Hotel. The salesman was out. A man named Joe True. While I waited for him to come back, I phoned the Bayway. They had no A. A. Allen registered. Joe True got back at two-thirty, scented with good bourbon. He was a jouncy, leathery little man who punctuated each comment with a wink and a snicker, as if he had just told a joke. It saddened him somewhat to learn I was not a potential cus-

tomer, but he brightened up when I offered to buy him a drink. We
went to a nearby place where he was extremely well known by all, and
they had his drink in front of him before we were properly settled on
the barstools.

"Frankly, I didn't know he was a live one," Joe True said. "You get
to know the look of people who buy boats like that one. That Mr.
Allen, he looked and acted more like hired crew, like he was lining
something up for his boss. Grease under his fingernails. A tattoo on his
wrist. A very hard-looking character, very brown and wide and powerful-looking. And smiling all the time. I showed him a lot of listings, and
he was so quick to talk price I began to take him serious. He settled on
that *Jessica III,* that was the name the original owner registered her at."

"A good boat?"

"A fine boat, Mr. McGee. She'd had a lot of use but she was maintained well. Twin 155's, and they'd been overhauled. A nice compromise between range and speed. Nicely appointed. Built in fifty-six if I
remember right. Good hull performance in a rough sea. We took it out.
He handled it and liked it. When we came back in, he scared hell out of
me. I thought we were going to peel away about fifty feet of dock. But
he hit the reverse just right, and I was up in the bow, and he put me
right beside a piling as gentle as a little girl's kiss. And when he checked
the boat over, he knew just what to look for. He didn't need any survey
made. And he bought it right. Twenty-four thousand even."

"Cash?"

Joe True shoved his glass toward the bartender and looked at me and
said, "You better tell me again what it is you're after."

"I'm just trying to locate him, Joe. As a favor for a mutual friend."

"I got a little nervous about that deal, and I told Mr. Kimby about
being nervous and he checked it out with his lawyer. No matter where
Allen got the money, nobody can come back on us."

"Why did the money make you nervous?"

"He didn't look or act like the kind of a man to have that kind of
money. That's all. But how can you tell? I didn't ask him where he got
it. Maybe he's some kind of eccentric captain of finance. Maybe he's
thrifty. What he had was five cashier's checks. They were all from
different banks, all from New York banks. Four of them were five thousand each, and one was twenty-five hundred. He made up the difference
in hundred-dollar bills. The agreement was we'd change the name the
way he wanted and handle the paper work for him and do some other

things for him, nothing major, get the dinghy painted, replace an anchor line, that sort of thing. While that was being done our bank said the checks were fine, so I met him at the dock and gave him the papers and he took delivery. That man never stopped smiling. Real pale curly hair burned white by the sun, and little bright blue eyes, and smiling every minute. The way he handled the boat, I finally figured he was actually buying it for somebody else, even though it was registered to him. Maybe some kind of a tax deal or something like that. I mean it looked that way because of the way those cashier's checks were spread around. He was dressed in the best, but the clothes didn't look just right on him."

"And you haven't seen him since?"

"Haven't seen him or heard from him. I guess he was a satisfied customer."

"How old would you say he is?"

Joe True frowned. "It's hard to say. If I had to guess, I'd say about thirty-eight. And in great shape. Very tough and quick. He jumped off that thing like a cat and he had the stern line and the spring line all rigged while I was making the bow line fast."

I bought Joe his third drink and left him there with his dear friends. Junior Allen was beginning to take shape. And he was beginning to look a little more formidable. He had left Candle Key in late February with something of value, and had gone to New York and managed to convert it into cash, all of it or some of it, whatever it was. Weeks later he had returned to Miami, bought himself a good hunk of marine hardware and gone back to Candle Key to visit the Atkinson woman. It had required considerable confidence to go back. Or recklessness. A man with a criminal record shouldn't flaunt money, particularly in an area where an angry woman might be likely to turn him in.

Yet, actually, the boat procedure was pretty good. It gave him a place to live. With papers in order and a craft capable of passing Coast Guard inspection, he wasn't likely to be asked too many embarrassing questions. People who build a transient life around a forty-foot cruiser are presumed innocent. I'd found the *Busted Flush* to be a most agreeable headquarters for the basically rebellious. You escape most of the crud, answer fewer questions, and you can leave on the next tide.

But there was one hitch, and perhaps Junior Allen wouldn't be aware of it. The tax people take a hearty interest in all registered craft over twenty feet. They like to make sure they weren't purchased with their money. A cash transaction like that one might intrigue some persistent little man up there in Jacksonville, and give him a heady desire to have a chat with Ambrose A. Allen, transient.

But first he would have to find him.

I wondered if I would find him first.

I visited the Bayway Hotel. It was a mainland hotel, small, quiet and luxurious in an understated way. The little lobby was like the living room in a private home. A pale clerk listened to my question and drifted off into the shadows and was gone a long time. He came back and said that A. A. Allen had stayed with them for five days last March and had left no forwarding address. He had given his address when registering as General Delivery, Candle Key. He had been in 301, one of their smallest suites. We smiled at each other. He smothered a yawn with a dainty fist and I walked out of his shadowy coolness into the damp noisy heat of the Miami afternoon.

The next question was multiple choice. I did not want to get too close to Junior Allen too soon. When you stalk game it is nice to know what it eats and where it drinks and where it beds down, and if it has any particularly nasty habits, like circling back and pursuing the pursuer. I did not know all the questions I wanted to ask, but I knew where to look for answers. Cathy, her sister, Mrs. Atkinson, and perhaps some people out in Kansas. And it might be interesting to locate somebody who had served with Sergeant David Berry in that long ago war. Apparently the Sergeant had found himself a profitable war. It was past four o'clock, and I kept thinking of questions I wanted to ask Cathy, so I headed on back toward my barge. I parked Miss Agnes handy to home, because I would need her that evening to go see Cathy Kerr.

I stripped to swim trunks and did a full hour of topsides work on the *Busted Flush,* taking out a rotted section of canvas on the port side of the sun deck, replacing it with the nylon I'd had made to order, lacing the brass grommets to the railing and to the little deck cleats, while the sun blasted me and the sweat rolled off. One more section to go and I will have worked my way all around the damned thing, and then I am going to cover the whole sun deck area with that vinyl which is a clever imitation of teak decking. Maybe, after years of effort I will get to the point where a mere forty hours a week will keep it in trim.

I acquired it in a private poker session in Palm Beach, a continuous thirty hours of intensive effort. At the end of ten hours I had been down to just what I had on the table, about twelve hundred. In a stud hand I stayed with deuces backed, deuce of clubs down, deuce of hearts up. My next three cards were the three, seven and ten of hearts. There were three of us left in the pot. By then they knew how I played, knew I had to be paired, or have an ace or king in the hole. I was looking at a pair of eights, and the other player had paired on the last card. Fours. Fours checked to the eights and I was in the middle, and bet the pot limit, six hundred. Pair of eights sat there and thought too long. He decided I wasn't trying to buy one, because it would have been too clumsy and risky in view of my financial status. He decided I was trying to look as if I was buying one, to get the big play against a flush, anchored by either the ace or king of hearts in the hole. Fortunately neither of those cards had showed up in that hand.

He folded. Pair of fours was actually two pair. He came to the same reluctant conclusion. I pulled the pot in, collapsed my winning hand and tossed it to the dealer, but that hole card somehow caught against my finger and flipped over. The black deuce. And I knew that from then on they would remember that busted flush and they would pay my price for my good hands. And they did, for twenty more hours, and there were many many good hands, and there was a great weight of old-time money in that little group. In the last few hours I loaned the big loser ten thousand against that houseboat, and when it was gone I loaned him ten more, and when that was gone I loaned him the final ten and the craft was mine. When he wanted another ten, with his little Brazilian mistress as security, his friends took him away and quieted him down and the game ended. And I named the houseboat in honor of the hand which had started my streak, and sold the old *Prowler* on which I had been living in cramped circumstances.

After the manual labor, I treated myself to a tepid tub and a chilly bottle of Dos Equis, that black Mexican beer beyond compare, and dressed for summer night life. Just at dusk Molly Bea came a-calling, tall glass in hand, tiddly-sweet, pinked with sunburn, bringing along a dark lustrous giggler to show her my adorable little old boat. The giggler was named Conny, and she was from Gnaw-luns rather than Takes-us, but she was a similar piece, styled for romps and games, all a girlish prancing, giving me to believe—with glance and innuendo—that she had checked me out with Molly Bea, given her total approval, then matched for me and won. She was prepared to move in with me and send Molly Bea back to the Tiger. After the inspection tour, I got rid of both of them, locked up and went off to a downtown place which sells

tourist steaks at native prices, and then went on out to the Mile
O'Beach, to the Bahama Room, your host Joey Mirris, featuring for
Our Big Summer Season, the haunting ballads of Sheilagh Morraine,
and Chookie McCall and her Island Dancers. Closed Mondays.

Joey Mirris was a tasteless brassy purveyor of blue material and
smutty sight gags. It was a pickup band, very loud and very bored.
Sheilagh Morraine had a sweet, true, ordinary little voice, wooden gestures and expressions, and an astounding 42-25-38 figure she garbed in
show gowns that seemed knitted of wet cobwebs. But Chook and her
six-pack were good. She planned the costumes, lighting, arrangements,
routines, picked the girls carefully and trained them mercilessly. They
were doing three a night, and the dancers were the ones bringing in the
business, and Adam Teabolt, the owner-manager, knew it.

The room will take about two and a quarter, and they had about seventy for the eight o'clock show. I found a stool at the end of the raised
bar, tried not to notice Mirris and Morraine, and then gave my full attention to the so-called Island Dancers. The wardrobe for the entire
seven could have been assembled in one derby hat. Under the blue
floods I saw Cathy Kerr working in perfect cadence with the group,
wearing a rather glassy little smile, her body trim and nimble, light and
muscular and quick. There is no flab on good dancers. There is no
room for it, and no time to acquire it. Effort coats the trained golden
flesh with little moist highlights. As always, the bored band did its best
for the Chook-troop, and part of the routine was a clever satire on all
sea-island routines.

After the eight o'clock show I sent a note back to Cathy and then
went to the hotel coffee shop. She joined me five minutes later, wearing
a dreary little blouse, a cheap skirt and her heavy stage makeup. We
had a corner table. Through the glass wall I could see the lighted pool
and the evening swimmers.

"I'm going to try to see if I can do anything, Cathy."

The brown eyes searched my face. "I surely appreciate it, Mr.
McGee."

"Trav. Short for Travis."

"Thank you, Trav. Do you think you can do anything?"

"I don't know. But we have to make some kind of agreement."

"Like what?"

"Your father hid something and Junior Allen found it. If I find out what it is or was and where he got it, maybe there is somebody it should go back to."

"I wouldn't want anything that was stole."

"If I can make recovery of anything, Cathy, I'll take my expenses off the top and split what's left with you, fifty fifty."

She thought that over. "I guess that would be fair enough. This way, I've got nothing at all."

"But you can't tell anyone we have this arrangement. If anybody asks you anything about me, I'm just a friend."

"I think maybe you are. But what about those expenses if you don't get anything back?"

"That's my risk."

"So long as I don't end up owing. Lord God, I owe enough here and there. Even some to Chookie."

"I want to ask you a few questions."

"You go right ahead, Trav."

"Do you know of anybody who served with your father in the Army?"

"No. The thing is, he wanted to fly. He enlisted to try to get to fly. But he was too old or not enough schooling or something. He enlisted in nineteen forty-two. I was six years old when he went away. He trained in Texas someplace, and finally he got into the . . . something about Air Transit or something."

"ATC? Air Transport Command?"

"That was it! Sure. And he got to fly that way, not flying the airplanes, but having a regular airplane to fly on. A crew chief he got to be. Over in that CBI place. And he did good because we got the allotment and after he was over there, those hundred-dollar money orders would come once in a while. Once there were three of them all at once. Ma saved what she could for when he got back, and the way it turned out, it was a good thing she did."

"But you don't know anybody he served with?"

She frowned thoughtfully. "There were names in the letters sometimes. He didn't write much. My mother saved those letters. I don't know if Christy threw them out when she died. Maybe they're still down at the house. There were names in them sometimes."

"Could you ride down there with me tomorrow and find out?"

"I guess so."

"I want to meet your sister."

"Why?"

"I want to hear what she has to say about Junior Allen."

"She'll say she told me so. She didn't like him much. Can I tell my sister what you're trying to do for us?"

"No. I'd rather you wouldn't, Cathy. Tell her I'm just a friend. I'll find some way to get her to talk about Allen."

"What can she tell you?"

"Maybe nothing. Maybe some things you didn't notice."

"It'll be good to see my Davie."

"Why was Allen sent to prison?"

"He said it was a big misunderstanding. He went in the Army and he was making it his career. He was in the Quartermaster, in the part that they have boats, like the Navy. But little boats. Crash boats, they call the ones he was on. And then he got into the supply part of it, and in nineteen fifty-seven they got onto him for selling a lot of government stuff to some civilian company. He said he did a little of it, but not as much as they said. They blamed it all on him and gave him a dishonorable discharge and eight years at Leavenworth. But he got out in five. That's where he was a cellmate of my daddy, and said he came to help us because my daddy would have wanted him to. That's the lie he told us."

"Where did he come from originally?"

"Near Biloxi. He grew up on boats, that's how the Army put him into the boats. He said he had no folks left there."

"And you fell in love with him."

She gave me a strange and troubled look. "I don't know as it was love. I didn't want him to have me like that, right there at the home place with my mother still alive then, and Davie there, and Christine and her two. It was shameful, but I couldn't seem to help myself. Looking back I can't understand how it could be. Trav, I had a husband, and there was one other man beside my husband and Junior Allen, but my husband and the other man weren't like Junior Allen. I don't know how to say it to a stranger without shaming myself more. But maybe it could help somehow to know this about him. The first time or so, he forced me. He would be tender and loving, but afterward. Saying he was sorry. But he was at me like some kind of animal, and he was too rough and too often. He said it had always been like that with him, like he couldn't help himself. And after a while he changed me, so that it didn't seem too rough any more, and I didn't care how many times he came at me or when. It was all turned into a dream I couldn't quite wake up from, and I went around feeling all soft and dreamy and stupid, and not caring a damn about what anybody thought, only caring that he wanted me and I wanted him. He's a powerful man, and all the time we were together he never did slack off. Do a woman that way and I think she goes off into a kind of a daze, because really it's too much, but there was no way of stopping him, and finally I didn't want to, because you get used to living in that dazy way. Then when he come back and moved in with that Mrs. Atkinson . . . I couldn't stop thinking how . . ." She shook herself like a wet puppy and gave me a shamefaced smile and said, "How to get to be a damn fool in one easy lesson. I was just something real handy for him while he was looking for what my daddy hid away. And all the time I thought it was me pleasing him." She looked at the coffee-shop clock. "I have to be going to get ready for the next show. What time do you want to go in the morning?"

"Suppose I pick you up about nine-thirty?"

"I'd rather I come to your boat about then, if that's okay with you."

"It's fine with me, Cathy."

She started to stand up and then sat back again and touched the back of my hand swiftly and lightly and pulled her fingers away. "Don't hurt him."

"What?"

"I wouldn't want to think I set anybody onto him that hurt him. My head knows that he's an evil man deserving any bad thing that can happen to him, but my heart says for you not to hurt him."

"Not unless I have to."

"Try not to have to."

"I can promise that much."

"That's all I wanted." She cocked her head. "I think maybe you're clever. But he's sly. He's animal-sly. You know the difference?"

"Yes."

She touched my hand again. "You be careful."

4

Cathy Kerr sat primly beside me on the genuine leather of old Miss Agnes as we drifted swiftly down through Perrine and Naranja and Florida City, then through Key Largo, Rock Harbor, Tavernier and across another bridge onto Candle Key. Her eagerness to see her child was evident when she pointed out the side road to me and, a hundred yards down the side road, the rock columns marking the entrance to the narrow driveway that led back to the old frame bay-front house. It was of black cypress and hard pine, a sagging weathered old slattern leaning comfortably on her pilings, ready to endure the hurricane winds that would flatten glossier structures.

A gang of small brown children came roaring around the corner of a shed and charged us. When they had sorted themselves out, I saw there were but three, all with a tow-headed family resemblance. Cathy kissed and hugged them all strenuously, and showed me which one was Davie. She handed out three red lollipops and they sped away, licking and yelping.

Christine came out of the house. She was darker and heavier than Cathy. She wore faded jeans hacked off above the knee, and a man's white T-shirt with a rip in the shoulder. She moved slowly toward us, patting at her hair. She did not carry herself with any of Cathy's lithe dancer's grace, but she was a curiously attractive woman, slow and brooding, with a sensuous and challenging look.

Cathy introduced us. Christine stood there inside her smooth skin, warm and indolent, mildly speculative. It is that flavor exuded by women who have fashioned an earthy and simplified sexual adjustment to their environment, borne their young, achieved an unthinking physical confidence. They are often placidly unkempt, even grubby, taking no interest in the niceties of posture. They have a slow relish for the physical spectrum of food, sun, deep sleep, the needs of children, the caresses of affection. There is a tiny magnificence about them, like the sultry dignity of she-lions.

She kissed her sister, scratched her bare arm, said she was glad to meet me and come on in, there was coffee made recent.

The house was untidy with tracked shell and broken toys, clothing and crumbs. There was a frayed grass rug in the living room, and gigantic Victorian furniture, the dark wood scarred, the upholstery stained and faded. She brought in coffee in white mugs, and it was dark, strong and delicious.

Christy sat on the couch with brown scratched legs curled under her and said, "What I was thinking, that Lauralee Hutz is looking for something, and she could be here days for twenty-five a week and I could maybe make forty-five waitress at the Caribbee, but it would mean getting there and back, and the garden is coming along good, and I got six dollars last week from Gus for crabs, so it don't seem worth it all the way around, getting along the way we are with what you send down, but it's lonely some days nobody to talk with but little kids."

"Did you fix up that tax money?"

"I took it in person, and Mr. Olney he showed me how it figures out a half percent a month from the time it was first due. I got the receipt out there in the breadbox, Sis."

"Christine, you do how you feel about the job and all."

She gave Cathy a small curious smile. "Max keeps stopping by."

"You were going to run him off."

"I haven't rightly decided," Christine said. She looked me over. "You work at the same place, Mr. McGee?"

"No. I met Cathy through Chookie McCall. I had an errand down this way, so I thought Cathy might like to ride down."

Cathy said abruptly, "Daddy's letters from in the Army, you throw them out going through Ma's things?"

"I don't think I did. What do you want them for?"

"Just to read over again."

"Where they'd be if anyplace, is in the hump-top trunk in that back bedroom, maybe in the top drawer someplace."

Cathy went off. I heard her quick step on the wooden stairs.

"You going around with her?" Christine asked.

"No."

"You married?"

"No."

"She's still legal married to Kerr, but she could say desertion and get loose in six months. A man could do a lot worse. She's strong and she's pretty and she's a worker. She's saddened now, but anybody make her happy, they'd see a different woman. She's a loving one, laughing and singing when she's happy."

"I guess Junior Allen saddened her."

She looked surprised. "You know all about him?"

"Most of it, I guess."

"She must like you to tell you. Cathy is older than me but younger. She doesn't see things about people. I wanted to run him off the place. All that laughing and smiling, and his eyes didn't smile. Then he got to her, loving her up so she couldn't think straight, and it was too late to run him off by then. Even too late to tell her he put his hands on me every chance he had, laughing at me when I called him names. I knew he was after something. I knew he was looking. But I didn't know what for or where it could be. It was a wicked way he did her, Mr. McGee, getting her to need him so bad, then walking out. Better for her if he never come anywhere near here again, but he come back with our money and moved in on a rich woman, and not a damn thing in the world anybody could do about it."

"Go to the police?"

"Police? Whatever he got was already stole one time. Police never did any favors for the Berry family. When you've got a daddy dies in prison, you don't look friendly on the police."

"When was the last time Allen was in the area?"

Suspicion changed her placid face, tightening it. "You wouldn't be some kind of police?"

"No. Absolutely not."

She waited out the fade of suspicion, gave a little nod. "He was coming and going, taking her off on that boat, staying there with her, and maybe a month ago, one day the boat was gone and she was there alone. There's a sale sign on that house and she stays pretty much inside the house and they say she's turned to drinking more so perhaps Junior Allen is gone for good."

"Perhaps that's just as well, for Cathy's sake."

"He shamed her. People knew what was going on. And they knew Kerr ran out on her. Junior Allen called her names and people heard it. They laugh about her. I clawed one face bone raw and they don't do their laughing in front of me. What Cathy doesn't need is any more trouble. You remember that. I don't think she can take one more little bit of any kind of trouble."

"I don't plan to give her any."

"She looks pretty good now. All slim as a girl." She sighed. "Me, I seem to keep right on widening out."

Cathy came rattling down the stairs with a crushed white box fastened with rubber bands. "They were down in the bottom," she said. "And there was this picture." She showed it to Christine and then brought it over to me. It was a snapshot. A powerful man sat grinning on the top step of the porch of the old house. A placid pretty woman in a print dress sat beside him. The man had his arm around a squinting, towheaded girl of about five. She was leaning against him. A younger girl was in her mother's lap, her fingers in her mouth.

"Old times," Cathy said wistfully. "Suppose somebody came to us that day and told all of us how things would be. You wonder, would it have changed a thing?"

"I wish that somebody would come along right now," Christine said. "I could use the information. We're due for good luck, Sis. The both of us."

I stood up. "I'll go along and do my errand and stop back for you, Cathy."

"Shall we wait lunch?" Christine asked.

"Better not. I don't know how long I'll be."

The town of Candle Key was a wide place on a fast road. The key was narrow at that point. The town was near the southwest bridge off the key. It had taken a good scouring in 1960 and had a fresh new look, modern gas stations, waterfront motels, restaurants, gift shops, marine supplies, boat yards, post office.

I stopped at the big Esso station and found the station manager at the desk marking an inventory sheet. He was a hunched, seamed, cadaverous man with dusty-looking black hair and his name was Rollo Urthis. He greeted me with the wary regard salesmen grow accustomed to.

"Mr. Urthis, my name is McGee. I'm trying to get a line on the present whereabouts of one Ambrose Allen. Our records show that he worked for you for several months."

"Junior Allen. Sure. He worked here. What's it all about?"

"Just routine." I took a piece of paper from my wallet, looked at it and put it back. "There's an unpaid hotel bill of two hundred and twelve dollars and twenty cents. At the Bayway Hotel in Miami, back in March. They put it in the hands of the agency I work for, and he registered there as coming from Candle Key."

His grin exposed a very bad set of teeth. "Now that must be just one of them little details that Mister Junior Allen overlooked. When you run acrosst him, he'll probably just pay you off out of the spare change he carries in his pocket and give you a big tip for your trouble, Mister."

"I'm afraid I don't understand, Mr. Urthis."

"He quit me in February and got rich all of a sudden."

"Did he inherit money?"

"I don't know as that is just the right word. People got different ideas where he got it. He was away for nearly a month and came back on a big cruiser he bought himself, new clothes and a gold wristwatch no thicker than a silver dollar. I'd say he made a woman give it to him. He's the kind can make women do things they might not want to do if he gave them time to think about it. He came here and moved right in with the Berry girls, big as life. Their ma was still alive then, last year. They had hard luck, both of them. Cathy is as nice a little woman as you'd want to know, but he got next to her pretty quick. When he got the money he dropped her and moved in on Mrs. Atkinson. She was a customer a long time, and I could have swore she wouldn't stand for anything like that. But she did. Lost me a customer too. God knows where he's at now. But maybe Mrs. Atkinson would know, if you could get her to talk to you about it. I hear she's touchy on the subject. Nobody around here has seen Junior Allen in better than a month I'd say."

"Was he a satisfactory employee, Mr. Urthis?"

"If he wasn't I wouldn't have kept him. Sure, he was all right. A quick-moving man, real good when we had a rush, and good at fixing things. The trade liked him. He smiled all the time, and he could always find something that needed doing around here. Maybe he was just a little bit too friendly with the women customers, the good-looking ones. Kidding around a little, but nobody complained. Frankly, I was sorry when he quit. The people you get these days, they don't want to work."

"Was he reliable in money matters?"

"I'd say so. I don't think he left owing anybody, and if he did, he sure was able to pay up when he got back. I think he got it off Mrs. Atkinson some way. If so, it would be up to her to complain, not me."

"Where could I find her?"

"See that big real estate sign up the road? Turn right just beyond it and go straight down to the water and turn right again, and it's the second house on the right, a long low white-colored house."

It was one of those Florida houses I find unsympathetic, all block, tile, glass, terrazzo, aluminum. They have a surgical coldness. Each one seems to be merely some complex corridor arrangement, a going-through place, an entrance built to some place of a better warmth and privacy that was never constructed. When you pause in these rooms, you have the feeling you are waiting. You feel that a door will open and you will be summoned, and horrid things will happen to you before they let you go. You cannot mark these houses with any homely flavor of living. When they are emptied after occupancy, they have the look of places where the blood has recently been washed away.

The yard was scrubby with dry weeds. A dirty white Thunderbird rested in the double carport. A new red and white sign in the yard said that Jeff Bocka would be happy to sell this residence to anyone. I stood at the formal entrance, thumbed a plastic button and heard an inside dingle. I heard a faint swift approaching tickety-clack of sandals on tile, and the white door was flung open, and I discarded all preconceived visions of Mrs. Atkinson.

She was a tall and slender woman, possibly in her early thirties. Her skin had the extraordinary fineness of grain, and the translucence you see in small children and fashion models. In her fine long hands, delicacy of wrists, floating texture of dark hair, and in the mobility of the long narrow sensitive structuring of her face there was the look of something almost too well made, too highly bred, too finely drawn for all the natural crudities of human existence. Her eyes were large and very dark and tilted and set widely. She wore dark Bermuda shorts and sandals and a crisp blue and white blouse, no jewelry of any kind, a sparing touch of lipstick.

"Who are you? What do you want? Who are you?" Her voice was light and fast and intense and her mouth trembled. She seemed to be on the narrow edge of emotional disaster, holding herself in check with the greatest effort. And about her was a rich and heavy scent of brandy, and an unsteadiness, the eyes too swift and not exactly in focus.

"Mrs. Atkinson, my name is Travis McGee."

"Yes? Yes? What do you want?"

I tried to look disarming. I am pretty good at that. I have one of those useful faces. Tanned American. Bright eyes and white teeth shining amid a broad brown reliable bony visage. The proper folk-hero crinkle at the corners of the eyes, and the bashful appealing smile, when needed. I have been told that when I have been aroused in violent directions I can look like something from an unused corner of hell, but I wouldn't know about that. My mirror consistently reflects that folksy image of the young project engineer who flung the bridge across the river in spite of overwhelming odds, up to and including the poisoned arrow in his heroic shoulder.

So I looked disarming. When they give you something to use, you use it. Many bank robbers look extraordinarily reliable. So you use your face to make faces with, play parts, pick up cues. In every contact with every other human in every day of your life, you become what you sense they want of you or, if you are motivated the other way, exactly what they do not want. Were this not so, there would be no place left to hide.

"I just wanted to talk to you about . . ."

"I won't show the house without an appointment. That was the arrangement. I'm sorry."

They learn that voice and that diction in those little schools they go to before they go on to Smith and Vassar and Wellesley.

"I want to talk to you about Junior Allen."

I could have listed maybe fifty possible reactions without coming close to the one I got. Her eyes dulled and her narrow nostrils flared wide and her mouth fell into sickness. She lost her posture and stood in an ugly way. "That's it, I suppose," she said in a dragging tone. "Certainly. Am I a gift? Or was there a fee?" She whirled and hurried away. She skidded and nearly fell when she turned left at the end of the foyer. I heard an unseen door bang. I stood there in the silence. Then I heard a muffled sound of retching, tiny and far off and agonizing. The noon sun blasted down upon whiteness. I stepped into the relative darkness of the house, into the cool breath of air conditioning. I closed the formal door.

She was still being sick. I went swiftly and quietly through the house.

It was as littered as Christine's house, but a different sort of litter. Glasses, dirty ashtrays, food untouched, clothing, things broken in violence. But you could not mark that cold house. In thirty seconds with a fire hose you could have it dripping and absolutely clean. There was no one else there. She was living in this big house like a sick frail animal in a cave.

I could hear water running. I rapped on the closed door.

"Are you all right?"

I heard a murmur I could not interpret. It had a vague sound of reassurance. I roamed around. The place offended me. There was a giant dishwasher in the kitchen. I found a big tray and went through the house collecting the glasses and plates and cups. It took three trips. I scraped stale food into the disposer. Housewife McGee. After I set the dishwasher to churning, I felt a little better.

I went back and listened at the door. There was no sound.

"Are you all right in there?"

The door opened and she came out and leaned against the wall just outside the bathroom door. She had a ghastly pallor and the rings around her eyes looked more smudged.

"Are you moving in?" she asked tonelessly.

"I just came here to . . ."

"This morning I looked at myself, and I thought maybe the process had to start somewhere, so I got terribly clean. I washed my hair and scrubbed and scrubbed, and stripped the bed and even found a drawer with clean clothing in it, for a wonder. So you're in luck, aren't you? Excellent timing, provided you wish to start clean."

"Mrs. Atkinson, I don't think you . . ."

She looked at me with a horrid parody of sensuality, a sick bright leer. "I suppose you know all of my specialties, dear."

"Will you listen to me!"

"I'm sure you don't mind if I have a drink first. I'm really much better after I have some drinks."

"I've never seen Junior Allen in my life!"

"I hope he told you I've gotten terribly scrawny and . . ." She stopped the hideous parody of enticement and stared at me. "What did you say?"

"I've never seen Junior Allen in my life."

She rubbed her mouth with the back of her hand. "Why did you come to me?"

"I want to help you."

"Help me what?"

"You said it yourself. The process has to start somewhere."

She stared at me without comprehension, and then with a savage doubt, and finally, slowly, with belief. She turned, sagging, and, before I could catch her, she fell to her knees, bare knees making a painful sound of bone against terrazzo. She hunched down against the baseboard and rubbed her face back and forth and began her howling, whooping sobs and coughings. I gathered her up. She shuddered violently at my touch. She was far too light. I took her to her bedroom. When I stretched her out on her freshly made bed, the sobbing stopped abruptly. She became as rigid as dry sticks, her eyes staring at me with glassy enormity, her bloodless lips sucked in. I took her sandals off and covered her with the spread. I fixed the blinds to darken the room, as those helpless eyes followed me. I brought a stool over and put it beside her bed and sat down and took her long frail cold hand and said, "I meant it. What's your name?"

"Lois."

"All right, Lois. Cry. Cry the hell out of it. Rip it all open. Let it go."

"I can't," she whispered. And suddenly she began to cry again. She yanked her hand free, rolled over, rolled her face into the pillow and began the harsh sobbing.

I had to make a guess about what would be right and what would be wrong for her. I had to take a risk. I based the risk on what I know of loneliness, of the need of closeness in loneliness. I stroked her, totally impersonal, the way you soothe a terrified animal. At first she would leap and buck at the slightest touch. After a while there was only a tremor when I touched her, and finally that too was gone. She hiccuped and at last fell down into sleep, curled and spent.

I searched the house until I found her keys. I locked up and left her in the darkened room. I checked the bus schedules and went and got Cathy and took her to where she could catch the bus which would get her home in time. I told her a little of it. There was no question in her mind about my obligation to stay.

5

The doctor's name was Ramirez. He looked like a Swede. He spent a long time with her.

Then he came out and sat at the breakfast bar to drink some of the bad coffee I'd made.

"How is she?"

"Where do you fit in this, McGee?"

"I just stopped to ask her some questions and she fell apart."

He stirred his coffee. "Samaritan, eh?"

"I suppose so."

"Her family should be notified."

"Suppose there isn't any?"

"Then she should be institutionalized. What's the financial situation?"

"I haven't any idea."

"Nice house. Nice car."

"Doctor, what's her condition?"

"Several things. Malnutrition. That plus a degree of saturation with alcohol so she's been having auditory hallucinations. But severe emotional shock is the background for both the other manifestations."

"Prognosis?"

He gave me a shrewd glance. "Fair. A little bit of nerve, a tiny bit of pride, that's all she has left. Keep her tranquilized. Build her up with foods as rich as she can take. Lots of sleep. And keep her away from whoever got her into such a condition."

"A man could do that to a woman?"

"Given a certain type of man and that type of woman, yes. A man like the man who was living with her."

"Did you know him?"

"No. I heard about him. First he was with Catherine Kerr, then with this one. A different social level, eh?"

"Should she talk about Allen?"

"If she's willing to. If she can trust anybody enough, it might be good for her."

"I wonder what happened."

"Things she could not accept. Things she could not live with."

"Not live with?"

"McGee, I do not think it is too dramatic to say you saved her life."

"But she might not trust me."

"Or anyone, ever. That too is a mental disorder. I don't think it's good for her to stay here."

"When can she leave?"

"I will stop by the same time tomorrow. I can tell you then. Give her one of these every four hours. You can stay here?"

"Yes."

"Eggnogs, rich soups, a little at a time, as much as she can hold down. If she gets very agitated, give her one of these. Encourage her to sleep. And talk. Tomorrow we will talk about a nurse. I think she has been physically abused, but I think she has a good constitution."

"Will anybody make any trouble about my staying here?"

"You are adults. You don't look like a fool, McGee. You don't have the look of the kind of murderous fool who'd try to make love to her in her condition. I take you on faith. It saves time. And if anybody does not like this temporary arrangement, I recommended it."

"I'll be too busy with the housework."

"She is exhausted. I think she will sleep a long time now. But it would be nice to be there when she wakes up."

While she was in deep sleep, I collected all the soiled clothing and bedding. I took it into town and dropped it off. I bought supplies. When I got back she was still in almost the same position, making small snores, evenly spaced, barely audible. It took me until dusk to polish the big house. I kept looking in at her.

Then I went in and she made a sound like a whispered scream. She was sitting up. I turned the lights on. Her eyes were huge and vague.

I stayed a cautious ten feet from her and said, "I am Trav McGee. You've been sick. Dr. Ramirez was here. He'll be back tomorrow. I'll stay in the house, so you'll be completely safe."

"I feel so far away. I didn't have any dreams. Unless . . . unless this is one."

"I'm going to fix you some soup. And bring you a pill."

"I don't want anything."

I arranged more agreeable lighting. She watched me. I had checked where things were kept. I found a sedate nightgown, a robe of Hong Kong silk, tossed them on the foot of the bed.

"If you're strong enough, Lois, get ready for bed while I fix the soup. The bathroom is clean now."

"What is going on? Who are you?"

"Mother McGee. Don't ask questions. Just accept."

I heated the canned soup, strengthened it with cream, fixed her one slice of toast with butter. When I came back she was propped up in bed. She was wearing the nightgown and a bed jacket. She had tied her tousled dark hair back, rubbed away the last trace of lipstick.

"I'm wobbly," she said in a small shy voice. "Can I have a drink?"

"That depends on how you do with the soup and toast."

"Soup maybe. Toast no."

"Can you feed yourself?"

"Of course."

"Take the pill."

"What is it?"

"Dr. Ramirez called it a mild tranquilizer."

I sat nearby. She spooned the soup up. Her hand trembled. Her nails were clean and broken. There was an old bruise, saffroned, on the side of her slender throat. She was too aware of my watching her and so I tried some mild chatter. Abstract theory by McGee. My tourist theory. Any Ohioan crossing that state line into Florida should be fitted with a metal box that rests against the small of the back. Every ninety seconds a bell rings and a dollar bill emerges part way from a slot in the top of the box. The nearest native removes it. That would take care of the tipping problem. At places where hundreds of them flock together, the ringing of bells would be continuous.

It was difficult to amuse her. She was too close to being broken. The best I could achieve was a very small quick smile. She managed two-thirds of the soup and two bites of toast. I set them aside. She slid down a little and yawned.

"My drink?"

"In a little while."

She started to speak. Her eyes blurred and closed. In a few moments her mouth sagged open and she slept. In sleep the intense strain was gone and she looked younger. I turned the bedroom lights out. An hour later the phone rang. Someone wanted to sell us an attractive building lot at Marathon Heights.

As she slept I searched for the personal data. I finally found the traditional steel box behind books in the living room. It opened readily with a bent paper clip. Birth certificate, marriage license, divorce decree, keys to a safe-deposit box, miscellany of family materials, income statements. I spread it out and pieced together her current status. She had accepted a settlement at the time of divorce three years ago. The house was a part of it. Her income was from a trust account in a bank in Hartford, Connecticut, a family trust setup whereby she received a little over seven hundred dollars a month and could not touch the principal amount. Her maiden name was Fairlea. There was an elder brother in New Haven. D. Harper Fairlea. On her hall table was a great stack of unopened mail. I checked it over and found that people were clamoring to have their bills paid, and in the stack I found her trust income checks, unopened, for May, June and July. Her personal checkbook was in the top drawer of the living-room desk, a built-in affair. She had not balanced it in some time, and I estimated she had a couple of hundred dollars in her account.

At nine-thirty I called D. Harper Fairlea in New Haven. They said he was ill and could not come to the phone. I asked to talk to his wife. She had a soft, pleasant voice.

"Mr. McGee, surely Lois could tell you that Harp had a severe heart attack some months ago. He's been home a few weeks now, and it is going to be a long haul. Really, I thought the very least she could do was come up here. He is her only blood relative, you know. And I have been wondering why we haven't heard from her. If she is in some sort of trouble and needs help, about all we can say is that we hope things will work out for her. We really can't give her any kind of assistance right now. We have three children in school, Mr. McGee. I don't even want to tell Harp about this. I don't want to give him something else to fret about. I've been inventing imaginary phone calls from Lois, inventing concern and telling him she is fine."

"I'll know better in a few days how she is and what will have to be done."

"I understood she has some nice friends down there."

"Not lately."

"What is that supposed to mean?"

"I think she gave up her nice friends."

"Please have her phone me when she's able. I'm going to worry about her. But there's just nothing I can do. I can't leave Harp now, and I just don't see how I can take her in."

No help there. She hadn't seemed very concerned about who I might be. I sensed that the two sisters-in-law had not gotten along too well. So it was no longer a case of waiting for somebody to come and take over. I was stuck, temporarily.

I made up a bed in the bedroom next to hers. I left my door and her door open. In the middle of the night I was awakened by the sound of glass breaking. I pulled my pants on and went looking. Her bed was empty. The nightgown and bed jacket were on the floor beside the bed. The nightgown was ripped.

I found her in the kitchen alcove, fumbling with the bottles. I turned on the white blaze of fluorescence and she squinted toward me, standing naked in spilled liquor and broken glass. She looked at me but I do not think she knew me. "Where is Fancha?" she yelled. "Where is that bitch? I hear her singing."

She was beautifully made, but far too thin. Her bones were sharp against the smoothness of her, her ribs visible. Except in the meagerness of hips and breasts, all the fatty tissue had been burned away, and her belly had the slight bloat that indicates starvation. I got her away from there. Miraculously, she had not cut her feet. She squirmed with surprising strength, whining, trying to scratch and bite. I got her back into her bed, and when she stopped fighting me, I got one of the other pills down her. Soon it began to take effect. I put the lights out. I sat by her. She held my wrist very tightly, and fought against the effects of the pill. She would start to slide away and then struggle back to semi-consciousness. I did not understand a lot of her mumbling. Sometimes she seemed to be talking to me, and at other times she was back in her immediate past.

Once, with great clarity, with a mature and stately indignation she said, "I will not *do* that!" Moments later she repeated it, but this time in the lisping narrow voice of a scared young child. "Oh, I will not *do* that!" The contrast came close to breaking my heart.

And then at last she slept. I cleaned up, hid the remaining liquor and went back to bed.

In the morning she was rational, and even a bit hungry. She ate eggs scrambled with butter and cream, and had a slice of toast. She napped for a little while, and then she wanted to talk.

"It was such a stupid thing, in the beginning," she said. "You live here all year around, and you want the natives to like you. You try to be pleasant. It's a small community after all. He was at the gas station. And terribly cheerful and agreeable. And just a little bit fresh. If I'd stopped him right in the beginning . . . But I'm not very good about that sort of thing. I guess I've always been shy. I don't like to complain about people. People who are very confident, I guess I don't really know how to handle the situations as they come up. It was just things he said, and the way he looked at me, and then one time at the gas station, I had the top down, he stood by the door on the driver's side and put his hand on my shoulder. Nobody could see him doing it. He just held his hand there and I asked him please not to do that and he laughed and took his hand away. Then he got more fresh, after that. But I hadn't reported him before, and I decided I would stop trading there, and I did. Then one day I was at the market and when I came out, he was sitting in my car and he asked me very politely if I could drop him off at the station. I said of course. I expected him to do something. I didn't know what. And if he did anything, I was going to stop the car and order him to get out. After all, it was broad daylight. The moment I got in and shut the door and began to start the car, he just reached over and . . . put his hand on me. And he was grinning at me. It was such . . . such an unthinkable thing, Trav, so horrible and unexpected that it paralyzed me. I thought I would faint. People were walking by, but they couldn't see. I couldn't move or speak, or even think what I should do. People like me react too violently when they do react, I guess. I shoved him away and shouted at him and ordered him out of the car. He took his time getting out, never stopping his smile. Then he leaned into the car and said something about how I'd give him better treatment if he was rich. I told him there was not that much money in the world. You know, there is something sickening about that curly white hair and that brown face and those little blue eyes. He said that when he made his fortune he would come back and see how I reacted, something like that, some remark like that."

The orderliness of that portion of the account was an exception. For the rest of it, her mind was less disciplined, her account more random. But it was a good mind. It had insight. Once, as she was getting sleepy, she looked somberly at me and said, "I guess there are a lot of people like me. We react too soon or too late or not at all. We're jumpy people, and we don't seem to belong here. We're victims, maybe. The Junior Allens are so sure of themselves and so sure of us. They know how to use us, how to take us further than we wish before we know what to do about it." She frowned. "And they seem to know by instinct exactly how to trade upon our concealed desire to accept that kind of domination. I wanted to make a life down here, Trav. I was lonely. I was trying to be friendly. I was trying to be a part of something."

Ramirez came in the early afternoon just after I had teased her into eating more than she thought she could. He checked her over.

He said to me, "Not so close to hysteria now. A complex and involved organism, McGee. All physical resource was gone. And just the nerves left, and those about played out. Maybe we can rest them a little now. You wouldn't think it, but there's an awesome vitality there."

I told him of my contact with the family, and of the wrestling match in the middle of the night.

"She may become agitated again, maybe not so much next time."

"How about a rest home?"

He shrugged. "If you've had enough, yes. But this is better for her. I think she can come back quicker this way. But she can become emotionally dependent upon you, particularly if she learns to talk it out, to you."

"She's been talking."

He stared at me. "Strange you should do all this for her."

"Pity, I guess."

"One of the worst traps of all, McGee."

"What can I expect?"

"I think as she gets further back from the edge she will become placid, listless, somnolent. And dependent."

"You said to get her away from here."

"I'll take a look at her tomorrow."

The thunderheads built high that Thursday afternoon, and after a long hot silence, the winds came and the rain roared down. The sound of the rain terrified her. She could hear, in the sound of the rain, a hundred people all laughing and talking at once, as though a huge cocktail party filled all the other rooms of the sterile house. She became so agitated I had to give her the second one of the quieting pills. She awakened after dark, and she had soaked the sheets and mattress pad with sweat. She said she felt strong enough to take a shower while I changed the bed for her. I had found one last set of clean sheets. I heard her call me, her voice faint. She was crouched on the bathroom floor, wet and naked and sallow as death. I bundled her into a big yellow terry robe and rubbed her warm and dry and got her into bed. Her teeth chattered. I brought her warm milk. It took her a long time to get warm. Her breath had a sour odor of illness. She slept until eleven and then ate a little and then talked some more. She wanted the light out when she talked, and wanted her hand in mine. A closeness. A comfort.

I heard more of it then. A vague outline. She had thought Junior Allen gone forever, and he had come back in the shining cruiser, wearing his brand-new resort clothes, curiously humble and apologetic and anxious for her esteem. He had tied up at her dock, just across the road from the house. She had told him to go away. She kept looking out the windows and saw him sitting disconsolate in his new boat in his new clothes, and at dusk she had gone out onto the dock, endured another profuse apology, then gone aboard for a tour of the cruiser. Once he had her aboard, had her below decks, he was the smiler again, crude and forceful, and he had taken her. She fought him for a long time, but he had been patient. There was no one to hear her. Finally in a kind of terrorized lethargy, she had endured him, knowing he was not quite sane, and thinking this would be the end of it. But it was not. He had kept her aboard with him for two days and two nights, and when he had sensed that she was too dazed and too exhausted and too confused to make even a token resistance, he had moved into the house with her.

"I can't really explain it," she whispered in the darkness. "There was just nothing that had gone before. The only past I knew was him. And he filled the present, and there wasn't any future. I didn't even feel revulsion toward him. Or think of him as a person. He was a force I had to accept. And somehow it began to be terribly important to please him—with the food I cooked for him, the drinks I made for him, the clothes I washed, the continual sex. It was easier to stay a little bit drunk. If I kept him pleased, even that kind of life was endurable. He turned me into an anxious thing, watching him every minute to be certain I was doing what he wanted me to do. I guess that is a kind of response." Her hand tightened in mine. "There was even a kind of physical response to him, not pleasure. A kind of horrid release, a breaking. He learned how to make that happen sometimes, and he'd laugh at me. Then we would go away on that boat and it would be the same, and come back here and it would be the same. I didn't even think of it ever ending. I was too busy getting through each hour as it came along."

She slept then. I went out into the night. The tropical earth was steamy-fresh, bugs chirring and tree toads yelping, and the bay a moony mirror. I sat on the end of her dock and blew smoke at the mosquitoes and wondered why I should be so cynical about her.

It was true that she was a sensitive and introspective woman, and equally true that Junior Allen was a cruel crude bastard, but I could not quite comprehend how his use of her could have brought her to such a state. In the Victorian tradition, it was the fate worse than death, but she was an adult female, and regardless of the method of approach, he had become her lover and had, in time, induced sensuous response in her. I thought of the failure of her marriage and wondered if perhaps she was merely a neurotic headed for breakdown anyway, and Junior Allen had merely hastened the process.

I watched the running lights of a boat heading down the channel, and I heard the grotesque yammering of one of the night birds, and the faraway sobbing of a lovelorn cat.

I went in and checked her in her deep sleep, and went to bed in the neighboring room.

6

She took a good breakfast in the morning and seemed well enough for me to leave her for a time. I went off in Miss Agnes and picked up the laundry and then I made a call on Jeff Bocka, the realtor whose sign stood in Lois Atkinson's yard.

He had a face and head as round and pink as a beach ball. He had that total and almost obscene hairlessness that some diseases cause, a baldness of skull, brows and eyelids. He had amber eyes and small amber teeth.

"Of course I can move that house. I can move it if I can show it, buddy. But I can't show it if that nutty broad screws it up. I made appointments. Twice. What happens? The place is a mess and she is a mess. The first time she is all right for ten minutes, then starts screaming at my clients. The second time she wouldn't even let us in. She's got the place free and clear. There's a recent survey. No cloud on the title. A sound house in a good location. Waterfront. I can move it for forty-five tomorrow, but nobody buys a house if they can't look at it, buddy." He shook his head. "When I get around to it, I take my sign off that lawn."

"When she moves out, if she still wants to sell, I'll leave the keys with you."

"How about the condition of it?"

"It will be okay."

"What do you mean, if she wants to sell?"

"If, on second thought, she's absolutely certain."

"She better move away. She had some friends here. Nice people. Until that gas jockey moved in with her and she started hitting the bottle."

"I guess that offends your sense of morality."

He showed me his little teeth. "This is a decent place."

"They all are, friend."

I walked away and left him standing in the doorway of his cinderblock office, the sunshine making silver highlights on his smooth pink skull.

Ramirez came in the afternoon and marveled at the improvement. She got dressed in the afternoon. She was very reserved. She looked sleepy and moved slowly. In the evening she had another bad spell. And again, in the darkness, she talked.

"I started to come back to life in spite of him, Trav. I seemed to realize that he was trying to destroy me, and I knew I would not be destroyed. I found a little quiet place way back inside myself, and no matter what he made me do, I could go back there and it didn't seem to matter. I began to feel that he had done his worst, and I was in some sense stronger than he was, and I would survive him, and get over him, and get free of him. I began to be able to lift my head and to think of ways of ending it. But . . . he couldn't let that happen, of course. He couldn't let me escape."

It was difficult for her to try to tell me how he had blocked all escape. It became incoherent. And there was much of it she could not remember, fortunately. He kept her drunk so she would be easier to manage, and lessen the chance of her going over the side when she was unguarded.

On that last cruise, Junior Allen had taken the boat over to Bimini. And there he had taken aboard a double-gaited little Haitian slut named Francha, and from there they had gone to a remote bay in the Berry Islands and anchored and stayed there a week, and completed the corruption and destruction of Lois Atkinson. She remembered nothing of the trip back to Candle Key. And there, in June, he had left for good, at his option, knowing he had left that gentle woman with all the explosive images and fragmentary memories that would kill her.

I speculated about motive after Lois had drifted off into sleep. There are men in this world who are compelled to destroy the most fragile and valuable things they can find, the same way rowdy children will ravage a beautiful home. Look at me, they are saying.

Lois, shy, lovely, sensitive, a graceful and cultivated woman, merely by the fact of her existence offered a challenge to Junior Allen. And she had challenged him further by defying him. Even though it meant the stupidity of returning to Candle Key after finding and taking what Sergeant David Berry had hidden, he had to meet that challenge and totally subdue a more delicate morsel than Cathy Kerr could ever be.

The worst crimes of man against woman do not appear on the statutes. A smiling man, quick and handy as a cat, webbed with muscle, armored with money, now at liberty in an unsuspecting world, greedy as a weasel in a hen house. I knew the motive. The motive was murder. And this symbolic killing might easily be followed by the more literal act.

Sly and reckless, compulsive and bold. The goat-god, with hoof and smile and hairy ears, satyr at the helm of the *Play Pen*.

Love him, understand him, forgive him, lead him shyly to Freud, or Jesus.

Or else take the contemporarily untenable position that evil, undiluted by any hint of childhood trauma, does exist in the world, exists for its own precise sake, the pustular bequest from the beast, as inexplicable as Belsen.

I kissed her sweaty temple and tucked the blanket around her narrow shoulder. Symbol of weakness. Symbol of the beast. But I could find no symbol for myself. McGee as avenging angel was a little too much to swallow. I hoped to temper vengeance with greed. Or conversely. Either way, it does simplify the rationalizations.

She began to gorge like a wolf. The anticipated placidity came, bringing small sweet absent smiles, yawns and drowsiness. She dressed and we took walks, and as the edges of bone quickly softened with new flesh, the night talks dwindled. I was in charge of a vegetable woman, mildly amiable, unquestioning, softly remote, an eater and a sleeper, a slow walker. Ramirez was paid off, offering no thoughts for the future. She phoned her sister-in-law, proclaiming that everything was peachy. With me she talked over the segments of a happy childhood. But she did not like the house and did not want the house, or the car. I organized her financial matters, and she signed the deposit slip and all the small checks for the anxious. She wanted to be elsewhere, but did not worry about where, or want the effort of planning anything. We packed. There was not much she wanted. Miss Agnes, half truck, accommodated it readily. I took the keys to Bocka, with the address where she could be reached. She signed the title and I sold her car, deposited the cash in her account. She signed the post office change of address card. I made the arrangements about the utilities. I took a last look through the house. She sat out in the car. I checked all the windows, turned the air conditioning off, slammed the front door.

As we drove away, she did not look back. She sat with a dreaming smile, her hands folded in her lap.

Other people go down to the keys and bring back shell ashtrays or mounted fish or pottery flamingos. Travis McGee brings back a Lois Atkinson. The souvenir fervor is the mainstay of a tourist economy.

"You can stay aboard my houseboat until you find a place."

"All right."

"Maybe you'd like to go back to New Haven to be near your brother."

"Maybe I would."

"You should be feeling well enough to travel pretty soon."

"I guess so."

"Would you rather I found you a place of your own right away?"

"It doesn't matter."

"Which would you rather do?"

The effort of decision brought her out of torpor. She made fists and her lips tightened. "I guess I have to be with you."

"For a little while."

"I have to be with you."

The patient becomes emotionally dependent upon the analyst. She said it without anxiety. She stated her fact, strangely confident I would accept that fact as completely as she did. In a little while she slumped over against the door and fell asleep. I felt indignant. How could she be so damned certain she had not given herself over into the hands of a Junior Allen of another variety? Where did all this suffocating trust come from? Here was a mature woman who did not seem to know that the wide world is full of monsters, even after one vivid example. I had the feeling that if I told her I was taking her to the cannibal isles to sell her for stew meat, she would wear the same Mona Lisa smile of total acceptance.

I am just not that trustworthy.

Below decks the *Busted Flush* was very hot and very stale and offensively damp. A power failure had kicked the air conditioning off. I had set the thermostat at eighty when I left, minimum power expenditure, just enough to keep it from getting the way it was. I reset it for sixty-five. It would be an hour before it was comfortable. I took her to a place where we could get a good lunch, and brought her back. She came aboard. I toted her gear aboard. She looked around, mildly and placidly interested. I stowed her and her gear in the other stateroom. She took a shower and went to bed.

I found nine days of mail clogging my box. I weeded it down to a few bills, two personal letters. I phoned Chook. She wanted to know where the hell I'd been. It pleased me that Cathy hadn't told her. I said I'd been staying with a sick friend. She gave me Cathy's number. I phoned her. She sounded very guarded, but said she was alone and told me I could come and see her, and told me how to find it. It was over in town, the top floor of a cheap duplex behind one of the commercial strips along Route One. Pizza, Guaranteed Retreads, Smitty's Sheet Metal, Bonded Warehouse. She lived beyond neon and the wind-whipped fragments of banners announcing forgotten sales.

It was stinking hot upstairs. All buff plaster and ragged wicker, straw and old bamboo. A big fan whizzed and whined by a window, blowing the warm air through. She wore sleazy shorts and a faded halter top. She explained that she shared the place with another dancer from the group and a girl who worked in the local television station. She had two card tables set up. She was stitching away on new costumes for the group. Extra money, she explained. She offered iced tea.

I sat in a wicker chair near the hot breath of the fan and told her about Mrs. Atkinson. Not all of it. She worked and listened. When I leaned back my shirt stuck to the wicker. It had become August while I wasn't looking. She moved around the tables, nipping and stitching, bending and turning, and I was too aware of the modeling of those good sinewy legs, a-gleam with sweat, and the rock-solid roundness of the dancer butt. What I didn't tell her about Lois, she seemed perfectly able to guess. She carried pins in her mouth. The material she worked with was gold and white.

"I thought you'd changed your mind," she said.

"No."

"There's no reason why you shouldn't, Trav." The pins blurred enunciation.

"Were there names and addresses in the letters?"

She straightened. "The ones there were, I put them separate. I can get them for you."

She brought them to me. I read them while she worked. She had a little blue radio turned low, the music merging with the noise of the fan. CMCA, Havana. Voice of the land of peace and freedom and brotherhood. No commercials. Nothing left to sell.

V-Mail, from a long-ago war.

Dear Wife: I have been well and hopping you are the same and the girls too have bought a money order and sending it along later do not try to save all instead buy what you need. I have had a lot of flight time this pass two months but for me it is all cargo work and not dangarous so dont worry about it none. It rains a lot this time of year, more than home even. Since Sugarman got sent elsewere, we have a new pilot his name is Wm Callowell from Troy New York, a first Lt. and a good safe flyer and he fits in okay with me and George so no worry on that acct. The food isn't much but I am eating good and feeling fine. You tell Cathy I am glad she likes her teacher, and kiss her for me and Christy too and a kiss for yourself as always your loving husb. Dave.

There were other names in other letters. Casual references, less complete. Vern from Kerrville, Texas. Degan from California. I wrote down all the fragments.

She sat with the showgirl brevities in her lap and stitched neatly and quickly. "I didn't know Mrs. Atkinson would be like that," she said thoughtfully.

"It wasn't anything she wanted to get involved in."

"No more'n me. She's beautiful." The brown-eyed look was quick. "You keeping her right there on your boat?"

"Until she feels better."

She crossed the room and put the costumes in a small suitcase and closed the lid. "Maybe she needs help more than I do."

"She needs a different kind of help."

"What are you going to do next?"

"Find out where your father got the money, if I can."

"What time is it?"

"A little after five."

"I've got to change and go out there."

"Have you got a ride?"

"I take a bus mostly."

"I can wait and take you on out."

"I don't like to be a trouble to you, Trav."

I waited. She showered quickly and came out of the bedroom wearing a pink blouse and a white skirt. In moments the blouse was damp and beginning to cling. I drove her on out to Teabolt's Mile O'Beach and went on back to Bahia Mar. My ward had arisen. She had slept so hard her eyes looked puffy, but she had acquainted herself with the equipment in my stainless steel galley, and she wore a pretty cotton dress, which hung just a little loosely on her, and she had taken two generous steaks out of the locker and set them out to thaw. She seemed a little more aware of the situation, shyly aware that she might be a nuisance.

"I could cook and clean and take care of laundry and things like that, and anything else you want me to do, Trav."

"If you feel up to it."

"I don't want to be a dead weight."

"Your job is to get well."

I guess I wasn't particularly gracious. Mine are bachelor ways, tending toward too much order and habit. Some affectionate little guest for a few days is one thing. A party cruise is another. But a lady in residence is potential irritation.

"I can pay my share," she said in a small voice.

"Oh, for God's sake!" I roared. She fled to her stateroom and silently closed the door.

In twenty minutes I felt sufficiently ashamed of myself to look in on her. She was diagonally across the big bed, sound asleep. I made a drink and carried it around until it was gone, and made another, and then went in and shook her awake.

"If you want to cook, it's time to cook."

"All right, Trav."

"Medium rare."

"Yes, dear."

"Don't be so damned humble!"

"I'll try."

After dinner, after she had cleaned up the galley, I brought her into the lounge and asked her if she felt well enough for questions.

"What about?"

"Junior Allen."

Her mouth twisted and she closed her eyes for a moment. She opened them and said, "You can ask questions."

But first I had to brief her. I had to make her understand why I was asking and what I wanted to know. She had heard village gossip about Junior Allen and the sisters. I gave her all of the facts, as I knew them.

For once her new placidity was impaired. She stared across at me through the lamplight. "He had a lot of cash with him when he came back. I didn't give him anything. So everything, the boat and everything, came from what he took from that place where he was living?"

"That's the only answer."

"But what could it have been?"

"Something he had to go to New York to get rid of."

"Travis, why are you so interested in all this?"

I tried to give her a reassuring smile, but from the look on her face it was not successful. "I am going to take it away from him," I said, in a voice not quite my own.

"I don't understand."

"And keep some of it and give Cathy her share."

"She's important to you?"

"As important as you are."

She thought that over. "Is . . . is this the sort of thing you do?"

"It's in the general area of the sort of thing I do, when I happen to need the money."

"But . . . he seems to be such a dangerous man. And maybe he's spent it all by now. And if he hasn't, how could you get anything away from him? I don't think you could, without killing him."

"I would think of that as a normal business risk, Lois."

The color she had regained drained out of her face. "How can you say such a terrible thing? You . . . you've been so good to me."

"What has that got to do with it?"

"But don't you see that . . ."

"I see that you are a damned fool, Lois. You took me at face value. You decided what sort of a person I am. If I can't match that image, it isn't my fault."

After a long silence she said, "Isn't it a waste?"

"Waste of what?"

"Of *you!* It seems degrading. Forgive me for saying that. I've seen those African movies. The lion makes a kill and then clever animals come in and grab something and run. You're so bright, Trav, and so intuitive about people. And you have . . . the gift of tenderness. And sympathy. You could be almost anything."

"Of course!" I said, springing to my feet and beginning to pace back and forth through the lounge. "Why didn't I think of that! Here I am, wasting the golden years on this lousy barge, getting all mixed up with lame-duck women when I could be out there seeking and striving. Who am I to keep from putting my shoulder to the wheel? Why am I not thinking about an estate and how to protect it? Gad, woman, I could be writing a million dollars a year in life insurance. I should be pulling a big oar in the flagship of life. Maybe it isn't too late yet! Find the little woman, and go for the whole bit. Kiwanis, P.T.A., fund drives, cook-outs, a clean desk, and vote the straight ticket, yessirree bob. Then when I become a senior citizen, I can look back upon . . ."

I stopped when I heard the small sound she was making. She sat with her head bowed. I went over and put my fingertips under her chin. I tilted her head up and looked down into her streaming eyes.

"Please don't," she whispered.

"You're beginning to bring out the worst in me, woman."

"It was none of my business."

"I will not dispute you."

"But . . . who did this to you?"

"I'll never know you well enough to try to tell you, Lois."

She tried to smile. "I guess it can't be any plainer than that."

"And I'm not a tragic figure, no matter how hard you try to make me into one. I'm delighted with myself, woman."

"And you wouldn't say it that way if you were."

"Spare me the cute insights."

She shivered and pulled herself together. "I'm grateful to you. I'll try to answer questions."

"What did he say about money?"

She tried. She sat as trim and obedient as a bright girl in class. He said he had all the money he would ever need. Yes, he had repeated that in different ways at different times. And said he would never have to use any of it to buy a woman. There was some hiding place aboard where he kept cash.

"And maybe something else," she said in an odd voice.

"What?"

"Let me think," she said. Her face was very still. She had that listening look people wear when they dig into small vague memories. "A crooked blue marble," she said. "It was such a hot day. Sickeningly hot because there was no wind at all. And all that glare off the water. I'd drunk too much. I was trying not to be sick. Their voices were a blur. They were always arguing about something, shouting at each other. He was showing her something, and it fell to the deck, a blue marble, and it rolled toward her across the teak. It rolled crooked. She pounced on it and popped it into her mouth, like a child. I guess she wasn't over eighteen, but she was as old as all the evil in the world. He was murderously angry and he went at her and she ran, laughing at him. He chased her all over the boat and when he had her cornered, she dived over the side. She floated, laughing and squealing at him. She was naked. She looked very dark in the water, and I could see her shadow shimmering on the white sand bottom. He ran and got a gun. It surprised me that it made such a small snapping noise, but the bullets spit the water up, close to her, and she came quickly to the boarding ladder and climbed aboard. He took her by the nape of the neck and she spat the blue marble into his hand. Then, still holding her, he beat her with his fist until she spent most of the rest of the day down in one of the bunks, whimpering. The marble was a very deep blue. He kept thinking about it and getting mad all over again. He would yell down there, cursing her. He went down once or maybe twice and struck her again." She stared at me with dead eyes and said, "I think I remember it because that was the longest time that they left me alone. Afterwards I kept thinking of the gun. I tried to find it, but I couldn't. When he caught me looking for it, he guessed, and he gave me to her and watched her beat me. She made it look as if she was beating me harder than she was. She wasn't sorry for me. She just didn't want to hurt me so badly I'd be of no use to her. She was terribly hard and chunky and strong. Her legs and thighs were like thick polished mahogany, and she laughed at nothing and she sang all the time in a hard screeching voice, in very bad French. In my empty house, before you came to me, Trav, I kept hearing her singing, as loudly as if she was in the next room."

Some of the old mad light came back into her eyes. "Do you want to hear me sing like Fancha?"

"Take it easy, honey."

"Would you like me to laugh and dance like Fancha?"

She had begun to tremble violently. I hurried to get the pills and brought her one of the strong ones. She didn't try to fight it. She was in bed and asleep in fifteen minutes.

After I had chased the ghastliness of Fancha out of my mind, I settled down to some planning. A trip out to Leavenworth had a deceptive plausibility. It is bad practice to try to question prison people. They live by the book. They need documentation and identification and proper authority. When you can't present it, they immediately wonder if you are there to try to help somebody slip out. I decided that was the last resort. I would chase down every other lead, and if they all dwindled to absolutely nothing, then I would go out there to Kansas and get the feel of it and try to con somebody.

Before I went to bed, I took a look at my ward. In the faint light she looked no more than nineteen, gentle, and unmarked by any ugliness.

7

In the morning I tried the William Callowells of Troy, New York.

Such chances run small. If he lasted out that war, and stayed out of a police action, and avoided civil disaster, maybe he could be a roamer, that address gone stale in a transient world.

Troy had a pair of them. William B. William M. The efficient operator took the numbers of both from Troy information, and I tried it by the alphabet. William B.'s home gave us another number. A girl said it was Double A Plastics, and three minutes later I had the wary voice of William B. A pilot in World War Two? Hell, no, he was twenty-six years old, and a chemical engineer and he had lived in Troy less than a year and knew there was another Wm. in the book, but knew nothing about him. Thanks so much. You are entirely welcome.

My LDO left the circuit open and I heard a woman answer the William M. number. She had a small unsteady voice. She responded in a very formal manner. "I regret to say that Mr. Callowell passed away last March."

I asked to speak to her. "Mrs. Callowell, I am sorry to hear about your husband."

"It was a blessing. I prayed for his release."

"I just wonder if he was the Mr. Callowell I'm trying to locate. Was he a pilot in World War Two?"

"My goodness no! You must mean my son. My husband was eighty-three years of age."

"Can I get in touch with your son, Mrs. Callowell?"

"Why, if you had called yesterday you could have talked to him. We had a wonderful visit."

"Where can I reach him?"

"The operator said you are calling from Florida. Is it terribly urgent?"

"I would like to reach him."

"Just a moment. I have it written down here. His home, of course, is in Richmond, Virginia. Let me see. Today is the . . . third, isn't it. He will be at the convention in New York City through Tuesday the ninth. At the Americana Hotel. I suppose you could reach him there, but he said there would be a great many meetings and he would be very busy."

"Thank you so much, Mrs. Callowell. By the way, where was your son's overseas duty?"

"In India. He has always wanted to go back and see the country again. He wrote such wonderful letters from there. I saved them all. Maybe one day he will have the chance."

I hung up and finished my half cup of tepid coffee. I phoned an airline. They had one at the right time. JFK Airport by 2:50 p.m. Lois seemed very disconcerted at the prospect of being left alone. She looked as if her teeth might chatter. Her eyes were enormous. I instructed her as I packed, and made her write down the briefing. Mail, laundry, phone, groceries, the manual switch to kick the air conditioner back on, garbage disposal, reliable local doctor, how to lock up, etc., television channels, cozy bookshelf, fire extinguishers, and a few small items of standard marine maintenance. She bit a pale lip and scribbled it all. She needed neither car nor bike. Everything, including the public beach, was walkable. Take the white pills every four hours. Take a pink one if you start to shake apart.

At the gangplank I kissed her like any commutation ticket husband, told her to take care of herself, scuttled toward Miss Agnes, slapping my hip pocket where the money and the credit cards were. The unemployed merit no credit cards. But I had a guarantor, a man for whom I had done a sticky and dangerous favor, a man whose name makes bank presidents spring to attention and hold their shallow breaths. The cards are handy, but I hate to use them. I always feel like a Thoreau armored with a Leica and a bird book. They are the little fingers of reality, reaching for your throat. A man with a credit card is in hock to his own image of himself.

But these are the last remaining years of choice. In the stainless nurseries of the future, the feds will work their way through all the squalling pinkness tattooing a combination tax number and credit number on one wrist, followed closely by the I.T. and T. team putting the permanent phone number, visaphone doubtless, on the other wrist. Die and your number goes back in the bank. It will be the first provable immortality the world has ever known.

Manhattan in August is a replay of the Great Plague of London. The dwindled throng of the afflicted shuffle the furnace streets, mouths sagging, waiting to keel over. Those still healthy duck from one air-conditioned oasis to the next, spending a minimum time exposed to the rain of black death outside.

By five minutes of four I was checked into the hotel. They had a lot of room. They had three conventions going and they still had a lot of room. Once inside the hotel, I was right back in Miami. Same scent to the chilled air, same skeptical servility, same glorious decor—as if a Brazilian architect had mated an air terminal with a manufacturer of cotton padding. Lighting, dramatic. At any moment the star of the show will step back from one of the eight (8) bars and break into song and the girlies will come prancing in. Keep those knees high, kids. Keep laughing.

Wm. M. Callowell, Jr., was not listed under his own name, but under the Hopkins-Callowell, Inc. suite, 1012–1018. I asked the desk which convention that was. "Construction," he said. "Like they make roads."

A man in the suite answered the phone with a young, hushed and earnest voice, and said he would check Mr. Callowell's agenda. He came back in a moment and said in an even more hushed voice, "Sir, he just this moment returned from a meeting. He's having a drink here now, sir."

"Will he be there long?"

"I would imagine at least a half hour."

I checked myself in a full-length mirror. I smiled at Mr. Travis McGee. A very deep tan is a tricky thing. If the clothing is the least bit too sharp, you look like an out-of-season ballplayer selling twenty pay life. If it is too continental, you look like a kept ski instructor. My summer city suit was Rotarian conservative, dark, nine-ounce orlon looking somewhat but not too much like silk. Conservative collar on the white shirt. Rep tie. A gloss on the shoes. Get out there and sell. Gleam those teeth. Look them square in the eye. You get out of it what you put into

it. A smile will take you a long way. Shake hands as if you meant it.
Remember names.

There were a dozen men in the big room. They had big voices and
big laughs and big cigars and big glasses of whisky. Junior executives
were tending bar for them, sidling in to laugh at the right time, not too
loudly, at all evidences of wit. They wore no badges. That is the key to
the small and important convention. No badges, no funny hats. Any
speakers they get are nationally known. And they order their food off
the full menu.

One of the juniors told me that Mr. Callowell was the one over there
by the big windows, with the glasses and mustache. William Callowell
was in his middle forties. Average size. Somewhat portly. It was difficult
to see what he looked like. He had a stand-up ruff of dense black hair,
big glasses with black frames, a black mustache, and he smoked a big
black pipe. There didn't seem to be enough skin showing. The only
thing unchangeably his was a wide fleshy nose with a visible pattern of
pores. He was talking with two other men. They stopped abruptly when
I was six feet away and they all stared at me.

"Excuse me," I said. "Mr. Callowell, when it's convenient I'd like a
word with you."

"You one of the new Bureau people?" one of his friends asked.

"No. My name is McGee. It's a personal matter."

"If it's that opening, this isn't the time or the place, McGee," Callowell said in a soft unfriendly voice.

"Opening? I gave up working for other people when I was twenty
years old. I'll wait in the hall, Mr. Callowell."

I knew that would bring him out fast. They have to know where you
fit. They have those shrewd managerial eyes, and they can look at a
man and generally guess his salary within ten percent either way. It is a
survival reaction. They're planted high on the side of the hill, and they
want to know what's coming up at them, and how fast.

He came lounging out, thumbing a new load into his pipe.

"Personal matter?"

"I came up from Florida this afternoon just to see you."

"You could have phoned and I would have told you I have too heavy
a load here."

"This won't take much time. Do you remember a crew chief named
Sergeant David Berry?"

It snapped him way back into the past. It changed his eyes and the set of his shoulders. "Berry! I remember him. How is he?"

"He died in prison two years ago."

"I didn't know that. I didn't know anything about that. Why was he in prison?"

"For killing an officer in San Francisco in nineteen forty-five."

"Good Lord! But what's that got to do with me?"

"I'm trying to help his daughters. They need help."

"Are you an attorney, Mr. McGee?"

"No."

"Are you asking me to help Berry's daughters financially?"

"No. I need more information about David Berry."

"I didn't know him very well or very long."

"Anything you can tell me will be helpful."

He shook his head. "It was a long time ago. I can't take the time right now." He looked at his watch. "Can you come back at eleven?"

"I'm registered here."

"That's better. I'll come to your room as near eleven as I can make it."

"Room seventeen-twenty, Mr. Callowell."

He rapped on my door at eleven-twenty. He'd had a full measure of good bourbon and a fine dinner and probably some excellent brandy. It had dulled his mind slightly, and he was aware of that dullness and was consequently more careful and more suspicious than he would have been sober. He refused a drink. He lowered himself into a comfortable chair and took his time lighting his pipe.

"I didn't catch what you do for a living, Mr. McGee."

"I'm retired."

He hoisted one black eyebrow. "You're young for that."

"I keep myself busy with little projects."

"Like this one?"

"Yes."

"I think I better know a little more about this project."

"Let's lay down the shovels, Mr. Callowell. I'm not on the make for anything you have. Berry came home rich from his little war. I'd like to find out how. And if I can find out, how, maybe I can get a little of it back for his girls. His wife is dead. All this will cost you is a little time. And a little remembering."

For a little while I thought he had gone to sleep on me. He stirred and sighed. "There were ways to get rich over there. They said it was even better earlier in the war. Berry had been there a long time before I came along. ATC. Flying C-46's out of Chabua in Assam. Passengers and cargo. Calcutta, New Delhi, and over the Hump to Kunming. Go sometimes to twenty-two thousand feet in those creaking laboring bastards, and then come down through the ice and get your one and only pass to lay it down at Kunming. I'd say I made twenty-five flights with Berry. No more. I didn't get to know him. Crews didn't stay together too long in that deal. The first one I had, my first airplane over there, quit. Structural failure, and the landing gear collapsed, and I slid it a long long way. Just three in a crew. They split us up. I got the ship Berry was on. Berry and George Brell, copilot. I was uneasy, wondering if Brell thought he should have been moved up. Their pilot wangled a transfer out."

"Sugarman?"

"That was the name! He was killed later. Brell didn't resent me. It worked out all right. Brell and Berry were competent. But they weren't friendly. Berry was pretty surly and silent, but he knew his job. I think he was sort of a loner. We had probably twenty-five flights together, probably ten of those round trips to China. Then one night we came up from Calcutta and I had let down to about a thousand feet when the starboard engine caught fire without any warning at all. It really went. Too much for the extinguisher system. I goosed it up to as much altitude as I dared, leveled it off and we went out one two three. Five seconds after my chute opened, the wing burned off and it went in like a rock, and five seconds after that I landed in a bed of flowers right in front of the station hospital and wrenched my ankle and knee. Very handy indeed. I hobbled in with my arm around a great big nurse. Berry and Brell visited me and thanked me and brought me a bottle, and I never saw them again."

"Did you hear any rumors about Berry making money?"

"I seem to remember hearing a few vague things. He was the type. Very tough and silent and cute."

"How would he have done it?"

"By then the most obvious way was by smuggling gold. You could buy it in Calcutta, and sell it on the black market in Kunming for better than one and a half times what you paid for it. And get American dollars in return. Or, take Indian rupees and bring them back and convert them into dollars at Lloyd's Bank. Or buy the gold with the rupees. It could be pretty flexible. But they were cracking down on it. It was a risk I didn't want to take. And I knew that if Berry or Brell was doing it, and got caught, there would be a cloud on me. So I kept my eyes open. You could do a lot with gold in China then. They had that runaway inflation going, and damn few ways to get the gold in there. You could even make a profit by smuggling rupee notes in large denominations into China. They say the Chinese used the rupees to trade with the Japs. The Japs liked the rupees to finance their espionage in India. Hell, the Chinese were trading pack animals to the Japs in return for salt. It was a busy little war. I think Berry was a trader. He had that native shrewdness. And I think he had the knack of manipulating people. Once I think he actually sounded me out, but there was nothing I could put my finger on. I must have given him the wrong answers."

"Was he close to George Brell?"

"Let's say a little closer than a sergeant and a lieutenant usually get, even in an air crew. They were together quite a while."

"Then Brell, if still living, is the next man to talk to."

"I know where you can find him."

"Really!"

He hesitated. It was the business syndrome. He had something somebody else wanted and he had to stop for a moment to consider what advantage might be gained. This reflex brought him all the way back from the jungly old war in the back alcove of memory, where he was Lieutenant Callowell, agile, quick and very concerned about the ways of hiding and controlling the fear he felt every day. He fell back into the portly disguise of William M. Callowell, cushioned with money and authority, shrewd builder and bidder, perhaps privately worried about impotence, audits and heart attacks. I could sense he did not often think of the war. There are middle-aged children who spend a part of every day thinking of their college or their war, but the ones who grow up to be men do not have this plaintive need for a flavor of past importance, and Callowell was one of these.

He relit his pipe, shifted his weight. "Two years ago there was a short article in *Newsweek* about our operation, in connection with the Interstate program. They used my picture. I got letters from people I hadn't heard from in years. Brell wrote me from Harlingen, Texas, sounding like a dear old flyboy buddy, which he wasn't. Letterhead stationery, thick parchment bond, tricky typeface. Brell Enterprises I think it was.

One inch of congratulations to me, and a yard of crap about how well he was doing, closing with the hope we could get together and talk over old times. I answered it with a very short cool note, and I've heard nothing since."

"You didn't like the man."

"For no reason I can put my finger on, McGee. We had dull, dirty, dangerous duty over there, but, after all, it was Air Transport Command. Brell was the tailored uniform type, with the hundred mission cap, and when we were in Calcutta he'd put on the right hardware and turn himself into a Flying Tiger and cut one hell of a swath through the adoring lassies. And he toted a thirty-eight with pearl grips instead of the regulation forty-five. And he didn't like to make landings. He would get very sweaty and overcontrol when he made landings."

"He would have the information on David Berry, then."

"If he's willing to talk. If he was in on it, on any cute money on the side, why should he talk to anybody about it?"

"I've leveled with you, Mr. Callowell, but I might try something else with Brell."

"And use my name in vain, McGee?"

"It might occur to me."

"I would advise against it. We have lawyers without enough to do. They get restless."

"I'll bear that in mind."

"I don't often do this much talking for so little reason, McGee. You have a nice touch. You're an eager listener. You smile in the right places. It puts people on. And, of course, you haven't leveled with me."

"How can you say such a thing!"

He chuckled and pulled himself to his feet. "End of session, McGee. Good night and good luck." At the door he turned and said, "I'll have you checked out, of course. Just for the hell of it. I'm a careful and inquisitive man."

"Can I make it easier by giving you my address?"

He winked. "Slip F-18. Bahia Mar. Lauderdale."

"Mr. Callowell, I am impressed."

"Mr. McGee, any reasonably honest man in the construction industry either sets up his own CIA or he goes broke." He chuckled again and trudged toward the elevators, trailing fragrant smoke.

8

In the morning I placed a station-to-station call to the number listed for George Brell in Harlingen. I got a lazy-toned switchboard operator who put me through to a sharp-voiced secretary who said that Mr. Brell was not in his office yet. As she had no way of knowing it was a long-distance call, I side-stepped her request for my name and said I would phone later.

Then I phoned my barge boat. After three rings, I heard her voice, small, tense, cautious. "Hello?"

"This is your night nurse speaking."

"Trav! Thank God."

"What's the matter? Is something wrong?"

"Nothing in particular. Just . . . I don't know . . . tension, I guess. I got so used to you being nearby. I hear sounds. And I jump. And I had bad dreams."

"Cook them out in the sun."

"I'm going to. On the beach, maybe. When are you coming back?"

"I'm going to Texas today."

"What?"

"There's a man there I want to see. I might be back there by Friday, but I'm not certain. Take your pills, honey. Don't agitate yourself. Eat, sleep and keep busy. You're smack in the middle of hundreds of boats and thousands of people."

"Trav, a woman phoned and she's very anxious to get in touch with you. She said it's an emergency. It sort of put her off stride to have a woman answer and say you're away. I said you might phone and she said to tell you to phone her. Miss McCall. With a very strange first name. I don't know if I have it right."

"Chookie."

"That's it."

I had her look in my book and give me the number. By the time I hung up, Lois sounded pretty good. I wondered if I had been a damn fool not to lock up my liquor supply, or at least to arrange to have somebody stay with her. Hurry home, Mother McGee. People have their acquired armor, made up of gestures and expressions and defensive chatter. Lois's had all been brutally stripped away, and I knew her as well anybody ever had or ever would. I knew her from filled teeth to the childhood apple tree, from appendix scar to wedding night, and it was time for her to start growing her new carapace, with me on the outside. I caught her raw, and did not care to be joined to her by scar tissue when healing began.

Chook's phone went to nine rings before she answered in the gritty rancor of interrupted sleep. But her voice changed when she recognized mine. "Trav! I phoned you last night. Who is that Mrs. Atkinson?"

"One of your more successful rivals."

"I mean really. Is she the one that whosis took on when he dropped Cathy?"

"Yes."

"Trav, I phoned about Cathy. She worked the first show last night. She seemed fine. And then they found her unconscious out on the beach there at the hotel. She'd been terribly beaten. Her face is a mess. Two broken fingers. They don't know yet if there's any internal injuries. She regained consciousness before they got her to the hospital. The police questioned her. She told them she went out to walk on the beach and somebody jumped her and beat her up. She couldn't give them a description. I talked to her next, after they'd given her a sedative. She acted very strange about it. I think it was him, Trav. She won't be able to work for two weeks anyway, maybe longer. She's really a mess."

"Does she want to talk to me?"

"She doesn't want to talk to anybody. It's in the paper today. Show girl assaulted on private beach. Mysterious assailant and so on."

"Are you going to see her today?"

"Of course!"

"I might not get back before Saturday. Look in on Lois Atkinson if you get a chance. Our friend left her in pretty sad shape. She's a lady."

"Oh, rally?"

"With ragged edges. You'll like her, I think. Make girl talk. Then I'll try to phone you tonight at the hotel, for a report on both of them."

"McGee's clinic?"

"The Junior Allen discard club. Take care."

A travel office at the hotel helped me find the best way to get to the Rio Grande Valley. A direct 707 out of Idlewild to Houston, a two-hour layover and then a feeder flight down to Harlingen with one stop at Corpus Christi. I had barely missed a better deal, and so I could take my time getting out to JFK Airport.

The flight took off with less than half the seats occupied. The whole country lay misty-bright, impersonal, under a summer high, and we went with the sun, making noon last a long time. The worst thing about having a hundred and eighty million people is looking down and seeing how much room there is for more. A stewardess took a special and personal interest in me. She was a little bigger than they usually are, and a little older than the norm. She was styled for abundant lactation, and her uniform blouse was not. She had a big white smile and she was mildly bovine, and I had the curious feeling I had met her before, and then I remembered where—in that valuable book by Mark Harris, *Bang the Drum Slowly,* the stewardess that "Author" runs into when he is on his way out to Mayo's. My stewardess perched on the edge of the seat beside me, back arched, smiling.

"Houston is going to be wicked hot," she said. "I am going to get me into that motel pool as fast as I can, and come out just long enough every once in a while to get a tall cold drink. Some of the kids just stay in the rooms, but I think they keep them too cold. It gives me the sinus. I layover here and go out at ten tomorrow, and somehow Houston is always a drag, you know?"

The mild misty blue eyes watched me and the mouth smiled and she waited for my move. You can run into the Tiger's Perpetual Floating House Party almost anywhere. At 28,000 feet, and at the same 800 fps muzzle velocity of a .45 caliber service pistol. Nobody leaves marks on anybody. You meet indirectly, cling for a moment and glance off. Then she would be that hostess in Houston and I would be that tanned one from Florida, a small memory of chlorinated pool water, fruit juice and gin, steak raw in the middle, and hearty rhythms in the draperied twilight of the tomb-cool motel cubicle, riding the grounded flesh of the jet-stream Valkyrie. A harmless pleasure. For harmless plastic people, scuffproof, who can create the delusion of romance.

But it is a common rudeness to refuse the appetizer without at least saying it looks delicious.

"I'd settle for Houston," I said with a manufactured wistfulness. "But I'm ticketed through to Harlingen."

The smile did not change and the eyes became slightly absent. She made some small talk and then swayed down the aisle, smiling, offering official services. Most of them find husbands, and some of them are burst or burned in lonely fields, and some of them become compulsively, forlornly promiscuous, sky sailors between the men in every port, victims of rapid transit, each flight merely a long arc from bed to bed.

I saw her later in the Houston terminal, stilting along, laughing and chattering into the face of a big florid youngster in a nine-gallon hat.

I was in Harlingen at a little after five, the sun high and blazing, the heat as wet and thick as Florida's. I rented an air-conditioned Galaxie and found a tall glassy motel with green lawns, pool and fountains, and checked into a shadowed icy room facing the pool. I showered and changed to sport shirt and slacks. I drove around. It was a village trying to call itself a city. Pale tall buildings had been put up in unlikely places for obscure reasons. It was linked to Brownsville by the twenty-five mile umbilicus of Route 77. The George Brell residence was at 18 Linden Way, Wentwood. Big plots, big sweeping curves of asphalt. Architectured houses, overhangs, patios, sprinklers, driveways and turnarounds pebbled in brown, traveler palms, pepper trees, Mexican gardeners, housewives in shorts, antique wrought-iron name signs. Number eighteen was blonde stone, glass, redwood, slate. Formal plantings. A black Lincoln and a white Triumph in the drive, a black poodle in a window of the house, glaring out at the world.

I went back among the common people and found a beer joint. Standard opening conversation gambit. "Sure hot." Standard answer. "Sure is."

The beer was so cold it had no taste. The juke played hill country laments. I found a talkative salesman. Local economy: Damned town had been too long at the mercy of the Air Force. Close the base, open the base, et cetera. Oranges and grapefruit were basic. Bad freeze year and everything goes to hell. Little winter tourist business building up pretty good. Padre Island and so forth. More transient traffic through into Mexico now the Mexicans fixed their damn road decent from Matamoros to Victoria. Quickest way from the States to Mexico City. He was talkative and cranky.

I got him into local success stories, and when he got onto George Brell I kept him there. "Old George is into a lot of things. His wife had some groves, and now he's got more. His first wife, dead now. God knows how many of those Beeg-Burger drive-ins he's got now. A dozen. More. And the real estate business, and warehouse properties, and the little trucking business he's started up."

"He must be a smart man."

"Well, let's say George is a busy man. He keeps moving. They say he's always in some kind of tax trouble, and he couldn't raise a thousand dollars cash, but he lives big. And he talks big. He likes a lot of people around him all the time."

"You said he married again?"

"Few years back. Hell of a good-looking girl, but I don't think she's more than maybe three years older than his oldest girl from his first wife. Built her a showplace house out in Wentwood Estates. Gerry, her name is."

My salesman had to get on home, and after he had gone I went back to a booth and phoned George Brell. It was ten to seven. I got him on the line. He sounded emphatic. I said I wanted to see him on a personal matter. He became wary. I said that Bill Callowell had suggested he might be able to help me.

"Callowell? My old pilot? Mr. McGee, you come right on out to the house right now. We're just sitting around drinking, and we'll have one ready for you."

I drove out. There were a half-dozen cars there. A houseman let me in. Brell came hurrying to me to pump my hand. He was a trim-bodied man in his late forties, dark and handsome in a slightly vulpine way, and I suspected he wore a very expensive and inconspicuous hairpiece. He looked the type to go bald early. He had a resonant voice and a slightly theatrical presence. He wore tailored twill ranch pants and a crisp white shirt with blue piping. Within ten seconds we were Trav and George, and then he took me out to a glassed back deck where the people were. A dozen of them, seven men and five women, casually dressed, friendly, slightly high. As he made the introductions he managed to give me the impression that all the men worked for him and he was making them rich, and all the women were in love with him. And he made it known to them that I was a dear friend of one of the most influential road builders in the country, a man who had flown desperate missions with George Brell, and had survived only because George was along. His wife, Gerry, was a truly stunning blonde in her middle twenties, tall and gracious, but with eyes just a little cold to match a smile so warm and welcoming.

We sat around on the sling chairs and leather stools, and talked the dusk into night. Two batches left, cutting the group down to five. They made it unthinkable not to stay to dinner. The Brells, a young couple named Hingdon and me. A little while before dinner, Brell took Hingdon off to discuss some business matter with him. Mrs. Hingdon went to the bathroom. Gerry Brell excused herself and went to see how the preparation of dinner was coming.

I went wandering. A harmless diversion. It was a big rambling house, obviously furnished by a decorator who had worked with the architect. And they had not been in it long enough to add those touches that would spoil the effect. There was a room off the living room, a small room with lights on inside. I saw a painting on the far wall of the small room that looked interesting. I listened and there was no sound of voices from the small room. I thought Hingdon and Brell might have gone in there. So I wandered in for a closer look at the painting. Just as I reached the middle of the room I heard a gasp and a scuffling noise. I turned and saw there were two people on a deep low couch to the right of the doorway. The couch had high sides, and I had not noticed them.

One was a pale-haired girl of about seventeen. She was slumped back in the couch against pillows. She had on short khaki shorts and a pale gray blouse unbuttoned to the waist. She had the long sprawled luxurious body of maturity, and she was breathing deeply, her face revealing that telltale slackness, the emptiness of prolonged sexual excitement. It was a child's mouth and a child's eyes set into a woman's face. Her lips were wet and her nipples swollen, and she was very slow in coming back from the dreamy land of eros. The boy was older, twenty possibly, and he was a massive brute, all hair and muscles and jaw corners and narrow infuriated eyes.

Left to my own devices, I would have gone very quietly away from there. But her warrior gave me no chance. "Why don't you knock, you silly son of a bitch?" he said in a gravelly voice.

"I didn't know it was a bedroom, boy."

He stood up, impressively tall and broad. "You insulted the lady."

The lady was sitting erect, buttoning her blouse. The lady said, "Deck him, Lew!" Sick him, Rover. He swarmed at me, obedient as any dog.

I am tall, and I gangle. I look like a loose-jointed, clumsy hundred and eighty. The man who takes a better look at the size of my wrists can make a more accurate guess. When I get up to two twelve I get nervous and hack it back on down to two oh five. As far as clumsiness and reflexes go, I have never had to use a flyswatter in my life. My combat expression is one of apologetic anxiety. I like them confident. My stance is mostly composed of elbows.

Lew, faithful dog, wanted it over right now. He hooked with both hands, chin on his chest, snorting, starting the hooks way back, left right left right. He had fists like stones and they hurt. They hurt my elbows and forearms and shoulders, and one glanced off the top of my shoulder and hit me high on the head. When I had the rhythm gauged, I counterpunched and knocked his mouth open with an overhand right. His arms stopped churning and began to float. I clacked his mouth shut with a very short left hook. He lowered his arms. I put the right hand in the same place as before and he fell with his mouth open and his eyes rolled up out of sight.

The little lady screamed. People came running. I massaged my right hand. "What's going on!" Brell yelled. "What the hell is going on!"

I was too angry for polite usage, for the living room turn of phrase. "I walked in here to look at the painting. I thought the room was empty. This crotch jockey had his little girl all turned on and steaming and they resented the interruption, and she told him to deck me. But it didn't work out."

Brell turned on the girl, anguish in his voice. "Angie! Is this true?"

She looked at Lew. She looked at me. She looked at her father. Her eyes were like stones. "What do you really care *who* gets laid around here *anyway!*" She sobbed and brushed by him and fled. After a stunned hesitation, he ran after her, calling to her. A door slammed. He was still yelling. A sports car rumbled and snorted and took off. Rubber yelped. It faded, shifting up through the gears.

"God love us," Gerry Brell said. She took a vase from the table and stood thoughtfully and dumped it on Lew's head, flowers and all. The Hingdons and I were busy trying not to look squarely at one another.

Lew pushed the floor away and sat up. He looked like a fat sad baby. His eyes were not properly focused.

Gerry sat on her heels beside him and put her hand on that meaty shoulder and shook him gently. "Sweetie, you better haul your ass out of here right now, because if I know George Brell, he's loading a gun right this minute."

The eyes focused, comprehended, became round and wide with alarm. He jumped up and without a glance at anyone or another word went running heavily and unsteadily out.

Gerry smiled at us and said, "Excuse me, please." She went off to find George.

Little Bess Hingdon stayed close to her big and rather solemn young husband as we went into the long living room. "Dear, I really think we should go."

"Just leave?" Hingdon said uncertainly.

There was a nice flavor about them, that scent of good marriage. Separated by a room of people, they were still paired, still aware of each other.

"I'll find Gerry," she said and went off.

Sam Hingdon looked curiously at me and said, "That Lew Dagg is a rough boy. Linebacker. One more year to go, and the pros are watching him."

"Like what did I hit him with?"

He grinned. "Something like that."

"Maybe he's out of condition. He should use the summer for a different kind of exercise. Is that Angie George's eldest?"

"Youngest. She's the only one left home. Gidge is the eldest. She's married to a boy in med school in New Orleans. Tommy's in the Air Force. They're Martha's children."

Bess came hurrying in, carrying her purse. "It's all right, honey. We can leave now. Good night, Mr. McGee. Hope we'll see you again."

I went out to the terrace and made myself a weak drink. I could hear Gerry and George yammering at each other. I could hear the music but not the lyrics. Fury and accusation. A pretty girl in dark braids and a uniform came onto the terrace and gathered up the debris of the cocktail snacks, gave me a shy glance and cat-footed away.

Finally George came out. He looked sour. He grunted at me, poured bourbon over one cube and downed it before the ice had a chance to chill it. He banged the glass down. "Trav, Gerry has a headache. She said to apologize. Jesus, what an evening!"

"Apologize to her for me. Tell her I didn't stop to think that could be your daughter when I spoke so rough. I was still angry. And about hitting that kid, he gave me no choice."

He stared at me with evident agony. "Just what were they doing, McGee?"

"I didn't actually see them doing anything. He had her blouse unbuttoned and her bra unhooked, but she had her shorts on."

"She doesn't even start college until fall. Goddamn that ape! Let's get out of here, Trav."

We went out and got into the Lincoln. He drove swiftly through a long maze of curving roads and slowed as we passed a house as conspicuous as his. I caught a glimpse of the Triumph. He speeded up. "Gerry said that's where she'd go. It's her closest girl friend."

He didn't speak again until we were on 77 heading south. "It's a hell of a thing for something like that to happen, the first time you're in my home."

"Worse for you than for me."

"How the hell am I supposed to keep an eye on her? That's Gerry's job and she's goofing it. She says she can't control her. She says Angie won't listen to her. I'm a busy man, goddamn it. I've got to send the kid away, but where? Where can you send them in August, for God's sake? There's no relatives to park her with. Did you hear what she said to me?" He banged the steering wheel with the heel of his hand. "What do you think, McGee? Do you think that ape is actually screwing my little girl?"

"I think you're driving too damned fast, George. And I don't think he is. Yet."

"Sorry. Why don't you think he is?"

"Because if he was, he would have had her off someplace where he could, without interruption. And from the look of her, that was the next step, George."

He slowed down a little more. "You know, that makes sense. Sure. He's probably trying to talk her into it. He's been hanging around for about a month. Trav, that's the second good turn you've done me tonight."

"And she doesn't care too much for the boy."

"How do you know?"

"When she ran out, he hadn't moved a muscle. She couldn't know but what I'd killed him."

"That's right! I'm feeling better by the minute. McGee, you must have a very nice punch."

"He's very easy to hit. And you're going too fast again."

We came into Brownsville. He took a confusing number of turns and put the car in a small lot on a back street. We walked half a block through the sultry night to the shabby entrance of a small private club, a men's club, with a comfortable bar and a good smell of broiled steak, and a cardroom with some intent poker players under the hooded green light.

We stood at the bar and he said, "A key for my friend, Clarence."

The bartender opened a drawer and took out a brass key and put it in front of me. "This is Mr. Travis McGee, Clarence. Trav, that key is good for life. Life memberships one dollar. Give Clarence the dollar." I handed it over. "Cash on the line here for everything. No fees, no assessments, no committees. And a good steam room."

We picked up our drinks and I followed George over to a corner table. "We can eat right here when we're ready," he said. He frowned. "I just don't know what the hell to do about that girl."

"Didn't Gidge and Tommy work out fine?"

It startled him. "Yes. Sure."

"Don't worry about her. She's a very lush-looking kid, George. And probably as healthy as she looks. Probably if you knew everything about Gidge and Tommy at the same age, your hair would turn white."

"By God, if you were twenty years older, McGee, I'd hire you to watchdog her for what's left of the summer."

"You wouldn't be able to trust me."

"Anyway, whatever you came to see me about, consider it done. I owe you that much."

"I want information."

"It's yours."

"How much did Dave Berry steal overseas, how did he steal it and how did he smuggle it back into the States?"

It twisted him into another dimension so suddenly it was like yanking him inside out. His face turned a pasty yellow. His eyes darted back and forth as though looking for a place to hide. He opened his mouth three times to speak and closed it each time. Then he said, spacing the words, "Are you a Treasury Department investigator?"

"No."

"What are you?"

"I just try to get along, this way and that. You can understand that."

"I knew a Sergeant David Berry once."

"Is that the way you want it?"

"That's the way it has to be."

"What are you scared of, George?"

"Scared?"

"You can't be scared of Berry. He's been dead two years."

It startled him, but not enough. "Dead? I didn't know that. Did they let him loose before he died?"

"No."

"There's no secret of the fact I had to testify for him. I hadn't gotten out yet. I had to go to the presidio where they tried him. I said I'd served with him for two years and that he was a good competent non-com. I said I'd seen him lose his temper a lot of times, but he'd never hurt anybody before. He'd been drinking. A jackass lieutenant with brand-new gold bars, never been out of the States, didn't like the way Dave saluted him. He made Dave stand on a street corner and practice. After about five minutes of that, Dave just hit him. And then kept picking him up and hitting him again. And then he took off. If only he'd hit him once, or if he hadn't run. . . . But I guess you know all about it."

"Why should I? I want to know how much, and how he got it and how he brought it back."

"I wouldn't know a thing about that, friend. Not a single stinking thing."

"Because you made it the same way and brought it back the same way, George?"

"I don't know what you're talking about, believe me."

"Because you can't be sure there isn't something official about this. Is that it?"

"McGee, I have had a lot of people asking a lot of questions for a long time, and they all get told the same thing. It was a good try, McGee. Let's eat." His morale came back fast.

It was midnight when we left the back-street club. He had a cocky, wary friendliness. As he unlocked the door of the Lincoln and swung it open, I chopped him under the ear with the edge of my hand, caught him and tumbled him in. And felt a gagging self-disgust. He was a semi-ridiculous banty rooster of a man, vain, cocky, running as hard as he could to stay in the same place, but he had a dignity of existence which I had violated. A bird, a horse, a dog, a man, a girl or a cat—you knock them about and diminish yourself because all you do is prove yourself equally vulnerable. All his anxieties lay there locked in his sleeping skull, his system adjusting itself to sudden shock, keeping him alive. He had pulled at the breast, done homework, dreamed of knighthood, written poems to a girl. One day they would tumble him in and cash his insurance. In the meanwhile it did all human dignity a disservice for him to be used as a puppet by a stranger.

He stirred once on the orderly trip back, and I found the right place on his neck for the thumb, and settled him back. Assured I was unobserved, I carried him into my chill nest, pulled the draperies, readied him for proof.

I stripped him, bound him, gagged him and settled him into the bottom of the shower stall. It was a hairpiece. I peeled it away and tossed it onto the lavatory counter. It crouched there like a docile, glossy little animal.

A naked man who cannot move or talk, and does not know whether it is night or day, and is not told where he is or how he got there, will break very quickly.

The cold water brought him awake, and I let it run until I was certain he was thoroughly awake. I sat on a stool just outside the shower stall. I turned the water off. He was shivering. He stared at me with a total malevolence.

"George, do you think any government agency would permit this kind of interrogation? I've got several ways of getting rid of you completely. All perfectly safe. You've been asleep a long time, George. A lot of people are looking for you. But they're looking in all the wrong places. Kidnapping is illegal, George. So we have to make a deal or I won't be able to let you go."

His eyes mirrored several new concerns, but he was telling himself he would never never give in.

"I'm after Berry's little package, and I need your help. When you're ready to talk, just nod your head. Your only other choice is to get boiled like a knockwurst." I reached up and turned on the hot water. Good motels keep it at about a hundred and eighty degrees, and it doesn't take long to get there. I gave him a short burst and a cloud of steam. He bucked himself off the floor and screamed into the towel, a small noise. His eyes were maddened and bulging and he forgot to nod.

I gave him a second blast, and when the steam cleared I could see him nodding vigorously. I gave him the third blast for insurance and he jumped nicely and nodded so hard he was rapping his head against the wall of the stall.

I reached in and took the gag away.

He groaned. "Jesus God, you've scalded me. What are you doing to me? My God, McGee, what are you trying to do?"

I reached my hand up and put it on the hot water lever.

"Don't!" he bawled.

"Keep your voice down, George. You're turning nice and pink. Now just talk to me. Tell me all about how you and Dave Berry worked it. And if something doesn't sound exactly right, I'll boil you a little, just for luck."

With a little coaching, he got through it pretty well. He and Berry had worked together from the beginning. At first it was Missionary Bonds, purchased in China, shipped back to a friend in the States to cash and send them the money to buy more. Double money on each deal. Then when that was closed out, it was the gold. They worked together, but kept the take separate. They didn't trust each other completely. But Berry was always making more than George Brell because he didn't spend an extra rupee on himself. He kept reinvesting it in gold. Berry found a goldsmith on Chowringhi Road in Calcutta who would cast facsimile structural parts for the aircraft out of pure gold. Berry would sand them a little, paint them with aluminum paint, screw them in place. A man in Kunming would melt them back into standard bars. This was after spot inspection was tightened up. When they were finally due to be shipped back on rotation, Brell had over sixty thousand American dollars, and he was certain that Dave Berry had at least three times that much. They took an R and R leave and hitched a flight down to Ceylon. It was Berry's idea. He had thought it all out, and had learned all he could about gem stones. The cash made Brell nervous. He followed Berry's lead. They spent the full ten days buying the most perfect gem stones they could find. Deep blue sapphires, star sapphires, dark Burmese rubies, star rubies. Some were too big to fit through the mouth of a standard-issue canteen. They cut the canteens open, put the gems inside and resoldered them. They poured melted wax over the stones to hold them in place. The wax hardened. They filled the canteens with water, hooked them on their belts and came home rich and nervous.

"I don't think they ever suspected Dave of a thing. He kept his mouth shut. But I did some hinting when I'd had a few drinks. They got onto me somehow. I went back home and hid them. I didn't dare touch them. I was on terminal leave, waiting to get out when I got called to the trial. After they sentenced him to life, I had a chance to be alone with him. I tried to make a deal with him. Tell me where his were. I'd take a reasonable cut for services rendered and see that his family got taken care of. Not a chance. He didn't trust me. He didn't trust anybody to be shrewd enough and smart enough. No, he was going to get out sooner or later, and he was going to handle it himself without any hitches, and then he could make it all up to his wife and girls.

"I didn't touch mine for three years. Then I had to have cash. There was some land I had to pick up. I could buy it right. I couldn't run the risk of selling them in this country. Martha and I took a vacation. We went to Mexico. I made contacts there. I took a screwing, but at least I felt safe. I got just a little over forty thousand. I brought it back in U.S. dollars, and I fed it into the businesses a little bit at a time. I was careful. But they came down on me, on a net worth basis, trying to make a fraud charge stick, saying there was unreported income. And it has cost me a hundred thousand dollars to keep from being convicted for that lousy forty thousand. I couldn't talk to you. I couldn't take the chance. There's no statute of limitations on tax fraud, and they could still jail me for never declaring the money I made overseas. I'm marked lousy in the files, and they are after me every year. They're never going to stop. Now, for God's sake, let me out of here."

After I untied him, I had to help him to his feet and half carry him into the bedroom. He sat on the edge of the bed and put his bald head down on his bare hairy knees and began to cry.

"I'm sick," he said. "I'm real sick, McGee."

He huddled and his teeth began to chatter. I tossed his clothes to him and he dressed quickly, his lips blue.

"Where are we?"

"About two miles from your house. We walked out of that club in Brownsville about three and a half hours ago. Nobody is looking for you."

He stared at me. "Do you know how you looked? You looked like you'd enjoy killing me."

"I didn't want to take too long over this, George."

"I couldn't hold out against what you were going to do."

"Nobody could, George."

He felt his bald head. "Where is it?"

"In the bathroom."

He tottered in. In a few moments he came out, hairpiece in place. But the haggardness of his face made it look more spurious than before. He sat again on the edge of the bed. We were oppressor and oppressed. Traditionally this is supposed to create enmity. But, so often, it does not. It had opened up too many conflicting areas of emotions. The violence was a separate thing, like a wind that had blown through, and we were left with an experience shared. He was anxious to have me know that he had acquitted himself well. I was eager to have him believe he had left me no other choice.

"You are a friend of Callowell's?"

"No."

"I wrote the stuffy son of a bitch a nice letter and got a brush-off."

"I traced you through him."

He didn't seem to hear me. "Callowell was so damn nervous about anything cute. He'd check that airplane. He'd check around, and right over his fat head some of the static line braces would be solid gold. I tried to kid with Dave about it. Dave didn't see anything funny. He was dead serious about everything. God, it warted him to send money home when he knew he could keep it and keep on doubling it. I kept spending too much. I had a private car in a private garage in Calcutta. I had a wife and two kids home too. But the difference between Dave and me, he was sure he'd live forever." He shivered violently. "Trav, you think you could get me home? I feel terrible."

I drove him home in the Lincoln. My rental was in his drive, and the Triumph was there, in the triple carport, beside a compact station wagon. I rolled the Lincoln into the empty space. Lights were on in the back of the house. I went into the big kitchen with him. There was a center island of stone, and copper pots aligned on a fruitwood wall.

Gerry Brell came into the light wearing a pink quilted robe with big white lapels, her blonde hair tousled, eyes squinting in the light.

"Honey, I don't feel so good," George said.

"He's having chills," I told her.

She took him off. At the doorway she turned and said, "Wait for me, Trav."

I looked in the refrigerators and found cold Tuborg in the second one. I leaned against the center island and drank it, feeling unreal. I walked on a fabric of reality but it had an uncomfortable give to it. You could sink in a little way. If you walked too much and came to a weak spot, you could fall through. I think it would be pretty black down there.

After fifteen minutes she came back to the kitchen, saw what I was having and got herself one. She had brushed her hair and her eyes were accustomed to the light.

She leaned against a bank of stainless steel sinks, facing me, and drank from the bottle and said, "He threw up. I turned on his electric blanket and gave him a sleeping pill."

"I think he's just emotionally upset."

"You've had a dandy introduction to the Brell family."

"Why did you ask me to stay?"

"Couldn't you just wait so we could work around to it instead of coming out with it like that?"

"I'm not at my best at four in the morning."

"Did you give him some bad news?"

"I don't know what you mean."

"George operates on the thin edge, and the edge is getting thinner all the time. I wanted to cut down the way we live, but he won't hear of it. Any little thing could tip the scales, and then the walls come tumbling down."

"How do you know that isn't exactly what I want?"

She looked rueful. "Then I made a bad guess about you. Did he say anything about me tonight?"

"No. But it's nice to know why you had me stay."

"What do you mean?"

"I hope you had a nice long talk with the girl when she got home."

"I guess I had to, didn't I? Not stepmother to child. That doesn't work, does it? Woman to woman. Call it an armed truce."

"The next time she makes a crack like that, Gerry, it might not go over his head."

"I think I made her understand that, if she loves her father, it would be a poor way to show it to give him a big broad hint about my infidelity. It's a hell of a confusing world, Mr. McGee. She's trying to throw herself away because she trusted me and I cheated on her father."

"Can she be sure of that?"

Her laugh was ugly. "Eyewitnesses are usually pretty positive. It happened back in June. Kids are so idealistic. How can I explain to her that it really didn't mean very much, that it was an old friend, sort of a sentimental, unplanned, old-times-sake sort of thing. I don't make a habit of that sort of thing. But ever since I heard the door open and turned my head and saw her there, pale as death before she slammed the door and ran, I've felt cheap and sick about it. We were getting fond of each other up until then. Now she thinks I'm a monster. Tonight she was trying to hurt me by hurting herself. I just hope George has forgotten what she said. His judgment is bad enough lately without something like that to cloud it."

"He didn't make any mention of what she said."

"Good. Could this thing with Angie have made him so sick?"

"I think it's probable."

She tilted her pretty head and studied me. "Trav, you seem so mild and sure of yourself, and maybe a little amused at us. Maybe you know enough about people to tell me what I should do about Angie."

"I'm not that sure of myself."

"I just wish there was a starting place. I can't reach her. She looks at me with hate. I just can't ever explain it to her."

"Are you a good human being, Gerry? I mean good in the sense that if you put everything in the scales, they'd tip that way?"

It startled her. "I don't know. I haven't thought of myself that way. I think I like the lush life a little too much. That's why I married George. I'm vain. I like men to admire me. I've got a coarse streak that comes out at the wrong times. But I do try to live up to . . . some kind of a better image of myself. And I try to improve. I came from nothing, Trav, from a little raggedy-ass spread in the Panhandle with too many kids and too few rooms. Dusted out, flooded out, burned out—we had it all. Until I got big enough to know that if I wore a tight skirt and red shoes, I could get the pretties I'd ached for, and then smart enough to know that the cheap approach gets the cheap pretties. This house and this life, they're big pretties, but the same old equation holds. I just don't know. Maybe I'm good, but that goddamn scale would hesitate a long time before tilting that way."

"Then tell the kid the whole thing. Lew proved she's old enough. Make her identify. Level with her. The saga of Gerry Brell, up to and including your little sentimental gesture, and how you feel about her. Don't hold anything back. Don't let George send her away. Keep her here until she knows it all and she can balance it out herself."

"She'll despise me."

"She already does."

She brooded for a few moments. "I'll do no sleeping tonight, I got to walk this one around, boy." She set the empty bottle aside and said, "I have the feeling I won't be seeing you again."

"I have to see George once more."

9

My motel windows were turning gray when I placed the overdue call to Chook. She was outraged, but when she calmed down she reported that Cathy lay listless on her hospital bed and answered questions in a small voice, in as few words as possible. And she liked Lois Atkinson. Very jumpy, sort of wild-eyed, but nice. They talked dance. Lois had studied ballet when she was little, but had grown too tall. And when was I coming back? That evening probably. Friday. The sun was visible from Florida, but it hadn't gotten to me. She was trying a replacement, temporary, for Cathy. The damned girl was fair, but she kept getting so winded you could hear her gasping forty feet away. Hurry home, darling McGee.

I slept until ten, arranged afternoon airline connections, then phoned my questions to a sly elderly angle-player in New York, an old friend, a quaint hustler of the unwary marks, a sometime dealer in everything from faked Braque to union dues, from gossip column items to guest shots. I said he would hear from me again.

I checked out and had a quick breakfast and went to George Brell's home. The pretty maid I had seen before had me wait inside the door while she checked with Mr. Brell. She came back and took me to him. He was propped up, reading the newspaper and drinking coffee. He was in a gigantic circular bed, with a pink canopy over it. In all the luxuriant femininity of that big bedroom, George looked shrunken and misplaced, like a dead worm in a birthday cake.

He threw the paper aside and said harshly, "Shut that door and pull that chair over here and sit down, McGee."

Pride quickly rebuilds the fallen walls. And refashions the past to fit its own requirements.

He started at me. "You're very cute, boy. I'd done a lot of drinking, and I was upset about Angie, and I was exhausted from all the deals I've been making lately."

"I certainly took advantage of you, George."

"I did a hell of a lot of talking, and some of it I can't even remember. I've got some kind of a flu bug."

"And I was pretty rough, George."

"I want to know where we stand, McGee."

"In what way?"

"I'm warning you, boy, the worst mistake you can make is try to use anything against me. I'm not about to try to buy you off, if that's what you're after. I can get rough too. Damned rough."

"Are you planning on getting rough anyway?"

"I'm thinking about it."

"I guess if those tax people knew exactly where to look, and what historical facts they could check out, they could come back at you with a little more ammunition, George."

He swallowed and fumbled a cigarette out of his pack and said, "You're not scaring me. Not a bit."

"I think we ought to forgive and forget the whole thing, George."

He boggled at me. "You're not here to clip me?"

"Frankly I don't think you've got enough to be worth clipping, even if I went in for that line of work."

"I'm a rich man!" he said indignantly.

"George, you just live rich. Two years from now, if you've got a pot left, I'll be astonished. All I wanted from you was information, and I had to be sure you weren't being shifty. I'm after what Dave brought back. So far all that's been found was what was left of the canteen. Not much, after eighteen years of tropical weather."

"Somebody got there first?"

"But they haven't had much of a start, George."

He tried a frail smile. "And that's all you wanted from me?"

"I tried to tell you that."

He sat up. "Any time you're in the Valley, Trav, this house is your house. You want to change your luck, I've got deals around here I just haven't had the time to work on. In ten years this area is going to be the most . . ."

"Sure, George."

He called to me as I reached the hall. I came back into the room. He moistened his lips. "If there should be any kind of trouble, and you have to do a lot of explaining . . ."

"I guess you better wish me luck."

He did and fell back into the percale pillows. As I started to find my way out, I looked back through the terrace glass toward the outdoor pool. Gerry and Angie were out there, standing on the far apron of the pool, talking intently, taking the sun before the day became too hot. Angie wore a conservative swim suit, and her stepmother wore a bikini. At that distance they looked of an age. After the promise of Gerry in clothing, her figure was a mild disappointment. She had high small breasts, and she was very long-waisted. The long limber torso widened into chunky hips and meaty thighs and short sturdy legs. As I watched them, Angie turned abruptly and started away. Gerry ran after her and caught her by the arm and stopped her. The girl stood in a sullen posture, her head lowered, as Gerry talked to her. Then she permitted herself to be led back to a sun cot. She stretched out, turning her face up toward the sun. The woman moved a white metal chair close and sat and talked down at the girl. Perhaps it was a trick of sunlight, but I thought I saw a silver gleam of moisture on the girl's cheek as I turned away.

This family was a circus act, balanced on a small platform atop a swaying pole, as the crowd goes *ahhhh,* anticipating disaster. A vain foolish man and a careless young wife and a tortured girl, swaying to the long drum roll. When it fell, the unmarked House Beautiful would sell readily, the Lincoln would be acquired by a Mexican dentist. Who would survive? George, perhaps, as he had the shortest distance to fall.

On the long east-southeast slant of the Houston-Miami jet flight, high over the blue steel silence of the Gulf, I thought of dour David Berry in the night, lifting away the big slabs of stone, tucking the shiny fortune down at the base of the pillar and replacing the stones, then waiting for his family to wake and find him. He had hoped for luck, stubbornly vowing to live and come back, knowing his women could not cope with the crafty problem of turning blue fire into money, knowing there was no one he could trust. Then Junior Allen had moved close to him, perhaps sensing a secret, chipping at it, prying.

Maybe, in his despair, David Berry had even considered trusting Junior Allen. But he had decided against it, or death came too quickly. But Allen knew it was there, and had lived there and thought and searched and finally found it.

A lump of wax like a huge blueberry muffin? All the rains and the heat and the salt damp had corroded the container away. And there would have been some bug with a taste for wax. Loose and gleaming probably, amid pale stalks and dirt, with Allen kneeling, his breath shallow and his heart thumping as he gathered them up.

Bugs would eat the wax. Chaw the old canvas. And one day there will be a mutation, and we will have new ones that can digest concrete, dissolve steel and suck up the acid puddles, fatten on magic plastics, lick their slow way through glass. Then the cities will tumble and man will be chased back into the sea from which he came. . . .

The large yellowed head lamps of Miss Agnes peered through dusk as I turned into Bahia Mar and found a slot a reasonable distance from the *Busted Flush*. There were lights on in my craft, a curiously homey look. Welcome traveler. I bing-bonged to save her unnecessary alarm, then stepped over the chain and went aboard, startling her when she pulled open the door to the lounge.

She backed away, smiling. "Hello. Or welcome home. Or something like that, Trav."

Three days had made an astonishing difference. Dark blue stretch pants patterned with ridiculous little yellow tulips. A soft yellow blouse with three-quarter sleeves. Hair shorter, face, arms and throat red-gold with new tan.

"Tourist!" I said.

"I thought maybe I wouldn't look so scrawny in this kind of . . ."

"Beach girl."

She drew herself up. "You think so? You think that's all there is to do?"

I had to be led around and I had to admire. Corridor walls scraped down and repainted a better color. New curtains in the head. A new set of stainless steel bowls for the galley. She said she would show me the topsides work by daylight, when I could appreciate it.

I put my suitcase in my stateroom and came back into the lounge and told her she was a useful guest. We stood smiling at each other and then she leapt at me, clutched me, wailed once, and went away, snuffling, keeping her back toward me.

"What's wrong?"

"I don't know."

"Come on now, Lois. What's wrong?"

She pulled herself together quickly. "Does something have to be wrong? Maybe I'm glad to have you back. I don't know."

She had started to rebuild the woman things, the artifice, the indirection, the challenge. It was her pride at work. She was healing and I was glad to see it, and I did not want to nudge the structure too heavily. It was too new.

"I'll fix your drink," she said. "I sold the house."

"Got the money?"

"Soon."

"Sorry?"

"About the house? It's just a house. I was hiding down there in that wretched little village because I thought I'd been a bad wife." She brought me my drink and handed it to me.

"Aren't you getting a little fat, dear?" I asked.

She beamed. "A hundred and seven this afternoon."

"What's right for you?"

"Oh, one eighteen, one twenty." She patted her hip. "After one twenty it all goes here."

"So if the hiding is over, what are you going to do?" It was a fool question, tangle-footed and unimaginative. And no way to take it back. It made her aware of obligation. She could handle day by day. If she kept her head down. I had rocked the fragile new structure. Those dark and pleasantly tilted eyes became haunted and she sucked at her lips and knotted her hands. "Not right now," I said, trying to mend it. "Some day."

"I don't know."

"How was New York, Trav? New York was hot, Lois. How was Texas, Trav? Texas was hot, Lois. Did you have any fun, Trav? I wouldn't call it fun, Lois. I wouldn't know what to call it."

She measured me out one half of a smile. "Oh, shut up."

"Do I take you out tonight?"

"Oh, no! I cook, really."

I looked at my watch. "I have a hospital visit to make. So schedule it for after I get back. Say forty minutes after I get back. Time to shower and change when I get back."

"Yes, master. Oh, I owe you six dollars and thirty cents on your phone bill."

"Those pants are pretty sexy, Mrs. Atkinson."

"I called Harp. I talked to Lucille. I didn't tell her hardly anything. Just that I'd been sick and things were better now."

"You're blushing, Mrs. Atkinson."

"Don't talk about these pants then. I bought them today. I don't feel very secure about them."

Cathy was in a six-bed ward. I pulled a chair close, kissed her on the forehead and sat beside her. I hoped she hadn't seen any dismay in my face. The sallow, thoughtful, rather pretty and fine-boned little face was gone. It was a stormy sunset, a ripe eggplant, a heavy mushroom. There was a single slit of brown eye to see with. Her left hand was splinted. "Hello," she said in a dead, fat-lipped voice. I stood up and yanked the curtains and sat down again and took her uninjured hand. It rested slack and warm and dry in mine.

"Junior Allen?" I said in a low voice.

"You don't have to mind about me, Mr. McGee."

"I thought it was Cathy and Trav. . . . Why did he do it?"

There is no way to read the expression of bruised meat. She watched me, hiding away back in there behind pain and indignity. "This part of it has got nothing to do with you."

"I want to know about it because you are my friend."

The slit eye was closed so long I began to wonder if she'd fallen asleep. She opened it. "He come there to the bar at the Bahama Room, and I messed up a routine awful when I saw him watching us. I don't know if it was an accident or he heard somehow or what. After, I hurried into my clothes and went out and he was gone. I went outside and saw him crossing the parking, and I ran after him. I caught him and said I wanted to talk with him. He said we didn't have anything to talk about. I said we could talk about money. That made him wonder. We walked through to the beach. Then I said that if he could just give me a little money out of what he got, maybe even just a thousand dollars, then I wouldn't make any trouble about any of the rest of it. He asked me what I would mean by trouble, and I said he found something that wasn't his, didn't he? He laughed once, short and nasty, and said I had no idea in the world what trouble was. So he reached quick and grappled holt of my neck with one hand, and pounded on my face with the other, and a couple of times he hit me in the belly. It all went dark while he was thumping on me, and I woke up in the ambulance. It . . . it doesn't hurt much now."

"Cathy, why didn't you tell the police?"

"I almost did."

"Why didn't you?"

"Not because I'm afraid of him beating on me again. But the whole thing might come out. And then I'd for sure never get a nickel back. And . . . it would have messed up what you're fixing to do, Trav. It could have messed you into a police thing."

What is there to do about one like that? I lifted her hand and kissed the roughened knuckles and said, "You are something, Cathy."

"I feel next door to nothing at all."

"Some good news anyway. There's no way to find out who the money ever belonged to, and no way to get it back to them anyway."

"What was hid there?"

"We'll talk when you get out of here."

"They won't tell me when. But I was on my feet some today. Hunched up and dizzy, but walked all the way to the john holding onto a lady. So maybe it won't be so long."

When I said good-by to her she said, "It was nice of you to come to visit me. Thank you very much."

I talked a long time with Lois that evening, giving her an edited version of my adventures. I went to bed. As I dropped off I could still hear her in the shower.

She came into my sleep and into my bed, awakening me with her mouth on mine, and strangely there was no shock or surprise in it. My subconscious had been aware that this would happen. A lady is a very special happening, so scented and delicate and breathless and totally immaculate. She wore a filmy something that tied at the throat and parted readily, presenting the warm length of her, the incredibly smooth texture of her, to my awakening embrace. Her breath was shuddering, and she gave a hundred quick small kisses. Her caresses were quick and light, and her body turned and glowed and glided and changed in her luxurious presentation of self, her mouth saying darling and her hair sweet in darkness, a creature in endless movement, using all of herself the way a friendly cat will bump and twine and nudge and purr. I wanted to take her on her basis, readying her as graciously as she had made herself ready, with an unhurried homage to all her parts and purposes, an intimate minuet involving offer and response, demand and delay, until the time when it would all be affirmed and taken and done with what, for want of a better name, must be called a flavor of importance.

But suddenly it was not going well. She would fall away from sweet frenzy, and then lift herself back up, but to a lesser peak. We were not yet joined. She was trying to hold onto all the wanting, but it kept receding, the waves of it growing smaller, her body becoming less responsive to each touch.

Finally she sobbed aloud and flung herself away, clenching her body into the foetal curl, posture of hiding, her back to me. I touched her. Her muscles were rigid.

"Lois, dear."

"Don't touch me!"

"Please, honey, you just . . ."

"Rotten, rotten, rotten!" she said in a small leathery howling voice, dragging the vowel sounds out.

I tried to stroke her. Her body was like wood, that great tension which comes with hysteria.

"Ugly rotten," she moaned. "You don't know the things, the ugly things. It can't ever be nice again. I let things happen. I did things. I stopped fighting."

"Give yourself time, Lois."

"*I . . . love . . . you!*" she wailed, protest and lament.

"You tried too soon."

"I wanted you."

"There's time."

"Not for me. I can't turn my mind off. It will always come back."

I laced my hands behind my head and thought about it. It was very touching. Such a total preparation. All plucked and perfumed, scrubbed and anointed, all tremulous with the reward for the heroic rescuer. Then, in the darkness, Junior Allen smirked at her and that sense of her own value, which a woman must have, was gone. She had packed and wrapped the gift with greatest care, labeled it with love, but suddenly it was a gift-wrapped flagon of slime. She had tried too soon, but had I tried to turn her away at the first touch, it might have been more traumatic than what had happened. I wondered if shock would be better than soothing.

"Terribly terribly dramatic, dear Lois."

"Uh?"

"So sad. Forever soiled, stained, lost, hopeless. The corrupted trollop of Candle Key. Gad, what drama!"

She uncurled herself slowly and cautiously, keeping her distance, furtively tucking the covering up under her chin. "Don't be a cruel disgusting bastard," she said in a flat voice. "At least try to have some empathy."

"For whom? A thirty-one-year-old adolescent, for God's sake? Do you think I'm so starved for a woman I take anything I can get? Sometimes I get a little foolish or a little depressed, and I do just that, but it leaves a bad taste. The bad taste comes from my being an incurable romantic who thinks the man-woman thing shouldn't be a contest on the rabbit level. The rabbits have us beat. My dear, if I thought you a bundle of corruptions, what feast is that for a romantic? No, dear Lois, you are sweet and clean from top to tippy toe, fresh and wholesome in every part, and pleasantly silly."

"*Damn* you!"

"I didn't tell you one little item, dear. It was Junior Allen who beat up Cathy. In her words, he grappled holt of her neck with one hand and pounded on her face with the other. Until she doesn't seem to have much of a face at the present time. And she didn't turn him in, not because she was scared, but because she thought because I'm trying to help her I might be brought into it somehow and the police might mess me up somehow. I keep stacking that up against your dramatics, and somehow you don't come out too well. Try it yourself and see."

She was silent for a long long time. I could not guess how she would respond, but I knew it was a critical moment, perhaps the moment upon which her whole future was balanced. And I despised myself right along with all other amateur psychiatrists, parlor sages, barstool philosophers.

"But I've been sick!" she said in a teeny, squeaky, ludicrous voice, and after a shocked moment I recognized it as the tag line of that ancient mouse joke, and I knew this girl would be well. My laughter exploded, and in a moment she joined in. Like children, we laughed ourselves into tears. It kept dying away and beginning again, and I was glad to see she did not water it down by trying to repeat it.

Then she got up, a pale and slender shape in darkness, and found the diaphanous wrap and floated it over her shoulders and was gone in silence, but for the small click of my door latch. Water ran. There was a thread of light under my door. After a long time it went out. I thought I knew by then how her mind would work, and I waited. The door made the smallest sound. The timid ghost drifted to me. And it began as before.

Often she faltered, and I brought her back. A lot of it was gentleness and waiting. And being kind. And telling her of her sweetness. At last there came the reward for patience, her tremendous inhalation broken into six separate fragments, her whole body listening to itself then, finding, being certain, and then taking with hunger.

Later she lay curled languid against my chest, her heart and breathing slow. "Wasn't too soon," she said, a blurred drone.

"No, it wasn't."

"Sweet," she said. "Ver' sweet." And she nestled down into the sleep of total exhaustion.

I could have gone to sleep at once if I could have convinced myself that everything was just peachy fine. But I felt I had maneuvered myself into a rather nasty little corner. Where does responsibility stop? Do you buy the cripple a shoeshine box and send it out into the traffic? I had the feeling I now owned this sleeping thing. True, it was a splendid specimen, good bones and a true heart. It could cook and adore and it had a talent for making love. Sew it into burlap and roll it in the mud and it would still be, unmistakably, a lady. You could take it anywhere.

But I wasn't built for owning, nor for anything which lasts. I could mend her spirit, only to go on and break her loving heart. And she would probably think it a poor bargain when the time came.

All the little gods of irony must whoop and weep and roll on the floors of Olympus when they tune in on the night thoughts of a truly fatuous male.

And I hold several international records.

10

I did not know how she would be in the mornnig. I could only hope that she would not be bubbly, girlish and coy.

She was pouring juice when I went into the galley, and she turned gravely to be kissed, knowing it her due. A little tilt to the dark head. A flicker of appraisal in slanted eyes.

"Temperature normal, pulse normal, patient starving," she said.

"What?"

"McGee's clinic. Morning report. I'm having poached."

"Scrambled medium."

"Yessir."

The breakfast was rather silent, but not with strain.

After pouring second coffees, she sat and looked at me and said, "I'm being a hell of a problem to you, Trav."

"I worry about it every minute."

"Thank you for patience and endurance. You have won the Lois Award."

"Hang it with my other plaques."

"I watched the dawn from your sun deck. It was a nice one, with thunderheads. I came to the astonishing conclusion that I better not try to give anything until I've built up something to give. Otherwise, it's just taking."

"In the morning I'm often anti-semantic."

"Any future aggression, if there is any, will have to be yours."

"Sounds valid."

"And if there isn't any, don't go around worrying about what I might be thinking. Last night I collected on my assurance. In advance."

"Okay."

"Finish your coffee and come see what unskilled labor has done to your barge."

The work was worth the admiration I gave it. I shooed her off to the beach, with all her gear. She was back in three minutes just to tell me that she couldn't guarantee she wouldn't get a little nutty from time to time, but she felt she was past the pill period, and then she headed back toward the beach, a lissome broad in her mirrored sunglasses, walking on good legs, and she was far younger than her years, yet old as the sea she approached.

The operator tracked down Harry in New York, from one number to the next.

"In answer to your questions, laddy boy, it is mostly a yes. A few months back some very fine items made an appearance here and there, you might say classic items, the kind you expect there should be a description, like perhaps on an insurance list. But they are clean, I am told. All Asiatic items, with, as usual, some of the faceted stuff cut freehand enough to take a smidgen off the value. They have appeared here and there and worked their way up through the Street, everybody taking the small edge a quality thing brings, and they are by now mostly in the hands of the top houses being mounted in ways worthy of them, and you can find one advertised in *The New Yorker* as a present, page eighty-one, a retail to curl the three hairs I have remaining. It was a goodly number of top items, a minimum of ten, and perhaps no more than fifteen, unless somebody is holding tight. As to source, laddy boy, on the Street I found a word here, a word there, adding up to a smiling savage man, not by any means a fool, unloading one at a time, without haste, for cash, known to slam one man against a wall, and having no trouble thereafter, claiming he'd be back often with more of the same."

"What did he walk away with?"

"Forty thousand minimum. These are important items, laddy boy. And he would wait so proof could be had they were not hot. Cash sets up a certain discount situation, of course, but he played one against another, and did well."

"Could you do as well if you had the same kind of merchandise? Five percent for your trouble?"

"You take my breath away. I might do even better. For ten."

"If I had them, we could dicker."

"You should not put such a strain on this ancient heart."

"Harry, can you get me a big blue star sapphire, say as big as the average he peddled, a fake that would slow an expert down for a few seconds?"

"There are only two kinds of fakes in that area, laddy boy, the very bad ones and the very good ones, and the good ones come high."

"How high?"

"Offhand, one large one."

"Can you rent me one or borrow one and airmail it to me?"

"Switching is very unhealthy."

"It isn't what I have in mind."

"I might be able to arrange it."

"That isn't the question. I have faith in you. Can you arrange it today?"

"Dear boy!"

"I would hate to have to deal with anyone else, particularly if I get hold of anything genuine later on."

"My arm is twisted."

And then, with a thumb in the Yellow Pages, I began checking the marinas. All this great ever-increasing flood of bronze, brass, chrome, Fiberglas, lapstreak, teak, auto pilots, burgees, Power Squadron hats, nylon line, all this chugging winking blundering glitter of props, bilge pumps and self-importance needs dockside space. The optimum image is the teak cockpit loaded soft with brown dazed girls while the eagle-eyed skipper on his fly bridge chugs *Baby Dear* under a lift bridge to keep a hundred cars stalled waiting in the sun, their drivers staring malignantly at the slow passage of the lazy-day sex float and the jaunty brown muscles of the man at the helm. But the more frequent reality is a bust gasket, *Baby Dear* drifting in a horrid chop, girls sunpoisoned and whoopsing, hero skipper clenching the wrong size wrench in barked hands and raising a greasy scream to the salty demons who are flattening his purse and canceling his marine insurance.

But they have to park.

And while the outboarders have infinite choice, those that can house forty-footers are merely legion. I made over an hour of phone calls with the simple query, "Had the *Play Pen* in there lately, forty-foot Stadel custom?"

The assumption was he'd put the damned thing somewhere handy when he'd visited the Mile O'Beach, but that assumption began to grow wan under the negative chorus. So somewhere unhandy, and I began to get into the toll call area, questing up and down the Waterway.

Lois came back from the beach. I sat glowering at the phone. She came back pinked, sun-dazed and slow moving, with spume-salted hair and a sandy butt, displaying upon a narrow palm, with a child's innocence, a small and perfect white shell, saying in a voice still drugged with sun and heat, "It's like the first perfect thing I ever saw, or the first shell. It's a little white suit of armor with the animal dead and gone. What does it mean when things look so clear and so meaningful? Silly little things."

I sat on a low stool, hating the phone.

"What's wrong?" she said, and leaned a hip against my shoulder, a weight oddly warm and heavy and luxurious for such slenderness. It was an uncontrived gesture and in a moment she was aware of it and moved away quickly, startled by herself.

"Where did Junior Allen like to tie up?"

She moved uneasily away, sat on a curve of the couch. "Little places, mostly. Not the great big marinas. I think he liked places where his boat would be biggest. A hose connection and power outlet and fuel. That's all he had to have. And privacy. He liked finger slips where he could tie up with the bow toward the main dock."

"I've been trying the small ones too."

"But after what he did to Mrs. Kerr, wouldn't he go away?"

"I would think so. But where was he beforehand? He couldn't have known that was going to happen. I'd assume he'd move along, thinking she would tell the police."

"Back to the Bahamas?"

"Maybe. I thought I could find where he was, and ask around and get some idea where he was headed. Did he ever say anything about things he wanted to do, or places he wanted to go?"

"He said something one time about going around the Gulf Coast and over to Texas."

"Oh fine."

"Trav, you know he could be tied up at some private place, like he was tied up at my dock."

"That's a lot of help too."

"You asked me. I'm trying to help."

She looked at me with gentle indignation. She was what we have after sixty million years of the Cenozoic. There were a lot of random starts and dead ends. Those big plated pea-brain lizards didn't make it. Sharks, scorpions and cockroaches, as living fossils, are lasting pretty well. Savagery, venom and guile are good survival quotients. This forked female mammal didn't seem to have enough tools. One night in the swamps would kill her. Yet behind all that fragility was a marvelous toughness. A Junior Allen was less evolved. He was a skull-cracker, two steps away from the cave. They were at the two ends of our bell curve, with all the rest of us lumped in the middle. If the trend is still supposed to be up, she was of the kind we should breed, accepting sensitivity as a strength rather than a weakness. But there is too much Junior Allen seed around.

"Find me that boat," I told her.

"What do you mean?"

"What specific or general thing do I have to know that will enable me to locate it?"

She stood up slowly and thoughtfully and went off to take her shower. I knew it was an emotional strain for her. She was trying to wipe every memory of that period out of her mind. And now I was forcing her to remember. They would be tangled memories, filtered through alcohol.

Suddenly she came racing into the lounge. She wore one of my big blue towels in sarong fashion, and had a white towel wrapped around her head. Her face looked narrow and intent. Her features looked more pointed.

"That last trip," she said. "I don't know if it will help. We stopped at some sort of a boat yard in Miami. I can't even remember the name. Something about a new generator. He kept complaining about the noise the generator made. They took up the hatches and got down in the bilge and did a lot of measuring. The man said it would take a long time to get the one Junior Allen wanted. It made him angry. But he ordered it anyway. He left a down payment on it. He ordered some kind of new model that had just been introduced."

She sat beside me and we looked at the Yellow Pages. She ran a slender fingertip down the listings. She stopped. "That's it. That's the one."

Robinson-Rand, down below Dinner Key, off the Ingraham Highway. Shipyard, storage. No job too large, no job too small.

"Maybe it hasn't come in yet," she said in a thin little voice. She shivered. "I'm scared, Trav. I hope it came in and he got it and went away. I hope you never find him."

I had bought Lois a lunch and sent her back to the houseboat. I parked Miss Agnes in Robinson-Rand's sizable lot. Even in the summer doldrums, it was a brisk place. Their storage areas looked full. They had long rows of covered slips, and two big in and out structures for small craft. The shop areas were in big steel buildings. Saws and welding torches and power tools were in operation, even on a Saturday afternoon, but I could guess it was only a skeleton crew working. They had a lot of big cradles and hoists, slips and ways. The office area was built against one end of one of the shop buildings, near a truck dock.

There was one girl working in the office, a plump, impersonal redhead with one eye aimed slightly off center.

"We're not really open," she said.

"I just wanted to check on a generator that was ordered, find out if it has come in yet."

She sighed as though I had asked her to hike to Duluth. "Who placed the order?" Sigh.

"A. A. Allen."

She got up and went over to a bank of file cabinets. She began riffling through cards. "For the *Play Pen?*" Sigh.

"That's right."

She took the card out and frowned at it. "Ordered June second. That's a Kohler 6.5A-23. Goodness, it should be in by now."

"Doesn't it say on the card?"

"No, it doesn't say on the card." Sigh. "All I can tell from the card is that it hasn't been delivered or installed." Sigh.

"Does the card say who handled the order?"

"Of course the card says who handled the order." Sigh. "Mr. Wicker. He isn't here today."

"Joe Wicker?"

"No. Howard Wicker. But people call him Hack."

"Do you keep a running list of the boats you have in?"

"Of course we keep a runnnig list of the boats we have in." Sigh. "Down at the dock office."

"Of course you keep a running list of the boats you have in. Down at the dock office. Thanks a lot."

She looked momentarily disconcerted. "Excuse me. The air conditioning isn't working right. And the phone keeps ringing. And people keep coming here." Sigh.

"I'm sorry too. Be of good cheer, Red."

She smiled and winked the crooked eye and went back to her gunfire typing.

I phoned the only listing for a Howard Wicker from a chilly saloon. A very small child answered and said "Hello." No matter what I said, it kept saying hello. I kept asking it to get its daddy and it kept saying hello, and I began to feel like Shelley Berman. Then the child gave a sudden howl of anguish and a woman with a tense exasperated voice came on the line.

Hack was out in the yard. Hold the line. The child came back on and started giving me the hello again. Tearfully.

"Yes?" Wicker said.

"Sorry to bother you on your day off. I understand you installed a Kohler 6.5A-23 on a forty-foot Stadel custom, and I'd like to know how it worked out."

"What? Oh. I don't know what you mean. It's a good rig. If there's room for it, and you don't hit over a seven thousand watt peak demand, it's going to be okay, isn't it?"

"I meant noise and vibration and so on."

"It's quiet enough for that rating. You're asking about a boat called the *Play Pen?*"

"I think that's the name."

"We got the generator in last Monday or Tuesday, and it hasn't been installed yet. They've phoned in a few times asking about it. I expect they'll phone in again this week. Then bring the boat around and we'll put it in. You want to see how the job goes, I could let you know. What have you got now?"

"An old Samson 10KW diesel. Manual and noisy. And big."

"It would depend on peak load, if you could get along with less."

I told him I would appreciate it if he'd give me a ring when the appointment with the *Play Pen* was set up. A collect call in Lauderdale. He wrote the number down and said he would.

"It won't be too long will it?" I asked. "The *Play Pen* is in the area?"

"Far as I know. He knows it's due about now."

I drove back through late afternoon heat. The world darkened, turned to a poisonous green, and somebody pulled the chain. Water roared down the chute. Rose-colored lightning webbed down. Water bounced knee high, silver in the green premature dusk, and I found a place to pull off out of the way and let the fools gnash each other's chrome and tin-work, fattening the body shops, busying the adjustors, clogging the circuit court calendars. The sign of the times is the imaginary whiplash injury.

Miss Agnes squatted, docile under the roar of rain, and I tried to pull Junior Allen into focus. Like the most untidy little hoodlum knocking over a Friendly Bob Adams Loan Office, he was on a short rein. Or reign. In these documented times, where we walk lopsided from the weight of identifications, only the most clever and controlled man can hope to exist long on a hijacked fortune. And Junior Allen was a felon. Maybe he was clever, but certainly not controlled. Returning to Candle Key to rape and corrupt the lonely woman who found him distasteful had been foolish. Bashing Cathy had been idiotic. Showing gems to the little Haitian bitch had been the act of a careless, overconfident man. He was a swaggering sailor with money in his pocket, and if he kept on being careless, neither he nor the money could last very long. Viewed in that light, his luck was impressive. His victims, thus far, had kept their mouths shut. Perhaps his present victim whoever she might be, might not be so obliging. And I might not have very much time.

A sulphur sun pierced the gloom, and the rain stopped and I drove to the hospital. She could look at me out of both eyes now, and the shape of her mouth looked more familiar. Chook had brought her a pretty new robe. With the nurse's permission, she moved from the bed into a wheelchair, and I pushed her to the sun room at the end of the corridor.

"Tomorrow I can go home," she said.

I moved a chair closer to her. Old bruises turn green and yellow. The old swelling kept her brown eyes pinched small. "Maybe I'm going to catch up with him soon, Cathy."

"What are you going to do?"

"Play it by ear."

"I'd like it fine if you could kill him some way you wouldn't get into trouble about it."

"I didn't know you were so savage about it."

"Savage? I'm not savage about it at all. The way that man does you, he's better dead. I was plain foolish, Trav. Even after everything, I was still hoping. You know? He'd find out it was best he should be back with me. Now wasn't that dumb? I couldn't even let myself know that was what I was wishing on. Then when he taken me and hammering me there in the dark, nobody to hear, not caring if he killed me dead, that killed it for good. I saw his face once when he'd spun me toward the palm tree lights, and he was smiling."

"Had he come looking for you?"

"He didn't say."

"Do you think he did?"

"I think it was just accident. There aren't so many places with a summer show, and a man roving around could come there and be as surprised as I was to see him. Trav, you be careful getting near him. He's mean as anything you like to find in a swamp."

"I'll be careful."

"I have the feeling he's not long for this world, and I don't want him taking you with him when he goes. I think when they had him locked away for five years, something went wrong with him. Something stopped. Something other people have. And he's sly. He must have tricked my daddy, and my daddy was real sly hisself, they say." She stared thoughtfully at me. "I guess you have to be a sly man too. Your face doesn't show much. But go careful with him, like as if he's a snake."

I got back to the *Busted Flush* at six-thirty. The rain had washed the sunset time to a lambent beauty. A fine east wind had driven the bug life inland. Scores of little groups were cocktailing aboard their craft, lazy-talking, working themselves into Saturday night. Buddy Dow, hired skipper of a big lunker owned by an insurance company in Atlanta, had aboard ten vacationing girls from the home office. He had enlisted two recruits and was despairingly in need of more. He tried to enlist me, and I paused for a moment to say no politely. He had them primed. A plain hello was a comedy line that set them all giggling. What Buddy calls the dog-ratio ran pleasantly low on this group. I had the feeling that if I got too close, greedy secretarial hands would haul me aboard, kicking and screaming. They all work toward a memorable vacation.

I went on along to my broad scow, and for a time it seemed as if she wasn't going to unlock it and let me inside. When she did, she went running to the couch and threw herself face down, rigid.

"What's the matter with you?"

An agony had blanched and dwindled her face. "He's here," she whispered.

"Junior Allen?"

"He saw me."

She was too upset to be very coherent, but I got it all out of her. She had gone down to the marine supply place to look for some kind of a small present for me. Just to give me a present. And she had wandered out onto the gas dock just beyond the offices and the tall control tower for the marina. And the *Play Pen* had been there, gassing up. Junior Allen had straightened up, stared at her, grinned at her, and she had fled.

"He didn't follow you?"

"No. I don't think so."

"Was he alone?"

"No."

"Who was with him?"

"I don't know. Young people. Three or four. I don't know. All I could see was him."

"What time was all this?"

"A-about quarter after five, I think."

11

Willy Lazeer is an acquaintance. His teeth and his feet hurt. He hates the climate, the Power Squadron, the government and his wife. The vast load of hate has left him numbed rather than bitter. In appearance it is as though somebody bleached Sinatra, skinned him, and made Willy wear him.

I knew he was off at six, and I knew it took him an hour of beer to insulate him against going home, and I knew where he would be loading up. I sat beside him at the bar. He gave me a mild, dim glance of recognition. His hour was almost up. I prodded his memory.

"*Play Pen. Play Pen.* Sure, I see that today."

"Forty-foot Stadel custom, white topsides, gray hull, blue line. Skippered by a rugged brown guy with white curly hair and small blue eyes and a big smile."

"So?"

"I was wondering where he's docked."

"How should I know, McGee? How the hell should I know?"

"But you do remember him?"

"He paid cash."

"Stopped a little after five?"

"So?"

"What kind of people did he have aboard, Willy?"

"Smart-ass kids."

"Tourists, college kids?"

He stared through me for a moment. "I knew one of them."

"One of the kids?"

"What the hell are we talking about? One of the kids. Yes. You know over the bridge on the right there, past where they're building is a place called Charlie Char-Broil."

"I know the place."

"I seen her there as a waitress. Young kid. They got their names on little badges. Hers is a funny one. Deeleen. I ain't seen her there a couple months. How come I remember her, she got snotty with me one time, bringing me the wrong order."

It was far as he could go with it.

I went back to Lois. She had a glass of bourbon that looked like a glass of iced coffee. Her smile was loose and wet and her eyes didn't track. I took it away from her and took her into her stateroom. She made little tired sighing sounds and lurched heavily against me. I tipped her onto the bed and took her shoes off. In three minutes she was snoring.

I locked up and went off on a Deeleen hunt.

Charlie Char-Broil smelled of burned grease, and she didn't work there anymore. But a friend named Marianne did, a pretty girl except for a rabbit mouth she couldn't quite manage to close. Nineteen, I guessed. Once she was convinced I wasn't a cop, she joined me in a back booth.

"Dee, she got fired from here when they changed the manager. The way it was, she did anything she damn pleased, you know? The manager we had, he was all the time taking her back in the storeroom, and finely somebody told the company. I told her it was the wrong way to act. She had a couple other jobs and they didn't last and I don't see her much anymore. I did see her. But, I don't know, some things can get too rough, you know what I mean? Fun is fun, but it gets too rough. What I found out, on a blind date she got for me, geez, it was a guy like could be my father, you know? And there was a hell of a fight and I found out she took money from him for me to show up. I ask her what she thinks I am anyhow. I think she's going to get in bad trouble, and I don't want to be around, you know."

"Where does she live?"

"Unless she's moved—she moves a lot—she's in the Citrus Inn. It's up like opposite Deerfield Beach, kind of an apartment-hotel kind of thing, sort of old and cruddy. In 2A up there, with a girl named Corry, that's where she was last I knew, getting her unemployment."

That was all the time she could spend with me. She slid out of the booth, patting at the blue and white skirt of her nylon uniform. She seemed to hear the total effect of her own words, and looked a little disconcerted. She was a strong-bodied girl whose rather long neck and small head made her look more delicately constructed than she was. Her fine silky hair was a soft brown with bleached streaks. "Don't get me wrong about Deeleen," she said. "I don't want you should think I'm trine to cut her up. The thing is, she had an unhappy love affair when she was just a kid."

"How old is she how?"

"Oh, she's twenty now." She hesitated. She was obligated to end our little chat with a stylized flourish. The way it's done in serial television. So she wet her little bunny mouth, sleepied her eyes, widened her nostrils, patted her hair, arched her back, stood canted and hip-shot, huskied her voice and said, "See you aroun', huh?"

"Sure, Marianne. Sure."

Bless them all, the forlorn little rabbits. They are the displaced persons of our emotional culture. They are ravenous for romance, yet settle for what they call making out. Their futile, acne-pitted men drift out of high school into a world so surfeited with unskilled labor there is competition for bag-boy jobs in the supermarkets. They yearn for security, but all they can have is what they make for themselves, chittering little flocks of them in the restaurants and stores, talking of style and adornment, dreaming of the terribly sincere stranger who will come along and lift them out of the gypsy life of the two-bit tip and the unemployment, cut a tall cake with them, swell them up with sassy babies, and guide them masterfully into the shoal water of the electrified house where everybody brushes after every meal. But most of the wistful rabbits marry their unskilled men, and keep right on working. And discover the end of the dream. They have been taught that if you are sunny, cheery, sincere, group-adjusted, popular, the world is yours, including barbecue pits, charge plates, diaper service, percale sheets, friends for dinner, washer-dryer combinations, color slides of the kiddies on the home projector, and eternal whimsical romance—with crinkly smiles and Rock Hudson dialogue. So they all come smiling and confident and unskilled into a technician's world, and in a few years they learn that it is all going to be grinding and brutal and hateful and precarious. These are the slums of the heart. Bless the bunnies. These are the new people, and we are making no place for them. We hold the dream in front of them like a carrot, and finally say sorry you can't have any. And the schools where we teach them nonsurvival are gloriously architectured. They will never live in places so fine, unless they contract something incurable.

I went north on the mainland route, past an endless wink and sputter of neon, through the perpetual leaf-fall and forest floor of asphalt, cellophane, candy wrappers, Kleenex, filter tips, ticket halves, Pliofilm and latex. One of Junior Allen's women lay wounded and the other lay drunk, and I was looking for a third.

The Citrus Inn was an old place, a three-story cube of cracked and patched Moorish masonry, vintage 1925, with three entrances, three sets of staircases, three stacks of small apartments. I was on a short, dead-end street in a commercial area. It was across the street from a large truck depot, and bracketed on one side by a shoestring marina and on the other by a BEER-BAIT-BOATS operation which had a tavern specializing in fried fish sandwiches. There was a narrow canal behind the three structures, sea-walled, stagnant.

The Citrus Inn had its own eroding dock, parallel to the sea wall. I had parked in front. I walked around the unlighted side of the Citrus Inn. I stopped abruptly and moved off into deeper shadows. There were two darkened old hulks tied up to the Citrus Inn dock. The third craft was lighted inside, and a weak dock light shone against the starboard side of it and into the cockpit. It shone on the life ring. The *Play Pen*. There were several of them in the cockpit. I couldn't see them distinctly. They had music going, the hesitating rhythms of Bossa Nova. A girl moved to it. Another girl laughed in a slurred sour way. A man said, in a penetrating voice, "Dads, we are just about now out of beer and that is a hell of a note, Dads. Somebody has got to trek way the hell to Barney's. You going to do us like this in the islands, Dads? You going to let us run out of the necessities of life once we get over there?"

Another man rumbled some kind of an answer, and a girl said something which the music obscured. In a few moments two of them came by me, heading for the tavern. I saw them distinctly when they clambered up onto the dock, a husky, sideburned boy with a dull fleshy face, and a leggy awkward girl in glasses.

As they passed me the girl said, "Shouldn't you buy it one time anyway, Pete?"

"Shut up, Patty. It makes Dads happy to spring for it. Why spoil his fun?"

I had my first look at Junior Allen. It wasn't much of a look. He was a shadowy bulk in the cockpit of the boat, a disembodied rumble of a voice. A single bark of laughter.

When I got back to the *Busted Flush,* Lois was still out. I sat her up. She whined at me, her head heavy, her eyes closed. I got her up and took her over to the beach and walked her until she had no breath for complaining. She trudged along, dutiful as a naughty child. I walked her without mercy, back and forth, until her head was clear, and then we sat on a public bench to give her time to catch her breath.

"I've got a ghastly headache," she said in a humble voice.

"You earned it."

"I'm sorry, Trav. Really. Seeing him . . . scared me so."

"Or gave you an excuse?"

"Don't be hateful."

"I just don't like to see you spoil what you're trying to do."

"It won't happen again."

"Do you mean that?"

"I don't know. I don't *want* it to happen again. But I keep thinking . . . he could come walking along this beach right now."

"Not tonight. He's busy."

"What!"

I told her how and where I had found him. With a sideburned boy named Pete, and three girls named Deeleen, Patty and Corry.

"From the little I heard, he's taking all of them or some of them on a cruise to the Bahamas. They think they're working him. They think they've found a very soft touch. They call him Dads."

"Can't those poor kids see what he is?"

"Cathy didn't. You didn't."

"What are you going to do?"

"Go see if I can make a date tomorrow afternoon."

"They might be gone."

"I think he'll wait until he gets the new generator installed."

"But what if he leaves with them in the morning?"

"If that seems too dreadful to you, Lois, you can always get drunk."

"You don't have to be so cruel."

"You disappointed me."

"I know. I'm sorry."

"How's your head now?"

"A little better, I think. Trav?"

"Yes, honey."

"Trav, I'm so hungry I could eat this bench."

When I took a look at the outdoors Sunday morning I knew they weren't going anywhere. It was a sparkling day. The wind had swung around and it was coming out of the northeast, hard and steady. A wind like that builds too much of a chop out in the Stream for anything the size of Junior Allen's cruiser. It would be running seven or eight feet out there, and very dirty.

I waited until noon and then drove up to the Citrus Inn. Apartment 2A was in the center section on the second floor. I wore a courting costume, summer version. T shirt, khaki slacks, baseball cap, straw shoes, an eager smile, and a bottle of good bourbon in a brown paper bag. I rapped on the scarred and ornate old wooden door, and rapped again, and a girl-voice yelled in an exasperated tone, "Just a minute!"

The latch rattled. The door opened an inch and a half, and I saw a tousle of dark hair and a segment of tan face and a cold green unfriendly eye. "Whaddya want?"

"I'm looking for Deeleen."

"She's not here."

"Are you Corry?"

"Who the hell are you?"

"A friend of a friend."

"Like who?"

"Marianne, works at Charlie Char-Broil."

"That silly bitch hasn't got any friends."

Had I done any pleading or begging, she would have slammed the door. So I stood easy, mildly smiling. It's a relaxed area. There is a code for all the transients. If you are presentable, unhurried, vaguely indifferent, it is a challenge. I was having better luck with this than I expected, up to this point. I wanted it to continue. If you push against hostility and suspicion, you merely increase it. In a few moments I saw a little less animosity.

"What's with this Marianne and you looking for Deeleen? I don't get it."

"I don't want to confuse you, Corry."

"There's some facts of life I should know?"

"I used to see Deeleen around there and never got to know her, and then she left and I was wondering about her, if she'd left town, and I asked around and Marianne said maybe she was still here. So this was an empty day, and I had this jug, so I thought I would come see. But if she's as friendly as you are, I guess it wasn't much of an idea."

She examined me for at least twenty silent seconds. "Stick around a minute," she said, and closed the door. It was ten minutes before she came out. She had stiffened her dark hair somehow until it looked like a Japanese wig. She wore a swim suit and an open cabana coat. The swim suit was a black and white sheath, the black faded and the white slightly grubby. Though flawed by a bulldog jaw and a little too much meat across the hips, she was reasonably presentable. She closed the door and smiled up at me and said, "You're practically a giant, huh? You got a name?"

"Trav."

"There's a kid in the apartment sleeping it off. She was whoopsing half the night from beer. Come on, I'll show you something."

I followed her down the short corridor to a back window overlooking the dock. A girl in a very brief bikini lay on a pad on the cabin roof of the *Play Pen*. I looked down at her over Corry's shoulder.

She looked up at me quizzically. "I don't blame you at all to come looking, she's built so cute, huh?"

"Tasty."

"But if she's absolutely the only idea you came up here with, honey, you can save yourself the trouble. She's all set up with the guy owns the boat."

"It's a lot of boat. Whose is it?"

"An old guy named Allen. We call him Dads. We're going to go far and wide on that boat, man. We're going to the Bahamas on that boat. Would you believe it, he says it's hard to find people to go cruising with you? Isn't that a crazy problem. But the way things are, honey, she won't play. It could screw up the boat ride." She turned toward me from the window with just the slightest hint of the stylized posture of the model, the small mechanics of display, seeking approval. "So?"

She had invited inspection and I gave it, then said, "You have to know when to change your ideas. You have to stay loose."

"The thing is," she said, "I wouldn't want you should have any terrible disappointment. I mean on account of Dee."

This was the small smoky game of appraisal and acceptance, offer and counteroffer. She had narrowed it down to that one response necessary to her esteem. So I responded as she wished. "If that was you down there in the sun, Corry, and Dee up here with me, then I could feel disappointed."

She smirked and beamed and preened, then linked my arm and took me down onto the dock. "Hey!" she said. Deeleen sat up, owlish in huge black glasses. "Where is everybody?" Corry asked as I helped her aboard.

"Dads took off someplace in Pete's car. Pete went down to see Mitch about if he's got the motor back on the little boat yet. Patty okay?"

"She's still sacked out up there."

Deeleen got up and came clambering slowly and cautiously down into the cockpit. At a thirty-foot distance she was a very attractive, ripe-bodied young girl. At close range the coarseness and the sleaziness of the materials used in construction were all too evident. Her tanned hide had a coarse and grainy look. Her crinkle of putty-colored hair looked lifeless as a Dynel wig. The strictures of the bottom half of the bikini cut into the belly-softness of too many beers and shakes, hamburger rolls and french fries. The meat of her thighs had a sedentary looseness. Her throat and her ankles and the underside her wrists were faintly shadowed with grime. There was a coppery stubble in her armpits, and a bristle of unshaven hair on her legs, cracked red enamel on her toenails. The breast band of the bikini was just enough askew to reveal a brown new-moon segment of the nipple of her right breast.

"Deeleen, I want you should meet Trav," Corry said.

"Hi," Deeleen said, looking me over. She had a broad mouth and a pink stain of lipstick on one front tooth. She was obviously awaiting further identification.

"That Marianne works at the Char-Broil, she told him one time we were out this way, and he came around. I was telling him about going on the cruise with Dads." It was very casual, but totally explicit. He came looking for you, but I told him the score and he settled for me.

Deeleen gave a little shrug of acceptance and slumped into a canvas chair, spraddled and hot. There was a little roll of fat around her waist. She hitched the bikini top up. High against the meat of the insides of her thighs a fringe of pubic hair escaped the scanty fabric which encased the plump and obvious pudendum. A few years ago she would have been breathtakingly ripe, and even now, in night light, with drinks and laughter, there would be all the illusions of freshness and youth and desirability. But in this cruelty of sunlight, in this, her twentieth year, she was a record of everything she had let them do to her. Too many trips to too many storerooms had worn the bloom away. The freshness had been romped out, in sweat and excess. The body reflects the casual abrasions of the spirit, so that now she could slump in her meaty indifference, as immunized to tenderness as a whore at a clinic.

"What's with squirrel-face Marianne?" she asked indifferently.

"Nothing new."

Corry shed her cabana coat, put canvas cushions on the wide transom and stretched out. They had stopped surveying me. I had passed inspection.

"Even with that wind it's almost too goddamn hot," Corry said. "Anybody figured out what we're going to do?"

"I'll wait'n see what Dads wants."

Corry turned more toward Dee, closing me out of the conversation. "Was it the way you figured?" she asked.

Dee gave a flat, mirthless laugh. "Only more so."

"Anybody want a drink?"

They both stared at me as though startled to find I was still there. "Sure," Deeleen said. "What is it?"

"Bourbon."

"Okay," Corry said.

"But he locked it when he took off," Dee said. "You can't get down where the ice and glasses and stuff is. Corry, you want to bring stuff down from upstairs?"

"It's after one," Corry said. "He can get some stuff from Barney, can't he?"

"Ask to buy some of the big paper cups," Dee told me. "And get a six-pack of Coke, huh?"

Barney's service was slow, and he overcharged me for the cups, Coke and ice. By the time I returned to the *Play Pen,* the girls had shuffled me and dealt me. Corry informed me of their approval and of the choice that had been made. She did it by rubbing the back of my neck while I fixed her drink. We moved back under the overhang, out of the direct weight of the sun. With the breeze, it was comfortable. As they began to get a little high, they included me more naturally in their conversation. We talked about the cruise. Pete arrived. He had a dead handshake, like a canvas glove full of hot sand. Corry gave him a key to 2A and he went up to see how Patty was. There was discussion about whether she would go on the cruise. She would have to lie to her folks.

Suddenly Junior Allen swung aboard, leaped, landed lightly. He was immaculate in white sport shirt, white slacks, pale blue yachting cap. I guessed he was nearing forty. I had not been prepared for him to look so powerful and so fit. He was broad, with shoulders so packed and corded with muscle they gave him a slightly simian posture, the impression enhanced by the extra-long weight and heft of brown tattooed arms, and the short legs, slightly bowed. He had a brown, seamed, knotty face, broad, smiling broadly, the smile squinching the small blue eyes. It was a friendly grin. It was a likable grin. It did not change in any way as he looked at me.

"Hello, kids," he said. His voice was a brassy rumble. He rumpled Dee's lifeless hair with a big brown paw. "Who we got aboard, little sweetheart?"

She was transformed. She was elfin, lisping, adoring, his ripe, dumpy little child. "This is Trav, darling. He's with Corry. Trav, this is Dads Allen. He's the one owns this boat. Hasn't it got a cute name?"

"It's a *very* cute name," I said.

He was quick. He caught my hand in exactly the way I didn't want him to catch it, and watched my mouth as he ground my knuckle bones.

"Glad you like it," he said. "Welcome aboard."

He took his keys out and unlocked the hatchway to the cabins. He pulled Dee to her feet, slapped her bare rump and said, "Little sweetheart, you go bring up some decent glasses and the vodka."

Little sweetheart snickered and arched and went below dutifully. Junior Allen sat where she had been, and patted Corry's bare knee and said, "What's your line of work, Trav?"

"Whatever I happen to find. A little charter boat work in season. Take boats north and south for the winter folks. Fry cook. Half-ass marine mechanic. You name it."

After little sweetheart brought his bottle and the glasses, he fixed himself a drink. He beamed at me. "These kids tell you about the trip? I'm going to take four of 'em over and show them the islands. Hell, I've got the boat, the time and the money. It's the least I can do."

Had I not known the history, I would have readily bought the image he was projecting. Fatuous, expansive idiot, hooked by the tired flesh of little sweetheart, taking her and three of her friends on the romantic tropic tour.

"Passenger list still open?" I asked, smiling back.

That changed his eyes but not his grin. "If Pete and I sleep in the two bunks forward, that leaves the main cabin for the gals. I can sleep six, but they got to be very good close friends." He roared with laughter. "Sorry we can't sign you on, buddy."

"I get to be the fifth wheel," Corry said bitterly.

"How so, girl?".

She stared coldly at him. "What's so complicated, Dads. You and Dee, Pete and Patty. And good old Corry. Hell, sign him on. I'll need somebody to talk to. Maybe you'll need somebody to run your boat."

"I never need any help with a boat," he said, smiling. "Or anything else, little sweetheart."

"I'm Corry. She's little sweetheart, Dads."

He patted her knee again and beamed at her. "You'll have fun. Don't you worry about it a minute."

"Always bitching about something," Dee said. "Always."

Pete and Patty came aboard. And within minutes I knew what Junior Allen was after. At first glance Patty was unattractive, an impression derived from the gawkiness and the glasses. They kidded her coarsely about getting sick, and she responded by clowning. The clowning was her defense. Her breasts were high and immature and sharp against the fabric of her blouse. Her legs were long and pale and lovely. There was a colt grace about her, a loveliness of gray eyes behind the heavy lenses, a ripe warm sensitivity of mouth. She was Lois, years ago, and in a different social stratum. She was wasted on the lout dullness of side-burned Pete. She was fresh and fragile and vulnerable. She was the obvious victim, and once he had the quartet where they could not escape him, it would require no great effort to turn the other three into accomplices. They were coarsened already. They would help Junior Allen teach their funny clown-girl the facts of life, help him take her down into nightmare where, finally, her clowning would do her no good at all.

We drank. His young pals called him Dads and patronized him. He grinned and grinned. Deeleen teased him. Corry kidded him. Pete ignored him. Junior Allen grinned and grinned and grinned. But some instinct made him wary of me. I would look toward him and see those little blue eyes studying me over that wide smile. He was a big old tom watching benignly as the mice cavorted. He didn't want another cat at the party. There wasn't enough for two.

But I did find out what I wanted to know. Pete said, in answer to a

question by Patty, that they would leave as soon as Junior Allen had
some work done on the boat. They would move their gear aboard and
go down to Miami where the work was to be done, and cross over to
Bimini from there. The cruise would last a week or ten days. Dads was
paying all expenses. Dads was a live one. Patty would tell her people
she was visiting a friend, a girl who lived in Jacksonville. Dads said
they'd probably be leaving Tuesday or Wednesday. Don't bring along a
lot of stuff. We'll be roughing it, kids.

We ate Barney's fish sandwiches. We switched to beer. In the late afternoon the group split up. Pete took Patty home. Dads and Dee stayed
aboard. I went up to the apartment with Corry. They were dingy rooms,
small, high-ceilinged, too many layers of paint on the walls, the rugs
dusty, the cheap furniture stained and scarred, the utilities primitive.
She had spent the last hour back in the sun. She was dazed with sun and
beer. She opened us two fresh beers and then went off to take a shower.
She gave me a book to look at. It was a thick portfolio of eight-by-ten
glamor shots of her, girlie shots, nude and semi-nude studies, with
tricky lighting effects. She had been a couple of years younger, I suspected, when they had been taken. Some were quite attractive, some
were remarkably tasteless, and the balance were perfectly standard—the
tawny back-lighted bulge of breasts and buttocks, and the standardized
glowing wet-mouthed smile of enticement. She said the photographer
friend had sold quite a lot of them to magazines. I could believe her.
The figure was standard adequate and so was the photographic technique. After I had finished the book and long after the shower had
stopped, I heard her calling me in a small voice. I went to the bedroom.
She had pulled the yellow shades down, making a dim golden light in
the shabby room. She lay naked on the bed with a black towel across
her loins. "Hello there, darling," she said. She wore the same smile as
in the photographs, but drowsier.

"Hello yourself."

Wrestler's jaw, sleepy green eyes, huge smooth brown thighs. She
yawned and said, "Less have a li'l love and a li'l nap, sweetie."

"Let me borrow a shower first."

"Sure. Sure, you go 'head. But hurry it up. I'm in such a wonnerful
mood, lover."

I went into the bathroom. It was a morass of stale towels and sour
swim suits, fetid and perfume-sweet, soapy and damp. It astonished me
not to find moss on the walls, mushrooms in the corners, ferns behind

the john. The stream of water was feeble and tepid. I made the shower last a long long time. I used the least damp towel I could find. I opened the bathroom door with great care, and as I had hoped and expected, she was making a regular little snare-drum snore, saying "Paah" with each exhalation. I dressed stealthily, tiptoed to the bed, removed the black towel and tossed it into the bathroom. I put my empty beer can on the floor next to hers. In the living room I found a postcard and a pencil stub. I wrote, "Corry, sweet: Even when you're half asleep, you're marvelous. I'll be in touch, honey." I put it on the bed on the far side of her and tiptoed out, grinning like an idiot. Or like Dads.

But the grin had the feel of a suture. These are the little losers in the bunny derby, but they lose on a different route than the Mariannes, or the ones you see in the supermarket on the nights when they double the green stamps, coming in junk cars, plodding the bright aisles, snarling at their cross sleepy kids. Deeleen and Corry save wistfulness for thoughts of the key clubs. They could be the center fold in anybody's sex book. You have to stay with the kicks. Age twenty and age twenty-one. The cats always show up. The phone always rings. Friends have friends. It isn't like anything was going to wear out, man. It isn't like they were going to stop having conventions. And you get a little tired or a little smashed or a little bored, so you throw a big fast busy fake and it is over in nothing at all. And learn the ways to work them for the little gifts here and there. Like maybe a cruise. Or the rent. Or a couple beach outfits by Cole. Friendship gifts. Not like you were really working at it. The ones work at it, there is always some character taking the money, and there can be police trouble and all that. You work waitress once in a while. The rest of it is dates, really. One date at a time. And some laughs, and if you're short, he can loan you. And other numbers to call when there's a whole bunch of guys.

This is the queasy shadowland, and they don't even work hard at that because they have never learned to work at anything. They turn sloppy, and when the youngness is gone, there isn't much left. Just the dead eyes and the small meaty skills and the feeling their luck went bad sometime when they weren't watching. Fifteen to twenty-five is the span, and they age quickly and badly. These are the bunnies who never find a burrow.

I got back to Lois in the hot blue dusk and she was extraordinarily docile. She wore a little navy blue dress with a starched white collar, and she had her dark hair flattened to severity. She gave the impression she was dedicating her life to sobriety and good works.

I forgave her all indiscretions, and her dark eyes glowed.

After dinner I told her about the cruise. I told her what I planned to do. We went over the plans, amending them, tightening them here and there. We did not talk of the end of it, even though the end was implicit in the things that had to happen before the end.

She kissed me a good-night with quick cool lips, a dark glance that swiveled demurely away.

In my bed I thought of the brutal leathery hands of Junior Allen. Behind the agreeable grin he was as uncompromising as a hammer. Beast in his grin-mask. A clever, twisted thing, hunting for that perversion of innocence, the horrification of gentleness which would feed his own emptiness.

And I began thinking of that gentleness nearby. I computed the distance with care. Twenty-one feet, perhaps, from bed corner to bed corner. Would it not be good for her spirit, her morale, to be desired? Left alone, would she become dubious of her own time of gentle aggression? And would not her fastidious litheness take away the heavy taste of the fleshy girls in the Citrus Inn? McGee, the Perfidious. Rationalizer. Womanizer. Gonadal argumentation. Go to sleep.

Was she on her left side? Her right side? Was she wakeful too? Were her eyes open in the same darkness, listening to the same whispery drone of the air conditioning? Was she wondering why I did not desire her?

Go to sleep, McGee, for God's sake. You want a permanent dependent?

I sat up. My heart was bumping and my breath was shallow. I went in there, moving as silently as a drift of smoke. She would be sleeping. I would turn right around and glide away from there.

I moved close to the bed, barely making out the dark spill of the pillowed hair, holding my breath to try to hear the cadence of her breathing. She made a small throaty sound of total contentment, of a perfect gladness, and reached and found my wrist and drew me to her, flipping the sheet and blanket aside, presenting herself so totally, guiding us with such an artful ease, that as I lay with her we were joined, her readiness and her long exultant shudder a confession of what her night thoughts had been. After a few moments she stilled us, so sweetly enclasped, saying, as she turned us, "Wait, darling. Please. The way we talked tonight. I could not really look at you. You couldn't really look at me. Because we couldn't say anything about the end of it. And that's a shadow. You know it is."

"There isn't any other choice."

"You know there is. I can charge him with rape. It's true enough, you know. I can testify. They can put him away."

"It won't look very good for you. Staying with him."

"Look good to whom? I care about my opinion of myself and your opinion of me. No one else. He terrorized me. I'm articulate. I can make anyone see how it was. And I can talk to Cathy and she will identify him as the man who beat her. Between the two of us, darling, we can make certain he'll be put away for a long time. Get the first part of it done, and before he can retaliate, we'll go to the police, Cathy and I."

"I don't think that's the way to . . ."

"I want it that way. Promise."

"But . . ."

She had her fingers laced at the nape of my neck. She gave me a hearty tug. "Promise!"

"You have me at a disadvantage."

"Ah, I have you at an advantage, McGee. Promise!"

". . . All right."

She pulled strongly. She rocked her wide mouth against my shoulder in a dainty, exacting, continuing, irresistible demand. And at last murmurously curled herself into sleep, the small love words falling away into heavy slumber. Once she was gone I had a little time to think of the promise. I looked at it coldly. It was a tactical stupidity. Junior Allen, once he was trapped, would spoil everything he could reach. He would try to make deals. And he would have the knowledge of Sergeant David Berry's fortune to bargain with, stolen, restolen, and stolen once again . . . if all went well for me.

Yet I knew I would keep the promise. Try to salvage something. She moaned in her sleep. Her long legs twitched. She was running from an old horror. I stroked her hair and kissed her eyes and she came half awake and sighed and settled back again.

If it all went wrong, would anyone ever be able to comfort Patty Devlan?

The small insured package from Harry arrived Monday morning. When I got back from the post office, Lois, excited and nervous, told me that Howard Wicker had called collect and left the message that the *Play Pen* was set up for a ten o'clock appointment Tuesday morning for installation of the new generator.

"It's moving so quickly," she said, wide-eyed.

I opened the package and took out the imitation gem. It was deep blue, big as a songbird's egg, with a bright and perfect star. I did a stupid thing. I bent and rolled it across the floor toward her. It rolled crookedly. Had it been a snake she could not have leaped back more violently, ashen and trembling, putting her hand to her throat, looking sick.

"Just like that," she whispered.

"Pick it up."

She hesitated a long moment, then reached and picked it up. Her color was coming back. She studied it and looked at me. "This really isn't real?"

"Not unless my friend made a horrible mistake."

"It's beautiful."

"Cornflower blue. Long ago they were thought to be love charms. It wouldn't fool an expert."

"Will it fool Junior Allen?"

"For just long enough, I think."

"My God, Trav, be careful!"

I took it away from her and wrapped it in some of the tissue from the small box and put it into my pocket.

She wore blue sailcloth shorts I had not seen before, a blouse with a narrow blue and white horizontal stripe. We had a connubial flavor this morning, but awkward. I had stayed the night with her, and when the early snarl of the fishermen leaving had awakened me, I had made love to her again. Without words. Afterward, she had rolled onto her stomach and wept, and could not say why and could not be soothed. She had showered first, and when I came out she was busy fixing breakfast, her mouth small, her face prim, her eyes evasive.

"What are you going to do?" I asked her.

"Just some lawyer things, about the sale of the house. It won't take long."

"Make it last. Keep busy. Keep your mind off this."

I offered her Miss Agnes, but she decided she would rather take a cab. She changed to a skirt and left. There is a cabstand up by the charter boat docks.

I looked at a chart and estimated that Junior Allen would cast off at about seven to be at Robinson-Rand by ten. With happy cruise passengers. Suddenly the careful plan seemed full of basic flaws. How could I be so certain he kept the loot aboard the *Play Pen?*

Logically, that was the best place for it. He was good with his hands. He'd had all the time in the world to prepare a hiding place. A forty-foot cruiser is a complex piece of equipment. It would take days to make a careful search of every inch of it. I'd had a good opportunity to study the layout, and saw no good reason why my shortcut wouldn't work. If the random factors didn't get too random. If they didn't get out of control. He'd had more luck than he deserved.

And I had done my homework on him. Know the man, know the terrain, know the values. Nothing had been wasted and, I hoped, nothing overlooked.

There is as much danger in overestimating as in underestimating the quality of the opposition.

A. A. Allen, Junior, came through as a crafty, impulsive and lucky man. He had gone after the sergeant's fortune with guile and patience, but now that he had begun to have the use of it, he was recklessly impatient to find his own rather perverse gratifications. Sanity is not an absolute term. Probably, in the five years of imprisonment, what had originally been merely a strong sexual drive had been perverted into a search for victims. He had indulged himself with erotic fantasies of gentle women, force, terror, corruption. Until, finally, the restolen fortune became merely a means to that end, to come out and live the fantasies.

Cathy was a victim. And then Lois Atkinson. And Patty Devlan was next. As if each satisfaction required that the next victim be more vulnerable, more open to terror. Taste is quickly jaded. Make a projection of his trend and his needs, and it might well end up with the jump-rope set, and then become murderous because smaller mouths would not stay closed.

Good old Dads. Would honey like a nice boat ride on the nice man's boat? Would sweetie like a nice ten-day nightmare?

The five of them aboard would, catalyzed by a total isolation and the brute heat of the islands in August, and by the closeness of flesh in a confined space, by the liquor, by the meaty and casual permissiveness of the girls from the Citrus Inn, finally embark on those permutations and interrelations which would fit Junior Allen's fantasies. Good old Dads would gradually take charge, and all the fragile alarms of Miss Patty would find no response in the sun-dulled and drink-dulled paganism of Corry and Deeleen and Pete, find among them no protective conspiracy to save her from that inevitable result of Junior Allen's sly maneuvering, that obligatory scene for her when good old Dads would, smiling, and with grotesque ham-handed imitation of tenderness, gather her squeaking and whimpering and pleading into the seaman's bunk for that thickened and driving instruction, that hammering indoctrination which would thrust her quickly along the road of not giving a damn, not for Pete, not for herself, not for any of the abandoned and gentle dreams. Poor frantic little clown-girl, hiding the loveliness behind the heavy lenses, the shrill guffaw, the exaggerated gawkiness. Have some nice candy, sweetheart, and go with the nice man in his nice car, and wave good-by to all your friends.

I had made a note of the phone number in the Citrus Inn apartment, and I phoned. Deeleen answered. "Who? Oh sure. Hi. You want Corry? Well, she isn't here. You want her, what you do is call that bitch after I've gone."

"What's the matter?"

"I've had it with her, boy. Believe me, I've had it. You should have hung around. It was a big evening. She got drunk and she got nasty. I'm telling you, we're splitting up."

"Is the cruise off?"

"Hell no! We're leaving from here six-thirty tomorrow morning, and go someplace to get some work done on the boat and leave from there and go to Bimini at night. In the moonlight. Like I told her, the only thing I want is come back and find her moved out. She says I should move out. Where does she get that? I found this place, didn't I? Who needs her? She likes to spoil everything for everybody. The thing was, she snuck off with Pete. He's a nice kid, but what's the point? She knew he's been trying to make out with Patty for months, God knows why, but that's their business, isn't it. She had to know it would bitch up the cruise and all. It was a mess around here last night, Patty crying her eyes out. So she busted up the trip sort of, but she didn't spoil it. That's what we decided last night after she came back to the boat with Pete, both of them stoned, and there was a big fight and they took off. Just Dads and Patty and me. And the hell with Corry and Pete. I don't know where they are, and nobody cares. The cruise'll get Patty's mind off him. The thing is, there'd have been no harm done if Pete gets from her what Patty won't give him yet, but she has to come back smashed and bragging about it in front of Patty."

"How did it all start, Dee?"

"I don't know. We were all just kidding around, rough kidding maybe, and Corry got sore at something Dads said, and then Pete got sore at something Patty said to Corry, and then Corry went away, and a little while later Pete slipped away."

My admiration for Junior Allen was reluctant. He had simplified things for himself. They could not know that they had been maneuvered, any more than Cathy had known in the beginning. So he could set off with his little putty-haired pig, and with the wan victim of the lover's quarrel and the betrayal.

"I was going to stop around a little later on, Dee, and have a bon voyage drink with you people."

"There's nobody here now but me, Trav. Dads is off picking up supplies. Patty went home. She's coming back tonight and stay here at the apartment so we can get off at six-thirty like Dads wants. My stuff is aboard already, so I'll probably sleep aboard tonight. Maybe Patty too, if she wants. What you could do, you could come around tonight because four would be better'n three for a bon voyage drink?"

"You don't think Corry will be back?"

"Man, I *know* she won't be back. She and Pete took off together, and they're shacked someplace. She's out of the picture, Trav. You know, I wisht Patty was more of a doll, and then maybe you'd like to come along, because now there's room. What you do, when you come around, you take a good look at her. It could turn out three's a crowd and she'll need comforting the way she feels now. She's really got a nice complexion. And she says things you would laugh yourself sick when she's feeling good."

"That would be up to Dads."

"You can come around and if you like the idea, then we can ask him, but it wouldn't be fair not telling you you don't make out with Patty. She's got a thing about it, scared or something. I don't know. Maybe it would be different, off on a cruise. The way I figure it, if you want to go, honey, I can make Dads do about anything I want. Come right down to it, this cruise was my idea in the first place."

"I guess he can afford it."

"A guy like that, he gets what he wants and I get what I want, so it works out nice, and he wants to keep it that way. You come around later on, huh?"

"I'll be there."

"You don't have to bring any bottle, honey. Dads has loaded cases of it aboard."

My lady returned. Tilty eyes, swirl of a white skirt, little beads of the hotness on her upper lip and at her hairline.

I took her hands. Swung her around. "You are a fine fine thing."

"What's happened to you?"

"I like lovely ladies. You are refreshing."

"I'm hot and sticky."

"And rich?"

"I mailed the check to the bank." I beamed at her. She asked me again. "What's going on?"

"It's the contrast, I think. Because you can cry and not know why. Because I was looking around and saw your toothbrush. And some diaphanous items dripping dry in our shower stall. And because you have tidy hips, and when you are very passionate, it is all of you trying to say what your heart is saying, not just an end in itself—which sounds like a vulgar pun and isn't at all."

"Have you been drinking?"

"I'm drunk with power. Phantom McGee strikes again. Junior

Allen is a stupid crafty man. And McGee is going to put him out of business."

She looked alarmed. "Darling, he's a terrible man."

"I am even more terrible in my wrath. How's this for glower?"

"Remarkable."

"No hairs in the sink and you put the butter away."

She looked owlish. "Are we engaged?"

"Ask me again, after we put this dull, foolish, sly fellow out of commission."

She swallowed. "We?"

"I need one very small assist from you."

She swallowed again. "And this act you're putting on is supposed to give me confidence?"

"Doesn't it?"

"Not very much."

"No danger for you."

"You know what just seeing him did to me."

"I know. Lois, he just isn't that ominous. Evil, but not ominous. Sly, but not prescient. Once he is off balance, he will stay off balance, and fall heavily. And the law will gather him in."

She sat, her face wan and thoughtful. "What do you want me to do, Travis?"

In the sultry blue dusk, the three of us lounged in the spacious cockpit of the *Play Pen,* kindly old lump-jawed, crinkle-eyed Dads Allen in his spotless whites, Deeleen slumped and placid in low-waisted short shorts and a narrow halter which provided a startling uplift, Fearless McGee in pale blue denims and an old gray sport shirt. McGee with a short sturdy pry bar taped to his leg, and an old white silk sock in his pocket, with a goodly heft of bird shot knotted into the toe of it.

A lazy hour of the day. Deeleen yawned and said, "Patty should be along any time." She lazily scratched her belly, her nails making a whispering, fleshy, sensuous sound. "How about Trav coming along with us, lover?"

"I don't know whether I want to," I said.

Dee snickered. "He wants another look at Patty, huh?"

"We haven't invited him yet," Junior Allen said.

"What I want to do over there," Deeleen said, "I want me one of those buckets with the glass in the bottom, and you look at the coral and fish and stuff. And I want to go shopping in Nassau. Are you going to stake me for a little shopping, lover?"

"All you can use," he said, his smile white in the night. Lights were reflected on the still black water of the sea-walled canal. Two kinds of music merged in the softness of the night.

"Geez, I wish we could take off tonight, as soon as Patty gets here," she said.

"How is she going to get here?" I asked.

"She's taking a cab, like to go to the bus station, but she isn't," Dee said. She tilted her glass. The ice rattled up against her lips. I had been trying to time the drinks, and this time her glass and mine were empty, and Junior Allen's was more than half full. I stood up and reached and took her glass and said, "Okay if I fix a couple?"

"Go ahead," he said.

I went below. There was a light on in the galley. Spotless galley. Pristine whites. Trim happy ship. I gave her a heavy shot and hoped it would cover the other taste. Twisted the two capsules open, spilled the powder, stirred it in. A powerful barbiturate. Even with the liquor, I was more than reasonably sure it would do her no harm. She was a young and healthy animal. Fifteen minutes after she got it down, she would become unbearably sleepy. It would knock her out for a good fourteen hours, and leave her dulled and lethargic for the following two days. I wondered with a certain irony if it wasn't practically what Junior Allen had all planned for her, and I was merely jumping the gun. Or maybe he had decided she would be a willing accomplice.

I put no liquor in mine.

She murmured thanks when I gave her the drink. I had observed her drinking habits. One swallow at a time, one minute between swallows, until it all was gone. The taste seemed to suit her.

A breeze moved the cruiser, nudged it gently against a piling.

"She oughta be here pretty soon," Dee said. "If she doesn't come, the hell with her, lover. Who needs her?"

"She'll be along," Junior Allen said.

"Just the three of us, we could have a ball," Dee said. "She's not much of a swinging thing. Who needs her?" She yawned. "And she'll be drag-assin' around, crying over Pete anyways."

Dusk had deepened into night, and I saw the stars, and two planes winking, and heard the cheeing of the night insects mingled with the sound of music.

Deeleen yawned vastly and said, "I can't keep my eyes open. Lover, I'm going to go sack out for a while." She stood up heavily. She looked at him and made a kissing sound. As she passed me, she dragged her fingertips across my cheek. She went below, wobbling along the narrow area between the bunks as though the *Play Pen* were in a choppy sea. She bent and rolled herself heavily onto a bunk. From where I sat, I could see a narrow path of light from the galley light stretching diagonally across her, across the downy small of her back, the deep crease of her waist and the high gluteal round of her hip. Sweet dreams, sweet girl. Slide way way down. Stay out of the action.

I talked with Junior Allen. He didn't have his mind on it. He was crouched in the brush, and he could taste lamb, and he was alerted for the first shy sound of the little hoofs coming along the trail. I gently and indirectly advanced the idea of my coming along, and he firmly closed the door. He got up and sprang nimbly onto the dock, snapped the weak dock light on, checked his lines, adjusted a fender and came aboard again, restless.

Suddenly a man came onto the dock out of the shadows. He wore a gaudy shirt, wrinkled pants and a bright red fishing hat.

"Anybody here name of Mister Allen?" he asked in a soft voice.

"I'm Allen."

The man fumbled in his shirt pocket and took out a piece of paper. He squatted on the edge of the dock and held it out and said, "Apex Taxi, Mister Allen. You're to call the lady at this here number."

Junior Allen snatched it and turned it toward the light and looked at it. "What lady? She give this to you?"

"No, sir. I got called over the radio and put it down on that paper. They say come here and find you and give it to you." He straightened up and hesitated for a moment, and then went back the way he had come.

"Probably from Patty," I said.

It was the spur he needed. He hesitated, and I could sense that he was considering ordering me ashore and locking up, locking Deeleen on the inside. I slumped deeply in the canvas chair and said, "If it isn't her, and she should come while you're off phoning, I'll tell her you'll be right on back."

"You do that," he said. He sailed up onto the dock and went off. He had a springy and muscular gait, like a Percheron in a spring pasture.

I counted to ten and then went below. I found the lights and turned them on. I went through that boat like a nervous whirlwind, yanking out the drawers and dumping them, pawing through stowage areas. I had little hope of finding a thing, but I wanted it to look like a thorough search. And as I yanked and scurried and spilled, I was pleading with Lois. "Keep him going, baby. Keep him hanging on the line. Keep him hooked." We had planned some interesting things to say to the monster. In spite of the racket I was making, Deeleen did not make a quiver.

I selected a spot very carefully, a lighted place where his glance would fall naturally, and I placed the fake sapphire precisely, right where it could have fallen from the hand of a hasty thief. I put a fifty-dollar bill on the cockpit deck where the interior lights shone out upon it. I turned the dock light out and snapped the switch off, breaking it. Then I clambered quickly to the cabin roof and flattened myself out on the far side of the dinghy. I checked my observation points. I could hold onto the safety rail and lean over and look through the port into the small forward cabin, or hitch back a few feet and look the same way into the larger cabin.

I thought I knew exactly what he would do, what he had to do under those circumstances. Lois had been very dubious about this part. And she had been worried about somebody coming along. But she had been wrong there, and would be wrong again, I knew.

I heard his hasty footsteps on the dock. I kept my head down. I heard the thump and felt it as he leaped down into the cockpit. I heard his grunt of consternation.

He would have to find out, and find out quickly. I leaned over cautiously and stared in, my head upside down. I saw him snatch the gem up, stare at it, shove it into his pocket. He whirled toward his marine radio rig, grasped the wooden drawer directly under the rig and pulled it all the way out. A strange resonant buzzing began. He reached back in the place where the drawer had been, and the buzzing stopped. He worked at something in there, and then pulled his arms out, a cloth bag in one hand and a small plastic bag of paper money in the other. He examined them. He stowed them away again, started the buzzer and replaced the drawer. As soon as the drawer was in place, the buzzing sound stopped. He went to the sleeping girl. He took her brutally by the hair, lifted her and wrenched her around. His back was to me. It was a very broad back. Her eyes opened, wide and absolutely vacant, and she seemed to stare so directly at me, I almost yanked myself away from the port. She closed her eyes again. He slapped her. They stayed closed. He dropped her.

Suddenly he reached into his pocket and took out the stone. He moved closer to the nearest light. His body seemed to tense, shoulders lifting. I pulled myself back up, sensing that he would whirl, that he would catch me.

I wormed my way toward the stern, onto the overhang, working the silk sock out of my pocket. The lights below began to go off quickly, one after the other. I had not counted on that. I closed my eyes tightly for several seconds and then opened them wide, trying to hurry night vision. I heard him coming. Moving swiftly. I wanted one good chance, and I had to take a risk to get it. I slid head and shoulders over the edge as he came out. He heard or sensed the movement and tried to turn, but I got him very nicely and solidly, better than I had expected. He took three wandering sideways steps and went down onto his hands and knees. I dropped, landing on toes and knuckles, and as he straightened, I gave it to him with more precision, more of a wrist-snapping impact. He went back down onto his hands, shaking his head, sighing. I marveled at the toughness of his skull. I snapped him behind the left ear and his arms quit and his face smacked the teak deck. For a moment, standing and breathing hard, I debated lashing him up. But after three of those, I guessed he would last more than long enough for my two chores, finding and taking his treasures, and disabling his boat.

The drawer arrangement was tricky. He had a battery buzzer back in there. I couldn't find his manual switch, so I yanked the wires loose. The compartment was directly behind the drawer, with a sliding lid. I shoved the money into one pocket. I jounced the cloth sack. It made a glassy clinking sound. It stirred an old memory. Glassies won in the schoolyard long ago, a heft marking many victories. I shoved the sack inside my shirt. They had a strange coolness through the cloth against my skin. A Himalayan coolness perhaps, cold as smuggled gold. Or cell bars. Or those small blue eyes above the lovable smile.

The boat would be no problem. Hoist a hatch, tear off a handful of wiring. But then I remembered the fake stone. If I couldn't send it back, Harry would want a lot more than it was worth. I squatted beside Junior Allen and felt it in his right trouser pocket. I worked my hand into the pocket. Suddenly he rolled against my hand, pinning it, rolled onto my wrist and arm and the leverage forced me down against the deck. Then he was on his back, my right arm under him. He hooked his left arm around my neck, pulled my head against his waist and began hammering me with his free hand. I had no leverage and no room to strike back. As my face began to break, and the world began to blur, I planted my knees and stuffed my other arm under him and heaved. It brought him up and turned him, and I ripped my right hand free of his pocket. He bounded up with a rubbery agility, and I barely saw the kick coming, and turned just enough to take it on the point of the shoulder. My left arm went numb. He was a jolly brawler. He kept low and balanced, snorting with each exhalation, and I hit him twice before he bowled me over and bore me down in a tangle of chairs and began the jolly business of rib cracking, gouging, kneeing and breaking everything loose he could reach. He clambered and straddled me, trapping my arms under his blocky legs, picked me up by the ears and banged my head back onto the teak. As the world went slow and dreamy, I got an arm loose and saw my hand way up there, the heel of it under his chin. He tried to hammer his clasped hands down onto my rigid arm, and would have snapped it nicely had I not gotten my feet braced and bucked him off. He was back at me like a cat, and he swung a hard chunk of wood from one of the smashed chairs. I caught the first one on the shoulder and I cleverly caught the next one right over the left ear. It broke a big white bell in my head, and he sidestepped, grunting for breath, and let me go down. I landed on my side, and he punted me in the belly like Groza trying for one from the midfield stripe.

I had that fractional part of consciousness left which gave me a remote and unimportant view of reality. The world was a television set at the other end of a dark auditorium, with blurred sound and a fringe area picture. Somewhere the happy smiler leaned against the rail and sucked air for a time. I couldn't have fluttered an eyelid if somebody had set me on fire. He began cleaning up the cockpit. He hummed to himself. I recognized the tune. "Love is a Many Splendored Thing." William Holden and Jennifer Jones. I remembered her going into the shallows of that bay in Hong Kong in that white swim suit. But I couldn't keep my mind on her. Every time Dads got in range of me, he kicked. In time to the music. Then he kicked me in the head. It faded that distant television set right out, right down to a little white dot and then that was gone too. . . .

. . . The little set came back to life. There was vibration. Marine rumble. Sound of the wake. Boat idling along. And a thin and hopeless little female voice nearby saying, "Oh, don't. Oh, don't any more. Oh, please don't any more please."

I was folded into a corner of the stern of the cockpit. I had to puzzle that voice out. Slowly. Dear little Patty. But she wasn't supposed to be around. I'd written her out of the script. And Junior went, "Ho, ho, ho." Like a jolly Santa. "You are a cute little ole button," he said. "You're a tasty bit."

I picked one eye and pumped it open. Right eye. It was like jacking up a truck. In the night radiance, Junior Allen was ho-ho-hoing Miss Patricia Devlan. He was crouched at her like a bear, and he had her butted back against the transom, both her thin wrists held behind her in one hand, and his other hand up under her skirt, lifting her onto tip-toe. They were close enough to fall on me.

Suddenly he turned and stared forward and grunted, released her and went up toward the wheel. A course correction, reset the automatic pilot, came back to the fun. But I did not want anyone ho-ho-hoing Miss Devlan. She was hunched over, sobbing. I came up with blinding speed—like one of those trick clothes drying racks being unfolded by a sleepy drunk. I was forty feet tall and one inch wide, with a head fashioned of stale gas. As Junior roared, I slooped one dead arm out and around the girl's waist, pulled her toward me and rocked right over backward with her, over the rail and down into the black bay water, tucking in all elbows and knees, feeling the wrench of the water, waiting to see how a prop would feel chopping meat.

We popped up in the turbulence, and I saw the running lights receding at a comforting pace. I looked around at shore lights, orienting myself. We were about one mile south of the kick in the head, in a place where the bay was wide, but the channel was fairly narrow. She tilted her pale child-face back, her hair pasted seal black to her head, and made a waffling sound of total hysteria. The boat stopped bubbling along and roared into a turn. I clopped Miss Devlan across the chops and shoved her in the best direction and yelled, "Swim, baby!"

She came out of it. She swam very well indeed. She pulled ahead of me. I felt as if I were swimming with four broken arms. And with each breath I could convince myself he was still kicking me in the stomach. We had a good angle of escape. We had to go fifty feet to get past the submerged spoil banks from the channel dredging. He had to come back about a hundred and fifty yards. I was hoping I could sucker him into jamming it aground. But I heard him throttle down sharply, then roar the engines again as he put it into reverse to sit dead in the water.

"Keep going," I yelled at her. "Angle a little left."

The spotlight hit us. She stopped swimming. I took two big strokes and reached her and bore her under. Pistols make a silly spatting sound over open water. And slugs hitting near you make a strange sound. *Tzzeee-unk. Tzzeee-unk.* I tried to kick us along and she got the idea. The underwater breaststroke felt as if it pulled my ribs free of my breastbone. I lost her. I grabbed some air and went down again and kept churning along. I peered up and saw no radiance, and came up and looked back. He was in a big curve, and he straightened out and went ramming south toward Lauderdale.

"Patty?" I yelled.

"H-here I am," she said, about ten feet behind me. She was standing in waist-deep water. I went to her and felt the lumpy edges of an oyster bar underfoot.

"He . . . he . . . he was going to . . ."

"But he didn't."

"He . . . he . . . he was going to . . ."

"He's gone. Pull yourself together."

I put an arm around her. She leaned her face against my chest and said, "Haw! Oh, God. Haw!"

"Come on, baby."

"I'm . . . I'm all right. He took my glasses off and threw them overboard. He said I'd never need them again. I c-can't hardly see without them."

"He's gone, Patty. And he's got his little chum with him, and they deserve each other. Get yourself collected, and then we'll swim to shore." Behind her, two hundred yards away, was the bright shore, loud with neon in the night. It made pink and green and blue highlights on her hair. I let her go. Her blouse was pasted to her peach-sized breasts. Except for the breasts, she looked about twelve. With them, she looked fourteen.

"How did you get into the act?" I asked her. "I phoned your mother and told her the damn fool thing you were planning to do."

"That was you? I . . . I went out my bedroom window. I didn't want to . . . miss the fun."

"He's a real fun fellow, old Dads is."

"Don't, please. He said I was the one he was really after. I went to the boat and everything was . . . so strange. You were lying there so still and bloody I thought you were dead. He told me to go below and wake Dee up. I tried, and I couldn't. I wanted to go home then. He said we were going to have a nice cruise, not to worry. He said you'd tried to rob him. He said he was going to turn you over to the police. He said you were just knocked out. He said that before he turned you in, he wanted to get your accomplice too. He told me to stay aboard and watch you, and give a yell if you woke up. He said he'd be hiding close by. I didn't like it, but I stayed there like he said. I was thinking about Pete and that girl, and I just didn't care what I did. Then a woman came. A tall pretty woman. She stood on the dock and she said in a loud voce, 'What have you people done to him? What have you done to Travis McGee?' She couldn't see you from there."

"Dear God! She was waiting for me in my car. She should have run when she knew something had gone wrong."

"He came out of nowhere and swooped her right up and jumped aboard with her. She started to scream and then she saw you and stopped. He let go of her and she just stood there, staring at you. While she wasn't moving . . . he . . . he hit her. With his fist. It was such a terrible blow it made me sick to my stomach. She fell like a rag doll and he picked her up and put her in a bunk. I got off. But he caught me and brought me back. He threw the lines off and started up. When he got out of that little canal he went real fast out to the main channel and real fast for a little while south down the channel, then he slowed it down and fixed it to steer itself and came back and threw my glasses away and started . . . doing things to me. I guess . . . I could have jumped overboard. But I couldn't think of anything . . . and then you . . ."

"Come on! Can you make it now? Come on, girl!"

We swam side by side. It all seemed so damned slow. I headed for the brightest clustering of lights. We ended up in the shells and shallows at the base of a five-foot sea wall. I got the top of it and wormed my way over it, reached down and got her wrists and yanked her up. She stumbled and fell into the damp night grass at the base of a coconut palm. I picked her up and herded her along with me, our rubber shoes squelching, breaths wheezing, strides unsteady. I had to get to a phone. My face felt like a multiple fracture. I steered us around a rock garden before we fell into it. It was a motel complex, and for reasons which defy the imagination it was named The Bearpath. They were doing a nice little summer business. The dance instructors were Bossa-Novaing a clutch of tourists, all of whom looked as if they did each other's hair for a living. Bidding was vicious in the cardroom. We came churning in, dripping and battered and winded.

Dapper little fellows came running toward us, wringing their hands, making shrill little cries of consternation.

"Phone!" I demanded.

"But you can't come in here like this . . ."

I grabbed the nearest handful of silk blazer and lifted it onto its tippy-toes, and he pointed a rigid arm at a salmon phone on a baby-blue counter. When I asked the switchboard girl to get me the County Sheriff's office, she asked in a voice wet with acid and postnasal drip if I was a guest of the hotel. I told her that if she delayed the call one more second, I would start throwing their guests through their window walls, as a gesture of impatience. Patty stood docile beside me, chin down, shoulders rounded, and her little rump tucked humbly under.

I got a deputy who was so bright and so quick it helped me pull myself together. I was aware of all the silence behind me, the stilled dancers, the frozen card games, the fellows in pastel silk. I described the boat. I said it had left the Citrus Inn maybe forty minutes ago, and was headed south, A. A. Allen, Junior, possibly psycho, in command. Young girl aboard, drugged and unconscious. Deeleen. Last name unknown. And a Mrs. Lois Atkinson, taken aboard against her will, and slugged. May plan to head out from Lauderdale to the Bahamas.

"What's your name and where are you calling from?"

"The Bearpath Motel. I have a girl here who needs attention, and needs to be taken home. A Miss Devlan . . ."

"We have an alert on a Patricia Devlan, eighteen, dark hair, slender build . . ."

"The same. In her case it was attempted kidnapping and attempted assault. You can pick her up here."

"What's your name?"

I hung up and gave a brief glance at the forty or fifty pairs of bulging eyeballs, and turned and found a way out. I went through some hedges and a flower bed and a parking lot. I had a vivid little silvery grinding in my chest with each breath. I headed toward commercial lights and oriented myself. Better than a mile back to Miss Agnes. Scout pace, they call it. Run fifty steps, walk fifty. The car was there. No key. But the spare was up under the dash in a little magnetic box.

I headed her for home. I heard myself sob. It was like a big hiccup. A sad brave wonderful gal who had trusted me. She'd trusted me. She'd trusted reliable old McGee. They had to stop trusting me. Damn them for trusting me. I blinked and drove and cursed McGee.

13

A dry shirt and pants made no remarkable improvement in my appearance. I trudged to the huge neighboring cruiser where my joyous friend, the Alabama Tiger, operates the world's only permanent floating house party. He had some hundred proof for immediate medication, asked me who had dragged me down a flight of stairs by the heels, and offered me the temporary loan of my choice among several eager amateur nurses. But I told him I would rather borrow the *Rut Cry*. He didn't ask why. He told me to take it. He likes to get up and fly. The *Rut Cry* is twenty-one feet of white water hull with big tanks and two big Mercs astern. It was moored alongside, gassed and ready. A chattering flock of the Tiger's girls helped me strip the weather canvas off it, and handled the lines and shoved me off, the fast motors burbling; then they stood and waved me their musical good-bys. I belted myself down into the foam rubber seat, found the switch for the running lights, spun the boat and took it out and down, under the bridge, past the Navy and on out into the Atlantic. Once clear of the channel chop, I figured a rough heading for Bimini and let it go. At forty it began leaping clear, banging my teeth, collapsing my spine, cavitating, slamming, roaring. It was punishment for past sins, sticking knives in every bruise. Once I put a bow corner under and came too close to tripping it over. I pulled it back down to thirty. When I was well clear of any possible traffic, I cut the running lights. Southeast wind. No chop in the Stream. Big long ones I could take on the quarter. I estimated his hull would give him a cruising speed of fifteen tops. I could run in one hour what he could run in two. So give him a two-hour head start, right at the sea buoy. No. Make it an hour and a half from that point. And I had cleared it at nine-fifteen. So at nine-fifteen I was twenty-two miles behind him. Forty-five minutes. Give him another ten miles by the time I got to that point. Twenty minutes more. By rough reckoning, if all the guesses were right, I could run up on him by ten-thirty.

So I ran until ten-thirty, then cut to dead slow and headed directly into the long shallows swells. I undid the two straps and stood up, my hand braced on the top of the wheel. Each time I was at the crest of a wave, I tried to sweep one segment of the horizon. Moonlight silvered the spill of water. I was too far off to pick up the Cat Cay light. My heart jumped when I saw lights east and north of my position, but after three good looks at them, I knew it was a southbound freighter staying clear of the Stream. I stared until I began to see things that weren't there.

I sat down again and leaned my forehead against the top of the wheel. My tongue found an unfamiliar place where a corner of a tooth was gone. The valiant slob. Goof McGee. This was like trying to fill a straight with a three-card draw. He could run without lights too. He was too canny to head this way. He had enough range for Cuba. Or he knew a nice little corner he could tuck it into, down near Candle Key.

The irony of the stars looked down at my grandstand play and dwindled me. One man in one small boat in the vasty night. In my despair I let the boat swing and a small wave broke and slapped and sprayed my face. Tears and sea water taste much the same.

The authorities wouldn't stoop to the idiocy of a night search. They would wait for dawn and bring the choppers out, along with some playmates from the C.A.P. And some of the reserve boys needing flight time.

Suddenly the silver was gone. I looked up and saw a haloed thunderhead obscuring the moon. There was lightning under it, low and blue against the sea. So I began my run back, taking it slow, taking the bad motion of the sea on the stern quarter, climbing the long slow hills and then scooting down the other side. I looked toward the storm. I could outrun it by giving myself a beating. I had a rough heading home. It didn't have to be on the nose. It's a big coast. Hardly anyone ever misses it. When you come in at night you pick out the huge pink haze of Miami and then adjust your course accordingly.

The lightning was almost continuous. And as I looked toward it, I picked up something out of the corner of my eye. Some sort of blob between me and the lightning. I thought I had imagined it, and then I saw it again. I spun and headed toward it. It was gone and then I picked it up again. No lights. Just an outline against lightning in the darkening night. I soon had it again, larger, too big to miss. I made a big swing to come up astern. The next flash of lightning was close and bright, bright enough to give me the after-image of the pale cruiser on the black sea.

The *Play Pen,* slower than I thought, way behind the estimated schedule, and picked up by a freak of light and vision.

I hung back off his stern quarter and adjusted my speed to his. I lay about two hundred yards off. He was between me and the storm. There was little chance he would pick me up unless he happened to be looking in that direction when the next bright flash occurred. He was doing ten knots, possibly to conserve fuel, and according to my compass, he was on a heading that would bring him in well south of Bimini. It seemed possible he might figure on getting inside, in on the Bahama Bank and dropping the hook, and then heading on for the Berry Islands at first light. Get his fuel at Frazier's Hog Cay, a good reach for him, but possible.

It made a nice problem. I couldn't run up on him without him hearing the snarl of the Mercs. Shoved into my belt was the little Czech automatic I had picked up when I had changed clothes. It would fire every time, with a little bit more accuracy than a garden hose. And at the moment of trying to get aboard, I would be very vulnerable.

There was a click of blinding lightning, an ozone stink, a hard slam of thunder; I heard the hiss of the rain coming, and suddenly it moved across him and he was gone. It came drenching down on me, and I turned toward him, giving it a little more speed, straining to see him. Suddenly the stern loomed up in the rain. I spun the wheel and reversed both motors and narrowly avoided slamming into him. I could ask for no better cover than the rain, than the sound and the blinding screen of it. He moved on, and I hurried after him, nearly losing him, catching up again. I fumbled and took a line out of the locker. I risked leaving the wheel and scrambled forward and made it fast to the bow cleat. I hurried back and came back on course, and held the other end of the line in my teeth. He was pulling a big mound of water behind him, but I felt that if I could slide past that, there was relatively flat water alongside of him. The rain felt as solid as hail, and it was surprisingly cold. Squinting ahead, I made two false starts, and then ran it up just where I wanted it. I killed the motors, leaped and caught the rail. And felt the little pistol slide down my pants leg and rap the top of my foot. But it was too late to change my mind. As I went over the rail, I saw him hunched at the wheel in the next gleam of lightning. I took a quick turn of the line around the rail an instant before the dead weight of the *Rut Cry* came against it. The line did not pop, as I half expected. It felt like half-inch nylon. I made it fast. I squatted low and looked for Junior Allen. The lightning came. He was gone. The wheel was turning.

Without warning, the drenching rain stopped. The *Play Pen* had begun to turn in a big circle to port, rolling badly when it entered the trough. I glanced over my shoulder. The *Rut Cry* was painfully visible, riding well, nose high on the hump of water the cruiser was dragging. And the damned moon came out. I was a black bug in a bright silver box. Something snapped twice. A finger flicked at my hair, a bee whirred by my ear. I rolled into the far corner of the cockpit. My hand landed upon the haft of a boat hook. I yanked it out of the clips, half rolled and hurled it like a spear at the dark entrance to the cabin. There was a grunt and a clatter and a soft curse. Then both engines slowed and chuckled and died and we lay dead in the water. The *Rut Cry* moved up and nudged the stern. We rocked. Gear creaked and rattled. I snatched up a chair we hadn't smashed during the earlier game, hurled it toward the darkness where I thought he was, and grasped the overhang of trunk cabin roof and swung myself up and crawled forward. I was in the open and in white moonlight, but he couldn't get to me without my seeing him.

The rain wind had moved the open boat out to the side, starboard, amidships, at the end of the nylon line. Holiday boat. Play pretty for the Tiger. I flattened myself out beside the overturned Fiberglas dinghy and, by touch, loosened the lashings which held it fast. I had no great plan. I wanted to create some more variables, trusting I could use them to my advantage. I wondered why he was so silent. It was unnerving. He had whipped me once, and I knew how brutally quick and strong he was. And I was not in as good shape as the last time. I could not recall doing him very much damage. But I couldn't let it come out the same way again. Not and live. I had made the mistake of thinking of him as a man, rather than an animal. He wasn't even a furry animal. He was reptilian. He had to be planning something.

Suddenly I realized that the *Rut Cry* was gliding slowly toward the cruiser. I inched forward and looked, and saw him bringing it in, a squat dark shape in the cockpit, outlined by the pale moonlight. He swung and snapped and as I yanked back like a turtle, a slug whined off the aerial into the night. Suddenly I realized what he could have been doing during all that silence. He could have been grabbing the wad of bills and bag of marbles out of his hidey hole. I had come out of no-where bearing the gift of a small fast boat and, presumably, enough gas to get back to the mainland. So *adios, compadre.* It made a nice solu-tion for him. He would know that I had gotten away, and things were going very sour for him. He could right it very neatly. He could head for a dark piece of the mainland, set the boat adrift, and live to play other games in other places. I could do him no more harm than I had already done. It would not matter to him whether he left me dead or alive aboard the *Play Pen.* Once he freed the line and dropped into the *Rut Cry,* his chances were damned good. I couldn't catch him.

I waited just as long as I dared. The *Play Pen* was in the trough, rocking and thrashing, taking white buckets of water into the cockpit whenever a crest hit the port side as it was rolling that way. It was a so-called self-bailing cockpit, which merely means that the cockpit deck is higher than the normal waterline, and the water runs on out the scuppers set low into the transom corners.

When the *Rut Cry* was alongside and had been there for about five seconds, I put my hands under the bow of the overturned dinghy and flipped it up and over and down into the cockpit, and went after it. It made a great *brong* and *boomp,* and came bouncing up off the teak, giv-ing him a glancing blow as it leaped out over the stern. It knocked him sprawling, and he dropped the coiled line from the *Rut Cry.* The line began to play out rapidly, as the wind, more effective in moving that hull than the hull of the bigger boat, began to push it off and away on the starboard side. I landed off balance, and timed the roll, and as he came up, I fell toward him, snapped both hands down onto the gun wrist as his arm started to swing around, and, against its resistance, went right on over it, clamping it, curling tight, like a kid doing a trick on a tree limb. I smacked the crown of my head onto the teak, legs swinging over, and felt something give in that arm just as I had to release it. We spilled into the tangled heap, awash in the stern starboard corner, both fighting to get loose. He went clawing and scrabbling after the end of the line as it moved on out over the starboard rail, and came within frantic reaching inches of it just before a wild roll to port rocked him back. In the moonlight I saw the white end of it yanked over the rail and off into the night as we rolled away from the slow pull of the drifting *Rut Cry*. I was kneeling, patting around in the water, reaching and feeling for the gun. His hands were empty, and I wondered if it had flipped overboard. He skidded on the seat of his pants, and for a moment the roll held him nailed against the port side. Water smashed in on him. I knew that he knew what he had to do. He had to take care of me and get the *Play Pen* moving and go downwind and get the smaller boat. I was the problem. My fingertips brushed the gun and I grabbed at it just as he used the roll to starboard to come at me. If he had come crawling he would have made it in time. But he got onto his feet to drive at me, and it gave me time to bring the gun up and fire once into his leathery paunch, and yank the trigger twice more without effect before he got his hands on me. He had begun a strange screaming, a whistling sound with each exhalation. It was not pain or fear. It was just a violent exasperation. If he was trying to stomp something that wouldn't lie still enough, he might make that same sound.

He grabbed me around the neck, but as I broke out of it, I realized the strength of his right arm was gone. He could use it, but it did not have that sickening power in it. I scuttled away from him and we were braced on hands and knees, nose to nose. The motion was too violent to risk standing up. We could not guard against each other. I had lost the gun. He used his left hand. I used my right. We traded blows as they do in cheap television, groaning with effort, a measured grunt-smack, grunt-smack, grunt-smack. I knew that if I could keep it up, time was on my side. He had a bullet in him. Probably he realized he was losing ground. I saw him reach his left hand into the front of his shirt. Another gun? A knife? In sudden fright, I tried to hit him hard enough to finish it, but he yanked his head back, cat-quick, and I missed and sprawled flat. As I rolled, I saw him bringing something down at my head, and I yanked away. It struck me a glancing blow and hit the teak deck and burst. Then there were all the jelly beans, rolling and spilling, scattering and fleeing in the moonlight, the bright treasure from the cloth sack. He gave a howl of dismay and began scrambling, pouncing, snatching at the round gem stones. Water smashed in, sweeping them inevitably toward the stern, out the scuppers, seeding the deep with riches. I think he forgot for a moment that he had to do something about me. I got low, as I had been taught, and timed the roll, and as he lifted up a little too far, I drove at him, shoulder into the pit of the belly, legs driving. I drove him back into the starboard rail as it dipped low, and he went over, grabbing at me, clawing at me. But I got hold of the rail and he missed it and went into the sea.

I don't know why I expected him to go down like a stone. I clung to the rail, gasping and gagging, and saw him pop up, snap the water out of his eyes, orient himself, and turn and start churning his way toward the *Rut Cry*. With a sprained arm, with a bullet in his gut, I could still believe he would make it. It was out there, rising and falling in the moonlight.

In a strange kind of panic, I groped for something to throw at him. The *Play Pen* was drifting in the same direction. He was not getting out of range very fast. There was a big Danforth anchor in the open storage locker in the center of the transom. I pulled it out, chain rattling on the shaft, got the shaft in both hands, braced myself, threw it out there as hard as I could in a high clanking arc. It landed on the back of his head and neck and shoulders just as a wave lifted him, and tumbled forward over his shoulder—and the sea was suddenly empty. The line which had been bent onto the chain whipped at my ankle. By instinct I stepped on it. I bent weakly and picked it up. I didn't have the strength to pull the anchor back in. I gave it a couple of turns around the starboard stern cleat. I kept looking for him. I couldn't believe that anything had ended him. I took a step to catch my balance, and stepped on something like a pebble. I picked it up and put it in my pocket. I pulled myself to the controls. I had to stop all that damned motion before I went out of my mind. I got the engines started, turned it into the wind and put it on dead slow, and jacked the Metal Marine pilot into gear. It took over the wheel, holding it there. My underlip was in two segments, and one was folded down, exposing my teeth on the left side. I put the running lights on. There was a flashlight in a bracket beside the instrument panel. I went below. The violent motion had spilled both women out of the bunks. They lay in the narrow aisle, both face down, Deeleen atop Lois. I heaved Deeleen back up onto the port bunk. She was deep in her sleep, long exhalations rattling in her throat.

I was gentler with Lois, kneeling, turning her, gathering her up. I put the light on her when she was on the bunk. Her face was the color of yeast. Her lips were blue and bloodless. The whole left side of her face was a dark bruise. I could not detect respiration, but when I laid my ear against her chest I thought I could hear a thin, small, slow sound, a thready struggle of the heart.

I covered them both with blankets, tucking them around their bodies, muttering to myself. My head seemed full of distances, of wraiths and mists, a wide and lonely country encased in a papery fragility of bone.

Find the Tiger's boat. Priority one. Look downwind. I went to the controls and took it out of pilot and swung it to take the sea dead astern, and stepped it up a little. Suddenly I remembered the damned anchor. I wasn't tracking well. It would be very clever to wind the line around a shaft. A towed anchor will swing up and bobble around in the wake. I put it back on pilot and went astern. I decided I would just release the line and let it go. I put the light back into the wake to see if I could see it. The wake made a smooth hump about forty feet back of the transom. Junior Allen rode that hump, face up out of the water, grinning at me.

Suddenly, as if to show off, as if to prove how well he had everything under control, he made a complete roll, exposing the metallic gleam of the anchor for an instant, then steadying again, face high, making little white bow waves that shot past his ears.

I could not move or think or speak. The known world was gone, and in nightmare I fought something that could never be whipped. I could not take the light off him. He rolled again. And then I saw what it was. His throat was wedged in that space between the flukes of the Danforth, and the edges of the points were angled up behind the corners of his jaw, the tension spreading his jowls into that grin. I got to the cleat, and with nerveless stumbling hands I freed the line. He disappeared at once as the anchor took him down. I hugged the rail and vomited. When I looked forward, eyes streaming, I suddenly saw I was coming too damned close to running the *Rut Cry* down. I sprang to the controls, circled it, came up on it slowly, got its line with a boat hook and made it fast to the center cleat in the transom.

I made an estimate of the course, guessed it at two-ninety, and, watching the *Rut Cry* to see how it rode, I slowly put it up to 2800 rpm. I went down and looked at the women. Lois's hands were limp and icy. I found a pulse in her throat with my lips. She was alive.

I turned on the ship-to-shore and transmitted on the Coast Guard emergency frequency. On my third try they came in loud and clear. I told them who I was and where I was, and something of the nature of the medical emergency. It was after midnight. My lip made my voice strange. I told them I did not think from the looks of the woman and the sea a copter pickup was feasible. They told me to stand by. They came back on, and at their request, I took the flashlight and lifted her eyelids and looked at her eyes. I told them one pupil was tiny and the other was very large. They told me to stand by again. I went topside to look around. I saw a glow of lights on the western horizon. I swung the flashlight beam around and spotted a little red gleam in the scupper. I picked it up. I found three more after that. Five all told, the only ones which hadn't been washed into the sea.

They came back on and gave me a five-degree course correction, having spotted me in some mysterious way, and told me to make all possible speed for Lauderdale, and come right to the Pier 66 gas dock where an ambulance would be waiting.

I gave it all it would take. The marine engines roared. At full throttle they turned close to 4500. I backed them off a little. The tanks were half full, I slammed toward home, steering it by hand, the Tiger's boat wallowing and swinging astern.

Red lights were revolving and blinking on the shiny vehicles parked at the gas dock. I laid it in close and a gang of people swarmed aboard with lines, yelling orders to each other. They came aboard and took the women off, giving them an equally gentle professional handling.

I rode to the hospital with them. They stitched my mouth, X-rayed me, taped my ribs, eased my nose back to a reasonably central position. While they were doing that to me, other people shaved her head and cut into her skull and released the cumulative pressure of the massive cerebral hemorrhage. The operation was a great success. Three days later the patient died of pneumonia, under oxygen, with me sitting there, staring in at her through the Pliofilm, willing every struggling breath she took, until finally she just did not take the next one. She settled smaller then, her face little and gray under the turban of gauze and adhesive.

14

What do you do when they turn all your lights out?

I guess you answer the questions. There were a lot of people and a lot of questions, because it was what they call an interesting problem of jurisdiction.

And though you do not really give a damn how much or how little you tell them, there is, after all, an instinctive caution which takes over and tends to simplify the answers you give. I had no idea where he had gotten his money. Cathy had no idea either. She just thought he might possibly be the same man who had beaten her up. I was her friend. I was just trying to check it out, and had gotten caught in the middle. And had had some luck.

Deeleen was as angry as a boiled squirrel for having slept through all the action. Patty made a resolute witness, precise, outraged and articulate.

I had a simple little story and told it forty times. Yes sir, I was pretty silly trying to find him in the dark out there in the ocean. He let me come aboard and then he knocked me out. I was getting up when he was trying to climb into the other boat. I saw him lose his balance and fall in. I saw him swimming, trying to catch the other boat, but it was drifting as fast as he could swim. I was too weak and dizzy to do anything. I think I heard him call out once. I got the big boat started and I went looking for him, but when I found the other boat, it was empty.

I soon created a massive disinterest on the part of the reporters. I talked very freely and at great length. I could do twenty minutes on the characteristics of the *Play Pen,* and another twenty on the hull design of the *Rut Cry.* I could give an hour lecture of setting compensated compass courses, and what the weather had been like out there. They listened until their eyes glazed and their jaws creaked when they yawned. I did not tell them of my night visions of Junior Allen down there, his neck wedged into the anchor, his heels high, dancing slowly in vagrant currents.

There are some other things you do when they turn your lights out. You learn how to use the darkness. Varieties of darkness. The darkness of hot sun on the beach, and intense physical effort. The small darkness of liquor. The small darkness of the Tiger's girls. But these do not work in any lasting way. The body mends, but a part of it took its last breath behind that glassine barrier.

Once in a while they show up to ask some more questions, but you are amiable, slightly stupid, and very polite. The sister-in-law had come down and gathered up what was left of the lady and had taken the remains north, for suitable burial in the family plot.

One day I realized I was nearly broke. And I had gone into this thing for the money. It was to laugh. Somewhere behind my heart I thought I heard her small amusement, a faint melody. Who are we laughing at, darling, it said.

So I took some of the last of the funds and went up to New York and sat in a cheap hotel room and made contact with Harry. I showed him what I had. His eyes glistened even while he tried to tell me they were junk. I gave him the one that looked least valuable to me. We settled for seven percent as his end. It took him a day and a half. He brought me back thirty-eight hundred and thirteen dollars. He got rid of two more the next day, one at a time, at a little over four thousand apiece for me. A full day for the next one. Five thousand and a bit. When I turned over the last one, I had a hunch I would not see him again, so I told him I had been holding out the cream of the little crop. He wanted to see it. I told him he could see it when he came back with the money for the fifth one. It made a serious problem for him. He did not know just how to manage his own greed. So he came back, again with a little over five thousand. He didn't look sufficiently disappointed when I told him there wasn't any more. So I knew he had covered all bets. I had covered mine too. Leaving Harry to batter his way out of the bathroom, I had the elevator boy, greased with a ten, take me to the basement where a slightly more expensive fellow, prearranged, led me out a back way into a narrow alley. Forty minutes later I was on a train to Philadelphia, and from there I arranged air transit to Florida.

On an afternoon in late September I had the brown-eyed, sad-eyed blonde come over to the *Busted Flush*. Draperies muted the light in the lounge. She wore a blue dress faded by many washings, and came shyly out of the blaze heat of the day into the coolness of the lounge, wearing her blue dress and her humble company manners, moving well on those shapely, sinewy dancer's legs.

"I call you and you trot right over, just like that, Cathy?"

"I guess so."

"You're a very humble gal, aren't you?"

"I don't know. I guess so. You tried to help out, Mister. I'm right sorry about that woman. I told you so before, I guess you remember. I'm sorry it had to come about that way."

Her shy oblique glance caught me and moved away. She looked down at her hands. I guess she knew about drunken men. Maybe she could understand the reasons for the drinks I had taken. Maybe she had heard it all in my voice when I had called her to come over.

"Your sympathy touches my heart," I said.

She sighed deeply. "You can talk ugly if it suits you. I don't mind. Seems like nothing comes out right for any person anymore these days."

She was sitting on the yellow couch. I picked up a small table and took it over and put it down in front of her. I went and locked the door and then went into the master stateroom and came out with the money. As I had planned, I put it in three piles on the table. A big pile and two slender ones.

"During the fun and games," I said, "Junior spilled the goodies. He got some back and went down with them. There was one time when I could have hauled him in, dead, and picked him clean, the wet money and what other stones he had, and let him sink again. I didn't have the stomach for it. In fact, I didn't even think of it. I got five stones. The rest went overboard. I sold them in New York. I got a total of twenty-two thousand six hundred and sixty-eight dollars for them. There's sixteen hundred and sixty-eight dollars in this pile right here."

She looked at it and looked up at me, eyes as attentive and obedient as a learning child.

"It will cover my expenses," I said. "I spent about that much. This pile is one thousand dollars. I'm taking it as a fee. That leaves twenty thousand in this pile. Yours."

"You said it would be half for you."

"Cathy, I'm not going to argue with you. It was a lousy recovery. It was peanuts. The fee is for self-respect. It's yours."

"I never could touch that much all at once in my lifetime. You should take half."

"Listen, you idiot woman! How do you know you're not being taken? Maybe I got it all from him. Why should you take my word about anything?"

"You did good. I didn't even know you got a thing. You keep half like we said."

I reached and grabbed her purse. I crammed the money into it and managed to fasten the catch. "I got all I want!"

"There's no call to yell. You want me to have it, I'll take it. And I thank you kindly, Travis."

I kicked the table out of the way and slumped onto the couch beside her. The damned humble, docile, forgiving woman. I wanted to beat her. I wanted to do some ugly thing that would destroy that mute earnestness, that anxiety to please me. I hooked a hand around her neck and pulled her over to me, stroked her body and kissed her roughly. I released her and she sagged back and moistened her lips and stared at me with a little frown between her brows.

"Well?" I said.

"If'n you're telling me you want me, and waiting that I should say yes or no, I guess it would be yes, if it would comfort you some, if you think it's what you want off me. I made bad trouble for you . . . and there isn't much I can do one way or another."

I got up and caught her wrist and pulled her along. She came willingly. I pushed her into the stateroom ahead of me. She looked around the room. I stumbled and sat on the bed. She undid a side zipper on that blue dress and gave me a quick and earnest look as she did so, teeth biting into her underlip, a boyish tousle of blonde hair falling across her forehead, her worried little frown still in place. She pulled the dress off over her head and hung it over the back of a chair. She balanced herself and slipped her shoes off. She wore very plain white nylon underthings, trim panties and a functional-looking bra.

"My God, Cathy," I said, "you're not under any compulsion." She looked blank. "You're not obligated."

"You're hurting, ain't you?" she said, and reached her arms behind her and unhooked the bra.

"Get dressed!"

"What?"

"It was a lousy idea. Get dressed and go."

I saw the tears come then, spilling, but not changing the expression of her face. "You got to know what you want," she said. "I'm not so much. I guess you know that. But drinking and all, you got to know or have somebody tell you."

I stretched out with my back to her. "I'm sorry," I said. "Just take off, will you?"

I listened for some sound. I guess she was standing there staring at me. Then she came around the bed and crawled on from the other side, came crawling into my arms, in just her little white pants, tugging and fitting my arms around her, hitching up so she could pull my face into the soft hollow of her throat. She smelled soapy-clean, and faintly of some flower perfume.

"Cathy, I didn't mean . . ."

"Hush up," she said. "It don't have to be that, I know. What you want to do, you want to smash and kick and fight. I know about that, honey. I know about something else too. You got to let go. It's hard to let go. God love you, I know that. A woman can cry it off some. But you listen. I'm just somebody close right now, for you to hold to, and that he'ps too. It don't matter what you want or don't want, or do or don't do. You just hang on close, and you try to let her go. She's gone. You got to let her go the rest of the way, with no blaming yourself. I'm here with you. Just somebody to be with. You can use me just to hang onto, or love me or whip me or cry some if you could. Or talk about her or anything. I'll be with you now. I'm off tonight. Now you think for a minute and say go or stay."

"I guess . . . stay."

"Sure, honey."

With her free hand, with strong fingers, she worked at the tension in the nape of my neck, in the muscles of my shoulders. I did not realize how tense I had been until from time to time I sighed and at each long exhalation I seemed to settle and soften against her.

In the last of daylight I took her hand and looked at it, at the weathered back of it, the little blue veins, the country knuckles. It seemed a very dear hand indeed. I kissed her, and felt the little ridge where they'd stitched my mouth. Her brown eyes glinted in the last of the light, and in a little while her breathing quickened. It was all strange and deep and sweet and unemphatic, as though it was an inescapable extension of that comforting closeness, as natural as all the rest of it.

In darkness she said in a murmurous voice, "With that money, I should be near my boy. It will last good and long down to Candle Key. I could spell Christine, watching over the kids. She wants a waitress job again, tired of being alone there. I can give notice. Honey, what you should do, you should come on down there in this boat and tie on up to our old dock down there. Put you to work, on handyman stuff that's piled up. With the other kids in school, we could maybe take Davie fishing in the skiff sometimes. What we could be . . . I guess . . . is a comfort to one another for a time down there, just sweet and close like this was, and we would know when it was time for you to leave. It wouldn't be no obligation to you, Travis."

And so we did. And I was mended as much as I could ever expect. And left finally, wondering if I was not perhaps the world's fool for not settling for that, for keeps.

On the late November day when I left, she grinned away tears, made our jokes which had become familiar to us, and stood on the dock holding the kid's hand, waving until I was past the island and out of sight.

Nightmare In Pink

For the six Kiwis

1

She worked in one of those Park Avenue buildings which tourists feel obligated to photograph. It's a nice building to visit, but they wouldn't want to live there.

She worked on the twentieth floor, for one of those self-important little companies which design packages for things. I arrived at five, as arranged, and sent my name in, and she came out into the little reception area, wearing a smock to prove that she did her stint at the old drawing board.

Nina Gibson. She was a bouffant little girl. I had seen a picture of her at age twelve. At twice that, she had changed. Mike had carried her picture in his wallet. Now she had a pile of blue-black curls, Mike's blue blue eyes, small defiant face, skin like cream. She had one of those hearty little figures typical of a certain type of small girl. The hand-span waist, and the rich solid swell of goodies above and below.

"You'll have to wait a little while," she said. "I'm sorry."

"Then when you come out the next time you smile and say hello."

"Should I? This isn't my idea, Mr. McGee."

"It's called a social amenity, Nina."

"There won't be many of those," she said, and went back into the mystic depths of her profession. I sat amid the cased displays of household words. Three cents' worth of squeeze bottles, plus two cents' worth of homogenized goo, plus prime-time television equals 28 million annual sales at 69 cents each. This is the heartbeat of industrial America. I sat and watched the receptionist. She was used to being watched, but she liked it. She was packaged too. One (1) receptionist, nubile, w/English accent, indefinitely tweedy, veddy country. The little company was up to date. They had one that looked as if she were sitting in a spring wind blowing off the moors, with her steed tethered in the hall.

Nina came out—gloved, pursed, be-hatted, wearing a fall suit a little too tailored for her structure—came out with a frail and indefinite-looking man and paused to argue with him, saying, "Freddie, if you show him three, he'll bog, and you know it, dear. That little mind can make a choice of the best of two, if the choice is obvious. So make the presentation of just Tommy's and Mary Jane's. They're the best and the worst so far, and he'll pick Tommy's and we're in."

Freddie shrugged and sighed and went back in. Nina nodded imperiously at me, and we went out and rode down in the musical elevator and walked a block and a half to a lounge in a muted little hotel where the prism spots gleamed down on an expensive assortment of coiffing and barbering, furs and tailored shoulders, sparkling glassware, lovely people maneuvering each other into this or that unspeakable thing by means of quiet smiles and quiet talk and deadly martinis. We found a banquette against a quiet wall, and she ungloved herself, leaned to the offered light, ordered a dry sherry.

She stared at me, mocking and defensive. "The fabulous Travis McGee. Fabulous means something about fables. I don't need any fables. Thank you so much."

"From a very old picture, I didn't think you'd be this pretty."

"I'm a darling girl."

I didn't want to be within fifteen hundred miles of this darling girl. I didn't want to be in this October city. I wanted to be back aboard my *Busted Flush* moored in Slip F-18, Bahia Mar, Lauderdale, my 52 feet of custom houseboat which I could fill with my favorite brand of darling girls, the brown untroubled ones, eager galley slaves, the hair-salty, rump-sandy, beer-opening, fish-catching, happy-making girls in sun-faded fabrics, sun-streaked hair. But Miss Nina looked at me out of her brother Mike's true blue eyes, and he had never asked me for anything else.

"I'll tell you a story," I said.

"Oh please do, sir," she said.

"There was a little matter of a thirty-six-hour pass, and our captain did not think he could spare us both. So Mike and I had some small games and wagers and I won, jeeped back, flew out, spent all those Japanese hours in a silk robe and in deep hot steaming water and on a pallet on a polished floor in a paper room with a darling girl whose name I couldn't say, and I called her Missy. She scrubbed me and fed me and loved me. She was five feet tall and giggled into her hands. And what made all the pleasure the sweeter was thinking of poor Mike stuck back there. So I flew back and jeeped back and they said he was dead. Either he had died at the aid station, or at the station hospital, or en route to the general hospital. Nobody was sure. Then they said he was still alive but would die. And now, of course, he is, like they say, the ward of a grateful republic, and he can't see and he can't walk, and it is a gala day when they wheel him into the sunshine for an hour, but through all those miracles of medical science, they kept Mike Gibson alive. The point of the story is guilt, Miss Nina. Guilt because I am glad it was Mike instead of remarkable, valuable old me. I don't want to be glad, but I am. Then there's another kind of guilt. I've visited him about once a year, on the average. Do I go to see him to prove to myself it happened to him instead of to me? Should I see him oftener, or not at all? I don't know. I do know one thing. The nurse wrote me he wanted to see me. I went there. He told me about your visit. He said find out. So, with your help or without it, Miss Nina, I find out."

"How terribly dear!" she said. "How ineffably buddy-buddy! I shouldn't have gone running to him with my little heartache, Mr. McGee. It was selfish of me. It upset him, and it didn't do me any particular good. How can he check up on anything anyway? Why don't you just invent some soothing little story for him and go down and tell it to him and then go back to your beach-bum career, whatever it is?"

"Because he may be all chopped up, but he's not stupid."

"It's too late now. Meddling won't do any good."

"Maybe there's some questions you both want answered."

For just a moment the vulnerability showed in her mouth and in her voice. "Answers? What good are answers? The boy is dead."

"I can poke around a little."

"You? Really now, Mr. McGee. You are spectacularly huge, and a tan that deep is almost vulgar, and you have a kind of leathery fading boyish charm, but this is not and never was a game for dilettantes, for jolly boys, for the favor-for-an-old-buddy routine. No gray-eyed wonder with a big white grin can solve anything or retrieve anything by blundering around in my life. Thanks for the gesture. But this isn't television. I don't need a big brother. So why don't you just go on back to your fun and games?"

"I will, when I'm ready."

"My fiancé is dead. Howard Plummer is dead." She glowered at me and banged the table with a small fist. "He's in the ground, dead. And he wasn't what I thought he was. And I'm trying to get over it, to get over losing him and to get over being a fool. So please don't stir it all—"

"What did you do with the money?"

It stopped her. She stared at me. "What money?"

"The money you started to tell Mike about."

"But I didn't tell him. I stopped myself."

"Nina, it was as good as telling him. He lies there and hears all the words you don't quite say. That's why I can't go back to him with a soothing story. What about the money?"

"It's nothing to do with you."

"It has now."

"Please don't try to be earnest and domineering, Mr. McGee. I am not going to lean on you."

"I've come blundering into your life, Nina, at Mike's request. Plummer was killed in August. The police investigated it. I can come stumbling onto the scene and tell them that Plummer had a good piece of cash tucked away and his girl friend has it now, and suggest that maybe there was some connection."

"You wouldn't *do* that!"

"Why not?"

"There wasn't any connection. That's stupid. It would just get me into a lot of trouble. My God, my brother asked you to come here to help me, not get me into a mess. I don't want any help."

"Miss Nina," I said, smiling my very best disarming smile, "let's get straightened away. Being a beach bum takes money. If you want to do it with flair. If the money comes in regularly, then you're working for it, and you lose your status. I have to come by it in chunks now and then, to protect my way of life. Now I don't really think I would have had much creative interest in the life and times of Nina Gibson if you hadn't given your brother the impression your boyfriend had been clipping a pretty good piece of money somehow. When I heard that, my ears lifted into little tufted points. Where there was some, there might be more. I like to ride to the rescue when I think that's where the money is."

She had herself a startled and agonizing reappraisal. With trembling hand she tried to sip from a glass already empty. I caught a suave passing eye and signaled another round.

"What are you anyway?" she whispered.

"Your friend and protector, Nina."

She tried to laugh. "This is really ironic, isn't it? Poor Mike, trying to take care of little sister, and he sicks a big bland monster on me."

"We're going to have a lot of nice talks, little sister."

She narrowed those very blue eyes. The lashes were very black, very dense, very long. "I don't want any nice talks. I know I was stupid about the money. I haven't touched it. I haven't told anybody about it. I almost told Mike, but that is as close as I've come to telling anyone." She glanced at our banquette neighbors and lowered her voice, leaned slightly toward me. "McGee, if I had thought for one moment there was any connection between Howie's death and that money, I would have told the police myself. And all the time he was giving me that righteous conversation about his honesty and his responsibility, he was stealing from Mr. Armister just like the rest of them. Finding that money just about broke my heart forever, McGee. I don't *want* it. I don't want that kind of money. I've thought of burning it. You can solve my little problem. I'll *give* it to you. You can take it and go away. It's quite a lot of money. Exactly ten thousand dollars."

"What makes you think he stole it?"

"Don't you think I've tried to think of every other possible way he could have gotten it? I was going to *marry* him. I *loved* him. I thought we knew everything about each other. I thought he was acting so strange because he was so worried about what they were doing to Mr. Armister. But after I found the money, I knew why he was acting strange. I'll *give* it to you, Mr. McGee. And you can go away and leave me alone."

Her control broke. Tears clotted the lashes. She rummaged her purse, found tissue, and honked into it. She gave me a despairing glance and went trotting off to the ladies' room.

I sipped my new drink and remembered Mike's troubled voice in the afternoon quiet of the wing of the veterans' hospital in North Carolina. "The thing is, Trav," he had said, "Nina was always loved. Maybe that's a bad thing. It gives people that terrible confidence that the world is going to give them the chance to fulfill themselves. Plummer sounded like the right kind of man. She opened her heart to him, all the way. The people who have always been loved have that awful capacity for giving. Now that he's dead, she can't forgive him. It's souring her. Trav, I can pay all expenses if you—"

"Expenses, hell."

"Was he a bum? Nina has always seen things as black or white. She's always been honest with herself. If you could just find out about that guy. Then make her understand why he did whatever he did. Otherwise I think she's going to destroy . . . that special something she's always had."

"She won't want me meddling around."

"Shake her up if you have to, Trav. The way she was when she came here, it bothers me. That's not Nina. All that bitterness. She's trying to hate herself. Maybe because she thinks she was a fool about Plummer."

"The very nicest girls get taken by the worst types, Mike."

"If that's the way it was, find out for sure. And see what you can do to help her get over it. But don't take too much time over it."

I hadn't liked the sound of that. But when I questioned him he said that he merely meant he didn't want to ask me to waste too much of my time on this kind of a personal favor. After I left him I had a few minutes with the nurse who had cared for him for several years, a muscular and colorless little woman. She looked up at me and her eyes slowly filled at my question, but she did not look away. She nodded her head abruptly. "They want to operate again. He asked them if they could hold off for a while."

"What are the odds?"

"Without it he won't last much longer, Maybe even if it's successful, he won't last long. But he's fooled everybody for a long time. Mike is a wonderful man. We all go to him with our troubles—even some of the doctors. And there's nothing we can ever do for him. I envy you, Mr. McGee, being able to do somethiing for him. They say he used to be bitter. But that was before my time. I love him. I have a husband I love too. Do you know what I'm trying to say?"

"I think so."

"When he's gone, I can't stay here. I couldn't."

"He's fooled everybody many times, Nurse."

She bobbed her head and turned and walked swiftly away, walking with her shoulders high as though hunched against an anticipated blow.

***

So here I was, shaking up little sister. The one so well-loved. She had slammed the door of the open heart. No room for help from a kindly stranger. But the threat of harm from a greedy stranger could lever her.

She came back, a little pink around the edges, but carrying herself proudly and well. She slid onto the bench and said, "I wasn't babbling. I meant it . . . about the money."

"Can you afford a gesture that expensive?"

"I'm on a good salary. There's nothing I want so badly I can't get along without it. But you have to keep your side of the bargain and leave me alone."

"Why is that so important?"

"A lot of people thought he was a very nice guy. I want to leave it that way. And I don't think I want to know any more than I know right now."

"I weaken a lot easier when I have the money in my hand, honey."

"Don't you believe me?"

"Let's go look at it. Or did you put it in a lockbox?"

She finished her sherry and put her glass down. "Any time you're ready, Mr. McGee."

"Trav."

She shrugged. "Trav, then. But there's not too much point in it. I don't plan to get to know you. I don't think Mike would want me to know you. I don't think he knows you."

"He used to. But people change."

"He shouldn't have guessed about the money. I started to tell him. I wish he hadn't guessed."

I finished my drink, beckoned for the check. "It brought me to you at a dead run, Miss Nina."

"How marvelous for me!"

2

She had a third-floor walkup on 53rd, a few doors from Second Avenue, a studio apartment with one bedroom. The hallway had a girlie flavor, hints of soap and perfume on the stale and dusty air. They tend to flock together. Once a few of them are established, they know when the next vacancy is coming up—and there is always a friend in need.

Nina Gibson was clean but not neat. Great stacks of decorator and craft and design magazines. Shelves of presentation designs that never quite worked out. A huge drawing table with Luxo lamps clamped onto it, like big gray metal grasshoppers. Art books. Big action paintings, Kline-like, but without Kline's sober weight and dignity. A great big pushpin wall with her working drawings stuck all over it. A ratty, unhoused assortment of high-fidelity components.

When they get you into their nest and the door is closed, they stiffen up. It is one of the syndromes of the new freedom, I guess. Man and woman in the living place, in the food and bed place. This is my cave and I live here. Stiffness and exaggerated informality and the laughter goes Ha Ha, as if written down that way. And too much of silence between the very ordinary comments. This is because, I think, the living place, just being there, focuses the attention on sexual speculations. In the living place they tuck themselves in and walk carefully. How would we be together? It is the great unasked question. Eyes get a little shifty. Excuses are made in a lofty tone, and the special advantages are pointed out in the brass voice of a Greek guide describing the ruined temples.

Nina said, "Excuse the mess. I do a lot of work here."

I gave an unwelcome blurt of laughter. She stared at me as if I'd lost my mind. But I couldn't tell her about the wild Freudian slip I had suddenly remembered. Years ago I had taken a shy girl to dinner. She had eaten like a wolf pack, even to having a second piece of coconut-cream pie. I had gone up to her place for the well-known nightcap. The girl she lived with was away for the weekend. We were feeling each other out, making chatty talk on one level, creating sensual tensions on another. I was deciding just when and how to make my pass, and she was wondering when it was coming and what to do about it—acceptance or rejection. She sighed and smiled and gave a little hitch to her skirt and said, "My goodness, I shouldn't have had that second piece of pants."

"Is something so terribly funny?" Nina demanded.

"No, I just—" I was saved by the telephone. She hurried to it and answered.

"Hello? Oh, hi, Ben. What? No. No, I'm sorry, I guess not. No, dear, it isn't like that. I'm on two more accounts now, and there just doesn't seem to be any time."

Her voice went on, polite, personal, unswervingly firm in rejection of whatever pitch Ben was making. I wandered over to the pushpin wall and looked at her work. One drawing of a jar was striking. It had a severe and classic beauty. She hung up and came over to me.

"Do you like that one?" she asked.

"Very much."

"You've got a pretty good eye, McGee. The client didn't like it. We go around telling each other that good taste will sell. Maybe it will, at the right time and the right place. But what is truly commercial is a kind of vulgarity upgraded just enough to look like good taste. And the best ones in the business are the ones who can toss that kind of crap off naturally, and really believe it's great."

I looked down at her thoughtful face. "The trouble with that jar, Nina, what's there to put in it?"

"You have a point. Wait right here." She went into the small bedroom and closed the door. I prowled the place. I looked at the books and the records. Aside from an unwholesome taste for string quartets, and a certain gullibility about predigested sociology, she passed the McGee test with about a $B+$. Hell, an $A-$. Maybe somebody had given her the Vance Packard books. He has the profitable knack of making what everybody has known all along sound like something new and astonishing. The same way Norman Vincent Peale invented Christianity and James Jones designed the M-1 rifle. I could relate all three to her handsome jug. Theirs was an upgraded vulgarity.

She came out suddenly and marched across to me and put ten thousand dollars into my hand. I sat on her couch and bounced it in my hand and took the two rubber bands off it. Three packs of used bills in the bank wrappers, initialed by whoever had done the wrapping. Two packs of fifty fifties. One pack of fifty hundreds. She stood in her pale gray blouse and her suit skirt, in her dark pumps and her nylons and her discontent, and looked at me with a small defiant face. This was her gesture of disappointing love, and it seemed a shame to bitch it for her. I riffled the edges of the bills in silence and snapped the rubber bands back on. I flipped the little brick of money at her head, and she dodged wildly and stuck one hand up and surprised herself by catching it.

She stared blankly at me. "What's wrong?"

I swung my legs up and stretched out on her couch, fingers laced at the nape of my neck. "It's a pretty little egg, honey, but I want to meet the goose."

She stomped her foot. "You son of a bitch!"

"It tempted me a little, but not enough. This goose seems to be named Armister."

"Get *out* of here!"

"Let's have a nice little talk."

In her fury she made an unwise lunge to yank me off the couch. I caught her wrists. She was a very strong little girl. She nearly got her teeth into my hand before I could get my forearm under her chin. She tried to kick, but she didn't have the room or the leverage. But she fought—grunting, writhing, flinging herself around until she landed in a sitting position, with a great padded thump, beside the couch. She slumped then, breathing hard in exhaustion, a tousle of the blue-black hair hiding one blue eye.

"Damn you!" she gasped. "Damn you, damn you, damn you!"

"Will you listen?"

"No!"

"It's all very simple. How about this guy, this wonderful marriageable Howard Plummer? What kind of a dreary excuse for a girl are you?"

"I'm not listening to you."

"The tiresome thing about you, honey, is that if he was still alive, you probably wouldn't listen to him either. Suppose you found the money and he was still alive. I can see the scene. Your eyes flash fire. Fists on your hips. A hell of a nasty tone of voice. Howie, darling, prove to me you're not a thief, and it better be good. Why, that poor slob really lucked out of marrying you, darling girl. Howie, darling, this little red smudge on your collar better be blood, you two-timing bastard. Howie, baby, don't you take a step outside our happy home without letting me know where you are every single minute."

"You . . . you filthy . . ."

"You poor righteous little prude. Poor Miss Prim."

"What are you trying to *do* to me?"

"Make you give your man the same break any court would give him. Innocent until proven guilty. And the court wouldn't have gone to bed with him before condemning him without a trial, baby."

I released her wrists. She belted me a good one, and a microsecond after it landed, I jarred her down to her heels with an open-handed blow. The blue eyes swarmed out of focus and came back, shocked and wide, and then the tears hit her. They choked her and ripped her up, and she leaned into me, grinding her face into the side of my knee. I stroked her hair. It was all spasms, as convulsive as trying to steady a vomiting drunk. I wondered if she had really cried since her Howie had died. She was ridding herself of poison, coughing it out. It took her a long time to slow down and begin to ride it with any kind of reasonable rhythm. I got up and boosted her onto the couch and went off and found her bathroom, brought her back a cold wet washcloth and a big soft dry towel. I sat on the floor beside the couch and patted her once in a while. She drifted into a limp exhaustion, punctuated by a hiccup now and again. She sighed and turned her face toward me. I swabbed it with the cold cloth and she dried it on the towel. She stared at me, quiet and solemn as a justly punished child.

"Trav. Trav, I've been horrible."

"So?"

"Don't you see? I didn't even give him a chance. He couldn't explain, and I didn't even give him a chance."

"Do you understand that, Nina?"

"N-No."

"You had to muffle the pain any way you could. Lessen the loss. By trying to believe he lied and cheated. But you couldn't really believe it. It's a proof of how much love there was."

"But it's so unfair to him."

"Not to him, honey. To his memory, maybe. Not to him."

"What . . . what can I do now?"

"There's just one thing we can do. It's what I came to do. It's what Mike sent me to do. Let's find out what happened."

"But you made me think it was just the money that . . ."

I pushed her hair back away from the other puffy eye. "Mike said I might have to shake you up."

She stared at me. She shook her head slowly from side to side. She made a mouth. "You two. You and Mike. How could you know more about me than I knew?"

"Is it a deal?"

Her smile was frail, but it was a smile. "We'll have a lot of nice little talks."

After she regained enough energy to check the larder, she told me how far and in what direction I had to go to find a delicatessen. When I returned, she had changed to baggy slacks and a big pink hairy sweatshirt. She had fixed her face and her hair and set a table for us by the window. She unloaded the sacks, accusing me of exotic and extravagant tastes. But she found herself hungrier than she had expected. Her voice was still husky from her tears, and I had left a small bruise along her left jaw.

After we had eaten and she had stacked the few dishes, we sat on the couch with drinks.

"I didn't even know he had been killed until noon of the next day," she said in a soft, thoughtful voice. "And I fell all apart. Those days are a blur. Sedatives, good friends standing by. I wanted to die too. It seemed such a horrid waste, to lose him that way. Sort of by mistake. Because somebody was greedy and scared and careless, some dirty sick animal out of nowhere. But I held myself together somehow. His sister flew out from California. There was a service here because of his friends here. She took care of his things, giving some away, giving me what she thought I'd like to have of his, closing his apartment. The body went back to Minnesota to be buried there in the family plot with his parents. I couldn't have stood going there and enduring another service. I think his sister understood. I hope she did. It wasn't until after she was gone that I remembered his things here. I was in such a daze. We weren't exactly living together. Just sort of. After we were married, we were going to live here and give up his apartment. It was handier for both of us. He had a key to here. And some personal things here. I didn't know exactly what he'd brought over. I'd already started taking up less room with my stuff to give him room. We knew what furniture of his we were going to bring over. I'd given him half my closet shelf. So finally I got the courage to go through the things he'd brought over, stopping every once in a while to lie down and cry myself sick. Over little things. I had to stand on a chair to reach the back of the shelf. The money was last. It was in the corner. It was wrapped in brown paper and tied with string. He died a week before my twenty-fourth birthday, Trav, and I didn't want to open it because I thought that if it was a gift for me hidden there, it would just break my heart so badly I'd never get over it. I sat on the bed and unwrapped it . . . and it was the money. And suddenly there was a coldness in my heart, and I suddenly decided that he . . . that he . . ."

"Easy, Nina."

"When you think you know everything about a person and . . ."

"We both know it was a defensive emotional reaction."

"I wish I was as certain as you are, Trav. Maybe I am a lousy little righteous prude."

"And maybe we find out it was just what you thought it was."

She nodded. She slipped her hand into mine. "I know. I've thought of that. But now I know I do have to find out. And for that I have . . . I have to thank you. What should we do about the money?"

"We'll know later what has to be done. If it's all right with you, I'll take it along and put it in the hotel safe. Now tell me about his work."

In a little while she began yawning, and I knew she'd given all she had to give, for one day. She found a heavy manila envelope and I sealed the money into it. She came with me to the door and, sleepy as a child, unthinkingly lifted her face for a kiss. Her mouth was soft. She backed away suddenly and put her hand to her throat.

"I wasn't trying to be . . ."

"Go to bed, Miss Nina. Go to sleep. Dream good dreams."

"I might. I just might."

3

After breakfast I made some phone calls and found out which precinct I should contact. I went to the precinct and stated my wishes. They looked it up. Their man who had worked the case, along with Homicide people who had covered it, was a Sergeant T. Rassko. I couldn't even find out that much until a Lieutenant Bree had questioned me with care and suspicion.

"I don't get the point," he kept saying, as he teetered and patted his stomach. "Whadaya tryna complish?"

I tried again. "Lieutenant, you know what a veteran is?"

"Don't get smart with me."

"This veteran is in a veterans' hospital. Ever since Korea. Blind and busted up. Plummer was going to marry this veteran's kid sister. I'm the veteran's best friend. He asked me to find out how Plummer got killed."

"Whadaya tryna complish? It was in the papers. You want to make out we're not doing a job around here? You want to tell us something we don't know already? I don't get the point."

"Lieutenant, please, imagine that you are a blind veteran in a hospital. Your sister's fiancé gets killed."

"Better than she should have married him, the one my sister married."

"Would you be satisfied with hearing somebody read you a little newspaper item, or would you want to have a friend go see where and how it happened and come and tell you about it?"

Comprehension began, twinkled, flowered into a smile. "Hey, you just want to tell him how it was covered, hey?"

"That's it."

"Let's see your identification again, McGee."

He studied my Florida driver's license. As he handed it back, the cop eyes took the practiced flickering inventory—tailoring, fabric, shirt collar, knuckles and fingernails, shoeshine, haircut—all the subtle clues to status.

"What kind of work you in, Mr. McGee?"

"Marine fabrications consultant."

"Yeah. You sit over there and I'll see what I can do." He walked heavily away, portly, white-haired, slow of wit. I sat on a worn bench and watched the flow of business. It is about as dramatic as sitting in a post office, and there are the same institutional smells of flesh, sweat, disinfectants, and mimeo ink. Two percent of police work is involved with blood. All the rest of it is a slow, querulous, intricate involvement with small rules and procedures, violations of numbered ordinances, complaints made out of spite and ignorance, all the little abrasions and irritations of too many people living in too small a space. The standard police attitude is one of tired, kindly, patronizing exasperation.

Thomas Rassko, Detective Sergeant, looked and acted like a young clerk in a fashionable men's store. Quiet, bored, indifferent, quietly dressed, pale, and cat-footed. Bree had cleared me, but I was obviously a waste of time. He led me to the visitor's chair beside a bull-pen desk, went away, and came back with a thin file packet.

He sat down and opened it and sorted the contents and said, "Deceased white male American age twenty-seven. Estimated time of death, between eleven and midnight on Saturday, August tenth. The body was found just inside the truck driveway to a warehouse at three eighteen West Nineteenth Street. There was a notification by the warehouse watchman at one thirty-five." He sorted some eight-by-ten glossies and handed me one. "This will give you the best idea of it."

Howard Plummer lay in the harshness of the electronic flash, face down on asphalt, close to a brick wall. He was turned slightly toward the wall, legs sprawled loose, one arm under him, the jacket of his pale suit hiked above the small of his back. Both side pockets of his pants and one hip pocket were pulled inside out.

"You could practically call it accidental death," Rassko said. "A standard mugging that went wrong. The way they work it, there are usually two of them. They pick somebody well-dressed, maybe a little bit smashed, and follow along close, and when the situation is right, no traffic, and a handy dark corner, the stronger of the two takes him from behind, an arm around the throat, yanks him into the dark corner, and the other one cleans him—wallet, watch, everything. By then, if he hasn't blacked out, they yank his pants down around his ankles, give him a hell of a shove and then run like hell. This Plummer was husky. Big enough to make them nervous, maybe. Or maybe he struggled too hard. Or maybe they were amateurs. Like sometimes we get sailors who get rolled and then try to take it back from anybody who comes along. That forearm across the throat can be very dangerous. They probably thought he had just blacked out, but the larynx was crushed. They let him drop and they ran, and he strangled to death."

"No leads at all?"

"This is a very low category of crime, Mr. McGee. Punk kids come in from way out—Queens, Brooklyn, even Jersey—so it isn't necessarily a neighborhood thing. Maybe they never even found out the guy died. They aren't newspaper readers. Our informants came up empty so far. There was nothing for the lab to go on. We couldn't find anybody who saw anything. We estimate he had about fifty dollars on him. His wallet never showed up. Nobody, not even his girl, could tell us the make wristwatch he was wearing, so we don't know if it was pawned."

"What was he doing in that neighborhood?"

Rassko shrugged. "It was a hot Saturday night. His girl had to go to some kind of business dinner at a hotel. He left his apartment about six. We couldn't trace him. Maybe he was just cruising. We don't know whether he was walking east or west when he got hit. Maybe he took a girl home and he was walking looking for a cab. Too bad. Nice fellow, I guess, good education, good job, and about to be married. Like I said, it's almost like accidental death. But it was no place for a well-dressed man to be walking alone at night, especially if he'd had a few drinks. That's asking for it."

"Did you have any trouble identifying him?"

"No. His name was written on the label in his suit, and the name was in the phone book. What we do to speed it up, we take a Polaroid flash of the face and send a man to check with the neighbors. The first contact verified the identity. I don't know where else we can go with it. Tomorrow or next year we may break somebody in connection with something else and hear all about this one, so we can close the file. There's only so much work you can do on a thing like this, and then it stops making sense to go further on account of the rest of the work load. But we don't forget it. We keep the live cases posted."

I thanked him for giving me so much time. I went out into the bright beautiful October day and walked slowly and thoughtfully back toward midtown. It was just past noon and the offices were beginning to flood the streets with a warm hurrying flow of girls. A burly man, in more of a hurry than I was, bumped into me and thrust me into a tall girl. They both whirled and snarled at me.

New York is where it is going to begin, I think. You can see it coming. The insect experts have learned how it works with locusts. Until locust population reaches a certain density, they all act like any grasshoppers. When the critical point is reached, they turn savage and swarm, and try to eat the world. We're nearing a critical point. One day soon two strangers will bump into each other at high noon in the middle of New York. But this time they won't snarl and go on. They will stop and stare and then leap at each other's throats in a dreadful silence. The infection will spread outward from that point. Old ladies will crack skulls with their deadly handbags. Cars will plunge down the crowded sidewalks. Drivers will be torn out of their cars and stomped. It will spread to all the huge cities of the world, and by dawn of the next day there will be a horrid silence of sprawled bodies and tumbled vehicles, gutted buildings, and a few wisps of smoke. And through that silence will prowl a few, a very few of the most powerful ones, ragged and bloody, slowly tracking each other down.

I went back to my sterile cheerful miracle-plastic automated rectangle set high in the flank of a new hotel. I shucked my jacket and lay cradled on foam, breathing air made by careful machines, supine in a sub-audio hum that silenced all the city sounds.

I thought of death and money and blue-eyed tears. And some other blue eyes gone blind. This emotional obligation did not fit me. I felt awkward in the uncomfortable role. I wished to be purely McGee, that pale-eyed, wire-haired girl finder, that big shambling brown boat-bum who walks beaches, slays small fierce fish, busts minor icons, argues, smiles, and disbelieves, that knuckly scar-tissued reject from a structured society who waits until the money gets low and then goes out and takes it from the taker, keeps half, and gives the rest back to the innocent. These matters can best be handled by the uninvolved.

But I was involved in this. While Missy, neck-deep in the steaming old stone bath, had been giggling and clasping Travis McGee within her sturdy little legs, somebody had blinded Mike Gibson and chopped him up.

I frowned at my sound-proofed ceiling and thought how they could improve the hotel service. Make the rounds—manager, technician, and chambermaid. Are you happy enough, sir? Not quite. Gather around the bed, open the little compartment in the headboard, pull out the joy tubes and slip them into the veins, unreel the joy wires and needle them into the happy-making part of the brain. Adjust the volume. Is that better, sir? Enormously. When are you leaving us, sir? Turn me off next Tuesday. Thank you, sir. Enjoy your stay in New York, sir. Happy hallucinations.

I detected the reason for my reluctance to make the next move. I was afraid that, through ignorance, I would blow the whole thing.

And the next move was Robert.

Nina had told me that if I could make him talk to me, he could tell me more about Howard Plummer's job than anyone else. Robert Imber. He worked in the Trust Department of a Fifth Avenue bank.

Robert received me in a junior shrine of his very own, a leathery little church-lighted opaque box, filled with a hush of money. He sat waxen in his dark suit, his pale little mouth sucked in, a steep and glossy wave in his dark brown hair. No one had ever called him Bob or Bobby. He was a Robert, brown-eyed and watchful.

"Yes, a dreadful dreadful thing," he said. "This city is a jungle. I hope Miss Gibson is . . . recovering. I really hardly know her. You see, I left Armister-Hawes almost a year ago, and that was about the time Howard began to go with Miss Gibson."

"I don't yet understand what Armister-Hawes is."

He blushed as though caught in dreadful error. "It isn't *really* Armister-Hawes. It used to be, years ago. It was an investment banking house with branches in London and Brussels and Lisbon. But it is still in those same charming old offices, and the brass plate at the entrance says Armister-Hawes and one gets in the habit. Really, it's just the headquarters from which the Armister financial affairs are handled."

"They need a headquarters for that?"

"Oh yes indeed, Mr. McGee. And quite a large staff. It's very *old* money, and quite a bit of money. There are the real estate holdings to manage, and quite a complex structure of holding companies, trusts, foundations, corporate investment entities, and several very active port-folios, of course. Charles McKewn Armister, the Fourth, as head of the present family, takes an active interest."

"Why did you leave?"

He studied me. He was so motionless, I wondered if he was breathing.

"I beg your pardon?"

"I wasn't trying to pry. I just thought it must have been very interesting work."

"Oh, it was. Excellent training, too. You get into so many ramifications of so many things. But this opportunity opened up for me. And there was the chance they wouldn't have been able to keep me on had I stayed. You see, I was junior to Howard Plummer."

"You mean they were cutting down?"

"Not exactly. It's rather difficult to explain it to a layman. They had embarked on a long-range program of cutting down on active manage-ment responsibilities. For example, a large office building can mean a great deal of paper work, leases, maintenance contracts, tax matters, and so on. They had begun to divest themselves of that sort of thing, a bit at a time. And they had begun to simplify the securities holdings, cutting down the number of transactions there too. And they had stopped going into new ventures."

"If that's the way it was going, I wonder why Howard didn't leave too."

"I have reason to believe he was considering it. But he was making quite good money. And he had a strong feeling of loyalty toward Mr. Armister. I imagine he would not have remained there much longer. He was a very sound man, Mr. McGee. Excellent investment judgment."

"Speaking as a layman, Mr. Imber, I wonder about one thing. If the policy changed, if they started selling off stuff, wouldn't it give some-body a better chance to siphon off some of that Armister money?"

His eyes bulged. "What an extraordinary thing to say!"

"Wouldn't it be possible?"

"Surely you are joking, Mr. McGee. You have no idea of the impos-sibility of doing anything like that. There is a practically continuous tax audit of transactions. There are checks and balances within the account-ing system. Mr. Armister is very alert. The head of the legal staff, Mr. Baynard Mulligan, is a very able and respected man. Mr. Lucius Pe-nerra, head of the accounting staff, is totally competent and respected.

And *nothing* of any importance happens without Mr. Armister's personal investigation and approval. No, Mr. McGee, it is not only rather stupid to make a formless accusation like that, it could even be dangerous. I suspect it always is dangerous to slander any important and respected organization."

"There would be no way to clip that outfit?"

"Absolutely none. How did we get into this subject?"

"One more question, Mr. Imber. Do you think the change of policy was smart?"

"That all depends."

"On what?"

"If you wish to take maximum advantage of a fortune of perhaps sixty or seventy millions of dollars, conserve it and increase it, while at the same time taking advantage of every tax break and every change in the economic climate, then the previous operation was better. But there are human values too. For example, Mr. Armister could have decided the work was too confining and restrictive. So he could seek a static rather than an active position. He might eventually have it in mind to cut down to the point where he could disband all operations and turn the holdings over to the trust departments of his banks. It might mean as much as a five percent change in his annual position, say three million dollars. That is what he would be in effect paying for the privilege of not taking risks."

"How old is he?"

"I would say he is about forty-four now. Inherited money is a terrible responsibility, Mr. McGee. It can become a crushing burden. Naturally I have no right to make guesses about what Mr. Armister wants or doesn't want."

"Did Howard ever complain about the new policy?"

"Why have you come to see me?"

"I wanted to find out about Howard's job."

"But why?"

"Miss Gibson is curious."

"Why should she be curious?"

"I wish I could tell you, Mr. Imber. But I gave my word."

"I certainly hope she isn't doubting Howard's honesty. He was a completely reliable man."

"Did he complain about the new policy?"

"Just once. Just before I left. Together we had worked out a very sound land-use program for a large tract in Maryland, and figured the investment needed to begin the first phase. Then Mr. Mulligan told Howard they had decided to put it on the market. It was a bitter disappointment. Howard tried to fight the decision but got nowhere. I remember him walking back and forth in front of my desk, cursing the entire organization." He looked at his watch. "I'm very sorry, but . . ."

I got up quickly. I thanked him for giving me the time. His handshake was abrupt, cold and strenuous. I glanced back at him as I went out his doorway. He was sitting erect, registering disapproval. I had slandered one of his gods. I was a reckless layman. And I suspected that he was annoyed with himself for talking perhaps too much and too freely. There is only one way to make people talk more than they care to. Listen. Listen with hungry earnest attention to every word. In the intensity of your attention, make little nods of agreement, little sounds of approval. You can't fake it. You have to really listen. In a posture of gratitude. And it is such a rare and startling experience for them, such a boon to ego, such a gratification of self, to find a genuine listener, that they want to prolong the experience. And the only way to do that is to keep talking. A good listener is far more rare than an adequate lover.

I had one useful source of information, if she was in the city. Constance Trimble Thatcher, age about seventy-two. She was the victim in a Palm Beach episode a few years ago. Though she was abnormally shrewd, a plausible sharpster had probed for a weak point and gouged her without mercy. I had discovered the con almost by accident, shaken it out of the operator, and taken it all back to her and explained my fee system. She had turned over half without a murmur, demanding only that I never let anyone know what a damned old fool she had been.

I gave my name and she came to the phone in person and demanded that I come see her immediately before her extremely dull cocktail guests arrived. I taxied up to her big old duplex overlooking the park. I waited in the foyer. The tall old rooms were full of Regency furniture, gold brocade, and fresh flowers. From the buffet preparations, I could guess she expected at least fifty.

She came trotting toward me, all smiles and pearls, piled white hair, green gown, and little yips of welcome. She pulled me into a small study off the foyer and closed the mahogany door. She held my hands and peered up at me and said, "McGee, McGee, you beautiful shifty scoundrel, if *only* I were thirty years younger."

"It's good to see you again, Mrs. Thatcher."

"What!"

"It's good to see you again, Connie."

She drew me over to the couch and we sat down. "I can't hope that you came to see an old lady just out of affection and old times, McGee. So there's something you want. And by the look of you, you haven't settled down yet and never will. You are a brigand, McGee."

"You never found me a nice girl, Connie."

"I sent you one, dear. But that was only for therapy."

"How is Joanie?"

"Back with her husband, but you would know that, wouldn't you, because it was your advice, so she told me. She's had her third child by now. Happy, they say. Was I a wicked old woman to send her to you?"

"You know you were."

"She needed a fling, and she could have fallen among thieves. She came back all aglow, McGee. I was eaten with jealousy. Tell me, what intrigue are you mixed up in now, and will you make any money?"

"What do you know about Charles McKewn Armister, the Fourth?"

She stared at me, head slightly cocked, one eye narrowed. It is easy to see how beautiful she must have been. "It's an interesting question," she said. "I know what there is to know."

"Which is why I came to you."

"When I was a little girl I fell off a horse—one of many many times—and his grandfather picked me up. And for a time I thought I would marry his father, a romantic fellow much given to kissing and writing love poems. But young Charlie has always been a stick. He was a very proper little boy. He married young. I think they were both twenty. Joanna Howlan he married. Money to money. They had summer places close together at Bar Harbor. A proper girl for him, I guess. One of those sturdy freckled girls, good at games, with a nice smile, and as proper as he. Two children of the marriage, a boy and a girl. The boy is twenty-two, I would guess, and off in some far place in the Peace Corps; the girl eighteen and in Holyoke." She scowled into space. "I don't know how to say it, McGee. Charlie and his wife have no flair for the use of money, at least not that much money. It's the cult of simplicity. They take all the magic out of it. Some kind of inverted snobbism, I guess. Social guilt. I just don't know. They have the old place on the Island, and an apartment in town, and a smallish place at Hobe Sound. They are quiet, gentle, careful, dull people and, like I said, very good at games. Tennis and sailing and such. Charlie works very hard, they say, tending the money, making it grow and giving it away properly. It's strange we should mention a fling before, because I hear that Charlie is having himself one."

"Hmmm?"

"At the time of life when you can most expect it from a man who marries young, McGee. He had some kind of a breakdown a year ago. One of those anxiety things. Now he and Joanna are separated, but no one has said anything about divorce. He has his own apartment in town. And he has created a drunken fuss in a few public places, bless him, after years of restraint. And I did hear something strange about the menage he's set up for himself." Her eyes clouded. "Let me think. When a woman forgets gossip, McGee, she is nearing the end of her road. What *was* it? Oh! I heard he is living with his lawyer and his secretary. Now *there* is a lurid arrangement for you!" She shook her head. "How could I have forgotten, dear boy? It might be handy, though. He would be right there to prepare releases, wouldn't he? The lawyer is Baynard Mulligan. I've met him. Quite amusing and attractive, really. A rather nice Virginia family, but I understand they lost their money when he was small. Let me see now. He married Elena Garrett when he was thirty and she was no more than nineteen. But it didn't work out at *all*. It lasted four years, I think. They say she became alcoholic. Now she's married to some little teacher person over at Princeton and has become very earnest and happy, and she's having child after child. Baynard didn't remarry. Let me see what else I know about Charlie Armister."

"You are fantastic, Connie, and I am grateful, but for the last five minutes I've heard your guests arriving."

"McGee, darling, the bar is in a perfectly obvious place, and this is a hideously boring batch, actually the sort of party I'd have the Armisters at, if they were together and in the city. I get all the dead ones together and let them amuse each other. It's better than inflicting them in little dabs on my lively friends. I'll go out there when I'm ready. Perhaps the most interesting thing about Charlie Armister is his sister-in-law, Joanna's elder sister. Give me a moment and I can tell you the exact name. Teresa Howlan Gernhardt . . . ah . . . Delancy Drummond. Terry, she is called. Very international, and she's a charming earthy bawd, and has a marvelous figure for her age. She must be forty-six. She's usually in Rome or Athens, but I've heard she's here now, probably to hold her sister's hand. It's remarkable two girls could be so unlike. McGee, darling, I do suppose you are brassy enough to go ask Terry about Charlie, and she's probably annoyed enough to tell you. Where would she be? Mmmm. Either at the Plaza or at the Armister apartment. Try them both, dear. But don't get the wrong apartment. The old one, the one where she'd be, is the one on East Seventy-ninth. I think Charlie's hideout is further down. Now, I think I must go join my guests, much as I dread it. And you *must* come back and tell me the scandalous reason why you should be interested in Charlie Armister. I won't tell a *soul*."

"The hell with Charlie. I'm interested in that secretary." We stood up. I bent and kissed her soft wrinkled cheek.

"Slip out swiftly, my dear, before any of these old battle wagons can clutch you and start honking at you. And phone me again soon."

I went out, smiling. The old elevator was rattling up the shaft so I took the stairs down. Constance Trimble Thatcher has her own kind of wisdom. There had been one morning when I had thought she had lost her mind. That was the morning Joanie had appeared at my gangplank looking pallid and jumpy and sacrificial in her resort wear. With trembling hand she had thrust a note at me. I saw her chin shaking as I looked at her after reading it. It was in Connie's oversized purple script, and all it said was, "Be very sweet to this dear exhausted harried child. Some utter idiots wanted to clap her into a rest home. But, as her godmother, I think I know better what she requires." The next day I had cast off and gone chugging down to the Keys bearing my wan, huddled, jittery passenger. Three weeks later I delivered her to the Miami airport for her flight back. She was ten pounds heavier, brown as walnuts, her hair bleached three shades lighter, her hands toughened by rowing, her muscles toned and springy. We kissed the long humid good-byes, and she laughed and cried—not in hysterics, but because she had good reasons for laughing and good reasons for crying, and we both knew just how she could pick up the pieces of her life and build something that would make sense. Captain McGee. Private cruises. Personalized therapy. And a little twinge of pain when the plane took off, pain for McGee, because she was too close to what-might-have-been. If there's no pain and no loss, it's only recreational and we can leave it to the minks. People have to be valued.

4

I discovered that Mrs. Drummond was in residence at the Plaza, but not in on this early Friday evening, so I took a taxi over to East 53rd. Nina was not home from the office. I whisked the soot off the wall by the entrance steps and sat and waited for her, and watched the office people bring their anxious dogs out. You could almost hear the dogs sigh as they reached the handiest pole. There was a preponderance of poodles.

This is the most desperate breed there is. They are just a little too bright for the servile role of dogdom. So their loneliness is a little more excruciating, their welcomes more frantic, their desire to please a little more intense. They seem to think that if they could just do everything right, they wouldn't have to be locked up in the silence—pacing, sleeping, brooding, enduring the swollen bladder. That's what they try to talk about. One day there will appear a super-poodle, one almost as bright as the most stupid alley cat, and he will figure it out. He will suddenly realize that his loneliness is merely a by-product of his being used to ease the loneliness of his Owner. He'll tell the others. He'll leave messages. And some dark night they'll all start chewing throats.

A six-foot girl walked slowly by leading a little gray poodle in a jeweled collar. He peered out at me from under his curls with his little simian eyes. She wore flowered stretch pants and a furry white sweater. She slanted a quick look of speculation at me. She went by. Her haunches moved with a weighty slowness in time to her strolling gait. The poodle stared back at me. Bug off, he said. There isn't enough love to go around. You are the familiar enemy.

"Classy neighborhood, huh?" Nina said.

I sprang up and said, "You sneaked up on me."

"We call that one the Snow Maiden. She has about forty sweaters. All tight. All white."

"It's a lot of girl."

"Waiting long? Come on up."

As we slowly climbed the stairs, she said, "I slept like a felled ox, Trav. I didn't even hear the alarm. And all day I've been just dragging around. If I'd put my head down for one minute, I'd have gone to sleep. Reaction or something."

"You blew a lot of old fuses last night."

"And burned out the wiring." She leaned against the wall and handed me her key and yawned. I let us in. The place was more orderly.

"Housework?" I said.

"A little bit last night. It was messy."

"I'll take you out to dinner tonight."

"Let me get out of my shoes and have a drink and think about it, dear. Fix me bourbon on ice, will you? You know where the things are. Knock and hand it in. A shower might wake me up."

"No sherry?"

She gave me a rueful smile. "I was on sherry because I was scared of what anything stronger would do to me. I was afraid of losing control. I'm a bourbon girl from way back."

She dragged her way into the bedroom and closed the door. I fixed drinks. When I rapped on the bedroom door, nothing happened. I could hear the shower. I went into the bedroom. Her clothing had been tossed on her unmade bed. The bathroom door was ajar. The shower roared. There was a warm, steamy, flowery scent of girl. I knocked on the bathroom door. In a moment a wet arm came out. I put the glass in the hand. It went back in.

"Thank you," she called. "You know what?"

"What?"

"I'm getting a bonus."

"That's nice."

"On the Marvissa account. We got it. They took my design. It was a competition. Five hundred dollars."

"Congratulations."

"And I was so tired, my only response was a weak and humble little smile. I'll be out in a few minutes, dear."

I went back into the living room. The heady scent of soapy girl seemed to follow me out. I ordered McGee to stop picturing her in the shower. I told him he had seen whole platoons of showering women, and scrubbed many a glossy back in his day, and this was a damned poor time for adolescent erotic fantasies. And the business of the drink had not been a tricky invitation. It had been a friendly innocence. This was Mike's kid sister. It would have a flavor of incest. And this wasn't what he had meant by shaking her up. So I paced, and smirked woodenly at her drawings, and wrenched my mind into other patterns.

At last she came out in feathery slippers and a long pink and black robe cinched tightly around the tininess of her waist, with a little mist of perspiration on her upper lip, and some of the ends of the blue-black hair dampened.

"I'll dress when we decide what kind of a place we're going."

"Sure. Refill?"

"Please."

So with new drinks, we sat and I told her about my day, Sergeant Rassko and Robert and Constance Trimble Thatcher. I made it complete. The Rassko thing was obviously a strain for her, so when I came to Robert I funnied him up more than he merited, and made her laugh a little. She was intrigued with Connie, and with the idea that so social and lofty a lady would be so gossipy with me.

"You must have some special credentials, Trav."

"I did her a favor once when she was very depressed. Her self-esteem was at a low ebb. She doesn't know many people like me. I guess I amuse her. And in some funny way, we're alike."

"You and Constance Trimble Thatcher?"

"We're both impatient with fraud. With all pretentious and phony people. She can afford to be. With me it's an extravagance."

"Am I phony?"

"You design the vulgar pots and sell them to the vulgar people. When you start believing them, you become fraudulent, Miss Nina. You make a plausible adjustment to the facts of life. I don't. And that isn't a virtue on my part. It's the disease of permanent adolescence. Honey, when you take your tongue out of your cheek, you become suspect."

"The Marvissa containers are hideous."

"Of course."

"But I'm proud of the bonus, Trav."

"Why not? Nina, once you accept the terms of the compromise, you'd be a damn fool not to do your best within those limitations. Beat them at their own game, and be proud you can."

"Okay, sir."

"Now. More questions about what Howie told you about the thievery."

"I told you, he only suspected it. He was very troubled about it. He said he couldn't prove anything. I asked him why not. He said I would have to take a course in accounting before he could even begin to explain it to me. But he tried to explain it. He said suppose you have a hundred buckets full of water and a hundred empty buckets, and all of a sudden you start pouring water back and forth from one to another as fast as you can. He said you could keep it moving around so fast that nobody would ever notice there was less and less total water all the time, and the only way it could be checked would be to stop the whole thing and carefully measure what was left."

"How about names?"

"He didn't like to talk about it to me. I'd always start pleading with him to quit. I kept telling him that if there was something nasty going on, he might get blamed or something. And I told him it was making him gloomy."

"What did he say about quitting?"

"He said that it was a good idea. In a little while. It irritated him that he couldn't sit down and have a serious talk with Mr. Armister. When he first went with them he said they used to talk things over, discuss future planning and so on. He said Mr. Armister had sound ideas. But then Mr. Armister got sort of . . . hearty and cheerful and indifferent. He said it had to be some kind of a high-level conspiracy, and he used to wonder if Mr. Armister was engineering it somehow, draining money out and hiding it away maybe in Switzerland for tax-evasion reasons. He said he guessed he was getting too nosy, because Mr. Mulligan kept hinting that it might be a good time for Howie to locate somewhere else, with a nice bonus and good letters of commendation."

"But he never found anything specific."

"Not that I know of."

"And what was he going to do if he did? Did he say?"

"No. But he used to look very grim and angry, as if he would go to the authorities or something if he found out. I loved him, Trav, but I have to say that Howie was just a little bit stuffy. He had very rigid ideas of right and wrong. He was . . . sort of repressed." She blushed slightly. "I believed that after we were married, I could sort of loosen him up."

I leaned back and said, "Sixty to seventy millions is a lot of water to pass from bucket to bucket. Quite a lot could get spilled. Ten percent would be six or seven million. Would you happen to know the name of the affectionate secretary?"

"Sure. Bonita Hersch. Howie couldn't stand her. She was Mr. Mulligan's secretary until Mr. Armister's secretary retired, and then she moved up."

"Why did he dislike her?"

"I guess because things changed there after she became Mr. Armister's secretary. You know how offices are. Or do you? They can be nice, everybody getting along, or it can get very formal. She built a wall around Mr. Armister and set the other people against each other. Trav?"

"Yes, Miss Nina."

"What do you *really* think about all this?"

I turned and looked into the intent blue eyes, thicketed with those long lashes, at the face small and young under the weight of blue-black curls.

"I think it is a lot of money. We're all still carnivorous, and money is the meat. If there's a lot of money and any possible way to get at it, I think people will do some strange warped things. Hardly anybody is really immune to the hunger, not if there's enough in view. I know I'm not."

"Is that one of those facts of life you were lecturing me about?"

"I was patronizing you, baby. I do a lot of talking. It makes me believe sometimes I know who I am. McGee, the free spirit. Such crap. All I've ever done is trade one kind of bondage for another. I'm the victim of my own swashbuckled image of myself. I'm lazy, selfish, and pretty shifty, Miss Nina. So I have to have an excuse structure. So I glamorize my deficiencies and lecture pretty little women about truth and beauty. Are you wise enough to understand that? If so, you are wise enough not to trip over my manufactured image."

"I think you are very strange."

"Don't get intrigued. It's not worth it. I'm a high-level beach bum. And I'm about as permanent as a black eye."

There is a time in all such things when eyes look into eyes, with vision narrowing and intensifying until there is nothing left but the eyes, searched and searching. This is a strange and tingling thing that narrows the breath—but it is a communication, and once it has happened there is an awareness beyond words.

She licked a dry mouth and half whispered, "I've run into doors. I've had my share of black eyes. I've gotten over them."

"Shut up."

"Mike said you were such a hell of a fine soldier."

"The result of a pertinent observation. I noticed that the better you were, the longer you lasted. Out of pure fright, I put my heart into it."

"Mike said you were going into business with your brother when you got back."

"When I got back, there wasn't any business. They had taken it away from him, and he had worked too hard at it, and he killed himself."

Blue eyes came closer and the voice was more of a whisper. "Mike said you have a strange thing about women."

"I happen to think they are people. Not cute objects. I think that people hurting people is the original sin. To score for the sake of scoring diminishes a man. I can't value a woman who won't value herself. McGee's credo. That's why they won't give me a playboy card. I won't romp with the bunnies."

With her lips two inches from mine and her lids looking heavy, she said, "Mike said it's a disaster to play poker with you."

"I live aboard my winnings. It's called the *Busted Flush*."

"Take me for a boat ride," she said, and rested her fists against my chest and fitted a soft sighing mouth to mine. It started in mildness, and lifted swiftly to a more agonizing sweetness of need than one can plausibly expect from a kiss. Her arms pulled, and she gave a wrenching gasp, and I held her away. She stared, blind and wide, then plunged up and wandered away, went over to her pushpin wall, and began idly straightening drawings.

"Trav?"

"We have to decide where to eat so you can get dressed."

"Trav?"

"Go; with the basic black, something suitable for baked mussels, pasta, a big garlic salad ice-cold, a bottle of Bardolino, espresso."

"Trav, damn it!"

"And shoes you can walk in, because we'll want to walk a little while after dinner and look at the lights and look at the people."

She turned and looked at me and shook her head in a sad exasperation and went into the bedroom and closed the door.

I held it all off until we were down to our second cups of the thick bitter coffee. I held it off by regaling her with folksy legends of the palm country, and bits of marina lore—such as my neighbor boat which housed the Alabama Tiger's perpetual floating house party, and how to catch a snook, and the best brand of rum in Nassau, and such like. I paused for moment.

"Trav?" she said, in that same old tone of voice, and I was locked into the intensity of her blue eyes and we were back with it.

"As you told me in the beginning, you are a darling girl. And a darling vulnerable girl, because somebody dimmed your lights back on August tenth, and because last night you whooped and coughed up enough of yourself to be equivalent to ten sessions on the couch and you want to transfer to me more than you should. You are just too damned willing to give all that trust and faith and affection, and it scares me. And when a damn fool shoots fish in a barrel, he also blows hell out of the barrel."

"Is that all?"

"When I think of more, I'll let you know."

"I don't need a den mother. I can take my own risks. For my own reasons."

"Just like a grown-up?"

"Oh shush. You don't do my vanity much good, McGee."

"Concentrate on your five-hundred-dollar bonus."

After long thought she gave a little shrug of acceptance. "So be it, den mother. What's your Saturday program?"

"Charlie Armister's sister-in-law. Terry Drummond. And hope to pick up some guide lines from her. Ready? Let's take that walk."

We walked a long amiable way on Fifth, making small jokes that seemed funnier than they probably were, and nightcapped with George at the Blue Bar at the Algonquin, and then taxied her home and held the cab. "Coward," she whispered, and gave me a child's simple kiss, and started up the stairs with a great burlesque comic show of exaggerated hip waving, turned and waved and grinned, and hurried on up.

5

I called Mrs. Drummond again on the house phone at ten minutes of eleven and she told me to come up. There was a man with her in the sitting room of the small suite. He had wire glasses, a tall forehead, and a deferential manner. She introduced him as Mr. King.

"What do you want to talk to me about?" she asked. She was tall and slender, and brown as a Navajo. She had dusty black hair pulled back into a careless bun. She wore tailored gray slacks, gold strap sandals, a silk shirt with three-quarter sleeves in an unusual shade of gray-green which enhanced the vivid and astonishing green of unusually large eyes. Her figure, as advertised, was taut and trim, tender and tidy as a young girl's. Even the backs of her slender hands were young. But the years had chopped her face. It was creased and withered and eroded into a simian brownness out of which the young green eyes stared. She had a deep drawling voice, barked rough by whiskey and smoking and living. She was smoking a cigarette, and her habits with it had a masculine look.

I glanced at King. She said, "Mr. King would like to know too."

Sometimes you have to take the risk very quickly, before you can scare yourself. "I want to know what's happening to Charlie Armister."

"Why, dear?"

"As a favor for a friend. And maybe, in all the confusion, some of that money will rub off on me."

"So you want to hustle him, dear?"

"Not to the exclusion of everything else, Mrs. Drummond."

She turned to King. "You can pop along now, sweetie."

"But I think I should . . ."

"Please."

"But in view of what he . . ."

She moved to him in a slow graceful stride, patted his cheek, took his shoulder, and turned him toward the door. "I'll be in touch."

He went with an obvious reluctance. She went over and sat on a small desk, slim legs swinging. She gave me her monkey grin.

"He's my lawyer. He's terribly protective. People get some terribly cute ideas, and I like to have him nearby when I make my little appraisal."

"Do I look that harmless?"

"No indeed, ducks. But old Connie Thatcher gave me a ring and said that if you should happen to come see me, you're a dear, and I should be nice. I was afraid you'd be one of those nice young men. I shouldn't underestimate Connie. She called you a brigand. Fix me a drink, dear. Two fingers of the Plymouth gin. One cube."

She watched me in silence as I fixed it and took it over to her. When I handed it to her, she caught me by the wrist with her free hand. Her fingers were thin and hot and strong. I automatically resisted her attempt to turn my wrist. She released me at once and grinned at me. I had the feeling I had won a claiming race, and before making her bid she had taken a look at my teeth.

"You're a powerful creature, Trav. Connie said people call you that. Please call me Terry. Aren't you drinking?"

"Not right now, thanks."

"I've offended you, haven't I?"

"Give me the blue ribbon and they can lead me back to my stall."

Her laugh was deep. "What would you expect of me, sweetie? Coyness, for God's sake? I'm a vulgar honest woman inspecting prime male. I don't see too many of your breed. They're either pretty boys or dull muscular oxen or aging flab. You move well, McGee. And I like deep-set gray eyes, hard stubborn jaws, and sensuous mouths. Aren't you a girl-watcher?"

"Of course."

"I'm too old for you, sweetie. But not too old to think of taking you to bed." She stuck a finger in her drink and stirred it and licked her finger. "Didn't Connie tell you I'm notoriously crude?"

"You certainly work at it, Terry."

For an instant the vivid green eyes narrowed, and then she laughed. "I'm supposed to be keeping *you* off balance, sweetie. It isn't supposed to work the other way."

"So let's call it a draw. I'm an acceptable stud, and from the neck down you're Miss Universe. And if there was ever any reason to go to bed, we'd probably find each other reasonably competent. But I came here to talk about Charlie."

"You *are* a bold bastard, aren't you?"

"Sure. And we're both emotional cripples, Terry. I've never married and you can't stay married, so perhaps all we've got is competence. And that makes a hell of a dry diet. Now how about Charlie?"

She sprang down from the desk, gave me a tearful savage glare, and ran into the bedroom and slammed the door as hard as she could.

I wandered over to the bar table and fixed myself a weak drink. I took it to the window and stood and watched the Saturday people strolling on the park walks. I picked through the magazines on the coffee table, and sat and leafed through one. There were some excellent color reproductions of three recent paintings by Tapies, work that had the burned, parched, textured, solemn, heartbreak look of his native Spain. I lusted to own one. I told myself I could bundle monkey-face into the sack and use her up, and she'd buy me one as a party favor. And she could buy all my clothes. In no time at all I too could look like a fag ski instructor. She could trundle me off to Athens. Teresa Howlan Gernhardt Delancy Drummond McGee. I wondered how many hours a day it cost her to keep that figure in such superb condition. Diet, steam, massage, exercise, lotions, hormones, dynamic tension. And lotsa lovin' —that most effective suppling agent of all. From the neck down she was Doriana Gray, dreading the magic moment when, overnight, every excess would suddenly become visible.

In twenty minutes she opened the door cautiously and stared out at me, brown face slightly puffed. "Oh," she said.

"Should I have left?"

"Don't be an idiot."

"Two fingers and one cube?"

"Please." She sat in a wing chair by the windows. I took her the drink. She looked up at me with a wan smile. "You know, McGee, you are sort of a walking emetic. You are a big rude finger down my throat."

I smiled at her. "You wouldn't settle for a standoff. You had to keep prodding, Terry."

"Okay. Now you're the dominant male. Now you're in charge. But people just don't talk to me like that."

"Because you're rich. Everybody you meet gives a damn about that. The rich are an alien race."

"And you don't give a damn?"

"Of course I do. But I can't con you and lick your pretty sandals simultaneously, honey."

"My God, you really and truly make me feel like a young girl again, Trav."

"It should be a relief to you to be able to drop the act you put on."

"I guess it is. Sort of. But what do I do for defense?"

"You go all demure."

"Jesus!" She gave her barking laugh. "Okay. We're friends. And if I'm not good at it, it's because I don't have many, and the ones I have are women." She held her hand out. I shook it. I sat on the couch. "Now we can talk about Charlie," she said.

"It will be a different kind of talk than it would have been."

"You're that smart too, aren't you? I mean smart in that way. Son of a gun. Charles McKewn Armister, the Fourth. He and my sister Joanna are the same age. And sort of the same kind of sturdy quiet smiling people. Built solemn sand castles. When they were twelve, thirteen, fourteen, in that range, she crewed for him, and they took about every cup the club put up. In tennis doubles they were almost unbeatable. Everybody knew they would be married and have healthy beautiful children, and everybody was right. I was a slimy child, two years older. When he was sixteen and I was eighteen, I tried to seduce him. I didn't really want him. It was just mischief. He always seemed sort of sexless to me. Maybe I was just curious. It took Charlie a hell of a long time to figure out what I was trying to do, and when the light dawned, he was aghast. He panicked. He fled. I thought I was terribly wicked that summer. I was merely silly and unhappy and reckless. And notorious. I had to buy an abortion in Boston, and got septic, and damn near died, so I wonder who that baby would have been, and who the others would have been if I could have had them. But this isn't about Charlie, is it?

"Back to Charlie. I never saw much of Charlie and Joanna. In my cluttered lousy life they seemed to be a nice far-off focus of sanity. I was the wild Howlan sister and she was the tame one. So now she sits stunned out there in that ugly gray castle on the Island, wondering if he's ever coming back. I go out there and get her drunk and make her talk it out. It always looked like such a terribly *normal* marriage. But it wasn't. I mean I would have thought Charlie would have been one of those bluff types, a cheerful clap on your haunch and seven minutes later they're snoring like a bison. I was married to one of those, God help me. He had about the same attitude toward sex as he had toward breakfast. He didn't particularly care what was served as long as he could have a healthy breakfast that didn't take too damned long. But my weepy drunken sister at last tells me that Charlie was hexed, probably by his cruel, romantic, cold son of a bitch of a father, just as I was by mine, but in the opposite direction. Charlie is all tied up in psychopathic knots about sex. Impotent a lot of the time. Scared of being impotent. Able to manage it only when he's very tired or slightly drunk. And they are so good and so dear to each other in all other ways. And such a healthy outdoorsy pair.

"A year ago he had a genuine breakdown. It was kept pretty quiet. He went into a private rest home. When he got out, he just didn't go back to Joanna. She saw him a few times. He seemed perfectly cheery, and a little too loud, and he made silly jokes. He said he was taking another apartment in town. He told her the usual check would be deposited in her account every month, and she should keep on having all the bills sent to the office. But she couldn't pin him down. She couldn't really communicate with him."

"How long was he in the rest home?"

"Two months and a half."

"Did she go to see him there?"

"She was told it would be better if she stayed away. They said it was an acute anxiety neurosis. I've been trying to dig into this damn fool situation, and I've been here two weeks, and I *still* haven't been able to see him. He doesn't go to any of his clubs anymore. He's in a five-bedroom apartment on East Seventy-first. His personal attorney, Baynard Mulligan, lives there with him. And his private secretary, Miss Bonita Hersch. They have a daytime maid, a live-in cook, and a chauffeur. He spends a couple of hours every working day at the office. I've left a dozen messages for him to call me. Nothing." She got up and went to the bar table and fixed herself another gin and ice.

She brought it over and sat beside me, turned to face me.

"Now I've made a damn fool of myself by telling a lot of very personal and private matters to an absolute stranger."

"But you stopped short."

"Did I?"

"Terry, you told the facts and left out the assumptions."

"Do I have to know how you fit into all this?"

"Not really."

She nodded. "Then you tell me what I'm assuming."

"You've thought it all over. You're reasonably shrewd. And you've known practically from birth that you are a target for every sharpie who comes along. So you develop an instinct. You know that something is wrong. It all adds up to one thing. Some people have managed to move in on Charlie Armister. They have gotten to him. They own him. Did you ever see a lamprey?"

"A what?"

"It's an eel. It hides in the weeds in the bottom of a lake. Sometimes it has to hide a long time. When a fat lake trout comes by, the eel shoots up and fastens its round mouth with a circle of teeth into the white belly of the fish. The fish struggles awhile, then goes on about its business, with eel in tow. It swims and feeds and lives for a long time, but it keeps getting thinner and weaker. When it dies, the eel leaves it and goes back into the weeds."

"Mulligan?"

"And Hersch and the necessary corps of assistants. It has to be a big and very delicate conspiracy. This isn't a hit-and-run operation. This is a symbiotic relationship."

"Do you think that is *really* happening?"

"First, they are now, and have been for almost a year, liquidating profitable operations and making no new capital investments. Secondly, a very earnest young man who worked there, and who was doggedly trying to find out what was going on, got himself mugged and killed in an alley two months ago."

She stared at me. "Are you insane?"

"The greater the profit, the greater the risk."

"But . . . but if they've got Charlie, we should go to the police at once!"

"Sure. What do we say?"

"We . . . we accuse Baynard Mulligan of conspiracy."

"And have him arrested?"

"Of course."

"And if we could force an audit somehow, we'd find the books in perfect balance. We'd find that every decision they've made can be justified. And Charlie would probably be furious. Mulligan would bring nine kinds of civil action against both of us. You see, whatever is happening, it probably isn't against Charlie's will. You can't safely control an unwilling man over a long period of time. They've hooked him on something and they've made him happy with it."

"Hooked him?"

"Maybe they've addicted him. For example, oral Demerol. It's a synthetic hard drug and perhaps twice as addictive as heroin. It would keep him buzzing and happy as a clam and dependent on the only source he knows."

"How ugly! How terrible!"

"But that's only a guess. I'm just saying that it's possible. With an unlimited supply they could keep him in good physical shape for a long long time. Long enough to shake a lot of leaves off the money tree, Terry."

"You've scared the hell out of me, Trav."

"I meant to. I don't want you getting reckless. I want them nice and confident."

"When did you decide this was going on?"

"As you were telling me all about Charlie."

"That was the last piece to the puzzle?"

"No. There's a few to go."

"What are you going to do? I want to help."

"I look for the weak link, Terry. Somebody who knows about it, and can be made to talk about it. I don't know how you can help. The best thing you can do is keep absolutely quiet."

She pursed her lips and nodded. "Yes. Yes, of course. But did you just sort of . . . stumble onto this, Trav?"

"My best friend's sister was engaged to the boy who was killed."

"Oh."

"I'm not used to the big rich. You can be my guide."

I saw the monkey grin again. "We're just like anybody else. Isn't that what Hemingway told Fitzgerald? We're just like anyone else, except we have more money. And I think you know how to handle us very nicely. Well, directly, if not nicely." She held her glass out to me. "More of the same, please."

I fixed it, and as I gave it to her I looked carefully to see if there was any effect from the others. The green eyes were clear and alert. The mouth had not loosened.

This was an international witch. A special segment of show business. A millioned girl had briefed me once upon a time. It is the iceberg analogy. The real-and-true school just under the surface, invisible. Perhaps like Charlie and Joanna Armister in the years of togetherness. And like old Connie. So that the ones you see, the ones that do a little flapping on the surface, they are the fringe kids. The almosts. The restless ones like Terry Drummond, and the dubious nobility, and the climbers, lounging on the faraway sun decks with their sexpot acquisitions of both sexes, squinting bored into the Rolleis of the social photographers. Farukers, my millioned girl called them, an in-group word for the ones who make vulgar and obvious uses of themselves and their money. So this green-eyed Terry was not quite classy. She had roamed too far and hard and wide, divorced too publicly, made too many scenes, kept her perennially girlish rump too busy. Once upon a time maybe there had been something touchingly lonely about her, a hidden vulnerability, but now it was so encapsulated by the scars of roaming that all she could do was fake the emotions she believed she could feel.

But she had lost no sensitivity to mood and opinion. She smiled and said, "Don't tell me you're that conventional, McGee."

"What do you mean?"

"Didn't I detect some dreary middle-class disapproval?"

"Middle-class curiosity."

"Darling, I've tried everything. Twice. Does that answer your question?"

The laugh was guttural and the eyes as old as Egypt.

"I was only wondering how you drink so much gin and stay girlish."

"Oh, that! Heavens. These are the only calories I get, darling. I gave up eating long ago. Twice a day my maid, my treasure, blends up a great goopy mess of protein and mineral and vitamin things and I choke it down. I'm balanced, dear. I'm inured. I'm in a continuous state of glowing health, slightly tiddly, but entirely aware and useful. I'm going riding at three today. Could you join me? And going to Connecticut for the weekend. We should be back by Monday noon, dear. It would give us time to discuss this whole dreadful mess."

"Sorry. There's only one thing to discuss. How do we break into the magic circle? What's the starting point? What's the cover story?"

She pursed her lips and laid a slender finger against the side of her nose. "Mmmm. What if I asked the Hersch person to lunch with me? As a secretarial type, the idea might enchant her. I could plead with her to send Charlie back to my sister. My word, I could even try to bribe her and see what happens! What do you think, Trav?"

"I think it might be interesting. I might join you, accidentally. But can I trust you not to let her suspect that you suspect that she is helping Mulligan pick Charlie clean?"

"Are you asking me if I'm capable of intrigue, dear?"

"That's about it."

"McGee, darling, you are looking at the woman who invented the word. I can be so devious I can hardly stand it."

"Gin and all?"

"Gin and all. Once upon a time I pried my third husband loose from a greedy bit of fluff by marrying her off to my second husband's younger brother, and then got them both out of the way by getting a dear friend to offer him a job in Brazil, and nobody ever realized I had anything to do with it."

"Remarkable."

"If I can't handle some meaty obvious little stenographic person, ducks, I should turn in my uniform."

"Do you think you can set it up for Monday?"

"I shall try."

"What if she says no?"

She looked amused. "Dear boy, if you were a twelve-year-old outfielder and Mickey Mantle invited you to lunch, would you turn him down?"

"It's a point."

She arched herself slightly. "I've spent my life in the major leagues."

6

Saturday afternoon I went and took a look at Armister's setup on East
71st. It was a relatively recent building, perhaps ten years old. It had a
canopy, a doorman, shallow planting areas carefully tended, a reception
desk, some pretentious pieces of bronze statuary in the paneled foyer. I
did not loiter. In places like that, the residents pay for insulation. The
staff has cold eyes. They have seen all the gimmicks and know how to
block them.

I found the right alley that led to the back of the building. A wide
ramp led down to the basement parking area. I walked down the ramp.
Big cars had a luxurious gleam under the ceiling lights. The service elevators were beyond a wire cage where an old man sat under a hooded
light. Over in the wash rack, a Negro was slowly and carefully polishing
a bottle-green Lancia.

"Can I help you?" the old man said.

"Yes, please. I'm supposed to pick up the Thayers' Mercedes. They
told you about it."

"What?"

"The black 300 SL. It's supposed to be ready to go."

"Thayer?"

"That's right."

"Mister, you must have the wrong place."

"Isn't this One twenty-one?"

"Yes, but we got no Thayer in the house at all."

"I wonder if I could use your phone."

"Sure thing. Come around."

I looked up Nina's number. I knew she was working at the office. I dialed. I let it ring ten times and hung up.

"Now I don't know what to do," I said. "They're in the country and wanted me to bring the car out."

"You sure it's East Seventy-first, mister?"

"That's what I was told."

"You just got the wrong place."

"Maybe I could wait a few minutes and try again."

"No long-distance calls."

"Of course not."

Two young girls came out of the service elevator. The Negro backed the Lancia out of the rack and brought it up for them. He put the top down. They went droning up the ramp and away. A package delivery man came whistling in, greeted the old man, and went up the stairs to the service entrance to the foyer. I moved casually to the other side of the cage and looked at the parking chart with the slots labeled with the names of the users.

"You won't find Thayer on there," the old man said.

"You've convinced me of that, friend. Which Armister is this?"

"Mr. Charles Armister."

I spotted another slot labeled Mulligan, not far from the Armister slot. Both had the apartment number beside the name. 9A.

My inspection of the chart was making him uneasy. I tried to call again. I hung up and said, "This is ridiculous."

His house phone rang. He picked it up and said, "Garage. Yes sir. Right away, sir." He hung up and called to the Negro. "Dobie, run that Highburn Cad around front on the double." He turned to me and said, "If he can start it. They haven't used that thing in six weeks."

That's what you wait and hope for, the opening the other man makes.

"Unless you have a chauffeur, a car is a nuisance in this town."

"We got about fifteen chauffeur-driven here. They're the ones get the use."

The Cadillac moved up the ramp, belching, missing a little.

"But that takes a lot of money."

"There's money in this house, mister. A man would like to cry, the amount of money there is in this house. Just take that name that caught your eye, that Armister. He could have ten chauffeurs and it wouldn't cramp him."

"But he struggles along with one, eh?"

"That's right. He's got Harris, the meanest son of a bitch I ever—" He stopped abruptly, hearing himself talk too much. He narrowed his eyes. "Isn't there any address for Thayer in that book?"

"Unlisted number."

He shifted in his chair. "They don't like people hanging around here, mister."

"Okay. Thanks for your help."

"Good luck to you."

I walked all the way down to Nina's Park Avenue office building. It had an echoing Saturday silence. I had my choice of automatic elevators. The music was turned off. After I had pounded on the corridor door a few times, a scrawny, smocked redhead let me in. She was smoking a small cigar. She led me back to Nina, to the cluttered workrooms where squeeze bottles germinate. Nina had a smutch on her chin. WQXR was blasting over a table radio—something dry, stringy, and atonal. I watched her work until she told me I made her nervous, and then I went off and drank tepid beer out of paper cups with the redhead, and we talked about new realism, using bad words.

Nina gathered me up and we went out into a day which had turned colder, the late afternoon sunlight showing a watery weak threat of winter. We went to the hotel lounge where we had first talked, and because we had become different people to each other, it made it a different place. It was nearly empty. We sat at a curve of the padded bar. My bourbon girl, unsmutched, with eyes of finest blue.

It astonished me that she could not get enough of Teresa Howlan Gernhardt Delancy Drummond. Voice, hair, clothing, every nuance of conversation. "*You* said *that* to *her!*" Horror. Consternation.

At first it amused me, and then it irritated me. "She didn't step down from Olympus, honey. She's just another restless woman, that's all. She never had to grow up. She was one hell of an ornament for a long time. Now not so much. And when there's no more studs, there'll be nothing left but green eyes, money, and gin. She's going to be a very tiresome, bad-tempered old woman."

"Why do you have to try to cut her down?"

"I'm not. Nina, really, don't act like a schoolgirl reading about a movie queen. Terry isn't worth that kind of awe."

"Stop patronizing me. Maybe I don't have your advantages, McGee.

I'm just a simple thing from Kansas with a degree from Pratt Institute. I'm naïve about the glamorous figures I read about in the papers."

"What are we quarreling about?"

"Just because I have a perfectly understandable curiosity—"

"She wore an emerald as big as a tea bag."

"What? With slacks?"

"In her navel, honey."

She stared at me and then laughed abruptly. "Okay, Travis. You win. I'll try to stop acting awed."

Cocktail-lounge business began to improve. I told her about checking the Armister apartment house, about all the careful insulation provided for the residents. We went out into the cool blue dusk and walked to her place. As we walked we made plans. I couldn't see any way to move any faster on the whole situation. I would wait for Terry's lunch with Bonita Hersch. So we had a Saturday night, and I would wait at her place while she changed, and then we would go to my hotel and I would leave her in one of the cocktail lounges while I changed. Some friends of hers were having a party in the Village, and we would take a look at it after dinner, stay if it pleased us, leave if it didn't.

Again we climbed her stairs. She took her key out but she didn't need it. The lock was intact, but the door frame was splintered. She pushed the door open, found the lights, and gave a cry of dismay. I pulled her back and made a quick search to be certain we weren't interrupting anybody at his work. The apartment had been carefully, thoroughly searched. Every drawer had been dumped, every cupboard emptied. She trotted about, giving little yelps of anger, dismay, and indignation. From what I could see, there was no vandalism. I grabbed her as she went by and shook her.

"Hey! Let me go!"

"Settle down. Check the valuables." She hurried into the bedroom. I followed her. All the drawers had been pulled out of the bureau, which was pulled away from the wall. She sat on the floor and began pawing through the heap of possessions. I put the drawers back in and pushed the bureau back against the wall. She found her red leather jewel case and opened it. She went through it hastily.

She stared up at me and and said, "Everything's here!"

"Are you sure?"

"Sure I'm sure. This is a solid-gold chain. Feel how heavy it is. It's worth two hundred dollars anyway. . . ." She gasped suddenly and ran into the tiny kitchen. Everything was scrambled. She scuffled around and found an envelope and looked into it and said, "Oh, damn! This is gone."

"What was it?"

"Something over two hundred dollars. Maybe about two-fifty. I was putting five-dollar bills in it, and when there were enough, I was going to buy a mink cape sort of thing. Damn!"

I made her check very carefully. She was so mad she wasn't very rational, but at last it was evident to both of us that the only thing taken was the money. The upholstered chairs had been tipped over, and the burlap ripped away from the springs. I put a chair on its legs and made her sit down and stop dithering. I examined the job with a reasonable amount of acquired competence. One learns by doing.

"Now hush a minute, Nina. It's no trick downstairs. You ring buzzers until somebody clicks the front door open. This door was no problem." I took a close look at the way it was broken. "Somebody worked a little pry bar into it and slowly crunched it open. It was fast and it was thorough, Nina."

"This is *my* place," she said fiercely. "Nobody has any right . . ."

"We've got a problem," I said.

"Nobody has any right to . . . What? *We've* got a problem?"

"Somebody is either stupid or they don't give a damn."

"What?"

"Normal burglary, they'd just hit the places where people keep valuables. Bedroom drawers, desk drawers, kitchen cupboards, closet shelves. They wouldn't upend your couch and yank the burlap loose. They were after that ten thousand."

"Over two months later?"

"Think of some other answer. They came across a little bit of cash and took that. Why not? Like finding a dime on the sidewalk. If they wanted to make it look as if you were being cleaned out by a standard burglar, they would have taken your few hundred dollars' worth of jewelry, your camera, your little radio, and put them in a trash can if they didn't want to risk handling them. If Plummer never left the ten thousand here, this would be a big fat mystery. And if you hadn't given it to me it would be gone now, and maybe with a hell of a lot less evidence of search around here. He would hit the obvious places first."

"What makes you so sure of all this?"

"I'm not. I'm just trying to make sense out of it. I can take it a little further, too."

"Yes?"

"As you say, over two months have gone by. Somebody knew Plummer had that ten thousand. His sister closing his apartment could have come across it and said nothing. That would be the normal reaction of most people. So whoever did this would have to have some good reason to assume the sister didn't have it, didn't take it back to California. Maybe his place was checked before she arrived."

"Like what they did here? I didn't hear anything like that."

"What shape were you in?"

She closed her eyes for a moment. "Lost. Utterly lost, Trav."

"Who would know?"

She stirred out of the memory of grief. "Danny. Danny Gryson. He was a rock."

She made a phone call. She caught him just as he was going out. She talked to him for several minutes, with sad overtones in her voice, hidden laments in a minor key. I fixed drinks for us. When she hung up she looked at me, bit her lip, tilted her head. "I better stop criticizing your guesswork, dear. Somebody got into Howie's place that Sunday and tore it all up. He couldn't see that anything in particular was missing. He just had time to put it back in shape before he had to go out to the airport and meet Grace. Danny's wife, Sally, was staying here with me, and by then I was loaded with pills. He didn't report it."

"That was damn foolish. Couldn't he see there might be a connection between that and Plummer being killed?"

"But Howie was mugged. And nobody knew anything about any money. And there was so much going on anyway."

I put the couch back on its legs and sat down. "Something doesn't fit, Nina. Something doesn't fit worth a damn."

"How, dear?"

"Plummer was threatening to upset a very big applecart. Millions. Assume he was taken out of the picture very cleverly. Why should very clever people who are stealing millions bitch up their own scheme by searching his apartment the very next day?"

"Maybe they thought he'd written up how it was being done or something and they were looking for that."

"Then why did somebody plunder this place two months later? No, honey. I think this is promising. I think we have a situation where control at the top is not too solid. The people running this are not going to give much of a damn about ten thousand dollars. But to one of the little people who are in on it, it could be a very tidy amount."

"Or somebody who was in it with Howie," she said in a small strained voice. I looked at her and saw the look of tears on the way.

"Come off it, Nina."

"I'm sorry. It's just that sometimes I . . ."

"Let's get to work."

It took a long time. She had a dime-store hammer and some brads. I did some temporary repairs on the door latch. I thumbtacked the burlap back on the undersides of the upholstered furniture. Once she had the kitchen back together, she laid out the rest of the things I had brought from the delicatessen. It was a buffet picnic while we brought order out of total chaos. She put records on. Folk music from Greece. Never-on-Sunday music. Most pleasant. Drinks and small spiced sturdy sandwiches and music and cooperative chores.

I waited for something to occur to her. I was stacking her books back on her shelves and she came into the living room and said, "Hey, we shouldn't get it looking too much better than it did before, Trav. That would be a terrible commentary on my—"

She stopped and I looked at her. She was frowning.

"Trav?"

"Yes, dear."

"Aren't we going to report this to the police?"

"No."

"But if I didn't know anything about any ten thousand dollars, wouldn't I report it to the police? I mean, it would be the natural thing to do."

"Yes, it would."

"So won't whoever searched this place wonder about whether I report it or not?"

"Probably."

"And if I don't, won't he think that's because I *do* know something about the ten thousand dollars?"

"It might work that way."

She sat on a stool nearby and held her clenched hands in her lap and looked at me with her dark brows raised. "What are you trying to do? Turn me into bait?"

"On a very small chance, yes. It took him two months to come looking. Maybe you'd have spent the hell out of it by now. And anyway, we can still report it. Leave a few drawers messed up."

She nibbled at the edge of her thumb. "But it might make things happen faster if we don't?"

"There's that small chance. And I'm not going to let anything happen to you, Nina."

She stood up. "So okay. Anyhow, nothing would happen, I mean about getting my mink money back. Lois downstairs, they really cleaned her out a year ago. Some of the furniture even. She was on her vacation."

She shrugged, turned in a slow circle of Greek dance, popping her fingers, and twirled on off into the bedroom. In a little while I went in and hauled the spilled mattress back up onto the bed. She finished a sandwich, licked her fingers, tried to give me a big wicked wink. But she wasn't a good winker. She couldn't close one without nearly closing the other. It made her look squinty and nearsighted.

When we had to pass in a narrow space, doing the chores of reassembling the place, she contrived to bump me with a round hip. She hummed with the music. She looked bemused and tricky and smug, darting her blue and challenging glances. When she would come to show me where something went, she would manage to press the heat of a mellow breast against my arm. She built the big awareness of girl. We were in the girl house, perfumed with girl, with blue eyes everywhere. The infrequent small talk bore no relation to what was going on, to what she was causing.

Finally she managed to trip and turn, and be caught just so, gasping, a silky weight, breath warm, eyes knowing, lips gone soft and an inch away, and not enough air in the room.

I straightened her back up and gave her a little push. "Now, Nina, damn it, just one goddam minute, damn it!"

"Oh boy," she said. "Ethics and everything. The little sister. You talk so many bold games, it gets confusing for a girl. I guess you think it would be a lousy thing to come here to take care of me, and then take care of me too many ways, huh? But there are all kinds of lousy things. How lousy is it you should be so stuffy you make me seem sort of cheap and obvious?"

"Don't get sore."

"I'm getting mad to keep from crying. I mean you're so stuck on this role you have to play. My God, I suppose I am the little sister, but I am also an adult, Trav. I told you before I've run into some doors and had my share of black eyes. I had a disaster marriage and very very fast annulment. But you have some kind of a boy scout oath with my brother, and . . . now I feel degraded and . . . damn it, get *out* of here!"

I laughed and caught her. She yawped and leaped about, saying in effect that the precious moment had passed, and the hell with it, and we couldn't retrieve the situation, it was spoiled, etc. etc. I stilled her mouth and each time she talked it was with a little less conviction, and finally she stood docile, trembling, taking huge noisy inhalations, her strong pale neck bent forward while, with clumsy fingers, I unlatched the little hook and eye at the back of her dress and stripped the zipper down. "This is n-n-nutty," she whispered. I told her that indeed it was. I made a silent excuse to Big Brother. I told him to give me credit for trying.

And then there was the sweet drugging time of resting, all unwound, all mysteries known, somnolent there in a narrow wedge of light from a bathroom door open a few inches. Time moves slowly then, as in an underwater world. She had hitched herself to rest upon me, so distributed that she seemed to have no weight at all. She had her dark head tucked under the angle of my jaw, her hands under me and hooked back over the tops of my shoulders, her deep breasts flattened against me, used loins resting astraddle my right thigh, a spent mild whiskery weight.

From time to time she would take a deep breath and let it out with little catchings, little pulsings of heat against my throat. With my eyes closed, I slowly and lightly stroked the smooth contours of her back, from the moist warmth of shoulders, down to the papery coolness of the small of her back, the deep curve where she was as narrow as a child, then on to the swelling fruit of hips, richer to the touch than to the eye. When I brought my hand back, if I flattened it, pressed more strongly against the small of her back, it would bring on a little reflexive pulse of her hips, a small clamping of her fingers, a quicker inhalation—all fading echoes of the way it had been.

I felt a fatuous satisfaction in having done so much for her. In spite of all the physical attraction we had felt for each other, there had been the first-time awkwardness about it, the sense of being with a stranger, of learning and guessing and wondering. And it should all have been like that, all half-measures and falterings, leading to the need for mutual reassurances afterward. But suddenly it had all locked and steadied and deepened for us. She was no myth-figure of frenzies and clawings.

Suddenly we had known all this together for a thousand years, and knew no strangeness in each other, and reached down to a deep, simple, powerful pace that released her time and time again until it became continuous for her, a vast lasting, a spending that seemed like forever.

"Golly, golly, golly," she said in a sighing whisper.

"Yes indeed."

"What hit me?"

"You're asking for a slightly bawdy answer, girl."

She chuckled and stretched against me like a cat. "Mmmm," she said. "I had some stage fright, you know. When you put the lights out and came back to me, I was wondering sort of what in the world was I doing here."

"Don't you know?"

She giggled. Then she said, "This is so nice. For afterward. Just holding and sweet and saying jokes. I can say anything to you. I can mention Howie. You don't mind if I mention Howie?"

"No."

"Afterward, it was kind of anxious with him. You know. Like when you have strangers to dinner, and you have to make sure after dinner that everything was all right. Nothing burned and nothing sour. And I wanted to be held afterward, but he always felt sort of wooden, as if it was something he had to do, and I felt unwelcome. You hold me as if you like holding me, darling. And, my God, I don't have to ask how it was. Not for me and not for you. My God, I don't ever have to wonder about it. If there is any more than that, they better not invent it, because people couldn't stand it."

She hitched up, shoved her black curls back, leaned on my chest, and kissed the end of my nose. "Maybe you are too damn smart," she said. "Maybe it's all a bunch of darn technique or something."

"Don't start doubting anything."

She scowled down at me, her face in the reflection of the light that angled across her white shoulder. "Do you understand I'm not a bum? I definitely made up my mind to make you hustle me into bed."

"Stop feeling insecure, Nina. You're losing the glow."

"There were three boys before Howie, and one was that horrid little marriage, but each time it was forever. And with Howie too. You know I always felt it would be cheap and nasty and degrading to just . . . make love with a man without it being all set up to be forever. I mean a woman makes deals, doesn't she? We want security, so we trade the body for the deal, and the pleasure gets thrown in as a bonus. But the one time in my life I feel . . . well, lewd and reckless and maybe a little bit self-destructive, it turns out to be the very most there ever was for me, more than I knew there could be, damn it. But this wasn't just for recreation. It was more than that. I'm not a tramp. But maybe I'm not what I thought I was, either."

She settled back the way she had been, tucking her hands under me. She sighed. "Talk, talk, talk. I just never felt so . . . so unwound and undone and sweetened. Oh boy, the constant miracle of me. Bores talk endlessly about themselves. Keep patting me. I don't want to lose the glow. I don't want to go back out into the cold world. Darling, *am* I talking too much?"

"No."

"If I stopped babbling would you like to have a nap?"

"No."

She lay in thoughtful stillness for a little time, then pulled her right arm free and rested her curled fist on my chest. "I want to keep on feeling good, but I'm beginning to get scared again. In a different way. Tell me everything is all right."

"I give too many lectures."

"You have to talk to me before you turn into a stranger again, dear."

"Reassurances? What do you want of me? Do you want me to buy back your self-respect by telling you I love you?"

She stiffened. She pushed herself up quickly. She sat, facing me, hugging her legs, her canted head resting on her knees, the round of her hip fitting into my waist. "That was kind of a cruel dirty cold thing to say, Trav."

"Shock treatment."

"What the hell good does it do?"

"By feeling insecure about our making love, Nina, you make the inference we are a pair of cheap people involved in some cheap pleasant friction. Pull on the pants and walk away, adding up the score. I think we're interested in each other, involved with each other, curious about each other. This was a part of exploring and learning. When it's good you learn something about yourself too. If the spirit is involved, if there is tenderness and respect and awareness of need, that's all the morality I care about. Take your choice, honey. It's up to you. You can look at us from the inside, and we can be Nina Gibson and Travis McGee, heightened and brightened and expanded by something close and rare and dear. Or you can look at it from the outside, and then it makes you that silly little broad I banged when I was up in New York. And it turns me into playboy McGee, smirking and winking. It turns an importance into a cruddy diversion."

She closed her eyes. In the path of bathroom light her face looked small and pale and still. Her hands were clasped. Her cheek still rested on her round knees. It is one of the lovely and classic postures of a woman.

She opened her eyes and said, "I think I can accept that, if I keep trying. But be patient. I've got a lot of cruddy old conservative traditional ideas about this kind of thing. I don't even know why I wanted to seduce you. I felt terribly wicked and reckless. If I say something now, will you promise not to take it the wrong way?"

"All right."

"I love you. And I'm not trying to buy back anything. Or claim anything. Or promote anything."

"Thank you, Nina."

She smiled. "That was the only right thing you could have said. You're welcome. Love is a gift, not a bargain. That's something to learn, I guess. But what could you have learned from me?"

"That a nineteen-inch waist is delicious."

"Please don't make jokes."

"I learned that I'm growing older."

"What do you mean by that?"

"There was a very special sweetness about you I couldn't identify, Nina. A sad, ceremonial, ritualistic sweetness. It became a kind of a love rite."

"I sensed a little of that, darling."

"And there was a strange feeling of familiarity, a haunted feeling. Now I know what made it so special, an odd little feeling that you might be my very last bittersweet girl, the last one I will ever know with such an unused flavor of innocence about her, an almost childish wonder and intensity. It made me feel that so much of your life is ahead of you, and I have used up so much of mine."

"Don't," she whispered. "I want you to be glad about me."

"I am. I don't go hunting for regret. Maybe when joy is a little conditional, it's sharper."

"Darling, I don't feel childish and I don't feel innocent, and God knows I'm a long long way from feeling unused. Don't patronize me. I really think of myself as grown up. I earn two hundred and fifteen dollars a week. I've buried the man I was going to marry. I wasn't a whimpering little ninny, was I? I made love like a grown woman. Please don't turn me into the symbolic girl in some sad little self-involved drama of McGee. As you said, I'm Nina Gibson. I'm not typical of anything but me. Ceremony? I guess I'm glad it was ceremonious for us. But no alligator tears, darling Trav. And if this doesn't sound too insane, I think I would like to go to that party. I want to put something in between us and us. I want a thinking time."

"Sure."

She uncurled and leaned and kissed me and then got up. She glanced at me. The shaft of light touched the outside of my right thigh, the ugliness of the long guttered scar—deep, puckered, banded with the white welts of shiny tissue.

She made a little whistling suck of air through her teeth, then reached and traced the length of the scar with her healing fingertips. That is the test of a total woman. The squeamish ones shy away with sick face. They are the half women, the cringing delicate ones, who are never worth a damn in bed. A complete woman, more than any man could ever be, is involved in the realities, the elemental dynamics of life, the blood and pain and mess of it, cleaning and healing. In this is all the enduring lustiness of their purposes and their needs. "They hurt you," she said. This, too, is one of the elemental statements of life.

"I used to have a romantic limp."

"I shouldn't wonder."

"It got infected, and I wasn't in a situation where I could get it treated."

"Why not?"

"Some people were looking for me."

"You could have lost your leg."

"They told me that, too."

It was a big loft apartment, hung with masks and action paintings, loud with chatter and Haitian beat, with meager lights, a sparse collection of junk furniture, scores of soiled pillows, forty or more guests. I found a place to stand, a wall to lean upon, a drink to hold. Half the guests, like Nina, had the little apologetic flavor of success of those who have moved uptown. The others had that boisterous defensive arrogance of the *in* group, with cryptic talk and compulsive disdain. Nothing had changed since I had last attended a party in that area, some four years before. I could identify the types—the fierce, sad, bearded young men and their bra-less girls in ballet shoes, the Petulant Fairy, the Orgiastic Dancer, the Symbolic Negro, the Brave Couples, the Jealous Dike, Next Year's Playwright, the Girl Who Would Throw Up Later On, the Symbolic Communist, the Traditional Nymphomaniac, the Eager Tourist, and the Wise Old Sculptor with Bad Breath.

I kept seeing my Nina, always on the far side of the room, in a dark green fuzzy-soft dress, a necklace of gold coins. I had zippered her into that dress, and made of that small ceremony a delaying game that nearly canceled our attendance. Whenever I met her blue glance across the room, we were as alone as if none of the others existed.

People kept drifting up and digging at me to see what manner of animal this might be. A bone-thin blonde with a big bite mark on her sallow neck came and leaned loosely upon me and said, "Cruddy bottles and tubes and pots. She had a teenyweeny li'l talent, but it was honest. Right? Where do you fit in, buster boy? You square as that other one, that investment type?"

"I'm in marine hardware," I said earnestly.

"You're in what, buster?"

"Leisure-time America has taken to the waterways. A boating America is a healthy America."

She unhooked herself and peered at me. "Oh dear Jesus," she said.

"We're launching a new line of nylon cleats in decorator colors."

She worked thin lips as though considering spitting, and then drifted away, scratching herself.

A round young man with blond bangs explained how he and a darling friend of his would each write exactly five pages of description of the same sexual experience, using the same typewriter and the same spacing, and then they would cut the pages in half, vertically, and paste them together, so that the left half of each page was written by a different person than the one who wrote the right half. Then a third darling friend would retype the ten-page manuscript, sticking in any bridge words that struck his fancy.

"It's the duality of it that makes it so magical," he said. "It's truly a complex of our images. Charles thinks we should publish, now that we have fifteen of them. We're selling shares at fifty dollars."

"I'm in marine hardware," I said.

"Oh?"

"Maybe you could try that system to write us some copy on our new imitation-teak decking."

"Surely you jest."

"You could check it out with the agency. They use some way-out stuff sometimes. You know. Like Picasso. Those guys."

"Like Picasso," he said faintly. "Those guys." He tottered off, fingering his bangs.

I met a few nice ones, Nina's special friends, a girl with good and steady eyes, and a wry and likable man who worked for a publishing house. They were properly protective of her, looking me over with great care, giving a dubious approval. I stalked Nina into a corner and said, "Had enough of this?"

"Let's see if we can last ten more horrible minutes."

"Five," I said, looking into blue, down into blue, teetering on the edge of blue depths.

She bit her lips and eyes widened. "Three," she said.

"Minutes or seconds?"

"Find my coat and I'll go say good-bye for us."

So we rolled home in taxi laughter and climbed the stairs, and with slow and loving care and myriad interruptions, I undressed her into the rowdy bed. We gamboled and romped like love-struck kids until we sobered into our ultimate ceremony and this time she called to me. "Trav, Trav, Trav-isssss!" It was a night of small entangled sleeps and awakenings. Our uses seemed to deepen the hunger rather than blunt or diminish it. We became more violently sensitized to each other, more skilled and knowing in the plunder. It is a rare thing, that infatuation which grows with each sating, so that those caresses which are merely affection and the gratitude of release and sleepy habit turn in their own slow time into the next overture, the next threshold, the next unwearied increment of heat and need, using and knowing, learning and giving, new signs and signals in a private and special language, freshened heats and scents and tastes, sweetened gasps of fitting thus, knowing this, learning of that, rediscovering the inexhaustible here, the remorseless now.

In an early sunlight of Sunday I dressed slowly. She lay foundered and pungent in the turmoiled bed, deep in her honeyed sleep. When I was ready to go, I sat on the edge of the bed and kissed her salty temple and a smudged eyelid. She murmured and slowly raised a hundred-weight of head and peered at me from a small sleep-sodden face. Then she lunged and hung soft arms around my neck, sagging heavily against me, and mumbled, "Doan go way."

"I'll be back."

"Um."

"You get some sleep, darling."

"Uh huh."

I kissed her and caressed her, and she began to stir at once into her sensitized response. I laughed and unlocked her arms and laid her back down. I covered her up, tucked her in, patted the high round mound of her hip. She murmured and was immediately asleep. I fixed the blinds to darken the room and left her there.

I decided to walk until I found a cruising cab, but after two blocks decided to walk all the way. There was a rasp of beard on my jaws and my eyes felt sandy. There is an odd feeling some would call the postcoital depression. I felt drab, as if my muscles were no longer firmly affixed to the bone, as if the bone itself had become leaden and weighty. Such a hunger, such a using up, seemed part of a pattern of betrayal. Betrayal of the blinded brother, and of a dead man I had never known, and of the girl herself. Perhaps that was the reason for sadness, the awareness of a merciless using. I had been strongly attracted by the strange freshness of her, her flavor of being unused, a kind of clear-eyed innocence. Virginity is a very relative term. Walking the empty streets I convinced myself that I had thoroughly eroded the very thing which had attracted me. It was a mournful and romantic concept. She had the look of a girl who had never spent such a night as the one just past. And her body had all the tastes and flavors of discovery. Every weary lover can, with just a little trouble, turn himself into an insufferable horse's ass. I had the impertinence to mourn my Nina's loss of innocence. Conventional McGee, guilty debaucher of girls. I fancied that when she awoke, when she remembered all, she might feel appalled and stricken by too many rude and undignified uses, efforts which by light of day she would think grotesque. The wearied lover becomes very stately and very indignant at himself. He is a Tory, despising his own bacchanal.

When I got up to my room the red light on my phone was blinking. The operator told me that Mrs. Drummond had called me several times, and that her last message was to return her call whenever I got back. It was twenty after eight.

The same maid I had talked to before answered the phone. A Gabor accent. I wondered if that was some kind of type-casting. She had me wait. I waited five minutes.

Terry Drummond barked into the phone. "Tomcatting, were you? Are you sober, sweetie?"

"Completely."

"The office pig is joining me for brunch, here at the hotel."

"What about Connecticut?"

"This is more interesting. Is there any chance she might know you or know anything about you?"

"No."

"Good. She is meeting me at ten. I want you to arrive at two thirty. To meet me. I'll tell her I'm expecting you. Then I shall make a horrible scene after you get there. Just follow my lead, sweetie. I am going to be a sickening bitch. It's a character bit I'm used to. Then I shall sweep out and leave you with the pig. I'll give her a bit of going-over too, so then you'll be fellow victims."

"What good does that do?"

"Are you certain you aren't drunk, sweetie? When we talked, you seemed like quite a clever shifty fellow. And terribly attractive in a sort of brown brutal way. You must be enormously successful with shopgirls and such. Why should the office pig be less vulnerable? Cozy up to her, sweetie. You would be a nice change for her, after poor Charlie. And we do want to find out what the hell is going on, don't we? Just bat those terrible pale gray eyes at her, and show your white teeth and bulge your muscles a little. She'll go all weak in the knees."

"Oh, naturally."

"Well . . . didn't I?"

"You have notoriously weak knees, Terry."

"You're *such* a bastard. See you here at two thirty."

I undressed. I showered long, rinsing away the subtle pungencies of love, hung out my do-not-disturb sign, left a call and toppled into bed.

7

My phone woke me a few minutes before my twelve-thirty call.

I answered it and Nina said, "Well?"

"Oh. Hi, darling."

"You have a girl over here. Remember?"

"What's your name again?"

"My name is I love you McGee."

"You sound pretty merry."

"I feel absolutely stupendous. I have deep black circles under my eyes, and I have this uncontrollable twitch, and I limp on both hind legs, and I never felt better in my life. And I miss you. Terribly. What have you been doing? Sleeping? What's the matter with you? No stamina?"

"When did you wake up?"

"Five minutes ago. And I'm about to take a great big steaming hot bath and wash my hair."

I told her about Terry's call, but I did not tell her Terry's suggestion about Bonita Hersch.

She was disappointed. I said I would make it just as soon as I could.

I paused at the entrance and looked into the brunch area. A lot of the tables had emptied. They were at a table on the right, over at the side. Terry spotted me and waved. She wore a casual tweed suit, a small brown hat, and looked smart and very much at ease. As I walked toward the table I looked at the other woman. There was a stiffness in her posture. She wore a black dress. Her fur was over the back of her chair. She wore a rather intricate hat atop a careful sculpturing of pumpkin-gold hair. From a distance she bore a rather striking resemblance to Princess Grace of Monaco. But as I neared the table I saw there was a coarseness in her face, features slightly heavier. She looked to be about thirty.

A waiter quickly moved a chair to the table. "Hello, darling," Terry cawed. "Bonita dear, this is Travis McGee; Trav, Miss Bonita Hersch. You're a few minutes late, darling."

"Sorry."

Her smile was wicked. "You're not too terribly attentive, dear. I'd hate to think that I bore you."

"You couldn't bore me, Terry," I said, and asked the waiter to bring me some coffee.

"Isn't he decorative, Bonita? Look at those monstrous shoulders. But he's really frightfully proper and dull and just a little bit stupid."

"Take it easy, Terry."

"My God, is that a command? Aren't we masterful today? Perhaps you bore me."

"Come off it, Terry, for God's sake."

"Am I embarrassing you, Trav? Gracious! Isn't it odd how the friends of one's friends never quite work out? Next time I see Bunny I shall tell her that you certainly lived up to the advance billing, but by the cold light of day, you depress me." She gathered her purse and cigarettes and stood up, looking at us with seamed monkey smile. I got slowly to my feet.

"Oh, stay right here, dear. Wait for your coffee and have a nice little chat with Bonita. You and she should get along marvelously. She's a dreary little typist who seems to think she's going to marry my sister's husband, poor thing. She's rather sexy in a crude way, don't you think? Have a charming time, dears."

She went swiftly away, smiling at friends, her stride vital and youthful.

"She is a terrible, terrible woman," Bonita said in an awed and trembling voice. "Nobody has ever talked to me like that before."

I took a more careful look at Bonita Hersch. Her grooming was almost too perfect. Every little golden hair was in place. Her eyes were a pale cold gray-blue. Under the disguise of lipstick, her upper lip was very thin and her under lip was full and heavy. Her hands were wide and rather plump, with short thick fingers.

"She was very rude to you, Miss Hersch."

"She invited me here."

"That makes it unforgivable."

"It certainly does. And she got everything wrong. Things aren't at all
. . . the way she said they are. Do you know her well?"

"Not very well. Somebody asked me to look her up. She's a spoiled
woman, Miss Hersch."

"I am not going to try to understand why she was rude." There was a
little more edge and authority in her voice, but it was a light-bodied
voice. It had a hushed and confidential quality about it.

"Let's try to forget Terry Drummond. I don't have to have that
coffee. Maybe we could go somewhere else and I could buy you a
drink?"

She turned those appraising eyes on me. A sharp pink tongue-tip was
momentarily visible at the corner of her mouth. She looked at a small
jeweled watch, lifting the ornamental cap with the edge of her thumb-
nail. "I think that would be very nice, Mr. McGee."

"Fine," I said. I stood up and took her chair. She stood up and
moved away from the table and waited for me to hang her fur wrap on
her shoulders. She had a long slender back. Her breasts were small and
high. The black dress was exquisitely fitted to her, particularly effective
in displaying the long ripe lines of her heavy and elegant and firmly
girdled hips. She smiled formal thanks, with a little flicker of darkened
eyelashes over her shoulder at me, and then walked out ahead of me,
walking with that very slight awkwardness, more illusion than reality, of
long-waisted women sensuously and consciously overripe in hip and
thigh. At each short stride the calves of her legs swelled round and
smooth under sheer nylon, making her ankles look more fragile than
they were.

She settled into the cab, in a spiced fragrance of her perfume, and
smiled and said, "If I might choose . . ."

"Of course."

"Driver, Armitage Inn, please. Lexington at Fif—"

"I know where it is, lady."

"As you interrupted me, driver, I was about to tell you to go to the
side entrance." There was a little silken whip in that voice, and it made
a nice little pop when she got her wrist into it.

Her morale was improving. I saw what was wrong about her. She was
just too bloody refeened.

"Do you live in the city, Mr. McGee?"

"Florida, Miss Hersch."

"Can we be . . . what did she call you. Trav? Trav and Bonita? I must warn you. Please do not call me Bonny. I wondered about your marvelous tan, Trav. Are you in business in Florida?"

"I'm a boat bum, Bonita."

"Oh?" I detected a faint chill.

"I have a custom houseboat down there. I live aboard. I get into a few little things now and then, but mostly I do as little as possible."

"It sounds like a lovely life." The chill was gone.

I could realize how bright Terry had been. She had put Bonita Hersch in such a bad light that the woman would feel obligated to correct the picture. And she had given me, by indirection, the sort of credentials which would make me seem both interesting and harmless to Bonita.

I had to admire her choice of a place. We were given a deep red-leather booth with sides high enough to assure privacy. There was inoffensive background music, lighting designed to make women lovelier, and excellent service.

She shook her head sadly. "That woman. What did she call me? A dreary typist. Now it seems amusing. I do type. Once upon a time I was a typist. But I've never felt particularly dreary. I'm an executive secretary—private secretary to Charles McKewn Armister. And I certainly do not care to marry anyone. Then I *would* feel dreary. Do you know, that implausible woman offered me a huge sum of money to send Mr. Armister back to his wife? She couldn't be more mistaken, really."

"What gave her the idea you could?"

"She misinterpreted a certain situation, Trav. In a way I can't blame her for that. I imagine a great many people have the same idea. But she could have listened to an explanation. You see, I live in Mr. Armister's apartment. But so does Mr. Baynard Mulligan, his personal attorney and the head of his legal staff. And a chauffeur. And a cook. It's quite large. There are five bedrooms and four baths in addition to the servants' quarters. I worked for Mr. Mulligan for several years. When Mr. Armister's secretary retired a year ago, I replaced her, at Mr. Mulligan's suggestion and with Mr. Armister's approval. I'm perfectly willing to admit that it is a strange arrangement, but I function as a housekeeper, in a sense. I run the staff and supervise the buying and the menu—that sort of thing. They are both very busy men. It's a convenience for them.

It costs me very little to live these days, but I must admit that I hated giving up my own little place. I'm actually starved for privacy, Trav. I would have loved to have had you see my precious little apartment."

"Then there never was anything between you and Charlie Armister?"

I was again aware of her calculating appraisal. "Nothing important or enduring. Just a little time of foolishness. It ended months ago. Proximity, I suppose. It can be so dangerous, you know. And Charlie is a dear, dear man. He made me forget one of my basic rules of behavior. A girl should never never never have an affair with the man she works for. It's such a stupid thing to do. It always has to end, you know, and then there's the terrible awkwardness of trying to work smoothly together, and usually the man gets rid of the secretary somehow. And it might mean a much less important job. I've seen that kind of thing happen far too often. So I've made it a rule. It seems Charlie was the exception. But we survived it nicely, without impairing the working relationship."

"That was fortunate."

"Yes indeed it was. I have a tremendous capacity for loyalty, Trav. I give the man I work for all my energy and competence. That's what I'm paid to do, to increase his working efficiency, protect him, advise him when he asks. There has to be . . . a rather formal flavor about it to make it work. Do you understand?"

"I think so."

"Any wise and ambitious woman will compartment her office life and her private life. I imagine Mrs. Drummond heard some rumor or other, and she must think it is still going on. But it isn't, of course. She could just as well try to bribe Martha, our German cook, to send Charlie back to Joanna."

"That marriage is on the rocks?"

"Apparently. He was terribly repressed, and now he's broken out and I don't believe he'll ever want to go back to the kind of life he led before. He's really a very happy man now."

"Is he going with anyone?"

"Trav! Remember what I said about loyalty? I really can't discuss the man I work for, can I?"

I swallowed the temptation to ask her what she had been doing. I smiled at her, thinking that this was as nasty a bit as I had come across in a long time. I could sense the ruthless pursuit of the career. And her equivalently ruthless pursuit of sexual gratification. This was the product of a dozen highly competitive offices, of skilled infighting, merciless intrigue.

Her heart was as cold as a stone at the bottom of a mountain lake.

Her bosses would remember her as a jewel. Her lovers would remember her as an enchanting mistress. She would embody all the cheap glamour techniques, the skillful arrangements of Sex-and-the-Single-Girl. She would pick her lovers the way an IBM sorter finds a new sales manager. Married men would suit her best. They weren't as likely to be a nuisance, create scenes and difficulties. I saw a succession of dapper and slightly puffy fellows with little black mustaches, gold bill clips, hard-top convertibles, and small stock options. They would all say Bonita is a good sport. Bonita knows how to make a man feel like a king. There were no hard feelings. We're still good friends. Very clever girl. Fastidious.

A precious little apartment and sexy hostess pajamas, candlelight and little taste treats cooked in shiny copper pots. Mild music and deft little conversational bits, and then after she had stacked the pots and dishes for her precious little maid to take care of the next day, she would delicately bower herself in silk and perfume, all coiffed and tidily diaphragmed, with the lights just so, and pull the poor dazzled son of a bitch, marveling at his luck, onto those deep soft hungry cannibal loins. Because when a girl does without, she gets a little edgy, and lots of authorities say it is sort of a beauty therapy, my dear, keeping the glands in order and all. It's good for the skin.

But if poor Harry the Mustache happened to work for the same outfit, and happened to get in her way or the way of her boss, she could open his throat with the same indifferent skill with which she had learned to cut radishes into precious little rosettes. And when one Harry would become too accustomed to her, and begin to take all that stylized graciousness for granted, with too little humble gratitude, she would skillfully shuck him and begin her patient search for the next one. From each she would absorb some special field of knowledge—wines or paintings, sports cars or antique glass—because she wants so terribly to become truly and totally sophisticated.

This was a guileful, perfumed monster. God only knows where they come from. They clump up in the big cities. Somehow they all manage to look quite a lot like each other. They consider themselves sophisticates. They buy growth stocks. They worry a lot about their breasts and about secretarial spread. The idea of ever having a baby is some kind of a grotesque joke. It would hurt. And then you'd be stuck with it. Their conversation is fantastically up to date. They get the very best of service everywhere they go. And when, at last, they begin to get a little scared, they go on the biggest and most careful hunt of all. The big game they are after has a triple listing—D and B, Social Register, and Who's Who. And with all their polished skills, they wrench the poor bastard away from his wife, nail him, and—in smug luxury—ruin all the years he has left.

Her smile was practiced and charming. Her makeup, hair styling, and dress design were carefully planned to enhance every good feature.

"Trav, dear, let's drink to dreary rich women like poor Terry. And to Sunday afternoons in October. And to finding new friends."

"And to privacy."

She made a rueful face. "That lovely thing which I ain't got. I really have to be alone a little while every day. It renews me, you know? I pity people who haven't enough resources to be able to be by themselves. In that huge apartment, I lock myself in my room and think and read. I read a great deal. It's the only way we have to lead more lives than one."

"That's a very interesting way of putting it, Bonita."

She arranged her face into a pretty little frown of thought. "I suppose we all feel trapped in one life. Sometimes it makes one want to do mad mad things. It's dreary to be circumspect *all* the time."

"Think up a madness."

"Sure," she said. She made her cold eyes sparkle. "Take a cab right now, to Kennedy. Buy a toothbrush, fly to Florida, and go off on your boat and hide away in the islands."

"I'll go check the flights."

"Darling, I do wish I could. I really do. But sometimes we all have to settle for a little less, don't we?"

It was a very personal voice. It was good for nuances. She was beginning to make me feel like a juicy bug on the end of a handy twig. Any minute now the sticky tongue would flick out and snare me and yank me into that greedy maw. She was managing it with great skill. She had fed me most of my lines.

"What will you settle for, Bonita?"

"Another drink, dear."

"That's a very minor request."

"Everything is relative, Trav. Everything should be sufficient to the moment, don't you think?"

"It seldom is."

"That's because most people never know exactly what they want. It's a great blessing, to always know exactly what you want."

"Do you?"

"You still didn't order that drink."

After I did, she said, "Will you be in town long?"

"Another few days. A week. Maybe a little more."

"Are you staying with friends?" I named my hotel. She looked disapproving. "Those new ones are so characterless."

"And completely anonymous. I like that kind of privacy."

"Are the rooms really nice? I picture them as little white boxes."

"They're quite comfortable."

She glanced down for a fraction of a second, and I knew that she had opened that jeweled watch. Her lips tightened slightly. I was being a dull pupil. I wondered if she'd take me by the ear and lead me, bellowing, back to my hotel room. She had the hunger, she had set the scene, and she was pressed for time. But I had suddenly forgotten my lines.

I saw her begin to wonder if I found her unattractive. The thought disturbed her. I had to take her off the hook. "I wish I could see that apartment you used to have."

"But I had to give it up, dear. It broke my heart. All my precious things in storage. And I can't show you the apartment where I live now. I'm . . . not really in a position to have guests. Surely you understand."

"Of course, Bonita." I was beginning to have a difficult time relating her to conspiracy, to large-scale theft, to possible murder. She was clear-eyed and healthy. The long round pale throat had a look of grace and strength. She was fragrant and purposeful, and she knew how to use her eyes and mouth to maximum effect. She sat there, humid and intent, leaning slightly forward, with a tilted smile, planted firmly on those glossy needful hips, readied for any opportunity to rationalize a brief Sunday-afternoon liaison as a bit of enchanting October madness, concealing with a hasty jerry-built scaffolding of romance the plain vulgar structure of itch. Her living arrangement had deprived her, apparently, and though she was more accustomed to the leisurely pursuits fashioned about the precious little apartment, she was obviously willing to gratify herself in a more casual fashion when opportunity arose. And, because of Terry, I had a suitable cachet. Once a reasonably attractive woman has accustomed herself to an almost masculine directness, her batting average can run unreasonably high. And such was her skill she had injected a thoroughly steamy overtone into the conversation without ever having committed herself in any way. Were I to dutifully trundle her off to the gold and white lobby and up to my plastic aerie, she would arrange to get herself kissed, then laugh fondly and patronizingly and chide me for being a dear silly boy, then put her black dress on a hanger and carefully turban her intricate hair with a towel to keep it from being mussed, and graciously, generously, coyly present herself for service, giving her explicit executive-secretarial instructions and requests in that light-bodied, musical, secretive voice. October madness, my dear. Everything sufficient to the moment. We all have to settle for what we can get. Eased and content, she would dress with great care, making a gay chatter all the while, and, at the door, pat my cheek fondly and call me a dear boy, quite confident I would never never forget this magical afternoon when a veritable princess had brightened my drab days with her impulsive generosity.

Playing it her way, a game for which I had no stomach, would end the relationship. Offending her would end it just as readily. If I were to learn anything from her, I had to achieve some kind of continuity.

"Bonita, I could prove that the rooms are not little white boxes, but I think Walker might wake up in a bad temper."

"Walker?"

"He was a little too tight to drive back to the country last night. Bunny's nephew."

"Oh?"

"Bunny Rodriguez. Terry mentioned her."

"Oh, yes, of course," she said with a little uncertain frown between her golden brows.

"When I left to meet Terry, he didn't look as if he would wake up until Monday." I smiled at her. "There's an old phrase: Had I but known."

She reached swiftly and patted my hand. "Tours of inspection are dull things at best, my dear. And we certainly don't want to disturb Walker, do we?"

"I could have him evicted."

"You're fun, Trav. I do like being with you."

"A pair of refugees from Terry Drummond. I suppose it's the money.

People with that kind of money are never quite real. I can't imagine Charles McKewn Armister as being quite real, Bonita."

"Oh he is, definitely. But he does have some unreal attitudes, I suppose. I remember while I was still working for Bay. That was well over a year ago, before Charles became ill. Charles came back from having lunch at one of his clubs one day, and he was very indignant. He was used to paying a dollar and a half for his lunch, and they had raised the price to a dollar sixty-five. He wrote an indignant letter to the house committee. I suppose he had lunch there twenty times a year. Twenty times fifteen cents comes to three dollars. And it was that same month that he and his wife gave seven hundred thousand dollars to Princeton. Out of foundation monies of course. But the contrast."

"Terry said he doesn't use his clubs any more."

There was a cold flicker in her pale blue eyes. "Not lately. You see, they are making huge changes in the investment setup of the Armister money. And when Charlie goes out, even if he went to a private club, there are just too many people who are too anxious to find out what the plans are, and suggest things and try to gain some advantage. After all, when you start moving some seventy millions of dollars about, people get some terribly clever ideas. It's part of my job to . . . to insulate Charlie from those people." She patted my hand again, more lingeringly. "But I don't want to talk shop, dear. This is a rare day off for me. It's practically a vacation. I should be back at the apartment by seven at the latest."

"And here it is quarter to four. Will I be able to see you again soon, Bonita?"

She looked rueful. "It's really terribly difficult, Trav. I'm at their beck and call."

"Aren't your evenings your own?"

"They should be. But it hasn't worked out that way. I do special work at the apartment for Baynard. One of the extra bedrooms is set up as an office now. This is a very busy time for all of us. But . . . you could give me a ring. At the office would be best."

I ordered us another round. The drinks were getting to her slightly, but they did not make her any less evasive when I tried to swing the conversation around to Charlie Armister.

Finally I said, "How much did Terry offer you to send Charlie back to Joanna?"

She bit her lip. "I suppose Terry would tell you anyway. Fifty thousand dollars. Isn't that absurd?"

I shrugged. "She's got it. And she loves her sister. Too bad you couldn't send him back."

"Charlie is a generous employer."

"Not that generous, is he?"

"No. But I have more than enough for my needs, Trav."

"Your expensive tastes?"

She smiled. "Clothes and furs. And nice surroundings. But if I had millions, I think I'd keep working. It's my life."

"Power hungry?"

"It's my weakness, dear. I love to have the little people jump when I want them to jump. I have an earnest little secretary of my own. Miss Angela Morse. She's a fat humble little thing, and she strives so hard to please. She gets all sweaty when I speak to her. But in a few years I might be able to really turn her into something."

I filed that away. A little later I was able to take another hack at Charlie-lore. She left a small opening and I said, "When he had his nervous breakdown, did he come right back and move into the apartment?"

"What nervous breakdown, dear?"

"All right. When he was sick."

"Yes, he wanted to stay in town. Baynard found the apartment. We moved in and got it all ready for him. He was very pleased with it."

"And then you and he had your little fling."

"Darling, you're going to make me terribly sorry I ever mentioned that. He couldn't spend much time at the office. I took things back for his signature and so on. And, as I said, it was proximity. Terry acted as if I were some horrible little slut trying to snag myself a rich man. I have more pride than that."

"That's obvious."

"Why do we keep talking about Charlie?"

"Maybe I'm jealous."

She took hold of my wrist, a firm pressure in her small plump hand. "You shouldn't be, dearie. It's been over for months. And I have been a veritable nun ever since."

"And Charlie has been a monk?"

"Hardly!"

"You sound very positive."

"Didn't I tell you he's recovering from a life of repression? He has whole acres of wild oats all saved up. So poor Baynard, to keep Charlie from making a fool of himself, or to keep some bitch from blackmailing him, has been . . . well, arranging things for him."

"Ladies of the evening?"

"It distresses poor Baynard. But from what little I have seen of a couple of them, they seem quite presentable. I guess if you pay enough they would be. They look like college girls who do some modeling on the side. I don't know what the source is, but apparently it's inexhaustible. Harris goes and picks them up in the Lincoln and brings them up the service elevator. They leave in the morning the same way. I imagine they are perfectly trustworthy. And it does keep him out of trouble. It seems so strange that—" She stopped abruptly and released my wrist. She stared at me. "I must be getting drunk, Trav. I shouldn't be saying these things."

"You're among friends."

She drew herself up. "Am I? Perhaps you're pumping me. How do I know that Terry Drummond didn't arrange this so you could pump me, dear?"

"You're getting to be paranoid."

"Hardly. I'm just naturally cautious. And very loyal. I told you how loyal I am. I am very very loyal to the man I work for. And I am very very loving to the man I *don't* work for."

"Baynard?"

"Don't be a dope. I meant it abstract."

"But you are a nun, you said."

"Yes indeed. Tragic, isn't it? But that's the way the ball bounces sometimes. Did I ask for this drink? How many does this make? Is it sinful to get smashed on Sunday, dear?"

"It's the best day."

She beamed and preened herself and fluttered her eyelashes. "What a man wants, he doesn't want *involvement*. You know? I know how a man thinks. I think like a man, darling. Does that seem strange?"

"Not at all."

"A man wants to have his fun and no regrets. Fair for one, fair for all. Right?"

"Right."

"Promiskus . . . promiscuous means like cheating on a man. I've always said, Bonita, you've got to be loving and loyal, because you don't want to be a tramp. Geez, I miss my darling li'l apartment so much. A girl should be a good sport. You know? God, I hate a teaser. That's false pretenses. Right?"

"Right."

"A man wants you gracious. Nice li'l private dinners and pretty, sexy clothes. Good cooking. Herbs. I use lots of herbs. And damned good in bed. That's what counts the most, let me tell you, sonny boy." She stopped again and her eyes widened. She wore a listening expression. Suddenly there were beads of moisture on her pale forehead.

"Scuse me," she said in a tiny voice and got up quickly and hurried away, leaning forward slightly from the waist. She was gone a long time. When she came back she looked slightly hollow-eyed. But sobered.

"I think you'd better take me home, dear."

At 121 East 71st, the doorman held the door for us. I walked her past the desk and back to the elevators. She smiled her weak apologetic thanks, touched my hand, and stepped in and pressed the button for the ninth floor.

I went to the desk. The pale clerk looked suspiciously at me through heavy glasses. "Yes sir?"

"Miss Hersch was feeling faint. I want to give her a chance to get up there and then phone up and see if she is all right."

He hesitated, nodded, lifted a house phone onto the counter. He plugged me into 9A and rang.

Bonita answered. "Yes?"

"Trav. I wanted to be sure you got up there all right."

"I'm all right. Sweet of you to phone."

"I'd like to see you again."

"Phone me at the office, dear. Thank you for the drinks and the nice talk."

I thanked the clerk and went out. The early dusk was arriving. There was a chill in the air. I exchanged weather pleasantries with the doorman and gave him a dollar to whistle me up a cab. I wanted him to remember me as the legitimate guest of a resident of his carefully guarded tower.

I knocked at Nina's door. She opened it, grabbed me, and hauled me in. After a devoted business of kissing, I held her at arm's length to admire her. She had her hair pulled back and tied. She wore a flowered blouse and sexy black stretch pants. She looked fresh as morning, dainty as lace, innocent as a field of lambs. She gave me a vast bawdy wink that screwed up half her face.

"It's the only way I can wink," she said. "Unless I hold the other eye shut. And that looks ridiculous. Where the hell have you been?"

"How are you for guilt and regrets?"

She looked blankly at me. "Guilt? Regrets? Heck, if I've decided not to be prim, why should you bring it up?"

"Just to be sure."

"I've invented fifty more things we can do. Darling, you're like owning the key to the candy store."

"You frighten me."

"Good! Where have you been?"

"With a female creature. Let me tell you about you. After being with her in an intimate bar, Miss Nina, you are exceptionally glorious. You are invaluable. You are honest and true."

"Of course."

"There is a very smart little male spider who first grabs a bug and wraps it up and then a-courting goes, hoping he can be done and away before the big savage female spider finishes eating the bug."

"Did you bring me a bug?"

"No."

"Pretty careless of you."

"One should take a bug to Bonita Hersch."

"Did you?"

"I didn't go near the web."

"If you ever do, McGee, I'll peel you with a dull knife and feed you to the snakes."

"You're very fierce today, Miss Gibson."

"Man, I'm plain savage. And healthy. And tired of waiting."

With no warning except a sudden expression of mischief, she leaped up at me, wrapped her arms high around my neck, and locked her legs around my waist. She put her teeth into the side of my neck and made a small and comfortable snarling sound. I strolled around with her as if she weren't there. I whistled a small tune, picked up a part of her Sunday paper and looked at it, went out into the kitchen and got a drink of water. Then I wandered in and sat on her bed. She brought her head around and put her nose against mine, her eyes wide and staring.

"Nina, dear! Where did you come from?"

"Wanna play owl?"

"Certainly. How do you play?"

"Just like this. Open your eyes wide too. First one blinks is a lousy owl."

She won three straight rounds of owl. I told her that if she played my rules, she wouldn't find it so easy to win. She said she'd play anybody's rules and still win. I said my game was called naked owl. She said she would be delighted to show me I was outclassed. We stacked the clothing on a chair. I won three straight rounds. She called me a dirty sneaking cheat, and said that if all I came around for was a bunch of kid games, I could go right back to Bonita. I said that the way this game had developed, it was no longer for kids. It was more like a game for the young adult. She said that if everybody would hold still for just one cotton-picking minute, she could win the final game and break the tie, because you couldn't play any kind of game well if your attention kept wandering.

She was a joy. She won by disconcerting me. She slowly crossed her big blue eyes and crowed with triumph when I laughed and blinked. We laughed until she got hiccups, and then she had to find out, in an experimental mood, if making love would cure hiccups. She said that if it would, it could become a lot more popular than blowing into a paper bag or drinking out of the wrong side of a glass.

On Monday morning as she was scrambling eggs, all dressed for work, she turned to me and said, "Hey!"

"What, honey?"

"I just remembered. It *did* cure those hiccups."

"Yes, but can we patent it?"

She grinned like an urchin. "Maybe not, but we sure know what to do about the next attack."

I patted her and said, "Miss Nina, modern medical science thinks in terms of prevention rather than cure."

She pondered that for a few moments and said, "You know, sweetheart, it's sort of awe inspiring to think that I may never have another case of hiccups as long as I live. It's the least you can do for me."

She was my joy. She served the eggs and put the pan under the faucet. Then she whirled and with a look of small despair said, "Please tell me, am I too goddam elfin for you?"

"What?"

"Too utterly disgustingly kittenish and prancy and cutey-cute. You know what I mean. Elfin, for God's sake. I just can't be a dignified lady in love—all sighs and swoons. Except for when it's *really* happening, sex with you makes me feel like all games and riots and jokes and prancing. Does it bug you, darling?"

"Not at all."

"I could try to be sort of glamorous."

"Come sit down and eat your eggs before they get cold, you fool woman."

"You do things and it starts me giggling. It's just a sort of a kind of joy, darling. But I don't really want to be a silly child bride to you."

"Clue me with giggles. Delight me with games. If you were my own device, girl, if I had invented you, geared you, shaped you, wired you for sound, I would have made you exactly what you are in every respect. Does that hold you?"

"Uh huh. But is love supposed to be . . . so much darned fun?"

"Until the prudes came on the scene, it probably always was."

She sat solemnly and ate scrambled eggs for a few minutes, glancing at me, wearing a slight frown.

"Trav?"

"Yes, dear."

"Then maybe what's wrong with me, I worry about enjoying it too much. I like every part of everything. Just even holding you while you sleep makes my heart turn over and over. I want to *be* you. I want us to be one creature, wearing one skin, knowing any pain or pleasure as if we were all of one part. Like once last night, a time when I couldn't reach you, I turned my head like this and kissed my own shoulder, and it made sense to me, and I laughed out loud, because it was our flesh I was kissing with one of our mouths."

I looked at her earnest and troubled face. "Nina, it isn't foolish or wicked to enjoy. Wickedness is hurting people on purpose. I love what you are and how you are and who you are. You give me great joy. And you make horrible coffee."

"I know. Isn't it foul?"

I walked her to work. As we parted she said, "I give you permission to sit on that railing and leer at the Snow Maiden while you wait for me."

"I have a thing about white sweaters."

"Then buy me one. Any fetishes you have, just let me know."

And she joined the throng pouring into the office building.

8

That Monday morning, after I had freshened up at my hotel, I retrieved Howie's money, took a thousand dollars out of the envelope, taped it up again, and had it put back in safekeeping.

Though I felt slightly helpless at penetrating the Currency Curtain the big rich erect around themselves—perhaps to guard them from such as me—I was considerably more confident of my ability to find my way around within the upper-level call-girl circuits. Perhaps, though I have never sought such services, this confidence is a clue to the social status of McGee. Once upon a time I had to unravel a situation in Chicago, and I guessed that it could not be too different in New York.

I could assume there would not be too many very fancy and expensive setups. I was not too much concerned about the private entrepreneurs—those little setups where two or three girls are close friends and have enough of the right kind of visiting-fireman contacts to establish themselves on a semipro basis. There would be hundreds of those in the city, and they would be too risky for Baynard Mulligan to approve of them. Those girls, not subjected to any outside control, can prove to be neurotic, alcoholic, thieving, or diseased. This would have to be a businesslike operation—discreet, reliable, trustworthy, thoroughly screened, and paying adequately for all necessary protection. I could not imagine there would be more than three truly expensive circuits in the city.

I hit it on the first day. I tried the Convention Manager of the hotel where I used to stay, before I became so well known there that I lost some essential freedom of movement. An assistant manager I knew introduced me to the Convention Manager. Even with an introduction he was very edgy and cautious. I told him I had three Venezuelan friends coming to town, and I wanted to line up three very superior girls—superior, entertaining, fashionable, and cooperative—price no object. He hedged and dithered and pretended helplessness, and finally told me I might try Arts and Talents Associates on West 38th Street, and ask for Mrs. Smith, but I was on my own and I could not use his name.

I phoned the place and asked for Mrs. Smith. She had a dull, tired, doughy voice. "Model service, Mrs. Smith speaking."

I said I wanted to employ a model and she asked me if I had an account with them. I said I didn't, but that I wished to open an account. She suggested I stop by and talk with her about it, and if I would be along soon, not to bother stopping at reception but come right to her office, Number 1113.

It was a big drab ugly rabbit warren of an office building, with noisy elevators, narrow littered corridors. I saw enough of Arts and Talents to see that it was large and busy and very probably entirely legitimate. Kids who looked like theater bums were in groups outside the main entrance to the eleventh-floor offices, drinking Coke and jabbering.

I knocked at 1113 and went in. It was a ten-by-ten office with a single narrow window, a big scarred desk, three phones, a bank of file cabinets, and Mrs. Smith, typing. She was very fat and she had blue hair, stone eyes, and a tiny mouth. She did not look evil. She merely looked tired and bored and clerical. She looked at me the way a butcher looks at a side of beef.

"I phoned about opening an account."

"Sit down, please. Excuse me one moment." She finished typing, her fat hands very deft, pulled the sheet out, and put it into a manila folder on her desk. She turned and faced me across the desk. "What is your name, please?"

"Maybe you could tell me what the routine is first."

She looked mildly pained. "Our client records are completely confidential. If we open an account for you, you'll be given a code number. There's no cross index to actual names. But I do have to see identification and approve issuing you a code number."

"My name is Travis McGee," I said, and handed her my Florida driver's license.

"Where are you staying in town?" I told her. She asked me to step into the hall until she called me back in. I had about a four-minute wait. She opened the door and nodded and I went back in.

"We don't generally open an account for anyone unless we have some verification from one of our other accounts. And we also have to know who recommended us."

"The man who recommended you asked me not to use his name. So I'd rather you wouldn't check back with him." She asked who it was. I told her.

"Are you acquainted with any of our other accounts?"

"I believe so. But this is a situation where I would rather not mention names. Would an address be of any help?"

"It might be."

"One twenty-one East Seventy-first. Apartment Nine A. I believe it is . . . a current account."

She swiveled around, turning her heavy back toward me. She opened a card drawer. In a few moments she closed it and turned back again. "Yes, of course," she said, and there seemed to be a definite decrease in wariness. "Did that party recommend us also?"

"That party would not be likely to make a specific recommendation, Mrs. Smith. But there were favorable comments about . . . this organization, indirectly."

"We handle small accounts on a cash basis only. And our minimum model fee is two hundred dollars. Will that be satisfactory?"

"Perfectly."

"I believe we can open an account for you. Would you write this number down, please?" I borrowed a pen and wrote it on the margin of one of my permanent credit cards: 90-17. Then she gave me an unlisted number to call, and I wrote that down too.

She rolled a five-by-eight file card into her typewriter and said, "The standard procedure is for you to call that number and give your account number and the time you wish to employ someone, and a number where we can call you back within the hour. I will now fill out your model card, and when you phone in we check this card and then determine availability, make the appointment for you, and call you back and give you the details. I'll have to ask you questions about your preferences so that I can complete this card for our records."

"Certainly."

"First, will this be just for normal modeling services? By that I mean you will be the only one involved, and there will be no extremely unusual requirements."

"Just normal by all means."

"Preferable age range?"

"Uh . . . twenty-two to twenty-six."

"Racial type?"

"I beg your pardon?"

"Nordic, Mediterranean, Asiatic, Exotic?"

"Nordic."

"Build?"

"Slim, reasonably tall."

"Any special requirements?"

"Well . . . reasonably bright and presentable."

"All the girls on our list are intelligent, very presentable, smartly dressed, and—with the exception of some of the Exotics—can be taken anywhere. Many of them have excellent jobs."

"Do you have a space on that card for a sense of humor?"

"You will find that our girls adapt themselves to whatever mood seems required of them. They are lovely girls. Did you say that you wished to employ a model for this evening?"

"If that's possible."

"We do prefer twenty-four-hour notice, but there is no particular problem on a Monday night." She turned and rolled her desk chair over to a low filing cabinet. I could see that she was shuffling and sorting photographs, checking them against a list. She turned back to the desk and spread out four eight-by-ten semigloss prints for me to examine. I was expecting cheesecake and was surprised to see that they were head and shoulder shots, studio glamour portraits by someone who knew how to use backlighting. Four very lovely girls, four blond heads, four sensitive faces. Each portrait had a complicated code number inked in the top right margin.

"These match the information on your model card. If at any time you care to alter your requirements, phone the number I gave you and give your account number and either request a change verbally or come up here and see what we have on file."

"You are certainly beautifully organized here, Mrs. Smith."

"Thank you. We've been in business for a very long time. We can't afford to be slipshod. One of our accounts has been coming in once a year for eleven years to select one of our girls to take on a lengthy cruise—usually thirty to forty days. We handle that on a flat fee of five thousand dollars, so you can readily understand that we must use the greatest care in both the selection of our accounts and the girls on our list. I must tell you that whichever of these girls you select will be asked to make a verbal report on any difficulties. If it is decided that you are not a satisfactory account, your number will be dropped. We owe that much to the girls."

"Of course."

"Which model appeals to you?"

"They're all beautiful. I was wondering, could you tell me if any of these were . . . employed on that other account I mentioned?"

"Why?"

"That's a good question. If one were I thought I'd pick her. Because, as I said, that other client or account—or whatever you call it—was so pleased. Could you check?"

"This is most unusual."

"I don't want to be a nuisance. I'd just feel better about it . . . this first time."

She looked at me with stone eyes and then shrugged. "It will take a few moments to cross-check it." It took longer than a few moments. She sighed heavily from time to time. As she went back to the photo file she said, "Our models also fill out an account-preference card. But I imagine you would be satisfactory to any of them." She turned back to the desk. "Here. None of those original four have been out on that account. These two have, and they match up with your card."

One had a rather ordinarily pretty face and the other looked more interesting. Her face was more angular, slightly vulpine, the upper lids quite plump. "That one," I said.

"You understand, of course, that you must have a place to take her to?"

"I understand."

"Would you wait outside again, please?"

It was a longer wait than before. When she called me in again, she said, "She will meet you this evening at quarter to seven at Satin House on West Forty-eighth. You'll recognize her from her picture. She would prefer it if you get there just a little earlier and sit at the bar so you can see her when she comes in. Her name is Rossa." She spelled it out for me. It was pronounced Raw-sah.

"Last name?"

"Our policy is to leave it up to the girls to give their last name if they so desire. If not, her name is Rossa Smith. She's an enchanting girl. Her model fee is two hundred and fifty dollars. We prefer that you have that amount ready, sealed in a small envelope, and give it to her whenever seems convenient. And I must ask you to leave two hundred dollars with me. It will be posted to your account. It's our protection in case at any time you fail to keep an appointment. Should that happen, we will have to ask you to post another deposit in the same amount before making another appointment. If you don't have the cash, you can bring it to me at any time before five today."

"I have it right here."

"Good. Thank you. If at any time you have any complaint about a model, we would appreciate your bringing it to our attention. I might say that such complaints are very very rare. You will be answered twenty-four hours a day at that number I gave you. Are there any other questions?"

"If I should like Rossa, can I ask for her again?"

"Yes, of course. Many accounts ask for specific girls." She curved her tiny mouth into a small smile. "I'm certain you'll find her most charming. Oh, I forgot to tell you, if at any time you wish to make up a party and require two or more girls, we will appreciate your stopping by and making arrangements in person rather than trying to do it over the phone."

"I understand. Uh . . . how high do the rates go?"

"Most are at two hundred and two-fifty. We have several at three hundred, a few at four hundred, and two at five hundred. But it varies, according to the size and quality of our list at any given time. There have been some at a thousand, but not recently."

"What makes it worth five hundred, Mrs. Smith?"

Her expression told me she thought it a vulgar question. "Those are girls who are very well known, due to television work usually. Some accounts prefer to be seen with girls who will be recognized in public. Generally they don't stay on our list long." Her smile was quite suddenly and surprisingly vicious. "They either go up, or they go down."

I bade her good day and walked out and found that it was raining, puddling the sidewalks with black city glop. There were no empty cabs in sight. I went to a corner drugstore. I looked at the pretty girls on the streets, hurrying through the rain. Though I knew it was absurd, they all looked quite different to me. I kept wondering if they were on somebody's list. Behind one fat doughy woman in one small cheap office, I could sense the rest of the organization—the recruiters to bring them in, the suave muscle to keep them in line. It wasn't a sorority. Mrs. Smith wasn't a house mother.

I phoned Terry Drummond from the drugstore. She bellowed hoarse curses at me for almost three minutes before I could quiet her down enough to apologize for not reporting to her about Bonita Hersch.

I made a detailed report. She chided me for being a coward. I said it hadn't been cowardice, merely revulsion. She said I might have learned something useful. I said that this way there was a better chance of seeing her again. She said she hadn't realized I was so fastidious. She stopped snarling at me when I gave her a hint of what I had in mind and said I would see her in about an hour.

It took a little longer than an hour. A bellhop took over the heavy carton and carried it up to Terry's suite for me. She watched with interest while I unpacked the tape recorder and set it up. It had a two-hour capacity at 3¾ ips, and the operation was very quiet. It fit nicely behind the skirts of the sofa, and there was a handy wall plug there for it. I placed it so it was easy to get at the controls from the side of the sofa. I ran the little nondirectional microphone up the back of the sofa and pinned it in place just out of sight. I turned it on and we experimented with it, adjusting the gain, talking in different parts of the room, playing the tape back. It would work fine if we could keep the girl in that half of the room. Terry was confident she could get her to sit on the sofa, the ideal place for a good pickup.

She had a lot of questions to ask, but not enough time to ask them before a late lunch date. It left me with time to kill. The rain had stopped. I had a sandwich and then I went down to take a look at the Armister layout. It was on a narrow side street in the financial district, a sooty old gray two-story building with ornate stonework around the cornices. There were three stone steps up to a dignified entrance doorway. A brass plate set into the stone at the side of the entrance said "Armister-Hawes" in fragile and ancient script worn thin by many polishings. There was a uniformed porter to keep things swept and polished, and to open the door for the people.

I found a pay phone in an office building a block away and called Nina and told her I might be fairly late, and to get herself fed and be patient.

"I'd hate to start before you got there," she said.

"It's a very old joke and I'm surprised you know it."

"I plan to be a constant source of surprises and consternations, McGee."

"Your record so far is excellent. How about your busted door. Did you phone the man?"

"It's being fixed today. What's so interesting you can't be home when I get there?"

"I've lined up a tall blonde."

"I don't think I'm keeping you busy enough, dear."

"Go on back to the old drawing board."

"I got my bonus. It's a pretty blue check. And I got pinched in the elevator again. Does that mean anything?"

"I'll tell you what it means when I see you late tonight."

As I hung up I had a tantalizing memory which for a moment I could not identify. Then I remembered the rude, random conversations I'd had on field telephones long ago with Mike Gibson. That memory was like taking an unexpected blow right over the heart. I wondered why Nina and I had not talked more about Mike. Maybe she sensed that it would make me feel strange and guilty. She did not want to be the picture of the twelve-year-old girl in Mike's wallet. I did not see how she could be. They could not be one and the same. No.

But I fed coins into the box and sent Mike a wire, for the nurse to read to him. EVERYTHING SHAPING UP BETTER THAN YOU THOUGHT. DETAILS SOON. I felt like a sneak when I sent it. "Shake her up if you have to, Trav," Mike had said. Thanks a lot, buddy.

I roamed back past Armister-Hawes, on the opposite side of the street, wondering if I could chance going in and saying hello to Bonita, wondering what good it would do. After I passed it, I glanced back just in time to see a big black Lincoln pull up in front. A huge, husky chauffeur in a blue-gray uniform got out slowly. I moved into a handy doorway and watched the scene. It was twenty minutes of four. He wandered around the car, stopped and took a handkerchief out, and rubbed a place on the window trim. The porter came out and they stood and talked idly. The porter kept glancing back through the glass doors. Suddenly he turned and hurried up the steps and pulled the door open, half bowing, smiling, touching his cap. Two men and a woman came out. The woman was Bonita Hersch, in a dark tailored office suit, with a puff of white at her throat. Both men looked tanned and fit, tailored and prosperous. One was tall and lean, with a long face and a long neck and sloping shoulders. He wore no hat. He had white hair, curled tightly and closely to his skull. The other man was shorter and broader. He wore a dark hat and a pale topcoat. The chauffeur was holding the rear door of the car open. The taller man walked slowly toward the car. The broader man stopped and said something to the porter. The porter responded. The man threw his head back and laughed. He punched the porter on the shoulder and then did a little dance step, fists up, in a parody of boxing. Bonita tugged at his arm. The man turned and went with her toward the car, laughing again. They got in and the chauffeur closed the door and hurried around the back of the car and got behind the wheel. The big gleaming car started up smoothly and moved away down the wet street.

I hurried over. The porter was just going back inside. He saw me and held the door for me. He was much older than he looked from a distance.

"Wasn't that Miss Hersch who just drove off?"

"Yes sir, her and Mr. Mulligan and young Mr. Armister. They're gone for the day now, sir."

"*Young* Mr. Armister?"

He looked embarrassed. "It's just a habit. He's the only Mr. Armister nowadays."

"Would Miss Morse still be here?"

"Oh yes sir, she won't be leaving till five or after. You go right straight down this main hall, sir, and turn left at the end, and her desk is there right out in the open outside Miss Hersch's office."

I thanked him and went back. Angela Morse was an overweight little sandy blonde with a nervous expression and a bad complexion. As she looked at me apprehensively, I told her that I knew I had just missed Miss Hersch, and I would like to leave a personal note for her, if she could give me something to write on. She gave me a pad and pen with fumbling haste.

I wrote, "Stopped by to buy you a coffee break only to find out you keep very executive hours. I'm wishing myself better luck next time. Trav."

She gave me an envelope for it, and I put the note in and gave it back, unsealed. She said she would put it on Miss Hersch's desk. She wore a navy-blue something with a white schoolgirl collar. The offices had a hushed and sepulchral flavor of money. The ceilings were high, the carpeting deep, the paneling dark and glossy and carved. Through an open door I could see into the rigid formality of a small conference room. Angela Morse's desk was set up in sort of an inner foyer, a wide formal central area onto which the other executive offices opened. There was a crystal chandelier, a small fireplace. A small display light shone on an oil painting in an ornate gilt frame. I suddenly realized that it certainly was not a reproduction of Manet haystacks. Perhaps a copy? I moved over and read the little plaque on the frame. Manet. The girl's electric typewriter stopped. It was a brash snickety little sound in that setting. I turned and she was looking at me, apparently wondering why I didn't leave.

"This is a handsome room," I said.

"It's kind of spooky, not getting hardly any daylight in here to work by."

"Do they use both floors?"

"No. I mean sort of. It's storage up there for supplies and all, and dead old files that go back a thousand years practically. And a dusty old apartment nobody has used in years."

"I thought it was a lot bigger organization."

"Counting everybody, there's twenty-three now. It used to be about thirty-five last year. But we don't manage as many properties now."

"I imagine Mr. Armister is a nice guy to work for."

She smiled. "Oh, he's real nice. He's kind of jolly and fun and all. He isn't at all stuffy like you'd think."

Jolly Charlie Armister. Just a rich bundle of fun. Fun with Bonita. Fun with the Arts and Talents.

I thanked her again and walked slowly down the center corridor, glancing into the offices on either side, at the mild sedate girls running the chuckling electric machinery that recorded the flux of money, at the quiet men making little marks on tabulated reports and talking in bank voices into phones and dictation equipment. It was the world's most dignified horse room. The basic commodity was the same.

After those offices, my hotel looked like something designed to be thrown away after use. The old city was being filled with these tall tasteless rectangles, bright boxes which diminished the people who had to live and work in them. People kennels. Disposable cubicles for dispensable people.

As I showered I wondered if perhaps these hideous new tax-shelter buildings, with people sealed into the sour roar of manufactured air, didn't play some significant part in creating New York's ever-increasing flavor of surly and savage bitterness—a mocking wise-guy stink of discontent. Ugliness creates more ugliness. So the buildings could contribute, and so could the narrow greed of the truly vicious little trade unions. Screw you, buster, I'm getting mine. Thirty-hour week. Twenty-five-hour week. Grind the last panicky dime out of the golden goose. So it's down to twenty-five hours, which figures to ten bucks an hour, and anybody gets smart—all you do is walk out again and tie up the whole crappy city. But even when you're working, what do you do with all those great raw boring horrible hunks of time? All those hours when if anybody looks at you just a little bit wrong, you want to smash them to pulp. Man, we got a strong union. We got this city right by the balls. But something is going wrong and nobody knows exactly what it is. You can read it in all the eyes you see.

9

The Satin House was jammed with glossy people in that kind of lighting which makes women look mysterious and men look stalwart. Smiles and glassware sparkled. Some huge suction yanked the smoke up and out. Soft acoustics blurred and merged all the shoulder-to-shoulder yakking. I got a stool at the very end of the bar near the door, my right shoulder against the wall, and a huge tailored back at my left blocking all vision in that direction. The bartenders made their deft moves between the gleaming bottle rack and the dark wood and red leather of the bar.

I kept a full drink in front of me, and I kept craning my head around to watch the door. She came in precisely on time, looking for no one, knowing in perfect confidence she would be looked for; tall, but not quite as tall as I had guessed from her face, slender in a dark green-gray wool dress, a mutation mink jacket that matched almost perfectly the taffy pallor of her hair, a hat that would have been hilarious worn by anyone without that look of remote and lovely calm, big lizard purse with silver clasp, lizard shoes.

I went to her quickly. "Rossa, you're right on time."

"Hello!" she said with a smile, with a warmth as subtle as her perfume.

"I'm Trav, and there's one tiny corner over there I've been hoarding."

I took her over. Broad-back had taken my stool. He was turned, facing his companion. "Excuse me," I said. He gave me a totally disinterested glance and went on talking to his friend.

"Excuse me," I said again. This time he did not even glance.

I was getting very tired of this city. I had heard his friend call him Bernie. I put my fingertips on his chin and turned his face around toward me. He clapped his hand on my wrist to pull my arm down. I was braced and he could have chinned himself on it without depressing it a quarter inch.

"Bernie," I said, "lift it off my stool or I am going to make a rude and terrible scene. I might bite one of your pretty ears right off." The bartender had moved close and I could sense the management behind me.

"Oh, were you sitting here?" he said. It was his most plausible decision. He got up. He went around and stood on the other side of his friend. He laughed very very heartily. He showed his shiny teeth when he laughed. Rossa slid onto my stool and asked for a sweet vermouth on the rocks. I wedged in beside the stool, arm on the bar, facing toward her.

"I don't really go around stirring up trouble," I said.

"I would have run," she said. "I am a sissy." She had a very slight accent, possibly Danish or Norwegian. When she had walked, when she had slid onto the stool, she had moved well, in a flowing and limber manner. Her face was angular and distinctive, with the planes and hollows of handsomeness rather than the round look of prettiness. Her brows were darker than her hair, arched highly in a habitual expression of mild query. Her upper lids were so full as to narrow and tilt her eyes, gray and as pale as mine. The skin texture of her face was very fine, and she used a slightly orange shade of lipstick on the full broad mouth.

"It's stuffy in here, Rossa. Should I check your jacket?"

"Do you want to stay very long in a place so crowded, Trav?" She tasted my name as she said it, with a slight hesitation.

"I guess not."

"Then I am fine, thank you. There's a place near for a drink, not so crowded, where we can both sit. Unless you have some other place you would rather go?"

"We'll try your place."

She wrinkled her nose in a small smile. "We will drink quickly and let Bernie have the stool, eh? Then he will be a big man again."

We walked a half block to another place. She had a nice long stride. There was a small blue booth for two along a dark wall. She chatted easily. She told me her name was Rossa Hendit, and she worked in an airlines ticket office on Fifth Avenue. She did not say which one. I could imagine some such name as Swenska or Nordway or Fiordlund, one of those little tiled places with a shiny engine in the window and pieces of ribbon leading to strange names on a map.

I told her I was from Florida. She had been to Miami several times. We talked climate, citrus, beaches, and sunburn lotion. She had no whore look or whore manner that I could detect. But there was a curious inadequacy about our easy conversation. We both knew there was an envelope of money in one of my pockets, and it would end up in her purse. This was a situation I had never been in before. It took me a long time to analyze it. Finally I realized that we could generate no particular tension between us because the result was preordained. She was a stately and beautiful girl, fashionable and bright, with shining eyes and a good mouth. But there was no spice of pursuit. A doe which runs up and stares down the gun barrel is not a sporting venture. There is an electric tension in the chase, in searching out the little clues and vulnerabilities, making those little adjustments which favor the hunter. The biggest question had been answered before we met. Mrs. Smith had been the one who said yes. The only remaining question was how she would be in bed. And from the look of her, and from the cost of her, I could be certain she would be smooth-skinned, sensuous, tasty, and just as active or as passive as anybody wanted her to be. She looked as if she had passionate capacity, but one would never know whether her responses would be genuine or faked. I guessed she had begun judging and appraising me from the first moment and was, and would continue to be, trying to react in all ways which would please me. She wished, or had been taught, to give full value.

At one point I glanced up quickly and surprised a different expression in her eyes—an absolute coldness, a bleak and total indifference which was gone the instant I saw it. And that, I thought, was the whore's look and the whore's secret, that monumental unconcern which insulated her. I knew in that moment that this sort of thing could never interest me. I had to have the involvement of the spirit. These tasty goods were for the other kinds of men: the ones for whom sex is an uncomplicated physical function one performs with varying degrees of skill with every broad and chick who will hold still for it; the men who are the cigar chompers, gin players, haunch grabbers; the loud balding jokesters with several deals going for them on the long-distance lines; the broad-bellied expense-account braggarts who grab the checks, goose the cocktail waitresses, talk smut, and run-run-run until their kidneys quit or their hearts explode.

And this savory and expensive chick had decorated the night places with them, and had lost track of the number of bald heads, lost track of the number of times she had, with the cigar smoldering on the night stand, skillfully drained their transient loins.

Into a small silence I said, "Have you been doing this long?"

The answer came so quickly and reasonably it had the ring of policy. "Dear, don't think of such things. You'll make us both unhappy. I work all day. I like to go out. I'm your date."

"It's just a little friendly curiosity, Rossa."

"Please, dear, with you I have been feeling that it is really a date. Let me keep pretending."

"You mean we're different, you and I?"

"Don't you feel that way about it too, darling?"

It was very skilled. As standard practice it would inflate the man's ego. Every man could be led to believe he was special. And at the end, with a great faked galloping climax, she would make him believe it forever. Every customer is unique.

"Perhaps. But I want to talk about it."

She pouted in a rather pretty way, and said, "How did a lovely girl like you get into anything like this? Isn't that a very trite question, Trav? Aren't you and I worth better conversation than that?"

"Do you know that old joke, what the lovely girl answers?"

"Surely. Just lucky, I guess. Darling, it is really very adolescent of you to want to pry. Just accept me. As if I was born an hour ago. Just for you."

"All clean and fresh and sweet and virginal."

She looked down at her hand. She examined the nails. It reminded me of Bonita Hersch's hand, except that the nails were longer. She looked across at me. This time the whore look was frank and apparent. Under all that tasty trimming was a basic coarseness which would gag a goat. I didn't have to know how she got into the business. It had been invented for her.

"If you can wait here an hour, someone will come who might suit you better. One of the newer ones, I think. Younger and possibly a little nervous about everything."

"I wasn't trying to offend you, Rossa."

"My dear fellow, it would stagger the imagination to think of any way you could possibly offend me. I was merely thinking of making things more agreeable for you."

"You are agreeable."

Suddenly her smile was dazzling. She was a fashion model facing into an imaginary spring breeze in a professional studio. "I will suit you very very well. Never fear. You are an exciting man, Trav. I shouldn't want to give you up at this point. Now we can forget all that and this will be a date for us. You came in to buy a ticket. You asked me to have a drink with you after work. I am a very proper girl and I am wondering if you are going to make me feel too reckless." She reached with a small gold lighter and lit my cigarette and then, as she started to hold the flame to her own, fumbled with it and it dropped into her lap and clattered onto the floor. She laughed and said, "See? You are actually making me a little bit nervous, darling."

I sat on my heels beside our small blue booth and peered under the table for the lighter. I saw the glint of it back against the wall and reached and picked it up, sat back in the booth, lit her cigarette with it, and handed it to her.

"Thank you, dear," she said, with a splendid imitation of fondness. We finished our drinks, ordered another.

I felt incomparably shrewd. I would take her to the Plaza. I would take her up to Terry's suite, and suddenly Rossa Hendit would discover that it was not the sort of evening she had anticipated. All we wanted from her was conversation about Charlie, and Terry was set up to pay well for it. The tape would furnish Terry's very good lawyer with enough background to enable him to go after a court order to get Charles McKewn Armister hospitalized for observation, with Joanna Armister signing the commitment papers. After they had taken him off whatever they had him on, Charlie would be able to blow the whole scheme sky high.

My date began to seem slightly absentminded. It was a quiet bar, and thinning out. She went to the ladies' room and seemed to be gone a long time.

Reality is a curious convention. It is the special norm for each of us. Based upon the evidences of our own senses, we have each established our own version of reality. We are constantly rechecking it with all sensory equipment. In the summer of 1958 I was in Acapulco when a major earthquake struck that area. I was awakened by the grating of roof tiles and a thousand dogs howling. I went barefoot to the window.

There was a cool tile floor under my bare feet. Suddenly I realized that the tile floor was rippling. There were waves in the solid tile, throwing me off balance. Such a thing could not be. Tile floors were solid. To have such a floor rippling in such a way destroyed the validity of all sensory impressions and gave me a feeling of black and primitive terror I had never felt before. I could no longer depend upon my evidences of reality.

She came back from the ladies' room. She sat and smiled at me. I said, "Let's get another drink up at the Plaza."

That is what my mind told my mouth to say. But the fit of the words in my mouth felt strange. I heard, like an after-echo, what I had said. "Let's get a down with the ending ever."

She was leaning toward me, with a narrow and curious avidity. "Darling," she said. "Darling, darling." It had an echo-chamber quality. She opened her mouth wide enough so that I could see the pink curl of her tongue as she formed the *d*.

I saw a tiny mark appear at her hairline, right in the center of her forehead. It moved slowly down her forehead, and as it did so the two flaps of flesh folded away at either side, bloody pink where they were exposed, displaying the hard white shine of ivory bone. The moving line parted her brows, bisected her nose and lips and chin, and the halved damp soft flesh fell away, leaving the white skull, the black sockets where the eyes had been. The jaws and teeth were exposed in a white death grin, but the jaw still worked and the pink tongue was still moist within that sepulchral dryness, curling, saying, "Darling, darling."

I closed my eyes tightly, both hands clamped on the edge of the table. Under my hands the table edge turned wet and soft and full of roundnesses. I squinted down, fighting for control, and with vision it turned back into a table edge. But as I closed my eyes again all the softness was under my hands. This was the earthquake terror again, roaring through my mind like a black wind. In some far corner of my mind I was trying to make an appraisal. She had dropped the lighter and kicked it over against the wall. It gave her time enough.

I tried to hang onto a tiny edge of reality. I knew the words. I wanted the whole room to hear the words. Call the police.

I heard the words come out. A wet, brutish howling. "Can Paul bury shit anything." My muscles were knotted. I risked a glance at the skull. She was gone. She seemed gone. I could not be sure she was gone. I could not be sure of anything.

Then the room tilted abruptly, thudding my shoulder against the wall. I tried to see them. They were in a half-circle standing on that steep slant, looking down into the booth, the tallest narrowest people I had ever seen, with tiny little heads no bigger than oranges. One of them was a policeman. "Hadda!" I yelled at him. "Hassa hadda," and began to vomit with fright. A snake looked at me out of a door in the cop's narrow belly.

Then there were white things, white grunting things, running at me and pulling, and I fought them in a dream, and was yanked and mashed face down and felt a little stinging bite in my buttock.

I rolled under a night sky and saw a thousand tiny peering faces at either side, atop tall in-leaning bodies. There was a thump, a sliding, a bang of doors. Motor roar. High city lights moving by. A sinking deepness, somebody close by, and fingers on my wrist. The thing I was in turned on its side and we went off into dark country, scraping swiftly along on the side, leaving a shower of sparks. . . .

For a long time I could not tell whether I was awake or asleep. I was in a bed in a white room. Daylight came through a window screened with heavy mesh. I could move my head, and that was all. I could see a white wall. Things kept happening to that wall. For a long time I could not stop them from happening. In sleep you cannot stop things from happening. Places would open in the wall. I could see into horrid places and see horrid things. Grotesque copulations. Huge rotting bugs. Ghastly things eating each other. Things would open the wall from the other side and come through and disappear as they got too close to the bed, and I would go rigid waiting for them to get me. Once hundreds of people started laughing at me. They were behind the bed where I could not see them. It was deafening.

After an interval of time I could not measure, I began to be able to exert control over the wall. I could close it up and make it white and blank. It was like making a fist with my mind. If I let the fist relax, the things would come again. After a long time I began to be able to relax the fist little by little without anything appearing. I became convinced that I was awake. Later I was able to make ghastly things appear only by an effort of will, a kind of reaching to make them happen. They lost color and solidity. Finally I could make nothing happen. I was in a white room. I was in bed. I could move only my head.

Two men came in. They stood by the bed and looked down at me.

One was in a business suit. He had a bald head and a young face. The other was tall, young and husky, dressed in white.

The one in the business suit said, "How do you feel?"

"Who are you?"

"I am Doctor Varn. I'd like to know if you are still hallucinating."

My mind seemed to take a long time to grasp the question and find the answer. "No. There aren't any things in the wall any more."

"Do you hear any strange sounds?"

"Not any more. Where am I?"

"Toll Valley Hospital, Mr. McGee, just south of New Paltz, New York. It is a private institution for the treatment of mental and nervous disorders."

"Why am I here?"

"Because you are ill, Mr. McGee. Jerry, please go tell Dr. Moore we can schedule Mr. McGee for hypnotherapy at two o'clock."

The one in white left. I heard the door close.

"I'm not sick."

"You were very ill, Mr. McGee. You were irrational and violent in front of witnesses, including an officer of the law. In New York State any officer of the law can commit you for observation if he is a witness to dangerous and irrational behavior, if in his opinion you are endangering public safety."

I wished my brain did not feel so slow and tired and muddy. "Then . . . wouldn't I go to a public hospital?"

"Usually, yes. But I have been treating you for some time now, Mr. McGee. When you began to behave oddly, your friend, Miss Hendit, became alarmed and phoned me. I arranged to have you brought out here."

"You have been treating me for some time?"

"According to my office files. My nurse can verify it, of course." He shook his head. "Until last evening, I really thought we were making progress."

He was so plausible it frightened me as badly as the things in the wall. I forced myself back toward reality. "What did that whore put into my drink?"

"That's an irrational question, Mr. McGee."

"So give me an irrational answer. Humor me."

"In the past several years we've made some very interesting discoveries regarding the relationship between blood chemistry and mental disorders. In order to get the extreme reaction you experienced, she would have had to give you quite a dangerous dosage of a complex chemical compound which can, in a normal human being, temporarily duplicate all the physical and mental and sensory symptoms of violent schizophrenia."

"But she didn't have to do that because I was already nuts."

He looked down at me with mild surprise and a certain amount of approval. "Mr. McGee, you have astonishing recuperative powers—mental and physical. You broke the arm of a very highly trained attendant."

"Good."

"I expected you to be slightly incoherent, but your word choice seems controlled. We can schedule you sooner than I expected."

"For that therapy you told him about?"

"Dr. Moore uses a combination of mild hypnotic drugs and hypnotic technique. You see, we need to know a great deal more about you, Mr. McGee. We are particularly interested in all of your activities during the past several days."

"I won't tell you a damned thing."

"That is an irrational statement. But perhaps I made an inaccurate statement. We are not particularly interested in your activities. We have a request for an accurate report of your activities. We are far more interested in your responses to the psychotomimetic drugs."

"The what?"

"Our resident organic chemist, Dr. Daska, had been achieving some interesting variations in the Hofmann formulae, creating more directive compounds in the psilocybin and D-lysergic acid diethylamide areas. The experimental compound the girl gave you has the lab designation of Daska-15. A single odorless tasteless drop. Approximately three millionths of an ounce, actually, in a distilled-water suspension. Harvard University's Center for Research in Personality has done some basic work in this area, but Daska can achieve more predictability. Daska-15 gives consistently ugly hallucinations, and mimics highly psychotic disturbances of the sensory areas, communication and so on." He seemed to have forgotten he was talking to me. His enthusiasm and dedication were apparent.

"What the hell kind of a place *is* this?" I demanded.

His young face firmed as he brought his attention back from the misty distances of research.

"Eh? Oh, this is the Mental Research Wing of Toll Valley Hospital, Mr. McGee. We're concerned with psychotomimetic techniques, surgical techniques, electrical and chemical stimulation of areas of the brain —in fact the whole range of the mechanical rather than the psychiatric approach to mental disorder."

"What the hell kind of a doctor are you? You know I don't belong here."

"We're making significant progress in several directions. Important progress." He seemed strangely apologetic, and anxious for me to understand.

"So what?"

"We have chimps and monkeys and rodents who didn't ask to come here either, Mr. McGee."

My mind was quickening a little. "Are you trying to tell me I'm some kind of an experimental animal?"

"All this work is generously supported by foundation money."

Were I a character in a funny paper, a light bulb would have appeared over my head. "One of the Armister foundations?"

He looked sad and apologetic. "Crash programs are essential in this area, Mr. McGee. It is . . . a very difficult thing to weigh a few isolated instances of . . . questionable ethical behavior against the greatest good for the greatest number. Also . . ." His voice trailed off into a troubled silence.

"Also what?"

"It would be illegal to attempt to solicit healthy volunteers. And the few cases we can get from the main hospital, with all necessary permissions, are generally so hopeless we can't accurately appraise results." He shrugged a mild sadness away and smiled down at me, his features clean and remarkably handsome under the sheen of his hairless head. "We're not monsters, Mr. McGee. There won't be anything as unpleasant as what you have already been through. Many of the Daska compounds have extremely pleasant side effects. This will merely be a case of taking you through the experimental series and then, under hypnotics, getting your detailed verbal report of the experience and sensations. You'll be physically checked and checked against the electroencephalograph and given a detailed multiphasic personality inventory test between each segment of the series to determine any area of deterioration."

"You are so comforting, Doctor. Was Charles Armister here?"

He hesitated and said, "He was with us for ten weeks." He looked at his watch. "I'll send in some medication, and some people to get you cleaned up and fed, Mr. McGee."

"You want to keep me healthy."

"Yes, of course," he said, and smiled and nodded and went out.

I had ten minutes alone. McGee, the suave shrewd operator. In retrospect I could marvel at the heights of blundering stupidity I had reached. It was as if a team of experts were systematically looting a bank, and I had come bumbling onto the scene to ask them how they were making out.

Certainly Mrs. Smith of Arts and Talents had checked with the other account. It gave them the time, place, and opportunity to get me out of their hair. Probably before that they had become aware of my buzzing around, drinking with Bonita, leaving her a note at the office, getting in contact with Terry Drummond, talking to the law about Howard Plummer, getting close to Plummer's fiancée. So when my buzzing became a little too annoying, they had swatted me. And I hadn't even taken the very elementary precaution of leaving some record of what I had learned, where it could get into the hands of the law.

Suddenly I felt a fear quite different from the terror of any distortion of reality. I was afraid for Nina Gibson and what they could do to her if she tried to do anything about my inexplicable disappearance.

A square sandy woman in white came in, bared my shoulder, held a hypo up to the light, then injected me in the shoulder muscle. She did not speak when spoken to. She swabbed the spot with alcohol before and after the injection and went away. In a little while I chuckled. I felt very very good. What the hell, let them have their fun. It was for the good of mankind. Way down in my mind a little lizard head of fright kept opening its cupboard and looking out, but I kept shoving it back. I locked the cupboard door. Two husky attendants came in. They got me up, took me out of the canvas jacket. I wanted to apologize for mussing my bed. I didn't want to be a burden to anybody. They were arguing with each other about the season bets they were going to make on pro football. I wanted to tell them a joke to make them laugh with me, but I couldn't think of one. They took me into an adjoining tiled bath. I stripped on request and they put me into a shower and gave me soap and a brush. I hummed as I showered. When I came out they gave me a coverall suit to wear, a light-green garment zippered from throat to crotch. It seemed the most wonderfully practical and comfortable thing I had ever worn. I couldn't understand why everyone didn't wear exactly the same thing. They gave me straw slippers. Instead of telling me what to do, they tended to give me a shove in the direction they wanted me to go. I didn't mind. They were busy talking to each other. One of them thought the Packers had a chance.

I sat on the bed. They put the wheeled tray in front of me. I had to eat everything with a hard rubber spoon. Everything was delicious. They stood by the screened window and talked. Whenever one would glance toward me, I would smile. But they didn't seem to notice the smile or want to be friends. That was all right too. When I was finished, one of them took me back into the bathroom and produced an electric razor. He watched me until he was certain I could use it properly. I was anxious to use it properly, to please him.

They took me down a hall. It was a gray hall, like ships I had been on. I had a quick look out one window and saw a nice place of lawns and trees, flowers and a parking lot far away, and some people strolling on the paths. It was a very nice place.

They took me to a room. Dr. Varn was there. I was glad to see him again. His friend was named Dr. Moore. He was a nice fellow too, a middle-sized man like Dr. Varn, but swarthy. They had me get into a lounging chair and then they fixed it so that I was very very comfortable. They darkened the room. Dr. Moore started a tiny light swinging in a circle above me. I watched the light. Dr. Moore told me I was very comfortable. He had a nice voice. Friendly. He was interested in me. I was very anxious to please him. In all that comfort I closed my eyes and folded back into myself, as if looking down into the blackness inside my head. I could hear my voice and his voice, and they were a little bit apart from me. I could tell Dr. Moore everything. It is good to have someone you can tell everything to. It is good to have someone who is concerned about you. I told him all my troubles, but they did not really seem very important any more. If anything was wrong, he would fix it.

10

It was night again. Lights came on in my room. Dr. Varn shook me, and I came awake suddenly. I rolled out of bed and came to my feet. Varn backed away. He had two attendants with him. A different pair. They looked wary and competent.

"Oh, you bastards," I said. "You sick dirty bastards."

"Mr. McGee, you can be reasonable or you can be unreasonable. If you are unreasonable, we'll put you under restraint. There is someone here to talk to you. There is something he wants you to do. And you have to be alert and awake to do what he wants. He is certain you will want to do it."

I slowly brought myself under control. I had nothing to gain by getting my hands on Varn.

"I'll be reasonable," I said. It was an effort.

"Come with me, please."

The attendants came too. There were small lights in the corridors, like battle lamps. We went down narrow concrete stairs. I was trying to learn as much as I could about the layout.

We went to a small visiting room. They herded me into a metal chair. It was bolted to the floor. They pulled a wide strap like a seat belt across my thighs and made it fast. When they started to fasten my arms to the arms of the chair, Varn told them not to bother. He sent one away. He told one to watch me. He went out and came back in a few moments with the same man I had seen getting into the Lincoln with Armister and Bonita Hersch.

He had a long face and a long neck. At first glance he looked frail. But sloping shoulders packed the fabric of the tailored suit, and his hands were big and knuckly, his wrists heavy. His white hair was curly, fitting the long skull closely—a dramatic cap of silver. He had a look of cool intelligence. Of importance.

He stood and, without taking his eyes off me, said, "Doctor, if you and your man would wait outside the door, please. I'll sing out if we have any difficulty in here. I don't think we will."

Varn and the attendant went out. The man said, "You do know who I am, of course."

"Baynard Mulligan."

He hitched himself onto a steel table and sat facing me, long legs swinging. "I will have to take Varn's word that you are highly intelligent. You've made belief a little difficult, McGee."

"I'm not used to such rarefied atmosphere, Mr. Mulligan."

"You could have figured certain things out for yourself, certain obvious equations. This venture is about ten times as profitable as anything you have ever heard of before. So it was planned for ten times as long, is conducted with ten times the care, and has ten times as many safeguards against interference. Fortunately there are not ten times as many people involved. That would increase the risk and diminish the return."

"How many are involved?"

"Nine of us, to a greater or lesser degree. Say five principals and four assistants. It's very complex."

"How are you making out?"

"We're on schedule. Not too much greed and not too little. A proper amalgam of boldness and caution. In addition to all operating expenses, we've diverted six millions of dollars to established number accounts in Zurich. We're under continuous tax audit, of course, which you might call the official seal of approval. Another eighteen months should see us home free—target twenty millions. That is just about the maximum amount we can cover with the faked portfolios and fictitious holdings. Not the maximum, actually. I always insist upon a safety factor. Our Mr. Penerra advises me that it will take years to discover through audit all the ways we managed it and covered our tracks. By then, of course, all five principals will be happily and comfortably distributed in extradition-proof areas. You see, when an applecart gets so big, McGee, one man is a fool to expect to tip it over. What's the matter? You look upset."

"You're telling me a lot."

"Yes, I guess you are reasonably bright. I wouldn't be telling you this if there was the slightest possible chance of your telling anyone else. I assure you, there is not the slightest possible chance. So, if you care to ask questions?"

"If this is such a careful, cautious, brilliant operation, how come you handled Plummer so stupidly? That's what brought me into it."

"I know. Bitter, heartbroken girl, and your duty to poor Mike and so on. Quite touching, actually. But you see, McGee, it was just a curious kind of irony. There was a slight lack of judgment involved. Plummer had a good head. He was becoming troublesome. I tried to talk him into resigning. Simplifying of our operations, no future, and so forth. Finally he agreed. I had offered him a five-thousand-dollar bonus at termination. He asked for ten. It seemed strange. He wanted it in cash. That was easily arranged. I thought I knew what he had in mind. Childish, really, but it could have worked. He planned to go to the tax people with it, claim something funny was going on but that he had no proof, and drop the cash on a desk and ask them why he could ask for and get a cash bonus in that amount if his suspicions were incorrect. We had him followed. We found out that he had arranged an appointment. We could not let him keep it, of course. We were set up to have him brought here, under very plausible circumstances. But before it could be finalized that same evening, the poor fellow was actually mugged. By person or persons unknown."

"You didn't have him killed?"

"Don't be a fool. It was an ironic accident. We're too bright and too civilized to be murderous, McGee. This is a business operation. If you have been thinking you would be killed, allow me to ease your mind."

"Do you expect to keep me here forever?"

"That would be too awkward and too expensive. McGee, we are actually in your debt. Things were going so smoothly that we became slightly careless. It was good for us to have you arrive on the scene. Through your efforts we have learned that Olan Harris—the chauffeur, and one of our assistants in this project—has been dangerously stupid. Searching those apartments is unforgivable. For ten thousand dollars he endangered a project concerned with two thousand times that amount. He said he just kept thinking about that money. He is already in residence in this wing. Varn is delighted to get him. He is as hardy a physical specimen as you are, McGee. Poor Varn keeps deploring the fact he can't publish his test findings."

"And is Miss Hersch here too?"

"You are quick, aren't you? She is not subject to that sort of disposal. Or, to be a little more accurate, perhaps, not subject to disposal until the operation is terminated. She is essential. Mr. Armister is dependent upon her. She handles him nicely. Miss Hersch is not exactly a principal, though she believes herself to be. Her behavior in this matter has been very regrettable. She is a snob, of course. She went running when Mrs. Drummond summoned her. She took you at face value. She got drunk. She told you too much, far too much. She admitted all this, admitted she had been foolish, and promised it would never happen again. She did not admit her attempt to arrange to have intercourse with you. But it became quite obvious from what you told Dr. Moore. She is contrite. But I think we can arrange a very suitable discipline for her. Very suitable. It should quiet any random urges she might have been feeling."

"What's going to happen to me?"

"Nothing, until we can be certain no one is going to make a fuss about you, McGee. Varn and Moore and Daska will run tests on you. You shouldn't suffer any damage from those. And when the time seems appropriate, you will be treated and released."

The very casualness of his tone made me feel chilled.

"That word 'treated' intrigues me."

"It has made Mr. Armister a very contented man, McGee."

"What has?"

"It's a minor surgery. It used to be used frequently in cases of acute anxiety, but it has been discredited these past few years. I can only give you my layman's idea of it, of course. Varn used to do a lot of them. They go in at the temples, I believe, with a long thin scalpel and stir up the frontal lobes. It breaks the old behavior patterns in the brain. With a normal adult it has very specific effects. It will drop your intelligence quotient about forty points, permanently. It will make you incontinent at first. They'll shift you over to one of the regular rooms for special care—toilet training, dressing and feeding yourself, that sort of thing. You will have a short attention span, but you will be able to make a living doing some kind of routine task under supervision. It does cure all repressions and inhibitions, McGee. You will become a very friendly earthy fellow. Very strong but quite casual sex impulses. You will eat well and sleep well, and you will have no tendency to fret or worry about anything. If somebody annoys you, you may react a little too violently, but other than that you should have no trouble with society. It will be a pleasant life, believe me. Mr. Armister is quite content. We keep him well-dressed and tanned and healthy, and see that he has a chance to satisfy all random desires. In return he signs his name wherever he is asked to. And he creates a nice impression. He isn't very rewarding to talk to for any great length of time, but he passes muster when he sits in on signings and conferences. Most important of all, McGee, you will have just small disorganized memories of all this, and no urge to do anything about anything you do happen to remember clearly. Mr. Armister remembers his wife and children, but has no urge to see them."

I could not speak. There were no words to convey my horror at what they had done to him. And wanted to do to me.

"Charlie is a powerful man," he said quietly. "He led a life of sexual repression and torment. Now he is extremely active, but without what Miss Hersch terms finesse. In the beginning we thought she could provide everything he would need. But after a month she begged off, and we agreed to supply Charlie with girls he could use. It's a minor expense compared with the return which comes from keeping him content. But now, I think, that as a sort of continuous act of contrition, Miss Hersch will assume her prior duties and functions. At any rate, there is something I wish you to do. We have checked you out of the hotel. I want you to write two letters. Varn will bring the necessary materials. You will write to Florida and arrange to have your boat sold and the money and your personal possessions shipped here."

"You're crazy as hell."

"And you will write to Miss Nina Gibson and tell her that you are not interested in pursuing this further, and wish her well, and quiet her suspicions. A nice, pleasant, and rather chilly brush-off. Actually, a note to Mike Gibson might be in order too. And one to Terry Drummond? I don't know. I'll have to think about that. She is just a little too important and well known to tangle with. Personally, I think she'll get bored and say the hell with it and go back to Greece."

"I will not write a damned word to anybody."

"Varn!"

The door burst open so quickly I knew my chances of trying anything were slim. And I had the feeling that in the last twenty-four hours I had lost a small edge of physical coordination. When Varn and the attendant saw nothing was wrong, the attendant stepped back into the hall and the door swung shut.

There was a flavor of wariness in Dr. Varn's approach toward Baynard Mulligan.

"Doctor, I would like you to brief Mr. McGee on the Doris Wrightson case."

"I don't believe that would be advisable," Varn said.

Mulligan ignored him. Looking at me, he said, "I can give you a layman's appraisal of her condition when she was brought in. She was a thirty-one-year-old spinster, shy, frail, and introverted, an office worker in poor physical condition. Chronic migraine headaches, a susceptibility to infections of the urinary tract, pains in the lower back. Her pulse was rapid and irregular. Emotionally she was tense, anxious, with poor social and emotional adjustments. She became very upset when office routine was disturbed. Though she was a good worker, she tired easily, and she would weep when spoken to harshly. And she had the strange idea that she was sent here for treatment merely because she had stumbled across some irregularity in the accounting system and had come to me, snuffling and wringing her hands, to accuse our Mr. Penerra of peculation." He turned to Varn. "Certainly, Doctor, she had many physical and emotional problems?"

"Yes. Of course."

"But Dr. Varn is obviously reluctant to discuss the experimental treatment, even though it was astonishingly successful."

"I do not believe we should . . ."

"Experimentations along this line have been conducted in the USSR for some years, didn't you tell me, Doctor?"

"But . . ."

"Everything else that is done here, McGee, can be classified as acceptable therapy. But in this country we have such a sentimental approach to the value of the human animal, that if this line of inquiry became known, mobs would probably appear to burn this place to the ground. It makes Dr. Varn nervous. Please tell Mr. McGee how Doris Wrightson was treated, Doctor."

The two men stared at each other in silent conflict. I saw a gleam of sweat on Varn's bald head. Suddenly Varn gave a small shrug of acceptance. In a perfectly flat voice he said, "After a complete series of tests, an electrode in the form of a very fine alloy wire was inserted into that area of the patient's brain—that deep area which can loosely be defined as the pleasure area. Proper location was achieved through trial and error. A transistorized field-current setup was then adjusted as to the volume of the signal to give a maximum stimulus. In effect this resulted in an intensified pleasure sensation, a simultaneous experiencing of all pleasures, emotional and physical. The patient was given physical tasks, within the limits of her capacities, with the equipment set up in such a manner that the completion of the task would close a contact and give a ten-second stimulus. It was discovered that once the patient had been started on such a cycle, she would continue of her own volition until totally exhausted. Following these procedures, we have made detailed observations of muscle generation, the psychology and physiology of sleep, nutrition, the pleasure phenomenon, and related matters."

"Could we see the patient, Doctor?" Mulligan said.

"She's resting now."

"Doctor, I can remain more convinced of the value of your programs here when I can be given a chance to observe results. Right now there is a list of equipment purchases on my desk for approval."

Varn went to the door and spoke to the man outside. Doris Wrightson was brought in a few minutes later. There was a scarf tied around her head. She wore a gray denim hospital dress that looked too small for her—loose at the waist, but tight across breasts and hips. She moved with a ponderous litheness—that odd gait of the perfectly conditioned athlete. Musculature squared her jaw. Her shoulders and neck were solid and heavy, packing the fabric of the dress. In repose her arms and legs had the roundness and illusion of softness of a woman, but at the slightest move, the slabbed muscles distorted contour, as explicit as an anatomical drawing. For a moment I could not think what she reminded me of, and then I saw it. She was precisely like one of the circus girls: one of those hard, chunky, quiet, amiable fliers—narrow-waisted, flat-bellied—with thighs like a warmed layer of thin foam rubber stretched over granite, and with such pectoral development that even the high round breasts are muscular. This was no sedentary office worker, nor could I imagine her as ever having been one. She said, "Hello, Doctor. Hello, Mr. Mulligan," and then stood off to one side, placid and incurious as a good dog. Though she was very pale, her skin had the moist luminous glow of perfect health, and the whites of her mild brown eyes were blue-white.

Varn said, "She's now at the point where, with a rig designed on the basis of a rowing machine, she will expend forty-eight-hundred foot pounds of energy a minute—fifty foot tons an hour—and maintain that rate for eight hours in two four-hour segments. It requires a five-thousand-calorie intake to keep her weight stabilized on that basis. As we keep increasing effort required, we alter the specific physical motions in order to avoid overdevelopment of any specific muscle areas."

"How do you feel, Doris?" Mulligan asked.

"I feel very good, thank you."

"All other physical problems have disappeared," Varn said. "Her normal heartbeat at rest is approximately fifty."

"Can you explain her emotional adjustment?"

"Only by inference," Varn said. "As you can see, she is placid and amiable and cooperative. Social interactions and interrelations no longer concern her. She is not anxious about how people react to her. She is totally unself-conscious. Her desire to please is based upon our ability to provide her with that pleasure stimulus which forms a compulsion so complete nothing else is of any particular concern to her. She takes pride in doing the hard tasks we set her, though, a pride a little apart from the reward of the pleasure stimulus."

"How about intelligence?" Mulligan asked.

"That's difficult. The conventions we use to measure intelligence are conditioned by emotional factors. The tests imply a wide range of emotional responses. She has one single emotional compulsion. My guess is that intelligence is unimpaired. But her indifference to anything other than the pleasure stimulus makes it difficult to measure. There seems to be an impairment of memory regarding everything which ever happened to her before she came here. Her skills seem unimpaired."

"What's your appraisal of the future?"

"I don't believe we're anywhere near the top limit of physical capability, even though her physical strength is astonishing right now. We're trying to keep her at that point of stasis where strength increases without any breakdown of muscle tissue. I would guess that the end point will be reached when the bone structure cannot take the stress involved."

"What will happen when you stop the experiment?"

"No!" Doris Wrightson cried, her face vivid with dismay.

Varn went quickly to her and said, "We're not going to stop, Doris. Don't be upset." He patted her shoulder. It was a gentling gesture, the way one pats the bulging shoulder of a nervous horse. She quieted quickly, less of the whites of her eyes showing, and he guided her to the door, turned her over to someone waiting there for her.

Varn came back and said, "That's the special problem, as you can see. When we have tried stopping for one day, she becomes very restless and anxious and difficult to manage. It is, in a sense, a very strong addiction. But, unlike other addictions, there is no change in the tolerance level. The exact same percentage increase in the strength of the stimulus now will cause her to faint as it did in the beginning. There is the same effect from an increase in duration."

"What are you going to do with her?"

"We'll face that when we come to it, Mr. Mulligan. Dr. Moore has several suggestions. We'll try the least radical ones first."

"Would you be interested in another female?"

The quickening of interest on Varn's handsome face turned my heart to ice. "It improves the validity of any experimental procedure to have another subject to use as a control," he said. "But . . . we would want to be very certain that . . . there would be no one on the outside to insist on visiting . . ."

"Just like Miss Wrightson? I think I can guarantee that."

"Wilkerson is very interested in setting up an experiment for agility rather than strength. He has the idea of a plate which the subject would have to touch to close the contact, and then he could put it a little higher each day . . ."

His patient impersonal explanation was lost in the roar of blood in my ears. In a little cold white tall room in the back of my mind, my Nina, in gray denim, with a wire in her head, with all of her world and her life focused down to a single recurrent ecstasy—crouched and sprang, crouched and sprang. . . .

Varn was gone. Mulligan studied me. "At a lunch counter, McGee, somebody can reach across her to get a paper napkin. It would be that simple. Moore's report says that you have a strong sexual-emotional attachment for the girl—a protective instinct, with a slight overtone of moralistic guilt. That last astonished me somewhat."

"You are a bastard, Mulligan."

"Dr. Varn's most bitter disappointment is that he cannot publish. But the fellow is endlessly curious. There are certain unpleasantly feral implications in turning people into hopelessly dependent compulsives, but who are we to say that a hundred years from now history might acclaim the good doctor as the one who found the way of turning man into super-man. From a beginning of rewarding strength or agility, why not reward the problem-solving ability, or artistic effort, or mind-reading? Or maybe it will be a world where all the dutiful clods wear their little wires, and men of high intelligence and ambition push the buttons. Our bald little doctor is properly nervous about this field of investigation, but he is careful about his security measures. He is inquisitive, not monstrous. And I am not without compassion."

"You are a legitimate maniac, Mulligan. You are the one they should lock up."

"Don't be childish. Years ago, when I was looking for exactly the right angle of approach, I realized it would be stupid to try to contrive enough fatal accidents to take care of people who might get in the way of a long-range, large-scale project. This has worked well. After these people were bribed and coerced into their first illegal, unethical, unprofessional act, they've had no choice but to be cooperative. I don't actually give a damn about their rationalizations. Charlie was their first project, you are the sixth, Olan Harris is the seventh, and Miss Gibson can be the eighth. I think you will write the letters, McGee. I think you will make every effort to make them plausible and convincing. I do not think you will try to be clever or tricky. As soon as you have written them, you are no longer a problem to me, and I shall probably never see you again. I may see you after your personality has been surgically adjusted, and you will probably remember me and feel a sense of antagonism. But you won't be dangerous."

"I'll be a very happy man."

"That's everybody's goal, isn't it?"

"Let them treat *you*, Mulligan."

"I am a happy man, my friend. I'm getting my gratification from finding a way past all the rules and restrictions and conventions of a dull and orderly society. I'm performing a theft of such dimensions it will be legend rather than theft. And, like our Dr. Varn, I am slightly bitter because I will never be able to publish the details of it. But books will be written about it. From the look of you, I think you are ready to write those letters."

I was, and I did.

11

I was woven into delicious clouds, high and ecstatic on softened hill-tops, taking the slow, sweet, aching suffusions of the warm slow drift of great masses of pure color, which moved across me and through me and changed in almost imperceptible ways. I was one, united to pure sensation, everything about me becoming a part of me, a fabulous unity, so that I knew at last the ultimate fact of all existence, knew it and knew that there were no words with which it could be expressed because it was beyond words. I rolled over and stretched my arms into a strange grass, more like hair than grass, metallic blue-green in color, springing out of the soft white earth-flesh; hair-grass thick as pencils, half as tall as a man, making a strange electric tingling wherever it touched my flesh. I rolled and saw leaning to me a golden reaching softness of limbs of ancient Martian trees—reaching, grasping gently, curling, caressing, taking me up and through brightness and then into a dusky feathery hollow between enormous breasts, into a stroking and fitting and long long gentle never-ending orgasm. . . .

Tiny bright light swinging and my voice in a darkened room.

Brush and soap and shower. "He was never worth a goddam until they moved him to linebacker."

Light in the room at night. Face at the grill in the door.

Pasty feel of electrodes at the temples, pen scratching a rhythmic line on a chart.

"Now, Travis, run in position until I tell you to stop."

Indifferent face in the night. Needle fang in my arm. Cool wipe of alcohol. Medicine smell. Off into drifting . . .

They wanted a manageable patient, a mild eagerness to cooperate. There were times when I felt I was fighting my way to the surface and then I would be pushed down again, down into the drifting. No problem to anybody. When I got close to the surface I would know that some terrible thing was going to happen, but I did not know what it was.

I do not know how they slipped up, or why they slipped up. Perhaps it was one of those little errors in routine, somebody skipping a medication indicated on the chart. But suddenly I came awake in the night. I did not know what night it was, or how much time had passed. I knew only that I was alert and terrified. Wisps of strange dreams and visions clotted the corners of my mind. The night light was sealed into the baseboard, guarded with a heavy grill. I looked out the door grill into a segment of empty gray corridor.

I paced the room and, at the first rattle of the latch, got quickly into bed. It was the square sandy nurse. She fixed the hypo in the dim light. When she bared my arm and bent over it, I hit her sharply on the shelf of the jaw, near the chin. She fell across me without a sound. I found the hypo when I shifted her cautiously. I got up and straightened her out and looked in her pockets. I found the little vial from which she filled the hypo. I injected her in the arm with what was in the hypo, then drew off more from the vial, sticking the needle through the soft rubber top, and gave her that. She had a split ring with two keys on it. I did not know what they fitted. She had left my door wedged open a few inches. She was on the floor on her back. Her mouth hung open. She began to snore. I rolled her onto her face. She stopped snoring. I shoved her under the bed. She slid easily on the gray vinyl flooring. I was in the short hospital gown I wore at night. They would bring me clean coveralls each morning. The door to the tiled bath was locked. I did not dare go out into the hallway. This might be the only chance I would have. They would know how to handle patients who got out into the corridors. They would have safe, practical, effective methods. They would never give me a second chance. There would be nothing left but the dreams and visions until they had finished their series, and then there would be a tiny blade shoved into my head, and after that I would never worry very much about anything.

The room door opened inward. It was held open by a rubber wedge. I listened. I heard nothing. I pulled the door halfway open and wedged it. The night-light made a fairly bright area just inside the door. I had to bait it with something. I used her keys. They caught the light. They would catch the eye of anyone passing. The normal reaction would be to pick them up. I waited alongside the door, where I could not be seen through the grill. I waited a long time. I heard someone coming. Scuff of a shoe. Faint rustle of clothing. I clenched my hands together. I heard a soft exclamation. The instant I saw a hand reaching for the keys, I jumped out and brought my clenched hands down on the nape of a neck, as hard as I could. He made too much noise tumbling onto the floor. I pulled him inside, wedged the door open an inch or so. I dragged him over beside the bed. I was going to inject him. But as I touched him, he gave a prolonged shudder and died. I worked his clothing off him and put it on. The legs and sleeves were short. I was worried about the shoes. I wanted shoes. But they were just big enough. I put him into the bed and covered him over. I felt in the pockets. There was a wallet. I took it to the light. He was Donald Swane. He had three keys. One of them was identical to one of the nurse's keys. I felt sorry for the poor dead son of a bitch. He had no way of knowing that some of the patients didn't belong there. Which ones do you believe?

He had eleven dollars, half a pack of Camels, a Zippo lighter, three keys, half a roll of clove Life Savers, and no weapon at all. Once upon a time I had tried to memorize the layout of the building. I couldn't remember much of it.

I didn't want to walk out of the room. It seemed like a safe place. I didn't know what was waiting outside. His shoes were quiet. They had rubber soles. I carried the hypo and vial in the pocket of the white jacket. I opened the door and looked up and down the corridor. It was empty. To my left I saw a red bulb burning over a doorway. I remembered there were stairs there. I walked swiftly, letting the door close behind me. I went through the stairway door. I had left his watch on his wrist. It was after four in the morning. I wanted to go down the stairs. As I started to go down, a door opened on the next flight down, and somebody started coming up. I went up. There was only one more flight. I waited until I was certain they were coming all the way up. I went out into a corridor very like the one on my floor below. I pulled a door open. It was a lab. A blue night-light shone on tubing and retorts, zinc benches, bottle racks. I made certain the door could be opened from the inside, and let it shut. I crouched against the door, straining my ears to hear any sound in the corridor. The door was too thick. I waited at least five minutes. Then I looked around the lab. The windows were steel casement windows, rigidly braced. They did not open far enough for me to get out. I was on the third floor. I could have risked a drop from that height.

I wanted a weapon. I searched the small lab. I found a short heavy length of pipe. I tied it into a towel. I looked into a big refrigerator. It was full of racks of small vials containing colorless fluid. They were marked in a D series. D-1 to D-17. Many of them had sub-numerals in parentheses. I took vials of D-15, three of them, and some of the other numbers. They were small. I had the idea that if I could get out of there, the vials would be some proof of what was being done there, provided they were the Daska compounds. Somehow I saw all the doctors I had not met as looking exactly like Varn, all handsome little bald fellows.

It felt reassuring to have a club in my hand. I expected alarm bells to go off at any moment. I thought they would have some way of sounding an alarm when a patient was loose. Perhaps a siren. The corridor was empty. I ran to the stairs and went racing down. I got down to the ground-floor level. The corridor there was much wider. I remembered a time, a lifetime ago, when I had been taken down to talk to Baynard Mulligan. It seemed a longer corridor than the ones upstairs. In the far distance I saw two nurses standing and talking. If I could not see their faces, they could not see mine. There had to be an exit in that direction, perhaps halfway between me and the nurses. I walked toward them, trying to move casually. Suddenly a man came out of a doorway forty feet in front of me and started walking toward me, looking at a piece of paper he held in his hand.

I pushed open the first door I came to and went in. I was in a kitchen area. Two men were working slowly and sleepily at a big range. A dull-looking girl stood at a work table yawning and slicing grapefruit into halves. There was a lot of stainless steel and steam racks. They all looked at me questioningly.

"You seen Don?" I asked.

"What the hell would he be doing in here? Go look in the dining room."

There was a long pass-through area at one end of the room. I could look through there into a big institutional dining area. I saw the swinging doors with push plates which had to lead there. I walked toward the doors.

"Don who?" the girl asked.

"Skip it."

The dining area was empty. There was a long counter with low stools and, beyond it, a cafeteria area adjacent to the pass-through. A busty redheaded girl in a blue nylon uniform stood at the work area behind the counter, slicing small boxes of dry cereal and placing the boxes into white bowls.

She glanced at me and said, "You want coffee, it's about three more minutes. I threw out the old, it tasted like battery acid, man." She gestured toward a huge gleaming urn that stood on the counter.

As I started to turn away, she said, "You new?"

"Brand new."

"Didn't take you long to get the coffee habit. It's like my husband says it's that way in the navy."

Find a door and walk out, I thought. And then what? Are there walls, gates, guards? It is way out in the country? Any way to get a car?

"Rest yourself while you wait, man."

I needed a diversion. I needed everybody looking in some other direction. I sat on a stool. The vials in my pocket clinked. I stared at the long distortion of my face in the shining urn. Why the hell not?

"Mind if I look in the top of that thing?"

"What for? You look at those tube things and you can tell, it's when they get dark enough."

"I was wondering how they make them now," I said. I got up onto the counter and pulled the lid.

"Hey!" she said.

"This is very interesting."

"Climb in and have a swim. You a nut or something?"

She turned back to her cereal. I thumped the rubber tops off the vials of D compound and dumped them in. Maybe they were harmless. Maybe they were cholera germs. Maybe heat changed them. It was too late to wonder about it. Scores slain in coffee poisoning. I wiped the counter with a paper napkin. I sat on a stool. She looked at me and her face was losing form, sliding and loosening like melting candy. I heard a strange prolonged chord of music in a minor key. The walls of the big room tilted inward toward me, and the edges of reality had turned pink.

"You feel okay?" she asked, out of a mouth that was sliding down her throat into the top of her uniform.

"Just a little residual hallucination."

"Huh? Oh."

"I'll be back for some of your delicious coffee, angel."

"You do that."

"Don't melt while I'm gone."

"Melt? It isn't hot in here, man."

The door kept receding as I walked toward it. It took me three or four hours to reach it. I went into the corridor. I found a storage room. I folded myself into a cement corner behind huge cartons of toilet paper, and held my fists against my eyes and tried to keep the whole world from melting away into a pink eternal nothing. In seven or eight months the world began to refocus and solidify. The musical chord died away, and I could hear clattering, shouts, a bell ringing. I got up and walked out into a vast confusion. I heard glass breaking. Two men were trying to hold a third man. He was screaming, spasming, throwing them all over the corridor. I edged by them. A woman stood braced with her back against the wall, eyes closed, expression dreamy, slowly driving her nails into her cheeks and yanking them out again, blood running onto her beige blouse. I walked by her. I reached the main entrance. The world was out there, beyond tall glass, a bright cool morning. A man on all fours was in a corner, trying to ram his way through, backing up and lunging forward like a big stubborn turtle trapped in a box. A girl sat spraddled on the floor. Her blouse was ripped to rags. Her empty eyes looked at me. She was sucking her thumb and slowly massaging her small loose breasts.

A man lay quite still just outside the main doors. I stepped over him. I heard sirens. I saw ambulances. People were running toward the building. They ignored me. I saw the parking lot and walked steadily toward it.

Off to my right I saw a fat woman running in a big circle as though she were running an imaginary base path. A big car came into the lot just as I got there. A man slammed the brakes on and piled out. "What the *hell* is going on?" he demanded. "What's happening in there?"

I turned him around and rapped him behind the ear with my length of pipe. When he fell, his car keys spilled out of his hand. I peeled his topcoat off and put it on. I took his car and drove away from there. Fifteen minutes later I was on the Thruway, heading south toward the city. Twenty minutes later the sides of the highway began to curl upward and turn pink and the musical sound began again. I had to pull off. It took twenty minutes to get from my lane to the shoulder. The car was barely moving. But when it reached the shoulder it began to leap up and down. I stopped it short of a tree and lay down on the seat with my arms wrapped around my head. My own face was melting off. I could feel it. I could hear it drip onto the seat upholstery.

Several months later the world resolidified and I drove on.

I drove down off the parkway at Forty-sixth. I drove over Forty-fourth and abandoned the car a couple of blocks short of Times Square. I walked south and found a sleazy hotel and paid five-fifty for a small sour room. I stretched out on the bed, still in the stolen topcoat, and waited for the edges of everything to start to turn pink again. I had noticed the clock in the lobby. It was quarter after ten. I wondered what year it was.

12

We are supposed to learn from our mistakes. I had walked into the Armister situation with all the jaunty confidence of a myopic mouse looking for a piece of cheese in the cobra cage.

But by the narrowest margin possible I had escaped spending the rest of my life as a very happy fellow working, perhaps, in a shoe factory over in Jersey.

I had to make some kind of a move now, but everything I could think of scared me. The Mulligan group had all kinds of weight and pressure. I was an escaped nut. A demonstrably murderous nut. And I had no proof of anything.

Charlie was my walking proof. Charlie was my boy. But I didn't see how I could get to within a thousand yards of him.

But maybe somebody else could, if they knew enough.

Like a loving wife?

I picked my phone up. A thin and adenoidal voice said, "You wanna make any outside calls, you got to leave the money at the desk. Twenty cents each, local calls."

I found my apprehensive way down and left a dollar and got back to safe refuge. Then I realized how stupid I was being. I had made all the mistakes I was permitted. I rubbed cold water on my face and studied my mirror image. The eyes looked strange. With the topcoat buttoned, the white jacket did not show. I had a crust of oneday beard. Noticeable, but not too bad.

I went down again and got change for my dollar and found the phone booths in the dim back of the stale lobby.

I tried the Plaza. Mrs. Drummond was not registered. They gave me a forwarding address in Athens.

I leaned against the phone for a little while. I got information. She looked up the Long Island number for Mr. Charles Armister, told me how to dial it and how much to feed the coin slots.

I got a soft-voiced woman with a pronounced accent. She told me Mrs. Armister was in the city. At the apartment. She gave me the phone number. I checked the book. It was the number listed for the other apartment, the one further uptown.

I dialed that one. Terry Drummond answered. That brassy sardonic voice was one of the world's better sounds.

"McGee! They bought you off, obviously. What's the matter, ducks? You want to see if you can get a better price from me? How'd you find me?"

"Nobody bought me off."

"Sweetie, it was perfectly obvious to me from your note that—"

"Shut up! I have something important to tell you, Terry. I don't know how much time I have. I wasn't bought off. They had me in a mental hospital."

"In a what?"

"Get a pencil and paper so you can write things down. I don't know how long I can last. I'll try to give you the cold facts."

"Hold on just a minute, Trav."

I waited. A softer voice came on the line and gave a cautious "Hello?"

It had a little of the quality of Terry's voice, but was far more subdued.

"Trav? Joanna is on the extension."

"This isn't the sort of thing she should hear, Terry."

"If it has anything to do with my husband, I want to hear it," Mrs. Armister said firmly.

"All right. I don't know how you can check these things out, but if you get good lawyers and get the authorities in on it, maybe you can move. Baynard Mulligan heads up a group which has stolen six million dollars so far from Charles Armister. There are nine of them. Mulligan, Penerra and Bonita Hersch, those are the only names I know. They plan to work at it for another eighteen months and build it up to twenty million and then skip. When anybody gets troublesome, they get put in the Mental Research Wing of the Toll Valley Hospital up across the river from Poughkeepsie. Write these things down. They've got people up there now who got in the way. Olan Harris, who was the chauffeur. A secretary named Doris Wrightson. And others whose names I don't know. They get them legally committed. They did that to me too. I escaped this morning. I killed a man getting out of there."

"Dear God," Terry rumbled.

"That's where Charles went when he—"

"Shut up, Joanna," Terry said.

"When Charlie was up there," I said, "they operated on him. They stuck a knife in his head. I think it's called a lobotomy. That made him easy to manage. They keep him happy, and he signs anything. But anybody who didn't know him before would think he was perfectly all right."

I heard a soft, weak, wailing cry of despair and Terry said sharply, "Pull yourself together, Jo!"

"Write down these names of doctors. God knows where they came from, or how they ever got licenses. Mulligan has them in the palm of his hand. He supports the experimental program. Varn, Moore, Daska, and Wilkerson. And listen. Don't go flying off in all directions. There's a hell of a mess out there right now, but if they can get it quieted down fast enough, and if you get in the way, you both could end up out there with little wires in your heads, and electric currents making you jump around like monkeys on a stick."

"Can this be true?" Joanna wailed.

"Sister, dear, I will vouch for McGee. He is a very rough type, and he sounds angry, and what he says explains a lot of very curious things. McGee, where are you? Can I help you? What do you need?"

"Money."

"Sweetie, I have the thousand dollars I was going to use to bribe that tart who never showed up. Will that help?"

"A lot. But get moving on this other stuff first. Listen. This is important for both of you. Don't eat out. Don't drink anything anywhere. Fix your own food and drink right there and don't let anybody near it. Don't even let anybody buy it for you."

"But why?"

"One drop of a tasteless, odorless substance can turn you into something they come after with a net. They worked it on me, maybe on Charlie, and probably on the others. It imitates insanity."

"Sweetie, this is priceless. I used to adore Fu Man Chu."

"You have a great sense of humor, Terry. You are as funny as a crutch."

"I'm sorry, Trav. It's just my image speaking."

"By now Mulligan knows I'm loose, I would imagine. He is going to be very anxious to find me and shut my mouth. And he can afford a lot of help. I need money, and then I need a place to go, a place for two people to go, if I can . . ."

"Sweetie, where are you?"

I drew such a blank I had to look at the tag on my room key. "The Harbon Hotel on West Forty-first. Room 303."

"You wait right there," she said and hung up.

But I was in a horrid haste to find the next number and fumble the next dime into the slot. I had thought the best thing to do would be to protect Nina by staying out of touch with her. But in telling Terry what Mulligan might do, I had realized Nina was the best possible weapon for him to use against me. He had proved that point once.

The cool British accent of the receptionist was an implacable barrier. She was teddibly sorry, Miss Gibson was in conference and could not be disturbed. I said it was life and death. She said that if I would leave my name and number, she would have Miss Gibson call me. I cursed her and she sighed and broke the connection. With my last dime I called back. With great gentleness I stressed the urgency of the situation. I begged her to have Miss Gibson phone Mr. Jones in Room 303 at the Harbon Hotel as soon as possible. I stressed the room number. I was certain the place was full of Joneses, miss and mister.

I bought a paper. The stairs tilted sideways. The railing felt like a wet snake. I shoved seven keys at seven keyholes and they all fitted and all turned, and I stumbled into a pink room and curled up on the bed, my knees against my chest. As I fought it, I thought with a sickening remorse of the people out there at Toll Valley—the man butting his head into a corner, the woman pulling bits of meat out of her face, the thumb sucker, the base runner—all of them so ruthlessly tumbled into that horrible place where reality was warped, where things came out of the wall. They were all innocents. They could not know that the private hospital was being used in a vicious way. They were staff, visitors, am-

bulatory patients—anybody entitled to go into the dining room and have
a cup of nightmare.

It dwindled away. All the pink unstable edges turned back to normal
hue and I straightened myself out, in post-hallucination depression. For
the ultimate in depressive experiences, try a little jolt of induced insanity while wearing a dead man's clothing in a cheap hotel room. Cold
air-shaft light came into the room, shining on the dusty sour rug, on a
blond bureau with missing knobs, on places on the headboard of the
bed where brown paint had been chipped and gouged away. Ten thousand people had left a stink of loneliness in this room. Here they had
paced, coughed, snapped their knuckle bones, spilled their drinks, taken
their pills, belched, sighed, wept, scratched, dreamed, vomited, smoked,
bragged, cursed, and groaned. In this room each had endured his or her
own special kind of sickness, felt despair, and either accepted or
inflicted something they called love.

I saw the paper where I had dropped it, just inside the door. I went
over and got it and took it back to the bed. While I had been in the
blurry world of induced dreams and visions, the other world had
trudged its way along to a November Tuesday. Education bill returned
to committee. Three injured in Birmingham bomb attack. Actress beats
narcotics rap. Seven dead in Freeway collision. Parklands sold to cam-
paign contributor. Truck strike in eighth week. Thirty-nine dead in jet
crash. Model claims fractured jaw in divorce action. Disarmament talks
stalled. Teacher accused of teen slayings. Earthquake in Peru. Launching failure. Tax cut stymied. . . .

I was back in the sane, reasonable, plausible world.

Terry Drummond rapped at my door and I let her in. She wore
fifteen thousand dollars' worth of glossy fur coat. Her brown simian
face wrinkled with distaste as she looked around. "God, what a scrimey
hole!" The coat swung open. The body of eternal girl was clad in gray
slacks and a wine-red cardigan. She stared at me. "And you look worn
around the edges, dear. And thinner. And where did you get that grim
grubby clothing?"

"Off the boy I had to kill to get out of there."

She swallowed and sat down quickly. "You do get damned explicit.
Maybe I'm not as used to the facts of life as I thought I was. But we did
hear Toll Valley Hospital very prominently mentioned over the noon
news broadcast."

"What did they say?"

"Something about mysterious poisoning, four dead in violent and unpleasant ways, and dozens injured, and dozens out of their mind, patients escaping and so on; and apparently the first batch of people who got there to quiet things down suddenly began to go just as mad as the rest of them. They said something about experimental drugs getting out of hand. It seems that there is still a state of horrible confusion up there, and all kinds of investigations being started, and experts roaring in from all over, and reporters and police and television and everything. Did you do all that, darling boy?"

I did not answer. Four dead. Four innocents.

"Trav?" she said in the softest voice I had ever heard her use.

I lifted my head and looked at her.

"Please don't look so terribly agonized. You did what you had to do. I'm sure of that. I've started things going. I believe what you said about them doing something terrible to Charlie out at that place. From the news report, it sounds as if you managed to destroy it. I'm not going to let anything happen to you on account of that, believe me. They were giving you drugs, weren't they?"

"They were giving me drugs."

"Then you cannot be held responsible. Which is worse, Trav, some deaths and injuries, or that place going on and on . . . *doing* things to people?"

"I can devise my own rationalizations, thanks."

"Don't be cold and cruel. Sweetie, I brought the money, but after I got Joanna calmed down, we had another idea. You want a safe place for two people? The other one would be your little Gibson girl you told me about? My dear Roger King is alerting all the legal troops. I am certain he can erect some sort of protective throng around the apartment at East Seventy-ninth. It's really quite vast, and Joanna brought in some of the staff from the Island. I don't think we'd need extra protection, but it would probably make you happier. So let's go on back to the apartment, and then I can go gather up your little friend, and we can all sit there and plan the utter destruction of creepy Baynard."

"How did you get here?"

"By taxi. He's sitting down there with his meter clicking."

"You just walked out of the apartment and took a cab."

"Of course," she said blankly.

"And nobody followed you?"

"My word, aren't we getting a bit paranoiac?"

My phone rang.

"Hello?"

"Trav! Oh, Trav, darling, thank God!"

"That letter I wrote you . . ."

"Was the most complete nonsense ever written. It was a cry for help. I was going out of my mind with worry. The moment I got it I went at once to—"

"We better do our talking later. Do exactly as I say, Nina. It's very important. Get out of there as soon as you can. If there is any kind of back exit or side exit, use it."

"But . . ."

"That place where we went, near your office, that first day. Go there. Wait for me there. Don't have a drink. Just wait for me. Don't talk to anybody. Just wait there alone."

"Trav, I . . ."

"Please!"

She agreed. I hung up, and turned and looked at Terry Drummond. Her odd green eyes looked damp. "It's important with that one?"

"Very."

"That makes me feel such a wistful old bag, ducks. Hold me a minute? I have a case of the horrors."

She came to me. I put my arms around the resiliency, the warmth of girl under that fur coat, and held her close. She tucked her brown puckered face into my neck and sighed.

"Well, hell," she said. "Let's go. Let's go pick up your young stuff and run for cover."

I shoved the sheaf of large bills into the wallet of the dead Donald Swane. I said, "We are going to cheat your cabby, Terry."

"We can't. I gave him a ten to hold him there. But I'll play your games, dear. We sneak out another way?"

"If you can bear it."

"I can."

"Terry, every once in a while I go off. I hallucinate. I have to fold. I don't know how long it lasts. But don't be scared. I come out of it. It seems to be a little bit less each time. If it happens in public, just keep people away from me and give me time to come out of it."

Her mouth looked pale. "All right, Trav."

There was no other way to leave. We went out the main entrance and turned away from the waiting cab. That coat was too damned conspic-uous. "Lady! Hey, lady!" We walked swiftly to the corner.

The panting driver caught up to us. "Hey, lady! You coming back to the cab?"

"Keep the change, my good man."

"But that guy is waiting for you in the cab."

"What guy?" she demanded.

"The one come out of the hotel after you went in, the one you told he should wait in my cab, lady."

He turned and pointed. We looked. A man was walking diagonally across 41st, heading in the opposite direction, moving swiftly.

"Hey, there he goes!" the driver said.

I grabbed Terry's arm and hustled her around the corner and walked her as fast as she could go. "Hey!" she said. "Hey, I apologize. For everything."

At the next corner I saw a cab discharging passengers. I ran her over to it and we piled in. He pulled his flag down. I said, "Make some turns here and there, driver. A very busy process server is trying to hand the lady a paper."

He started up and said, "You looked in a hurry. But the way I see it, what's the use? Sooner or later you get nailed."

"I'd like to make it later," Terry said.

The driver was good. He judged the lights so as to be the last car around each corner as the light changed. He angled crosstown and downtown, and said, "Unless he rented a whirlybird, friend, he's no-where."

I gave him the block on Park I wanted. Terry said in a low voice, "I never saw that man before in my life. What was he going to do to me?"

I made a grim joke. "Process you," I said. She put her hand on her throat. "And they'll have to process Charlie too. If he's dead, nobody can prove what was done to him. Nobody can test him."

Her eyes looked like green glass. "You can't be serious."

"He's part of the proof."

She waited in the cab. I went in to get Nina. She was on the left of the entrance. There was a man sitting on either side of her. She looked pale and strained. The two men looked deft and deadly and competent. I paused. The men's trim shaven faces began to turn into bristly dog faces, dogs in dark suits, in pink light, with a white kitten between them. Dimly I realized that it was emotional stress which was bringing this on, time after time. I could curl up on the floor and hold my fists against my eyes. I staggered, and launched myself through the pink light, straining toward the nearest dog, yelling to Nina in a great cracked, croaking voice, "Run! Run!" I could give her that much. She had not asked for any part of this. I didn't want her in gray denim with wires in her head. I would rather be eaten by the dogs.

I caught a dog throat, hurled a dog body wide and far, whirled in pinkness to dive past the kitten, was cracked, and foundered, and was dwindled down to black flow, to a dark puddled sinking nothing. . . .

13

I awoke naked between crisp sheets in a big shadowy bedroom. There was a lamp with a blue shade in a far corner. The blue light made little gleamings of richness on the corners and edges of things. I could hear a faint whisper of night traffic. I turned my head slowly. A far door was ajar. There was a brighter light beyond it. My head felt strange. I lifted my hand and touched my head and felt gauze and tape.

I wondered if I was now a very happy fellow. This would be the lion's den, of course. The quiet and spacious luxury of the inner sanctum, where Mulligan and Hersch kept a pet named Charlie Armister. Marvelous talent for organization.

I lay and wondered how happy I was. How uninhibited. Maybe Mulligan could use me as chauffeur, replacing the greedy and unreliable Harris. But a job like that would require initiative. I would need supervision. Maybe they had gathered us all up and made us all very happy. Terry and Joanna. And Nina.

Then I knew I was not happy at all. I could remember every fraction of every instant with her, every kiss and contour.

No matter what the bastards did, McGee would keep trying. He would keep on clattering on in there, banging the rusty armor, spurring the spavined old steed, waving the mad crooked lance. I rolled up and sat on the edge of the bed. The rug was thick and soft against bare feet. I could see a dressing table, a faint gleam of bottles and jars aligned against the mirrors. I saw a small white fireplace, stood up, swayed for a moment, and tottered over to it. There was a rack of shiny fireplace tools. Brass. I selected the poker. As I turned, I saw myself in a mirrored door. Big brown spook with a surgical turban. I tottered and brandished my weapon and whispered, "Tally ho."

I prowled silently to the door that was ajar. It was a bathroom done in pink, gold, and white. It was empty. I wrapped a big towel around my waist and knotted it. I went back through the bedroom and put my ear against the closed door. I could hear a low distant murmur of voices. I opened the door cautiously. It opened onto a dim carpeted hallway. At the end of the hallway was a living room. I could see a segment of it, a drift of smoke, a tailored male shoulder. Several men seemed to be talking at once. Plotting. I heard the rattle of ice in a glass.

The hell with them. I would burst among them and see how many skulls I could crack before they wore me out. I took the brass poker in both hands. I took a deep breath. I headed for that big room, and just as I got there, I let out the war cry of a thousand disreputable years of McGee. As I yelled, the towel knot came undone. The towel slipped and wrapped around my ankles. I plunged free and went stumbling across the room in wild, head-down run. I ran into the glass doors of a huge breakfront desk loaded with porcelains, crashed, rebounded, cracked myself across the mouth with the handle of the poker, lay dazed and sprawling and looked up into the frozen astonishment on the faces of a dozen men, and on the face of Terry Drummond, and on the face of Nina Gibson, and on the old, worn, dignified face of Constance Trimble Thatcher.

"Whose apartment *is* this?" I managed to ask in a humble voice.

The man in charge sat by my bed and gave small guarded explanations. He did not want to say anything he did not have to say. His name was Beggs. His face was almost entirely nose, with a little mouth tucked under the bottom edge of it, and little eyes crowded up against each side of it.

"We had been making a quiet investigation for some time," he said.

"Who is we?"

"A cooperative venture between interested agencies. Certain small irregularities came to our attention. When Miss Gibson went to the Bureau with your letter, they turned her over to us and she told us what she knew. It . . . uh . . . became a matter of greater urgency. We decided she should have protection at all times. The two men with her were the two you assaulted."

"How did I do?"

"Splendidly, until you fell and hit your head on the edge of the table. Mrs. Drummond insisted you be brought here."

"Now what?"

"What do you mean?"

"What are you doing about all this great urgency?"

"Everything is going reasonably well."

"Don't I have the right to know what's going on?"

"What right? For blundering around endangering people?"

"The inherent God-given right of every total damned fool, Mr. Beggs."

A little smile curled in the deep shadow of the nose.

"What particularly concerns you?"

"What about Charlie?"

"You do have rather a nice instinct for these things. Mrs. Drummond conveyed to me your fears about Mr. Armister, and so we dated our blank warrants and went in two hours ago. We had to break in. There was a suicide note, in his handwriting, beside him, and an empty bottle which had contained sleeping pills. There was no one else there. They pumped him out and gave him stimulants and began walking him. He's quite confused about what happened. He is at the hospital now. His wife is with him."

"What about Mulligan?"

"We believe we will locate him."

"And Bonita Hersch?"

"Apparently Miss Hersch and Mr. Penerra are in the company of Mr. Mulligan. We have two other men in custody, and they seem to have the feeling that the others ran out on them. They may give us some excellent suggestions as to where to look. We believe that Mulligan and company delayed a little too long before trying to leave. Over-confidence, probably."

I hesitated before asking the next question. "Toll Valley?"

"What about it?"

"Is it out of business?"

"Hardly. It is a perfectly reliable place. But their Mental Research Wing has been closed down, and all staff persons, those who are well enough at the moment, charged with illegal practices, administering unauthorized medicines, performing unnecessary operations—that sort of thing. I imagine it will be a very lengthy investigation, and public interest may well die down before it is settled one way or another."

"Dr. Varn?"

"Killed himself at two o'clock this afternoon."

"There were some other people out there. . . ."

He took out a small black pocket notebook. "Olan Harris, George Raub, John Benjamin, and Doris Wrightson. Yes. They have been moved to other institutions for intensive care. They were all employed by Armister interests in one way or another. I'm in hopes they can be made well enough to testify. If you have no other questions . . ."

"What about what happened out there?"

The little eyes sighted along that nose. They were as unreadable as raisins. "Apparently there was some sort of mixup where experimental compounds were accidentally used in their commissary department. There was such confusion I doubt if we will ever know exactly what happened. It is even possible that Dr. Varn did it purposely, on an experimental basis."

"There were deaths?"

"Four. One was apparently from heart disease. One fell into a fountain and drowned. One woman stabbed herself with a serving fork. And an attendant apparently died of a fall."

"Is there any record of . . . my escaping from out there?"

"I don't know what you are talking about. There is no record of your ever having been out there, Mr. McGee. Mrs. Thatcher, who is, by the way, an old friend, assures me that there would certainly never be any reason for you to have been sent to such a place. She thinks you are unstable, but not in any particularly mental way."

"Testimony?"

"From you, Mr. McGee? I think not. I think we can struggle along without you. When we organize these matters, we like to be able to call upon witnesses who will stay within the areas we propose to prosecute."

It puzzled me for a moment, and then I said, "Oh! Charlie."

He nodded his approval. "Of course. What purpose would be gained? We will have enough without that. We don't seek sensational press coverage in these matters. The courts will appoint trustees to make audits and sort everything out and manage the money henceforth. And we do expect that some recovery of monies will be made. If we can lay hands on Mr. Mulligan, I expect he will be glad to arbitrate the matter."

"He should be gutted and broiled."

"You are very savage, but I imagine that disbarment, poverty, and total anonymity will be a far more galling fate for Mr. Mulligan."

Someone knocked on the door. Beggs went to the door. He spoke in low tones to someone for a little while and then came back and stood beside my bed. "We expect to take Penerra off a Mexico City flight when it stops in Houston. And Canadian authorities have the Hersch woman. Apparently Mulligan tricked her and abandoned her in Montreal."

"How about Mulligan?"

"She may have some useful information for the man I am sending up there. The report says she is very upset."

"What do you want of me?"

"Mr. McGee, we would all take it as a great favor to everyone concerned if you would gather your strength and go back to Florida where you came from, and keep your mouth shut. As a matter of fact, if you do not keep your mouth shut, I will subpoena you for every single court action arising from this whole mess, and it may take from three to five years to clean up, and I shall call you every time and let you sit and listen to what my people have to listen to, year after year. I assure you, Mr. McGee, that no one has ever made a more dreadful threat to you, or meant it more sincerely."

He smiled, swiveled the bulk of his nose around, and followed it out of the bedroom.

Terry came in and talked. Nina came in and talked. Servants brought dinner on a tray. Terry brought wine. Terry and Nina and I talked. The doctor came back and looked me over. He wanted to know what had happened to my mouth. Terry told him I had engaged in mortal combat with a breakfront desk. And lost. He looked at her with great suspicion and told me I was ridiculously, impossibly, grotesquely healthy. But to get a lot of rest. He left pills, very small lavender ones. I took two. I washed them down with wine. Terry talked. Nina talked. I began to yawn. . . .

In the stilly depths of night and sleep came a perfumed silken sliding, a warmth, a closeness and cautious caress. "Nina?" I said.

"Yes darling," she whispered.

A slow writhing luxurious warmth under shortie wisp of sheerness. Head tucked into my neck. A long slow arousing, coming from the pill sleep into the needs of love. It was a sweet hypnosis, without haste. When she was shudderingly readied, and I was turning to take her, too many little things added up to an almost subliminal wrongness. Something about the scents of her, something about lengths and textures, something about a less springy feel of her hair against my cheek, something about the way she avoided kissings, something about the deep sweep of curves which did not seem right in my hands, even something about the catch of her breath in response. I stopped and pinned her and ran my hand over her hair and her face. My fingertips felt the soft little serrations on her face.

"Terry!" I whispered.

She hitched herself at me frantically. "Never mind," she said in a gritty whisper. "It's way too late now. Do it. Come on, damn you!" And she tried in a convulsive grasping to join us. I broke her arms and legs away from me, and struggled away from her and stood up and went over to the other side of the room and sat, trembling, on the bench of the dressing table.

I sat and listened to all the foul growling words she could think of to call me. She raved her low-voiced threats. "Jo was going to be generous, and I'll make sure you won't get a dime. And I'll tell that cheap busty little girl of yours that you laid me. Who the hell do you think you are?"

"Are you through?"

"God, what a priss you are. You don't deserve an honest-to-God woman. Little shopgirls. That's your speed, McGee. You can be a big hero to them. Come back here and prove you're a man."

"Are you through?"

She did not answer. I saw a pale stirring, and then the shape of her, indistinct, sitting on the edge of the bed. In her normal wry mocking tone she said, "Hell, I guess it was worth a try."

"I'm sorry, Terry."

"Am I that repulsive to you?"

"You know better than that."

"Then, just between friends, what put you off?"

"After I knew it was you?"

"After you knew it was me."

"When I knew it was you, I knew it wasn't Nina. That's about the only answer I can give you."

After a silence she said, "I guess that's the only answer there is. In some nutty way I guess I have to admire you. You are a strange animal, McGee. I'm not used to your kind. I don't think I've ever bedded another man who could have quit right then and there."

"It wasn't exactly easy."

"Thank you, ducks. That's some help. But, you know, you have left me in one hell of a condition."

"Go take a cold shower."

"There's romance for you. Well, I got tricky, and it didn't work, and I have only myself to blame."

I saw paleness move toward the door. She stopped at the door and said, "I hereby accuse you of probably being a pretty good man."

"Thank you."

"And I am not a very nice woman."

"You are probably nicer than you are willing to admit, Teresa."

"Ho, ho, ho," she said and went out and the latch clicked as she quietly closed the door.

I went back to the bed. It was scented with her. My heart was still running a little fast. I laughed at myself silently. Mocking and derisive. I had defended my honor. Righteous prig. I knew what I should have done. Once I had suspected who it really was, kept my damned mouth shut. Saved astonishment until later. How many times do you find yourself in bed with a legend? The three unholy McGees—the one I try not to be, and the one I wish I was, and the one I really am. Going ahead with it would have been the one I guess I try not to be. But sometimes I wish there was less clown in the one I really am. I go about getting walloped with bladders, and setting my own nose on fire. Maybe I want to be a true hero. But whenever I hear that word, the only hero I can think of is Nelson Eddy, yelling into Jeanette's face. And wearing his Yogi Bear hat.

While considering a cold shower for myself, I dropped back into sleep.

14

Though their doctor lauded my health, I was not too content with it. The head wound was not too bad. I had hit the Formica edge a slashing glancing blow across the hairline in front, and a four-inch flap of scalp had had to be stitched back into position. A few days later I acquired a pair of black eyes of such a deep hue and generous area that I resembled a large uneasy raccoon.

It wasn't physical damage which bothered me. It was psychic damage. We are all in a state of precarious balance, and it is difficult to realize how delicate that balance is until it is upset—either by emotions or clever chemistry. You do not quite trust all the perfectly reliable messages of the senses.

I found that I had a bigger emotional swing than I wanted. I would become vastly elated for no reason, and deeply depressed without warning. And sometimes I felt ludicrously close to girlish tears. The governor was out of kilter. I told myself I could not go about reacting like a Smith College sophomore, but I could not shake the feeling of emotional convalescence, of not being entirely certain of what I might do next. Though I stopped hallucinating, the world had lost its stability. It would give a vivid little hitch from time to time, like a brief cosmic hiccup.

I met Charles McKewn Armister and his wife. They were similar physical types—stocky, sandy, fit, outdoor people. Her attitude toward him was gentle and loving, protective and slightly apprehensive. They had employed a husky male chauffeur-nurse-valet-attendant to stay close to him and keep him out of mischief. Had I not known about him, I would have thought him a perfectly normal club-man bore. He had hearty and trivial conversation. He seemed in perpetual good spirits.

He pumped my hand and said, "We're indebted to you. Yes sir. Pretty ugly mess. Knew old Bay for years. Never thought he'd try any hanky-panky. Got some good chaps running the show now. Reliable. Like Jo says, it's time for me to relax and enjoy myself. Travel, do some sailing, sharpen up the old tennis, hey old girl?" He put his arm around his wife's waist, gave her a hearty hug, slid his freckled hand down to her matronly rear, and gave her such a massive pinch she leaped into the air, eyes bulging.

"Charles!" she said. He laughed heartily.

He looked at me, smiling, and said, "They won't let me take a drink. Imagine that? They say I get too noisy. Matter of fact, I don't miss it. A man doesn't have to drink to feel good, does he?"

"Charles?"

"What, my dear? What?"

She looked at him with the loving earnest patience of a mother coaching a child. "Weren't you going to ask Mr. McGee something?"

"What? Oh yes, of course. Why don't you and little what's-her-name come stay with us for a bit out at the Island? Rest and recuperation, fellow. And recreation. Glad to have you. Indebted to you."

And with the smiling, absentminded unconcern of any minor league outfielder, he reached his hand to the front of his beautifully tailored trousers and scratched his crotch.

"Uh. Thank you very much. But Miss Gibson and I are going down to North Carolina to see her brother. Perhaps some other time."

"Any time at all, fellow. Give us a ring any time."

"Charles, dear," Joanna said, "would you like to go down with Wade now and wait for me in the car?"

"What? Of course, old girl. Certainly."

Terry said, "I'll be out day after tomorrow to stay a few days, Charlie." She stepped to him to kiss him on the cheek. He chuckled, and before she could evade him, put his hands on her breasts and gave them a simultaneous squeeze like a clown honking a pair of rubber horns, and, still chuckling, went out through the door Wade was holding for him. The moment they were gone, the sisters flew into each other's arms, and clung and wept, making their small soft sisterly sounds. I went to the windows and stood with my back to them, heard murmurous mutual comfortings, snifflings, nose blowings.

"Mr. McGee?" Joanna said. I turned toward them. They were under control, smiling, eyes slightly reddened. She dug into her purse and took out a folded envelope and held it out to me. As I took it, she said, "This is a token of our appreciation for trying to help my sister and me, and Charles of course, and some small restitution for what you . . . had to endure at the hands of a man we once loved and trusted."

"You don't have to do this."

"I want to. It's out of my own funds. They say we won't be able to touch anything of Charles's for quite a long time, until it is all straightened out. I talked this over with my attorney, and he suggested that for tax purposes we both consider it as a gift. I will send you the same amount next year, and the same amount the year after. He said it would be better for both of us that way."

"I feel a little strange about this."

"For God's sake, why should you?" Terry said rudely. "If it wasn't for you, Charlie, bless him, would be dead. This broad is loaded and she's grateful. And you are permanently unemployed, by choice, aren't you, McGee? What's with this hesitation? You seem to be rejecting all kinds of little gifts lately." She winked broadly at me.

I put the envelope in my pocket. Nobody had been able to find the stuff they had checked out of my hotel. So I was wearing gift clothing. Gift from Nina. I had given her the measurements—44 extra-long, 35 waist, 35 inseam, shoes 13 C, shirts 17-35—and she had scurried around harassing people to cuff the pants, and had even bought one of Abercrombie's better suitcases to put the gear in. She bought far more than I had wanted, but aside from slightly hairier fabrics than I would have chosen, everything was fine.

Joanna put her hand in mine. Her eyes were shiny. She said good-bye and went down to join her jolly, happy, uncomplicated husband.

"If he wants to keep busy," I said to Terry, "he can always run for office."

"Oh, you are very very funny. When is the little designer coming after you?"

"Her name is Nina. Three o'clock. What are you going to do?"

"Today, or from now on? Today I am going to go out and buy, buy, buy. Gaudy, expensive, ridiculous things. I am going to bully the clerks, make scenes, and buy, buy, buy. It's my therapy, darling. As to from now on, I shall get sister settled down, then go back to Athens, then down to Montevideo for Christmas with a flock of other professional houseguests, then Mexico in the spring, and summer near Cannes, and from then on plans are a bit vague. I expect I shall go right on being Terry Drummond."

There was a touching look of vulnerability about her.

"Good luck to Terry Drummond," I said.

"Sweetie, if you try to feel sorry for me, I shall hit you flush in the mouth."

I took the envelope out and opened it and looked at the figure on the check. It was a ridiculous figure. It was unreal. I tucked it away, resisting the temptation to take it out for another look to see if I could have misread it.

After our baggage was checked aboard, and while we waited for the flight to be announced, I told Nina about the envelope at the hotel. I had gone there on the off chance, and found they still had it. I had to sign an affadavit about the loss of the receipt, and then tell them exactly what was in it, so they could check the contents—with my approval.

"It belongs to you," I said.

"I keep hoping I can have a lot of time with him before they operate, Trav."

"It's more cash than I usually carry around, honey."

"Do you think Mike is scared of the operation?"

He wasn't scared. The time we spent there was strange. We had a rental car and two rooms in a motel about six miles from the hospital. In the morning we would have breakfast in the motel restaurant and then I would drive her to the hospital. We would both spend a little time with Mike, and then I would leave her there. It was cold gray November weather, with low clouds and a frequent misty rain. I had the days to myself. I had my own devils to wrestle. I worked at getting myself back into shape. When I forced exercises to the limit of endurance, I would think of the circus-girl look of Doris Wrightson and wonder what they were doing with her, and how they managed to keep that sensation out of the public press.

At four thirty I would go back and sit and talk with them for a half hour and then take Nina back to the motel. We did not talk much. She seemed remote. We were not lovers. I had kissed her, but sensed a flavor of remoteness in her acceptance. She was too focused on her brother and, perhaps, on those evaluations of herself which came from all their talk. He was the only blood-closeness she had left.

Nightmares awoke me. In sleep, the things would come out of the walls again. The worst ones were the shiny ones which rattled.

She had those three days with him, and at the end of the third day, before they began to prep him for the operation scheduled for the following morning, after she had kissed him and wished him luck, he asked me to stay a moment. "Man-talk," he told her.

"She's gone?"

"She's gone, Mike."

There was a smile on his ruined gaunted face. "Kid sister. We had to break through that. We had to find each other as people. I'm glad there was time for that."

"So is she."

"Big brother. Shattered hero. She had to look behind all that and find out who I am. Without the deification impulse. Just a guy. Now we like each other for the right reasons, Trav."

"These Gibsons are good folks."

"You're uneasy. You think I'm going to saddle you with kid sister forever. We talked about you two."

"Mike, I swear, the way it happened between us wasn't . . ."

"Don't insult me with that crap, Sergeant. She's a woman. She's capable of making choices. And neither of you are very effete or bloodless. It got her over that Plummer thing. And over the bitterness. She's in love with you."

"Are you sure of that?"

"More sure than she is. She's suspicious of it. She thinks it might be physical infatuation. But now that I know her, I don't think she could be a purely physical person in any relationship. There would have to be more, or it wouldn't work for her. But she knows, just as I know, that it would be a very foolish business to try to permanently halter McGee. You are too much of a maverick, Sergeant. Too roving and restless. Maybe a little too self-involved."

"I could be getting over that, Mike."

"Are you volunteering to marry my sister, you cad?"

"What the hell, Mike?"

"Don't get jumpy, boy. I asked you to stay behind so I could make certain that out of a lot of vague guilts, if I don't make it through this cutting session, you two idiots won't make a sentimental and emotional gesture and get yourselves stuck with each other. Marriage makes a lousy memorial. Pack her along with you, with my blessing, boy, and use her well. Otherwise the two of you will be walking around with steam coming out of your ears. Six months from now, if it still percolates, then make a decision independent of guilt or memorials to me. If it is yes, I shall stare down in disbelief from Valhalla."

"Twenty years from now, you silly bastard, we will probably be running here to get some advice from you about your teen-age nephews and nieces. Bad advice."

He held his hand out toward me. I took it.

"McGee, deserve the girl. And afterwards, be someone for her to run to when she gets bruised. And when she does want to get married, you be my eyes—you take a good long searching look at the son of a bitch, and pry her loose if he can't cut it."

They kept him under the knife for six hours and sent him back alive. Barely. He lasted for two days, and had a few moments of drugged consciousness, and when he went there was a gloom around that great big place that you could feel. They said the words and put him in the ground, and I took the pale and hollow-eyed and silent girl down to Lauderdale, to Slip F-18, Bahia Mar, and installed her aboard the *Busted Flush,* my fifty-two-foot barge-type houseboat, diesel powered, offensively luxurious in all the right areas, and reasonably shipshape topsides. A frantic phone call had barely kept it from being sold out from under me. I gorged a frail bank account with Joanna's check. I introduced Nina around to the permanent characters, the Alabama Tiger and Captain Johnny Dow and all the rest of them. She made a good impression. I set her to work keeping house(boat) and as a deck hand. I browned her on the beach, and told her gaudy lies and stories to make her smile, and kept her so active and busy that her slight office softness was trimmed down to firm and lovely flesh. But all I could do was admire it. She had her own stateroom. She was not morose. She was not brooding. She was just very quiet and thoughtful, a little time of the deadness of the spirit. Sometimes there was as awkwardness between us when something accidental, some physical contact, would remind us that we were, quietly and deliberately, restricting our relationship to a casual basis.

I couldn't seem to throw off the nightmares. I felt very edgy at times.

The *Busted Flush* never got so much earnest and dedicated maintenance. And I kept worrying about Christmas. It was coming along soon and I knew it would be rough for her.

She was the one who found the small item in the back of the *Miami News*. Mr. Baynard Mulligan had been given three years for embezzlement and tax evasion. He was appealing. The prosecution's case had been weakened when Mr. Mulligan had married one of the key witnesses against him, a Bonita Hersch, the secretary who had aided him in his raid on the Armister fortune, and who had been instrumental in his apprehension. Another secretary, a Doris Wrightson, had given testimony very damaging to Mulligan.

With the first genuine glint of humor I had seen in a long time, Nina said, "I'll bet he'll end up wishing he'd settled for twenty years."

I studied her. We were in stasis. We both needed to be jolted out of this strange drabness of spirit which was spoiling the game.

I said, "Let's cruise this thing down to the Keys, honey."

She looked startled. "Do you know how to run it, all alone?"

"I'll have you to help."

"That's pretty scary. I don't know anything about ropes and compasses and things."

"We'll blunder along."

I really think it was a fish who brought my love back to me—a fleet, six-pound, goggle-eyed bonefish. Cool wind and weather had cleared away the bugs. We went chugging down Florida Bay. Once she stopped being apprehensive, she became almost nonchalant at taking her trick at the wheel, reading the charts, spotting the markers. And one misty morning partway down, she discovered fish. She had never fished in her life. She was using one of my spinning outfits. The hard wrench at the line electrified her. It was a new world. She became a very intent, a very beady-eyed, a very dedicated fisherman. She lost some good ones and chewed herself out, and never made the same mistake more than twice. This was the first real sparkle of interest I had seen since Mike had died.

We went down into the Content Keys and found a sheltered cove and established residence. When we needed anything, we would take the dinghy and wind up the little limey outboard and chug on in to Ramrod. It was a quiet Christmas. I gave her a spinning outfit of her own, with a little pink plastic tackle box and a gaudy array of lures. She was enchanted. She gave me two bottles of excellent brandy, a superior yachts-man's hat, and a little transistor radio to replace the one she had man-aged to drop over the side. Merry Christmas. Merry Platonic Christmas to all.

On a reasonably warm January afternoon, after we had taken a swim, she took the dinghy out alone to fish the flats. I was having a bad day. I stayed aboard. I had awakened exhausted by nightmares, listless, and without appetite. I tried to get some sun while she was fishing, but ended up pacing my top deck, wondering if the emotional damage which made me so edgy was permanent. Then I heard her whooping. She was standing up in the dinghy. There was some great commotion going on out there. I ran and got the glasses and put them on her. She was keeping the rod tip high, and as she circled toward me I could see that her face was practically bulging with intensity, determination, and excitement. At about the moment I realized she had a reasonably good bonefish on, she lost her balance and fell out of the dinghy without foundering it. But she didn't drop the rod. She scrambled up. The water came just below her waist. She turned a grinning face toward the *Busted Flush* and whooped again. I watched her work him, and get him close, and move cautiously to the dinghy, make about four false tries, and then swoop up that gleaming silver length with the landing net. She piled aboard, did some bailing, and then came chugging home. I made the dinghy fast and then helped her over the rail. Her little blue sunsuit was sodden.

"Hey, isn't he glorious! Isn't he the damnedest thing? He went a thousand miles an hour! Around and around and around. What is he? Can we eat him?"

"He's a bonefish, and he's a nice one, and it is early for them around here. We can't eat him."

"No?"

"No."

She bit her lip, dropped to her knees, and worked him out of the net. His gills were working. She grasped him around the middle, lowered him and carefully dropped him into the water. He floated on his side, tail making weak movements. "Hurry along," she told him. "Go on about your business, Bonefish. You are a nifty fish. Go warn your rela-tives there's a girl around here named Gibson who's going to raise hell with your whole clan." He slowly righted himself, and gave a more

powerful flicker of that tail, and went angling slowly down and away.
"Come back yourself, any time," she called.

And she spun, joyous, grabbed me with round tan arms and fishy
hands, pasted wet sunsuit against me, gave me a happy noisy kiss.

"Congratulations," I said, and kissed her in return.

She looked at me speculatively. The next kiss was longer. Her face
changed and softened. "Bit on a little white dude," she said dreamily.

"Little crabs are better."

The next kiss was imperative. I swung her up and took her below. It
was all back for us, more than before—a deeper, richer, and more demanding hunger.

February, March, and into the loveliness of April.

Sometimes we moved to other coves, other beaches. Always private.
We had no need for anyone else. She could sleep in my arms and sense
the looming presence of nightmare and waken me, quiet me, soothe me.
And little by little they went away. There was laughter aboard. And a
vastly diminished laundry problem. Clothes were for when you got cold,
or thought you heard a boat coming, or when you had to go ashore.
There were a thousand permutations and combinations of love. By day
and by night, very quick and very lengthy, comical and saddened,
bawdy and spiritual, simple and complicated, mild and stormy. It
seemed that we could never wear away that hard enduring edge of need,
that the pace would never slacken.

But at last of course it did. A little less compulsive magic, but more
of something else. The product of love and of the ten million words of
history and revelation we spoke to each other. One day there was the
unspoken awareness that we had to get back to the world. On a trip to
Key West she had purchased, almost apologetically, tools of her trade.
She began to do a little more drawing each day. And her lust for
bonefish dwindled.

We sat topside one evening, holding hands, watching a vast fiery sunset. She was silent for a long time.

"Trav?"

"Yes, darling."

"I don't want you to think . . . I mean, I don't want to seem
like . . ."

"Hush," I told her, and raised that small and valuable hand to my   N34 lips, kissed her fingertips and palm. "We'll take our time getting back to Lauderdale. How about five days?"

"How did you know?"

"The same way you knew it was time."

"And two days there, and then put me on a plane, darling. And don't let me look back, because if you do I won't be able to leave you. You knew I would?"

"When you were ready. Yes."

"I'll always love you. Can you understand that?"

"Yes, but don't ever try to make anyone else understand it, Nina."

"It will always be too private to tell."

And so it was an April magic, going back. Hauntingly sweet, because we knew this was the end of it. There was nostalgia in each caress.

Perhaps those weeks of us were, in one sense, a memorial. People have built imposing structures out of far meaner materials. I cherished her and celebrated her, and we restored each other.